the ecco anthology of

contemporary
american
short fiction

An Imprint of HarperCollins*Publishers*

the ecco anthology of

contemporary american short fiction

selected by

joyce carol oates

and

christopher r. beha

HARPER ● PERENNIAL

An extension of this copyright page begins on page 755.

HarperCollins books may be purchased for educational, business, or sales promotional use. For information, please e-mail the Special Markets Department at SPsales@harpercollins.com.

FIRST EDITION

Designed by Justin Dodd

Library of Congress Cataloging-in-Publication Data is available upon request.

ISBN 978-0-06-166158-7

20   OV/LSC   15 14

CONTENTS

PREFACE

"Art, a master once observed, is never theoretical"—So the un-named narrator of Steven Millhauser's elegantly composed allegory of the artist's relationship to his art "The New Automaton Theater" tells us. It's a compelling irony of Millhauser's provocative story that it presents a theory of art—of mimesis—through its very spec-ificity, and suggests the impossibility of explaining, paraphrasing, analyzing, and even comprehending art in terms other than itself: "Nothing short of attendance at the Neues Zaubertheater can con-vey the startling, disturbing quality of the new automatons."

So too with the forty-eight stories of this collection, of which nearly all were written and published in the twenty-first century and reflect something of the dazzling variety of the contemporary scene: styles, tones, subjects, settings, points of view (including, in our highly politicized era, differing and subtly contentious po-litical perspectives). Of the forms of literature none is more supple, more flexible and open to aesthetic variation than the short story; its very brevity is an inspiration to the writer to experiment in ways that would be impractical—if not fatal—in the longer novel form. No literary form is more ideally suited to the challenge of story-telling through unique and idiosyncratic voices, in which "charac-ter" is revealed in the telling, swiftly and dramatically:

Earlier today, me and Cut drove down to South River and bought some
more smoke. The regular pickup, enough to last us through the rest of
the month. The Peruvian dude who hooks us up gave us a sampler of his
superweed (Jewel luv it, he said) and on the way home, past the Hydrox
factory, we could have sworn we smelled cookies baking right in the
back seat.

—Junot Díaz, "Aurora"

I cringe from the heat of the night on my face. I feel as bare as open
flesh. Tonight I am much older than the twenty-five years that I have
lived. The night is the time I dread most in my life. Yet if I am to live, I
must depend upon it.

—Edwidge Danticat, "Night Women"

Next night, walking out where it happened, I found her little red bow.
    I brought it in, threw it down on the table, said: My God my God.
    Take a good look at it and also I'm looking at it, said Uncle Matt.
And we won't ever forget it, am I right?

—George Saunders, "The Red Bow"

My first day as an escort, my first "date" had only one leg. He'd gone
to a gay bathhouse, to get warm, he told me. Maybe for sex. And he'd
fallen asleep in the steam room, too close to the heating element. He'd
been unconscious for hours, until someone found him. Until the meat
of his left thigh was completely and thoroughly cooked.

—Chuck Palahniuk, "Escort"

Such abrupt and edgy story openings are characteristic of our era,
in which the tradition of the finely crafted short story in the mode of
Henry James, James Joyce, Anton Chekhov, Ernest Hemingway, and
others has been complemented by a vernacular urgency that would
seem to spring from nonliterary sources like the stage monologue or
performance art. Certainly the more traditional story continues to
be written, and very beautifully written, by contemporary writers

as varied as John Updike, Russell Banks, Rick Bass, E. L. Doctorow, Thomas McGuane, and Deborah Eisenberg, among others in this volume; and there are ingeniously conceived stories in which a distinctly moral perspective prevails beneath virtuosity of form, as in Richard Bausch's "1–900" (a transcript of a lonely man's protracted phone call with a female sex-worker), Tobias Wolff's "Bullet in the Brain" (the final, accelerating minutes of a man's life), and David Foster Wallace's "Incarnations of Burned Children" (a parents' nightmare, in miniature) .

Ours is not a time of self-conscious literary experimentation, like the 1960s and 1970s, yet unsettling short fiction continues to be written, adhering more to recognizable forms such as romantic comedy (Aimee Bender's "Off"), stand-up comedy (Lydia Davis's "Television"), and the crime-mystery story (Louise Erdrich's "Disaster Stamps of Pluto" and David Means's "Sault Ste. Marie") than to elaborately extended novel-length fictions. The reader is likely to be provocatively disoriented by the matter-of-fact distortions of *the real* in such fabulist tales as Stuart Dybek's "Death of the Right Fielder," Richard Burgin's "The Identity Club," and Elizabeth McCracken's "Some Terpsichore," yet the ethical concerns of these stories are as crucial as those of more explicit "realistic" stories like those by Doug Unger, Pinckney Benedict, Michael Chabon, Sheila Kohler, and Ben Fountain. The perimeters of *the real* are not ostensibly challenged by such stories as Greg Johnson's "Double Exposure" and Richard Ford's "Reunion," but it is helpful to know who "Sylvia Plath" is to fully appreciate Johnson's story, as it is helpful to know John Cheever's short story "Reunion," with its similar setting in Grand Central Station, New York City, to fully appreciate Ford's artful variant. And there is the riddlesome mystery-crime-fable "The Paperhanger," by William Gay, a unique prose fiction that eludes all definition.

Through most of the twentieth century, the sexual frankness of such stories as Edmund White's "Cinnamon Skin," Mary Gaitskill's "The Girl on the Plane," Antonya Nelson's "Stitches,"

Adam Haslett's "City Visit," Annie Proulx's "People in Hell Just Want a Drink of Water," and others in this collection would have distracted readers from the serious ethical questions the stories raise, as the ethnicity of Sherman Alexie's "The Toughest Indian in the World," Jhumpa Lahiri's "Once in a Lifetime," John Edgar Wideman's "Who Invented the Jump Shot," and Edward P. Jones's "Old Boys, Old Girls" would have marginalized these stories among many "mainstream" Caucasian-American readers. Now it might be argued that it is the socially "marginalized"—our evermore literate and self-expressive ethnic minorities—that can lay claim to seeing contemporary American society most vividly.

In recent decades memoir and memoirist fiction—that is, fiction that simulates memoir as a literary strategy—have more or less replaced formal literary experimentation. Readers distrustful of "difficult" fiction are rarely rebuffed by the conversational, confessional mode that makes of the explicit a virtue and resists over-subtlety; reading, the reader becomes an immediate confidante, an intimate friend. In stories as diverse as Lorrie Moore's "Paper Losses," Ann Beattie's "Lavande," Amy Hempel's "To Those of You Who Missed Your Connecting Flights Out of O'Hare," Denis Johnson's "Emergency," Maile Meloy's "Ranch Girl," and Tim O'Brien's "On the Rainy River," as well as those by Edmund White and Junot Díaz, it is likely to be the forthright memoirist tone that rivets the reader, while in stories of hyper-domestic-realism like Matthew Klam's "Adina, Astrid, Chipewee, Jasmine" and Charles Baxter's "Poor Devil," it is likely to be the accumulation of prosaic detail, the poetic appropriation of the not-very-poetic, that most powerfully convinces. All of these are fictions of brilliant specificity, the very antithesis of "theory."

It was both a challenge and a pleasure to assemble, with the highly capable assistance of Christopher Beha, the stories in this volume. What Christopher and I most regret is having to leave out so many excellent stories—enough stories for another volume, or nearly! Several much-admired stories could not be included because of their length while in other cases we could not secure permission for reprinting. All forms of art are generated by the wish to make of the perishable something imperishable and of the merely finite and local something that might be called "universal"—a quixotic goal perhaps, but an admirable one. So too the anthologist hopes to bring together in a reasonably permanent structure the very best and most representative work of his or her era, as in *The Ecco Anthology of Contemporary American Short Fiction.*

—JOYCE CAROL OATES, February 2008

the ecco anthology of

contemporary
american
short fiction

THE TOUGHEST INDIAN IN THE WORLD

Sherman Alexie

A Spokane/Coeur d'Alene Indian, Sherman Alexie grew up on the Spokane Indian Reservation in Wellpinit, Washington, about fifty miles northwest of Spokane, Washington. He is the author of four novels and several volumes of poetry, as well as the story collections *The Lone Ranger and Tonto Fistfight in Heaven*, *The Toughest Indian in the World*, and *Ten Little Indians*. Alexie's young adult novel, *The Absolutely True Diary of a Part-Time Indian*, received the 2007 National Book Award in Young People's Literature. He lives in Seattle, Washington, with his wife and two sons.

Being a Spokane Indian, I only pick up Indian hitchhikers. I learned this particular ceremony from my father, a Coeur d'Alene, who always stopped for those twentieth-century aboriginal nomads who refused to believe the salmon were gone. I don't know what they believed in exactly, but they wore hope like a bright shirt.

My father never taught me about hope. Instead, he continually told me that our salmon—our hope—would never come back, and though such lessons may seem cruel, I know enough to cover my heart in any crowd of white people.

"They'll kill you if they get the chance," my father said. "Love you or hate you, white people will shoot you in the heart. Even after all these years, they'll still smell the salmon on you, the dead salmon, and that will make white people dangerous."

All of us, Indian and white, are haunted by salmon.

When I was a boy, I leaned over the edge of one dam or another—perhaps Long Lake or Little Falls or the great gray dragon known as the Grand Coulee—and watched the ghosts of the salmon rise from the water to the sky and become constellations.

For most Indians, stars are nothing more than white tombstones scattered across a dark graveyard.

But the Indian hitchhikers my father picked up refused to admit the existence of sky, let alone the possibility that salmon might be stars. They were common people who believed only in the thumb and the toot. My father envied those simple Indian hitchhikers. He wanted to change their minds about salmon; he wanted to break open their hearts and see the future in their blood. He loved them.

IN 1975 or '76 or '77, driving along one highway or another, my father would point out a hitchhiker standing beside the road a mile or two in the distance.

"Indian," he said if it was an Indian, and he was never wrong, though I could never tell if the distant figure was male or female, let alone Indian or not.

If a distant figure happened to be white, my father would drive by without comment.

That was how I learned to be silent in the presence of white people.

The silence is not about hate or pain or fear. Indians just like to believe that white people will vanish, perhaps explode into smoke, if they are ignored enough times. Perhaps a thousand white families are still waiting for their sons and daughters to return home, and can't recognize them when they float back as morning fog.

"We better stop," my mother said from the passenger seat. She was one of those Spokane women who always wore a purple bandanna tied tightly around her head.

These days, her bandanna is usually red. There are reasons, motives, traditions behind the choice of color, but my mother keeps them secret.

"Make room," my father said to my siblings and me as we sat on the floor in the cavernous passenger area of our blue van. We sat on carpet samples because my father had torn out the seats in a sober rage not long after he bought the van from a crazy white man.

I have three brothers and three sisters now. Back then, I had four of each. I missed one of the funerals and cried myself sick during the other one.

"Make room," my father said again—he said everything twice—and only then did we scramble to make space for the Indian hitchhiker.

Of course, it was easy enough to make room for one hitchhiker, but Indians usually travel in packs. Once or twice, we picked up entire all-Indian basketball teams, along with their coaches, girlfriends, and cousins. Fifteen, twenty Indian strangers squeezed into the back of a blue van with nine wide-eyed Indian kids.

Back in those days, I loved the smell of Indians, and of Indian hitchhikers in particular. They were usually in some stage of drunkenness, often in need of soap and a towel, and always ready to sing.

Oh, the songs! Indian blues bellowed at the highest volumes. We called them "49s," those cross-cultural songs that combined Indian lyrics and rhythms with country-and-western and blues melodies. It seemed that every Indian knew all the lyrics to every Hank Williams song ever recorded. Hank was our Jesus, Patsy Cline was our Virgin Mary, and Freddy Fender, George Jones, Conway Twitty, Loretta Lynn, Tammy Wynette, Charley Pride, Ronnie Milsap, Tanya Tucker, Marty Robbins, Johnny Horton, Donna Fargo, and Charlie Rich were our disciples.

We all know that nostalgia is dangerous, but I remember those days with a clear conscience. Of course, we live in different days now, and there aren't as many Indian hitchhikers as there used to be.

NOW, I drive my own car, a 1998 Toyota Camry, the best-selling automobile in the United States, and therefore the one most often stolen. *Consumer Reports* has named it the most reliable family sedan for sixteen years running, and I believe it.

In my Camry, I pick up three or four Indian hitchhikers a week. Mostly men. They're usually headed home, back to their reservations or somewhere close to their reservations. Indians hardly ever travel in a straight line, so a Crow Indian might hitchhike west when his reservation is back east in Montana. He has some people to see in Seattle, he might explain if I ever asked him. But I never ask Indians their reasons for hitchhiking. All that matters is this: They are Indians walking, raising their thumbs, and I am there to pick them up.

At the newspaper where I work, my fellow reporters think I'm crazy to pick up hitchhikers. They're all white and never stop to pick up anybody, let alone an Indian. After all, we're the ones who write the stories and headlines: HITCHHIKER KILLS HUSBAND AND WIFE, MISSING GIRL'S BODY FOUND, RAPIST STRIKES AGAIN. If I really tried, maybe I could explain to them why I pick up any Indian, but who wants to try? Instead, if they ask I just give them a smile and turn back to my computer. My coworkers smile back and laugh loudly. They're always laughing loudly at me, at one another, at themselves, at goofy typos in the newspapers, at the idea of hitchhikers.

I dated one of them for a few months. Cindy. She covered the local courts: speeding tickets and divorces, drunk driving and embezzlement. Cindy firmly believed in the who-what-where-when-why-and-how of journalism. In daily conversation, she talked like she was writing the lead of her latest story. Hell, she talked like that in bed.

"How does that feel?" I asked, quite possibly the only Indian man who has ever asked that question.

"I love it when you touch me there," she answered. "But it would help if you rubbed it about thirty percent lighter and with your thumb instead of your middle finger. And could you maybe turn the radio to a different station? KYZY would be good. I feel like soft jazz will work better for me right now. A minor chord, a C or G-flat, or something like that. Okay, honey?"

During lovemaking, I would get so exhausted by the size of her erotic vocabulary that I would fall asleep before my orgasm, continue pumping away as if I were awake, and then regain consciousness with a sudden start when I finally did come, more out of reflex than passion.

Don't get me wrong. Cindy is a good one, cute and smart, funny as hell, a good catch no matter how you define it, but she was also one of those white women who date only brown-skinned guys. Indians like me, black dudes, Mexicans, even a few Iranians. I started to feel like a trophy, or like one of those entries in a personal ad. I asked Cindy why she never dated pale boys.

"White guys bore me," she said. "All they want to talk about is their fathers."

"What do brown guys talk about?" I asked her.

"Their mothers," she said and laughed, then promptly left me for a public defender who was half Japanese and half African, a combination that left Cindy dizzy with the interracial possibilities.

Since Cindy, I haven't dated anyone. I live in my studio apartment with the ghosts of two dogs, Felix and Oscar, and a laptop computer stuffed with bad poems, the aborted halves of three novels, and some three-paragraph personality pieces I wrote for the newspaper.

I'm a features writer, and an Indian at that, so I get all the shit jobs. Not the dangerous shit jobs or the monotonous shit jobs. No. I get to write the articles designed to please the eye, ear, and heart. And there is no journalism more soul-endangering to write than journalism that aims to please.

So it was with reluctance that I climbed into my car last week and headed down Highway 2 to write some damn pleasant story about some damn pleasant people. Then I saw the Indian hitchhiker standing beside the road. He looked the way Indian hitchhikers usually look. Long, straggly black hair. Brown eyes and skin. Missing a couple of teeth. A bad complexion that used to be much worse. Crooked nose that had been broken more than once. Big, misshapen ears. A few whiskers masquerading as a mustache. Even before he climbed into my car I could tell he was tough. He had some serious muscles that threatened to rip through his blue jeans and denim jacket. When he was in the car, I could see his hands up close, and they told his whole story. His fingers were twisted into weird, permanent shapes, and his knuckles were covered with layers of scar tissue.

"Jeez," I said. "You're a fighter, enit?"

I threw in the "enit," a reservation colloquialism, because I wanted the fighter to know that I had grown up on the rez, in the woods, with every Indian in the world.

The hitchhiker looked down at his hands, flexed them into fists. I could tell it hurt him to do that.

"Yeah," he said. "I'm a fighter."

I pulled back onto the highway, looking over my shoulder to check my blind spot.

"What tribe are you?" I asked him, inverting the last two words in order to sound as aboriginal as possible.

"Lummi," he said. "What about you?"

"Spokane."

"I know some Spokanes. Haven't seen them in a long time."

He clutched his backpack in his lap like he didn't want to let it go for anything. He reached inside a pocket and pulled out a piece of deer jerky. I recognized it by the smell.

"Want some?" he asked.

"Sure."

It had been a long time since I'd eaten jerky. The salt, the gamy taste. I felt as Indian as Indian gets, driving down the road in a fast car, chewing on jerky, talking to an indigenous fighter.

"Where you headed?" I asked.

"Home. Back to the rez."

I nodded my head as I passed a big truck. The driver gave us a smile as we went by. I tooted the horn.

"Big truck," said the fighter.

I HAVEN'T lived on my reservation for twelve years. But I live in Spokane, which is only an hour's drive from the rez. Still, I hardly ever go home. I don't know why not. I don't think about it much, I guess, but my mom and dad still live in the same house where I grew up. My brothers and sisters, too. The ghosts of my two dead siblings share an apartment in the converted high school. It's just a local call from Spokane to the rez, so I talk to all of them once or twice a week. Smoke signals courtesy of U.S. West Communications. Sometimes they call me up to talk about the stories they've seen that I've written for the newspaper. Pet pigs and support groups and science fairs. Once in a while, I used to fill in for the obituaries writer when she was sick. Then she died, and I had to write her obituary.

"How far are you going?" asked the fighter, meaning how much closer was he going to get to his reservation than he was now.

"Up to Wenatchee," I said. "I've got some people to interview there."

"Interview? What for?"

"I'm a reporter. I work for the newspaper."

"No," said the fighter, looking at me like I was stupid for thinking he was stupid. "I mean, what's the story about?"

"Oh, not much. There's two sets of twins who work for the fire department. Human-interest stuff, you know?"

"Two sets of twins, enit? That's weird."

He offered me more deer jerky, but I was too thirsty from the salty meat, so I offered him a Pepsi instead.

"Don't mind if I do," he said.

"They're in a cooler on the backseat," I said. "Grab me one, too."

He maneuvered his backpack carefully and found room enough to reach into the backseat for the soda pop. He opened my can first and handed it to me. A friendly gesture for a stranger. I took a big mouthful and hiccupped loudly.

"That always happens to me when I drink cold things," he said.

We sipped slowly after that. I kept my eyes on the road while he stared out the window into the wheat fields. We were quiet for many miles.

"Who do you fight?" I asked as we passed through another anonymous small town.

"Mostly Indians," he said. "Money fights, you know? I go from rez to rez, fighting the best they have. Winner takes all."

"Jeez, I never heard of that."

"Yeah, I guess it's illegal."

He rubbed his hands together. I could see fresh wounds.

"Man," I said. "Those fights must be rough."

The fighter stared out the window. I watched him for a little too long and almost drove off the road. Car horns sounded all around us.

"Jeez," the fighter said. "Close one, enit?"

"Close enough," I said.

He hugged his backpack more tightly, using it as a barrier between his chest and the dashboard. An Indian hitchhiker's version of a passenger-side air bag.

"Who'd you fight last?" I asked, trying to concentrate on the road.

"Some Flathead," he said. "In Arlee. He was supposed to be the toughest Indian in the world."

"Was he?"

"Nah, no way. Wasn't even close. Wasn't even tougher than me."

He told me how big the Flathead kid was, way over six feet tall and two hundred and some pounds. Big buck Indian. Had hands as big as this and arms as big as that. Had a chin like a damn buffalo.

The fighter told me that he hit the Flathead kid harder than he ever hit anybody before.

"I hit him like he was a white man," the fighter said. "I hit him like he was two or three white men rolled into one."

But the Flathead kid would not go down, even though his face swelled up so bad that he looked like the Elephant Man. There were no referees, no judge, no bells to signal the end of the round. The winner was the Indian still standing. Punch after punch, man, and the kid would not go down.

"I was so tired after a while," said the fighter, "that I just took a step back and watched the kid. He stood there with his arms down, swaying from side to side like some toy, you know? Head bobbing on his neck like there was no bone at all. You couldn't even see his eyes no more. He was all messed up."

"What'd you do?" I asked.

"Ah, hell, I couldn't fight him no more. That kid was planning to die before he ever went down. So I just sat on the ground while they counted me out. Dumb Flathead kid didn't even know what was happening. I just sat on the ground while they raised his hand. While all the winners collected their money and all the losers cussed me out. I just sat there, man."

"Jeez," I said. "What happened next?"

"Not much. I sat there until everybody was gone. Then I stood up and decided to head for home. I'm tired of this shit. I just want to go home for a while. I got enough money to last me a long time. I'm a rich Indian, you hear? I'm a rich Indian."

The fighter finished his Pepsi, rolled down his window, and pitched the can out. I almost protested, but decided against it. I kept my empty can wedged between my legs.

"That's a hell of a story," I said.

"Ain't no story," he said. "It's what happened."

"Jeez," I said. "You would've been a warrior in the old days, enit? You would've been a killer. You would have stolen everybody's god-damn horses. That would've been you. You would've been it."

I was excited. I wanted the fighter to know how much I thought of him. He didn't even look at me.

"A killer," he said. "Sure."

WE DIDN'T talk much after that. I pulled into Wenatchee just before sundown, and the fighter seemed happy to be leaving me.

"Thanks for the ride, cousin," he said as he climbed out. Indians always call each other cousin, especially if they're strangers.

"Wait," I said.

He looked at me, waiting impatiently.

I wanted to know if he had a place to sleep that night. It was supposed to get cold. There was a mountain range between Wenatchee and his reservation. Big mountains that were dormant volcanoes, but that could all blow up at any time. We wrote about it once in the newspaper. Things can change so quickly. So many emergencies and disasters that we can barely keep track. I wanted to tell him how much I cared about my job, even if I had to write about small-town firemen. I wanted to tell the fighter that I pick up all Indian hitchhikers, young and old, men and women, and get them a little closer to home, even if I can't get them all the way. I wanted to tell him that the night sky was a graveyard. I wanted to know if he was the toughest Indian in the world.

"It's late," I finally said. "You can crash with me, if you want."

He studied my face and then looked down the long road toward his reservation.

"Okay," he said. "That sounds good."

We got a room at the Pony Soldier Motel, and both of us laughed at the irony of it all. Inside the room, in a generic watercolor hanging above the bed, the U.S. Cavalry was kicking the crap out of a band of renegade Indians.

"What tribe you think they are?" I asked the fighter.

"All of them," he said.

The fighter crashed on the floor while I curled up in the uncomfortable bed. I couldn't sleep for the longest time. I listened to the fighter talk in his sleep. I stared up at the water-stained ceiling. I don't know what time it was when I finally drifted off, and I don't know what time it was when the fighter got into bed with me. He was naked and his penis was hard. I felt it press against my back as he snuggled up close to me, reached inside my underwear, and took my penis in his hand. Neither of us said a word. He continued to stroke me as he rubbed himself against my back. That went on for a long time. I had never been that close to another man, but the fighter's callused fingers felt better than I would have imagined if I had ever allowed myself to imagine such things.

"This isn't working," he whispered. "I can't come."

Without thinking, I reached around and took the fighter's penis in my hand. He was surprisingly small.

"No," he said. "I want to be inside you."

"I don't know," I said. "I've never done this before."

"It's okay," he said. "I'll be careful. I have rubbers."

Without waiting for my answer, he released me and got up from the bed. I turned to look at him. He was beautiful and scarred. So much brown skin marked with bruises, badly healed wounds, and tattoos. His long black hair was unbraided and hung down to his thin waist. My slacks and dress shirt were folded and draped over the chair near the window. My shoes were sitting on the table. Blue light filled the room. The fighter bent down to his pack and searched for his condoms. For reasons I could not explain then and cannot explain now, I kicked off my underwear and rolled over on my stomach. I could not see him, but I could hear him breathing heavily as he found the condoms, tore open a package, and rolled one over his penis. He crawled onto the bed, between my legs, and slid a pillow beneath my belly.

"Are you ready?" he asked.

"I'm not gay," I said.

"Sure," he said as he pushed himself into me. He was small but it hurt more than I expected, and I knew that I would be sore for days afterward. But I wanted him to save me. He didn't say anything. He just pumped into me for a few minutes, came with a loud sigh, and then pulled out. I quickly rolled off the bed and went into the bathroom. I locked the door behind me and stood there in the dark. I smelled like salmon.

"Hey," the fighter said through the door. "Are you okay?"

"Yes," I said. "I'm fine."

A long silence.

"Hey," he said. "Would you mind if I slept in the bed with you?"

I had no answer to that.

"Listen," I said. "That Flathead boy you fought? You know, the one you really beat up? The one who wouldn't fall down?"

In my mind, I could see the fighter pummeling that boy. Punch after punch. The boy too beaten to fight back, but too strong to fall down.

"Yeah, what about him?" asked the fighter.

"What was his name?"

"His name?"

"Yeah, his name."

"Elmer something or other."

"Did he have an Indian name?"

"I have no idea. How the hell would I know that?"

I stood there in the dark for a long time. I was chilled. I wanted to get into bed and fall asleep.

"Hey," I said. "I think, I think maybe—well, I think you should leave now."

"Yeah," said the fighter, not surprised. I heard him softly singing as he dressed and stuffed all of his belongings into his pack. I wanted to know what he was singing, so I opened the bathroom door just as he was opening the door to leave. He stopped, looked at me, and smiled.

"Hey, tough guy," he said. "You were good."

The fighter walked out the door, left it open, and walked away. I stood in the doorway and watched him continue his walk down the highway, past the city limits. I watched him rise from earth to sky and become a new constellation. I closed the door and wondered what was going to happen next. Feeling uncomfortable and cold, I went back into the bathroom. I ran the shower with the hottest water possible. I stared at myself in the mirror. Steam quickly filled the room. I threw a few shadow punches. Feeling stronger, I stepped into the shower and searched my body for changes. A middle-aged man needs to look for tumors. I dried myself with a towel too small for the job. Then I crawled naked into bed. I wondered if I was a warrior in this life and if I had been a warrior in a previous life. Lonely and laughing, I fell asleep. I didn't dream at all, not one bit. Or perhaps I dreamed but remembered none of it. Instead, I woke early the next morning, before sunrise, and went out into the world. I walked past my car. I stepped onto the pavement, still warm from the previous day's sun. I started walking. In bare feet, I traveled upriver toward the place where I was born and will someday die. At that moment, if you had broken open my heart you could have looked inside and seen the thin white skeletons of one thousand salmon.

LOBSTER NIGHT

Russell Banks

Russell Banks is the founding president of Cities of Refuge North America and a member of the American Academy of Arts and Letters and the American Academy of Arts and Sciences. His work has been translated into twenty languages and has received numerous international prizes and awards. He lives in upstate New York.

Stacy didn't mean to tell Noonan that when she was seventeen she was struck by lightning. She rarely told anyone and never a man she was attracted to or hoped soon to be sleeping with. Always, at the last second, an alarm in the center of her brain went off, and she changed the subject, asked a question, like, "How's your wife?" or, "You ready for another?" She was a summertime bartender at Noonan's, a sprawling log building with the main entrance and kitchen door facing the road and three large, plate-glass, dining-room windows in back and a wide, redwood deck cantilevered above the yard for taking in the great sunset views, of the Adirondack Mountains. The sign said NOONAN'S FAMILY RESTAURANT, but in fact it was a roadhouse, a bar that—except in ski season and on summer weekends when drive-by tourists with kids mistakenly pulled in for lunch or supper—catered mostly to heavy drinkers from the several nearby hamlets.

The night that Stacy told Noonan about the lightning was also the night she shot and killed him. She had rented an A-frame at off-season rates in one of the hamlets and was working for Noonan only till the winter snows blew in from Quebec and Ontario. From May to November, she usually waited tables or tended bar in one or another of the area restaurants and the rest of the year taught alpine skiing at Whiteface Mountain. That was her real job, her profession, and she had the healthy, ash blond good looks of a poster girl for women's Nordic sports: tall, broad-shouldered, flat-muscled, with square jaw and high cheekbones. Despite appearances, however, she viewed herself as a plain-faced, twenty-eight-year-old ex-athlete, with the emphasis on *ex-*. Eight years ago, she was captain of the nationally ranked St. Regis University downhill ski team, only a sophomore and already a star. Then in the Eastern Regionals she pushed her luck, took a spectacular, cartwheeling spill in the giant slalom, and shattered her left thigh. The video of the last ten seconds of her fall was still being shown at the front of the sports segment on the evening news from Plattsburgh.

A year of physical therapy, and she returned to college and the slopes, but she'd lost her fearlessness and, with it, her interest in college, and dropped out before fall break. Her parents had long since swapped their house for an RV and retired to a semipermanent campground outside Phoenix; her three older brothers had drifted downstate to Albany for work in construction; but Stacy came back anyhow to where she'd grown up. She had friends from high school there, mostly women, who still thought of her as a star: "Stace was headed for the Olympics, y'know," they told strangers. Over time, she lived briefly and serially with three local men in their early thirties, men she called losers even when she was living with them—slow-talking guys with beards and ponytails, rusted-out pickup trucks, and large dogs with bandannas tied around their necks. Otherwise and most of the time, she lived alone.

Stacy had never tended bar for Noonan before this, and the place was a little rougher than she was used to. But she was experienced and had cultivated a set of open-faced, wise-guy ways and a laid-back manner that protected her from her male customers' presumptions. Which, in spite of her ways and manner, she needed: she was a shy, northcountry girl who, when it came to personal matters, volunteered very little about herself, not because she had secrets, but because there was so much about herself that she did not yet understand. She did understand, however, that the last thing she wanted or needed was a love affair with a man like Noonan— married, twenty years older than she, and her boss. She was seriously attracted to him, though. And not just sexually. Which was why she got caught off guard.

IT WAS late August, a Thursday, the afternoon of Lobster Night. The place was empty, and she and Noonan were standing hip to hip behind the bar, studying the lobster tank. Back in June, Noonan, who did all the cooking himself, had decided that he could attract a better class of clientele and simplify the menu at the same time if during the week he offered nightly specials, which he advertised on a chalkboard hung from the Family Restaurant sign outside. Monday became Mexican Night, with dollar margaritas and all the rice and refried beans you can eat. Tuesday was Liver 'n' Onions Night. Wednesday was Fresh Local Corn Night, although, until mid-August, the corn came, not from Adirondack gardens, but from southern New Jersey and Pennsylvania by way of the Grand Union supermarket in Lake Placid. And Thursday—when local folks rarely ate out and therefore needed something more than merely special—was designated Lobster Night. Weekends, he figured, took care of themselves.

Noonan had set his teenage son's unused tropical fish tank at the end of the bar, filled it with water, and arranged with the Albany wholesaler to stock the tank on his Monday runs to Lake Placid with a dozen live lobsters. All week, the lobsters rose and sank in the cloudy tank like dark thoughts. Usually, by Tuesday afternoon, the regulars at the bar had given the lobsters names like Marsh and Redeye and Honest Abe, local drinking, hunting, and bar-brawling legends, and had handicapped the order of their execution. In the villages around, Thursday quickly became everyone's favorite night for eating out, and soon Noonan was doubling his weekly order, jamming the fish tank, and making Lobster Night an almost merciful event for the poor crowded creatures.

"You ought to either get a bigger tank or else just don't buy so many of them," Stacy said.

Noonan laughed. "Stace," he said. "Compared to the cardboard boxes these guys've been in, the fish tank is lobster heaven. Four days of swimmin' in this, they're free range, practically." He draped a heavy hand across her shoulder and drummed her collarbone with a fingertip. "They don't know the difference, anyhow. They're dumber than fish, y'know."

"You don't know what they feel or don't feel. Maybe they spend the last few days before they die flipping out from being so confined. I sure would."

"Yeah, well, I don't go there, Stace. Trying to figure what lobsters feel, that's the road to vegetarianism. The road to vegans-ville."

She smiled at that. Like most of the Adirondack men she knew, Noonan was a dedicated, lifelong hunter—mainly of deer, but also of game birds and rabbits, which he fed to his family and sometimes put on the restaurant menu as well. He shot and trapped animals he didn't eat, too—foxes, coyotes, lynxes, even bear—and sold their pelts. Normally, this would disgust Stacy or at least seriously test her acceptance of Noonan's character. She wasn't noticeably softhearted when it came to animals or sentimental, but shooting and trapping creatures you didn't intend to eat made no sense to her. She was sure it was cruel and was almost ready to say it was sadistic.

In Noonan, though, it oddly attracted her, this cruelty. He was a tall, good-looking man in an awkward, rough-hewn way, large in the shoulders and arms, with a clean-shaven face and buzz-cut head one or two sizes too small for his body. It made him look boyish to her, and whenever he showed signs of cruelty—his relentless, not quite good-natured teasing of Gail, his regular waitress, and the LaPierre brothers, two high-school kids he hired in summers to wash dishes and bus tables—to her he seemed even more boy-ish than usual. It was all somehow innocent, she thought. It had the same strange, otherworldly innocence of the animals that he liked to kill. A man that manly, that *different* from a woman, can actually make you feel more womanly—as if you were of a different species. It freed you from having to compare yourself to him.

"You ever try that? Vegetarianism?" Noonan asked. He tapped the glass of the tank with a knuckle, as if signaling one of the lob-sters to come on over.

"Once. When I was seventeen. I kept it up for a while, two years, as a matter of fact. Till I busted up my leg and had to quit college." He knew the story of her accident; everyone knew it. She'd been a local hero before the break and had become a celebrity afterwards. "It's hard to keep being a vegetarian in the hospital, though. That's what got me off it."

"No shit. What got you *on* it?"

That's when she told him. "I was struck by lightning."

He looked at her. "Lightning! Jesus! Are you kidding me? How the hell did *that* happen?"

"The way it always happens, I guess. I was doing something else at the time. Going up the stairs to bed, actually, in my parents' house. It was in a thunderstorm, and I reached for the light switch on the wall, and, Bam! Just like they say, a bolt out of the blue."

"But it didn't kill you," Noonan tenderly observed.

"No. But it sure could've. You could say it *almost* killed me, though."

"But it didn't."

"Right. But it *almost* killed me. That's not the same as 'it didn't kill me.' If you know what I mean."

"Yeah, but you're okay now, right? No lingering aftereffects, I mean. Except, of course, for your brief flirtation with the veg-world." He squeezed the meat of her shoulder and smiled warmly.

She sighed. Then smiled back—she liked his touch—and tried again: "No, it really changed me. It did. A bolt of lightning went through my body and my brain, and I almost died from it, even though it only lasted a fraction of a second and then was over."

"But you're okay now, right?"

"Sure."

"So what was it like, getting hit by lightning?"

She hesitated a moment before answering. "Well, I thought I was shot. With a gun. Seriously. There was this loud noise, like an explosion, and when I woke up, I was lying at the bottom of the stairs, and Daddy and Mom were standing over me like I was dead, and I said, 'Who shot me, Daddy?' It really messed with my mind for a long time. I tried to find out if anybody else I knew had been struck by lightning, but nobody had. Although a few people said they knew someone or heard of someone who'd been hit and survived it. But nobody I ever met myself had been through it. I was the only person I knew who'd had this particular experience. Still am. It's strange, but when you're the only person you know who's gone through something that's changed you into a completely different person, for a while it's like you're on your own planet, like if you're a Vietnam vet and don't know anyone else who was in Vietnam, too."

"I can dig it," Noonan said somberly, although he himself had not been in Vietnam.

"You get used to it, though. And then it turns out to be like life. I mean, there's you, and there's everybody else. Only, unlike the way it is for everybody else, this happened to me in a flash, not over years and so slow you don't even realize how true it is. Know what I mean?"

"How true what is?"

"Well, just that there's you, and there's everybody else. And that's life."

"Sure, I can understand that." He turned away from the tank and looked into Stacy's blue eyes. "It's the same for me. Only with me it was on account of this goddamned bear. Did I ever tell you about the bear that tore my camp down?"

She said, "No, Noonan. You didn't."

"It's the same thing, like getting struck by lightning and afterwards feeling like you're a changed man." It was years ago, he said, when he was between marriages and drinking way too much and living in his hunting camp up on Baxter Mountain because his first wife had got the house in the divorce. He got drunk every night in town at the Spread Eagle or the Elm Tree or the old Dew Drop Inn, and afterwards, when he drove back to Baxter Mountain, he'd park his truck at the side of the road, because the trail was too rough even for a four-by-four, and walk the two miles through the woods to his camp. It was a windblown, one-room cabin with a sleeping loft and a woodstove, and one night, when he stumbled back from the village, the place had been trashed by a bear. "An adolescent male, I figured, it being springtime, who'd been kicked out of his own house and home. Not unlike myself. I had a certain sympathy for him, therefore. But he'd wrecked my cabin looking for food and had busted a window going out, and I knew he'd come back, so I had to take him down."

The next evening, Noonan blew out his kerosene lantern, climbed into the sleeping loft with a bottle of Jim Beam, his Winchester 30.06, and his flashlight, and waited. Around midnight, as if brushing away a cobweb, the bear tore off the sheet of polyurethane that Noonan had tacked over the broken window, crawled into the cabin, and made for the same cupboard he'd emptied the night before. Noonan, half-drunk by now, clicked on his flashlight, caught the startled bear in its beam, and fired, but only wounded him. Maddened with pain, the bear roared and stood on his hind legs, flinging his forelegs in the air right and left, and before Noonan could fire again, the animal had grabbed onto a timber that held up the loft and ripped it from its place, tearing out several other supporting timbers with it, until the entire cabin was collapsing around Noonan and the wounded bear. The structure was feeble anyhow, made of old cast-off boards tacked together in a hurry twenty years ago, never rebuilt, never renovated, and it came down upon Noonan's head with ease. The bear escaped into the night, but Noonan lay trapped under the fallen roof of the cabin, unable to move, his right arm broken, he assumed, and possibly several ribs. "That's when it happened," he said.

"What?" Stacy dipped a dozen beer mugs two at a time into cold water, pulled them out, and stuck them into the freezer to frost for later on.

"Just like you said. It changed my life, Stace."

"No kidding. How?" She refilled the salt shakers on the bar.

"Well, I stopped drinking, for one thing. That was a few years later, though. But I lay there all that night and most of the next day. Until this beautiful young woman out looking for her lost dog came wandering by. And, Stace" he said, his voice suddenly lowered, "I married her."

She put her fists on her hips and checked him out. "Seriously?"

He smiled. "Well, yeah, sort of. I'd actually known her a long time beforehand, and she'd visited me a few times at my camp, let us say. But, yeah, I did marry her . . . eventually. And we were very happy. For a while."

"Uh-huh. For a while."

Noonan nodded, smiled, winked. Then bumped her hip with his and said, "I gotta get the kitchen set up. We can pursue this later, Stace. If you want."

She didn't answer. She started slinging bottles of beer into the darkness of the cooler, and when she next looked up, he was gone, and a pair of road workers were coming through the door, hot and sunburned and thirsty.

THE DAY had been clear with wispy fantails of clouds in the east, promising a soft, late-summer sunset over the mountains for the folks dining out at Noonan's Family Restaurant. It was unusually busy that evening, even for Lobster Night. Depressed by a quarrel earlier with her pregnant daughter over money, Gail fell quickly behind in her orders and, after being yelled at, first by her hungry customers in the dining room and then by Noonan in the kitchen, where seven or eight bright red lobsters on their platters awaited pickup, she broke down and ran sobbing into the ladies' room. She came out, but only after Stacy went after her and promised to help in the dining room, where fifteen kids from three unrelated French Canadian families were banging their silverware rhythmically against their glasses. Back in the kitchen, halfway into the supper hour, Donny LaPierre threw down his dish towel and told Noonan to take his job and shove it, he didn't graduate high school just to get treated like an idiot for minimum wage. His younger brother Timmy, who would graduate the following year, high-fived Donny and said, "Whoa! Way cool, DL," and the two walked out together.

Noonan stood at the door and bellowed, "Don't even *think* about gettin' paid for this week!" and the boys gave him the finger from the parking lot and laughed and started hitching to Lake Placid.

Eventually, Gail and Stacy, between them, got everyone satisfactorily served, and the diners and their children quieted down, and order was restored, even in the kitchen—where Noonan, almost grateful for the chance to do it right, took over the dishwasher's job himself. At the bar, four bored, lonely regulars, men of habit, were drinking and smoking cigarettes and watching Montreal lose to the Mets on television. Stacy gave them a round on the house for their patience, and all four smiled and thanked her and resumed watching the game.

In the fish tank, the one last lobster bumped lazily against the glass. Stacy wiped down the bar and came to a slow stop by the tank. She leaned down and gazed into what she believed was one of the lobster's eyes—more of a greenish knob than an eyeball, anatomically absurd to her—and tried to imagine what the world of Noonan's Family Restaurant looked like through that knob and the thirty-gallon cell of cloudy water surrounding it and beyond that the lens of the algae-stained glass wall. It probably looks like an alien planet out here, she thought. Or incomprehensibly foreign, like some old-time Chinese movie, so you don't even know what the story's about, who's the good guy and who's the bad guy. Or maybe, instead of an actual place or thing, to a lobster it looks like only an idea out here. That scared her.

There must be some kind of trade-off among the senses, she reasoned, like with blind and deaf people. If one sense is weak, another must be strong, and vice versa. Lobsters, she figured, probably couldn't see very well, living as they did way at the dark bottom of the sea. To distinguish food from friend and friend from foe, they would need powerful senses of smell and hearing. She brought her face up close to the glass and almost touched it with her nose. The lobster bobbled and jiggled just beyond, as if struggling to use its weak eyes and tank-impaired hearing and olfactory senses to determine if Stacy was a thing that could eat it or breed with it or be eaten by it. So much in the life of any creature depends upon being able to identify the other creatures accurately, Stacy thought. In the tank, and out of it, too. And this poor beast, with only its ridiculous eyes to depend upon, was lost; was wholly, utterly, lost. She reached toward the lobster, as if to pat it, to comfort and reassure it that she would not eat it, and she could not breed with it, and would not make a decent meal for it, either.

Noonan's large hand dropped unseen from above, as if through dark water, and came to rest upon hers. She turned, startled, and there was his face a bare few inches away, his large, blood-shot, brown eyes and his porous, peach-colored skin with black whiskers popping through like lopped-off stalks, soft caves of nostrils, red lips, tobacco-stained teeth, wet tongue. She yanked her hand away and stepped back, bringing him into a more appropriate and safe focus, with the bar between them like a fence, keeping him out or her in, she wasn't sure, but it didn't matter, as long as they were on opposite sides of it.

"You scared me!" she said.

He leaned across the bar and smiled indulgently. Behind her, the men drank beer and watched baseball. She heard the crowd at the ballpark chitter in anticipation of the pitch. From the dining room came the low rumble of families distributing food among themselves and their hushed commentaries as they evaluated its quality and the size of their portions, praise and disappointment voiced equally low, as if both were gossip, and the clink of their forks and knives, gulps, chomps, an old man's sudden laugh, the snap of lobster claws and legs breaking.

"Stace, soon's you get the chance, c'mon out to the kitchen. There's something I want to tell you." He turned and abruptly strode to the dining room, spoke a moment to Gail, sympathetically offering to let her go home early, Stacy guessed, getting rid of witnesses, and gathered up a tub of dirty dishes left behind by Timmy LaPierre. As Noonan disappeared into the kitchen, he glanced over at Stacy, and though a stranger would have thought him expressionless, she saw him practically speaking with his face, saw him using it to say in a low, cold voice, "Stace, as soon as we're alone here tonight, I'm going to take you down."

She decided to force the issue, to go back to the kitchen right now, before Gail left, while there was still a fairly large number of people in the dining room and the four guys at the bar, and if Noonan said what she expected him to say and did what she expected him to do, then she would walk out the door just like the LaPierre boys had, take off in her car, the doors locked and windows up, the wheels spinning, kicking gravel, and squealing rubber as she left the parking lot and hit the road to Lake Placid.

Who the hell did he think he was, anyhow, coming on to her like that, him a married man, middle-aged, practically? Sure, she had been attracted to him from the first time she saw him, when he interviewed her for the job and had made her turn and turn again, while he sat there on the barstool and looked her over with genuine interest, almost with innocence, as if she were a bouquet of wildflowers he'd ordered for his wife. "Turn around, Stace. Let me see the other side." She had actually liked his suddenness, his fearless, impersonal way of telling her exactly what he wanted from her, instructing her to wear a tight, white T-shirt and black jeans or shorts to work in and to be friendly with the customers, especially the males, because he wanted return business, not one-night stands, and men will come back and stay late again and again, if they think the pretty girl behind the bar likes them personally. She had smiled like a coconspirator when he told her that and said, "No problema, Mr. Noonan."

"Hey, you can call me Charlie, or you can call me Noonan. Just don't call me at home, and never call me Mister. You're hired, Stace. Go change the dress and be back here by six."

But all that was before she told him about having been struck by lightning. Until then, she had thought it was safe to flirt with him, he was married, after all; and he was so unlike the losers she usually hooked up with that she had decided it was harmless as well as interesting to be attracted to him, nothing could come of it, anyhow; and wasn't it intelligent, after all, for a young woman to want a successful older man's attention and approval? Wasn't that how you learned about life and who you were?

Somehow, this afternoon everything had changed. She couldn't have said how it had changed or why, but everything was different now, especially between her and Noonan. It wasn't what he had done or not done or even anything he had said. It was what she had said.

A woman who has been struck by lightning is not like other people. Most of the time Stacy could forget that fact, could even forget what that horrible night had felt like, when she was only seventeen and thought that she had been shot in the head. But all she had to do was say the words, reestablish the fact, and the whole thing came back in full force—her astonishment, the physical and mental pain, and the long-lasting fear, even to today, that it would happen to her again. The only people who say lightning never strikes twice in the same place have never been struck once. Which was why she was so reluctant to speak of it.

But Noonan had charmed her into speaking of it, and all at once, there it was again, as if a glass wall had appeared between her and other people, Noonan especially. The man had no idea who she was. But that wasn't his fault. It was hers. She had misled him. She had misled herself. She checked the drinks of the customers at the bar. Then, to show Gail where she was headed, she pointedly flipped a wave across the dining room and walked back to the kitchen.

When she entered, Noonan was leaning against the edge of the sink, his large, bare arms folded across his chest, his head lowered: a man absorbing a sobering thought.

Stacy said, "What'd you want to tell me?" She stayed by the door, propping it open with her foot.

He shook his head as if waking from a nap. "What? Oh, Stace! Sorry, I was thinking. Actually, Stace, I was thinking about you."

"Me?"

"Yeah. Close the door. Come on in." He peered around her into the dining room. "Is Gail okay? She's not crying or anything anymore, is she?"

"No." Stacy let the door slide shut behind her. The exhaust fan chugged above the stove, and the dishwasher sloshed quietly next to the sink, tinkling the glasses and silverware inside and jiggling the plates. On a shelf by the rear door, a portable radio played country-and-western music at low volume—sweetly melancholic background music. There was a calming order and peacefulness to the kitchen, a low-key domesticity about it that, even though the room was as familiar to her as the kitchen of her rented A-frame, surprised Stacy. She felt guilty for having been so suspicious of Noonan and so quick to judge and condemn him. He was an ordinary man, that's all, a basically harmless and well-intended man; she had no reason to fear him. She liked his boyish good looks, didn't she? and enjoyed his smoky, baritone voice and unapologetic northcountry accent, and she was pleased and flattered by his sudden flashes of intimacy. "What did you want to tell me, Noonan?" she repeated, softly this time, invitingly.

He leaned forward, eyes twinkling, mischief on his mind, and looked right and left, as if not wishing to be overheard. "What do

you say we cook that last lobster and split it between ourselves?"
He gave her a broad smile and rubbed his hands together. "Don't
tell Gail. I'll boil and chill the sucker and break out the meat and
squeeze a little lime juice over it, and we'll eat it later, after we close
up, just the two of us. Maybe open a bottle of wine. Whaddaya say?"
He came up to her and put his arm around her shoulder and steered
her toward the door. "You go liberate the animal from its tank, and
I'll bring the kettle to a roiling boil, as they say."

"No." She shrugged out from under his arm.

"Huh? What d'you mean, 'No'?"

"Just that. No. I don't want a quiet little tête-à-tête out here with
you after we close. I don't want to make it with you, Noonan! You're
married, and I resent the way you act like it doesn't matter to you.
Or worse, me! You act like your being married doesn't matter to
me!"

Noonan was confused. "What the fuck? Who said anything
about making it? Jesus!"

She exhaled heavily. "I'm sorry," she said. "You're right. I don't
know what you've got in mind, Noonan. Really. I don't know why I
said all that. I'm just . . . I'm scared, I guess."

"You? Scared? Hah!" She was young and beautiful and healthy,
she was an athlete, a woman who could pick and choose among men
much younger, more available, better-looking, and richer than he.
What did she have to be scared of? Not him, that's for sure. "Man,
you are one screwed up broad, let me tell you." He shook his head
slowly in frustration and disgust. "Look, I don't give a shit you don't
want to join me in a whaddayacallit, a tête-à-tête. Suit yourself. But
I am gonna eat me some lobster anyhow. Alone!" he said, and he
sailed through the door into the dining room.

Stacy slowly crossed the kitchen to the back door, last used by
the LaPierre brothers on their way to the parking lot and road beyond. It was a screened door, and moths and mosquitoes batted
against it and swarmed around the yellow bulb on the wall outside.
On this side of the restaurant, it was already dark. Out back, where

the building faced west and the mountains, the sky was pale orange, with long, silver-gray clouds tinged with purple floating up high and blood red strips of cloud near the horizon. She decided she'd better return to the bar. There would be a few diners, she knew, who would want to take an after-dinner drink onto the deck and watch the sunset.

Before she could get out the door, Noonan, his face dark with confused anger, strode back into the kitchen, carrying the last lobster in his dripping wet hand. The lobster feebly waved its claws in the air, and its thick, armored tail curled in on itself and snapped back in a weak, hopeless attempt to push Noonan away. "Here, you do the honors!" Noonan said to Stacy and held the lobster up to her face. With his free hand, he flipped the gas jet below the slow-boiling lobster pot to high. "Have you ever boiled a live lobster, Stacy? Oh, it's a real turn-on." He leered, but it was an angry leer. "You're gonna love it, Stacy, especially the way it turns bright red as soon as you drop it into the boiling water. It won't sink right away, of course, because it's still alive and will struggle to climb out of the pot, just like you would. But even while it's trying to get out of the boiling water, it'll be turning red, and then it'll slow in its struggle, and you'll see it give up, and when that happens, it's dead and cooked and ready to be eaten. Yumm!"

He pushed the lobster at her, and it flailed its claws in her face, as if it were her hand clamped onto its back, not Noonan's. She didn't flinch or back away. She held her ground and looked into what passed for the animal's face, searching for an expression, some indicator of feeling or thought that would guide her own feelings and thoughts. But there was none, and when she realized there could be none, this pleased her, and she smiled.

"It's getting to you, right?" Noonan said. "I can tell, it's a turn-on for you, right?" He smiled back, almost forgiving her for having judged him so unfairly, and held the lobster over the pot of boiling water. Steam billowed around the creature's twisting body, and Stacy stared, transfixed, when from the dining room she heard the rising voices of the diners, their loud exclamations and calls to one another to come and see, hurry up, come and see the bear!

Stacy and Noonan looked at each other, she in puzzlement, he with irritated resignation. "Shit" he said. "This has got to be the worst goddamn night of my life!" He dropped the lobster into the empty sink and disappeared into the pantry, returning to the kitchen a few seconds later with a rifle cradled in his arm. "Sonofabitch, this's the last time that bastard gets into my trash!" he declared and made for the dining room, with Stacy following close behind.

She had never seen a black bear close-up, although it was not uncommon to come upon one in the neighborhood, especially in midsummer, when the mountain streams ran dry and sent the normally shy creatures to the lower slopes and valleys, where the humans lived. Once, when driving back to college after summer vacation, she thought she spotted a large bear crossing the road a hundred yards ahead of her, and at first had assumed it couldn't be a bear, it must be a huge dog, a Newfoundland, maybe, moving slowly, until it heard her car coming and broke into a swift, forward-tilted lope and disappeared into the brush as she passed. She wasn't sure she hadn't imagined it. She stopped the car and backed up to where the animal had entered the brush, but there was no sign of its ever having been there, no broken weeds or freshly fallen leaves, even.

This time, however, she intended to see the bear up close, if possible, and to know for sure that she did not imagine it. When she got to the dining room, everyone, Gail and the regulars from the bar included, was standing at the windows, gazing down at the yard in back where the land sloped away from the building, pointing and murmuring small noises of appreciation, except for the children, who were stilled by the sight, not so much frightened by the bear as in awe of it. The adults seemed to be mainly pleased by their good luck, for now they would have something novel to report to their friends and family when they returned home. This would become the night they saw the bear at Noonan's.

Then Stacy saw Noonan and several other diners, all of them men, out on the deck. They, too, stared down into the yard below the dining room and in the direction of the basement door, where Noonan stashed his garbage and trash barrels in a locked, wooden, latticework cage. The men were somber and intent, taut and almost trembling, like hunting dogs on point.

Stacy edged up to the window. Behind the distant mountains, the sun was gloriously setting. Its last golden rays splashed across the neatly mowed yard behind the restaurant and shone like a soft spotlight upon the thick, black-pelted body of the bear. It was a large, adult male, over six feet tall on his hind legs, methodically, calmly, ripping away the sides and top of the lattice cage, sending torn boards into the air like kindling sticks, working efficiently, but at the bear's own placid pace, as if he were utterly alone and there were no audience of men, women, and children staring down at him from the dining-room windows overhead, no small gang of men out on the deck watching him like a hunting party gathered on a cliff above a watering hole, and as if Noonan were not lifting his rifle to his shoulder, aiming it, and firing.

He shot once, and he missed the bear altogether. He fired a second time.

The bear was struck high in the back, and a tuft of black hair flew away from his chest where the bullet emerged, and the crowd in the dining room groaned and cried out, "He's shooting it! Oh, God, he's shooting it!" A woman screeched, "Tell him to stop!" and children began to bawl. A man yelled, "For God's sake, is he nuts?" Gail looked beseechingly at Stacy, who simply shook her head slowly from side to side, for she could do nothing to stop him now. No one could. People shouted and cried, a few sobbed, and children wailed, and Noonan fired a third time. He hit the bear in the shoulder, and the animal spun around, still standing, searching for the source of this terrible pain, not understanding that he should look up, that the man with the rifle, barely fifty yards away, was positioned out of sight above him and, because of his extreme anger, because of his refusal to be impersonal in this grisly business, was unable to kill him, and so he wounded the poor creature again and again, in the chest, in a paw, and shot him through the muzzle, until finally the bear dropped to all fours and, unsure in which direction to flee, tumbled first away from the restaurant downhill toward the woods, when, hit in the back, he turned and came lumbering, bleeding and in pain, straight toward the deck, where Noonan fired one last shot, hitting the bear this time in the center of his forehead, and the bear rolled forward, as if he had tripped, and died.

Rifle in hand, Noonan stomped in silence past the departing crowd, his gaze fixed rigidly on something inside, a target in his mind of a silhouetted bear. No one spoke to him or caught his eye as he passed; no one looked at his back, even, when he strode into the kitchen and the door swung shut behind him. The men who had stood with him on the deck outside were ashamed now to have been there. Making as little of it as possible, they joined their wives and friends, all of whom were lined up at the cash register, paying Gail, leaving cash on the table, or paying Stacy at the bar, and quickly heading for the parking lot and their cars. There were a few stunned, silent exceptions, older kids too shocked to cry or too proud, but most of the children were weeping, and some wailed, while the parents tried vainly to comfort them, to assure them that bears don't feel pain the same way humans do, and the man who shot the bear had to shoot it, because it was damaging his property, and not to worry, we will never come to this restaurant again, no matter what.

When everyone had left, Gail walked slowly from the dining room to the bar, where she took off her apron, folded it carefully, and set it on a barstool. "That's it for me," she said to Stacy. With trembling hands, she knocked a cigarette loose from the pack and lighted it and inhaled deeply. "Tell him he can mail me my pay," she said. "The fucker." She started for the door and then abruptly stopped. Without turning around, she said, "Stacy? Why the hell are you staying?"

"I'm not."

In a voice so low she seemed to be talking to herself, Gail said, "Yes, girl, you are." Then she was gone.

Stacy flipped off the lights in the bar and dining room one by one, unplugged the roadside sign, and locked the front entrance. When she pushed open the door to the kitchen, Noonan, standing at the far end of the long, stainless steel counter, looked up and scowled at her. He had cooked the last lobster and was eating it, eating it off the counter and with his hands: broken shells and the remains of its shattered carcass lay scattered in front him. He poked a forefinger into the thick, muscular tail and shoved a chunk of white meat out the other end, snatched it up, and popped it into his mouth.

"Eight fucking shots it took me!" he said, chewing. "That's what I get for stashing that goddamn pissant .22 here instead of laying in a real gun!" He waved contemptuously with the back of his hand at the rifle propped against the counter, and with his other hand pushed more lobster meat into his mouth. His face was red, and he was breathing rapidly and heavily. "I missed the first shot, y'know, only because I was so pissed off I didn't concentrate. But if I'd had a real gun, that second shot would've done the job fine. By God, tomorrow I'm bringing in my 30.06!" he declared.

Stacy picked up the .22 rifle and looked it over. She slid it into shooting position against her right shoulder and aimed along the barrel through the screened door and the fluttering cluster of moths to the outside lamp.

"Is it still loaded?" she asked.

"There's four rounds left, so don't fuck with it." He yanked the spindly legs off the underbelly of the lobster and sucked the meat from each and dropped the emptied tubes, one by one, onto the counter in front of him.

Slowly, Stacy brought the rifle around and aimed it at Noonan's skull. "Noonan," she said, and he turned.

"Yeah, sure."

She closed her eyes and pulled the trigger and heard the explosion, and when she opened her eyes, she saw in the middle of Noonan's broad, white forehead a dark hole the size of a dime, which instantly expanded to a quarter, and his large body jerked once as if electrocuted and flipped backwards, his astonished face gone from her sight altogether now, and she saw instead, the back of his head and a hole in it the size of a silver dollar. His body, like a large, rubberized sack of water, fell to the floor, spinning away from her as it descended and ending flat on its back, with Noonan's wide open eyes staring at the pot rack above the counter. Blood pumped from the hole in the rear of his skull onto the pale green linoleum and spread in a thickening, dark red puddle slowly toward her feet.

She lay the rifle on the counter beside the broken remains of the lobster and crossed to the stove, where the pot of water was still boiling and shut off the gas flame. Slowly, as if unsure of where she was, she looked around the room, then seemed to make a decision, and perched herself on a stool next to the walk-in refrigerator. She leaned her head back against the cool, stainless steel door and closed her eyes. Never in her life, never, had Stacy known the relief she felt at that moment. And not since the moment before she was struck by lightning had she known the freedom.

A RATTLING Ford pickup truck stopped beside the darkened roadside sign, and the LaPierre brothers, Donny and Timmy, leaped from the truck bed to the side of the road. "Hey, good luck with ol' Noonan, you little assholes!" the driver said, and he and a male passenger in the cab cackled with laughter. Two beery, expansive carpenters, they were cousins of the LaPierres, heading home to their wives and kids late from the bars of Lake Placid. They waved cheerfully to the boys and pulled away.

Donny and Timmy crunched across the gravel parking lot. The kitchen light and the lamp outside were still on, and when the boys were halfway across the lot, they saw Stacy through the screened door seated on the stool by the big walk-in fridge. She was asleep, it looked like, or maybe just bored out of her mind listening to one of Noonan's dumb hunting stories.

"You think he's screwing Stacy?" Timmy asked.

"C'mon, man. Stacy's a babe. And he's ancient, man," Donny said. "It's cool she's still here, though," he added. "She likes us, and he'll hire us back just to look good."

"I wouldn't mind a little of that myself."

"A little of what?"

"Stacy, man!"

Donny punched his younger brother on the shoulder. "Yeah, well, you'll hafta wait your turn, little fella!" He laughed. He waved away the swarming cloud of moths and pulled the screened door open. Timmy entered first, and Donny, hiding his fading grin behind his hand, followed.

THE HERMIT'S STORY

Rick Bass

Rick Bass is the author of many acclaimed works of fiction and nonfiction. His first short story collection, *The Watch*, set in Texas, won the PEN/Nelson Algren Award, and his 2002 collection, *The Hermit's Story*, was a *Los Angeles Times* Best Book of the Year. Bass's stories have also been awarded the Pushcart Prize and the O. Henry Award and have been collected in *The Best American Short Stories*.

An ice storm, following seven days of snow; the vast fields and drifts of snow turning to sheets of glazed ice that shine and shimmer blue in the moonlight, as if the color is being fabricated not by the bending and absorption of light but by some chemical reaction within the glossy ice; as if the source of all blueness lies somewhere up here in the north—the core of it beneath one of those frozen fields; as if blue is a thing that emerges, in some parts of the world, from the soil itself, after the sun goes down.

Blue creeping up fissures and cracks from depths of several hundred feet; blue working its way up through the gleaming ribs of Ann's buried dogs; blue trailing like smoke from the dogs' empty eye sockets and nostrils—blue rising as if from deep-dug chimneys until it reaches the surface and spreads laterally and becomes entombed, or trapped—but still alive, and drifting—within those moonstruck fields of ice.

Blue like a scent trapped in the ice, waiting for some soft release, some thawing, so that it can continue spreading.

It's Thanksgiving. Susan and I are over at Ann and Roger's house for dinner. The storm has knocked out all the power down in town—it's a clear, cold, starry night, and if you were to climb one of the mountains on snowshoes and look forty miles south toward where town lies, instead of seeing the usual small scatterings of light—like fallen stars, stars sunken to the bottom of a lake, but still glowing—you would see nothing but darkness—a bowl of silence and darkness in balance for once with the mountains up here, rather than opposing or complementing our darkness, our peace.

As it is, we do not climb up on snowshoes to look down at the dark town—the power lines dragged down by the clutches of ice—but can tell instead just by the way there is no faint glow over the mountains to the south that the power is out: that this Thanksgiving, life for those in town is the same as it always is for us in the mountains, and it is a good feeling, a familial one, coming on the holiday as it does—though doubtless too the townspeople are feeling less snug and cozy about it than we are.

We've got our lanterns and candles burning. A fire's going in the stove, as it will all winter long and into the spring. Ann's dogs are asleep in their straw nests, breathing in that same blue light that is being exhaled from the skeletons of their ancestors just beneath and all around them. There is the faint smell of cold-storage meat—slabs and slabs of it—coming from down in the basement, and we have just finished off an entire chocolate pie and three bottles of wine. Roger, who does not know how to read, is examining the empty bottles, trying to read some of the words on the labels. He recognizes the words *the* and *in* and *USA*. It may be that he will never learn to read—that he will be unable to—but we are in no rush; he has all of his life to accomplish this. I for one believe that he will learn.

Ann has a story for us. It's about a fellow named Gray Owl, up in Canada, who owned half a dozen speckled German shorthaired pointers and who hired Ann to train them all at once. It was twenty years ago, she says—her last good job.

She worked the dogs all summer and into the autumn, and finally had them ready for field trials. She took them back up to Gray Owl—way up in Saskatchewan—driving all day and night in her old truck, which was old even then, with dogs piled up on top of one another, sleeping and snoring: dogs on her lap, dogs on the seat, dogs on the floorboard.

Ann was taking the dogs up there to show Gray Owl how to work them: how to take advantage of their newfound talents. She could be a sculptor or some other kind of artist, in that she speaks of her work as if the dogs are rough blocks of stone whose internal form exists already and is waiting only to be chiseled free and then released by her, beautiful, into the world.

Basically, in six months the dogs had been transformed from gangling, bouncing puppies into six wonderful hunters, and she needed to show their owner which characteristics to nurture, which ones to discourage. With all dogs, Ann said, there was a tendency, upon their leaving her tutelage, for a kind of chitinous encrustation to set in, a sort of oxidation, upon the dogs leaving her hands and being returned to someone less knowledgeable and passionate, less committed than she. It was as if there were a tendency for the dogs' greatness to disappear back into the stone.

So she went up there to give both the dogs and Gray Owl a check-out session. She drove with the heater on and the windows down; the cold Canadian air was invigorating, cleaner. She could smell the scent of the fir and spruce, and the damp alder and cottonwood leaves beneath the many feet of snow. We laughed at her when she said it, but she told us that up in Canada she could taste the fish in the water as she drove alongside creeks and rivers.

She got to Gray Owl's around midnight. He had a little guest cabin but had not heated it for her, uncertain as to the day of her arrival, so she and the six dogs slept together on a cold mattress beneath mounds of elk hides: their last night together. She had brought a box of quail with which to work the dogs, and she built a small fire in the stove and set the box of quail next to it.

The quail muttered and cheeped all night and the stove popped and hissed and Ann and the dogs slept for twelve hours straight, as if submerged in another time, or as if everyone else in the world were submerged in time—and as if she and the dogs were pioneers, or survivors of some kind: upright and exploring the present, alive in the world, free of that strange chitin.

SHE SPENT a week up there, showing Gray Owl how his dogs worked. She said he scarcely recognized them afield, and that it took a few days just for him to get over his amazement. They worked the dogs both individually and, as Gray Owl came to understand and appreciate what Ann had crafted, in groups. They traveled across snowy hills on snowshoes, the sky the color of snow, so that often it was like moving through a dream, and, except for the rasp of the snowshoes beneath them and the pull of gravity, they might have believed they had ascended into some sky-place where all the world was snow.

They worked into the wind—north—whenever they could. Ann would carry birds in a pouch over her shoulder and from time to time would fling a startled bird out into that dreary, icy snow-scape. The quail would fly off with great haste, a dark feathered buzz bomb disappearing quickly into the teeth of cold, and then Gray Owl and Ann and the dog, or dogs, would go find it, following it by scent only, as always.

Snot icicles would be hanging from the dogs' nostrils. They would always find the bird. The dog, or dogs, would point it, Gray Owl or Ann would step forward and flush it, and the beleaguered bird would leap into the sky again, and once more they would push on after it, pursuing that bird toward the horizon as if driving it with a whip. Whenever the bird wheeled and flew downwind, they'd quarter away from it, then get a mile or so downwind from it and push it back north.

When the quail finally became too exhausted to fly, Ann would pick it up from beneath the dogs' noses as they held point staunchly, put the tired bird in her game bag, and replace it with a fresh one, and off they'd go again. They carried their lunch in Gray Owl's day-pack, as well as emergency supplies—a tent and some dry clothes—in case they should become lost, and around noon each day (they could rarely see the sun, only an eternal ice-white haze, so that they relied instead only on their internal rhythms) they would stop and make a pot of tea on the sputtering little gas stove. Sometimes one or two of the quail would die from exposure, and they would cook that on the stove and eat it out there in the tundra, tossing the feathers up into the wind as if to launch one more flight, and feeding the head, guts, and feet to the dogs.

Seen from above, their tracks might have seemed aimless and wandering rather than with the purpose, the focus that was burning hot in both their and the dogs' hearts. Perhaps someone viewing the tracks could have discerned the pattern, or perhaps not, but it did not matter, for their tracks—the patterns, direction, and tracing of them—were obscured by the drifting snow, sometimes within minutes after they were laid down.

Toward the end of the week, Ann said, they were finally running all six dogs at once, like a herd of silent wild horses through all that snow, and as she would be going home the next day there was no need to conserve any of the birds she had brought, and she was turning them loose several at a time: birds flying in all directions; the dogs, as ever, tracking them to the ends of the earth.

It was almost a whiteout that last day, and it was hard to keep track of all the dogs. Ann was sweating from the exertion as well as the tension of trying to keep an eye on, and evaluate each dog, and the sweat was freezing on her as if she were developing an ice skin. She jokingly told Gray Owl that next time she was going to try to find a client who lived in Arizona, or even South America. Gray Owl smiled and then told her that they were lost, but no matter, the storm would clear in a day or two.

They knew it was getting near dusk—there was a faint dulling to the sheer whiteness, a kind of increasing heaviness in the air, a new density to the faint light around them—and the dogs slipped in and out of sight, working just at the edges of their vision.

The temperature was dropping as the north wind increased— "No question about which way south is," Gray Owl said, "so we'll turn around and walk south for three hours, and if we don't find a road, we'll make camp"—and now the dogs were coming back with frozen quail held gingerly in their mouths, for once the birds were dead, the dogs were allowed to retrieve them, though the dogs must have been puzzled that there had been no shots. Ann said she fired a few rounds of the cap pistol into the air to make the dogs think she had hit those birds. Surely they believed she was a goddess.

They turned and headed south—Ann with a bag of frozen birds over her shoulder, and the dogs, knowing that the hunt was over now, once again like a team of horses in harness, though wild and prancy.

After an hour of increasing discomfort—Ann's and Gray Owl's hands and feet numb, and ice beginning to form on the dogs' paws, so that the dogs were having to high-step—they came in day's last light to the edge of a wide clearing: a terrain that was remarkable and soothing for its lack of hills. It was a frozen lake, which meant— said Gray Owl—they had drifted west (or perhaps east) by as much as ten miles.

Ann said that Gray Owl looked tired and old and guilty, as would any host who had caused his guest some unasked-for inconvenience. They knelt down and began massaging the dogs' paws and then lit the little stove and held each dog's foot, one at a time, over the tiny blue flame to help it thaw out.

Gray Owl walked out to the edge of the lake ice and kicked at it with his foot, hoping to find fresh water beneath for the dogs; if they ate too much snow, especially after working so hard, they'd get violent diarrhea and might then become too weak to continue home the next day, or the next, or whenever the storm quit.

Ann said that she had barely been able to see Gray Owl's outline through the swirling snow, even though he was less than twenty yards away. He kicked once at the sheet of ice, the vast plate of it, with his heel, then disappeared below the ice.

Ann wanted to believe that she had blinked and lost sight of him, or that a gust of snow had swept past and hidden him, but it had been too fast, too total: she knew that the lake had swallowed him. She was sorry for Gray Owl, she said, and worried for his dogs—afraid they would try to follow his scent down into the icy lake and be lost as well—but what she had been most upset about, she said—to be perfectly honest—was that Gray Owl had been wearing the little daypack with the tent and emergency rations. She had it in her mind to try to save Gray Owl, and to try to keep the dogs from going through the ice, but if he drowned, she was going to have to figure out how to try to get that daypack off of the drowned man and set up the wet tent in the blizzard on the snowy prairie and then crawl inside and survive. She would have to go into the water naked, so that when she came back out—if she came back out—she would have dry clothes to put on.

The dogs came galloping up, seeming as large as deer or elk in that dim landscape against which there was nothing else to give the viewer a perspective, and Ann whoaed them right at the lake's edge, where they stopped immediately, as if they had suddenly been cast with a sheet of ice.

Ann knew the dogs would stay there forever, or until she released them, and it troubled her to think that if she drowned, they too would die—that they would stand there motionless, as she had commanded them, for as long as they could, until at some point—days later, perhaps—they would lie down, trembling with exhaustion—they might lick at some snow, for moisture—but that then the snows would cover them, and still they would remain there, chins resting on their front paws, staring straight ahead and unseeing into the storm, wondering where the scent of her had gone.

Ann eased out onto the ice. She followed the tracks until she came to the jagged hole in the ice through which Gray Owl had plunged. She was almost half again lighter than he, but she could feel the ice crackling beneath her own feet. It sounded different, too, in a way she could not place—it did not have the squeaky, percussive resonance of the lake-ice back home—and she wondered if Canadian ice froze differently or just sounded different.

She got down on all fours and crept closer to the hole. It was right at dusk. She peered down into the hole and dimly saw Gray Owl standing down there, waving his arms at her. He did not appear to be swimming. Slowly, she took one glove off and eased her bare hand down into the hole. She could find no water, and, tentatively, she reached deeper.

Gray Owl's hand found hers and he pulled her down in. Ice broke as she fell, but he caught her in his arms. She could smell the wood smoke in his jacket from the alder he burned in his cabin. There was no water at all, and it was warm beneath the ice.

"This happens a lot more than people realize," he said. "It's not really a phenomenon; it's just what happens. A cold snap comes in October, freezes a skin of ice over the lake—it's got to be a shallow one, almost a marsh. Then a snowfall comes, insulating the ice. The lake drains in fall and winter—percolates down through the soil"—he stamped the spongy ground beneath them—"but the ice up top remains. And nobody ever knows any different. People look out at the surface and think, *Aha, a frozen lake.*" Gray Owl laughed.

"Did you know it would be like this?" Ann asked.

"No," he said. "I was looking for water. I just got lucky."

Ann walked back to shore beneath the ice to fetch her stove and to release the dogs from their whoa command. The dry lake was only about eight feet deep, but it grew shallow quickly closer to shore, so that Ann had to crouch to keep from bumping her head on the overhead ice, and then crawl; and then there was only space to wriggle, and to emerge she had to break the ice above her by bumping and then battering it with her head and elbows, struggling like some embryonic hatchling; and when she stood up, waist-deep amid sparkling shards of ice—it was nighttime now—the dogs barked ferociously at her, but they remained where she had ordered them. She was surprised at how far off course she was when she climbed out; she had traveled only twenty feet, but already the dogs were twice that far away from her. She knew humans had a poorly evolved, almost nonexistent sense of direction, but this error—over such a short distance—shocked her. It was as if there were in us a thing—an impulse, a catalyst—that denies our ever going straight to another thing. Like dogs working left and right into the wind, she thought, before converging on the scent.

Except that the dogs would not get lost, while she could easily imagine herself and Gray Owl getting lost beneath the lake, walking in circles forever, unable to find even the simplest of things: the shore.

She gathered the stove and dogs. She was tempted to try to go back in the way she had come out—it seemed so easy—but she considered the consequences of getting lost in the other direction, and instead followed her original tracks out to where Gray Owl had first dropped through the ice. It was true night now, and the blizzard was still blowing hard, plastering snow and ice around her face like a mask. The dogs did not want to go down into the hole, so she lowered them to Gray Owl and then climbed gratefully back down into the warmth herself.

The air was a thing of its own—recognizable as air, and breathable as such, but with a taste and odor, an essence, unlike any other air they'd ever breathed. It had a different density to it, so that smaller, shallower breaths were required; there was very much the feeling that if they breathed in too much of the strange, dense air, they would drown.

They wanted to explore the lake, and were thirsty, but it felt like a victory simply to be warm—or rather, not cold—and they were so exhausted that instead they made pallets out of the dead marsh grass that rustled around their ankles, and they slept curled up on the tiniest of hammocks, to keep from getting damp in the pockets and puddles of water that still lingered here and there.

All eight of them slept as if in a nest, heads and arms draped across other ribs and hips; and it was, said Ann, the best and deepest sleep she'd ever had—the sleep of hounds, the sleep of childhood. How long they slept, she never knew, for she wasn't sure, later, how much of their subsequent time they spent wandering beneath the lake, and then up on the prairie, homeward again, but when they awoke, it was still night, or night once more, and clearing, with bright stars visible through the porthole, their point of embarkation; and even from beneath the ice, in certain places where, for whatever reasons—temperature, oxygen content, wind scour—the ice was clear rather than glazed, they could see the spangling of stars, though more dimly; and strangely, rather than seeming to distance them from the stars, this phenomenon seemed to pull them closer, as if they were up in the stars, traveling the Milky Way, or as if the stars were embedded in the ice.

It was very cold outside—up above—and there was a steady stream, a current like a river, of the night's colder, heavier air plunging down through their porthole—as if trying to fill the empty lake with that frozen air—but there was also the hot muck of the earth's massive respirations breathing out warmth and being trapped and protected beneath that ice, so that there were warm currents doing battle with the lone cold current.

The result was that it was breezy down there, and the dogs' noses twitched in their sleep as the images brought by these scents painted themselves across their sleeping brains in the language we call dreams but which, for the dogs, was reality: the scent of an owl *real*, not a dream; the scent of bear, cattail, willow, loon, *real*, even though they were sleeping, and even though those things were not visible, only over the next horizon.

The ice was contracting, groaning and cracking and squeaking up tighter, shrinking beneath the great cold—a concussive, grinding sound, as if giants were walking across the ice above—and it was this sound that awakened them. They snuggled in warmer among the rattly dried yellowing grasses and listened to the tremendous clashings, as if they were safe beneath the sea and were watching waves of starlight sweeping across their hiding place; or as if they were in some place, some position, where they could watch mountains being born.

After a while the moon came up and washed out the stars. The light was blue and silver and seemed, Ann said, to be like a living thing. It filled the sheet of ice just above their heads with a shimmering cobalt light, which again rippled as if the ice were moving, rather than the earth itself, with the moon tracking it—and like deer drawn by gravity getting up in the night to feed for an hour or so before settling back in, Gray Owl and Ann and the dogs rose from their nests of straw and began to travel.

"You didn't—you know—*engage?*" Susan asks, a little mischievously.

Ann shakes her head. "It was too cold," she says.

"But you would have, if it hadn't been so cold, right?" Susan asks, and Ann shrugs.

"He was an old man—in his fifties—he seemed old to me then, and the dogs were around. But yeah, there was something about it that made me think of . . . those things," she says, careful and precise as ever.

They walked a long way, Ann continues, eager to change the subject. The air was damp down there, and whenever they'd get chilled, they'd stop and make a little fire out of a bundle of dry cattails. There were little pockets and puddles of swamp gas pooled in place, and sometimes a spark from the cattails would ignite one of those, and those little pockets of gas would light up like when you toss gas on a fire—explosions of brilliance, like flashbulbs, marsh pockets igniting like falling dominoes, or like children playing hopscotch—until a large enough flash-pocket was reached—sometimes thirty or forty yards away—that the puff of flame would blow a chimney-hole through the ice, venting the other pockets, and the fires would crackle out, the scent of grass smoke sweet in their lungs, and they could feel gusts of warmth from the little flickering fires, and currents of the colder, heavier air sliding down through the new vent-holes and pooling around their ankles. The moon-light would strafe down through those rents in the ice, and shards of moon-ice would be glittering and spinning like diamond-motes in those newly vented columns of moonlight; and they pushed on, still lost, but so alive.

The small explosions were fun, but they frightened the dogs, so Ann and Gray Owl lit twisted bundles of cattails and used them for torches to light their way, rather than building warming fires, though occasionally they would still pass though a pocket of meth-ane and a stray ember would fall from their torches, and the whole chain of fire and light would begin again, culminating once more with a vent-hole being blown open and shards of glittering ice tum-bling down into their lair . . .

What would it have looked like, seen from above—the orange blurrings of their wandering trail beneath the ice; and what would the sheet of lake-ice itself have looked like that night—throbbing with ice-bound, subterranean blue and orange light of moon and fire? But again, there was no one to view the spectacle: only the travelers themselves, and they had no perspective, no vantage from which to view or judge themselves. They were simply pushing on from one fire to the next, carrying their tiny torches.

They knew they were getting near a shore—the southern shore, they hoped, as they followed the glazed moon's lure above—when the dogs began to encounter shore birds that had somehow found their way beneath the ice through small fissures and rifts and were taking refuge in the cattails. Small winter birds—juncos, nut-hatches, chickadees—skittered away from the smoky approach of their torches; only a few late-migrating (or winter-trapped) snipe held tight and steadfast; and the dogs began to race ahead of Gray Owl and Ann, working these familiar scents—blue and silver ghost-shadows of dog muscle weaving ahead through slants of moonlight.

The dogs emitted the odor of adrenaline when they worked, Ann said—a scent like damp, fresh-cut green hay—and with nowhere to vent, the odor was dense and thick around them, so that Ann wondered if it too might be flammable, like the methane—if in the dogs' passions they might literally immolate themselves.

They followed the dogs closely with their torches. The ceiling was low—about eight feet—so that the tips of their torches' flames seared the ice above them, leaving a drip behind them and transforming the milky, almost opaque cobalt and orange ice behind them, wherever they passed, into wandering ribbons of clear ice, translucent to the sky—a script of flame, or buried flame, ice-bound flame—and they hurried to keep up with the dogs.

Now the dogs had the snipe surrounded, as Ann told it, and one by one the dogs went on point, each dog freezing as it pointed to the birds' hiding places, and Gray Owl moved in to flush the birds, which launched themselves with vigor against the roof of the ice above, fluttering like bats; but the snipe were too small, not powerful enough to break through those frozen four inches of water (though they could fly four thousand miles to South America each year and then back to Canada six months later—is freedom a lateral component, or a vertical one?), and as Gray Owl kicked at the clumps of frost-bent cattails where the snipe were hiding and they burst into flight, only to hit their heads on the ice above them, they came tumbling back down, raining limp and unconscious back to their soft grassy nests.

The dogs began retrieving them, carrying them gingerly, delicately—not caring for the taste of snipe, which ate only earthworms—and Ann and Gray Owl gathered the tiny birds from the dogs, placed them in their pockets, and continued on to the shore, chasing that moon, the ceiling lowering to six feet, then four then to a crawlspace, and after they had bashed their way out and stepped back out into the frigid air, they tucked the still-unconscious snipe into little crooks in branches, up against the trunks of trees and off the ground, out of harm's way, and passed on, south—as if late in their own migration—while the snipe rested, warm and terrified and heart-fluttering, but saved, for now, against the trunks of those trees.

Long after Ann and Gray Owl and the pack of dogs had passed through, the birds would awaken, their bright, dark eyes luminous in the moonlight, and the first sight they would see would be the frozen marsh before them, with its chain of still-steaming vent-holes stretching back across all the way to the other shore. Perhaps these were birds that had been unable to migrate owing to injuries, or some genetic absence. Perhaps they had tried to migrate in the past but had found either their winter habitat destroyed or the path so fragmented and fraught with danger that it made more sense—to these few birds—to ignore the tuggings of the stars and seasons and instead to try to carve out new lives, new ways of being, even in such a stark and severe landscape: or rather, in a stark and severe period—knowing that lushness and bounty were still retained with that landscape, that it was only a phase, that better days would come. That in fact (the snipe knowing these things with their blood, ten million years in the world) the austere times were the very thing, the very imbalance, that would summon the resurrection of that frozen richness within the soil—if indeed that richness, that magic, that hope, did still exist beneath the ice and snow. Spring would come like its own green fire, if only the injured ones could hold on.

And what would the snipe think or remember, upon reawakening and finding themselves still in that desolate position, desolate place and time, but still alive, and with hope?

Would it seem to them that a thing like grace had passed through, as they slept—that a slender winding river of it had passed through and rewarded them for their faith and endurance?

Believing, stubbornly, that that green land beneath them would blossom once more. Maybe not soon; but again.

If the snipe survived, they would be among the first to see it. Perhaps they believed that the pack of dogs, and Gray Owl's and Ann's advancing torches, had only been one of winter's dreams. Even with the proof—the scribings—of grace's passage before them—the vent-holes still steaming—perhaps they believed it was a dream.

Gray Owl, Ann, and the dogs headed south for half a day until they reached the snow-scoured road on which they'd parked. The road looked different, Ann said, buried beneath snowdrifts, and they didn't know whether to turn east or west. The dogs chose west, and Gray Owl and Ann followed them. Two hours later they were back at their truck, and that night they were back at Gray Owl's cabin; by the next night Ann was home again.

She says that even now she still sometimes has dreams about being beneath the ice—about living beneath the ice—and that it seems to her as if she was down there for much longer than a day and a night; that instead she might have been gone for years.

It was twenty years ago, when it happened. Gray Owl has since died, and all those dogs are dead now, too. She is the only one who still carries—in the flesh, at any rate—the memory of that passage.

Ann would never discuss such a thing, but I suspect that it, that one day and night, helped give her a model for what things were like for her dogs when they were hunting and when they went on point: how the world must have appeared to them when they were in that trance, that blue zone, where the odors of things wrote their images across the dogs' hot brainpans. A zone where sight, and the appearance of things—*surfaces*—disappeared, and where instead their essence—the heat molecules of scent—was revealed, illuminated, circumscribed, possessed.

I suspect that she holds that knowledge—the memory of that one day and night—especially since she is now the sole possessor—as tightly, and securely, as one might clench some bright small gem in one's fist: not a gem given to one by some favored or beloved individual but, even more valuable, some gem found while out on a walk—perhaps by happenstance, or perhaps by some unavoidable rhythm of fate—and hence containing great magic, great strength.

Such is the nature of the kinds of people living, scattered here and there, in this valley.

1-900

Richard Bausch

Richard Bausch is the author of ten novels and seven volumes of short stories. His work has appeared in *The New Yorker, The Atlantic, Esquire, Playboy, GQ, Harper's,* and other publications, and has been featured in numerous best-of collections, including *The O. Henry Prize Stories, The Best American Short Stories,* and *New Stories from the South.* In 2004 he won the PEN/Malamud Award for Short Fiction.

If you are calling to talk to one of us hot girls, are using a *Touch-Tone* phone, and you have your credit information handy, please press 1 now. We can hardly wait to talk to you.

. . .

Please punch in your credit card number, followed by the pound key.

. . .

Don't go anywhere because we're desperate for your hot love.

. . .

This is Marilyn, and I'm soooo hot to give you my—
Excuse me, Marilyn?
Oh, yes, baby, let me have your big—
My name's John, okay?

. . .

Okay?
You sound nervous, John. You shouldn't be. I'm gonna do whatever you want me to, baby, and it's gonna be so *hot.*

Well, I am a little nervous.

There's nothing to be nervous *about*, honey. I'm lying here naked, just thinking of you, John. That's what I'm doing right now. And I'm thinking of taking your—

Uh, listen, um, Marilyn—wait. *Wait*. Please. Do you think we— could we—is there any way we could talk about some other things first? I mean, I wonder if we could kind of get to know each other a little. Or anyway *seem* to get to know each other. Like, can we—talk around a little? You know, just generally? I've come to the conclusion that I need something a little less blunt right-away-into-it kind of thing, you know, and as long as I'm paying for the minutes, I'd think that would be all right. That is all right—right? Is that all right?

John, are you gonna talk, honey, or do you want me to?

I thought we'd both talk. You know, have a—have a conversation about things in general kind of thing, and, um, lead up to it. That appears to be what I require right now.

Oh, but I'm all *ready* for you, honey—

I know but *I'm* not ready yet. I need to talk a little.

. . .

Is your real name Marilyn?

. . .

Hello?

. . .

I mean, you know *my* real name.

Is this a crank call?

No, please. Don't hang up. I'd really like to talk to you. I'm not ugly or anything, or weird. I'm five feet eleven inches tall and I weigh a hundred sixty pounds in my stocking feet, as my father used to say, and I have dark blond hair—dishwater blond, I believe they call it. And I'm not saving newspaper articles about assassinations, or collecting body parts, you know. None of that, and I don't keep files on famous people and I'm not a disgruntled postal worker or anything at all like that—

Whoa, honey, slow down.

—I'm thirty-two and married, though my wife and I are

separated. We have two kids, a boy and a girl, twelve and nine—

Let me get a word in, baby. Don't you want me to talk? Is this your idea of conversation?

I'm sorry.

Honey, I want to tell you what I'm *doing* right now while I think of you, and listen to your sexy sweet voice—

Right, but I wanted to talk a little first. Converse a little.

Really.

Do you—do you have any children?

I'm sorry, baby, I can't answer that. Ask me about what I'm *doing* right now.

Well—first. I was only—I'm curious. I mean I wondered how this works.

But I want to get it *on* with you, baby. Come on, don't make me wait. I'm touching something right now, thinking of you.

Look, I really would like it if we just talk a little before we get intimate.

Intimate. You're kidding, right?

Well, you know what I mean.

. . .

I'm still paying for it, right?

Sure, that's right—it's your dime, baby.

So, Marilyn—where'd you go to school?

. . .

Hello?

You're kidding.

Can you tell me where you went to school?

Um, around.

More than one school? College?

. . .

Hello? Was it college?

John, I really can't get that personal.

A second ago you were telling me about touching yourself. I just want to know if you went to college.

Okay, it's been nice talking to you, sexy—

Oh, don't hang up. Really. I'm paying for the call. I just asked if you went to college. I have to feel like I know you at least a little bit before we get to the other stuff.

Look, sweetie, this isn't a date or anything.

But I'd like to feel that it's something close to it. Isn't this supposed to be about what I need, and am willing to pay for? What's the difference if it's all just talking, right? I mean that's not too much to ask for a dollar a minute, is it?

It's ninety-nine cents a minute.

Well, but that's a dollar. That's a thing my wife and I used to fight about. She'd look at something in the store and see eight dollars and ninety-nine cents and she'd think it was eight dollars. I had to remind her about it a lot. My wife and money, that was like a land-war-in-Asia kind of thing.

Excuse me?

We kept throwing more money at everything because we couldn't believe what we'd already wasted was wasted. That had a lot to do with why we kept on going in Vietnam. We couldn't believe we'd wasted so much life. We couldn't let it mean nothing. You—you get the point of that?

You want to talk about fucking Vietnam? Are you a vet or something?

I'm too young to be a vet. I'm interested in history, kind of thing. You like history, Marilyn?

Uh, no. I'm not into that.

My wife is, big time. As in the history of men keeping women down. The whole oppressive history of women-getting-screwed-by-men kind of thing. That's my wife.

Is that why you're separated?

We're separated because she decided I wasn't with the program anymore. Which was true, I guess. The program was basically about the improvement of John T. Bailey, E-S-Q. The perfection of that item, you might say, by a series of continual reminders of everything wrong with him.

It's kind of pushy, isn't it, reminding somebody about their faults.

I wouldn't call it pushy, no. Not exactly. The fact was, there is what you might call a lot of area for improvement. But it used to irritate me, I'll admit that.

And you want to talk about it?

Well, we could, I suppose.

Like I said, it's your dime.

Are *you* married?

No.

How old are you?

Look, honey, what did you call us for? This is *phone sex*.

But couldn't it be, like, phone *friendship* for a little while? Just a minute or two?

Man, I keep thinking this is some sort of prank or something.

It's not. I promise it's not. I'm not the type who plays pranks. I don't even think it's funny when other people do it.

Well.

I went to college. I went to West Texas State and majored in history. I didn't learn much. Don't get involved in a land war in Asia. Where did you go?

High school. I'm putting myself through college, now, and I can talk you through a heavenly experience, too. I can make you *hot*, and bring you off like a rocket.

Why are you going to college? I mean what do you hope to get out of it?

An education.

Is that just to get a better job, or pursue a career, or do you desire to be educated as in somebody who possesses a knowledge of the arts of civilization?

You talk funny, John.

Are you in search of knowledge and cultivation of your spirit?

All that.

Really.

Sure, why not?

You want part of the American Dream.

Okay.

But what is the American Dream, anyway? Going to art galleries, or owning-a-big-car-and-having-a-house-with-a-swimming-pool kind of thing? I mean, I think the American Dream is getting on television and being famous.

Is that what you want, John?

No, I'm saying that's the American Dream. I've got a little boy who wants to grow up to be famous. That's what he says he wants. He doesn't have the slightest idea how or why or what he'll end up doing, and none of that matters to him. He just wants to be famous. He wants everybody to know his name. That's his big dream. I think there's a lot of people out there like my son, only these're grown people.

I don't want to be famous.

Are you seeing anyone?

. . .

It's just a harmless question, Marilyn.

I'm with *you* now, honey.

But are you seeing anyone?

How are you going to get anything out of it if I talk about who I'm seeing, John?

Well, are you?

Okay, sure. Yes. I am.

Does he know you do this?

Maybe. Look, I think we ought to get down to something soon, baby. I'm so *hot* for you.

My wife didn't play around on me or anything, and I was faithful to her. You've probably figured out that I've never called one of these 900 lines before. I guess that's pretty evident. We had a good life, Kate and me. Her name is Kate. She likes sex, too. We both like it. I'm not one of those types who's never had any loving before, you know? But something got between us. A—a lethargy.

Lethargy.

It means—

I know what it means, honey. Are you telling me you couldn't get it up?

Oh, hell no. No, we really didn't have any trouble that way. Not any. We excited each other. She's really very adventurous in bed. We were great that way. But she's a better person than I am, that's pretty clear. We lived a little selfishly, too. I think that's what did us in. But we had fun in bed.

Tell me what she'd say to you, honey. I can make you feel her.

No, that isn't it. I'm telling you this to get to know you. You know a little about me. My wife and I hit this—this lethargic place. I should say straight out that I tend to excess, I admit that. I have a habit of getting a little too much to drink now and then, and I used to do some other kinds of substances. She did, too. We had a lot of easy money and we were a pair, let me tell you. She used to keep a big brick of cocaine in her dresser drawer.

Yikes.

It's true. But most of that is over, and we'd mostly got past all that, and I thought we were doing fine—especially, sexually, as I said. We were interested in each other for sex, you see, but there were these other areas—

What other area is there, when you get down to it, lover?

Well, just—you know—at the level of talk. I found that her voice irritated me.

And what was her problem with you?

Oh, lots of things. Lots of things that it isn't anybody's business to know.

. . .

I'm sorry, that didn't sound right. I don't mean anything by it.

Man, this is your money.

You ever find that somebody's *voice* gets on your nerves, Marilyn?

I guess.

Does my voice irritate you?

No.

You have to say that, though, right?

I don't *have* to say anything, lover.

How old are you?

Oh, baby, I'm old enough. And young enough. How old are you?

I'm thirty-two. I already said. So, now, what about you?

. . .

Hello? Tell me—come on, you can do that.

We're not allowed to tell our age, lover. I'm of age. I'm old enough for anything you want.

I do like the sound of your voice. You have a very lovely voice.

Oh, I haven't even *started*, honey. You don't seem to want to give me a chance.

Yes, but isn't it a relief not to have to go through the spiel?

Excuse me?

The routine. All that moaning and groaning and sex-detail-talk kind of thing to get some poor lonely stranger off over long distance. I'm in South Carolina, for instance. Where are you?

Close as your ear.

But where—really?

Washington, D.C.

Are you in a room with other girls talking on phones? I'm picturing you sitting at one of those consoles with all the plugs and the lines, and ear phones on, like an operator.

No, honey—I'm home in bed. I really am. And I'm naked, and I've go my hand on my—

How many calls like this do you handle a day?

I've *never* handled a call like this. I mean I *am* new, and maybe these people take calls like this every day, but it hasn't happened to me yet.

I really don't want to cause you any discomfort.

I'm *fine*. Are *you* all right?

Well, that's a question, there, Marilyn. That might take a little time to answer.

Do you want me to listen, honey?

You said *these people* a second ago. So there are others there with you, taking the calls?

I meant the other girls who work for this service. Look, this is a *service*.

I'm sorry. Really, I'm—uh, I'm curious. I wanted to talk. I mean I *do* want to get to the sex, too, you know, but I just—since it can't matter to you, really, and might even be a bit of a relief from the types you usually get, and you're still getting paid the going rate.

. . .

Nobody's ever asked to talk to you—just as yourself first?

Nobody yet.

I'm the first.

What did you mean about the types I usually get?

Well, what type of person makes this kind of call?

Wouldn't *you* be in a better position to answer that, John?

I've never made this type of call before.

Why do I get the feeling you make this kind of call every day?

No, really. This is a first for me.

Well, I'm not interested in being your friend or listening to your troubles, you know, John? Usually I do most of the talking on these calls. And I wouldn't want to listen to people tell their troubles all day for any amount of money. That does not strike me as my idea of having a good time. That does not sound like a good time at all to me.

I didn't mean to complain, actually. Just to be honest, so you could know a little about me and feel that it's all right to say a few small things about yourself and then we would know each other, and when we got down to the sex it would be so much more like the real thing.

The real—what?

Don't be mad, Marilyn. Don't you get a lot of guys who are curious about it?

Not all that many, no. It's pretty straightforward usually. Some heavy breathing and I say a few things and it's over.

Do you get perverts?

. . .

I guess that wasn't a fair question.

Look, are you one of those reporter types looking for a story?

No, I'm a separated father of two living alone in an apartment with most of the furniture gone and a lot of disarray I don't need. My wife and kids are hundreds of miles north, with the lion's share of the furniture, and last night I went out and got stinking and came back here and I've been lying here thinking about calling my sister, who is a perfect shit and a prig, and I decided instead to call you.

To unload your troubles.

No, and I'm sorry I said anything about it. If that bothers you I won't say another thing about it. I'm just trying to have a real conversation before we get going on things. I need that, or I can't get any pleasure out of it at all, and as we established at the beginning I *am* paying for this.

. . .

I didn't mean that the way it sounded, there, Marilyn.

Why is your sister such a prig, honey?

She's the type who says *I told you so.* Do you know the type?

I've known a few of those, yeah.

Brothers or sisters?

Sure.

You're being automatic now, I can hear it in your voice. You're not paying attention.

Yeah.

Yeah, you're not paying attention? Or yeah, you're being automatic.

Your voice is nice, baby, and I like the sound of it.

You do.

Why don't you think about how it might be to cozy up together here. I'd love to see you.

I murdered my grandmother and put her in the freezer, this morning.

Serves her right.

What?

I said it serves her right.

You *are* listening.

Trying to.

So what're you studying in college, Marilyn? What's your major?

Oh, do you want to do this or not, honey?

I just want to know what your major is.

I told you, we're not supposed to get that personal.

You're so far away. How is telling me what you're majoring in personal?

You know what, man? This is weird. This is positively weird.

It's unconventional. You're already doing something rather radically unconventional, so why not be unconventional with the conventions of *this*, which is so unconventional. Why not tell me something that's bothering you? I told you about my impending divorce, and my toot, and my shit of a sister, who won't take me in and whose husband threw me downstairs last night so that I almost broke my neck and who *told me* for years that I was messing up in a big way and when the mess finally caught up with me and I had to go see her she said I *told you so* all over again just in case I'd missed it the first two hundred seventy-seven thousand times she'd said it.

Did you say her husband threw you downstairs?

Harv's his name. A prince of a guy. A cupcake, old Harv.

I'd stay away from Harv, lover.

That's what my sister said. And after I went down the stairs, I got the message—I'm to stay away from old Harv. And you know what Harv does for a living? Harv's a veterinarian. He spends all day taking care of dogs and cats. Got a heart of gold, old Harv. Cries-at-sad-movies kind of thing. A sweetheart. Kindness personified, that guy.

Do you like *pussy*cats, lover?

They're fine if I don't have to live with one. Do you live with one?

I've got three of them.

I'm allergic. I have allergies that bother me when I'm around them.

I don't have any allergies.

Well, now there—that wasn't too much trouble, was it? I know a little something about you now. You live with three cats and you don't have any allergies.

Do you want me to start now, baby?

Not yet, not yet. Not like that. It's got to be natural, you know.

Natural.

I'm sober, too, Marilyn. Believe it or not. This is a very sober phone call.

Why don't you tell me what you're wearing?

Aren't I supposed to ask you that?

Okay. Ask, lover. I think I already said I'm not wearing anything.

Well, but I wanted to know one problem you're having in your life—something we could commiserate about, maybe.

You know what, John? I really don't have that many problems right now. I'm not desperate, or unhappy or lonely, particularly. I'm going to school and this is a job. And I usually do most of the talking, and I like to talk, so that's all right, too.

But it's not real talk. It's the same things over and over.

There's only a few things to say, right?

Doesn't that get old? That must get awful boring for you.

But there's usually somebody soooo *interested* on the other end of the line. Do you ever tell a joke, John? Do you tell jokes?

I see your point.

It's usually so easy. These guys who call are fast. You know what I'm saying? Most of them have already got a start on it.

But nobody's laughing.

That isn't what the desired result is, though, right?

The whole thing sounds a little pathetic to me. Do they ever ask you to say you love them?

Sure, some do. Now and then one does. That's a pretty harmless thing to ask.

And you don't mind doing that.

I'm talking on a telephone, lover.

Any of them ever scare you?

It's usually pretty friendly, and like I say, I do most of the talking. There's one guy who calls to say what he'd like to do to me—an obscene phone caller. Before we were around, he probably upset a lot of nice little housewives.

What do you see in the future for yourself? You think you'll ever be a nice little housewife, as you put it?

Are you writing a book?

I wondered if you plan on getting married someday, that's all.

Sure, why not? And what's wrong with using the word *housewife*?

I think you ought to ask my wife that one. Oh, boy, do I. I would love to see what she'd say to that one, I really would.

She's not a housewifey type?

Let us say she is not a housewifey type, yes. Let us just say that. Let us use that as the starting point of any conversations that arise about my, um, er, um, wife. She is not a housewifey type lady.

Okay.

So you plan on being a housewifey type someday.

Why not? Sure.

Kid?

I hope so—someday.

I've got two kids. I don't get to see them very often these days. What's your major?

I haven't decided.

Do you like a drink now and then?

Sure.

I'm bothering you, right? Don't deny it because I can hear it in your voice.

Is my voice starting to irritate you?

You know what irritated Kate about me?

Your voice?

Now *you're* making fun. You've got me on the speakerphone, right?

I don't have a speakerphone, John. What irritated Kate about you?

Well, she called it the convoluted nature of my mind. My—my thoughts. She said I twisted things around in my head until they started to hurt me and then I'd blame her for it. She said I was the most morbid, convoluted son of a bitch she ever saw, and she wasn't even yelling when she said it. Do I seem convoluted to you?

I wouldn't say that, lover.

I like it better when you say my name.

Okay—John.

Are you younger than thirty-two?

Yes.

And Marilyn is your real name.

Well, actually—

Please tell me what your real name is, Marilyn. Your first name. I told you mine.

How do I know you told me your real name?

It's on my credit card.

Honey, they just punch the name through and open the line for me.

Well, John is my real name. Now please tell me yours.

. . .

What harm can it do?

It's Sharon.

Hi, Sharon.

Hi.

Do you like sports, Sharon?

I play tennis.

I never played tennis. I'm a swimmer.

I swim, too.

Did you compete?

I was second team in high school.

I won a few medals in college, Sharon.

No kidding.

I started out pretty fast. That's where I met Kate. We dated for almost five years.

Couldn't make up your minds.

Well, we lived together.

Oh.

You know what happened to me the other day, Sharon? I was in New York, chasing my wife and the kids—did I tell you she took them and ran off? I chased them all the way up to Boston and then came back. She's got all the help and the ammunition. The law on her side, and lawyers and I'm a convoluted son of a bitch. And my own sister thinks I'm a wash, to use her ridiculous phrase. Anyway, the other day I was on this street corner in New York, down near the Village, and these two prostitutes were there waiting for the light to change. And I stood next to them, waiting. There wasn't much traffic to speak of. But they stood there. I wanted to say to them—I wanted to ask them why they chose to obey *that* particular law, you know? Why they were in compliance with the traffic law there and not in compliance with the several other laws they were breaking. Does this make sense to you? I mean I got arrested for beating down a door and it was like I was a criminal or something—or dangerous. Kate took out this peace bond on me, and it's like I'm on parole.

You think too much.

That's what Kate used to say, too.

Well, maybe you should listen to her.

I did. I did a lot—all the time. But then there was the fact that her voice started getting on my nerves. My convoluted mind started getting on hers.

I don't know what to tell you, lover.

Did you ever have a relationship fall apart?

. . .

Maybe not a marriage.

Actually, John, I've been in and out of relationships. I just haven't found the right one. I think the one I have now might be the right one, only—

Only what?

Nothing.

No, you were going to tell me something. That was sweet—come on, Sharon.

Well, he never actually says the words, you know—that—that he loves me. I don't believe I'm telling you this.

And it's important to you that he say it.

Okay—yeah. Right. It is. Wouldn't you wonder about it if you were seeing someone and you said *I love you* to them all the time and they never said it back?

I love you, Sharon.

. . .

Like that?

Well, it would be him saying it. He's very nice and I like being with him. But sometimes he—he seems to be avoiding it as a subject.

I love you, Sharon.

. . .

I love you. I really do—I feel the warmest sense of affection toward you now. Right now it's the truest thing in my whole mistake of a life.

Okay.

No, I mean it.

I said *okay,* lover. I don't think you should keep going on about it.

That's what Kate used to say.

. . .

Is he good to you?

As a matter of fact, he is. In every other way, he is.

Did you ever have a boyfriend who knocked you around?

No, and I wouldn't either.

Kate's father was like that. A military guy—with a mean streak. He was always coming up with things to be critical about. Kate grew up with him yelling at her and hitting her. Did you ever have anything like that, growing up?

No, thank God.

Well, it does something to a person. Kate is just as likely to react violently to something as she is anything else. I've never laid a hand on her, of course. I kicked a door in to see my children. Just to lay eyes on them one time, you know. But when she gets mad she tends to think of finding ways to cause you physical pain. She'll hit at you or throw something. It's scary as hell sometimes. She's always been the strong one, and she knows it. Not physically, of course. But inside—the one with the iron. The one with the highly developed *critical sense.* And I do love her, you know. It's not like you can turn that kind of thing on and off, like a faucet sort of thing.

Different people can do different things, lover.

Yeah, sure—do you come from good parents?

Uh-huh.

I don't mean it as anything but curiosity about someone I'm very fond of, Sharon.

Oh, and I'm growing fond of you, too, baby. Oooh, I'd like to have you touch me—

Not yet, wait. Just a little more general talk. I really feel something for you now.

Me, too. I'm getting all *hot*—

Are your parents still living?

. . .

Come on, just a little more.

Okay. My parents are still living.

You get along with them?

I never saw much of my father growing up. He and my mother got a divorce when I was small—I was only about five. My mother is fine. She lives in perfect blindness in Chicago.

By that do you mean she doesn't know what you're doing to put yourself through school?

Among other things.

Such as?

She's a devout Catholic. I'm not.

Were you ever?

When I was young I guess, sure.

Divorce is hard on a child. I'm worried about my own children. What they think of their father chasing after them like that, banging down doors. They've got to know that means I feel my love for them passionately.

I guess.

I'll tell you, Sharon—I'm about at the end of my self. I mean I've reached down and I've reached down and called up all the reserves and there's nothing left. My family's gone. I think she's got my own children afraid of me. Imagine that.

You just have to be patient and stick it out, John.

Well, that's a bromide, Sharon. That's not worthy of you.

. . .

Hello?

I haven't hung up. *Yet.*

Yeah, well anyway, I guess I've proved to myself that I'm not totally off the deep end—I can have a normal conversation.

. . .

Somewhat normal.

What's funny, lover?

Funny?

You laughed just then, didn't you?

I love you, Sharon. Does it make you feel good to hear it?

Not really, no. It has to be *him* saying it.

Can't you use your imagination a little?

You're the one who's supposed to be doing that.

What's to imagine? You'll provide the material, right?

Okay, if you say so.

I'm sorry, don't be upset with me, Sharon. I'm harmless, really. And I do feel this tremendous affection for you.

Why don't you say that to Kate?

. . .

Hello?

That was kind of you, to think of that, Sharon, really.

Thanks.

I really do feel this huge affection for you now. It's strange.

Well, I like you, too.

You know what, Sharon? I wish I could see you. In fact, I'd like to have you sitting on my lap naked.

Oh, well—

I would. I'd like to nibble the lobes of your ears and get into a bathtub with you and wash you all over. I'd like to put my tongue in your—

Okay, wait—hold it. Hold on, John. *This* is where you want to start in on the sex?

Why can't you just let it happen naturally?

You're kidding me, right?

I'm serious as hell, Sharon.

Look, you know what? I don't feel right about this now. And if you *are* a reporter, report that one. I don't like you saying that stuff to me now.

But—hell, Sharon, what do I really know about you? I don't know you *that* well. Come *on*. I just asked a few general questions. It was just conversation.

Well, it's got me spooked, and I'd just as soon leave it there.

Okay, then let's go on talking about my miserable personal life awhile, until you feel like going ahead. You start, when you're ready. Talking the line—when it seems right for you.

I started a *couple* of times, John—and you stopped me.

The next time, I promise I won't stop you.

But—see, I don't think it's going to seem right for me now. I mean I don't feel it now, and I wouldn't be very convincing, I'm not feeling all that good now, to tell you the truth. I think I feel a migraine coming on.

Let me get this straight—you have a *headache?*

I don't have a headache. Migraines don't always have to be headaches. I get them like light shows in my eyes, and the only thing for it is to lie down until the light show stops. But that isn't the point, really. The point is I don't feel right about this now.

You actually require yourself to feel something on these calls?

You know what I mean, lover.

What're you, an actress?

Okay. Sure.

You're an actress.

That's what I said, yes.

. . .

Hello?

I love you, Sharon.

No, I can't. Sorry. Call the number back—you'll get somebody else.

But I want *you*.

Well, you can't have me, okay? I'm not available.

. . .

I mean it's just too weird.

So what you're telling me now is that you've more or less decided not to do your job. Is that right? Do you believe it's right—just like that to decide you're not gonna do your job?

I'm not really interested in worrying about what's *right*, now, John.

But we did have an agreement.

Hey, thanks for calling.

Please don't hang up, Sharon. That's no way to end this.

I really have to go, now.

Okay, you do the talking, how about that? I won't say anything. Just do the spiel.

I can't, now. That's what I'm trying to tell you.

Please?

I've been thinking about you all night and I'm here on my warm silk-sheeted bed and lying back in the pretty red light and thinking about you and wishing you were here with me right now kissing me where I like it, John, and—

Can't you put a little feeling into it?

This is the shit, John. This is what you get for the money.

It's not very convincing. It's not as good as you sounded before.

It's the best I can do right now under the circumstances.

Damn.

Do you want me to go on?

I don't think it would do any good.

. . .

So what do we do now, there, Sharon?

You should've let me stay Marilyn. I'm better as Marilyn.

Okay, Marilyn. I love you, Marilyn. If I call the number again, can I ask for Marilyn and will they put me through to you?

They might.

It's a strange world, there, Marilyn.

Only if you let yourself think about it too much. To me, it makes a perfect kind of sense. Now I really do have to go.

Hey.

Yeah?

You were sweet, Marilyn.

You, too.

I know it wasn't as good for you as it was for me.

You take care of yourself, John. And try to be happy.

Thanks, kid. That's excellent advice. I know this isn't an advice line, but thanks anyway, it's kind of you to offer it.

Bye, John.

Now *there's* the note you want—that's sexy as hell the way you said that. If you could manage that tone the next time I call, it would be perfect. Do you think you could manage that tone the next time I call if I ask for Marilyn and they put me through to you?

. . .

Hello?

POOR DEVIL

Charles Baxter

Charles Baxter was born in Minneapolis and graduated from Macalester College in Saint Paul. After completing graduate work in English at the State University of New York at Buffalo, he taught for several years at Wayne State University in Detroit. In 1989 he moved to the
Department of English at the University of Michigan–Ann Arbor and
its MFA program. He now teaches at the University of Minnesota. Baxter is the author of four novels, four collections of short stories, three
collections of poems, and a collection of essays on fiction.

My ex-wife and I are sitting on the floor of what was once our
living room. The room is empty now except for us. This place
is the site of our marital decline, and we are performing a ritual
cleansing on it. I've been washing the hardwood with a soapy
disinfectant solution, using a soft brush and an old mop, working toward the front window, which has a view of the street.
My hands smell of soap and bleach. We're trying to freshen the
place up for the new owners. The terms of sale do not require
this kind of scouring, but somehow we have brought ourselves
here to perform it.

We're both battered from the work: Emily fell off a kitchen stool
this morning while washing the upstairs windows, and I banged
my head against a drainpipe when I was cleaning under the bathroom sink. When I heard her drop to the floor, I yelled upstairs to

ask if she was okay, and she yelled back down to say that she was, but I didn't run up there to check.

When my wife and I were in the process of splitting up, the house itself participated. Lamps dismounted from their tables at the slightest touch; pictures plummeted from the wall, the glass in their frames shattering, whenever anyone walked past them. Destruction abounded. You couldn't touch anything in here without breaking it. The air in the living room acquired a poisonous residue from the things we had said to each other. I sometimes thought I could discern a malignant green mist, invisible to everyone else, floating just above the coffee table. We excreted malice, the two of us. The house was haunted with pain. You felt it the minute you walked in the door.

Therefore this cleaning. We both like the young couple who have bought the house, smiling, just-out-of-school types with one toddler and another child on the way. We want to give them a decent chance. During our eight years together Emily and I never had any kids ourselves, luckily—or unluckily. Who can say?

Anyway, now that we've been cleaning it, our former dwelling seems to have calmed down. The air in the living room has achieved a settled, stale quietude, as if we never lived here. The unhappiness has seeped out of it.

Emily is sitting on the floor over in the corner now, a stain in the shape of a Y on her T-shirt. She's taking a breather. I can smell her sweat, a vinegary sweetness, quite pleasant. She's drinking a beer, though it's only two in the afternoon. She's barefoot, little traces of polish on her toenails. Her pretty brown hair, always one of her best features, is pulled back by a rubber band in the sort of ponytail women sometimes make when they're housecleaning. Her face is pink from her exertions, and on her forehead she has a bruise from where she fell.

She's saying that it's strange, but the very sight of me causes her sadness—a complicated sadness, she informs me, inflecting the adjective. She's smiling when she says it, a half smile, some grudges mixed in with this late-term affability. She takes a swig of the beer. I can see that she's trying to make our troubles into a manageable comedy. I was Laurel; she was Hardy. I was Abbott; she was Costello. We failed together at the job we had been given: our marriage. But I don't think this comedic version of us will work out, even in retrospect. She tells me that one of my mistakes was that I thought I knew her, but no, in fact I never really knew her, and she can prove it. This is old ground, but I let her talk. She's not speaking to me so much as meditating aloud in the direction of the wall a few feet above my head. It's as if I've become a problem in linear algebra.

My general ignorance of her character causes her sorrow, she now admits. She wonders whether I was deluded about women in general or about her in particular. To illustrate what I don't know about her, she begins to tell me a story.

But before she can really get started, I interrupt her. "'Sorrow,'" I say. "Now there's a noun from our grandparents' generation. Nobody our age uses words like that anymore except you. Or 'weary.' You're the only person I know who has ever used that word. I'm weary, you'd say, when you didn't look weary at all, just irritable. And 'forbearance.' I don't even fucking know what forbearance is. 'Show some forbearance'—that was a line you used. Where did you find those words anyway?"

"Are you done?" she asks me. We're like a couple of tired fighters in the fifteenth round.

"What's wrong with saying 'I'm bummed'?" I ask her. "Everyone else says that. 'I'm bummed.' 'I'm down.' 'I'm depressed.' 'I'm blue.' But you—you have a gift for the . . . archaic." I am trying to amuse her and irritate her at the same time, so I wink.

"I wasn't depressed back then," she says. "I was sad. The two aren't the same." I scuttle over to where she is sitting and take a swig from the beer can she's been clutching. Only the beer is gone. I take a swig of air. Okay; we may be divorced, but we're still married.

Before I met her, but after she had dropped out of college, Emily moved to the Bay Area. This was quite a few summers after the

Summers of Love, which she had missed—both the summers and the love. She rented a cheap basement apartment in Noe Valley, one of those places with a view of the sidewalk and of passing shoes, and during the day she worked in a department store, the Emporium, in the luggage department.

I interrupt her. "I know this," I say. "I know this entire story."

"No, you don't," Emily tells me. "Not this one." One of her co-workers was a guy named Jeffrey, a pleasant fellow most of the time, tall and handsome, though with an occasional stammer, and, as it happens, gay. He proved himself an effective salesman, one of those cheerful and witty and charming characters you buy expensive items from, big-ticket items, out of sheer delight in their company.

This co-worker, Jeffrey, befriended Emily soon after she had moved to San Francisco. An amateur guide and historian of tourist spots and dives, he showed her around the city, took her to the wharf and the Tenderloin District. He loved the city; he had had his first real taste of a possible future life there in that city, a potential hereafter of happiness. My wife-to-be and this Jeffrey rode BART over to Berkeley once and had a sidewalk vegetarian lunch—mock-duck tacos, she says—at a seedy little restaurant devoted to higher consciousness. On another day he drove her to Mount Tam in his rattly old blue VW. He'd brought sandwiches and wine and some pastry concoction he had made himself, as a picnic offering. They ate their picnic in the shade of a tree, the FM radio in his car serenading them with Glenn Gould. Why did he go to all this trouble? Emily says he was just being a friend, and then she pauses. "His boyfriend had left him a month before," she says, looking at her bare feet on the floor of our empty living room. "So he was lonely. And he was one of those gay men who have a latent hetero thing going on." How did she know this? She shrugs. She could tell by the way he looked at her sometimes. On a few rare occasions he looked at her the way a man looks at a woman.

It's true, I haven't heard this story. "So?" I ask.

So one day Jeffrey didn't show up for work. Or the next day or the day after that. He was sick, of course, with pneumonia, and after he recovered he came back to work for a few days and then disappeared again for another two weeks. Everyone knew he had the plague, and this was before all the antiretroviral drugs broke through to the population at large, so at work everyone avoided the subject of Jeffrey, someone they all liked.

By this time I am looking out the front window at our street. This is a nondescript neighborhood of similarly designed brick semi-colonials like ours, and as I watch, I see a guy in a Santa Claus suit come jogging by.

"Look," I say. "It's Rolf, from down the block. He's wearing that goddamn Santa Claus suit again."

Emily glances out, lifting herself halfway. "He must not be taking his meds."

"It's not that," I tell her. "He thinks it's better for visibility than a running outfit. Drivers see him right away. 'You don't accidentally hit Santa,' he told me once. At least he hasn't tied on the white beard. At least he's not wearing the cap."

"Who're you kidding?" Emily asks me. "The guy's bipolar. The Santa comes out in him whenever he gets manic."

"You could do worse," I say to her. "You've done worse."

We sit there looking at each other for a moment, unsmiling. Neither of us says anything, and I hear the furnace come on. The light flaring through the window has that burnished autumnal warmth. The furnace creates a low hum. Outside in the yard the leaves could be raked, but I'm not going to do that now.

"What happened to Jeffrey?" I ask, after another long pause. "He died, right?"

No, but he was in one of the Kaiser hospitals, where Emily went to see him. He didn't look good. "Wasted" is probably the right word. She tried to cheer him up, but he resisted her efforts. Still, he had one request. He wanted her to take some pictures of him, as a memento of how handsome he was despite his illness. He thought his looks had trumped the virus somehow. Beauty had staged its victory over infirmity, he thought. So she did it. She bought a camera and took some pictures of her friend sitting up in the chair next to the hospital bed, out of his hospital clothes and in his best: black jeans, leather jacket, etc. "You probably didn't know it," he said as she took his picture, "but I'm an aristocrat." He posed as if he were a rake and a bit of a snob, smiling an old-money smile.

But when the film was developed, the pictures proved unshowable: his skin wasn't just sallow, it was waxlike. His face seemed rigid, a staring mask. She didn't know what to do with these pictures. Ten years ago retouching photographs digitally wasn't as easy as it is now. But if the guy could tell lies to himself when looking in the mirror, she thought, maybe he could tell himself the same lies when he saw these photographs.

She arrived at his apartment—he was convalescing at home by now—and sat down next to him at the dinette table. One by one the pictures were laid out like playing cards, like the hand he'd been dealt. With his reading glasses on, Jeffrey looked at these images of himself. As it happened, the pneumonia had hung on for a while and he had lost a considerable amount of muscle tone; in the photos his cheekbones were garishly visible, and his eyes, despite his smile, had that peering-into-the-void anguish—there, I used that word—that you see on the faces of the near-dead. So Jeffrey was sitting there, looking down at these photographs of his death sentence, and he began to cry.

Emily tried to console him, but he turned away from her, shaking his head. He went into his bedroom, got dressed, and told her that they were going for a ride in the blue VW. He asked her to drive. He said that he had to have his hands free.

He directed her down toward the Presidio and then onto the Golden Gate Bridge, and when they were about midway across the bridge, he took the photographs and held them up one by one outside the window. The wind seized these portraits of him; some of them fluttered over the side of the bridge into the bay, and some of them just lay there on the gridded pavement for other cars to drive over. Dust to dust. Emily told him that he could be ticketed for littering, but he didn't listen to her; he was too busy getting rid of these snapshots. "They won't arrest me," he shouted over the road noise. "Not after they get a good look at me."

Then he instructed Emily to drive up the coast so that they could go whale watching. However, it was the wrong season: no whales that time of year. After a couple of hours they pulled over at a roadside rest area within sight of the Pacific. The two of them got out of the car. Though no whales were visible, Jeffrey, leaning against his car and staring out at the water, said he saw some. For the next half hour he described the whales swimming by, all the shapes and sizes and varieties of them, whale after whale, under the surface. He was like an encyclopedia entry: here were the humpback whales, and there the bottle-nosed, and the pilot and the beluga, the right whales and the blue. When he was finished with this harmless hallucinatory description, he got back into the car, and my wife—that is, then my wife-to-be and now my ex-wife—drove him back home, to his apartment on Clement. When they got back to his place, he was distracted and confused, so she undressed him and put him to bed, Good Samaritan that she is. And then—and this is the part I couldn't have imagined—she got into bed with him and put her arms around him until he fell asleep.

She's still sitting here in the living room, looking at me in silence, still unsmiling. The point of this story is that she loved this man—loved him, I think the phrase is, to death.

"No," I say, "you're absolutely right. You never told me that story." My heart is pounding slightly, and I have to work to sound calm. "So you loved him. What happened to this Jeffrey?" I ask her.

She looks at me. "Duh," she says. She removes her foot from my grasp. I hadn't realized I was holding on to it. I wonder what else she might have done for him that she hasn't told me, but I don't ask. "The thing is," she says, "I often dream about him. And these dreams—I often wake up from them, and they're terrible dreams, no comfort at all." She looks at me and waits. "They're really insane dreams," she says.

"How are they insane?"

"Oh," she says, "let's not spoil it with words." But I know my wife, and what she means is that in these dreams she is still lying next to him. She glances out the window. "There goes Santa again." She laughs. It's not a good laugh—more like a fun-house laugh. I get up, make my way to the kitchen, open the refrigerator, take out two beers (we've cleaned out the refrigerator except for a twelve-pack), and bring one of them back to her. I open the other one and gaze out the window, but Santa has turned the corner and is no longer visible, to my great disappointment. It's getting to be late afternoon, the time of day when you could use some Santa and aren't going to get it.

I take a good slug of the beer before I say, "No, you never told me that story. My God. Maybe it's true. Maybe we didn't know each other. Can you imagine that? We were married and we never knew the first thing."

"Spare me your irony," she says.

"I'm not being ironic. I'm telling you what you told me. But the thing is, your story isn't about you except on the sides, by comparison. You're a minor saintly character in that story. You're just the affable friend," I say, which isn't true, because that's not what the story has been about. I'm feeling a little competitive now, in this singing contest we're having. "After all, I've known plenty of people I've never described to you."

"I've heard that before," she says.

"Well, no, you haven't," I say. "Not exactly."

I am not an admirable man, and my character, or lack of character, accounts for my presence on this living-room floor on this particular day. If I am unadmirable, however, I am not actually bad, in the sense that evil people are bad. If I were genuinely and truly bad, my ex-wife wouldn't be sitting here on the floor with me, her ex-husband, after we'd cleaned the house for the next occupants.

My trouble was that after our first two years together, I couldn't concentrate on her anymore. I was distracted by what life was throwing at me. I couldn't be—what is the word?—faithful, but actually that was the least of it, because unfaithfulness is a secondary manifestation of something we don't have a word for.

When I met Emily, I was a clerk in a lighting store; I sold lighting fixtures. I suppose this was a pretty good job for someone who majored in studio art during college. I know something about light. My little atelier was filled with life-study drawings and rolled-up canvases of nakedness. That was pretty much what I did: nudes, the human body—the place where most artists start, though I never got past it.

I was always drawing and painting one particular woman, and, of course, it wasn't Emily. It was never Emily. The model was a woman I had seen for about two minutes waiting in line for coffee at one of those bookstore cafés. She had an ankle bracelet, and I could describe her to you top to bottom, every inch. I could do that, trust me—just take my obsession on faith. She had come into my life for two minutes, and when, that afternoon, I couldn't forget her, I began to draw her. The next day I drew her again, and the next week I began a painting of her, and a month after that I did another painting of her, and so on and so on.

One Saturday—this was about two years after we were married—Emily came into my studio, sometime in midafternoon. I had college football playing on the radio. As usual, I was painting the woman I once saw standing in line at this bookstore café. Emily asked me again who this person was, and I told her again that it was just someone I caught a glimpse of once. It didn't matter who she was—she was just this person. Which was, of course, untrue. She wasn't just a person. Emily stared at what I was doing with the canvas, and then she unbuttoned her blouse and hung it on a clothes hook near the door. She took off her shoes and socks and stood there with her bra and jeans still on, and then she unzipped the jeans and unclasped the bra and off they went, onto the littered floor. Finally the underpants went, and she was in the altogether, standing in my studio just under the skylight, the smell of turpentine in the room. I interrupted what I was doing and eventually went over to her and took her in my arms, but that turned out to be the wrong response—so wrong that I can date the decline of our marriage from that moment. What I was supposed to do was look at her. I was supposed to draw her; I was supposed to be obsessed by her; and finally, I was supposed to be inspired by her.

But that's not how everyday love works. "I want to be your everything," Emily once said to me, and I cringed.

The next time we made love, she was crying. "Please draw me," she said. "Dennis, please please please draw me."

"I can't," I said. Although I may not be a great artist, I was not going to draw her just because she asked me to. She was my companion. We were getting through this life day by day, the two of us. I loved her, I'm sure, and she loved me, I'm sure of that, too; but she has never inspired me, and I have never been obsessed by her. All the things that followed, including the affairs, both hers and mine, were small potatoes compared with that: I couldn't draw her in good faith.

At night I would hug her and kiss her and tell her that I loved her, my flesh pressed against her flesh, but that just made her cry all the more. The poisons in the house grew. Emily was not my everything, not my muse and inspiration. I never knew why she wanted that role, but she did, and because she wanted it, and I couldn't lie to her about how she could never be what she said she wanted to be, I could fold my arms around her as we stood or lay quietly together but it was never enough. And because it was never enough, it was hateful.

We were like two becalmed sailing ships carrying sailors from different countries who shouted curses at each other as we drifted farther and farther apart.

"No, right, sure, of course," she says, standing up and stretching. "Two ships." She turns toward me and loosens her hair so that it falls lightly over her shoulders and so that I can see her do it. Her eyes are glittery with a momentary thrill of distaste for me. No more housework today. "Right. You just told me stories and listened to the radio and painted your dream girl." She looks at me. "If you had been Picasso, everyone would have forgiven you."

Now, late in the afternoon, we go walking toward the park, a way of recovering our equilibrium before we get into our separate cars and drive off toward our separate residences. Anyone seeing us strolling past the piles of bright leaves on the sidewalk, the last light of the sun in our eyes, might think we were still a couple. Emily's wearing a little knitted red cap and a snug brown jacket, and she's squinting against the sun's rays; and because we are also facing a cool breeze from the west, her eyes fill with moisture—I refuse at this moment to think of it as tears—that she must wipe away before she says anything to me.

"It's true," she says. "Sometimes I forget the nicest things you did for me. Like that time you bought me flowers for my birthday."

"Which birthday was this?" I ask. The sun is in my eyes, too.

"It doesn't matter," she says. "What matters is that you walked into the house with these six red roses clutched in your hand, and I smiled, and I saw from the puzzlement on your face that in your absent-minded way you had forgotten that you had bought roses for me and that you were holding them in your hand at that very moment. Imagine! Imagine a guy who buys roses for his wife and then carries them into the house and still forgets that that's what he's doing. Imagine being so fucking absent-minded. It's a form of male hysteria."

"Watch your language," I say, kidding her. "It's true," I say. "I was presenting you with roses that I had forgotten about."

"And what it meant," Emily tells me, as if I hadn't said anything, "was that your instincts, your—I don't know what you would call it . . . your unconscious still loved me, even if your conscious mind

didn't. I thought, My husband, Dennis, still loves me. Despite everything. You could absent- mindedly get me roses on my birthday
without knowing what you were doing. Somewhere in there you
were still kindly disposed toward me. Your little love light was still
shining, before its last flickerings."

We arrive at the park. On our side of it is a small playground
with a slide, a climbing structure, swings. One little boy is still
playing, while his mother sits on a bench and reads the paper, but
now, in the dusk, she's squinting in order to make out the print. She
calls to her son, but he won't return to her quite yet. He won't follow her orders. Emily sits down in one of the swings, and I sit down
next to her. She puts her shoes in the patch of dirt and slowly begins
to swing herself back and forth. Behind us the woods seem to be
breathing in and out.

"I liked childhood," Emily says to me softly. "I liked being a kid.
A lot of the other girls wanted to grow up, but I didn't. They wanted
to go out on dates, the excitement of all that—boys, cars, sex, the
whole scene. But not me. I didn't want to launch my little ship into
adolescence. I didn't want my periods to start. I didn't want what
was about to happen to happen. I had this dread of it. I wanted to
stay a kid forever. I thought being an adult was the awful afterlife
of childhood."

I can't remember ever being afraid of growing up, so I don't say
anything in response. Even at this late date Emily can still surprise
me with what she says.

"And it was awful. I mean, it is awful. It's terrible, but of course
you can learn to live with it, and it's okay after a while even if it's
terrible, and besides, what choice do you have?"

"No choice," I say to her. The woman on the bench calls to her
son again, and this time he comes down to where she's sitting, and
he stands by her side and puts his hand on her arm as a signal that
he's ready. She nods, briefly looking at him. Then she folds her
paper, stands up, and takes his hand. These gestures are of such
gentle, subtle sweetness that they feel like a private language to me,

and my mind clouds up, given the weight of the day, given my own situation.

"You know," I say to Emily, as I swing back and forth in my swing, "I've been getting postcards. Anonymous postcards."

"Dennis," Emily tells me, "I don't have time for another story. I have to get home. I have a date tonight, if you can believe it."

"No, listen," I say. "They've been arriving in the mail every few days. They're anonymous—I don't know who's sending them. Not to work but to my home address, the apartment. And they have these picture-postcard photographs on the flip side—Miami Beach, the Bahamas, the Empire State Building, the usual. But on the message side it's something else."

"Dennis, really," she says, "I have to go." But she's still sitting there, in the playground, in her swing. "I have to get ready," she says, in a flat, neutral tone.

But I'm going to finish, and I say, "And what it is, these messages—they're always handwritten, always in blue ink, always in large letters, uppercase, all of them. Short, punchy sentences. Condemnations of me. Judgments." I hold up my hand to suggest a headline, even though the words have to fit on postcards. '"Your work has come to nothing.' 'Your life is a disaster.' 'Someone is watching you.' 'Aren't you ashamed of yourself?' Now, who do you suppose would send postcard messages like that?"

She looks over at me in the gathering dusk with a genuine expression of surprise, and I understand the moment I see her face that it's not Emily who has been sending me these postcards. All along I thought it would be her idea of retribution, these insane postcards. But she hasn't been mailing them, and this sends a brief shudder through me. Perhaps I knew all along. After all, I would know her handwriting even if she tried to disguise it. We're almost twins that way.

"If you're thinking it was me," Emily says, "think again. It wasn't."

'"You are a perpetual outcast,' another postcard said. And last week I got one that said, 'Have you no remorse?'"

"Well," Emily says after a pause, "whoever is sending them must know you. That's a good word—'remorse.' I could have used that word on you. A flea-market word, one of my grandparent words. You never used a word like that. Must be one of your little girlfriends sending these messages. Somebody who's a little obsessed with you, Dennis."

"Some poor devil," I say.

"Yes," she says, "a poor devil. That sounds about right." She gets up out of the swing and goes over to the climbing structure. "Which one do you suppose it is?"

"Well," I say, "I don't know." But actually I think I do know. Once, this woman and I were at dinner together, a woman who in her day had done a lot of drugs—the ones that give you dimestore visions. And out of nowhere she said, "I can see all your thoughts, you know. I can see them, and you don't even have to say them aloud, because I know what they are." She was holding her wineglass, this woman, and it had been a good evening until then, but when she said she could see my thoughts, it seemed time to get out of there. She sat up straight. "God and his archangels have taken a real dislike to you," she said, as I was motioning for the waiter. "They have a gun pointed at your head. I just think I should tell you that."

"She really said that?" Emily asks, coming down from the play structure. "That God and his archangels had a gun pointed at your head?"

"Yeah," I say. "Those were her exact words. But I can't imagine anyone's being obsessed with me. I have such a . . ." I can't think of the phrase.

"Where do you find these girls, Dennis?" she asks.

"Where everybody finds them. In the street, and so on."

"You should look in different places."

"I don't know any different places." What are Emily and I talking about? I've completely lost the thread.

"No," she says, "I suppose you don't." She waits. "Did you see that woman and her little boy? Did you see how . . . I don't know, how calm they were with each other? God, I loved seeing that. That calm. It makes you want to be a kid again. Of course, I always want that anyway."

I take her hand, and we walk back.

When we get to the house, my ex-wife is about to unlock her car and drive away, but she's left her purse in the kitchen. So together the two of us go in the front door, into the foyer, and step into the living room. They're completely dark—it's night by now—and only the streetlight is spraying a little bit of illumination into the room, barely enough to see by.

"Close your eyes," Emily says. "Could you find your way around in this place with your eyes closed? I bet you could."

"Of course," I say.

So I close my eyes and hold my arms out in the dark, and I walk all around the room where the lamps and tables and chairs once were where Em and I once lived, and I go into the dining room, still with my eyes closed, and I walk into the kitchen, past the counter and the dishwasher and then back out, taking my steps one at a time through these spaces I've come to know so intimately. While I'm walking through this dark house where Emily and I tried to stage our marriage, I have this image of Santa jogging—no, sprinting—away from me, and I probably have a grim look. It's right about then that I'm back in the living room and I bump up against Emily, whose arms have also been out in this game we're playing. In the story that I don't tell, we excuse ourselves but then, very slowly and tenderly, we are inspired by each other at last, and we embrace, and all the bad times fall away, and we kiss, and we mutter our apologies—our longstanding, whispered, complicated remorse—and perhaps we sink to the floor, and we make love in the dark empty living room, on the floor, understanding that maybe it will not be the last time after all. And as we make love, Emily makes her utterly familiar trembling cry when she comes.

That's the story I don't tell, because it doesn't happen, and couldn't, and would not, because I am unforgivable, and so is she.

Two poor devils—what we don't feel is remorse, the word on that postcard. We bump into each other, two blind staggerers, two solitudes, and then, yes, we apologize. And that's when Emily goes into the kitchen, her eyes open, but still in the dark house that she knows, as they say, by heart, and she picks up her purse from where she has left it, and she comes out, sailing past me, and maybe she half turns in the dark and blows me a kiss. But probably she doesn't.

She closes the front door behind her, absent-mindedly locking it, locking me into the house. And it's then, and only then, that I speak up. "Good-bye, honey," I say.

LAVANDE

Ann Beattie

Ann Beattie has published seven novels and seven collections of stories. She has been included in three O. Henry Award collections and John Updike's *Best American Short Stories of the Century*. She has received an award in literature from the American Academy of Arts and Letters, a Guggenheim Fellowship, and the PEN/Malamud Award for Short Fiction. She and her husband, the artist Lincoln Perry, divide their time between Maine and Key West, Florida.

Some time ago, when my husband went to stay at the American Academy in Rome in order to do research, I accompanied him because I had never seen the Roman forum. I had a book Harold had given me for my birthday that showed how the ruins looked in the present day, and each page also had its own transparent sheet with drawings that filled in what was missing, or completed the fragments that remained, so you could see what the scene had looked like in ancient times. It wasn't so much that I cared about the Forum; in retrospect, I wonder whether Rome, itself, hadn't seemed like a magical place where my eye could fill in layers of complexity— where I could walk the streets, daily performing my personal magic act.

At dinner our first night there, we were introduced to other visitors, and here is where the story starts: they were the parents of a young man to whom our daughter, Angela, had briefly been engaged at the end of her senior year at Yale—so briefly that I had never met his parents, though Harold and Donald Stipley had a passing acquaintance. The engagement itself had not lasted the summer, and though Harold and I were never sure why they became engaged, let alone why they called it off, we remembered that period as the time when bright, energetic, pretty Angela began to sink into lethargy and pessimism, foregoing graduate study at UCLA and choosing, instead, to work at a salad shop on Madison Avenue. ("Salad shop" does not do it justice, but Harold always called it that, so that is the way I think of it.) This was in the mid 80's, when many people in New York City had money, and for a while the salad shop did very well. Things fell apart a year or so later when her partner, a man she had met at Yale, fell in love and re-located the business to Philadelphia. Angela would not consider moving. She lived in a second floor walk-up in Chelsea and had a dog named Busy Man, who was in love with the dog next door, Benito (a female dog; I don't know the explanation of the name). When Harold suggested that Angela go along on the Philadelphia venture, she responded caustically: "Should I also buy snow shoes and go to Alaska, if he moves there next?" She intended to find other employment, she told her father heatedly. But she did not— whether because she failed in her search, or because she never seriously set about the task, I don't know—and before the year was over, it became apparent to us that Angela had a problem with drugs and alcohol. At Thanksgiving, she left a rolled cigarette on the edge of the bathroom counter, and at Christmas she did not show up at all, arriving two days later with alcohol on her breath and a friend who stole Harold's Waterman pen, his sterling silver business card case, and even a pair of Hermès suspenders.

If you are smiling, that is because we were the people to hate in the eighties, Harold and I: stuffy people who never set foot in a disco, drank moderately and altered our alcohol preference with the season, and listened almost exclusively to classical music. Harold requested that the family doctor speak to Angela, but instead of keeping her appointment, she went to his office on Park Avenue and left a canister of tennis balls with the receptionist, along with a gift card that said, "Carry on."

Then (details interchangeable with the problems of so many others who have been in our situation) began the late night phone calls accusing us of things we never did, followed by requests for money. At first, it was paying her rent. Later—though it was for drugs, we knew—it was a "down payment on a car." How was she going to garage a car in Manhattan? Well, maybe at night she could stick it up her father's ass, she suggested. We did not hear from her at all for six or seven months, then came home one day to find her sitting in the living room, reading a magazine. She was dressed nicely in a blue skirt and white blouse and blazer and said that she now worked as a secretary for a firm on Wall Street. She asked for a loan to pay the rent until she got her first paycheck. Harold agreed to lend her the money if he could sleep on her fold-out couch. What he thought I was going to do while he was camped out, I don't know, but clearly he thought it would be a way of monitoring her. There was a long, loud argument—much of it ridiculous accusations by Angela—followed by (another opportunity for me to provoke a smile) her shutting herself in the bathroom and shoving Harold's silk bathrobe into the toilet. She also left her pumps behind, opening the door and running from the apartment in her stockings. It would be funny to anyone, if it was not their child. Some time during this period, she gave her dog away.

At any rate, there we were in Rome, years later, being served pasta—delicious hand-formed ravioli stuffed with unusual ingredients, served with a simple brown butter sauce—when Donald Stipley was joined at the table, a bit late, by his wife. She immediately exclaimed that we had a connection, though it seemed Donald had not realized his son had ever been engaged. He asked twice if his wife was sure it had been an engagement. She was adamant, and I backed her up, though she remembered the ring in far more detail than I. Donald and Harold took to shrugging and laughing a bit nervously, suggesting that the whole matter was nothing they knew much about. In the back of my mind and perhaps in the back of Harold's was the question: had Angela been all right then or, even earlier than we knew, had something already been going dreadfully wrong? We discussed the qualities of Chuck Close's portrait of Alex Katz in the room outside the dining area. In winter, Donald Stipley's wife exclaimed, there was nowhere she would rather be than in front of the fireplace at the American Academy. Oh, perhaps Paris, she admitted, when her husband raised an eyebrow. They seemed to get along well, in that comfortable but vigilant way married people pay attention to each other after living together for years.

The next day, at the guard's gate in front of the lovely McKim, Mead and White main building, I ran into her again. The guard was calling a cab for her. Her name was Lavande. She had on a Chanel suit, black with white trim, and fashionable black boots with a higher heel than I'd been able to wear for years. Her pearl choker was certainly real, with pearls tinged ever-so-slightly pink, to compliment her complexion. The night before, when she'd discussed Andrea's engagement ring, my eyes had fallen to her own hand: an emerald-cut diamond in a wide band, either white gold or platinum, with baguettes at either side. She was on her way to shop near the Spanish Steps. Wouldn't I like to come along? I was a bit tired from my trudge up the steep steps from Trastevere, but yes, I decided; yes, I would go along.

In the cab, we talked about Rome, and I mentioned the book that had made me so curious I'd come along. She said she had never seen such a book. We walked to the American Express office, where she paid a bill, then decided to have an espresso before shopping. "To think we might have been related, all these years," she said, "and that we still might never have met, if not for a book you looked at." I agreed that life was often a cat's cradle of attachments and missed connections. "You don't often accompany your

husband on trips?" she said. No, I told her: as an art historian, so
much of his day was spent in research, and I hated just tagging
along, biding time. She said—how, exactly, did she put it?—that
she was always expected to accompany Donald. The trick was to
pack light, she said, and to bring Woolite. This hardly explained
the perfect condition of her suit, but seasoned travelers did have
their short-cuts and secrets, of course. Even her purchases were
small and lightweight: a gorgeous camisole; a pink cashmere
scarf. I asked if her son had married. I remember the moment I
spoke, where we were walking, even that a little wind had blown
up, so that I'd seen some grey in her almost-auburn hair. She
stopped, seemed momentarily puzzled, then said, "Oh, let's have
our own connection, let's not have it depend on *children*." Well,
yes, I thought; why move inevitably toward a discussion of the
pain Angela had caused her father and me? Lavande even spontaneously squeezed my hand, and I remember thinking how nice a
gesture that was. How girlish it made me feel. At a news stand, she
bought the International Herald Tribune and I watched her out
of the corner of my eye to see if she was surprised that I bought
"Hello!" magazine. Instead, she squealed with delight, as if I'd
done something slightly wicked. I felt young, would be the way I'd
describe the afternoon later, to Harold. His response those times
I said that was always the same: "You're younger than me, so you
mustn't complain." Did he ask whether the subject of Angela and
their son had come up again? I think I remember that he seemed a
bit disappointed I'd gathered no more information about the past
from Lavande.

They stayed a week, but because of Harold's schedule and my
own ineptitude with the buses, we did not see them every day. The
only other time I spent alone with Lavande was after she put a note
under our door inviting me to a "girls' afternoon" of herbal tea
she'd brewed and a cucumber masque from a homeopathic phar-
macy she'd discovered not far from the Academy. After they left I
went looking for the *plarmacia* and wondered what other things she

might have bought. I found some tiny scissors, almost as lovely as jewelry, and couldn't resist buying those. Back then, of course, you could still travel with such things on airplanes. I also bought rose-water, mixed with something unusual, such as lemon verbena: an after-shave spray, a beautiful little bottle closed with sealing wax and narrow silver cord that I gave to Harold, who would appreciate the packaging, if not the contents.

The evening before they departed I wrote my name on one of Harold's business cards, and she gave me—on a perforated page torn from a small notebook—her information, writing only her first name and a New York and Connecticut phone number. Both numbers turned out to belong to someone else, who had never heard of her. *Westport,* she had written with calligraphic swashes. Instead of writing Manhattan, she had written: *Upper East Side.*

"IT'S ONE of the things I love about you," Harold said. "How could you be this astonished that someone you hardly knew gave you a made-up phone number? It's a well known trick of dating, though I suppose it happens far more often to men."

"But why would she do it?" I said. "If it had been one phone number, I'd have thought she wrote a wrong numeral."

"Good it was two, then! That way, you got the point."

"Why would you want me to be disappointed?" I said.

"Well, truth be told, I thought there was something strange about her. Not the best person for a friendship, perhaps. I don't expect either of us thought they'd become close to us, did we?"

Sometimes I was not sure if Harold was obfuscating, or being entirely direct. In a way, I could understand Angela's frustration. Her father could be maddening when he was reading, as he so often was, and one didn't have his full attention. I was allowed to persist, even when he was busy; she had been trained not to.

"Harold, it's just very strange that someone who seemed friendly would provide false information."

"Well, people are strange," he said. "Did you see how she ate the edges of the ravioli and left the good part? Picked at her entire dinner."

"Oh?" I said.

He nodded. Still, I knew I did not have his full attention. Since it was the newspaper and not a book he was reading, I decided to ask one more question. "Did he give you a business card?" I said.

"What's that? I don't remember."

"Might you look in your wallet?"

He rolled his eyes, slid forward and extracted his wallet from his trouser pocket. He made quite a show of examining every piece of paper. Then, he found the business card and handed it to me, saying, "You're acting like a teenager, refusing to take the hint."

I could remember his frustration when Angela was a teenager, and he'd tried to instruct her in nuance, subtleties, social subtexts. How quiet she'd been, before she began to argue.

"If she'd wanted you to call her, she would have provided the correct numbers," Harold said. "You will embarrass yourself less if you write, and accept silence for an answer."

I wrote, and she was silent.

A YEAR later, Angela became engaged to her psychiatrist. We hadn't known she had a psychiatrist, but then, we hadn't known for much too long about her earlier substance abuse problems. We were also confused—deliberately, by her, we thought—about where she lived. She had another dog, a little pug-looking thing, named Mr. Jones. She and the psychiatrist, Dr. Mark Clifford, paid us a visit to announce the happy news. They passed the little dog back and forth as if they were playing "hot potato" in slow motion.

Angela came into the kitchen to help me make coffee. Usually she avoided being alone with me, as if I conspired to put her in chains, but I had liked Mark Clifford instantly, and I think her relief made her feel warmly toward me. The minute I spoke to her in the kitchen, though, I realized that I'd said the wrong thing and risked alienating her: "When you were engaged before, Angela, was that a real engagement, or one of those sort of, you know, loose engagements that people had at the time?"

"Excuse me?" she said.

"I shouldn't bring it up, I quite like Mark Clifford, but I don't remember things as clearly as I once did, and I was just wondering—"

"Loose," she said.

"Oh, really?" I said, surprised she'd answered at all.

She was a tall girl—almost as tall as her father. She had lovely eyes and brows, but she'd inherited my mouth, so that it seemed she regarded everything slightly grimly.

"You don't remember his name, do you? Your only daughter, her first great love, and you don't remember his first name."

She'd provoked me enough that the name suddenly sprang into my mind: *Steven*. I stabbed with it, eppe.

"Good for you," she said. "Yes, Steven. He was bi. I guess in the long run your conservative upbringing had an effect. You know what bi means, right?"

"Bi-sexual," I said.

She nodded. "And do you get the joke about what Mark and I named the dog?"

I thought about it and shook my head no.

"It's a Dylan song. 'Something's happening, and you don't know what it is, do you, Mr. Jones?' "

I smiled. "I see," I said. Recently, Harold and I had watched Martin Scorsese's documentary on Dylan—whose name I suppose I should have known had been selected, not given. I'd been surprised that Harold thought the documentary so fascinating. Though he said he found it informative about America's sub-culture at a particular time, I'd noticed his foot tapping to many songs. I, myself, had liked Joan Baez's perspective, and her sense of humor.

"That's great," she said. "You get that it's funny. I won't press my luck with your husband."

"Oh, Angela, your father loves you," I said. "He's fifteen years older than I, and from a very different background."

"Yeah, repressed rich WASP snobs," she said. "His background is that you drop the maid off at the bus stop and think you're a hero for going out of your way. Do you know how to make coffee? Can I help?"

"Of course I do," I said, flustered. "Our Melita broke, and it's just taking me a moment to remember—"

She walked over to where I stood and opened the top flap. She filled an empty vase from the dish drainer with water and poured it in the back. That was Angela: always grabbing what was at hand, always improvising. Her father used to maintain that was part of the reason she got in so much trouble. I measured coffee into the filter and pushed the little drawer into place.

"What's your interest in ancient history?" she said.

"Ancient history?" I asked.

"My engagement to Steven. I wasn't suggesting you were an archaeologist."

"Hardly that," I said. "A few trips to accompany your father on business, is about it."

She was standing there with her arms folded across her chest, looking at me. She said: "Steven Stipley. I wonder if he's sorted out his own sexuality. His mother used to dress him like a girl. He showed me a baby album filled with pictures of him in long hair, wearing dresses and Mary Janes. When his father left, she started calling Steven 'Sally.'"

"Left them?" I said. "But we met the Stipleys. They were to-gether, at the American Academy. And I have to tell you, Angela, that she did not strike me as the sort of woman—"

"You look like a wet bird about to shake its feathers mightily," she said. She had found the tin of cashews, opened it, and begun eating. She laughed, amused at her observation.

"What I mean," I said, "is that all reports are not to be believed, or at the very least, you might be overstating the case. I know many mothers find it difficult to send their sons for a first hair cut."

"Whew," she said, pulling out a kitchen chair and sitting down. "Didn't you hear me? Can I be any clearer? She dressed him as a girl, and when I met him, he couldn't have sex unless he had on womens' jewelry, or womens' underwear. What I'm saying is that—"

"I understand what you're saying, but I'm telling you that Dr. Jekyll and Mr. Hyde aside . . ."

"She rhymes! She laughs! *She gets everything.*"

"Whether you wish to cut me off or not, Angela, I'm telling you that I do not believe Lavande dressed her son as a girl."

"Lavande! You met the *mistress*. You've outdone me and met the famous Lavande! Steven's mother died when he was thirteen. He prayed every night she'd die, and when he was thirteen, she did. Then his father sent him to boarding school. Groton. It was the one thing he could talk to Harold about. Don't you remember?"

"No," I said miserably.

"You met Lavande," Angela said, relinquishing her mocking for true fascination. "She was a runway model in Paris. Steven had a picture of her from some fashion magazine: Gorgeous. Legs a mile high. So the great Donald Stipley—who wouldn't listen to what his son had to say any more than you would, by the way . . . he finally married her?"

Well, what did I know? She had on a diamond ring, but had Donald actually said that she was his wife, when he'd introduced her? Whether he'd married her or not was a technicality; he was lucky to have her as a companion, because she'd been sophisticated and confiding and *fun*—we had had such fun looking in the shops near the Spanish Steps, we'd been like schoolgirls, free for the day. She had pointed out birds, and known their names in Italian. Returning to the Academy, we had seen what looked like a water spout of black birds in the sky, taking every imaginable shape as they flew.

Angela was pouring the coffee into mugs. It seemed in all ways inferior to espresso—standing at the coffee shop with Lavande, who whispered that Italians thought Americans were too stupid to know that if they sat, instead of standing at the counter, the coffee would be twice the price. Since she took cabs and wore expensive clothes, I'd been surprised, at first, that she thought about what she spent, but I'd quickly understood: it was the principle, not the money.

I REALIZED I'd had it in the back of my mind to go to the Forum with Lavande only when Harold said he had a free hour the next morning, so we should go together. Of course, there was no reason not to go with him: he knew that too much information bored me, but was usually clever enough to present a detail or anecdote that would lead me to ask questions. I knew some things from the guidebook I'd flipped through in the Academy living room, and of course I'd also been fascinated by my birthday book, with its transparent pages. Rome had ruled the civilized world for almost five hundred years, but then, when the empire fell, the Forum had been forgotten. It was buried in river mud and cows had grazed there in the Middle Ages.

I was surprised, though, that so very little remained. It was good I'd read something about it, because it seemed to me more like a deserted battlefield than a place that had once been the center of the world. We stood by what Harold said was the Arch of Septimius Severus. Below, a tour guide led a group of Asians through the ruins. "Well, they had a good run, I have to say. Five hundred years, give or take," Harold said. "Lucky it was buried, or there'd be less to see than is here. Horrible, the things carried out before there were any restrictions. Still, it's very moving, don't you think?" Since he had walked a bit ahead of me, he didn't really expect an answer. None of the Asians seemed to be couples; standing here and there, I could rarely match one with another with any certainty. I thought Asians were always taking pictures . . . but then, the tour guide stopped speaking, and many cameras were raised. A man in a camouflage hat sat at a French easel, painting something in the direction of—Harold said—the Arch of Titus. "In that direction is the Temple of Vesta, and the house of the Vestal Virgins," Harold said. "Eternal flame isn't just an idea of our century, you know. The Virgins were its keepers—over there, guarding the eternal flame." The sun was weak in the sky. The area quite crowded. "You need a permit to paint here. A *permesso*," Harold said. "Not that the need will arise for you or me." He winked. I smiled. Harold was in his element when he was outdoors, in a historic place; he was being nice to refrain from giving me a history lesson.

Someone was handing Harold his camera, pantomiming in the universal language. He'd selected the right person: Harold was an accomplished photographer. He took a step back, made some adjustment to the camera, gave the universal nod for "I'll take the picture now." How sophisticated all this would have seemed to the Romans. A camera? Tourists? They were just Vestal Virgins, guarding the flame that would become extinguished.

I had no idea why the Spanish Steps, where Lavande and I had shopped, were called the Spanish Steps, but asking would reveal that my mind was not on what was being shown to me. Harold had returned the camera and was waiting for me with his arm slightly outstretched; he lightly guided me on with his hand cupped around my elbow.

FOR OUR anniversary, Harold booked tickets on a cruise ship. Early August found us in JFK, in the first class lounge, spending an hour or so having coffee and reading the paper before boarding the plane for Miami. We now had a grandchild, Emily, whom we adored. Since retiring the previous year, Harold traveled infrequently. We had bought a house in Maine, two hours away from Angela and Mark—close enough, but still far enough away—and they had kindly moved into our house to tend the garden for the two weeks we'd be gone (though Harold maintained that Mr. Jones would do more damage digging than our abandoning the plants and seedlings).

I was cradling a mug of coffee in both hands when I noticed someone wearing a pair of very fashionable high heels walk past, and looked up to see that it was Lavande. After my conversation in the kitchen the day Angela announced her engagement, I had more or less stopped thinking about Lavande, though the moment I saw her I realized that I had assumed, somehow, I would see her again. She was gone and could have stayed gone forever: she had not seen us; Harold had not seen her; her husband was nowhere in sight. But yes he was . . . at the opposite side of the lounge, a hand reached up from behind a tall chair back, and she handed him a cup of coffee. *Donald Stipley.* It popped back into my mind. Her name, I had most certainly not forgotten.

I might have expected to feel angry, but instead I felt almost pre-ternaturally calm. Those times I had thought of her, I'd wondered—with no expectation of an answer—whether she might have found herself in a situation she knew little or nothing about to this day—Donald's first marriage, his crazy wife, the child—or whether they both knew everything, and had put it behind them.

I watched her sit down, seeing only her profile, and that indistinct without my distance glasses. It came to me, then, that she did not know—that her behavior toward me had been only about being his mistress, so that she must have felt badly when his wife died prematurely, though she didn't know the extent of it—what other suffering had taken place. If I'd been Harold's second wife and he'd had a child, would I have wanted that child out of the picture, in boarding school? It was possible that I would have, though I thought that was based on the fact that I hadn't been very effective or able to communicate well as a parent. What would Harold have done if he'd discovered I was quite crazy, and that I had some perverse scenario in which I'd involved Angela? He would have every reason to hate me. It seemed impossible, but probably everyone marries thinking such a thing impossible. It was a shame, however well things had turned out, that as a child Angela had thought the slightest criticism was contempt toward her, and that she thought in stereotypes, so that her father and I could do nothing right, being of a particular time and class.

"Harold," I said, "Donald Stipley and Lavande are on the other side of the lounge. We must go say hello."

Harold was immersed in the book he'd brought to read on the plane: "On Beauty and Being Just." The small book almost disappeared in his big hands. "Do what?" he said, looking up.

"Across the way," I said. "It's Donald Stipley and Lavande."

He turned in their direction. "Well, for heaven's sake. Not friends of mine, mere acquaintances," he said.

I stood. "Come with me," I said. "She acted like my friend in Rome and—"

"God! This again!" he said. "Yes, I remember the situation."

He tucked the cover flap in the book to mark his place, but did not stand, and two things quickly occurred to me: first, that his lower back had ached for days, and that he wanted to pretend that the two of them were of no consequence so he would not have to rise; next, that he really was a historian, and once he had decided how something was—in this case, not mysterious—he had satisfied his curiosity. I could arouse his interest, but I would never, ever be able to bring myself to tell him the tawdry things Angela had told me in the kitchen.

As I walked toward them, I sensed Harold behind me, the way you sometimes sense shadows you do not see. I felt that he had risen and was going to appear at my side, and I was right. He walked more quickly than I would have expected. He stood beside me as I said, "Lavande."

She looked up, half-glasses on the bridge of her nose, her hair falling in perfect waves to her shoulders. She smiled, momentarily confused. She put down her coffee and stood to take my hand. The ring had been joined by another couple of bands. Diamonds sparkled.

"Rome," she said simply. I suppose she had forgotten my name. "Darling," she said to the man in the chair. "You remember our friends from Rome." Since Donald Stipley only frowned, she looked at Harold, with an expression that was pleading. What he had to understand, what we both had to acknowledge, was that Donald Stipley was old, frail, handicapped. She had said loudly into his hearing aid that we were their friends from Rome.

To my surprise, Donald Stipley erupted. "Harold! Put 'er there," he said. He raised his left arm slowly. Harold took his hand for a firm shake, then more or less guided the arm back to the chair rest. Donald's right arm remained across his chest, immobile.

I felt panicked, as if I didn't have much time. "Why?" I said to her, just as suddenly as Donald had spoken.

"Why?" Harold echoed quickly, as if coming to my rescue. "Well, Don, I don't know about you, but when you get to be our age, it's why not, isn't it?"

Donald Stipley nodded and laughed. A bit of drool rolled to his chin. Lavande leaned forward with a napkin. "Excuse us," she said quietly. Then she turned to me. "Because if you must know, I didn't think I'd have a life in which I could ever see you again. I'm not his wife, and on the Rome trip we'd decided to separate. On the flight back, he had a small stroke. Then two others."

It was clear Donald had heard every word. He lowered the napkin to his lap. He said: "I never told you you had to go."

"All but," she said.

"Let bygones be bygones," Harold said. He took me by the elbow. "Good flight," he said. "Lovely to see you again."

"How *can* you, Harold?" I said, shaking off his hand, and in that second I knew exactly the frustration Angela had felt all her life, diminished by his exquisite manners, his implacable sense of timing, which meant whatever was necessary to maintain the status quo.

"Because we're all too old, and it's too late," he said quietly. "You got your answer."

What went unsaid was that nothing could console me, I had needed a friend so very much.

OFF

Aimee Bender

Aimee Bender is the author of three books: *The Girl in the Flammable Skirt*, which was a *New York Times* Notable Book; *An Invisible Sign of My Own*, which was a *Los Angeles Times* pick of the year; and *Willful Creatures*, which was nominated by *The Believer* as one of the best books of the year. Her short fiction has been published in *Granta, GQ, Harper's, Tin House, McSweeney's, The Paris Review*, and elsewhere, as well as heard on PRI's *This American Life* and *Selected Shorts*. She has received two Pushcart prizes and was nominated for the Tiptree Award in 2005. She lives in Los Angeles and teaches creative writing at the University of Southern California.

At the party I make a goal and it is to kiss three men: one with black hair, one with red hair, the third blond. Not necessarily in that order. I'm alone at the party and I have my drink in a mug because by the time I got here, at the ideal moment of lateness, the host had used all her bluish glasses with fluted stems that she bought from the local home-supply store that all others within a ten-block radius had bought too because at some inexplicable point in time, everybody woke up with identical taste. I see two matching sweaters and four similar handbags. It's enough to make you want to buy ugly except other people are having that reaction too and I spot three identically ugly pairs of shoes. There's just nowhere to hide. I know the host here from high-school time and she likes to invite me to things because for one, she feels sorry for me and for two, she finds me entertaining and blushes when I cuss. It's how we flirt.

About half the people here are in couples. I stand alone because I plan on making all these women jealous, reminding them how incredible it is to be single instead of always being with the same old same old except tonight I am jealous too because all their men are seeming particularly tall and kind on this foggy wintery night and one is wearing a shirt a boyfriend of mine used to own with that nubby terry-cloth material recycled from soda cans and it smells clean from where I'm standing, ten feet away, and it's not a good sign when something like a particular laundry detergent can just like that undo you.

From here, against the wall, I can survey the whole living room. TV, couch, easy plant. The walls are covered with pastel posters of gardens by famous painters who rediscovered light and are now all over address books and umbrellas and mugs. Is it really worth it to dead earless van Gogh that his painting now holds some person's catalog of phone numbers? Is that what he wanted when he fought through personal hell to capture the sun in Arles? I used to paint and I would make landscapes that were peaceful and my teacher would stroll through the easels and praise me and say, "What a lovely cornfield, dear," but she never looked hard enough because if you did you would see that each landscape had something bad in it and that lovely was the wrong word to use: I made that cornfield, true, but if you looked closely, there was a glinting knife hanging from each husk. And I made a beach scene with crashing waves and a crescent moon and then this loaded machine gun lying on the sand by a towel; and then I made a mountain town with quaint stores and tall pine trees and people walking around except for that one man wrapped in dynamite walking over to the guy with the cigarette lighter standing by the drinking fountain.

The terrible thing is that the teacher never figured it out. And she saw all three paintings. She actually thought the guy in dynamite was wearing some strange puffy suit and that the corn was just very glinty. She said the machine gun was a nice kite. When the evaluation sheets came around, I said she was useless and should be fired.

The couples are shifting positions and I'm ready now and I find that redhead first. Lucky for me he is drunk already and sitting in a chair with pretzels and he's talking to no one because he's on break from being social because he is so drunk. I saunter over and ask him to help me look for my purse in the bedroom. "I lost my purse," I say to him. "Help." He blinks, eyelids heavy with the eye shadow of alcohol, and then he follows me into the bedroom which is covered with people's items: twenty-five coats and half as many purses. I am rich but I consider stealing some of the stuff because they are so trusting, these people, and I feel like wrecking their trust. But where would I stash a coat? We are looking around for my make-believe purse because I don't use a purse at all; when I go out, I just carry keys and slip one one-hundred-dollar bill into the arch of my shoe and let the night unroll from there. We're mumbling in the bedroom and I pretend I'm drunker than I am and then I ask him, right there, among all the coats, if he thinks I'm pretty. His eyes are bleary and he smiles and says, "Yeah, yeah." We're standing by the bed, and I lean over and I kiss him then, really gentle because at any minute he could throw up all over me, and his lips are dry and we spend a few minutes like that, gentle kisses on his dry lips, and then he starts to laugh and I am offended. "Why are you laughing?" I ask, and he laughs more, and I sort of push him and pick up one of the better coats on the bed, with a shiny lined inside of burgundy, and I put it on for a second even though I'm not cold and I ask him again why he laughed and he says, "We went to grade school together," and I say, "We did? We did?" and he tells me his name and then he tells me my name and I apologize because I don't remember him. "I remember you because you were the one with the inheritance," he says, and I tell him I was really good at painting too and he says, "Really? I don't remember that."

So I am through with him.

I take off the coat and throw it back on the bed and then head to the door.

"Wait, why did you kiss me?" he asks, and I know it is taking a big effort for him to string this sentence together because he is so drunk. "Let's go out sometime," he slurs. "I just laughed because it's funny, it's funny. To kiss someone you knew as a kid. It's funny."

I turn around and he looms above me and I can see the freckles on his collarbone and that means he has a chest of freckles and a back of freckles and knees of freckles and freckled inner thighs and I was the best artist in grade school for several years until that dumb girl moved here from Korea, and he is laughing more because he knew me as a little kid and is remembering something and I barely remember what it was like to be a little kid so it seems rude that he would recall something about me that I couldn't myself. If I can't remember it, then it should mean no one else can either.

"No," I tell him. "I don't want to go out with you, ever."

And I'm back in the main room. I return to the same wall. The redhead follows me out and collapses back into that chair, staring, but I ignore him and look at the table of food instead. The guacamole dip is at half, and there are little shit-green blobs on the tablecloth. The brie is a white cave. The wineglasses are empty except for that one undrinkable red spot at the bottom. I go refill my glass and the redhead closes his eyes in the chair. One down.

The blond is next, and he is someone I used to date and in fact only broke up with around three months ago so I think it'll be easy; I find him in the corner talking to two other guys and I glide over and because I am me I am wearing an incredible dress tonight; this one looks almost like it is made of metal; it has this slinky way of falling all over my hips and I feel like an on faucet in it and of course I am the most dressed up at the party, I always am, but that's the whole point, so when the host inevitably looks down at her everybodyownsthemjeans at the front door and says, "Oh, but it's not a formal party," I smile at her with as many teeth as I can fit and wink and say, "That's fine, that's fine, I just felt like wearing this tonight."

Inevitably, the next time I see that same host she has more lipstick on or a new glittering necklace her mother bought her but lady she is dust next to me inside this silverness. I am now almost right behind the blond man who broke up with me because he didn't feel loved and it was true, I did not love him, but he is the type to never go out with someone for a long time anyway so we would've broken up soon regardless and I just gave us a good excuse. I am next to him by now and I tell him we need to talk and could we go in the bathroom? He is confused for a minute but then agrees, and says "Hang on" to his friends who shake their heads because they remember me well and think he's being stupid and they're right but we go into the bathroom and I say, "Adam, I have a goal to kiss you tonight," and he says, "C'mon, is that what this is about?" and I tell him to come here but he has his hand on the doorknob but also he's not gone yet. "You're incredible," he says, shaking his head, and I feel mad, what does he mean, it's not a compliment, and he's out the door. And he's out the door, then. I'm alone in the bathroom and I'm sitting on the sink and my butt is falling a little into the sink part, faucet on faucet, and I turn around to myself in the medicine-cabinet mirror and check my teeth and they are bright and white because last week I bought a new tooth cleaner and it's working and my eyeliner isn't smeared because I bought the new eyeliner that swears it won't smear or you can sue the company, and I'm sitting there plotting my next blond when Adam comes back into the bathroom with determination and closes the door firmly. "You're just playing with me, aren't you?" he says, and I say, "Yeah," and he sighs a little. "At least you're honest," he says, and I say, "Thanks, I try to be honest, I do, that is one of my good qualities." He waits there by the door and I hop off the sink to go to him, stand and face him, and he's not running away so I'm moving in and then we're kissing, that easy, and his lips are the same ones I know well, in fact he was my longest boyfriend so I know his lips better than anyone's, and his upper lip is much thinner than his lower lip which I always liked and I kiss that pillow at the bottom and we kiss and it gets more, we keep kissing and I remember just what it's like and I am suddenly feeling like I miss him and I am remembering everything of what it's like to be with him and I am forgiving him for everything and we're still kissing and his teeth and his smell and we've been kissing too long now, it's gone on long enough, so I pull away. He has lipstick on the edges of his mouth. "Okay," I say, "thank you, okay." He looks shook up but also wants more and he has the same feeling I do; he felt the room change into a different room during that kiss but I'm trying to get it back to being the first room, the one where I know it all. His hands are all over my silver dress slipsliding around and the bathroom door opens, it's some lady who wants to use the bathroom and she sees us and blushes and I'm glad I don't know her because I don't want the whole party to know I'm in the bathroom kissing a blond while I still have a black-haired man to finish the night with. Adam is wiping the lipstick off now and his hand is still on my dress, on my hip; "You're a cold woman," he says to me, and then his hand is gone and he leaves and I am left in there again and I know I am not a cold woman because the whole point of why it was hard for him to leave just then is because I am a not-cold woman but I resent the lie anyway. I check myself in the mirror again and my skin has sharpened and the teeth and eyeliner are all still good and I am thinking about him for a minute, thinking about how when he came inside me and I came outside him he would say something like "This is it," and I'd think, It's the end of the world, and then we'd finish up and be sweating and hot and the world would still be there, like it had swung up and met us. And when we slept then it was so deep it really could've been the end of the world with sirens and megaphones and panicked TV people and I know at least for myself I wouldn't have even noticed.

I exit the bathroom after I've used it and the lady who interrupted is standing there and she is embarrassed and I am not and I step on her foot as I walk out and she says, "Oops, sorry," like all women do and I am mad at that because it was my fault so why is she apologizing? and I hate that she said "Oops" in that little meek voice and now I'm in a bad mood. And I still have one flavor to go. It's an hour later now and the guacamole is gone and the brie is all shell and these stupid people don't know that the white part of brie is important to the taste, that it doesn't count if you only eat the mushy inside, that the French would leave en masse if they came to this party and saw the Americans carving out their cheese like cave dwellers, but the party people only like easy cheese, and easy jeans, and they are all sipping from their fluted glasses and I get re-fill number three or four and the wine is making my bones loose and it's giving my hair a red sheen and my breasts are blooming and my eyes feel sultry and wise and the dress is water. Adam is back with his friends and he won't look at me and they are sheltering him like a little male righteous wall and the redhead is gone by now or passed out somewhere and I am looking for black hair, looking, looking, and you'd think it'd be easy considering something like four-fifths of the entire earth has black hair and I do find one prospect but he seems harsh and too talkative so I pass him up and I find a cute black guy but he seems to be one of the married ones and I am trying to keep this as simple as possible and I'm looking, still looking, then bingo: it's the tallest man in the room. He has sharp black hair over his ears and glasses and a swarthiness and he is the smarty guy and he is talking to a woman who is clearly entranced by him, but remember: I am a column of mercury, and this woman is wearing a blouse and khaki pants, drinking water from a mug imprinted with water lilies. The deal is done.

She is telling him about her job at a pet hospital. She is a vet of sorts. Every person on earth likes a vet except me, because I think there are too many animals in the first place. And when these vets keep saving the sick animals, we are just stuck with more.

"These are from the last cat," she is saying, holding up her arm which is covered with raised tracks.

He nods, observes. I, however, am not interested in her fake drug habit look-alike war wounds. I bet a thousand dollars she grew up with a dog who had a name with a γ or an *ie* at the end. I had a dog once, a big dog, a Great Dane, and I named him Off so when I called him, I said "Off!" and he came bounding over. It really fucked with people's heads. At the dog park no one got it. They kept trying to figure out how I did that, if I was okay, what was happening. I was laughing all the time at the dog park. I wore dresses there too and I think people brought their friends to see me, like I was a sight in the city, a tourist attraction. If I was forty it'd be a problem but I'm not so they adore me. Off died early because he was a purebred but I didn't put him to sleep, I kept him company and stroked his big forehead until I saw his eyes shut on their own. I had him cremated. I sprinkled most of his ashes into my plants, but fed a few of the remaining ones to the cat next door because she had always been tormented by Off's size and I thought it was a little bit of sweet vindication.

It's nearly midnight, and I'm waiting for the man here to say something so I can form my game plan. Adam is talking to a woman now and I can tell he is appearing extra animated to get my goat. I can only see the woman's butt from here, but it's very flat and Adam is an ass man so I'm not worried. I don't shrivel up into wiggly jealousy. Instead I feel like thrusting through all the women here, stepping on all those dainty toes, releasing a chorus of "Oops, sorries," a million apologies for something I did wrong.

The vet is still talking. "Last week," she is saying, "the sweetest beagle came in with some kind of dementia and I had to put him to sleep . . ."

"That must be tough," he says, "to put a dog to sleep."

I'm underneath the yellow-and-pink floral painting. Fuck me, I'm thinking. She is taking too damn long. At the door, one of the couples is saying goodbye to the host. Her hand is on his elbow. The host looks dampened; I think somebody broke her stereo.

And suddenly, in a wash, I am feeling low. I am feeling like there is nothing in this whole party for me and I want everyone to leave now. I'm thinking about how when I filled out the evaluation for the painting teacher, and I said she should be fired, I made sure to sign my name. I've given some money to the university—not enough to get a building named after me, but close. And when the next session rolled around and I looked for her name in the catalog, I couldn't find it anywhere. My final painting for the class was that—the catalog page without her name in it.

"Oh," she had said, "isn't that a delightful picture of the sea."

I slump a little on the wall. The red-haired man is back, asleep in his chair. Vet says, "I feel like I'm a prison guard or something with all this lethal-injection stuff."

And then the man says something about how he worked in a prison once and he saw a lethal injection once and it was the worst thing he'd ever seen and I perk up then, rejuvenated, because that's all I need to know; I figure now if he worked in a prison then he has sympathy with people who are trapped or bad and just like that my plan is set.

So I smile at both of them as I move away from the wall in a silvery wave and he notices me then, how can he not, and he nods and khaki vet is off talking again and I interrupt and say, "I have to do something," and the vet is surprised that I can talk and gives me a snotty look down her I-never-got-past-my-childhood-dream nose, and I say, to him only, "Hey, if I'm not back here in a couple minutes, will you check on me?"

He nods, unsure what I mean. She slivers her eyes at me. I open mine wide back, because eye slivering is for old hags. I'm not sure about the details of my plan yet but I step past Adam who is still talking to that unfuckable woman with no ass and I go into the bedroom. I'm planning on stealing something, but I'm not sure what to steal that would make him come find me. I survey the bed. I could steal all the wallets but it seems too unoriginal and detailed so I decide to do the thing I wanted to do with the red-haired man and that is to steal all the coats. I lean over and scoop them together, wool ones and tweed ones and velvet ones and cotton ones, and pick them up in a huge stack, my arms a belt, so heavy they make me stagger, and I go inside the bedroom closet with them and shut the door until I am smothered with coats. It's hot in here, and it smells like shoe polish. I arrange myself underneath the billion coats and then I wait for either the black-haired man to remember to hunt for me or someone else to get ready to leave the party. After just a few minutes, there are footsteps in the bedroom and it's two people and they're ready to bundle up for outdoors and go back to where they live and of course they cannot find their coats and it's winter and they are certain they brought coats. So they leave the room and return to the host and I can hear her quizzical voice going up. "Coats? Bedroom." Her tone is always so sincere. In high school her mother wouldn't let her shop at certain stores because they were too expensive and too slutty and so I would take her shopping and buy her a blue leather miniskirt or a sheer black slip and she would try them on at my house in the ultra-mirrored bathroom and model and pose. She refused to wear them out. She just wore them for me. She has this compact body and looked sporty in everything and I told her compliment after compliment and we never touched but she still always blushed like crazy. There was this one dress of white feathers and she looked like a whole different genre of person inside it. It would've made my entire high school worthwhile if she'd worn that to her prom but she could hardly leave the bathroom and her face was bright red so that between her and the dress I was reminded of a peppermint. I never took those outfits back to the store; I kept them for a few of her visits and when she seemed bored of them or started to guilt-trip me and ask how much they cost, I gave them to Goodwill. Goodwill, for good reason, loved me. And my head is leaning back on a soft coat of lamb's wool and I can hear the talking outside getting louder and I'm thinking that the reason I kept going out with Adam in the first place was because when I showed him my painting of the ocean in my living room, on our second date, when I was wearing peach velvet, long sleeves, super plunging low neck, he looked at it for about one second and said, "Lady, you are screwed UP." And even though I was a little bit insulted, I was also ridiculous with gratitude and I took off my clothes right there, in one smooth movement, unzipped that peach velvet to show a different kind of peach, a different kind of velvet. Within seconds he was kissing my shoulders and my side and the inside of my knee and he told me to stay standing for a while then and I felt like the tallest person ever born. And by now the couple is back in the bedroom and the party is filtering into the bedroom because they know something is wrong and they are all wondering where all the coats are and someone is getting upset, someone with an expensive coat and I reach out my hand and grope around until I find it. Cashmere. It smells like a woman, like expensive perfume, but not as rich as me; me, I buy perfume so expensive it doesn't smell like anything but skin. And they are panicking and someone is saying how the pocket of her coat has her keys in it and she's asking, "Who is missing? Who took the coats?" and I am touching the pocket with the keys, it's near my foot, and I hear Adam call my name and I am quiet but he is thinking, It's her, she is somewhere hiding with coats, and he excuses himself from flat butt but I don't want to see him ever again, I want the black-haired man to find me so I can kiss him and get home already. I close my eyes, hoping that when he opens the closet he will find me sleeping and I'll wake, disoriented; I'll tell him in a delightfully raspy voice that I was cold and needed a blanket and he will think I'm a nut or drunk but also he will be moved somehow and we'll start kissing in the bottom of the closet and he will have intuitive knowledge about my mouth, and I am hearing footsteps approach the closet, heavy ones, male ones, nearby, someone is approaching the closet and it's opening a crack and then it's open but I can't see who's there because my eyes are closed and then it's the black-haired man, it is, I can tell because he says "Oh," and I recognize his deep voice. I reach up a hand because I want to drag him in here—I am stuck, I am bad, it's jail, it's just like you like—but instead, he calls out, "Hey! I Found The Coats!" really loud, and then I pretend to wake up and say "Oh, hi, what? I was just cold," and the host comes by and when she sees me it's like I'm her troublesome dog-pet and she says "I'm so sorry," and the black-haired man points me out and says, "Here You Are, Miss," like he's a bellhop locating luggage and I explain how I was cold and the coat couple reach in the closet as if I'm not even in it and fuss around and retrieve their coats and then they're off and everyone else is taking their coats really fast in case I'm somehow going to eat them and it's a time-limit thing and coat after coat is picked up until I'm coat-less and just myself in my dress and I feel truly cold now and bare and small and then Adam is standing there in the crowd, and he says, "I'll take it from here," and I think that's so fatherly of him it makes me feel sort of sick also because it makes me feel sort of good and the host asks what I was doing, and for the third or fourth time I say I was cold, I just thought I'd be warmer with all these coats. I make my eyes blurry. And she buys it. She thinks I'm that plain drunk from her affordable-yet-delicious wine. And the black-haired man buys it too and nods but then turns around and goes back to the other room to talk to the vet. He leaves the drunk crazy lady behind and returns to the conservative animal lover. And it's just Adam there now, standing with his familiar face—who knows I wasn't cold or drunk, standing there as everyone clears out and he tells me to get up and pulls me when I don't and sits me on the bed. We stare at the wall together. And I'm thinking how I didn't reach my goal and that the whole strawberry/vanilla/chocolate trio isn't nearly as good with just two flavors, and he is sitting there thinking something else, I have no idea what, and he isn't touching me but I can hear him breathing. In the other room, people are leaving. The hidden coats scared them and they took it as some kind of cue that the party was over. Everyone is trickling out and thanking the host and whispering about me and she continues to be ultra-sincere, even when some complainer says something about a wrinkle in her coat, in a mad voice. Oops, I think. Sorry. I stare at the wall directly ahead. There's a painting of a desert hung up. It's in a simple wood frame and in it there's just a row of cacti and then the sun setting in the distance and who needs weapons when they're cacti. That's all I'm looking at when Adam takes my hand.

MERCY

Pinckney Benedict

Pinckney Benedict grew up on his family's farm in southern West Virginia. His stories have appeared in *Esquire, Zoetrope: All-Story, StoryQuarterly, Ontario Review, The O. Henry Prize Stories, New Stories from the South,* the Pushcart Prize series, *The Oxford Book of American Short Stories,* and elsewhere.

The livestock hauler's ramp banged onto the ground, and out of the darkness they came, the miniature horses, fine-boned and fragile as china. They trit-trotted down the incline like the vanguard of a circus parade, tails up, manes fluttering. They were mostly a bunch of tiny pintos, the biggest not even three feet tall at the withers. I was ten years old, and their little bodies made me feel like a giant. The horses kept coming out of the trailer, more and more of them every moment. The teamsters that were unloading them just stood back and smiled.

My old man and I were leaning on the top wire of the southern fence-line of our place, watching the neighbor farm become home to these exotics. Ponies, he kept saying, ponies ponies ponies, like if he said it enough times, he might be able to make them go away. Or make himself believe they were real, one or the other.

I think they're miniature horses, I told him. Not ponies. I kept my voice low, not sure I wanted him to hear me.

One faultless dog-sized sorrel mare looked right at me, tossed its head, and sauntered out into the thick clover of the field, nostrils flaring. I decided I liked that one the best. To myself, I named it Cinnamon. If I were to try and ride it, I thought, my heels would drag the ground.

Horses, ponies, my old man said. He had heard. He swept out a dismissive hand. Can't work them, can't ride them, can't eat them. Useless.

Useless was the worst insult in his vocabulary.

We were angus farmers. Magnificent deep-fleshed black angus. In the field behind us, a dozen of our market steers roamed past my old man and me in a lopsided wedge, cropping the sweet grass. They ate constantly, putting on a pound, two pounds a day. All together like that, they made a sound like a steam locomotive at rest in the station, a deep resonant sighing. Their rough hides gleamed obsidian in the afternoon sun, and their hooves might have been fashioned out of pig iron.

The biggest of them, the point of the wedge, raised his head, working to suss out this new smell, the source of this nickering and whinnying, that had invaded his neighborhood. His name was Rug, because his hide was perfect, and my old man planned to have it tanned after we sent him off to the lockers in the fall. None of the other steers had names, just the numbers in the yellow tags that dangled from their ears. Rug peered near-sightedly through the woven-wire fence that marked the border between his field and the miniature horses', and his face was impassive, as it always was.

The teamsters slammed the trailer's ramp back into place and climbed into the rig's cab, cranked up the big diesel engine, oily smoke pluming from the dual stacks. The offloaded horses began to play together, nipping at one another with their long yellow teeth, dashing around the periphery of the field, finding the limits of the place. Cinnamon trailed after the others, less playful than the rest. Rug lowered his head and moved on, and the wedge of heavy-shouldered angus moved with him.

Another livestock van pulled into the field, the drivers of the two trucks exchanging casual nods as they passed each other. I was happy enough to see more of them come, funny little beggars, but I had a moment of wondering to myself how many horses, even miniature ones, the pasture could sustain.

More of the midgets, my old man said. What in hell's next? he asked. He wasn't speaking to me exactly. He very seldom addressed a question directly to me. It seemed like he might be asking God Himself. What? Giraffes? Crocodiles?

THIS VALLEY was a beef valley from long before I was born. A broad river valley with good grass, set like a diamond in the center of a wide plateau at twenty-four hundred feet of altitude. For generations it was Herefords all around our place, mostly, and Charolais, but our angus were the sovereigns over them all. My grandfather was president of the cattlemen's association, and he raised some trouble when the Beefmasters and Swiss Simmentals came in, because the breeds were unfamiliar to him; and my old man did the same when the place to our east went with the weird-looking hump-backed lop-eared Brahmas. But they got used to the new breeds. They were, after all, beefers, and beef fed the nation; and we were still royalty.

Then the bottom fell out of beef prices. We hung on. Around us, the Charolais and Simmentals went first, the herds dispersed and the land sold over the course of a few years, and then the rest of them all in a rush, and we were alone. Worse than alone. Now it was swine to the east, and the smell of them when the wind was wrong was enough to gag a strong-stomached man. The smell of angus manure is thick and honest and bland, like the angus himself; but pig manure is acid and briny and bitter and brings a tear to the eye. And the shrieking of the pigs clustered in their long barns at night, as it drifted across the fields into our windows, was like the cries of the damned.

Pigs to the east, with a big poultry operation beyond that, and sheep to the north (with llamas to protect them from packs of feral dogs), and even rumors of a man up in Pocahontas County who wanted to start an ostrich ranch, because ostrich meat was said to be low in fat and cholesterol, and ostrich plumes made wonderful feather dusters that never wore out.

The place to our west wasn't even a farm anymore. A rich surgeon named Slaughter from the county seat had bought the acreage when Warren Kennebaker, the Charolais breeder, went bust. Slaughter had designed it like a fortress, and it looked down on our frame house from a hill where the dignified long-bodied Charolais had grazed: a great gabled many-chimneyed mansion that went up in a matter of months; acres of slate roof, and a decorative entrance flanked by stone pillars and spear-pointed pickets that ran for three or four rods out to each side of the driveway and ended there; and gates with rampant lions picked out in gold. That entrance with its partial fence made my old man angrier than anything else. What good's a fence that doesn't go all the way around? he asked me. Keeps nothing out, keeps nothing in.

Useless, I said.

As tits on a bull, he said. Then: Doctor Slaughter, Doctor Slaughter! he shouted up at the blank windows of the house. He thought her name was the funniest thing he had ever heard. Why don't you just get together and form a practice with Doctor Payne and Doctor Butcher?

There was no Doctor Payne or Doctor Butcher; that was just his joke.

Payne, Slaughter, and Butcher! he shouted. That would be rich.

THE HORSES started testing the fence almost from the first. They were smart, I could tell that from watching them, from the way they played tag together, darting off to the far parts of the pasture to hide, flirting, concealing their compact bodies in folds of the earth and leaping up to race off again when they were discovered, their hooves drumming against the hard-packed ground. They galloped until they reached one end of the long field, then swung around in a broad curve and came hell-for-leather back the way they had gone, their coats shaggy with the approach of winter and slick with sweat. I watched them whenever I had a few moments free from ferrying feed for the steers.

I would walk down to the south fence and climb up on the sagging wire and sit and take them in as they leaped and nipped and pawed at one another with their sharp, narrow hooves. I felt like they wanted to put on a show for me when I was there, wanted to entertain me. During the first snow, which was early that year, at the end of October, they stood stock still, the whole crew of them, and gaped around at the gently falling flakes. They twitched their hides and shook their manes and shoulders as though flies were lighting all over them. They snorted and bared their teeth and sneezed. After a while, they grew bored with the snow and went back to their games.

After a few weeks, though, when the weather got colder and the grass was thin and trampled down, the horses became less like kids and more like the convicts in some prison picture: heads down, shoulders hunched, they sidled along the fence line, casting furtive glances at me and at the comparatively lush pasturage on our side of the barrier.

The fence was a shame and an eyesore. It had been a dry summer when it went in, five years before when the last of the dwindling Herefords had occupied the field, and the dirt that season was dry as desert sand, and the posts weren't sunk as deep as they should have been. They were loose like bad teeth, and a few of them were nearly rotted through. I was the only one who knew what bad shape it was getting to be in. My old man seldom came down to this boundary after the day the horses arrived, and nobody from the miniature horse farm walked their border the way we walked ours. We didn't know any of them, people from outside the county, hardly ever glimpsed them at all.

It wasn't our problem to solve. By long tradition, that stretch was the responsibility of the landowner to the south, and I figured my old man would die before he would take up labor and expense that properly belonged with the owners of the miniature horses.

CINNAMON, THE sorrel, came over to me one afternoon when I was taking a break, pushed her soft nose through the fence toward me, and I promised myself that the next time I came I would bring the stump of a carrot or a lump of sugar with me. I petted her velvet nose and she nibbled gently at my fingers and the open palm of my hand. Her whiskers tickled and her breath was warm and damp against my skin.

Then she took her nose from me and clamped her front teeth on the thin steel wire of the fence and pulled it toward her, pushed it back. I laughed. Get away from there, I told her, and smacked her gently on the muzzle. She looked at me reproachfully and tugged at the wire again. Her mouth made grating sounds against the metal that set my own teeth on edge. She had braced her front legs and was really pulling, and the fence flexed and twanged like a bow string. A staple popped loose from the nearest post.

You've got to stop it, I said. You don't want to come over here, even if the grass looks good. My old man will shoot you if you do.

HE SURPRISED me watching the horses. I was in my usual place on the fence, the top wire biting into my rear end, and he must have caught sight of me as he was setting out one of the great round hay bales for the angus to feed from. Generally I was better at keeping track of him, at knowing where he was, but that day I had brought treats with me and was engrossed, and I didn't hear the approaching rumble of his tractor as it brought the fodder over the hill. When he shut down the engine, I knew that I was caught.

What are you doing? he called. The angus that were following the tractor and the hay, eager to be fed, ranged themselves in a stolid rank behind him. I kicked at Cinnamon to get her away from me, struggled to get the slightly crushed cubes of sugar back into my pocket. Crystals of it clung to my fingers. He strode down to me, and I swung my legs back over to our side of the fence and hopped down. It was a cold day and his breath rolled white from his mouth.

You've got plenty of leisure, I guess, he said. His gaze flicked over my shoulder. A number of the miniature horses, Cinnamon at their head, had peeled off from the main herd and were dashing across the open space. What makes them run like that? he asked. I hesitated a moment, not sure whether he wanted to know or if it was one of those questions that didn't require an answer.

They're just playing, I told him. They spend a lot of time playing.

Playing. Is that right, he said. You'd like to have one, I bet. Wouldn't you, boy? he asked me.

I pictured myself with my legs draped around the barrel of Cinnamon's ribs, my fingers wrapped in the coarse hair of her mane. Even as I pictured it, I knew a person couldn't ride a miniature horse. I recalled what it felt like when she had thrust her muzzle against my hand, her breath as she went after the sugar I had begun bringing her. Her teeth against the wire. I pictured myself holding out a fresh carrot for her to lip into her mouth. I pictured her on our side of the fence, her small form threading its way among the stern gigantic bodies of the angus steers. I knew I would be a fool to tell him I wanted a miniature horse.

Yes sir, I said.

He swept his eyes along the fence. Wire's in pretty bad shape, he said. Bastards aren't doing their job. Looks like we'll have to do it for them.

He shucked off the pair of heavy leather White Mule work gloves he was wearing and tossed them to me. I caught one in the air, and the other fell to the cold ground. You keep the fence in shape then, he said. The staples and wire and stretcher and all were in the machine shed, I knew.

Remember, my old man said as he went back to his tractor. First one that comes on my property, I kill.

———————

ON THE next Saturday, before dawn, I sat in the cab of our beef hauler while he loaded steers. There were not many of them; it would only take us one trip. I couldn't get in among them because I didn't yet own a pair of steel-toed boots, and the angus got skittish when they were headed to the stockyard. I would have helped, I wanted to help, but he was afraid I would get stepped on by the anxious beeves and lose a toe. He was missing toes on both feet. So he was back there by himself at the tailgate of the truck, running the angus up into it, shouting at them.

Rug was the first, and my old man called the name into his twitching ear—Ho, Rug! Ho!—and took his cap off, slapped him on the rump with it. Get up there! he shouted. I watched him in the rearview mirror, and it was hard to make out what was happening, exactly, because the mirror was cracked down its length, the left half crazed into a patchwork of glass slivers. The other angus were growing restive, I could tell that much, while Rug balked.

My old man never would use an electric prod. He twisted Rug's tail up into a tight, painful coil, shoving with his shoulder, and the big steer gave in and waddled reluctantly into the van. The truck shifted with his weight, which was better than a ton. The rest followed, the hauler sinking lower and lower over the rear axle as they clambered inside. My old man silently mouthed their numbers, every one, as they trundled on board, and he never looked at their ear tags once. He knew them.

When they were all embarked, when for the moment his work was done, his face fell slack and dull, and his shoulders slumped. And for a brief instant he stood still, motionless as I had never seen him. It was as though a breaker somewhere inside him had popped, and he had been shut off.

I MADE my daily round of the southern fence, patching up the holes the horses had made, shoveling loose dirt into the cavities they carved into the earth, as though they would tunnel under the fence if I wouldn't let them break through it. They were relentless and I had become relentless too, braiding the ends of the bitten wire back together, hammering bent staples back into the rotting posts. The sharp end of a loose wire snaked its way through the cowhide palm of the glove on my right hand and bit deep into me. I cursed and balled the hand briefly into a fist to stanch the blood, and then I went back to work again.

The field the horses occupied was completely skinned now, dotted with mounds of horse dung. Because the trees were bare of leaves, I could see through the windbreak to the principal barn of the place, surrounded by dead machinery. I couldn't tell if anyone was caring for them at all. I don't believe a single animal had been sold. Their coats were long and matted, their hooves long untrimmed, curling and ugly. A man—I suppose it was a man, because at this distance I couldn't tell, just saw a dark figure in a long coat—emerged from the open double doors of the barn, apparently intent on some errand.

Hey! I shouted to him. My voice was loud in the cold and silence. The figure paused and glanced around. I stood up and waved my arms over my head to get his attention. This is your fence!

He lifted a hand, pale so that I could only imagine that it was ungloved, and waved uncertainly back at me.

This is your fence to fix! I called. I pounded my hand against the loose top wire. These here are your horses!

The hand dropped, and the figure without making any further acknowledgment of me or what I had said turned its back and strolled at a casual pace back into the dark maw of the barn.

MOST DAYS I hated them. I cursed them as they leaned their slight weight against the fence, their ribs showing. I poked them with a sharp stick to get them to move so that I could fix the fence. They would shift their bodies momentarily, then press them even harder into the wire. The posts groaned and popped. I twisted wire and sucked at the cuts on my fingers to take the sting away. I filched old bald tires from the machine shed and rolled them through the field and laid them against the holes in the fence. The tires smelled of dust and spider webs. This was not the way we mended fence on our place—our posts were always true, our wire stretched taut and un-corroded, our staples solidly planted—but it was all I could think of to keep them out. The horses rolled their eyes at me.

And I tossed them old dry corn cobs that I retrieved from the crib, the one that we hadn't used in years. The horses fell on the dry husks, shoving each other away with their heads, lashing out with their hooves, biting each other now not in play but hard enough to draw blood. I pitched over shriveled windfallen ap-ples from the stunted trees in the old orchard behind the house. I tried to get the apples near the sorrel, near Cinnamon; but as often as not the pintos shunted her aside before she could snatch a mouthful.

YOU KNOW why we can't feed them, don't you? my old man asked me. We were breaking up more of the great round bales, which were warm and moist at their center, like fresh-baked rolls. The angus, led not by Rug now but by another, shifted their muscular shoul-ders and waited patiently to be fed. I could sense the miniature horses lining the fence, but I didn't look at them.

They'd eat us out of house and home, he said. Like locusts.

Behind me, the hooves of the horses clacked against the frozen ground.

ONE MORNING, the fence didn't need mending. It had begun to snow in earnest the night before, and it was still snowing when I went out to repair the wire. The television was promising snow for days to come. Most of the horses were at the fence, pressing hard against it but not otherwise moving. Some were lying down in the field be-yond. I looked for the sorrel, to see if she was among the standing ones. All of them were covered in thick blankets of snow, and it was impossible to tell one diminutive shape from the next. Each fence post was topped with a sparkling white dome.

I walked the fence, making sure there was no new damage. I took up the stick I had used to poke them and ran its end along the fence wire, hoping its clattering sound would stir them. It didn't. Most of them had clustered at a single point, to exchange body heat, I suppose. I rapped my stick against the post where they were gathered, and its cap of snow fell to the ground with a soft thump. Nothing. The wire was stretched tight with the weight of them.

I knelt down, and the snow soaked immediately through the knees of my coveralls. I put my hand in my pocket, even though I knew there was nothing there for them. The dry cobs were all gone, the apples had been eaten. The eyes of the horse nearest me were closed, and there was snow caught in its long delicate lashes. The eyes of all the horses were closed. This one, I thought, was the sorrel, was Cinnamon. Must be. I put my hand to its muzzle but could feel nothing. I stripped off the White Mule glove, and the cold bit immediately into my fingers, into the half-healed cuts there from the weeks of mending fence. I reached out again.

And the horse groaned. I believed it was the horse. I brushed snow from its forehead, and its eyes blinked open, and the groaning continued, a weird guttural creaking and crying, and I thought that such a sound couldn't be coming from just the one horse, all of the horses must be making it together somehow, they were crying out with a single voice. Then I thought as the sound grew louder that it must be the hogs to the east, they were slaughtering the hogs and that was the source of it, but it was not time for slaughtering, so that couldn't be right either. I thought these things in a moment, as the sound rang out over the frozen fields and echoed off the surrounding hills.

At last I understood that it was the fencepost, the wood of the fencepost and the raveling wire and the straining staples, right at the point where the horses were gathered. And I leaped backward just as the post gave way. It heeled over hard and snapped off at ground level, and the horses tumbled with it, coming alive as they fell, the snow flying from their coats in a wild spray as they scrambled to get out from under one another.

The woven-wire fence, so many times mended, parted like tissue paper under their combined weight. With a report like a gunshot, the next post went over as well, and the post beyond that. Two or three rods of fence just lay down flat on the ground, and the horses rolled right over it, they came pouring onto our place. The horses out in the field roused themselves at the sound, shivered off their mantles of snow, and came bounding like great dogs through the gap in the fence as well. And I huddled against the ground, my hands up to ward off their flying hooves as they went past me, over me. I knew that there was nothing I could do to stop them. Their hooves would brain me, they would lay my scalp open to the bone.

I was not touched.

The last of the horses bolted by me, and they set to on the remains of the broken round bale, giving little cries of pleasure as they buried their muzzles in the hay's roughness. The few angus that stood nearby looked on bemused at the arrivals. I knew that I had to go tell my father, I had to go get him right away. The fence—the fence that I had maintained day after day, the fence I had hated and that had blistered and slashed my hands—was down. But because it was snowing and all around was quiet, the scene had the feel of a holiday, and I let them eat.

WHEN THEY had satisfied themselves, for the moment at least, the horses began to play. I searched among them until finally I found the sorrel. She was racing across our field, her hooves kicking up light clouds of ice crystals. She was moving more quickly than I had ever seen her go, but she wasn't chasing another horse, and she wasn't being chased. She was teasing the impassive angus steers, roaring up to them, stopping just short of their great bulk; turning on a dime and dashing away again. They stood in a semicircle, hind ends together, lowered heads outermost, and they towered over her like the walls of a medieval city. She yearned to charm them. She was almost dancing in the snow.

As I watched her, she passed my old man without paying him

the least attention. He wore his long cold-weather coat. The hood was up, and it eclipsed his face. He must have been standing there quite a while. Snow had collected on the ridge of his shoulders, and a rime of frost clung to the edges of his hood. In his hand he held a hunting rifle, his Remington .30-06. The lines of his face seemed odd and unfamiliar beneath the coat's cowl, and his shoulders were trembling in a peculiar way as he observed the interlopers on his land. I blinked. I knew what was coming. The thin sunlight, refracted as it was by the snow, dazzled my eyes, and the shadows that hid him from me were deep.

At last, the sorrel took notice of him, and she turned away from the imperturbable angus and trotted over to him. He watched her come. She lowered her delicate head and nipped at him, caught the hem of his coat between her teeth and began to tug. His feet slipped in the snow. Encouraged by her success, she dragged him forward. I waited for him to kill her. She continued to drag him, a foot, a yard, and at last he fell down. He fell right on his ass in the snow, my old man, the Remington held high above his head. The sorrel stood over him, the other horses clustered around her, and she seemed to gloat.

The Remington dropped to the ground, the bolt open, the breech empty. Half a dozen bright brass cartridges left my old man's hand to skip and scatter across the snow. The hood of his coat fell away from his face, and I saw that my old man was laughing.

THE LOVE OF MY LIFE

T. C. Boyle

T. Coraghessan Boyle is the author of nineteen books of fiction, including, most recently, *After the Plague*, *Drop City*, *The Inner Circle*, *Tooth and Claw*, and *Talk Talk*. His stories have appeared in most of the major American magazines, including *The New Yorker*, *Harper's*, *Esquire*, *The Atlantic*, *Playboy*, *The Paris Review*, *GQ*, *Antaeus*, *Granta*, and *McSweeney's*, and he has been the recipient of a number of literary awards. He has been a member of the English Department at the University of Southern California since 1978. Boyle lives near Santa Barbara with his wife and three children.

They wore each other like a pair of socks. He was at her house, she was at his. Everywhere they went—to the mall, to the game, to movies and shops and the classes that structured their days like a new kind of chronology—their fingers were entwined, their shoulders touching, their hips joined in the slow triumphant sashay of love. He drove her car, slept on the couch in the family room at her parents' house, played tennis and watched football with her father on the big thirty-six-inch TV in the kitchen. She went shopping with his mother and hers, a triumvirate of tastes, and she would have played tennis with his father, if it came to it, but his father was dead. "I love you," he told her, because he did, because there was no feeling like this, no triumph, no high—it was like being immortal and unconquerable, like floating. And a hundred times a day she said it too: "I love you. I love you."

They were together at his house one night when the rain froze
on the streets and sheathed the trees in glass. It was her idea to take
a walk and feel it in their hair and on the glistening shoulders of
their parkas, an otherworldly drumming of pellets flung down out
of the troposphere, alien and familiar at the same time, and they
glided the length of the front walk and watched the way the power
lines bellied and swayed. He built a fire when they got back, while
she towelled her hair and made hot chocolate laced with Jack Daniel's. They'd rented a pair of slasher movies for the ritualized comfort of them—"Teens have sex," he said, "and then they pay for it
in body parts"—and the maniac had just climbed out of the heating vent, with a meat hook dangling from the recesses of his empty
sleeve, when the phone rang.

It was his mother, calling from the hotel room in Boston where
she was curled up—shacked up?—for the weekend with the man
she'd been dating. He tried to picture her, but he couldn't. He even
closed his eyes a minute, to concentrate, but there was nothing there.
Was everything all right? she wanted to know. With the storm and
all? No, it hadn't hit Boston yet, but she saw on the Weather Channel that it was on its way. Two seconds after he hung up—before she
could even hit the Start button on the VCR—the phone rang again,
and this time it was her mother. Her mother had been drinking.
She was calling from a restaurant, and China could hear a clamor of
voices in the background. "Just stay put," her mother shouted into
the phone. "The streets are like a skating rink. Don't you even think
of getting in that car."

Well, she wasn't thinking of it. She was thinking of having Jeremy to herself, all night, in the big bed in his mother's room. They'd
been having sex ever since they started going together at the end of
their junior year, but it was always sex in the car or sex on a blanket
or the lawn, hurried sex, nothing like she wanted it to be. She kept
thinking of the way it was in the movies, where the stars ambushed
each other on beds the size of small planets and then did it again
and again until they lay nestled in a heap of pillows and blankets,

her head on his chest, his arm flung over her shoulder, the music fading away to individual notes plucked softly on a guitar and everything in the frame glowing as if it had been sprayed with liquid gold. That was how it was supposed to be. That was how it was going to be. At least for tonight.

She'd been wandering around the kitchen as she talked, dancing with the phone in an idle slow saraband, watching the frost sketch a design on the window over the sink, no sound but the soft hiss of the ice pellets on the roof, and now she pulled open the freezer door and extracted a pint box of ice cream. She was in her socks, socks so thick they were like slippers, and a pair of black leggings under an oversized sweater. Beneath her feet, the polished floorboards were as slick as the sidewalk outside, and she liked the feel of that, skating indoors in her big socks. "Uh-huh," she said into the phone. "Uh-huh. Yeah, we're watching a movie." She dug a finger into the ice cream and stuck it in her mouth.

"Come on," Jeremy called from the living room, where the maniac rippled menacingly over the Pause button. "You're going to miss the best part."

"Okay, Mom, okay," she said into the phone, parting words, and then she hung up. "You want ice cream?" she called, licking her finger.

Jeremy's voice came back at her, a voice in the middle range, with a congenital scratch in it, the voice of a nice guy, a very nice guy who could be the star of a TV show about nice guys: "What kind?" He had a pair of shoulders and pumped-up biceps too, a smile that jumped from his lips to his eyes, and close-cropped hair that stood up straight off the crown of his head. And he was always singing—she loved that—his voice so true he could do any song, and there was no lyric he didn't know, even on the oldies station. She scooped ice cream and saw him in a scene from last summer, one hand draped casually over the wheel of his car, the radio throbbing, his voice raised in perfect synch with Billy Corgan's, and the night standing still at the end of a long dark street overhung with maples.

"Chocolate. Swiss chocolate almond."

"Okay," he said, and then he was wondering if there was any whipped cream, or maybe hot fudge—he was sure his mother had a jar stashed away somewhere, *Look behind the mayonnaise on the top row*—and when she turned around he was standing in the doorway.

She kissed him—they kissed whenever they met, no matter where or when, even if one of them had just stepped out of the room, because that was love, that was the way love was—and then they took two bowls of ice cream into the living room and, with a flick of the remote set the maniac back in motion.

IT WAS an early spring that year, the world gone green overnight, the thermometer twice hitting the low eighties in the first week of March. Teachers were holding sessions outside. The whole school, even the halls and the cafeteria, smelled of fresh-mowed grass and the unfold-ing blossoms of the fruit trees in the development across the street, and students—especially seniors—were cutting class to go out to the quarry or the reservoir or to just drive the back streets with the sunroof and the windows open wide. But not China. She was hitting the books, studying late, putting everything in its place like pegs in a board, even love, even that. Jeremy didn't get it. "Look, you've already been ac-cepted at your first-choice school, you're going to wind up in the top ten G.P.A.-wise, and you've got four years of tests and term papers ahead of you, and grad school after that. You'll only be a high-school senior once in your life. Relax. Enjoy it. Or at least *experience* it."

He'd been accepted at Brown, his father's alma mater, and his own G.P.A. would put him in the top ten percent of their graduat-ing class, and he was content with that, skating through his final semester, no math, no science, taking art and music, the things he'd always wanted to take but never had time for—and Lit., of course, A.P. History, and Spanish 5. "*Tú eres el amor de mi vida*," he would tell her when they met at her locker or at lunch or when he picked her up for a movie on Saturday nights.

"*Y tú también*," she would say, "or is it '*yo también*'?"—French was her language. "But I keep telling you it really matters to me, because I know I'll never catch Margery Yu or Christian Davenport, I mean they're a lock for val and salut, but it'll kill me if people like Kerry Sharp or Jalapy Seegrand finish ahead of me—you should know that, you of all people—"

It amazed him that she actually brought her books along when they went backpacking over spring break. They'd planned the trip all winter and through the long wind tunnel that was February, packing away freeze-dried entrées, Power Bars, Gore-Tex windbreakers and matching sweatshirts, weighing each item on a handheld scale with a dangling hook at the bottom of it. They were going up into the Catskills, to a lake he'd found on a map, and they were going to be together, without interruption, without telephones, automobiles, parents, teachers, friends, relatives, and pets, for five full days. They were going to cook over an open fire, they were going to read to each other and burrow into the double sleeping bag with the connubial zipper up the seam he'd found in his mother's closet, a relic of her own time in the lap of nature. It smelled of her, of his mother, a vague scent of her perfume that had lingered there dormant all these years, and maybe there was the faintest whiff of his father too, though his father had been gone so long he didn't even remember what he looked like, let alone what he might have smelled like. Five days. And it wasn't going to rain, not a drop. He didn't even bring his fishing rod, and that was love.

When the last bell rang down the curtain on Honors Math, Jeremy was waiting at the curb in his mother's Volvo station wagon, grinning up at China through the windshield while the rest of the school swept past with no thought for anything but release. There were shouts and curses, T-shirts in motion, slashing legs, horns bleating from the seniors' lot, the school buses lined up like armored vehicles awaiting the invasion—chaos, sweet chaos—and she stood there a moment to savor it. "Your mother's car?" she said, slipping in beside him and laying both arms over his shoulders to pull him to her for a kiss. He'd brought her jeans and hiking boots along, and she was going to change as they drove, no need to go home, no more circumvention and delay, a stop at McDonald's, maybe, or Burger King, and then it was the sun and the wind and the moon and the stars. Five days. Five whole days.

"Yeah," he said, in answer to her question, "my mother said she didn't want to have to worry about us breaking down in the middle of nowhere—"

"So she's got your car? She's going to sell real estate in your car?"

He just shrugged and smiled. "Free at last," he said, pitching his voice down low till it was exactly like Martin Luther King's. "Thank God Almighty, we are free at last."

It was dark by the time they got to the trailhead, and they wound up camping just off the road in a rocky tumble of brush, no place on earth less likely or less comfortable, but they were together, and they held each other through the damp whispering hours of the night and hardly slept at all. They made the lake by noon the next day, the trees just coming into leaf, the air sweet with the smell of the sun in the pines. She insisted on setting up the tent, just in case—it could rain, you never knew—but all he wanted to do was stretch out on a gray neoprene pad and feel the sun on his face. Eventually, they both fell asleep in the sun, and when they woke they made love right there, beneath the trees, and with the wide blue expanse of the lake giving back the blue of the sky. For dinner, it was étouffée and rice, out of the foil pouch, washed down with hot chocolate and a few squirts of red wine from Jeremy's bota bag.

The next day, the whole day through, they didn't bother with clothes at all. They couldn't swim, of course—the lake was too cold for that—but they could bask and explore and feel the breeze out of the south on their bare legs and the places where no breeze had touched before. She would remember that always, the feel of that, the intensity of her emotions, the simple unrefined pleasure of living in the moment. Woodsmoke. Duelling flashlights in the night.

The look on Jeremy's face when he presented her with the bag of finger-sized crayfish he'd spent all morning collecting.

What else? The rain, of course. It came midway through the third day, clouds the color of iron filings, the lake hammered to iron too, and the storm that crashed through the trees and beat at their tent with a thousand angry fists. They huddled in the sleeping bag, sharing the wine and a bag of trail mix, reading to each other from a book of Donne's love poems (she was writing a paper for Mrs. Masterson called "Ocular Imagery in the Poetry of John Donne") and the last third of a vampire novel that weighed eighteen-point-one ounces.

And the sex. They were careful, always careful—*I will never, never be like those breeders that bring their puffed-up squalling little red-faced babies to class,* she told him, and he agreed, got adamant about it even, until it became a running theme in their relationship, the breeders overpopulating an overpopulated world and ruining their own lives in the process—but she had forgotten to pack her pills and he had only two condoms with him, and it wasn't as if there was a drugstore around the corner.

IN THE fall—or the end of August, actually—they packed their cars separately and left for college, he to Providence and she to Binghamton. They were separated by three hundred miles, but there was the telephone, there was E-mail, and for the first month or so there were Saturday nights in a motel in Danbury, but that was a haul, it really was, and they both agreed that they should focus on their course work and cut back to every second or maybe third week. On the day they'd left—and no, she didn't want her parents driving her up there, she was an adult and she could take care of herself—Jeremy followed her as far as the Bear Mountain Bridge and they pulled off the road and held each other till the sun fell down into the trees. She had a poem for him, a Donne poem, the saddest thing he'd ever heard. It was something about the moon. *More than moon*, that was it, lovers parting and their tears swelling like an ocean till the girl—the woman, the female—had more power to raise the tides than the moon itself, or some such. More than moon. That's what he called her after that, because she was white and round and getting rounder, and it was no joke, and it was no term of endearment.

She was pregnant. Pregnant, they figured, since the camping trip, and it was their secret, a new constant in their lives, a fact, an inescapable fact that never varied no matter how many home pregnancy kits they went through. Baggy clothes, that was the key, all in black, cargo pants, flowing dresses, a jacket even in summer. They went to a store in the city where nobody knew them and she got a girdle, and then she went away to school in Binghamton and he went to Providence. "You've got to get rid of it," he told her in the motel room that had become a prison. "Go to a clinic," he told her for the hundredth time, and outside it was raining—or, no, it was clear and cold that night, a foretaste of winter. "I'll find the money—you know I will."

She wouldn't respond. Wouldn't even look at him. One of the *Star Wars* movies was on TV, great flat thundering planes of metal roaring across the screen, and she was just sitting there on the edge of the bed, her shoulders hunched and hair hanging limp. Someone slammed a car door—two doors in rapid succession—and a child's voice shouted, "Me! Me first!"

"China," he said. "Are you listening to me?"

"I can't," she murmured, and she was talking to her lap, to the bed, to the floor. "I'm scared. I'm so scared." There were footsteps in the room next door, ponderous and heavy, then the quick tattoo of the child's feet and a sudden thump against the wall. "I don't want anyone to know," she said.

He could have held her, could have squeezed in beside her and wrapped her in his arms, but something flared in him. He couldn't understand it. He just couldn't. "What are you thinking? Nobody'll know. He's a doctor, for Christ's sake, sworn to secrecy, the doctor-patient compact and all that. What are you going to do, keep it?

Huh? Just show up for English 101 with a baby on your lap and say, 'Hi, I'm the Virgin Mary'?"

She was crying. He could see it in the way her shoulders suddenly crumpled and now he could hear it too, a soft nasal complaint that went right through him. She lifted her face to him and held out her arms and he was there beside her, rocking her back and forth in his arms. He could feel the heat of her face against the hard fiber of his chest, a wetness there, fluids, her fluids. "I don't want a doctor," she said.

And that colored everything, that simple negative: life in the dorms, roommates, bars, bullshit sessions, the smell of burning leaves and the way the light fell across campus in great wide smoking bands just before dinner, the unofficial skateboard club, films, lectures, pep rallies, football—none of it mattered. He couldn't have a life. Couldn't be a freshman. Couldn't wake up in the morning and tumble into the slow steady current of the world. All he could think of was her. Or not simply her—her and him, and what had come between them. Because they argued now, they wrangled and fought and debated, and it was no pleasure to see her in that motel room with the queen-size bed and the big color TV and the soaps and shampoos they made off with as if they were treasure. She was pigheaded, stubborn, irrational. She was spoiled, he could see that now, spoiled by her parents and their standard of living and the socioeconomic expectations of her class—of his class—and the promise of life as you like it, an unscrolling vista of pleasure and acquisition. He loved her. He didn't want to turn his back on her. He would be there for her no matter what, but why did she have to be so *stupid?*

BIG SWEATS, huge sweats, sweats that drowned and engulfed her, that was her campus life, sweats and the dining hall. Her dormmates didn't know her, and so what if she was putting on weight? Everybody did. How could you shovel down all those carbohydrates, all that sugar and grease and the puddings and nachos and all the rest, without putting on ten or fifteen pounds the first semester alone? Half the girls in the dorm were waddling around like the Doughboy, their faces bloated and blotched with acne, with crusting pimples and whiteheads fed on fat. So she was putting on weight. Big deal. "There's more of me to love," she told her roommate, "and Jeremy likes it that way. And, really, he's the only one that matters." She was careful to shower alone, in the early morning, long before the light had begun to bump up against the windows.

On the night her water broke—it was mid-December, almost nine months, as best as she could figure—it was raining. Raining hard. All week she'd been having tense rasping sotto voce debates with Jeremy on the phone—arguments, fights—and she told him that she would die, creep out into the woods like some animal and bleed to death, before she'd go to a hospital. "And what am I supposed to do?" he demanded in a high childish whine, as if he were the one who'd been knocked up, and she didn't want to hear it, she didn't.

"Do you love me?" she whispered. There was a long hesitation, a pause you could have poured all the affirmation of the world into.

"Yes," he said finally, his voice so soft and reluctant it was like the last gasp of a dying old man.

"Then you're going to have to rent the motel."

"And then what?"

"Then—I don't know." The door was open, her roommate framed there in the hall, a burst of rock and roll coming at her like an assault. "I guess you'll have to get a book or something."

By eight, the rain had turned to ice and every branch of every tree was coated with it, the highway littered with glistening black sticks, no moon, no stars, the tires sliding out from under her, and she felt heavy, big as a sumo wrestler, heavy and loose at the same time. She'd taken a towel from the dorm and put it under her, on the seat, but it was a mess, everything was a mess. She was cramping. Fidgeting with her hair. She tried the radio, but it was no help, nothing but songs she hated, singers that were worse. Twenty-two miles to Danbury, and the first of the contractions came like a sei-zure, like a knife blade thrust into her spine. Her world narrowed to what the headlights would show her.

Jeremy was waiting for her at the door to the room, the light be-hind him a pale rinse of nothing, no smile on his face, no human expression at all. They didn't kiss—they didn't even touch—and then she was on the bed, on her back, her face clenched like a fist. She heard the rattle of the sleet at the window, the murmur of the TV: *I can't let you go like this*, a man protested, and she could picture him, angular and tall, a man in a hat and overcoat in a black-and-white world that might have been another planet, *I just can't.* "Are you—?" Jeremy's voice drifted into the mix, and then stalled. "Are you ready? I mean, is it time? Is it coming now?"

She said one thing then, one thing only, her voice as pinched and hollow as the sound of the wind in the gutters: "Get it out of me."

It took a moment, and then she could feel his hands fumbling with her sweats.

Later, hours later, when nothing had happened but pain, a parade of pain with drum majors and brass bands and penitents crawling on their hands and knees till the streets were stained with their blood, she cried out and cried out again. "It's like *Alien*," she gasped, "like that thing in *Alien* when it, it—"

"It's okay," he kept telling her, "it's okay," but his face betrayed him. He looked scared, looked as if he'd been drained of blood in some evil experiment in yet another movie, and a part of her wanted to be sorry for him, but another part, the part that was so commanding and fierce it overrode everything else, couldn't begin to be.

He was useless, and he knew it. He'd never been so purely sick at heart and terrified in all his life, but he tried to be there for her, tried to do his best, and when the baby came out, the baby girl all slick with blood and mucus and the lumped white stuff that was like something spilled at the bottom of a garbage can, he was thinking of the ninth grade and how close he'd come to fainting while the teacher went around the room to prick their fingers one by one so they each could smear a drop of blood across a slide. He didn't faint now. But he was close to it, so close he could feel the room dodging away under his feet. And then her voice, the first intelligible thing she'd said in an hour: "Get rid of it. Just get rid of it."

OF THE drive back to Binghamton he remembered nothing. Or practically nothing. They took towels from the motel and spread them across the seat of her car, he could remember that much . . . and the blood, how could he forget the blood? It soaked through her sweats and the towels and even the thick cotton bathmat and into the worn fabric of the seat itself. And it all came from inside her, all of it, tissue and mucus and the shining bright fluid, no end to it, as if she'd been turned inside out. He wanted to ask her about that, if that was normal, but she was asleep the minute she slid out from under his arm and dropped into the seat. If he focused, if he really concentrated, he could remember the way her head lolled against the doorframe while the engine whined and the car rocked and the slush threw a dark blanket over the windshield every time a truck shot past in the opposite direction. That and the exhaustion. He'd never been so tired, his head on a string, shoulders slumped, his arms like two pillars of concrete. And what if he'd nodded off? What if he'd gone into a skid and hurtled over an embankment into the filthy gray accumulation of the worst day of his life? What then?

She made it into the dorm under her own power, nobody even looked at her, and no, she didn't need his help. "Call me," she whispered, and they kissed, her lips so cold it was like kissing a steak through the plastic wrapper, and then he parked her car in the student lot and walked to the bus station. He made Danbury late that night, caught a ride out to the motel, and walked right through the Do Not Disturb sign on the door. Fifteen minutes. That was all it took. He bundled up everything, every trace, left the key in the box at the desk, and stood scraping the ice off the windshield of his car while the night opened up above him to a black glitter of sky. He never gave a thought to what lay discarded in the Dumpster out back, itself wrapped in plastic, so much meat, so much cold meat.

HE WAS at the very pinnacle of his dream, the river dressed in its currents, the deep hole under the cutbank, and the fish like silver bullets swarming to his bait, when they woke him—when Rob woke him, Rob Greiner, his roommate, Rob with a face of crumbling stone and two policemen there at the door behind him and the roar of the dorm falling away to a whisper. And that was strange, policemen, a real anomaly in that setting, and at first—for the first thirty seconds, at least—he had no idea what they were doing there. Parking tickets? Could that be it? But then they asked him his name, just to confirm it, joined his hands together behind his back, and fitted two loops of naked metal over his wrists, and he began to understand. He saw McCaffrey and Tuttle from across the hall staring at him as if he were Jeffrey Dahmer or something, and the rest of them, all the rest, every head poking out of every door up and down the corridor, as the police led him away.

"What's this all about?" he kept saying, the cruiser nosing through the dark streets to the station house, the man at the wheel and the man beside him as incapable of speech as the seats or the wire mesh or the gleaming black dashboard that dragged them forward into the night. And then it was up the steps and into an explosion of light, more men in uniform, stand here, give me your hand, now the other one, and then the cage and the questions. Only then did he think of that thing in the garbage sack and the sound it had made—its body had made—when he flung it into the Dumpster like a sack of flour and the lid slammed down on it. He stared at the walls, and this was a movie too. He'd never been in trouble before, never been inside a police station, but he knew his role well enough, because he'd seen it played out a thousand times on the tube: deny everything. Even as the two detectives settled in across from him at the bare wooden table in the little box of the overlit room he was telling himself just that: *Deny it, deny it all.*

The first detective leaned forward and set his hands on the table as if he'd come for a manicure. He was in his thirties, or maybe his forties, a tired-looking man with the scars of the turmoil he'd witnessed gouged into the flesh under his eyes. He didn't offer a cigarette ("I don't smoke," Jeremy was prepared to say, giving them that much at least), and he didn't smile or soften his eyes. And when he spoke his voice carried no freight at all, not outrage or threat or cajolery—it was just a voice, flat and tired. "Do you know a China Berkowitz?" he said.

And she. She was in the community hospital, where the ambulance had deposited her after her roommate had called 911 in a voice that was like a bone stuck in the back of her throat, and it was raining again. Her parents were there, her mother red-eyed and sniffling, her father looking like an actor who's forgotten his lines, and there was another woman there too, a policewoman. The policewoman sat in an orange plastic chair in the corner, dipping her head to the knitting in her lap. At first, China's mother had tried to be pleasant to the woman, but pleasant wasn't what the circumstances called for, and now she ignored her, because the very unpleasant fact was that China was being taken into custody as soon as she was released from the hospital.

For a long while no one said anything—everything had already been said, over and over, one long flood of hurt and recrimination— and the antiseptic silence of the hospital held them in its grip while the rain beat at the windows and the machines at the foot of the bed counted off numbers. From down the hall came a snatch of TV dialogue, and for a minute China opened her eyes and thought she was back in the dorm. "Honey," her mother said, raising a purgatorial face to her, "are you all right? Can I get you anything?"

"I need to—I think I need to pee."

"Why?" her father demanded, and it was the perfect non sequitur. He was up out of the chair, standing over her, his eyes like cracked porcelain. "Why didn't you tell us, or at least tell your mother—or Dr. Fredman? Dr. Fredman, at least. He's been—he's like a family member, you know that, and he could have, or he would have . . . What were you *thinking*, for Christ's sake?"

Thinking? She wasn't thinking anything, not then and not now. All she wanted—and she didn't care what they did to her, beat her, torture her, drag her weeping through the streets in a dirty white dress with "Baby Killer" stitched over her breast in scarlet letters—was to see Jeremy. Just that. Because what really mattered was what he was thinking.

THE FOOD at the Sarah Barnes Cooper Women's Correctional Institute was exactly what they served at the dining hall in college, heavy on the sugars, starches, and bad cholesterol, and that would have struck her as ironic if she'd been there under other circumstances—doing community outreach, say, or researching a paper for her sociology class. But given the fact that she'd been locked up for more than a month now, the object of the other girls' threats, scorn, and just plain *nastiness*, given the fact that her life was ruined beyond any hope of redemption, and every newspaper in the country had her shrunken white face plastered across its front page under a headline that screamed MOTEL MOM, she didn't have much use for irony. She was scared twenty-four hours a day. Scared of the present, scared of the future, scared of the reporters waiting for the judge to set bail so that they could swarm all over her the minute she stepped out the door. She couldn't concentrate on the books and magazines her mother brought her or even on the TV in the rec room. She sat in her room—it was a room, just like a dorm room, except that they locked you in at night—and stared at the walls, eating peanuts, M&M's, sunflower seeds by the handful, chewing for the pure animal gratification of it. She was putting on more weight, and what did it matter?

Jeremy was different. He'd lost everything—his walk, his smile, the muscles of his upper arms and shoulders. Even his hair lay flat now, as if he couldn't bother with a tube of gel and a comb. When she saw him at the arraignment, saw him for the first time since she'd climbed out of the car and limped into the dorm with the blood wet on her legs, he looked like a refugee, like a ghost. The room they were in—the courtroom—seemed to have grown up around them, walls, windows, benches, lights and radiators already in place, along with the judge, the American flag and the ready-made spectators. It was hot. People coughed into their fists and shuffled their feet, every sound magnified. The judge presided, his arms like bones twirled in a bag, his eyes searching and opaque as he peered over the top of his reading glasses.

China's lawyer didn't like Jeremy's lawyer, that much was evident, and the state prosecutor didn't like anybody. She watched him—Jeremy, only him—as the reporters held their collective breath and the judge read off the charges and her mother bowed her head and sobbed into the bucket of her hands. And Jeremy was watching her too, his eyes locked on hers as if he defied them all, as if nothing mattered in the world but her, and when the judge said "First-degree murder" and "Murder by abuse or neglect," he never flinched.

She sent him a note that day—"I love you, will always love you no matter what, More than Moon"—and in the hallway, afterward, while their lawyers fended off the reporters and the bailiffs tugged impatiently at them, they had a minute, just a minute, to themselves. "What did you tell them?" he whispered. His voice was a rasp, almost a growl; she looked at him, inches away, and hardly recognized him.

"I told them it was dead."

"My lawyer—Mrs. Teagues?—she says they're saying it was alive when we, when we put it in the bag." His face was composed, but his eyes were darting like insects trapped inside his head.

"It was dead."

"It looked dead," he said, and already he was pulling away from her and some callous shit with a camera kept annihilating them with flash after flash of light, "and we certainly didn't—I mean, we didn't slap it or anything to get it breathing. . . ."

And then the last thing he said to her, just as they were pulled apart, and it was nothing she wanted to hear, nothing that had any love in it, or even the hint of love: "You told me to get rid of it."

THERE WAS no elaborate name for the place where they were keeping him. It was known as Drum Hill Prison, period. No reform-minded notions here, no verbal gestures toward rehabilitation or behavior modification, no benefactors, mayors or role models to lend the place their family names, but then who in his right mind would want a prison named after him anyway? At least they kept him separated from the other prisoners, the gangbangers and dope dealers and sexual predators and the like. He was no longer a freshman at Brown, not officially, but he had his books and his course notes, and he tried to keep up as best he could. Still, when the screams echoed through the cellblock at night and the walls dripped with the accumulated breath of eight and a half thousand terminally angry sociopaths, he had to admit it wasn't the sort of college experience he'd bargained for.

And what had he done to deserve it? He still couldn't understand. That thing in the Dumpster—and he refused to call it human, let alone a baby—was nobody's business but his and China's. That's what he'd told his attorney, Mrs. Teagues, and his mother and her boyfriend, Howard, and he'd told them over and over again: "*I didn't do anything wrong.*" Even if it was alive, and it was, he knew in his heart that it was, even before the state prosecutor presented evidence of blunt-force trauma and death by asphyxiation and exposure, it didn't matter, or shouldn't have mattered. There was no baby. There was nothing but a mistake, a mistake clothed in blood and mucus. When he really thought about it, thought it through on its merits and dissected all his mother's pathetic arguments about where he'd be today if she'd felt as he did when she was pregnant herself, he hardened like a rock, like sand turning to stone under all the pressure the planet can bring to bear. Another unwanted child in an overpopulated world? They should have given him a medal.

It was the end of January before bail was set—three hundred and fifty thousand dollars his mother didn't have—and he was released to house arrest. He wore a plastic anklet that set off an alarm if he went out the door, and so did she, so did China, imprisoned like some fairy-tale princess at her parents' house. At first, she called him every day, but mostly what she did was cry—"I want to see it," she sobbed. "I want to see our daughter's *grave*." That froze him inside. He tried to picture her—her now, China, the love of his life—and he couldn't. What did she look like? What was her face like, her nose, her hair, her eyes and breasts and the slit between her legs? He drew a blank. There was no way to summon her the way she used to be or even the way she was in court, because all he could remember was the thing that had come out of her, four limbs and the equipment of a female, shoulders rigid and eyes shut tight, as if she were a mummy in a tomb . . . and the breath, the shuddering long gasping rattle of a breath he could feel ringing inside her even as the black plastic bag closed over her face and the lid of the Dumpster opened like a mouth.

He was in the den, watching basketball, a drink in his hand (7Up mixed with Jack Daniel's in a ceramic mug, so no one would know he was getting shit-faced at two o'clock on a Sunday afternoon), when the phone rang. It was Sarah Teagues. "Listen, Jeremy," she said in her crisp, equitable tones, "I thought you ought to know—the Berkowitzes are filing a motion to have the case against China dropped."

His mother's voice on the portable, too loud, a blast of amplified breath and static: "On what grounds?"

"She never saw the baby, that's what they're saying. She thought she had a miscarriage."

"Yeah, right," his mother said.

Sarah Teagues was right there, her voice as clear and present as his mother's. "Jeremy's the one that threw it in the Dumpster, and they're saying he acted alone. She took a polygraph test day before yesterday."

He could feel his heart pounding the way it used to when he plodded up that last agonizing ridge behind the school with the cross-country team, his legs sapped, no more breath left in his body. He didn't say a word. Didn't even breathe.

"She's going to testify against him."

OUTSIDE WAS the world, puddles of ice clinging to the lawn under a weak afternoon sun, all the trees stripped bare, the grass dead, the azalea under the window reduced to an armload of dead brown twigs. She wouldn't have wanted to go out today anyway. This was the time of year she hated most, the long interval between the holidays and spring break, when nothing grew and nothing changed—it didn't even seem to snow much anymore. What was out there for her anyway? They wouldn't let her see Jeremy, wouldn't even let her talk to him on the phone or write him anymore, and she wouldn't be able to show her face at the mall or even the movie theater without somebody shouting out her name as if she was a freak, as if she was another Monica Lewinsky or Heidi Fleiss. She wasn't China Berkowitz, honor student, not anymore—she was the punch line to a joke, a footnote to history.

She wouldn't mind going for a drive, though—that was something she missed, just following the curves out to the reservoir to watch the way the ice cupped the shore, or up to the turnout on Route 9 to look out over the river where it oozed through the mountains in a shimmering coil of light. Or to take a walk in the woods, just that. She was in her room, on her bed, posters of bands she'd outgrown staring down from the walls, her high school books on two shelves in the corner, the closet door flung open on all the clothes she'd once wanted so desperately she could have died for each individual pair of boots or the cashmere sweaters that felt so good against her skin. At the bottom of her left leg, down there at the foot of the bed, was the anklet she wore now, the plastic anklet with the transmitter inside, no different, she supposed, than the collars they put on wolves to track them across all those miles of barren tundra or the bears sleeping in their dens. Except that hers had an alarm on it.

For a long while she just lay there gazing out the window, watching the rinsed-out sun slip down into the sky that had no more color in it than a TV tuned to an unsubscribed channel, and then she found herself picturing things the way they were an eon ago, when everything was green. She saw the azalea bush in bloom, the leaves knifing out of the trees, butterflies—or were they cabbage moths?—hovering over the flowers. Deep green. That was the color of the world. And she was remembering a night, summer before last, just after she and Jeremy started going together, the crickets thrumming, the air thick with humidity, and him singing along with the car radio, his voice so sweet and pure it was as if he'd written the song himself, just for her. And when they got to where they were going, at the end of that dark lane overhung with trees, to a place where it was private and hushed and the night fell in on itself as if it couldn't support the weight of the stars, he was as nervous as she was. She moved into his arms, and they kissed, his lips groping for hers in the dark, his fingers trembling over the thin yielding silk of her blouse. He was Jeremy. He was the love of her life. And she closed her eyes and clung to him as if that were all that mattered.

THE IDENTITY CLUB

Richard Burgin

Richard Burgin is the author of twelve books, most recently the story collection *The Conference on Beautiful Moments*. *The Identity Club: New and Selected Stories* was listed in the *Times Literary Supplement* as one of the best books of 2006. Burgin was the founding editor of *Boston Review* and *New York Arts Journal* and is the founding and current editor of the literary journal *Boulevard*.

Sometimes you meet someone who is actually achieving what you can only strive for. It's not exactly like meeting your double, it's more like seeing what you would be if you could realize your potential. Those were the feelings that Remy had about Eugene. In appearance they were similar, although Eugene was younger by a few years and taller by a few inches. But they each had fine dark hair, still untouched by any gray and they each had refined facial features, especially their delicate noses. Eugene's body, however, was significantly more muscular than Remy's.

At the agency in New York where Remy had worked for three years writing ad copy, Eugene was making a rapid and much talked about ascent. A number of Remy's other colleagues openly speculated that Eugene was advancing because he was a masterful office politician. But when Remy began working with him on an important new campaign for a client who manufactured toothpaste, he saw that wasn't true at all. Eugene had a special kind of brilliance, not just for writing slogans or generating campaign ideas, but a deep insight into human motivations and behavior that he knew how to channel into making people buy products. Rather than being a master diplomat, Remy discovered that Eugene was aloof almost to the point of rudeness, never discussed his private life and rarely showed any signs of a sense of humor. Yet Remy admired him enormously and wondered if Eugene, who Remy thought of as one of the wisest men he knew (certainly the wisest young man) might be a person he could confide in about The Identity Club and the important decision he had to make in the near future.

All of these thoughts were streaming through Remy's mind after work one night in his apartment when the phone rang. It was Poe calling to remind him about The Identity Club meeting that night. Remy nearly gasped as he'd inexplicably lost track of time and now had only a half hour to meet Poe and take a cab with him to the meeting.

The club itself had to be, almost by definition, a secretive organization that placed a high value on its members' trustworthiness, dependability and punctuality. Its members assumed the identities—the appearance, activities and personalities (whenever they could) of various celebrated dead artists they deeply admired. At the monthly meetings, which Remy enjoyed immensely and thought of as parties, all members would be dressed in their adopted identities drinking and eating and joking with each other. As soon as he stepped into a meeting he could feel himself transform as if the colors of his life went from muted grays and browns to glowing reds and yellows and vibrant greens and blues. To be honest with himself, since moving to New York from New England three years ago, his life before the club had been embarrassingly devoid of both emotion and purpose. How lucky for him, he often thought, that he'd been befriended by Winston Reems— now known by club members as Salvador Dali, a junior executive at his agency who hadslowly introduced him to the club.

This month's meeting was at the new Bill Evans (who had patterned himself after the famous jazz pianist) apartment, and since Remy enjoyed music he was particularly looking forward to it. He had also been told that Thomas Bernhard, named for the late Austrian writer, would definitely be there as well. As Bernhard was renowned for being a kind of hermit it was always special when he did attend a meeting and it made sense that as a former professional musician he would go to this one.

Quickly Remy dried off from his shower and began putting on new clothes. He thought that tonight promised to be an especially interesting mix of people, which was one of the ostensible ideas of the organization, to have great artists from the different arts meet and mingle, as they never had in real life. The decision facing Remy, which he'd given a good deal of thought to without coming any closer to a conclusion, was who he was going to "become" himself. He was considered at present an "uncommitted member" and had been debating between Nathanael West and some other writers. Nabokov, whom he might have seriously considered, had already been taken. At least, since he still had a month before he had to commit, he didn't have to dress in costume—though he rather looked forward to that. Remy had been a member for four months and it was now time for him to submit to a club interview to help him decide whose identity he was best suited for. Sometimes these interviews were conducted by the entire membership, which reminded Remy of a kind of Intervention, other times by the host of that evening's meeting or by some other well-established member. The new member was never informed in advance, as these "probings" were taken very seriously and the club wanted a spontaneous and true response.

One of the reasons Remy was having difficulty choosing an identity—and why he felt some anxiety about the whole process—was that he'd kept secret from the club his hidden contempt, or at least ambivalence, about the advertising business and his disappointment with the emptiness of his own life as well. No wonder he found refuge in art and in imagining the lives that famous artists led. He'd heard other members confess to those exact sentiments but the public admission of these feelings would be difficult for Remy. He thought it was the inevitable price he had to pay to get his membership in the club, and along with Eugene (whose importance to him Remy also kept secret) the club was his only interest in life, the only thing worth thinking about.

Poe was waiting for him in front of his brownstone, dressed, as Remy expected, in a black overcoat with his long recently dyed dark hair parted in the middle, the approximate match of his recently dyed mustache.

"I'm sorry I'm so late," Remy said.

Poe stared at him. "Something is preoccupying you," he said.

"You're right about that," Remy said, thinking of Eugene and wishing he could somehow be at the party.

"Do you mind if we walk?" Poe said. "There's something in the air tonight I crave, although I couldn't say exactly what it is. Some dark bell-like sound, some secret perfumed scent coming from the night that draws me forward . . . besides," he said, with a completely straight face, as he took a swallow of some kind of alcohol concealed in a brown paper bag, "it will be just as fast or just as slow as a taxi."

"Fine," Remy said, who felt he was hardly in a position to object. In the club Remy suspected that members assumed their identities with varying degrees of intensity. Clearly Poe was unusually committed to his to the point where he had renounced his former name, become a poet, short story writer and alcoholic, and given up dating women his age. Because he worked mostly at home doing research on the Internet he was able to be in character pretty much around the clock.

"You need to focus on your choice," Poe said, "you have an important decision facing you and not much time to make it."

"I hope I'll know during the probing," Remy said, "I hope it will come to me then."

"Listen to your heart, even if it makes too much noise," Poe said, smiling ironically.

They walked in silence the rest of the way, Poe sometimes putting his hands to his ears as if Roderick Usher were reacting to too strident a sound. As they were approaching the steps to Evans's walkup, from which they could already hear a few haunting chords on the piano, Poe turned to Remy and said, "Are you aware that we're voting on the woman issue tonight?"

"Yes, I knew that."

Poe was referring to the question of whether or not The Identity Club, which was currently a de facto men's club, would begin to actively recruit women. Remy had sometimes thought of the club as practicing a form of directed reincarnation, but did that mean that in the next world the club didn't want to deal with any women?

"I'm going to vote that we should recruit them. How can we fully be who we've become without women? I need them for my poetry, and to love of course. I think the organization should try to increase our chances to meet them not isolate us from them."

"I completely agree with you," Remy said.

They rang the bell and Dali opened the door, bowing grandly and pointing towards a dark, barely furnished, yet somehow chaotic apartment.

"It's Bill Evans's home. I knew it would be a mess," Poe said quietly to Remy, drinking again from his brown paper bag.

Evans was bent over the piano, head characteristically suspended just above the keys, as he played the coda of his composition "RE: Person I Knew." He also had long dark hair but was clean-shaven. From the small sofa, the only one in the room, Erik Satie shouted "Bravo! Encore!" Remy couldn't remember seeing any photographs of the composer but he judged his French to be authentic. As a tribute to his admirer, Evans played a version of Satie's most famous piano piece "Gymnopedie" which Remy recalled the former Evans had recorded on his album Nirvana. This was the first time Remy had heard the new Bill Evans play and while he was hardly an Evans scholar he thought it sounded quite convincing. The harmony, the soft touch and plaintive melodic lines were all there (no doubt learned from a book that had printed Evans's solos and arrangements) though, of course, some mistakes were made and the new Evans's touch wasn't as elegant as the first one's. Still, Remy could see that the new Evans's immersion into his identity had been thorough. Remy had recently seen a video of the former Evans playing and could see that the new one had his body movements down pat. Could he, Remy, devote himself as thoroughly to the new identity he would soon be assuming?

"Encore, encore," said Satie again and now also Cocteau, who had joined his old friend and collaborator on the sofa. Continuing his homage to his French admirers, Evans played "You Must Believe In Spring" by the French composer Michael Legrand. When it ended Remy found himself applauding vigorously as well and becoming even more curious about the former life of the new Evans. All he knew was that he'd once been a student at Juilliard and was involved now in selling computer parts. He wished he'd paid more attention when he talked with him five months ago at the meeting but now it was too late, as members were not allowed to discuss their former identities with each other once they'd committed to a new one.

After a brief rendition of "Five," Evans took a break and Remy slowly sidled up to him, wishing again that Eugene were there. Though he was often aloof, when the situation required Eugene always knew just what to say to people. What to say and not a word more, for Eugene had the gift of concision, just as Evans did on the piano.

"That was beautiful playing," Remy finally said.

"Thanks, man," Evans said, slowly raising his head and smiling at him. Like the first Bill Evans, his teeth weren't very good and he wore glasses.

"I know how hard it is to keep that kind of time, and to swing like that without your trio."

"I miss the guys but sometimes when I play alone I feel a one-ness with the music that I just can't get any other way."

It occurred to Remy that Evans had had at least four different trios throughout his recording career and that he didn't know which trio Evans was "missing" because he didn't know what stage of Evans's life the new one was now living. Perhaps sensing this, Evans said, "When Scotty died last year I didn't even know if I could continue. I couldn't bring myself to even look for a new bassist for a long time or to record either. And when I did finally go in the studio again a little while ago, it was a solo gig."

Remy now knew that for Evans it was about 1962 since Scott La-Faro, his young former bassist, had died in a car accident in 1961.

"Do you play, man?" Evans asked.

"Just enough to tell how good you are," Remy said.

"So there's no chance you could become a musician?"

"No, no, I couldn't do it."

"I know the choice facing you is difficult."

"It is. It really is," Remy said, touched by the note of sympathy in Evans's voice.

"Do you do any of the other arts?"

"Not with anything like your level of skill or Dali's or any of the other members, for that matter. I write a little at my job . . . but you could hardly call it art. There's a man, a rising star at my ad agency named Eugene, who's working on a campaign with me now who has the most original ideas and comes up with the most brilliant material, who really is an artist. If he were here, instead of me, he could become George Bernard Shaw or Oscar Wilde."

"Have you spoken to him about the club?"

"No, no. I don't really know him that well. I mean he barely knows I exist."

"Anyway, I've been speaking to some of the other members and there's definitely growing support to include men of letters in the club, you know, critics of a high level like Edmund Wilson or Marshall McLuhan."

"Oh no, I'm not nearly smart enough to be Edmund Wilson or McLuhan either. I figure if I become a member it will be as a novelist. I was thinking of Nathanael West, or maybe James Agee."

"Either way you'd have to go young, man."

Remy looked at Evans to be sure he was joking but saw that he looked quite serious. A chilling thought flitted through his mind. Did the committed members have a secret rule that they had to die at the same age their "adopted artists" did? And if so, was it merely a symbolic death of their identity or their actual physical death duplicated as closely as possible? Was The Identity Club, which he'd thought of as devoted to a form of reincarnation, then, actually devoted in the long run to a kind of delayed suicide? Of course this was probably a preposterous fantasy, still, he couldn't completely dismiss it.

"But you'll have to die young too then," Remy said, remembering that Bill Evans had died at 51. He said this with a half smile so it could seem he was joking. Evans looked around himself nervously before he answered.

"I find that Zen really helps me deal with the death thing."

Remy took a step back and nodded silently. His head had begun to hurt and after he saw that Evans wanted to play again he excused himself to use the bathroom. Once there, however, he realized that he'd forgotten to bring his Tylenol. He opened the mirrored cabinet, was blinded by a variety of pharmaceuticals but found nothing he could take. He closed the cabinet and heard Evans playing the opening chorus of "Time Remembered," one of his best compositions. The music was startlingly lovely but then partially drowned out by a loud coughing in the hallway. Remy turned and saw Thomas Bernhard, face temporarily buried in a handkerchief.

"Are you looking for something?" Bernhard said in a German accent.

"I have a headache."

"How fragile we are yet how determined. So you are looking for . . . ?"

"Some Tylenol."

"Ah! You have a headache and I have some Tylenol," Bernhard said, withdrawing a small bottle from the cavernous pocket of his corduroy sports jacket.

"Since my illness I am nothing but pills, my kingdom for a pill. Here . . ." he said, handing Remy the bottle.

Remy took two and swallowed them.

"Thanks a lot," he said. Bernhard nodded, and half bowed in a gently mocking way.

"So, have you decided to become Nathanael West or not?"

"I understand that I'd have to die quite young then and quite violently," Remy said, laughing uncertainly.

Bernhard's eyes had a heightened, almost shocked expression. Then he started coughing loudly and persistently again. Remy waited a half minute, finally saying, "Why don't you drink some water?" He got out of the bathroom area, half directing Bernhard to the sink and returned to the living room.

"Is he alright?" Poe said, meeting him in the hallway. He was drinking from a half empty wine bottle.

"Yes, I think so," Remy said. But I'm not, he said to himself. For the first time he felt profoundly uncomfortable at a club meeting. The pressure of having to make his identity decision was oppressive and worse still were the dark fears he now had about the club's policies. The original conceit of the club had amused him in the titillating way he liked to be amused, but if he were right about his suspicions, then the club was far more literal about its directed reincarnation than he'd realized. If he were right about the death rule, to commit to an identity was to select all aspects of your fate including when you would die. And what if one changed one's mind and didn't want to cooperate after committing, what then?

The pain in Remy's head was excruciating and at the first polite opportunity he excused himself, heaping more praise on Evans for the wonderful evening before he closed the door . . . and shuddered.

He decided not to return the phone calls he got from three club members over the next two days. To say anything while he was uncertain what to do about The Club could be a mistake. On the one hand he'd been profoundly upset by what he thought he might have discovered about its policies, on the other hand the club was the nucleus of what social life he had and would be very difficult to give up. Besides his job, The Identity Club was his only consistent base of human contact.

Remy began to throw himself into the new campaign with more passion than he'd ever shown at the agency. Largely due to Eugene's contributions, it was succeeding and, as expected, it was Eugene who benefited the most from it with the agency higher-ups. It was not that Eugene worked harder than Remy; it was simply that he could accomplish twice as much with less effort because he was so talented in the field. Still, Remy didn't begrudge him his success. Instead his interest in Eugene grew even stronger as he continued to watch and study him. He felt if he could become Eugene's friend and confide in him, then Eugene might know just what he should do about The Identity Club.

As Remy suspected, Eugene led a highly ritualized existence in the work place. It wasn't difficult to arrange a "chance meeting" at the elevator banks and to quickly ask him to have a drink in a way he couldn't refuse. They went to a bar on Restaurant Row—Remy feeling happier than he had in days. But once outside the agency Eugene seemed tense and remote, and sitting across from him at the bar he avoided eye contact and spoke sparsely in a strangely clipped tone that forced Remy to become uncharacteristically aggressive.

"We're all so grateful for the work you did on the campaign. It was just amazing," Remy said. Eugene nodded and said a muted thank you. It was as if Remy had just said to him "nice shirt you're wearing."

"I'm really proud to have you as a colleague," Remy added for good measure.

Again Eugene nodded, but this time said nothing and Remy began to feel defeated and strangely desperate. He waited until their eyes locked for a moment then said, "Do you know what The Identity Club is?" The immediate reddening of Eugene's face told Remy that he did.

"What makes you think that I would know?"

"I know some of the key members in the club came from our agency."

Eugene raised his eyebrows but still said nothing.

"In fact, I'm a member myself or a potential member."

"Then what is it you think I would know about the club that you wouldn't know already?"

"Fair enough," Remy said, clearing his throat and finishing his beer.

"I'll be a little more candid. I'm a member in that I've been attending the meetings but I'm not a completely committed member. I've been trying to decide whether to commit to the club completely and since I respect you and admire your judgment so much I thought I would ask you about it."

"I tend to avoid organizations that have a strong ideology, especially ones that try to convert you to their world view. I think they are unappetizing and often dangerous."

"Why is it dangerous?" Remy asked.

"Any organization that asks you to alter your life, or to jeopardize it and in many cases to give it up is to be avoided like the plague. Is, in fact, the plague . . . I'm just making this as a general statement, OK? I'm not saying anything about your club specifically," Eugene said hurriedly, looking away from Remy when he tried to make eye contact with him again.

"Thank you for your advice."

"It wasn't advice about anything specific. Remember that. It was just a general observation on the nature of organizations."

"Thank you for your observations then. I appreciate it and will keep it completely confidential."

Eugene seemed more relaxed then but five minutes later excused himself, saying he had to leave for another appointment. Remy could barely make himself stand when Eugene left, he felt so frozen with disappointment. When he did begin to move he felt strangely weightless, like a dizzy ghost passing down a dreamlike street. It was as if for the first time the universe had revealed its essential emptiness to him and he was completely baffled by it. In his life before New York there had always been some kind of support for him. First his parents, when he was a child, of course. Perhaps he left them too soon. Then his teachers when he went to school where he also met his friends who were now dispersed around the country as he was, though none of them had landed in New York. The Identity Club had filled that void, he supposed, although not completely or else Eugene wouldn't have been so important to him. But now it was clear that Eugene wanted little to do with him and it was also becoming increasingly clear (from the meeting at Evans's house to the dark advice of Eugene) that there were real problems, some of them perhaps dangerous, with the club. But how could he bear to leave it? The truth was he could hardly bring himself to focus on these problems, much less think them through in any systematic way. He could barely bring himself to get to work on time, dressed properly and able to smile, and could hardly remember that in the past he had always prided himself on being neat, on time, and amiable—the ultimate team player. After work, the next day, he went directly home as if there were some awful menace on the streets he had to flee.

In his apartment he found it difficult to sit still, and nearly impossible to sleep. He began pacing from wall to wall of his apartment, feeling oddly like a gorilla in a cage, even to the point where he thought he felt fur on his back.

Then, finally, a change. The phone rang in his cage, he picked it up for some reason, following some ape-like impulse, and heard the voice of Bill Evans saying, "I've got to talk to you, man."

"Yes, go ahead."

"Not on the phone. Are you free now?"

Remy thought of the dark streets and wasn't sure how to answer.

"It's important."

"OK," Remy said.

"You know Coliseum Books on 59th Street?"

"Yes."

"Meet me there in half an hour. I'll be in the mystery section."

Remy hung up and continued pacing rapidly for a minute, like a gorilla doing double time. Then he stopped and began wondering if he should call a cab or not—would it really be any safer? And as he thought, the cage around him disappeared, as did his feeling of having fur and an ape persona. He was so happy about that he decided to run the twenty blocks to the bookstore, keeping his mind as thought-free as possible although he did feel a low but persistent level of anxiety the whole way.

As promised, Evans was in the mystery section in a long black overcoat looking at or pretending to look at a book by Poe with his black-rimmed glasses. Their eyes met quickly, Evans, looking around himself, half nodding, but waiting until Remy was next to him before he spoke in a low voice barely louder than a whisper.

"We can talk here, man."

"What is it?" Remy said. He wanted to say more but couldn't, as if all those silent hours in the aquarium made him forget how to talk.

"There're some things I think you don't know, that I want you to know."

"What things?"

"About the Club and its ideas. When I was talking to you at the last meeting you looked confused when I was referring to my trio, like you didn't know how old I was."

"But then I figured it out."

"Yah, cause I talked about Scotty's death and the record I made a year later. You figured it out cause you know about my career. But let me lay it out to you in simple terms cause you're going to have to make an important commitment at the next meeting and when you make it it's like a complete life commitment. When you take on a new identity there are a lot of rewards, but also a lot of demands. You have to do a tremendous amount of research too and you have to have a lot of strength to leave your old self completely behind. In that sense you have to kill your old self and its old life. The only thing you can keep is your job but you have to do your job the way Nathanael West would, if you go ahead and decide to become him. That's why it takes so much courage and faith as well as work—time spent in a library, or whatever, doing as much research on him as you can. And finally, well let me ask you how old you are?"

"Twenty-nine," Remy said in a voice now barely above a whisper, as well.

"OK, man. You'll live the life West did at 29, you'll take on his life in chronological order, so when you turn 30 West will turn 30 until . . ."

"Until when?"

"Until he dies, man. I wanted you to understand that. That's where the courage and faith part come in."

"But he died so young."

"Like I said, I'm gonna pass pretty soon too, but I'm also going to play jazz piano more beautifully than anyone's ever played it— that's the reward part—and besides, as long as the club exists I'll be reincarnated again somewhere down the line."

"But you'll be dead."

"No man, I'll be Bill Evans reincarnated. I might have to wait a number of years but like my song says, 'We will Meet Again,'" Evans said with an ironic smile.

Remy looked down at the floor to get his bearings.

"Do all the members understand this when they make their commitment?"

"Don't worry about the other members. Just focus on yourself."

"But what if I lack the courage and vision to do this, to . . ."

"Have you been studying the club literature, especially the parts about reincarnation?"

"Not as much as I should have. Look, Bill, what if I decide I can't go through with this and just want to withdraw my membership?"

"I wouldn't advise that," Evans said with unexpected sternness. "I really think it's too late for that in your case."

Instinctively Remy took a step back—his face turning a shade of white that, in turn, made Evans's eyes grow larger and more intense.

"Do you realize the invaluable work we're doing?"

"Yes, no," Remy said.

"We're saving the most important members of the human race—allowing their beauty to continue to touch humanity."

"But you're killing them again. Why not give the, give yourself, for example, a chance to live longer to see what you could do with more time?"

Evans shook his head from side to side like a pendulum.

"You can't go against Karma, man. We have to accept our limits." Remy took another step back and Evans extended his arm and let his hand rest on his shoulder.

"This world is as beautiful as it can get. You have to accept it. You know, like the poet said 'death is the mother of beauty.'"

"It sounds more like a suicide club than an identity club," Remy blurted.

"Sometimes when something is really important or beautiful you have to die for it, like freedom. Isn't that why all the wars are fought?"

"But most wars are stupid and preventable."

"Death isn't preventable, man. We know this. Every bar of every tune I play knows this. It's like we accept this unstated contract with the world when we're born, that we understand we'll have to die but we'll live out our destiny anyway."

"But all of science and medicine is trying to extend life, to defeat death."

"They'll never succeed, man. We know that, that's why we're a club of artists. Death and reincarnation is stronger than freedom. You have to give your life to forces that are bigger than you. Isn't that the unstated contract we all understand once we realize what death is? Isn't that humility the biggest part about what being a man is, man?"

Remy bowed his head, surprised that Evans was such a forceful speaker, and spoke with such complete conviction to the point where he had almost moved himself to tears. But all Remy felt was a desire to flee, to hide under his blanket and have The Identity Club, the agency and New York itself all turn out to be a hideous dream.

"As a matter of fact I took a risk seeing you like this and laying it all out for you."

"I appreciate that and I'll never tell anyone what we spoke about. I won't mention it to anyone at the agency, I promise. The agency is really a key player in all of this, isn't it?"

"I can't really get into that."

Remy nodded and felt a chill spread over him.

"Again, thank you for meeting me and for everything you told me, which, of course, I'll keep completely confidential," Remy said. He thought he should shake hands with Evans then, but couldn't bring himself to do it, instead found himself backing away from him.

"Remember how important beauty is and courage," Evans said, looking him straight in the eye.

"I'll remember everything you told me."

"See you at the next meeting then."

"Yes," Remy said, "I'll see you then."

He walked out of the store dreading the streets, feeling someone from the club might be following him. It was entirely possible that Evans might have tipped off somebody and had them tail him or perhaps had already informed someone at the agency. Had he made Evans feel he would cooperate and go forward with his membership? He could only hope so.

It was cold, even for New York in December. The wind was unusually strong and seemed to blow through him as if he were hollow. It was odd how people often said that because New York had so many people you often felt anonymous or alone but to Remy that night, the abundance of people simply increased the odds that one of them was following him. And if he thought about it he could always feel that someone was, simply because it was numerically impossible to keep track of everyone walking near him.

In his apartment again, Remy went back to the aquarium and to his fish-like movements through it. He hated the aquarium, especially since he felt so feverish, but it kept him from thinking, which would be still worse. He must have stayed in it pacing for hours, sleeping only for an hour or two on his sofa in the early morning. Fortunately he had saved up all his sick days and could now call the secretary at the agency and tell her, quite honestly, that he was too ill to come in.

After making the call, Remy went to his room and lay down, too dizzy to keep moving around. But as soon as his head hit the pillow he was assailed by a steady procession of thoughts, images, and snatches of dialogue about the club. He saw the hard look in Evans's eyes as he said, "I really think it's too late for that." The worried look (the first time he'd ever seen that expression on Eugene's face) as he said "I'm just making this as a general statement, OK? I'm not saying anything about your club specifically." He saw the horrified expression in Bernhard's eyes in the hallway and heard his coughing fit again. He should have waited till the fit ended, he thought, and gotten some kind of definitive answer from him. Then he saw an image of Poe's face as he stood in front of his apartment the night of Evans's party, heard him say again "something is preoccupying you." Was Poe in on it too? Should he try to inform him? It seemed some members knew more than others. Perhaps there really was a secret membership within the membership that had the real knowledge of what The Identity Club truly believed and what it was prepared to do to enforce its beliefs.

Remy stayed in his apartment the entire day, eating Lean Cuisines and canned soup. Intermittently he tried watching TV or listening to the radio but everything reminded him of the club as if all the voices he heard on TV and the radio were really members of the club. He no longer was as frightened of the streets the next morning since nothing had proved to be more torturous than the last sleepless hours in his apartment. Instead, he was almost happy to return to the agency and certainly eager to immerse himself in work. Somewhat to his surprise he found himself whistling a bouncy jingle in the elevator, which, in fact, was the theme song for the new toothpaste campaign he'd worked on with Eugene.

The mood in the office was decidedly different, however. The receptionist barely acknowledged him, and when he looked at her more closely, appeared to be wiping tears from her eyes. Little groups of silent, stone-like figures were whispering in the hallway as if they were in a morgue. Remy took a few steps forward towards his office, hesitated, then walked back to the receptionist's desk and stared at her until she finally looked at him.

"What happened?" Remy said.

"It's Eugene," she said tearfully. "He died last night. Here, it's in the paper," she said, handing him a *Daily News*.

"Oh my God," Remy said, immediately tucking the newspaper inside his briefcase and walking soldier-straight down the rest of the hall until he reached his office where he could close his door and lock it. On page seven he found out everything he needed to know. Eugene had fallen to his death from the balcony of his midtown Manhattan apartment. At this point, the article said, "It was yet to be determined if foul play was involved."

Remy let the paper drop on his desk, looked out his window at the maze of buildings and streets below and shivered. Everything was suddenly starting to fall into place like the pieces of a monstrous puzzle. That so many people in the club came from the agency, that Eugene was so obviously nervous when he obliquely spoke against it, that Evans said he was "taking a risk" talking to him two days ago at Coliseum Books. Obviously, Eugene's death was no accident. He'd been punished for trying to dissuade potential members from joining, either for the warnings he gave him, Remy, or perhaps for other warnings to other people in the agency Remy didn't know about.

He nearly staggered then from the pain of losing Eugene, who'd meant so much to him and could have meant so much more not only to him but also to the world, but when he looked out the window his mood turned to terror so complete it virtually consumed his pain.

What had he done? He'd locked himself in a prison near a window on the 27th floor—but surely the higher-ups in the agency had master keys that could open it and ways to open the window and arrange his fall or some other form of execution.

There was no time to do anything but leave the building, no time even to go home, for his apartment would be the most dangerous place of all, and so no time to pack anything either. The world had suddenly shrunk to the cash in his pockets, the credit card in his wallet, and the clothes on his back. His goal now was simply to get a taxi to the airport and then as far away from New York as he could. He picked up his briefcase and overcoat, then stopped just short of the door and put them down on the floor. To leave his office with briefcase in hand, much less wearing his overcoat, might well look suspicious. He had to appear as if he were merely getting a drink of water or else going to the bathroom, then take ten extra steps and reach the elevator.

He counted to seven, his lucky number, and then opened his door thinking that he could probably buy a coat in the airport. The huddle of stone-like figures was gone. He walked directly towards the elevators, eyes focused straight ahead to reduce the chance of having to talk to someone. Then he saw an elevator open and his boss, Mr. Weir, about to get out. Before their eyes could meet, Remy turned left, opened a door and ran down a flight of stairs, then down two more flights. He thought briefly of running all the way down to the street, but if someone spotted him he'd be too easy a target. Besides, he was quite sure no one from the agency worked on the 24th floor. He stopped running, opened the new stairway door, and forced himself not to walk too fast towards the elevators. Once there he pressed the button and counted to seven again, after which an empty elevator (an almost unheard of event) suddenly appeared.

On the ride down he thought of different cities—Boston, Philadelphia, Washington D.C.—where he had relatives. But would it be a good idea to contact any of them? He had the feeling that the agency not only knew where his parents and other relatives lived, but where his friends lived too. It would be better to make a clean break from his past and reinvent himself—assume a new identity, as it were, and go with that for a while.

Outside the wind had picked up and it was beginning to snow slightly. Fortunately a cab came right away.

"To LaGuardia," he said to the driver, who was rough shaven and seemed unusually old for the job. Seeing the older man, Remy thought, the old are just the reincarnation of the young. In fact, strictly speaking, each moment of time you reincarnated yourself since you always had to attain a balance between your core, unchanging self and your constantly changing one. But when he tried to think of this further, his head started to hurt. Looking out the window to distract himself he noticed a black line of birds in the sky and thought of Eugene's falling and then thought he might cry. A man was a kind of reincarnation of a bird, a bird of a dinosaur and so on. But it really was too difficult to think about, just as infinity itself was. That was why people wanted to shape things for themselves; it was much too difficult otherwise. And, that's why the club members wanted to act like God because it was much too difficult to understand the real God.

Remy's eyes suddenly met the driver's and a fear went through him. He thought the driver looked like someone from the agency so as soon as the taxi slowed down at the airport, Remy handed him much more money than he needed to and left the cab without waiting for his change. Then he ran into the labyrinth of the airport trying to find a plane as fast as he could and like those birds he'd just seen in the sky fly away into another life.

SON OF THE WOLFMAN

Michael Chabon

Michael Chabon is the author of two story collections and seven novels, including *The Yiddish Policemen's Union* and *The Amazing Adventures of Kavalier & Clay*, which won the 2001 Pulitzer Prize for fiction. He lives in Berkeley, California, with his wife, the novelist Ayelet Waldman, and their children.

When the man charged with being the so-called Reservoir Rapist was brought to justice, several of the women who had been his victims came forward and identified themselves in the newspapers. The suspect, eventually convicted and sentenced to fifteen years at Pelican Bay, was a popular coach and math instructor at a high school in the Valley. He had won a state award for excellence in teaching. Two dozen present and former students and players, as well as the principal of his school, offered to testify in behalf of his good character at his trial. It was the man's solid position in the community, and the mishandling of a key piece of evidence, that led some of his victims to feel obliged to surrender the traditional veil of anonymity which the LAPD and the newspapers had granted them, and tell their painful stories not merely to a jury but to the world at large. The second of the Reservoir Rapist's eight victims, however, was not among these women. She had been attacked on August 7, 1995, as she jogged at dusk around Lake Hollywood. This was the perpetrator's preferred time of day, and one of three locations he favored in committing his attacks, the other two being the Stone Canyon and Franklin Reservoirs; such regular habits led in the end to his capture, on August 29. A day before the arrest, the faint pink proof of a cross, fixed in the developing fluid of her urine, informed the Reservoir Rapist's second victim, Cara Glanzman, that she was pregnant.

Cara, a casting agent, was married to Richard Case, a television cameraman. They were both thirty-four years old. They had met and become lovers at Bucknell University and at the time of the attack had been married since 1985. In their twelve years together, neither had been unfaithful to the other, and in all that time Cara had never gotten pregnant, neither by accident nor when she was trying with all of her might. For the past five years this unbroken chain of menses had been a source of sorrow, dissension, tempest, and recrimination in Cara and Richard's marriage. On the day she was raped, in fact, Cara had called an attorney friend of her best friend, just to discuss, in a vague, strangely hopeful way, the means and procedures of getting a divorce in California. After the attack her sense of punishment for having been so disloyal to Richard was powerful, and it is likely that, even had she not found herself pregnant with Derrick James Cooper's child, she would never have counted herself among the women who finally spoke out.

The first thing Cara did after she had confirmed the pregnancy with her obstetrician was to make an appointment for an abortion. This was a decision made on the spur of the moment, as she sat on the crinkling slick paper of the examining table and felt her belly twist with revulsion for the blob of gray cells that was growing in her womb. Her doctor, whose efforts over the past five years had all been directed toward the opposite end, told her that he understood. He scheduled the operation for the following afternoon.

Over dinner that night, take-out Indian food, which they ate in bed because she was still unwilling to go out at twilight or after dark, Cara told Richard that she was pregnant. He took the news with the same sad calm he had displayed since about three days after the attack, when he stopped calling the detective assigned to the case every few hours, and dried his fitful tears for good. He gave Cara's hand a squeeze, then looked down at the plate balanced on the duvet in the declivity of his folded legs. He had quit his most recent job in midshoot, and for the three weeks that followed the attack had done nothing but wait on Cara hand and foot, answering her every need. But beyond sympathetic noises and gentle reminders to eat, dress, and keep her appointments, he seemed to have almost nothing to say about what had happened to Cara. Often his silence hurt and disturbed her, but she persuaded herself that he had been struck dumb by grief, an emotion which he had never been able adequately to express.

In fact Richard had been silenced by his own fear of what might happen if he ever dared to talk about what he was feeling. In his imagination, at odd moments of the day—changing stations on the radio, peeling back pages of the newspaper to get to the box scores— he tortured and killed the rapist, in glistening reds and purples. He snapped awake at three o'clock in the morning, in their ample and downy bed, with Cara pressed slumbering against him, horrified by the sham of her safety in his arms. The police, the lawyers, the newspaper reporters, the psychotherapists and social workers, all were buffoons, moral dwarves, liars, contemptible charlatans and slackers. And, worst of all, he discovered that his heart had been secretly fitted by a cruel hand with thin burning wires of disgust for his wife. How could he have begun to express any of this? And to whom?

That evening, as they ate their fugitive supper, Cara pressed him to say something. The looping phrase of proteins that they had tried so hard and for so long to produce themselves, spending years and running up medical bills in the tens of thousands of dollars, had finally been scrawled inside her, albeit by a vandal's hand; and now tomorrow, with ten minutes' work, it was going to be rubbed away. He must feel something.

Richard shrugged, and toyed with his fork, turning it over and over as if looking for the silver mark. There had been so many times in the last few years that he had found himself, as now, on the verge of confessing to Cara that he did not, in his heart of hearts, really want to have children, that he was haunted by an unshakable sense that the barrenness of their marriage might, in fact, be more than literal.

Before he could get up the courage to tell her, however, that he would watch her doctor hose the bastard out of Cara's womb tomorrow not only with satisfaction but with relief, she leapt up from the bed, ran into the bathroom, and vomited up all the matar paneer, dal saag, and chicken tikka masala she had just eaten. Richard, thinking that this would be the last time for this particular duty, got up to go and keep her hair from falling down around her face. She yelled at him to close the door and leave her alone. When she emerged from the bathroom she looked pale and desolate, but her manner was composed.

"I'm canceling the thing tomorrow," she told him.

At that point, having said nothing else for so long, there was nothing for him to say but, automatically, "I understand."

PREGNANCY SUITED Cara. Her bouts of nausea were intense and theatrical but passed within the first few weeks, leaving her feeling purged of much of the lingering stink and foul luster of the rape. She adopted a strict, protein-rich diet that excluded fats and sugars. She bought a juice machine and concocted amalgams of uncongenial fruits and vegetables, which gave off a smell like the underparts of a lawn mower at the end of a wet summer. She joined a gym in Studio City and struck up a friendship there with a woman who played a supporting character on a very bad sitcom and who was due a day before Cara. She controlled what entered her body, oiled and flexed and soaked it in emollients, monitored its emissions. It responded precisely as her books told her that it would. She put on weight at the recommended rate. Secondary symptoms, from the mapping of her swollen breasts in blue tracery to mild bouts of headaches and heartburn, appeared reassuringly on schedule.

For a time she marveled at her sense of well-being, the lightness of her moods, the nearly unwrinkled prospect that every day presented. In the wake of that afternoon at Lake Hollywood, which might have reduced her to nothing, she grew; every day there was more of her. And the baby, in spite of the evil instant of its origin—the smell of hot dust and Mexican sage in her nostrils, the winking star of pain behind her eyes as her head smacked the ground—she now felt to be composed entirely of her own materials and shaped by her hand. It was being built of her platelets and antibodies, strengthened by the calcium she took, irrigated by the eight squeeze bottles of water she daily consumed. She had quit her job; she was making her way through Trollope. By the end of her second trimester she could go for days on end without noticing that she was happy.

Over the same period of six months, Richard Case became lost. It was a measure, in his view, of the breadth of the gulf that separated Cara and him that she could be so cheerfully oblivious of his lostness. His conversation, never expansive, dwindled to the curtness of a spaghetti western hero. His friends, whose company Richard had always viewed as the ballast carried in the hold of his marriage, began to leave him out of their plans. Something, as they put it to each other, was eating Richard. To them it was obvious what it must be: the rapist, tall, handsome, muscled, a former All-American who in his youth had set a state record for the four hundred hurdles, had performed in one violent minute a feat that Richard in ten loving years had not once managed to pull off. It was worse than cuckoldry, because his rival was no rival at all. Derrick Cooper was beneath contempt, an animal, unworthy of any of the usual emotions of an injured husband. And so Richard was forced, as every day his wife's belly expanded, and her nipples darkened, and a mysterious purplish trail was blazed through the featureless country between her navel and pubis, into the awful position of envying evil, coveting its vigor. The half-ironic irony that leavened his and his friends' male amusements with an air of winking put-on abandoned him. For a month or two he continued to go with them to the racetrack, to smoke cigars and to play golf, but he took his losses too seriously, picked fights, sulked, turned nasty. One Saturday his best friend found him weeping in a men's room at Santa Anita. After that Richard just worked. He accepted jobs that in the past he would have declined, merely to keep himself from having to come home. He gave up Dominican cigars in favor of cut-rate cigarettes.

He never went with Cara to the obstetrician, or read any of the many books on pregnancy, birth, and infancy she brought home. His father had been dead for years, but after he told his mother what manner of grandchild she could expect, which he did with brutal concision, he never said another word to her about the child on the way. When his mother asked, he passed the phone to Cara, and left the room. And when in her sixth month Cara announced her intention of attempting a natural childbirth, with the assistance of a midwife, Richard said, as he always did at such moments, "It's your baby." A woman in the grip of a less powerful personal need for her baby might have objected, but Cara merely nodded, and made an appointment for the following Tuesday with a midwife named Dorothy Pendleton, who had privileges at Cedars-Sinai.

That Monday, Cara was in a car accident. She called Richard on the set, and he drove from the soundstage in Hollywood, where he was shooting an Israeli kung fu movie, to her doctor's office in West Hollywood. She was uninjured except for a split cheek, and the doctor felt confident, based on an examination and a sonogram, that the fetus would be fine. Cara's car, however, was a total loss—she had been broadsided by a decommissioned hearse, of all things, a 1963 Cadillac. Richard, therefore, would have to drive her to the midwife's office the next day.

She did not present the matter as a request; she merely said, "You'll have to drive me to see Dorothy." They were on the way home from the doctor's office. Cara had her cellular telephone and her Filofax out and was busy rearranging the things the accident had forced her to rearrange. "The appointment's at nine."

Richard looked over at his wife. There was a large bandage taped to her face, and her left eye had swollen almost shut. He had a tube of antibiotic ointment in the pocket of his denim jacket, a sheaf of fresh bandages, and a printed sheet of care instructions he was to follow for the next three days. Ordinarily, he supposed, a man cared for his pregnant wife both out of a sense of love and duty and because it was a way to share between them the weight of a burden mutually imposed. The last of these did not apply in their situation. The first had gotten lost somewhere between a shady bend in the trail under the gum trees at the north end of Lake Hollywood and the cold tile of the men's room at Santa Anita. All that remained now was duty. He had been transformed from Cara's husband into her houseboy, tending to all her needs and requests without reference to emotion, a silent, inscrutable shadow.

"What do you even need a midwife for?" he snapped. "You have a doctor."

"I told you all this," Cara said mildly, on hold with a hypnotist who prepared women for the pain of birth. "Midwives stay with you. They stroke you and massage you and talk to you. They put everything they have into trying to make sure you have the baby naturally. No C-section. No episiotomy. No drugs."

"No drugs." His voice dropped an octave, and though she didn't see it she knew he was rolling his eyes. "I would have thought the drugs would be an incentive to you."

Cara smiled, then winced. "I like drugs that make you feel something, Richie. These ones they give you just make you feel nothing. I want to feel the baby come. I want to be able to push him out."

"What do you mean, 'him'? Did they tell you the sex? I thought they couldn't tell."

"They couldn't. I . . . I don't know why I said 'him.' Maybe I just . . . everyone says, I mean, you know, old ladies and whatever, they say I'm carrying high . . ."

Her voice trembled, and she drew in a sharp breath. They had come to the intersection, at the corner of Sunset and Poinsettia, where four hours earlier the bat-winged black hearse had plowed into Cara's car. Involuntarily she closed her eyes, tensing her shoulders. The muscles there were tender from her having braced herself against the impact of the crash. She cried out. Then she laughed. She was alive, and the crescent mass of her body, the cage of sturdy bones cushioned with fat, filled with the bag of bloody seawater, had done its job. The baby was alive, too.

"This is the corner, huh?"

"I had lunch at Authentic. I was coming up Poinsettia."

It had been Richard who discovered this classic West Hollywood shortcut, skirting the northbound traffic and stoplights of La Brea Avenue, within a few weeks of their marriage and arrival in Los Angeles. They had lived then in a tiny one-bedroom bungalow around the corner from Pink's. The garage was rented out to a palmist who claimed to have once warned Bob Crane to mend his wild ways. The front porch had been overwhelmed years before by a salmon pink bougainvillea, and a disheveled palm tree murmured in the backyard, battering the roof at night with inedible nuts. It had been fall, the only season in Southern California that made any lasting claim on the emotions. The sunlight was intermittent and wistful as retrospection, bringing the city into sharper focus while at the same time softening its contours. In the afternoons there was a smoky tinge of eastern, autumnal regret in the air, which they only later learned was yearly blown down from raging wildfires in the hills. Cara had a bottom-tier job at a second-rate Hollywood talent agency; Richard was unemployed. Every morning he dropped her off at the office on Sunset and then spent the day driving around the city with the bulging Thomas Guide that had been her wedding gift to him. Though by then they had been lovers for nearly two years, at times Richard did not feel that he knew Cara at all well enough to have actually gone and married her, and the happy panic of those early days found an echo whenever he set out to find his way across that bland, encyclopedic grid of boulevards. When he picked Cara up at the end of the day they would go to Lucy's or Tommy Tang's and he would trace out for her the route he had taken that day, losing himself among oil wells, palazzos, Hmong strip malls, and a million little bungalows like theirs, submerged in bougainvillea. They would drink Tecate from the can and arrive home just as the palmist's string of electric jalapeños was coming on in her window, over the neon hand, its fingers outspread in welcome or admonition. They slept with the windows open, under a light blanket, tangled together. His dreams would take him once more to El Nido, Bel Air, Verdugo City. In the morning he sat propped on a pillow, drinking coffee from a chipped Bauer mug, watching Cara move around the bedroom in the lower half of a suit. They had lived in that house for five years, innocent of Cara's basal temperature or the qualities of her vaginal mucus. Then they had moved to the Valley, buying a house with room for three children that overlooked the steel-bright reservoir. The Thomas Guide was in the trunk of Richard's car, under a blanket, missing all of the three pages that he needed most often.

"I can't believe you didn't see it," he said. "It was a fucking hearse."

For the first time she caught or allowed herself to notice the jagged, broken note in his voice, the undercurrent of anger that had always been there but from which her layers of self-absorption, of cell production, of sheer happy bulk, had so far insulated her.

"It wasn't my fault," she said.

"Still," he said, shaking his head. He was crying.

"Richard," she said. "Are you . . . what's the matter?"

The light turned to green. The car in front of them sat for an eighth of a second without moving. Richard slammed the horn with the heel of his hand.

"Nothing," he said, his tone once again helpful and light. "Of course I'll drive you anywhere you need to go."

———

MIDWIVES' EXPERIENCE of fathers is incidental but proficient, like a farmer's knowledge of bird migration or the behavior of clouds. Dorothy Pendleton had caught over two thousand babies in her career, and of these perhaps a thousand of the fathers had joined the mothers for at least one visit to her office, with a few hundred more showing up to do their mysterious duty at the birth. In the latter setting, in particular, men often revealed their characters, swiftly and without art. Dorothy had seen angry husbands before, trapped, taciturn, sarcastic, hot-tempered, frozen over, jittery, impassive, unemployed, workaholic, carrying the weight of all the generations of angry fathers before them, spoiled by the unfathomable action of bad luck on their ignorance of their own hearts. When she called Cara Glanzman and Richard Case in from the waiting room, Dorothy was alert at once to the dark crackling effluvium around Richard's head. He was sitting by himself on a love seat, slouched, curled into himself, slapping at the pages of a copy of *Yoga Journal*. Without stirring he watched Cara get up and shake Dorothy's hand. When Dorothy turned to him, the lower half of his face produced a brief, thoughtless smile. His eyes, shadowed and hostile, sidled quickly away from her own.

"You aren't joining us?" Dorothy said in her gravelly voice. She was a small, broad woman, dressed in jeans and a man's pin-striped oxford shirt whose tails were festooned with old laundry tags and spattered with blue paint. She looked dense, immovable, constructed of heavy materials and with a low center of gravity. Her big plastic eyeglasses, indeterminately pink and of a curvy elaborate style that had not been fashionable since the early 1980s, dangled from her neck on a length of knotty brown twine. Years of straddling the threshold of blessing and catastrophe had rendered her sensitive to all the fine shadings of family emotion, but unfit to handle them with anything other than tactless accuracy. She turned to Cara. "Is there a problem?"

"I don't know," said Cara. "Richie?"

"You don't know?" said Richard. He looked genuinely shocked. Still he didn't stir from his seat. "Jesus. Yes, Dorothy, there is a little problem."

Dorothy nodded, glancing from one to the other of them, awaiting some further explanation that was not forthcoming.

"Cara," she said finally, "were you expecting Richard to join you for your appointment?"

"Not—well, no. I was supposed to drive myself." She shrugged. "Maybe I was hoping . . . But I know it isn't fair."

"Richard," said Dorothy, as gently as she could manage, "I'm sure you want to help Cara have this baby."

Richard nodded, and kept on nodding. He took a deep breath, threw down the magazine, and stood up.

"I'm sure I must," he said.

They went into the examination room and Dorothy closed the door. She and another midwife shared three small rooms on the third floor of an old brick building on a vague block of Melrose Avenue, to the west of the Paramount lot. The other midwife had New Age leanings, which Dorothy without sharing found congenial enough. The room was decorated with photographs of naked pregnant women and with artwork depicting labor and birth drawn from countries and cultures, many of them in the Third World, where the long traditions of midwifery had never been broken. Because Dorothy's mother and grandmother had both been midwives, in a small town outside of Texarkana, her own sense of tradition was unconscious and distinctly unmillenarian. She knew a good deal about herbs and the emotions of mothers, but she did not believe, especially, in crystals, meditation, creative visualization, or the inherent wisdom of pre-industrial societies. Twenty years of life on the West Coast had not rid her attitude toward pregnancy and labor of a callous East Texas air of husbandry and hard work. She pointed Richard to a battered fifth-hand armchair covered in gold Herculon, under a poster of the goddess Cybele with the milky whorl of the cosmos in her belly. She helped Cara up onto the examination table.

"I probably should have said something before," Cara said. "This baby. It isn't Richie's."

Richard's hands had settled on his knees. He stared at the stretched and distorted yellow daisies printed on the fabric of Cara's leggings, his shoulders hunched, a shadow on his jaw.

"I see," said Dorothy. She regretted her earlier brusqueness with him, though there was nothing to be done about it now and she certainly could not guarantee that she would never be brusque with him again. Her sympathy for husbands was necessarily circumscribed by the simple need to conserve her energies for the principals in the business at hand. "That's hard."

"It's extra hard," Cara said. "Because, see . . . I was raped. By the, uh, by the Reservoir Rapist, you remember him." She lowered her voice. "Derrick James Cooper."

"Oh, dear God," Dorothy said. It was not the first time these circumstances had presented themselves in her office, but they were rare enough. It took a particular kind of woman, one at either of the absolute extremes of the spectrum of hope and despair, to carry a baby through from that kind of beginning. She had no idea what kind of a husband it took. "I'm sorry for both of you. Cara." She opened her arms and stepped toward the mother, and Cara's head fell against her shoulder. "Richard." Dorothy turned, not expecting Richard to accept a hug from her but obliged by her heart and sense of the proprieties to offer him one.

He looked up at her, chewing on his lower lip, and the fury that she saw in his eyes made her take a step closer to Cara, to the baby in her belly, which he so obviously hated with a passion he could not, as a decent man, permit himself to acknowledge.

"I'm all right," he said.

"I don't see how you could be," Dorothy said. "That baby in there is the child of a monster who raped your wife. How can you possibly be all right with that? I wouldn't be."

She felt Cara stiffen. The hum of the air-conditioning filled the room.

"I still think I'm going to skip the hug," Richard said.

The examination proceeded. Cara displayed the pale hemisphere of her belly to Dorothy. She lay back and spread her legs, and Dorothy, a glove snapped over her hand, reached up into her and investigated the condition of her cervix. Dorothy took Cara's blood pressure and checked her pulse and then helped her onto the scale.

"You are perfect," Dorothy announced as Cara dressed herself. "You just keep on doing all the things you tell me you've been doing. Your baby is going to be perfect, too."

"What do you think it is?" Richard said, speaking for the first time since the examination had begun.

"Is? You mean the sex?"

"They couldn't tell on the ultrasound. I mean, I know there's no way to really know for sure, but I figured you're a midwife, maybe you have some kind of mystical secret way of knowing."

"As a matter of fact I am never wrong about that," Dorothy said. "Or so very rarely that it's the same as always being right."

"And?"

Dorothy put her right hand on Cara's belly. She was carrying high, which tradition said meant the baby was a boy, but this had nothing to do with Dorothy's feeling that the child was unquestionably male. It was just a feeling. There was nothing mystical to Dorothy about it.

"That's a little boy. A son."

Richard shook his head, face pinched, and let out a soft, hopeless gust of air through his teeth. He pulled Cara to her feet, and handed her her purse.

"Son of the monster," he said. "Wolfman Junior."

"I have been wrong once or twice," Dorothy said softly, reaching for his hand.

He eluded her grasp once more.

"I'm sort of hoping for a girl," he said.

"Girls are great," said Dorothy.

———

CARA WAS due on the fifth of May. When the baby had not come by the twelfth, she went down to Melrose to see Dorothy, who palpated her abdomen, massaged her perineum with jojoba oil, and told her to double the dose of a vile tincture of black and blue cohosh which Cara had been taking for the past week.

"How long will you let me go?" Cara said.

"It's not going to be an issue," Dorothy said.

"But if it is. How long?"

"I can't let you go much past two weeks. But don't worry about it. You're seventy-five percent effaced. Everything is nice and soft in there. You aren't going to go any two weeks."

On the fifteenth of May and again on the seventeenth, Cara and a friend drove into Laurel Canyon to dine at a restaurant whose house salad was locally reputed to contain a mystery leaf that sent women into labor. On the eighteenth, Dorothy met Cara at the office of her OB in West Hollywood. A nonstress test was performed. The condition of her amniotic sac and its contents was evaluated. The doctor was tight-lipped throughout, and his manner toward Dorothy Cara found sardonic and cold. She guessed that they had had words before Cara's arrival or were awaiting her departure before doing so. As he left to see his next patient, the doctor advised Cara to schedule an induction for the next day.

"We don't want that baby to get much bigger."

He went out.

"I can get you two more days," said Dorothy, sounding dry and unconcerned but looking grave. "But I'm going out on a limb."

Cara nodded. She pulled on the loose-waisted black trousers from CP Shades and the matching black blouse that she had been wearing for the past two weeks, even though two of the buttons were hanging loose. She stuffed her feet into her ragged black espadrilles. She tugged the headband from her head, shook out her hair, then fitted the headband back into place. She sighed, and nodded again. She looked at her watch. Then she burst into tears.

"I don't want to be induced," she said. "If they induce me I'm going to need drugs."

"Not necessarily."

"And then I'll probably end up with a C-section."

"There's no reason to think so."

"This started out as something I had no control over, Dorothy. I don't want it to end like that."

"Everything starts out that way, dear," said Dorothy. "Ends that way, too."

"Not this."

Dorothy put her arm around Cara and they sat there, side by side on the examining table. Dorothy relied on her corporeal solidity and steady nerves to comfort patients, and was not inclined to soothing words. She said nothing for several minutes.

"Go home," she said at last. "Call your husband. Tell him you need his prostaglandins."

"Richie?" Cara said. "But he . . . he can't. He won't."

"Tell him this is his big chance," Dorothy said. "I imagine it's been a long time."

"Ten months," said Cara. "At least. I mean unless he's been with somebody else."

"Call him," Dorothy said. "He'll come."

Richard had moved out of the house when Cara was in her thirty-fifth week. As from the beginning of their troubles, there had been no decisive moment of rupture, no rhetorical firefight, no decision taken on Richard's part at all. He had merely spent longer and longer periods away from home, rising well before dawn to take his morning run around the reservoir where the first line of the epitaph of their marriage had been written, and arriving home at night long after Cara had gone to sleep. In week thirty-four he had received an offer to film a commercial in Seattle. The shoot was scheduled for eight days. Richard had never come home. On Cara's due date, he had telephoned to say that he was back in L.A., staying at his older brother Matthew's up in

Camarillo. He and Matthew had not gotten along as children, and in adulthood had once gone seven and a half years without speaking. That Richie had turned to him now for help filled Cara with belated pity for her husband. He was sleeping in a semiconverted garage behind Matthew's house, which he shared with Matthew's disaffected teenage son Jeremy.

"He doesn't get home till pretty late, Aunt Cara," Jeremy told her when she called that afternoon from the doctor's office. "Like one or two."

"Can I call that late?"

"Fuck yeah. Hey, did you have your baby?"

"I'm trying," Cara said. "Please ask him to call me."

"Sure thing."

"No matter how late it is."

She went to Las Carnitas for dinner. Strolling mariachis entered and serenaded her in her magic shroud of solitude and girth. She stared down at her plate and ate a tenth of the food upon it. She went home and spent a few hours cutting out articles from *American Baby*, and ordering baby merchandise from telephone catalogs in the amount of five hundred and twelve dollars. At ten o'clock she set her alarm clock for one-thirty and went to bed. At one o'clock she was wakened from a light uneasy sleep by a dream in which a shadowy, hirsute creature, bipedal and stooped, whom even within the dream itself she knew to be intended as a figure of or stand-in for Derrick James Cooper, mounted a plump *guitarrón*, smashing it against the ground. Cara shot up, garlic on her breath, heart racing, listening to the fading echoes in her body of the twanging of some great inner string.

The telephone rang.

"What's the matter, Cara?" Richard said, for the five thousandth time. His voice was soft and creased with fatigue. "Are you all right?"

"Richie," she said, though this was not what she had intended to say to him. "I miss you."

"I miss you, too."

"No, I . . . Richie, I don't want to do this without you."

"Are you having the baby? Are you in labor now?"

"I don't know. I might be. I just felt something. Richie, can't you come over?"

"I'll be there in an hour," he said. "Hold on."

Over the next hour Cara waited for a reverberation or renewal of the twinge that had awakened her. She felt strange; her back ached, and her stomach was agitated and sour. She chewed a Gaviscon and lay propped up on the bed, listening for the sound of Richard's car. He arrived exactly an hour after he had hung up the telephone, dressed in ripped blue jeans and a bulging, ill-shaped, liver-colored sweater she had knit for him in the early days of their marriage.

"Anything?" he said.

She shook her head, and started to cry again. He went over to her and, as he had so many times in the last year, held her, a little stiffly, as though afraid of contact with her belly, patting her back, murmuring that everything would be fine.

"No it won't, Richie. They're going to have to cut me open. I know they will. It started off violent. I guess it has to end violent."

"Have you talked to Dorothy? Isn't there some, I don't know, some kind of crazy midwife thing they can do? Some root you can chew or something?"

Cara took hold of his shoulders, and pushed him away from her so that she could look him in the eye.

"Prostaglandins," she said. "And you've got them."

"I do? Where?"

She looked down at his crotch, trying to give the gesture a slow and humorous Mae West import.

"That can't be safe," Richard said.

"Dorothy prescribed it."

"I don't know, Cara."

"It's my only hope."

"But you and I—"

"Come on, Richie. Don't even think of it as sex, all right? Just think of that as an applicator, all right? A prostaglandin delivery system."

He sighed. He closed his eyes, and wiped his open palms across his face as though to work some life and circulation into it. The skin around his eyes was crepey and pale as a worn dollar bill.

"That's a turn-on," he said.

He took off his clothes. He had lost twenty-five pounds over the past several months, and he saw the shock of this register on Cara's face. He stood a moment, at the side of the bed, uncertain how to proceed. For so long she had been so protective of her body, concealing it in loose clothing, locking him out of the bathroom during her showers and trips to the toilet, wincing and shying from any but the gentlest demonstrations of his hands. When she was still relatively slender and familiar he had not known how to touch her; now that she loomed before him, lambent and enormous, he felt unequal to the job.

She was wearing a pair of his sweatpants and a T-shirt, size extra large, that featured the face of Gali Karpas, the Israeli kung fu star, and the words TERMINATION ZONE. She slid the pants down to her ankles and lifted the shirt over her head. Her brassiere was engineered like a suspension bridge, armor plated, grandmotherly. It embarrassed her. Under the not quite familiar gaze of her husband, everything about her body embarrassed her. Her breasts, mottled and veined, tumbled out and lay shining atop the great lunar arc of her belly, dimpled by a tiny elbow or knee. Her pubic bush had sent forth rhizoids, and coarse black curls darkened her thighs and her abdomen nearly to the navel.

Richard sat back, looking at her belly. There was a complete miniature set of bones in there, a heart, a pleated brain charged with unimaginable thoughts. In a few hours or a day the passage he was about to enter would be stretched and used and inhabited by the blind, mute, and unknown witness to this act. The thought aroused him.

"Wow," Cara said, looking at his groin again. "Check that out."

"This is weird."

"Bad weird?" She looked up at Richard, reading in his face the unavoidable conclusion that the presence of the other man's child in her body had altered it so completely as to make her unrecognizable to him. A stranger, carrying a stranger in her womb, had asked him into her bed.

"Lie back," he said. "I'm going to do this to you."

"There's some oil in the drawer."

"We won't need it."

She lowered herself down onto her elbows and lay, legs parted, looking at him. He reached out, cautiously, watching his hands as they assayed the taut, luminous skin of her belly.

"Quickly," she said, after a minute. "Don't take too long."

"Does it hurt?"

"Just—please—"

Thinking that she required lubrication after all, Richard reached into the drawer of the nightstand. For a moment he felt around blindly for the bottle of oil. In the instant before he turned to watch what his hand was doing, his middle finger jammed against the tip of the X-Acto knife that Cara had been using to cut out articles on nipple confusion and thrush. He cried out.

"Did you come?"

"Uh, yeah, I did," he said. "But mostly I cut my hand."

It was a deep, long cut that pulsed with blood. After an hour with ice and pressure they couldn't get it to stop, and Cara said that they had better go to the emergency room. She wrapped the wound in half a box of gauze, and helped him dress. She threw on her clothes and followed him out to the driveway.

"We'll take the Honda," she said. "I'm driving."

They went out to the street. The sky was obscured by a low-lying fog, glowing pale orange as if lit from within, carrying an odor of salt and slick pavement. There was no one in the street and no sound except for the murmur of the Hollywood Freeway. Cara came around and opened the door for Richard, and drove him to the nearest hospital, one not especially renowned for the quality of its care.

"So was that the best sex of your life or what?" she asked him, laughing, as they waited at a red light.

"I'll tell you something," he said. "It wasn't the worst."

THE SECURITY guard at the doors to the emergency room had been working this shift for nearly three years and in that time had seen enough of the injuries and pain of the city of Los Angeles to render him immobile, smiling, very nearly inert. At 2:47 on the morning of May 20 a white Honda Accord pulled up, driven by a vastly pregnant woman. The guard, who would go off duty in an hour, kept smiling. He had seen pregnant women drive themselves to have their babies before. It was not advisable behavior, certainly, but this was a place where the inadvisable behaviors of the world came rushing to bear their foreseeable fruit. Then a man, clearly her husband, got out of the passenger side and walked, head down, past the guard. The sliding glass doors sighed open to admit him. The pregnant woman drove off toward the parking lot.

The guard frowned.

"Everything all right?" he asked Cara when she reappeared, her gait a slow contemplative roll, right arm held akimbo, right hand pressing her hip as though it pained her.

"I just had a really big contraction," she said. She made a show of wiping the sweat from her brow. "Whew." Her voice sounded happy, but to the guard she looked afraid.

"Well, you in the right place, then."

"Not really," she said. "I'm supposed to be at Cedars. Pay phone?"

He directed her to the left of the triage desk. She lumbered inside and called Dorothy.

"I think I'm having the baby," she said. "No, I'm not. I don't know."

"Keep talking," said Dorothy.

"I've only had three contractions."

"Uh-huh."

"Contractions hurt."

"They do."

"But, like, a lot."

"I know it. Keep talking."

"I'm calling from the emergency room." She named the hospital. "Richard cut his hand up. He . . . he came over . . . we . . ." A rippling sheet of hot foil unfurled in her abdomen. Cara lurched to one side. She caught herself and half-squatted on the floor beside the telephone cubicle, with the receiver in her hand, staring at the floor. She was so stunned by her womb's sudden arrogation of every sensory pathway in her body to its purposes that, as before, she forgot to combat or work her way through the contraction with the breathing and relaxation techniques she had been taught. Instead she allowed the pain to permeate and inhabit her, praying with childish fervor for it to pass. The linoleum under her feet was ocher with pink and gray flecks. It gave off a smell of ashes and pine. Cara was aware of Dorothy's voice coming through the telephone, suggesting that she try to relax the hinge of her jaw, her shoulder blades, her hips. Then the contraction abandoned her, as swiftly as it had arrived. Cara pulled herself to her feet. Her fingers ached around the receiver. There was a spreading fan of pain in her lower back. Otherwise she felt absolutely fine.

"You're having your baby," Dorothy said.

"Are you sure? How can you tell?"

"I could hear it in your voice, dear."

"But I wasn't talking." Though now as she said this she could hear an echo of her voice a moment earlier, saying, *Okay . . . okay . . . okay.*

"I'll be there in twenty minutes," Dorothy said.

When Cara found Richard, he was being seen by a physician's assistant, a large, portly black man whose tag read COLEY but who introduced himself as Nordell. Nordell's hair was elaborately braided and beaded. His hands were manicured and painted with French tips. He was pretending to find Richard attractive, or pretending to pretend. His hand was steady, and his sutures marched across Richard's swollen fingertip as orderly as a line of ants. Richard looked pale and worried. He was pretending to be amused by Nordell.

"Don't worry, girlfriend, I already gave him plenty of shit for you," Nordell told Cara when she walked into the examination room. "Cutting his hand when you're about to have a baby. I said, boyfriend, this is not your opera."

"He has a lot of nerve," said Cara.

"My goodness, look at you. You are big. How do you even fit behind the wheel of your car?"

Richard laughed.

"You be quiet." Nordell pricked another hole in Richard's finger, then tugged the thread through on its hook. "When are you due?"

"Two weeks ago."

"Uh-huh." He scowled at Richard. "Like she don't already have enough to worry about without you sticking your finger on a damn X-Acto knife."

Richard laughed again. He looked like he was about to be sick.

"You all got a name picked out?"

"Not yet."

"Know what you're having?"

"We don't," said Cara. "The baby's legs were always in the way. But Richard would like a girl."

Richard looked at her. He had noticed when she came into the room that her face had altered, that the freckled pallor and fatigue of recent weeks had given way to a flush and a giddy luster in her eye that might have been happiness or apprehension.

"Come on," said Nordell. "Don't you want to have a son to grow up just like you?"

"That would be nice," Richard said.

Cara closed her eyes. Her hands crawled across her belly. She sank down to the floor, rocking on her heels. Nordell set down his suturing clamp and peeled off his gloves. He lowered himself to the floor beside Cara and put a hand on her shoulder.

"Come on, honey, I know you been taking those breathing lessons. So breathe. Come on."

"Oh, Richie."

Richard sat on the table, watching Cara go into labor. He had not attended any but the first of the labor and delivery classes and had not the faintest idea of what was expected of him or what it now behooved him to do. This was true not just of the process of parturition but of all the duties and grand minutiae of fatherhood itself. The rape, the conception, the growing of the placenta, the nurturing and sheltering of the child in darkness, in its hammock of woven blood vessels, fed on secret broth—all of these had gone on with no involvement on his part. Until now he had taken the simple, unalterable fact of this rather brutally to heart. In this way he had managed to prevent the usual doubts and questions of the prospective father from arising in his mind. For a time, it was true, he had maintained a weak hope that the baby would be a girl. Vaguely he had envisioned a pair of skinny legs in pink high-topped sneakers, crooked upside down over a horizontal bar, a tumbling hem conveniently obscuring the face. When Dorothy had so confidently pronounced the baby a boy, however, Richard had actually felt a kind of black relief. At that moment, the child had effectively ceased to exist for him: it was merely the son of Cara's rapist, its blood snarled by the same abrading bramble of chromosomes. In all the last ten months he had never once imagined balancing an entire human being on his forearm, never pondered the depths and puzzles of his relationship to his own father, never suffered the nightly clutch of fear for the future that haunts a man while his pregnant wife lies beside him with her heavy breath rattling in her throat. Now that the hour of birth was at hand he had no idea what to do with himself.

"Get down here," said Nordell. "Hold this poor child's hand."

Richard slid off the table and knelt beside Cara. He took her warm fingers in his own.

"Stay with me, Richie," Cara said.

"All right," said Richard. "Okay."

While Nordell hastily wrapped Richard's finger in gauze and tape, a wheelchair was brought for Cara. She was rolled off to admissions, her purse balanced on her knees. When Richard caught up to her a volunteer was just wheeling her into the elevator.

"Where are we going?" Richard said.

"To labor and delivery," said the volunteer, an older man with hearing aids, his shirt pocket bulging with the outline of a pack of cigarettes. "Fourth floor. Didn't you take the tour?"

Richard shook his head.

"This isn't our hospital," Cara said. "We took the tour at Cedars."

"I wish I had," Richard said, surprising himself.

When the labor triage nurse examined Cara, she found her to be a hundred percent effaced and nearly eight centimeters dilated.

"Whoa," she said. "Let's go have you this baby."

"Here?" Cara said, knowing she sounded childish. "But I . . ."

"But nothing," said the nurse. "You can have the next one at Cedars."

Cara was hurried into an algae-green gown and rolled down to what she and the nurse both referred to as an LDR. This was a good-sized room that had been decorated to resemble a junior suite in an airport hotel, pale gray and lavender, oak-laminate furniture, posters on the walls tranquilly advertising past seasons of the Santa Fe Chamber Music Festival. There was a hospital smell of airconditioning, however, and so much diagnostic equipment crowded around the bed, so many wires and booms and monitors, that the room felt cramped, and the effect of pseudoluxury was spoiled. With all the gear and cables looming over Cara, the room looked to Richard like nothing so much as a soundstage.

"We forgot to bring a camera," he said. "I should shoot this, shouldn't I?"

"There's a vending machine on two," said the labor nurse, raising Cara's legs up toward her chest, spreading them apart. The outer lips were swollen and darkened to a tobacco-stain brown, gashed pink in the middle, bright as bubble gum. "It has things like combs and toothpaste. I think it might have the kind of camera you throw away."

"Do I have time?"

"Probably. But you never know."

"Cara, do you want pictures of this? Should I go? I'll be right back. Cara?"

Cara didn't answer. She had slipped off into the world of her contractions, eyes shut, head rolled back, brow luminous with pain and concentration like the brow of Christ in a Crucifixion scene.

The nurse had lost interest in Richard and the camera question. She had hold of one of Cara's hands in one of hers, and was stroking Cara's hair with the other. Their faces were close together, and the nurse was whispering something. Cara nodded, and bit her lip, and barked out an angry laugh. Richard stood there. He felt he ought to be helping Cara, but the nurse seemed to have everything under control. There was nothing for him to do and no room beside the bed.

"I'll be right back," he said.

He got lost on his way down to the second floor, and then when he reached two he got lost again trying to find the vending machine. It stood humming in a corridor outside the cafeteria, beside the men's room. Within its tall panel of glass doors, a carousel rotated when you pressed a button. It was well stocked with toiletry and sanitary items, along with a few games and novelties for bored children. There was one camera left. Richard fed a twenty-dollar bill into the machine and received no change.

When he got back to the room he stood with his fingers on the door handle. It was cold and dry and gave him a static shock when he grasped it. Through the door he heard Cara say, "Fuck," with a calmness that frightened him. He let go of the handle.

There was a squeaking of rubber soles, rapid and intent. Dorothy Pendleton was hurrying along the corridor toward him. She had pulled a set of rose surgical scrubs over her street clothes. They fit her badly across the chest and one laundry-marked shirttail dangled free of the waistband. As Dorothy hurried toward him she was pinning her hair up behind her head, scattering bobby pins as she came.

"You did it," she said. "Good for you."

Richard was surprised to find that he was glad to see Dorothy. She looked intent but not flustered, rosy-cheeked, wide-awake. She gave off a pleasant smell of sugary coffee. Over one shoulder she carried a big leather sack covered in a worn patchwork of scraps of old kilims. He noticed, wedged in among the tubes of jojoba oil and the medical instruments, a rolled copy of *Racing Form.*

"Yeah, well, I'm just glad, you know, that my sperm finally came in handy for something," he said.

She nodded, then leaned into the door. "Good sperm," she said. She could see that he needed something from her, a word of wisdom from the midwife, a pair of hands to yank him breech first and hypoxic back into the dazzle and clamor of the world. But she had already wasted enough of her attention on him, and she reached for the handle of the door.

Then she noticed the twenty-dollar cardboard camera dangling from his hand. For some reason it touched her that he had found himself a camera to hide behind.

She stopped. She looked at him. She put a finger to his chest. "My father was a sheriff in Bowie County, Texas," she said.

He took a step backward, gazing down at the finger. Then he looked up again.

"Meaning?"

"Meaning get your ass into that room, deputy." She pushed open the door.

The first thing they heard was the rapid beating of the baby's heart through the fetal monitor. It filled the room with its simple news, echoing like a hammer on tin.

"You're just in time," said the labor nurse. "It's crowning."

"Dorothy. Richie." Cara's head lolled toward them, her cheeks streaked with tears and damp locks of hair, her eyes red, her face swollen and bruised looking. It was the face she had worn after the attack at Lake Hollywood, dazed with pain, seeking out his eyes. "Where did you go?" she asked him. She sounded angry. "Where did you go?"

Sheepishly he held up the camera.

"Jesus! Don't go away again!"

"I'm sorry," he said. A dark circle of hair had appeared between her legs, surrounded by the fiery pink ring of her straining labia. "I'm sorry!"

"Get him scrubbed," Dorothy said to the nurse. "He's catching the baby."

"What?" said Richard. He felt he ought to reassure Cara. "Not really."

"Really," said Dorothy. "Get scrubbed."

The nurse traded places with Dorothy at the foot of the bed, and took Richard by the elbow. She tugged the shrink-wrapped camera from his grasp.

"Why don't you give that to me?" she said. "You go get scrubbed."

"I washed my hands before," Richard said, panicking a little.

"That's good," said Dorothy. "Now you can do it again."

Richard washed his hands in brown soap that stung the nostrils, then turned back to the room. Dorothy had her hand on the bed's controls, raising its back, helping Cara into a more upright position. Cara whispered something.

"What's that, honey?" said Dorothy.

"I said Richard I'm sorry too."

"What are you sorry about?" Dorothy said. "Good God."

"Everything," Cara said. And then, "Oh."

She growled and hummed, snapping her head from side to side. She hissed short whistling jets of air through her teeth. Dorothy glanced at the monitor. "Big one," she said. "Here we go."

She waved Richard over to her side. Richard hesitated.

Cara gripped the side rails of the bed. Her neck arched backward. A humming arose deep inside her chest and grew higher in pitch as it made its way upward until it burst as a short cry, ragged and harsh, from her lips.

"Whoop!" said Dorothy, drawing back her arms. "A stargazer! Hi, there!" She turned again to Richard, her hands cupped around something smeary and purple that was protruding from Cara's body. "Come on, move it. See this."

Richard approached the bed, and saw that Dorothy balanced the baby's head between her broad palms. It had a thick black shock of hair. Its eyes were wide open, large and dark, pupils invisible, staring directly, Richard felt, at him. There was no bleariness, or swelling of the lower eyelids. No one, Richard felt, had ever quite looked at him this way, without emotion, without judgment. The consciousness of a great and irrevocable event came over him; ten months' worth of dread and longing filled him in a single unbearable rush. Disastrous things had happened to him in his life; at other times, stretching far back into the interminable afternoons of his boyhood, he had experienced a sense of buoyant calm that did not seem entirely without foundation in the nature of things. Nothing awaited him in the days to come but the same uneven progression of disaster and contentment. And all those moments, past and future, seemed to him to be concentrated in that small, dark, pupilless gaze.

Dorothy worked her fingers in alongside the baby's shoulders. Her movements were brusque, sure, and indelicate. They reminded Richard of a cook's, or a potter's. She took a deep breath, glanced at Cara, and then gave the baby a twist, turning it ninety degrees.

"Now," she said. "Give me your hands."

"But you don't really catch them, do you?" he said. "That's just a figure of speech."

"Don't you wish," said Dorothy. "Now get in there."

She dragged him into her place, and stepped back. She took hold of his wrists and laid his hands on the baby's head. It was sticky and warm against his fingers.

"Just wait for the next contraction, Dad. Here it comes."

He waited, looking down at the baby's head, and then Cara grunted, and some final chain or stem binding the baby to her womb seemed to snap. With a soft slurping sound the entire child came squirting out into Richard's hands. Almost without thinking, he caught it. The nurse and Dorothy cheered. Cara started to cry. The baby's skin was the color of skimmed milk, smeared, glistening, flecked with bits of dark red. Its shoulders and back were covered in a faint down, matted and slick. It worked its tiny jaw, snorting and snuffling hungrily at the sharp first mouthfuls of air.

"What is it?" Cara said. "Is it a boy?"

"Wow," said Richard, holding the baby up to show Cara. "Check this out."

Dorothy nodded. "You have a son, Cara," she said. She took the baby from Richard, and laid him on the collapsed tent of Cara's belly. Cara opened her eyes. "A big old hairy son."

Richard went around to stand beside his wife. He leaned in until his cheek was pressed against hers. They studied the wolfman's boy, and he regarded them.

"Do you think he's funny-looking?" Richard said doubtfully. Then the nurse snapped a picture of the three of them, and they looked at her, blinking, blinded by the flash.

"Beautiful," said the nurse.

NIGHT WOMEN

Edwidge Danticat

Edwidge Danticat was born in Haiti and moved to the United States when she was twelve. She is the author of several books, including *Breath, Eyes, Memory*, an Oprah Book Club selection; *Krik? Krak!*, a National Book Award finalist; *The Farming of Bones*, an American Book Award winner; and, most recently, *Brother, I'm Dying*, a National Book Critics Circle Award winner. She is also the editor of *The Butterfly's Way: Voices from the Haitian Dyaspora in the United States* and *The Beacon Best of 2000: Great Writing by Men and Women of All Colors and Cultures*.

I cringe from the heat of the night on my face. I feel as bare as open flesh. Tonight I am much older than the twenty-five years that I have lived. The night is the time I dread most in my life. Yet if I am to live, I must depend on it.

Shadows shrink and spread over the lace curtain as my son slips into bed. I watch as he stretches from a little boy into the broom-size of a man, his height mounting the innocent fabric that splits our one-room house into two spaces, two mats, two worlds.

For a brief second, I almost mistake him for the ghost of his father, an old lover who disappeared with the night's shadows a long time ago. My son's bed stays nestled against the corner, far from the peeking jalousies. I watch as he digs furrows in the pillow with his head. He shifts his small body carefully so as not to crease his Sunday clothes. He wraps my long blood-red scarf around his neck, the one I wear myself during the day to tempt my suitors. I let him have it at night, so that he always has something of mine when my face is out of sight.

I watch his shadow resting still on the curtain. My eyes are drawn to him, like the stars peeking through the small holes in the roof that none of my suitors will fix for me, because they like to watch a scrap of the sky while lying on their naked backs on my mat.

A firefly buzzes around the room, finding him and not me. Perhaps it is a mosquito that has learned the gift of lighting itself. He always slaps the mosquitoes dead on his face without even waking. In the morning, he will have tiny blood spots on his forehead, as though he had spent the whole night kissing a woman with wide-open flesh wounds on her face.

In his sleep he squirms and groans as though he's already discovered that there is pleasure in touching himself. We have never talked about love. What would he need to know? Love is one of those lessons that you grow to learn, the way one learns that one shoe is made to fit a certain foot, lest it cause discomfort.

There are two kinds of women: day women and night women. I am stuck between the day and night in a golden amber bronze. My eyes are the color of dirt, almost copper if I am standing in the sun. I want to wear my matted tresses in braids as soon as I learn to do my whole head without numbing my arms.

Most nights, I hear a slight whisper. My body freezes as I wonder how long it would take for him to cross the curtain and find me.

He says, "Mommy."

I say, "*Darling.*"

Somehow in the night, he always calls me in whispers. I hear the buzz of his transistor radio. It is shaped like a can of cola. One of my suitors gave it to him to plug into his ears so he can stay asleep while Mommy *works*.

There is a place in Ville Rose where ghost women ride the crests of waves while brushing the stars out of their hair. There they woo strollers and leave the stars on the path for them. There are nights that I believe that those ghost women are with me. As much as I know that there are women who sit up through the night and undo patches of cloth that they have spent the whole day weaving. These women, they destroy their toil so that they will always have more to do. And as long as there's work, they will not have to lie next to the lifeless soul of a man whose scent still lingers in another woman's bed.

The way my son reacts to my lips stroking his cheeks decides for me if he's asleep. He is like a butterfly fluttering on a rock that stands out naked in the middle of a stream. Sometimes I see in the folds of his eyes a longing for something that's bigger than myself. We are like faraway lovers, lying to one another, under different moons.

When my smallest finger caresses the narrow cleft beneath his nose, sometimes his tongue slips out of his mouth and he licks my fingernail. He moans and turns away, perhaps thinking that this too is a part of the dream.

I whisper my mountain stories in his ear, stories of the ghost women and the stars in their hair. I tell him of the deadly snakes lying at one end of a rainbow and the hat full of gold lying at the other end. I tell him that if I cross a stream of glass-clear hibiscus, I can make myself a goddess. I blow on his long eyelashes to see if he's truly asleep. My fingers coil themselves into visions of birds on his nose. I want him to forget that we live in a place where nothing lasts.

I know that sometimes he wonders why I take such painstaking care. Why do I draw half-moons on my sweaty forehead and spread crimson powders on the rise of my cheeks. We put on his ruffled Sunday suit and I tell him that we are expecting a sweet angel and where angels tread the hosts must be as beautiful as floating hibiscus.

In his sleep, his fingers tug his shirt ruffles loose. He licks his lips from the last piece of sugar candy stolen from my purse.

No more, no more, or your teeth will turn black. I have forgotten to make him brush the mint leaves against his teeth. He does not know that one day a woman like his mother may judge him by the whiteness of his teeth.

It doesn't take long before he is snoring softly. I listen for the shy laughter of his most pleasant dreams. Dreams of angels skipping over his head and occasionally resting their pink heels on his nose.

I hear him humming a song. One of the madrigals they still teach children on very hot afternoons in public schools. *Kompè Jako, domé vou?* Brother Jacques, are you asleep?

The hibiscus rustle in the night outside. I sing along to help him sink deeper into his sleep. I apply another layer of the Egyptian rouge to my cheeks. There are some sparkles in the powder, which make it easier for my visitor to find me in the dark.

Emmanuel will come tonight. He is a doctor who likes big buttocks on women, but my small ones will do. He comes on Tuesdays and Saturdays. He arrives bearing flowers as though he's come to court me. Tonight he brings me bougainvillea. It is always a surprise.

"How is your wife?" I ask.

"Not as beautiful as you."

On Mondays and Thursdays, it is an accordion player named Alexandre. He likes to make the sound of the accordion with his mouth in my ear. The rest of the night, he spends with his breadfruit head rocking on my belly button.

Should my son wake up, I have prepared my fabrication. One day, he will grow too old to be told that a wandering man is a mirage and that naked flesh is a dream. I will tell him that his father has come, that an angel brought him back from Heaven for a while.

The stars slowly slip away from the hole in the roof as the doctor sinks deeper and deeper beneath my body. He throbs and pants. I cover his mouth to keep him from screaming. I see his wife's face in the beads of sweat marching down his chin. He leaves with his body soaking from the dew of our flesh. He calls me an avalanche, a waterfall, when he is satisfied.

After he leaves at dawn, I sit outside and smoke a dry tobacco leaf. I watch the piece-worker women march one another to the open market half a day's walk from where they live. I thank the stars that at least I have the days to myself.

When I walk back into the house, I hear the rise and fall of my son's breath. Quickly, I lean my face against his lips to feel the calming heat from his mouth.

"Mommy, have I missed the angels again?" he whispers softly while reaching for my neck.

I slip into the bed next to him and rock him back to sleep.

"Darling, the angels have themselves a lifetime to come to us."

TELEVISION

Lydia Davis

Lydia Davis's story collections include *Samuel Johnson Is Indignant,* a *Village Voice* favorite; *Almost No Memory,* a *Los Angeles Times* Best Book of the Year; and *Varieties of Disturbance,* a National Book Award finalist. The acclaimed translator of *Swann's Way,* by Marcel Proust, and the recipient of a 2003 MacArthur Fellowship, Davis is on the faculty at the State University of New York at Albany, where she is also a fellow of the New York State Writers Institute.

1.

We have all these favorite shows coming on every evening. They say it will be exciting and it always is.

They give us hints of what is to come and then it comes and it is exciting.

If dead people walked outside our windows we would be no more excited.

We want to be part of it all.

We want to be the people they talk to when they tell what is to come later in the evening and later in the week.

We listen to the ads until we are exhausted, punished with lists: they want us to buy so much, and we try, but we don't have a lot of money. Yet we can't help admiring the science of it all.

How can we ever be as sure as these people are sure? These women are women in control, as the women in my family are not.

Yet we believe in this world.

We believe these people are speaking to us.

Mother, for example, is in love with an anchorman. And my husband sits with his eyes on a certain young reporter and waits for the camera to draw back and reveal her breasts.

After the news we pick out a quiz show to watch and then a story of detective investigation.

The hours pass. Our hearts go on beating, now slow, now faster.

There is one quiz show which is particularly good. Each week the same man is there in the audience with his mouth tightly closed and tears in his eyes. His son is coming back on stage to answer more questions. The boy stands there blinking at the television camera. They will not let him go on answering questions if he wins the final sum of a hundred and twenty-eight thousand dollars. We don't care much about the boy and we don't like the mother, who smiles and shows her bad teeth, but we are moved by the father: his heavy lips, his wet eyes.

And so we turn off the telephone during this program and do not answer the knock at the door that rarely comes. We watch closely, and my husband now presses his lips together and then smiles so broadly that his eyes disappear, and as for me, I sit back like the mother with a sharp gaze, my mouth full of gold.

2.

It's not that I really think this show about Hawaiian policemen is very good, it's just that it seems more real than my own life.

Different routes through the evening: Channels 2, 2, 4, 7, 9, or channels 13, 13, 13, 2, 2, 4, etc. Sometimes it's the police dramas I want to see, other times the public television documentaries, such as one called *Swamp Critturs*.

It's partly my isolation at night, the darkness outside, the silence outside, the increasing lateness of the hour, that makes the story on television seem so interesting. But the plot, too, has something to do with it: tonight a son comes back after many years and marries his father's wife. (She is not his mother.)

We pay a good deal of attention because these shows seem to be the work of so many smart and fashionable people.

I think it is a television sound beyond the wall, but it's the honking of wild geese flying south in the first dark of the evening.

You watch a young woman named Susan Smith with pearls around her neck sing the Canadian National Anthem before a hockey game. You listen to the end of the song, then you change the channel.

Or you watch Pete Seeger's legs bounce up and down in time to his *Reuben E. Lee* song, then change the channel.

It is not what you want to be doing. It is that you are passing the time.

You are waiting until it is a certain hour and you are in a certain condition so that you can go to sleep.

There is some real satisfaction in getting this information about the next day's weather—how fast the wind might blow and from what direction, when the rain might come, when the skies might clear—and the exact science of it is indicated by the words "40 percent" in "40 percent chance."

It all begins with the blue dot in the center of the dark screen, and this is when you can sense that these pictures will be coming to you from a long way off.

3.

Often, at the end of the day, when I am tired, my life seems to turn into a movie. I mean my real day moves into my real evening, but also moves away from me enough to be strange and a movie. It has by then become so complicated, so hard to understand, that I want to watch a different movie. I want to watch a movie made for TV, which will be simple and easy to understand, even if it involves disaster or disability or disease. It will skip over so much, it will skip over all the complications, knowing we will understand, so that major events will happen abruptly: a man may change his mind though it was firmly made up, and he may also fall in love suddenly. It will skip all the complications because there is not enough time to prepare for major events in the space of only one hour and twenty minutes, which also has to include commercial breaks, and we want major events.

One movie was about a woman professor with Alzheimer's disease; one was about an Olympic skier who lost a leg but learned to ski again. Tonight it was about a deaf man who fell in love with his speech therapist, as I knew he would because she was pretty, though not a good actress, and he was handsome, though deaf. He was deaf at the beginning of the movie and deaf again at the end, while in the middle he heard and learned to speak with a definite regional accent. In the space of one hour and twenty minutes, this man not only heard and fell deaf again but created a successful business through his own talent, was robbed of it through a company man's treachery, fell in love, kept his woman as far as the end of the movie, and lost his virginity, which seemed to be hard to lose if one was deaf and easier once one could hear.

All this was compressed into the very end of a day in my life that as the evening advanced had already moved away from me . . .

AURORA

Junot Díaz

Junot Díaz is the author of a novel, *The Brief Wondrous Life of Oscar Wao*, winner of the Pulitzer Prize and the National Book Critics Circle Award, and a story collection, *Drown*, for which he received the PEN/ Malamud Award. His fiction has appeared in *The New Yorker*, *The Paris Review*, and *The Best American Short Stories*. Born in the Dominican Republic and raised in New Jersey, Díaz lives in New York City and is a professor of writing at the Massachusetts Institute of Technology.

Earlier today me and Cut drove down to South River and bought some more smoke. The regular pickup, enough to last us the rest of the month. The Peruvian dude who hooks us up gave us a sampler of his superweed (Jewel luv it, he said) and on the way home, past the Hydrox factory, we could have sworn we smelled cookies baking right in the back seat. Cut was smelling chocolate chip but I was smoothed out on those rocky coconut ones we used to get at school.

Holy shit, Cut said. I'm drooling all over myself.

I looked over at him but the black stubble on his chin and neck was dry. This shit is potent, I said.

That's the word I'm looking for. Potent.

Strong, I said.

It took us four hours of TV to sort, weigh and bag the smoke. We were puffing the whole way through and by the time we were in bed we were gone. Cut's still giggling over the cookies, and me, I'm just waiting for Aurora to show up. Fridays are good days to expect her. Fridays we always have something new and she knows it.

We haven't seen each other for a week. Not since she put some scratches on my arm. Fading now, like you could rub them with spit and they'd go away but when she first put them there, with her sharp-ass nails, they were long and swollen.

Around midnight I hear her tapping on the basement window. She calls my name maybe four times before I say, I'm going out to talk to her.

Don't do it, Cut says. Just leave it alone.

He's not a fan of Aurora, never gives me the messages she leaves with him. I've found these notes in his pockets and under our couches. Bullshit mostly but every now and then she leaves one that makes me want to treat her better. I lie in bed some more, listening to our neighbors flush parts of themselves down a pipe. She stops tapping, maybe to smoke a cigarette or just to listen for my breathing.

Cut rolls over. Leave it bro.

I'm going, I say.

She meets me at the door of the utility room, a single bulb lit behind her. I shut the door behind us and we kiss, once, on the lips, but she keeps them closed, first-date style. A few months ago Cut broke the lock to this place and now the utility room's ours, like an extension, an office. Concrete with splotches of oil. A drain hole in the corner where we throw our cigs and condoms.

She's skinny—six months out of juvie and she's skinny like a twelve-year-old.

I want some company, she says.

Where are the dogs?

You know they don't like you. She looks out the window, all tagged over with initials and *fuck you*'s. It's going to rain, she says.

It always looks like that.

Yeah, but this time it's going to rain for real.

I put my ass down on the old mattress, which stinks of pussy.

Where's your partner? she asks.

He's sleeping.

That's all that nigger does. She's got the shakes—even in this light I can see that. Hard to kiss anyone like that, hard even to touch them—the flesh moves like it's on rollers. She yanks open the drawstrings on her knapsack and pulls out cigarettes. She's living out of her bag again, on cigarettes and dirty clothes. I see a t-shirt, a couple of tampons and those same green shorts, the thin high-cut ones I bought her last summer.

Where you been? I ask. Haven't seen you around.

You know me. Yo ando más que un perro.

Her hair is dark with water. She must have gotten herself a shower, maybe at a friend's, maybe in an empty apartment. I know that I should dis her for being away so long, that Cut's probably listening but I take her hand and kiss it.

Come on, I say.

You ain't said nothing about the last time.

I can't remember no last time. I just remember you.

She looks at me like maybe she's going to shove my smooth-ass line back down my throat. Then her face becomes smooth. Do you want to jig?

Yeah, I say. I push her back on that mattress and grab at her clothes. Go easy, she says.

I can't help myself with her and being blunted makes it worse. She has her hands on my shoulder blades and the way she pulls on them I think maybe she's trying to open me.

Go easy, she says.

We all do shit like this, stuff that's no good for you. You do it and then there's no feeling positive about it afterwards. When Cut puts his salsa on the next morning, I wake up, alone, the blood doing jumping jacks in my head. I see that she's searched my pockets, left them hanging out of my pants like tongues. She didn't even bother to push the fuckers back in.

A WORKING DAY

Raining this morning. We hit the crowd at the bus stop, pass by the trailer park across Route 9, near the Audio Shack. Dropping rocks all over. Ten here, ten there, an ounce of weed for the big guy with the warts, some H for his coked-up girl, the one with the bloody left eye. Everybody's buying for the holiday weekend. Each time I put a bag in a hand I say, Pow, right there, my man.

Cut says he heard us last night, rides me the whole time about it. I'm surprised the AIDS ain't bit your dick off yet, he says.

I'm immune, I tell him. He looks at me and tells me to keep talking. Just keep talking, he says.

Four calls come in and we take the Pathfinder out to South Amboy and Freehold. Then it's back to the Terrace for more foot action. That's the way we run things, the less driving, the better.

None of our customers are anybody special. We don't have priests or abuelas or police officers on our lists. Just a lot of kids and some older folks who haven't had a job or a haircut since the last census. I have friends in Perth Amboy and New Brunswick who tell me they deal to whole families, from the grandparents down to the fourth-graders. Things around here aren't like that yet, but more kids are dealing and bigger crews are coming in from out of town, relatives of folks who live here. We're still making mad paper but it's harder now and Cut's already been sliced once and me, I'm thinking it's time to grow, to incorporate but Cut says, Fuck no. The smaller the better.

We're reliable and easygoing and that keeps us good with the older people, who don't want shit from anybody. Me, I'm tight with the kids, that's my side of the business. We work all hours of the day and when Cut goes to see his girl I keep at it, prowling up and down Westminister, saying wassup to everybody. I'm good for solo work. I'm edgy and don't like to be inside too much. You should have seen me in school. Olvídate.

ONE OF OUR NIGHTS

We hurt each other too well to let it drop. She breaks everything I own, yells at me like it might change something, tries to slam doors on my fingers. When she wants me to promise her a love that's never been seen anywhere I think about the other girls. The last one was on Kean's women's basketball team, with skin that made mine look dark. A college girl with her own car, who came over right after her games, in her uniform, mad at some other school for a bad layup or an elbow in the chin.

Tonight me and Aurora sit in front of the TV and split a case of Budweiser. This is going to hurt, she says, holding her can up. There's H too, a little for her, a little for me. Upstairs my neighbors have their own long night going and they're laying out all their cards about one another. Big cruel loud cards.

Listen to that romance, she says.

It's all sweet talk, I say. They're yelling because they're in love.

She picks off my glasses and kisses the parts of my face that almost never get touched, the skin under the glass and frame.

You got those long eyelashes that make me want to cry, she says. How could anybody hurt a man with eyelashes like this?

I don't know, I say, though she should. She once tried to jam a pen in my thigh, but that was the night I punched her chest black-and-blue so I don't think it counts.

I pass out first, like always. I catch flashes from the movie before I'm completely gone. A man pouring too much scotch into a plastic cup. A couple running towards each other. I wish I could stay awake through a thousand bad shows the way she does, but it's OK as long as she's breathing past the side of my neck.

Later I open my eyes and catch her kissing Cut. She's pumping her hips into him and he's got his hairy-ass hands in her hair. Fuck, I say but then I wake up and she's snoring on the couch. I put my hand on her side. She's barely seventeen, too skinny for anybody but me. She has her pipe right on the table, waited for me to fall out before hitting it. I have to open the porch door to kill the smell. I go back to sleep and when I wake up in the morning I'm laying in the tub and I've got blood on my chin and I can't remember how in the world that happened. This is no good, I tell myself. I go into the sala, wanting her to be there but she's gone again and I punch myself in the nose just to clear my head.

LOVE

We don't see each other much. Twice a month, four times maybe. Time don't flow right with me these days but I know it ain't often. I got my own life now, she tells me but you don't need to be an expert to see that she's flying again. That's what she's got going on, that's what's new.

We were tighter before she got sent to juvie, much tighter. Every day we chilled and if we needed a place we'd find ourselves an empty apartment, one that hadn't been rented yet. We'd break in. Smash a window, slide it up, wiggle on through. We'd bring sheets, pillows and candles to make the place less cold. Aurora would color the walls, draw different pictures with crayons, splatter the red wax from the candles into patterns, beautiful patterns. You got talent, I told her and she laughed. I used to be real good at art. Real good. We'd have these apartments for a couple of weeks, until the supers came to clean for the next tenants and then we'd come by and find the window fixed and the lock on the door.

On some nights—especially when Cut's fucking his girl in the next bed—I want us to be like that again. I think I'm one of those guys who lives too much in the past. Cut'll be working his girl and she'll be like, Oh yes, damelo duro, Papi, and I'll just get dressed and go looking for her. She still does the apartment thing but hangs out with a gang of crackheads, one of two girls there, sticks with this boy Harry. She says he's like her brother but I know better. Harry's a little pato, a cabrón, twice beat by Cut, twice beat by me. On the nights I find her she clings to him like she's his other nut, never wants to step outside for a minute. The others ask me if I have anything, giving me bullshit looks like they're hard or something. Do you have anything? Harry's moaning, his head caught between his knees like a big ripe coconut. Anything? I say, No, and grab onto her bicep, lead her into the bedroom. She slumps against the closet door. I thought maybe you'd want to get something to eat, I say.

I ate. You got cigarettes?

I give her a fresh pack. She holds it lightly, debating if she should smoke a few or sell the pack to somebody.

I can give you another, I say and she asks why I have to be such an ass.

I'm just offering.

Don't offer me anything with that voice.

Just go easy, nena.

We smoke a couple, her hissing out smoke, and then I close the plastic blinds. Sometimes I have condoms but not every time and while she says she ain't with anybody else, I don't kid myself. Harry's yelling, What the fuck are you doing? but he doesn't touch the door, doesn't even knock. After, when she's picking at my back and the others in the next room have started talking again, I'm amazed at how nasty I feel, how I want to put my fist in her face.

I don't always find her; she spends a lot of time at the Hacienda, with the rest of her fucked-up friends. I find unlocked doors and Dorito crumbs, maybe an un-flushed toilet. Always puke, in a closet or on a wall. Sometimes folks take craps right on the living room floor; I've learned not to walk around until my eyes get used to the dark. I go from room to room, hand out in front of me, wishing that maybe just this once I'll feel her soft face on the other side of my fingers instead of some fucking plaster wall. Once that actually happened, a long time ago.

The apartments are all the same, no surprises whatsoever. I wash my hands in the sink, dry them on the walls and head out.

CORNER

You watch anything long enough and you can become an expert at it. Get to know how it lives, what it eats. Tonight the corner is cold and nothing is really going on. You can hear the dice clicking on the curb and every truck and souped-up shitmobile that rolls in from the highway announces itself with bass.

The corner's where you smoke, eat, fuck, where you play selo. Selo games like you've never seen. I know brothers who make two, three hundred a night on the dice. Always somebody losing big. But you have to be careful with that. Never know who'll lose and then come back with a 9 or a machete, looking for the re-match. I follow Cut's advice and do my dealing nice and tranquilo, no flash, not a lot of talking. I'm cool with everybody and when folks show up they always give me a pound, knock their shoulder into mine, ask me how it's been. Cut talks to his girl, pulling her long hair, messing with her little boy but his eyes are always watching the road for cops, like minesweepers.

We're all under the big streetlamps, everyone's the color of day-old piss. When I'm fifty this is how I'll remember my friends: tired and yellow and drunk. Eggie's out here too. Homeboy's got himself an Afro and his big head looks ridiculous on his skinny-ass neck. He's way-out high tonight. Back in the day, before Cut's girl took over, he was Cut's gunboy but he was an irresponsible mother-fucker, showed it around too much and talked amazing amounts of shit. He's arguing with some of the tígueres over nonsense and when he doesn't back down I can see that nobody's happy. The corner's hot now and I just shake my head. Nelo, the nigger Eggie's talking shit to, has had more PTI than most of us have had traffic tickets. I ain't in the mood for this shit.

I ask Cut if he wants burgers and his girl's boy trots over and says, Get me two.

Come back quick, Cut says, all about business. He tries to hand me bills but I laugh, tell him it's on me.

The Pathfinder sits in the next parking lot, crusty with mud but still a slamming ride. I'm in no rush; I take it out behind the apartments, onto the road that leads to the dump. This was our spot when we were younger, where we started fires we sometimes couldn't keep down. Whole areas around the road are still black. Everything that catches in my headlights—the stack of old tires, signs, shacks—has a memory scratched onto it. Here's where I shot my first pistol. Here's where we stashed our porn magazines. Here's where I kissed my first girl.

I get to the restaurant late; the lights are out but I know the girl in the front and she lets me in. She's heavy but has a good face, makes me think of the one time we kissed, when I put my hand in her pants and felt the pad she had on. I ask her about her mother and she says, Regular. The brother? Still down in Virginia with the Navy. Don't let him turn into no pato. She laughs, pulls at the nameplate around her neck. Any woman who laughs as dope as she does won't ever have trouble finding men. I tell her that and she looks a little scared of me. She gives me what she has under the lamps for free and when I get back to the corner Eggie's out cold on the grass. A couple of older kids stand around him, pissing hard streams into his face. Come on, Eggie, somebody says. Open that mouth. Supper's coming. Cut's laughing too hard to talk to me and he ain't the only one. Brothers are falling over with laughter and some grab onto their boys, pretend to smash their heads against the curb. I give the boy his hamburgers and he goes between two bashes, where no one will bother him. He squats down and unfolds the oily paper, careful not to stain his Carhartt. Why don't you give me a piece of that? some girl asks him.

Because I'm hungry, he says, taking a big bite out.

LUCERO

I would have named it after you, she said. She folded my shirt and put it on the kitchen counter. Nothing in the apartment, only us naked and some beer and half a pizza, cold and greasy. You're named after a star.

This was before I knew about the kid. She kept going on like that and finally I said, What the fuck are you talking about?

She picked the shirt up and folded it again, patting it down like this had taken her some serious effort. I'm telling you something. Something about me. What you should be doing is listening.

I COULD SAVE YOU

I find her outside the Quick Check, hot with a fever. She wants to go to the Hacienda but not alone. Come on, she says, her palm on my shoulder.

Are you in trouble?

Fuck that. I just want company.

I know I should just go home. The cops bust the Hacienda about twice a year, like it's a holiday. Today could be my lucky day. Today could be our lucky day.

You don't have to come inside. Just hang with me a little.

If something inside of me is saying no, why do I say, Yeah, sure?

We walk up to Route 9 and wait for the other side to clear. Cars buzz past and a new Pontiac swerves towards us, a scare, streetlights flowing back over its top, but we're too lifted to flinch. The driver's blond and laughing and we give him the finger. We watch the cars and above us the sky has gone the color of pumpkins. I haven't seen her in ten days, but she's steady, her hair combed back straight, like she's back in school or something. My mom's getting married, she says.

To that radiator guy?

No, some other guy. Owns a car wash.

That's real nice. She's lucky for her age.

You want to come with me to the wedding?

I put my cigarette out. Why can't I see us there? Her smoking in the bathroom and me dealing to the groom. I don't know about that.

My mom sent me money to buy a dress.

You still got it?

Of course I got it. She looks and sounds hurt so I kiss her. Maybe next week I'll go look at dresses. I want something that'll make me look good. Something that'll make my ass look good.

We head down a road for utility vehicles, where beer bottles grow out of the weeds like squashes. The Hacienda is past this road, a house with orange tiles on the roof and yellow stucco on the walls. The boards across the windows are as loose as old teeth, the bushes around the front big and mangy like Afros. When the cops nailed her here last year she told them she was looking for me, that we were supposed to be going to a movie together. I wasn't within ten miles of the place. Those pigs must have laughed their asses off. A movie. Of course. When they asked her what movie she couldn't even come up with one.

I want you to wait out here, she says.

That's fine by me. The Hacienda's not my territory.

Aurora rubs a finger over her chin. Don't go nowhere.

Just hurry your ass up.

I will. She put her hands in her purple windbreaker.

Make it fast Aurora.

I just got to have a word with somebody, she says and I'm thinking how easy it would be for her to turn around and say, Hey, let's go home. I'd put my arm around her and I wouldn't let her go for like fifty years, maybe not ever. I know people who quit just like that, who wake up one day with bad breath and say, No more. I've had enough. She smiles at me and jogs around the corner, the ends of her hair falling up and down on her neck. I make myself a shadow against the bushes and listen for the Dodges and the Chevys that stop in the next parking lot, for the walkers that come rolling up with their hands in their pockets. I hear everything. A bike chain rattling. TVs snapping on in nearby apartments, squeezing ten voices into a room. After an hour the traffic on Route 9 has slowed and you can hear the cars roaring on from as far up as the Ernston light. Everybody knows about this house; people come from all over.

I'm sweating. I walk down to the utility road and come back. Come on, I say. An old fuck in a green sweat suit comes out of the Hacienda, his hair combed up into a salt-and-pepper torch. An abuelo type, the sort who yells at you for spitting on his sidewalk. He has this smile on his face—big, wide, shit-eating. I know all about the nonsense that goes on in these houses, the ass that gets sold, the beasting.

Hey, I say and when he sees me, short, dark, unhappy, he breaks. He throws himself against his car door. Come here, I say. I walk over to him slow, my hand out in front of me like I'm armed. I just want to ask you something. He slides down to the ground, his arms out, fingers spread, hands like starfishes. I step on his ankle but he doesn't yell. He has his eyes closed, his nostrils wide. I grind down hard but he doesn't make a sound.

WHILE YOU WERE GONE

She sent me three letters from juvie and none of them said much, three pages of bullshit. She talked about the food and how rough the sheets were, how she woke up ashy in the morning, like it was winter. *Three months and I still haven't had my period. The doctor here tells me it's my nerves. Yeah, right. I'd tell you about the other girls (there's a lot to tell) but they rip those letters up. I hope you doing good. Don't think bad about me. And don't let anybody sell my dogs either.*

Her tía Fresa held on to the first letters for a couple of weeks before turning them over to me, unopened. Just tell me if she's OK or not, Fresa said. That's about as much as I want to know.

She sounds OK to me.

Good. Don't tell me anything else.

You should at least write her.

She put her hands on my shoulders and leaned down to my ear. You write her.

I wrote but I can't remember what I said to her, except that the cops had come after her neighbor for stealing somebody's car and that the gulls were shitting on everything. After the second letter I didn't write anymore and it didn't feel wrong or bad. I had a lot to keep me busy.

She came home in September and by then we had the Pathfinder in the parking lot and a new Zenith in the living room. Stay away from her, Cut said. Luck like that don't get better.

No sweat, I said. You know I got the iron will.

People like her got addictive personalities. You don't want to be catching that.

We stayed apart a whole weekend but on Monday I was coming home from Pathmark with a gallon of milk when I heard, Hey macho. I turned around and there she was, out with her dogs. She was wearing a black sweater, black stirrup pants and old black sneakers. I thought she'd come out messed up but she was just thinner and couldn't keep still, her hands and face restless, like kids you have to watch.

How are you? I kept asking and she said, Just put your hands on me. We started to walk and the more we talked the faster we went.

Do this, she said. I want to feel your fingers.

She had mouth-sized bruises on her neck. Don't worry about them. They ain't contagious.

I can feel your bones.

She laughed. I can feel them too.

If I had half a brain I would have done what Cut told me to do. Dump her sorry ass. When I told him we were in love he laughed. I'm the King of Bullshit, he said, and you just hit me with some, my friend.

We found an empty apartment out near the highway, left the dogs and the milk outside. You know how it is when you get back with somebody you've loved. It felt better than it ever was, better than it ever could be again. After, she drew on the walls with her lipstick and her nail polish, stick men and stick women boning.

What was it like in there? I asked. Me and Cut drove past one night and it didn't look good. We honked the horn for a long time, you know, thought maybe you'd hear.

She sat up and looked at me. It was a cold-ass stare.

We were just hoping.

I hit a couple of girls, she said. Stupid girls. That was a *big* mistake. The staff put me in the Quiet Room. Eleven days the first time. Fourteen after that. That's the sort of shit that you can't get used to, no matter who you are. She looked at her drawings. I made up this whole new life in there. You should have seen it. The two of us had kids, a big blue house, hobbies, the whole fucking thing.

She ran her nails over my side. A week from then she would be asking me again, begging actually, telling me all the good things we'd do and after a while I hit her and made the blood come out of her ear like a worm but right then, in that apartment, we seemed like we were normal folks. Like maybe everything was fine.

A HOUSE ON THE PLAINS

E. L. Doctorow

E. L. Doctorow was born in New York City on January 6, 1931. He is
the author of *The Book of Daniel*, *Ragtime*, *World's Fair*, *Billy Bathgate*,
The Waterworks, and *City of God*. He has published two short story
collections, *Lives of the Poets* and *Sweet Land Stories*, and two collections of essays. Doctorow is a recipient of a Guggenheim Fellowship,
a National Book Award, two National Book Critics Circle Awards, two
PEN/Faulkner Awards, the Commonwealth Award, the William Dean
Howells Medal from the American Academy of Arts and Letters, and a
presidentially conferred National Humanities Medal. His latest novel,
The March, won the 2006 PEN/Faulkner Award and the National Book
Award.

Mama said I was thenceforth to be her nephew, and to call her Aunt
Dora. She said our fortune depended on her not having a son as old
as eighteen who looked more like twenty. Say Aunt Dora, she said. I
said it. She was not satisfied. She made me say it several times. She
said I must say it believing she had taken me in since the death of her
widowed brother, Horace. I said, I didn't know you had a brother
named Horace. Of course I don't, she said with an amused glance at
me. But it must be a good story if I could fool his son with it.

   I was not offended as I watched her primp in the mirror, touching her hair as women do, although you can never see what afterwards is different.

With the life insurance, she had bought us a farm fifty miles
west of the city line. Who would be there to care if I was her flesh
and blood son or not? But she had her plans and was looking ahead.
I had no plans. I had never had plans—just the inkling of something, sometimes, I didn't know what. I hunched over and went
down the stairs with the second trunk wrapped to my back with
a rope. Outside, at the foot of the stoop, the children were waiting
with their scraped knees and socks around their ankles. They sang
their own dirty words to a nursery rhyme. I shooed them away and
they scattered off for a minute hooting and hollering and then of
course came back again as I went up the stairs for the rest of the
things.

Mama was standing at the empty bay window. While there is
your court of inquest on the one hand, she said, on the other is
your court of neighbors. Out in the country, she said, there will
be no one to jump to conclusions. You can leave the door open,
and the window shades up. Everything is clean and pure under
the sun.

Well, I could understand that, but Chicago to my mind was the
only place to be, with its grand hotels and its restaurants and paved
avenues of trees and mansions. Of course not all Chicago was like
that. Our third floor windows didn't look out on much besides the
row of boardinghouses across the street. And it is true that in the
summer people of refinement could be overcome with the smell of
the stockyards, although it didn't bother me. Winter was another
complaint that wasn't mine. I never minded the cold. The wind in
winter blowing off the lake went whipping the ladies' skirts like a
demon dancing around their ankles. And winter or summer you
could always ride the electric streetcars if you had nothing else to
do. I above all liked the city because it was filled with people all a-
bustle, and the clatter of hooves and carriages, and with delivery
wagons and drays and the peddlers and the boom and clank of the
freight trains. And when those black clouds came sailing in from
the west, pouring thunderstorms upon us so that you couldn't hear

the cries or curses of humankind, I liked that best of all. Chicago could stand up under the worst God had to offer. I understood why it was built—a place for trade, of course, with railroads and ships and so on, but mostly to give all of us a magnitude of defiance that is not provided by one house on the plains. And the plains is where those storms come from.

Besides, I would miss my friend Winifred Czerwinska, who stood now on her landing as I was going downstairs with the suitcases. Come in a minute, she said, I want to give you something. I went in and she closed the door behind me. You can put those down, she said of the suitcases.

My heart always beat faster in Winifred's presence. I could feel it and she knew it too and it made her happy. She put her hand on my chest now and she stood on tiptoes to kiss me with her hand under my shirt feeling my heart pump.

Look at him, all turned out in a coat and tie. Oh, she said, with her eyes tearing up, what am I going to do without my Earle? But she was smiling.

Winifred was not a Mama type of woman. She was a slight, skinny thing, and when she went down the stairs it was like a bird hopping. She wore no powder or perfumery except by accident the confectionary sugar which she brought home on her from the bakery where she worked behind the counter. She had sweet, cool lips but one eyelid didn't come up all the way over the blue, which made her not as pretty as she might otherwise be. And of course she had no titties to speak of.

You can write me a letter or two and I will write back, I said.

What will you say in your letter?

I will think of something, I said.

She pulled me into the kitchen, where she spread her feet and put her forearms flat on a chair so that I could raise her frock and fuck into her in the way she preferred. It didn't take that long, but even so, while Winifred wiggled and made her little cat sounds I could hear Mama calling from upstairs as to where I had gotten.

We had ordered a carriage to take us and the luggage at the same time rather than sending it off by the less expensive Railway Express and taking a horsecar to the station. That was not my idea, but exactly the amounts that were left after Mama bought the house only she knew. She came down the steps under her broad-brim hat and widow's veil and held her skirts at her shoe tops as the driver helped her into the carriage.

We were making a grand exit in full daylight. This was pure Mama as she lifted her veil and glanced with contempt at the neighbors looking out from their windows. As for the nasty children, they had gone quite quiet at our display of elegance. I swung up beside her and closed the door and at her instruction threw a handful of pennies on the sidewalk, and I watched the children push and shove one another and dive to their knees as we drove off.

When we had turned the corner, Mama opened the hatbox I had put on the seat. She removed her black hat and replaced it with a blue number trimmed in fake flowers. Over her mourning dress she draped a glittery shawl in striped colors like the rainbow. There, she said. I feel so much better now. Are you all right, Earle?

Yes, Mama, I said.

Aunt Dora.

Yes, Aunt Dora.

I wish you had a better mind, Earle. You could have paid more attention to the Doctor when he was alive. We had our disagreements, but he was smart for a man.

THE TRAIN stop of La Ville was a concrete platform and a lean-to for a waiting room and no ticket-agent window. When you got off, you were looking down an alley to a glimpse of their Main Street. Main Street had a feed store, a post office, a white wooden church, a granite stone bank, a haberdasher, a town square with a four-story hotel, and in the middle of the square on the grass the statue of a Union soldier. It could all be counted because there was just one of everything. A man with a dray was willing to take us. He drove past a few other streets where first there were some homes of substance and another church or two but then, as you moved further out from the town center, worn looking one-story shingle houses with dark little porches and garden plots and clotheslines out back with only alleys separating them. I couldn't see how, but Mama said there was a population of over three thousand living here. And then after a couple of miles through farmland, with a silo here and there off a straight road leading due west through fields of corn, there swung into view what I had not expected, a three-story house of red brick with a flat roof and stone steps up to the front door like something just lifted out of a street of row houses in Chicago. I couldn't believe anyone had built such a thing for a farmhouse. The sun flared in the windowpanes and I had to shade my eyes to make sure I was seeing what I saw. But that was it in truth, our new home.

Not that I had the time to reflect, not with Mama settling in. We went to work. The house was cobwebbed and dusty and it was rank with the droppings of animal life. Blackbirds were roosting in the top floor, where I was to live. Much needed to be done, but before long she had it all organized and a parade of wagons was coming from town with the furniture she'd Expressed and no shortage of men willing to hire on for a day with hopes for more from this grand good-looking lady with the rings on several fingers. And so the fence went up for the chicken yard, and the weed fields beyond were being plowed under and the watering hole for stock was dredged and a new privy was dug, and I thought for some days Mama was the biggest employer of La Ville, Illinois.

But who would haul the well water and wash the clothes and bake the bread? A farm was a different life, and days went by when I slept under the roof of the third floor and felt the heat of the day still on my pallet as I looked through the little window at the remoteness of the stars and I felt unprotected as I never had in the civilization we had retreated from. Yes, I thought, we had moved backward from the world's progress, and for the first time I wondered about Mama's judgment. In all our travels from state to state and with all the various obstacles to her ambition, I had never thought to question it. But no more than this house was a farmer's house was she a farmer, and neither was I.

One evening we stood on the front steps watching the sun go down behind the low hills miles away.

Aunt Dora, I said, what are we up to here?

I know, Earle. But some things take time.

She saw me looking at her hands, how red they had gotten.

I am bringing an immigrant woman down from Wisconsin. She will sleep in that room behind the kitchen. She's to be here in a week or so.

Why? I said. There's women in La Ville, the wives of all these locals come out here for a day's work who could surely use the money.

I will not have some woman in the house who will only take back to town what she sees and hears. Use what sense God gave you, Earle.

I am trying, Mama.

Aunt Dora, goddamnit.

Aunt Dora.

Yes, she said. Especially here in the middle of nowhere and with nobody else in sight.

She had tied her thick hair behind her neck against the heat and she went about now loose in a smock without her usual women's underpinnings.

But doesn't the air smell sweet, she said. I'm going to have a screen porch built and fit it out with a settee and some rockers so we can watch the grand show of nature in comfort.

She ruffled my hair. And you don't have to pout, she said. You may not appreciate it here this moment with the air so peaceful and the birds singing and nothing much going on in any direction you can see. But we're still in business, Earle. You can trust me on that.

And so I was assured.

———

BY AND by we acquired an old-fashioned horse and buggy to take us to La Ville and back when Aunt Dora had to go to the bank or the post office or provisions were needed. I was the driver and horse groom. He—the horse—and I did not get along. I wouldn't give him a name. He was ugly, with a sway back and legs that trotted out splayed. I had butchered and trimmed better looking plugs than this in Chicago. Once, in the barn, when I was putting him up for the night, he took a chomp in the air just off my shoulder.

Another problem was Bent, the handyman Mama had hired for the steady work. No sooner did she begin taking him upstairs of an afternoon than he was strutting around like he owned the place. This was a problem as I saw it. Sure enough, one day he told me to do something. It was one of his own chores. I thought you was the hired one, I said to him. He was ugly, like a relation of the horse—he was shorter than you thought he ought to be with his long arms and big gnarled hands hanging from them.

Get on with it, I said.

Leering, he grabbed me by the shoulder and put his mouth up to my ear. I seen it all, he said. Oh yes. I seen everything a man could wish to see.

At this I found myself constructing a fate for Bent the handyman. But he was so drunkly stupid I knew Mama must have her own plan for him or else why would she play up to someone of this ilk, and so I held my ideas in abeyance.

In fact I was by now thinking I could wrest some hope from the wide loneliness of this farm with views of the plains as far as you could see. What had come to mind? A sense of expectancy that I recognized from times past. Yes. I had sensed that whatever was going to happen had begun. There was not only the handyman. There were the orphan children. She had contracted for three from the do-good agency in New York that took orphans off the streets and washed and dressed them and put them on the train to their foster homes in the midland. Ours were comely enough children, though pale, two boys and a girl with papers that gave their ages, six, six, and eight, and as I trotted them to the farm they sat up behind me staring at the countryside without a word. And so now they were installed in the back bedroom on the second floor, and they were not like the miserable street rats from our neighborhood in the city. These were quiet children except for the weeping they were sometimes given to at night, and by and large they did as they were told. Mama had some real feeling for them—Joseph and Calvin and the girl, Sophie, in particular. There were no conditions as to what faith they were to be brought up in nor did we have any in mind. But on Sundays, Mama took to showing them off to the Methodist church in La Ville in the new clothes she had bought for them. It gave her pleasure, and was besides a presentation of her own pride of position in life. Because it turned out, as I was learning, that even in the farthest reaches of the countryside, you lived in society.

And in this great scheme of things my Aunt Dora required little Joseph, Calvin, and Sophie to think of her as their mama. Say Mama, she said to them. And they said it.

WELL, so here was this household of us, ready made, as something bought from a department store. Fannie was the imported cook and housekeeper, who by Mama's design spoke no English but understood well enough what had to be done. She was heavyset, like Mama, with the strength to work hard. And besides Bent, who skulked about by the barns and fences in the sly pretense of work, there was a real farmer out beyond, who was sharecropping the acreage in corn. And two mornings a week a retired county teacher woman came by to tutor the children in reading and arithmetic.

Mama said one evening: We are an honest to goodness enterprise here, a functioning family better off than most in these parts, but we are running at a deficit, and if we don't have something in hand before winter the only resources will be the insurance I took out on the little ones.

She lit the kerosene lamp on the desk in the parlor and wrote out a Personal and read it to me: "Widow offering partnership in prime farmland to dependable man. A modest investment is required." What do you think, Earle?

It's okay.

She read it again to herself. No, she said. It's not good enough. You've got to get them up off their ass and out of the house to the Credit Union and then on a train to La Ville, Illinois. That's a lot to do with just a few words. How about this: "Wanted!" That's good, it bespeaks urgency. And doesn't every male in the world thinks he's what is wanted? "Wanted—Recently widowed woman with bountiful farm in God's own country has need of Nordic man of sufficient means for partnership in same."

What is Nordic? I said.

Well that's pure cunning right there, Earle, because that's all they got in the states where we run this—Swedes and Norwegies just off the boat. But I'm letting them know a lady's preference.

All right, but what's that you say there—"of sufficient means"? What Norwegie off the boat'll know what that's all about?

This gave her pause. Good for you, Earle, you surprise me sometimes. She licked the pencil point. So we'll just say "with cash."

WE PLACED the Personal in one paper at a time in towns in Minnesota, and then in South Dakota. The letters of courtship commenced, and Mama kept a ledger with the names and dates of arrival, making sure to give each candidate his sufficient time. We always advised the early-morning train when the town was not yet up and about. Beside my regular duties, I had to take part in the family reception. They would be welcomed into the parlor, and Mama would serve coffee from a wheeled tray, and Joseph, Calvin, and Sophie, her children, and I, her nephew, would sit on the sofa and hear our biographies conclude with a happy ending, which was the present moment. Mama was so well spoken at these times I was as apt as the poor foreigners to be caught up in her modesty, so seemingly unconscious was she of the great-heartedness of her. They by and large did not see through to her self-congratulation. And of course

she was a large, handsome woman to look at. She wore her simple
finery for these first impressions, a plain pleated gray cotton skirt
and a starched white shirtwaist and no jewelry but the gold cross
on a chain that fell between her bosoms and her hair combed upward and piled atop her head in a state of fetching carelessness.

I am their dream of heaven on earth, Mama said to me along
about the third or fourth. Just to see how their eyes light up standing
beside me looking out over their new land. Puffing on their pipes,
giving me a glance that imagines me as available for marriage—
who can say I don't give value in return?

Well that is one way to look at it, I said.

Don't be smug, Earle. You're in no position. Tell me an easier
way to God's blessed Heaven than a launch from His Heaven on
earth. I don't know of one.

AND SO our account in the La Ville Savings Bank began to compound
nicely. The late summer rain did just the right thing for the corn,
as even I could see, and it was an added few unanticipated dollars
we received from the harvest. If there were any complications to
worry about it was that fool Bent. He was so dumb he was dangerous. At first Mama indulged his jealousy. I could hear them arguing
upstairs—he roaring away and she assuring him so quietly I could
hardly hear what she said. But it didn't do any good. When one of
the Norwegies arrived, Bent just happened to be in the yard, where
he could have a good look. One time there was his ugly face peering
through the porch window. Mama signaled me with a slight motion of her head and I quickly got up and pulled the shade.

It was true Mama might lay it on a bit thick. She might coquette
with this one, yes, just as she might affect a widow's piety with
that one. It all depended on her instinct of the particular man's
character. It was easy enough to make believers of them. If I had
to judge them as a whole I would say they were simple men, not
exactly stupid, but lacking command of our language and with
no wiles of their own. By whatever combination of sentiments

and signatures, she never had anything personal intended but the business at hand, the step-by-step encouragement of the cash into our bank account.

The fool Bent imagined Mama looking for a husband from among these men. His pride of possession was offended. When he came to work each morning, he was often three sheets to the wind and if she happened not to invite him upstairs for the afternoon siesta, he would go home in a state, turning at the road to shake his fist and shout up at the windows before he set out for town in his crouching stride.

Mama said to me on one occasion, The damned fool has feelings.

Well that had not occurred to me in the way she meant it, and maybe in that moment my opinion of the handyman was raised to a degree. Not that he was any less dangerous. Clearly he had never learned that the purpose of life is to improve your station in it. It was not an idea available to him. Whatever you were, that's what you would always be. So he saw these foreigners who couldn't even talk right not only as usurpers but as casting a poor light on his existence. Was I in his position, I would learn from the example of these immigrants and think what I could do to put together a few dollars and buy some farmland for myself. Any normal person would think that. Not him. He just got enough of the idea through his thick skull to realize he lacked the hopes of even the lowest foreigner. So I would come back from the station with one of them in the buggy and the fellow would step down, his plaid suit and four-in-hand and his bowler proposing him as a man of sufficient means, and it was like a shadow and sudden chilling as from a black cloud came over poor Bent, who could understand only that it was too late for him—everything, I mean, it was all too late.

And finally, to show how dumb he was, what he didn't realize was that it was all too late for them, too.

————————

THEN EVERYTHING green began to fade off yellow, the summer rains were gone, and the wind off the prairie blew the dried-out top-soil into gusty swirls that rose and fell like waves in a dirt sea. At night the windows rattled. At first frost, the two little boys caught the croup.

Mama pulled the Wanted ad back from the out-of-state papers, saying she needed to catch her breath. I didn't know what was in the ledger, but her saying that meant our financial situation was improved. And now, as with all farm families, winter would be a time for rest.

Not that I was looking forward to it. How could I with nothing to do?

I wrote a letter to my friend Winifred Czerwinska, in Chicago. I had been so busy until now I hardly had the time to be lonely. I said that I missed her and hoped before too long to come back to city life. As I wrote, a rush of pity for myself came over me and I almost sobbed at the picture in my mind of the Elevated trains and the moving lights of the theater marquees and the sounds I imagined of the streetcars and even of the lowings of the abattoir where I had earned my wages. But I only said I hoped she would write me back.

I think the children felt the same way about this cold countryside. They had been displaced from a greater distance away, in a city larger than Chicago. They could not have been colder huddled at some steam grate than they were now with blankets to their chins. From the day they arrived they wouldn't leave one another's side, and though she was not croupy herself, Sophie stayed with the two boys in their bedroom, attending to their hackings and wheezes and sleeping in an armchair in the night. Fannie cooked up oatmeal for their breakfasts and soup for their dinners, and I took it upon myself to bring the tray upstairs in order to get them talking to me, since we were all related in a sense and in their minds I would be an older boy orphan taken in, like them. But they would not talk much, only answering my friendly

questions yes or no in their soft voices, looking at me all the while
with some dark expectation in their eyes. I didn't like that. I knew
they talked among themselves all the time. These were street-
wise children who had quickly apprised themselves of the lay
of the land. For instance, they knew enough to stay out of Bent's
way when he was drinking. But when he was sober they followed
him around. And one day I had gone into the stable, to harness
the horse, and found them snooping around in there, so they were
not without unhealthy curiosity. Then there was the unfortunate
matter of one of the boys, Joseph, the shorter darker one—he had
found a pocket watch and watch fob in the yard, and when I said
it was mine he said it wasn't. Whose is it then, I said. I know it's
not yours, he said as he finally handed it over. To make more of an
issue of it was not wise, so I didn't, but I hadn't forgotten.

Mama and I were nothing if not prudent, discreet, and in full
consideration of the feelings of others in all our ways and means,
but I believe children have a sense that enables them to know
something even when they can't say what it is. As a child I must
have had it, but of course it leaves you as you grow up. It may be
a trait children are given so that they will survive long enough to
grow up.

But I didn't want to think the worst. I reasoned to myself that
were I plunked down so far away from my streets among strangers who I was ordered to live with as their relation, in the middle
of this flat land of vast empty fields that would stir in any breast
nothing but a recognition of the presiding deafness and dumbness
of the natural world, I too would behave as these children were
behaving.

AND THEN ONE stinging cold day in December, I had gone into town
to pick up a package from the post office. We had to write away to
Chicago for those things it would not do to order from the local
merchants. The package was in, but also a letter addressed to me,
and it was from my friend Winifred Czerwinska.

Winifred's penmanship made me smile. The letters were thin and scrawny and did not keep to a straight line but went slanting in a downward direction, as if some of her mortal being was transferred to the letter paper. And I knew she had written from the bakery, because there was some powdered sugar in the folds.

She was so glad to hear from me and to know where I was. She thought I had forgotten her. She said she missed me. She said she was bored with her job. She had saved her money and hinted that she would be glad to spend it on something interesting, like a train ticket. My ears got hot reading that. In my mind I saw Winifred squinting up at me. I could almost feel her putting her hand under my shirt to feel my heart the way she liked to do.

But on the second page she said maybe I would be interested in news from the old neighborhood. There was going to be another inquest, or maybe the same one reopened.

It took me a moment to understand she was talking about the Doctor, Mama's husband in Chicago. The Doctor's relatives had asked for his body to be dug up. Winifred found this out from the constable who knocked on her door as he was doing with everyone. The police were trying to find out where we had gone, Mama and I.

I hadn't gotten your letter yet, Winifred said, so I didn't have to lie about not knowing where you were.

I raced home. Why did Winifred think she would otherwise have to lie? Did she believe all the bad gossip about us? Was she like the rest of them? I thought she was different. I was disappointed in her, and then I was suddenly very mad at Winifred.

Mama read the letter differently. Your Miss Czerwinska is our friend, Earle. That's something higher than a lover. If I have worried about her slow eye being passed on to the children, if it shows up we will just have to have it corrected with surgery.

What children, I said.

The children of your blessed union with Miss Czerwinska, Mama said.

Do not think Mama said this merely to keep me from worrying about the Chicago problem. She sees things before other people see them. She has plans going out through all directions of the universe—she is not a one-track mind, my Aunt Dora. I was excited by her intentions for me, as if I had thought of them myself. Perhaps I had thought of them myself as my secret, but she had read my secret and was now giving her approval. Because I certainly did like Winifred Czerwinska, whose lips tasted of baked goods and who loved it so when I fucked into her. And now it was all out in the open, and Mama not only knew my feelings but expressed them for me and it only remained for the young lady to be told that we were engaged.

I thought then her visiting us would be appropriate, especially as she was prepared to pay her own way. But Mama said, Not yet, Earle. Everyone in the house knew you were loving her up, and if she was to quit her job in the bakery and pack a bag and go down to the train station, even the Chicago police, as stupid as they are, they would put two and two together.

Of course I did not argue the point, though I was of the opinion that the police would find out where we were regardless. There were indications all over the place—not anything as difficult as a clue to be discerned only by the smartest of detectives, but bank account transfers, forwarding mail, and such. Why, even the driver who took us to the station might have picked up some remark of ours, and certainly a ticket-seller at Union Station might remember us. Mama being such an unusual-looking woman, very decorative and regal to the male eye, she would surely be remembered by a ticket-seller, who would not see her like from one year to the next.

Maybe a week went by before Mama expressed an opinion about the problem. You can't trust people, she said. It's that damn sister of his, who didn't even shed a tear at the grave. Why, she even told me how lucky the Doctor was to have found me so late in life.

I remember, I said.

And how I had taken such good care of him.

Which was true, I said.

Relatives are the fly in the ointment, Earle.

MAMA'S NOT being concerned so much as she was put out meant to me that we had more time than I would have thought. Our quiet lives of winter went on as before, though as I watched and waited she was obviously thinking things through. I was satisfied to wait, even though she was particularly attentive to Bent, inviting him in for dinner as if he was not some hired hand but a neighboring farmer. And I had to sit across the table on the children's side and watch him struggle to hold the silver in his fist and slurp his soup and pity him the way he had pathetically combed his hair down and tucked his shirt in and the way he folded his fingers under when he happened to see the dirt under his nails. This is good eats, he said aloud to no one in particular, and even Fannie, as she served, gave a little hmph as if despite having no English she understood clearly enough how out of place he was here at our table.

Well as it turned out there were things I didn't know, for instance that the little girl, Sophie, had adopted Bent, or maybe made a pet of him as you would any dumb beast, but they had become friends of a sort and she had confided to him remarks she overheard in the household. Maybe if she was making Mama into her mama she thought she was supposed to make the wretched bum of a hired hand into her father, I don't know. Anyway, there was this alliance between them that showed to me that she would never rise above her unsavory life in the street as a vagrant child. She looked like an angel with her little bow mouth and her pale face and gray eyes and her hair in a single long braid, which Mama herself did every morning, but she had the hearing of a bat and could stand on the second-floor landing and listen all the way down the stairs to our private conversations in the front parlor. Of course I only knew that later. It was Mama who learned that Bent was putting it about to his drinking cronies in town that the Madame Dora they thought was such a lady was his love slave and a woman on the wrong side of the law back in Chicago.

Mama, I said, I have never liked this fool, though I have been holding my ideas in abeyance for the fate I have in mind for him. But here he accepts our wages and eats our food then goes and does this?

Hush, Earle, not yet, not yet, she said. But you are a good son to me, and I can take pride that as a woman alone I have bred in you the highest sense of family honor. She saw how troubled I was. She hugged me. Are you not my very own knight of the roundtable? she said. But I was not comforted. It seemed to me that forces were massing slowly but surely against us in a most menacing way. I didn't like it. I didn't like it that we were going along as if everything was hunky dory, even to giving a grand Christmas Eve party for the several people in La Ville who Mama had come to know—how they all drove out in their carriages under the moon that was so bright on the plains of snow that it was like a black daytime, the local banker, the merchants, the pastor of the First Methodist church, and other such dignitaries and their wives. The spruce tree in the parlor was imported from Minnesota and all alight with candles and the three children were dressed for the occasion and went around with cups of eggnog for the assembled guests. I knew how important it was for Mama to establish her reputation as a person of class who had flattered the community by joining it, but all these people made me nervous. I didn't think it was wise having so many rigs parked in the yard and so many feet tromping about the house or going out to the privy. Of course it was a lack of self-confidence on my part, and how often was it Mama had warned me nothing was more dangerous than that, because it was translated into the face and physique as wrongdoing, or at least defenselessness, which amounted to the same thing. But I couldn't help it. I remembered the pocket watch that the little sniveling Joseph had found and held up to me swinging it from its fob. I sometimes made mistakes, I was human, and who knew what other mistakes lay about for someone to find and hold up to me.

But now Mama looked at me over the heads of her guests. The children's tutor had brought her harmonium and we all gathered around the fireplace for some carol singing. Given Mama's look, I sang the loudest. I have a good tenor voice and I sent it aloft to turn heads and make the La Villers smile. I imagined decking the halls with boughs of holly until there was kindling and brush enough to set the whole place ablaze.

JUST AFTER the New Year a man appeared at our door, another Swede, with his Gladstone bag in his hand. We had not run the Wanted ad all winter and Mama was not going to be home to him, but this fellow was the brother of one of them who had responded to it the previous fall. He gave his name, Henry Lundgren, and said his brother Per Lundgren had not been heard from since leaving Wisconsin to look into the prospect here.

Mama invited him in and sat him down and had Fannie bring in some tea. The minute I looked at him, I remembered the brother. Per Lundgren had been all business. He did not blush or go shy in Mama's presence, nor did he ogle. Instead, he asked sound questions. He had also turned the conversation away from his own circumstances, family relations and so on, which Mama put people through in order to learn who was back home and might be waiting. Most of the immigrants, if they had family, it was still in the old country, but you had to make sure. Per Lundgren was close mouthed, but he did admit to being unmarried and so we decided to go ahead.

And here was Henry, the brother he had never mentioned, sitting stiffly in the wing chair with his arms folded and the aggrieved expression on his face. They had the same reddish fair skin, with a long jaw and thinning blond hair, and pale woeful-looking eyes with blond eyelashes. I would say Henry here was the younger by a couple of years, but he turned out to be as smart as Per, or maybe even smarter. He did not seem to be as convinced of the sincerity of Mama's expressions of concern as I would have liked. He said his brother had made the trip to La Ville with other stops planned afterwards to two more business prospects, a farm some twenty miles west of us and another in Indiana. Henry had traveled to these places, which is how he learned that his brother never arrived for his appointments. He said Per had been traveling with something over two thousand dollars in his money belt.

My goodness, that is a lot of money, Mama said.

Our two savings, Henry said. He comes here to see your farm. I have the advertisement, he said pulling a piece of newspaper from his pocket. This is the first place he comes to see.

I'm not sure he ever arrived, Mama said. We've had many inquiries.

He arrived, Henry Lundgren said. He arrived the night before so he will be on time the next morning. This is my brother. It is important to him, even if it costs money. He sleeps at the hotel in La Ville.

How could you know that? Mama said.

I know from the guest book in the La Ville hotel where I find his signature, Henry Lundgren said.

MAMA SAID, All right, Earle, we've got a lot more work to do before we get out of here.

We're leaving?

What is today, Monday. I want to be on the road Thursday the latest. I thought with the inquest matter back there we were okay at least to the spring. This business of a brother pushes things up a bit.

I am ready to leave.

I know you are. You have not enjoyed the farm life, have you? If that Swede had told us he had a brother, he wouldn't be where he is today. Too smart for his own good, he was. Where is Bent?

She went out to the yard. He was standing at the corner of the barn peeing a hole in the snow. She told him to take the carriage and go to La Ville and pick up a half a dozen gallon cans of kerosene at the hardware. They were to be put on our credit.

It occurred to me that we still had a goodly amount of our winter supply of kerosene. I said nothing. Mama had gone into action, and I knew from experience that everything would come clear by and by.

And then late that night, when I was in the basement, she called downstairs to me that Bent was coming down to help.

I don't need help, thank you, Aunt Dora, I said, so astonished that my throat went dry.

At that they both clomped down the stairs and back to the potato bin where I was working. Bent was grinning that toothy grin of his as always, to remind me he had certain privileges.

Show him, Mama said to me. Go ahead, it's all right, she assured me.

So I did, I showed him. I showed him something to hand. I opened the top of the gunnysack and he looked down it.

The fool's grin disappeared, the unshaven face went pale, and he started to breathe through his mouth. He gasped, he couldn't catch his breath, a weak cry came from him, and he looked at me in my rubber apron and his knees buckled and he fainted dead away.

Mama and I stood over him. Now he knows, I said. He will tell them.

Maybe, Mama said, but I don't think so. He's now one of us. We have just made him an accessory.

An accessory?

After the fact. But he'll be more than that by the time I get through with him, she said.

We threw some water on him and lifted him to his feet. Mama took him up to the kitchen and gave him a couple of quick swigs. Bent was thoroughly cowed, and when I came upstairs and told him to follow me, he jumped out of his chair as if shot. I handed him the gunnysack. It was not that heavy for someone like him. He held it in one hand at arm's length as if it would bite. I led him to the old dried up well behind the house, where he dropped it down into the muck. I poured the quicklime in and then we lowered some rocks down and nailed the well cover back on, and Bent the handyman he never said a word but just stood there shivering and waiting for me to tell him what to do next.

Mama had thought of everything. She had paid cash down for the farm but somewhere or other got the La Ville bank to give her a mortgage and so when the house burned, it was the bank's money. She had been withdrawing from the account all winter, and now that we were closing shop, she mentioned me the actual sum of our wealth for the first time. I was very moved to be confided in, like her partner.

But really it was the small touches that showed her genius. For instance, she had noted immediately of the inquiring brother Henry that he was in height not much taller than I am. Just as in Fanny the housekeeper she had hired a woman of a girth similar to her own. Meanwhile, at her instruction, I was letting my dark beard grow out. And at the end, before she had Bent go up and down the stairs pouring the kerosene in every room, she made sure he was good and drunk. He would sleep through the whole thing in the stable, and that's where they found him with his arms wrapped like a lover's arms around an empty can of kerosene.

THE PLAN was for me to stay behind for a few days just to keep an eye on things. We have pulled off something prodigious that will go down in the books, Mama said. But that means all sorts of people will be flocking here and you can never tell when the unexpected arises. Of course everything will be fine, but if there's something more we have to do you will know it.

Yes, Aunt Dora.

Aunt Dora was just for here, Earle.

Yes, Mama.

Of course, even if there was no need to keep an eye out you would still have to wait for Miss Czerwinska.

This is where I didn't understand her thinking. The one bad thing in all of this is that Winifred would read the news in the Chicago papers. There was no safe way I could get in touch with her now that I was dead. That was it, that was the end of it. But Mama had said it wasn't necessary to get in touch with Winifred. This remark made me angry.

You said you liked her, I said.

I do, Mama said.

You called her our friend, I said.

She is.

I know it can't be helped, but I wanted to marry Winifred Czerwinska. What can she do now but dry her tears and maybe light a candle for me and go out and find herself another boyfriend.

Oh, Earle, Earle, Mama said, you know nothing about a woman's heart.

BUT ANYHOW, I followed the plan to stay on a few days and it wasn't that hard with a dark stubble and a different hat and a long coat. There were such crowds nobody would notice anything that wasn't what they'd come to see, that's what a fever was in these souls. Everyone was streaming down the road to see the tragedy. They were in their carriages and they were walking and standing up in drays—people were paying for anything with wheels to get them out there from town—and after the newspapers ran the story, they were coming not just from La Ville and the neighboring farms but from out of state in their automobiles and on the train from Indianapolis and Chicago. And with the crowds came the hawkers to sell sandwiches and hot coffee, and peddlers with balloons and little flags and whirligigs for the children. Someone had taken photographs of the laid out skeletons in their crusts of burlap and printed them up as postcards for mailing, and these were going like hotcakes.

The police had been inspired by the charred remains they found in the basement to look down the well and then to dig up the chicken yard and the floor of the stable. They had brought around a rowboat to dredge the water hole. They were really very thorough. They kept making their discoveries and laying out what they found in neat rows inside the barn. They had called in the county sheriff and his men to help with the crowds and they got some kind of order going, keeping people in lines to pass them by the open barn doors so everyone would have a turn. It was the only choice the police had if they didn't want a riot, but even then the oglers went around back all the way up the road to get into the procession again—it was the two headless remains of Madame Dora and her nephew that drew the most attention, and of course the wrapped bundles of the little ones.

There was such heat from this population that the snow was gone from the ground and on the road and in the yard and behind the house and even into the fields where the trucks and automobiles were parked everything had turned to mud so that it seemed even the season was transformed. I just stood and watched and took it all in, and it was amazing to see so many people with this happy feeling of spring, as if a population of creatures had formed up out of the mud especially for the occasion. That didn't help the smell any, though no one seemed to notice. The house itself made me sad to look at, a smoking ruin that you could see the sky through. I had become fond of that house. A piece of the floor hung down from the third story where I had my room. I disapproved of people pulling off the loose brickwork to take home for a souvenir. There was a lot of laughing and shouting, but of course I did not say anything. In fact I was able to rummage around the ruin without drawing attention to myself, and sure enough I found something—it was the syringe for which I knew Mama would be thankful.

I overheard some conversation about Mama—what a terrible end for such a fine lady who loved children was the gist of it. I thought as time went on, in the history of our life of La Ville, I myself would not be remembered very clearly. Mama would become famous in the papers as a tragic victim mourned for her good works whereas I would only be noted down as a dead nephew. Even if the past caught up with her reputation and she was slandered as the suspect widow of several insured husbands, I would still be in the shadows. This seemed to me an unjust outcome considering the contribution I had made, and I found myself for a moment resentful. Who was I going to be in life now that I was dead and not even Winifred Czerwinska was there to bend over for me.

Back in town at night, I went behind the jail to the cell window where Bent was and I stood on a box and called to him softly, and when his bleary face appeared, I ducked to the side where he couldn't see me and I whispered these words: "Now you've seen it all, Bent. Now you have seen everything."

I STAYED in town to meet every train that came through from Chicago. I could do that without fear—there was such a heavy traffic all around, such swirls of people, all of them too excited and thrilled to take notice of someone standing quietly in a doorway or sitting on the curb in the alley behind the station. And as Mama told me, I knew nothing about the heart of a woman, because all at once there was Winifred Czerwinska stepping down from the coach, her suitcase in her hand. I lost her for a moment through the steam from the locomotive blowing across the platform, but then there she was in her dark coat and a little hat and the most forlorn expression I have ever seen on a human being. I waited till the other people had drifted away before I approached her. Oh my, how grief-stricken she looked standing by herself on the train platform with her suitcase and big tears rolling down her face. Clearly she had no idea what to do next, where to go, who to speak to. So she had not been able to help herself when she heard the terrible news. And what did that mean except that if she was drawn to me in my death she truly loved me in my life. She was so small and ordinary in appearance, how wonderful that I was the only person to know that under her clothes and inside her little rib cage the heart of a great lover was pumping away.

WELL THERE WAS a bad moment or two. I had to help her sit down. I am here, Winifred, it's all right, I told her over and over again and I held my arms around her shaking, sobbing wracked body.

I wanted us to follow Mama to California, you see. I thought, given all the indications, Winifred would accept herself as an accessory after the fact.

DEATH OF THE RIGHT FIELDER

Stuart Dybek

Stuart Dybek is the author of three books of fiction, *Childhood and Other Neighborhoods*, *The Coast of Chicago*, and *I Sailed with Magellan*, as well as two collections of poetry, *Brass Knuckles* and *Streets in Their Own Ink*. His work has appeared in numerous publications, including *The New Yorker*, *Harper's*, *The Paris Review*, and *The Atlantic*.

After too many balls went out and never came back we went out to check. It was a long walk—he always played deep. Finally we saw him, from the distance resembling the towel we sometimes threw down for second base.

It was hard to tell how long he'd been lying there, sprawled on his face. Had he been playing infield, his presence, or lack of it, would, of course, have been noticed immediately. The infield demands communication—the constant, reassuring chatter of team play. But he was remote, clearly an outfielder (the temptation is to say out-*sider*). The infield is for wisecrackers, pepper-pots, gum-poppers; the outfield is for loners, onlookers, brooders who would rather study clover and swat gnats than holler. People could pretty much be divided between infielders and outfielders. Not that one always has a choice. He didn't necessarily choose right field so much as accept it.

There were several theories as to what killed him. From the start the most popular was that he'd been shot. Perhaps from a passing car, possibly by that gang calling themselves the Jokers, who played sixteen-inch softball on the concrete diamond with painted bases in the center of the housing project, or by the Latin Lords, who didn't play sports, period. Or maybe some pervert with a telescopic sight from a bedroom window, or a mad sniper from a water tower, or a terrorist with a silencer from the expressway overpass, or maybe it was an accident, a stray slug from a robbery, or shoot-out, or assassination attempt miles away.

No matter who pulled the trigger it seemed more plausible to ascribe his death to a bullet than to natural causes like, say, a heart attack. Young deaths are never natural; they're all violent. Not that kids don't die of heart attacks. But he never seemed the type. Sure, he was quiet, but not the quiet of someone always listening for the heart murmur his family repeatedly warned him about since he was old enough to play. Nor could it have been leukemia. He wasn't a talented enough athlete to die of that. He'd have been playing center, not right, if leukemia was going to get him.

The shooting theory was better, even though there wasn't a mark on him. Couldn't it have been, as some argued, a high-powered bullet traveling with such velocity that its hole fuses behind it? Still, not everyone was satisfied. Other theories were formulated, rumors became legends over the years: he'd had an allergic reaction to a bee sting, been struck by a single bolt of lightning from a freak, instantaneous electrical storm, ingested too strong a dose of insecticide from the grass blades he chewed on, sonic waves, radiation, pollution, etc. And a few of us liked to think it was simply that chasing a sinking liner, diving to make a shoestring catch, he broke his neck.

There *was* a ball in the webbing of his mitt when we turned him over. His mitt had been pinned under his body and was coated with an almost luminescent gray film. There was the same gray on his black, high-top gym shoes, as if he'd been running through lime, and along the bill of his baseball cap—the blue felt one with the red C which he always denied stood for the Chicago Cubs. He may have been a loner, but he didn't want to be identified with a loser. He lacked the sense of humor for that, lacked the perverse pride that sticking for losers season after season breeds, and the love. He was just an ordinary guy, .250 at the plate, and we stood above him not knowing what to do next. By then the guys from the other outfield positions had trotted over. Someone, the short-stop probably, suggested team prayer. But no one could think of a team prayer. So we all just stood there silently bowing our heads, pretending to pray while the shadows moved darkly across the outfield grass. After a while the entire diamond was swallowed and the field lights came on.

In the bluish squint of those lights he didn't look like someone we'd once known—nothing looked quite right—and we hurriedly scratched a shallow grave, covered him over, and stamped it down as much as possible so that the next right fielder, whoever he'd be, wouldn't trip. It could be just such a juvenile, seemingly trivial stumble that would ruin a great career before it had begun, or ham-per it years later the way Mantle's was hampered by bum knees. One can never be sure the kid beside him isn't another Roberto Clemente; and who can ever know how many potential Great Ones have gone down in the obscurity of their neighborhoods? And so, in the catcher's phrase, we "buried the grave" rather than contrib-ute to any further tragedy. In all likelihood the next right fielder, whoever he'd be, would be clumsy too, and if there was a mound to trip over he'd find it and break *his* neck, and soon right field would get the reputation as haunted, a kind of sandlot Bermuda Triangle, inhabited by phantoms calling for ghostly fly balls, where no one but the most desperate outcasts, already on the verge of suicide, would be willing to play.

Still, despite our efforts, we couldn't totally disguise it. A fresh grave is stubborn. Its outline remained visible—a scuffed bald spot that might have been confused for an aberrant pitcher's mound ex-cept for the bat jammed in the earth with the mitt and blue cap fit over it. Perhaps we didn't want to eradicate it completely—a part of us was resting there. Perhaps we wanted the new right fielder, whoever he'd be, to notice and wonder about who played there before him, realizing he was now the only link between past and future that mattered. A monument, epitaph, flowers, wouldn't be necessary.

As for us, we walked back, but by then it was too late—getting on to supper, getting on to the end of summer vacation, time for other things, college, careers, settling down and raising a family. Past thirty-five the talk starts about being over the hill, about a graying Phil Niekro in his forties still fanning them with the knuckler as if it's some kind of miracle, about Pete Rose still going in headfirst at forty, beating the odds. And maybe the talk is right. One remembers Willie Mays, forty-two years old and a Met, dropping that can-of-corn fly in the '73 Series, all that grace stripped away and with it the conviction, leaving a man confused and apologetic about the boy in him. It's sad to admit it ends so soon, but everyone knows those are the lucky ones. Most guys are washed up by seventeen.

THE GIRL WHO LEFT HER SOCK ON THE FLOOR

Deborah Eisenberg

Deborah Eisenberg is the author of the short story collections *Transactions in a Foreign Currency*, *Under the 82nd Airborne*, *All Around Atlantis*, *The Stories (So Far) of Deborah Eisenberg*, and *The Twilight of the Superheroes*. Eisenberg is also the author of a play, *Pastorale*, which was produced by Second Stage in New York in 1982, and has written for *The New Yorker*, *Bomb*, and *The Yale Review*. She is the recipient of a Whiting Writers' Award, a Guggenheim Fellowship, the Rea Award for the Short Story, and three O. Henry Awards.

Jessica dangled a sock between her thumb and forefinger, studied it, and let it drop. "There are times," she said, "one wearies of rooming with a pig."

Pig. Francie checked to see what page she was on and slammed *World History* shut. "Why not go over to the nice, clean library?" she said. "You could go to the nice, clean library, and you could think nice, clean thoughts. I'll just root around here in the homework." She pulled her blanket up and turned to the window, her eyes stinging.

Faint, constant crumblings and tricklings . . . Outside, spring was sneaking up under the cradle of snow in the valley, behind the lacy gray air that veiled everything except the girl, identifiable as hardly more than the red dot of her jacket, who was winding up the hill toward the dorm.

Jessica sighed noisily and dumped a stack of clothing into a drawer. "I will get to that stuff, please, Jessica," Francie said, "if you'll just kindly leave it."

Jessica gazed sorrowfully at Francie's ear, then bent down to retrieve a dust-festooned sweatshirt from beneath Francie's bed.

"You know," Francie said, "there are people in the world— not many, but a few—to whom the most important thing is not whether there happens to be a sock on the floor. There are people in the world who are not afraid to face reality, to face the fact that the floor is the natural place for a sock, that the floor is where a sock just naturally goes when it's off. But do we fearless few have a voice? No. No, these are words which must never be spoken—true, Jessica? This is a thought which must never be thought."

It was Cynthia in the red jacket, the secretary, Francie saw now—not one of the students. Cynthia wasn't much older than the seniors, but she lived in town and never came to meals. "Right, Jessica?" Francie said.

There was some little oddness about seeing Cynthia outside the office—as if something were leaking somewhere.

"Jessica?" Francie said. "Oh, well. *'But the poor, saintly girl had gone deaf as a post. The end.'*"

Jessica's voice sliced between Francie and the window. "Look, Francie, I don't want to trivialize your pain or anything, but I'm getting kind of bored over here. Besides which, I am not your personal maid."

"Oink oink," Francie said. "Grunt, grunt. *'Actually, not the end, really, at all, because God performed a miracle, and the beautiful deaf girl could hear again, though everything from that moment on sounded to her as the gruntings of pigs.'*"

"*As* the gruntings of pigs?" Jessica demanded. "Sounded *as* gruntings?"

"Oink oink," Francie said. She opened *World History* to page 359 again. "An Artist's Conception of the Storming of the Bastille." Well, and who were "Editors Clarke & Melton," for that matter, to be in charge of what was going on? To decide which, out of all the things that went on, were *things that had happened*? Yeah, "World History: The Journey of Two Editors and Their Jobs." Why not a picture of people trapped in their snooty boarding school with their snooty roommates? "Anyhow, guess what, next year we both get to pick new roommates."

"If we're both still here," Jessica said. "Besides, that's then—"

"What does *that* mean?" Francie said.

"You don't have to shout at me all the time," Jessica said. "Besides, as I was saying, that's then and this is now. And if I were you, I'd stop calling Mr. Klemper 'Sex Machine.' Sooner or later someone's going to—"

But just then the door opened, and the girl, Cynthia, was standing there in her red jacket. "Frances McIntyre?" Cynthia said. She stared at Francie and Jessica as though she had forgotten which one Francie was. And Francie and Jessica stared back as though they had forgotten, too. "Frances McIntyre, Mrs. Peck wants to see you in the Administration Building."

Jessica watched, flushed and round-eyed, as Francie put on her motorcycle jacket and work boots. "You're going to freeze like that, Francie," Jessica said, and then Cynthia held the door open.

"Francie—" Jessica said. "Francie, do you want me to go with you?"

Francie had paused on the threshold. She didn't turn around, and she couldn't speak. She shook her head.

What had she done? What had been seen or heard or said? Had someone already told Mr. Klemper? Was it cutting lacrosse? Had she been reported smoking again in back of the Science Building? Because if she had she was out. Out. Out. End. The end of her fancy scholarship, the end of her education, the end of her freedom, the end of her future. No, the beginning of a new future, her real future, the one that had been lying in wait for her all along, whose snuffly breathing she could hear in the dark. She'd live out her days as a checkout girl, choking on the toxic vapors of household cleaners and rotting baked goods, trudging home in the cold to rot, herself, in the scornful silence of her bulky, furious mother. Her mother, who had slaved to give ungrateful Francie this squandered opportunity. Her mother, who wouldn't tolerate a sock on the floor for as long as one instant.

Mrs. Peck's bleached blue eyes stared at Francie as Francie stood in front of her, shivering, each second becoming more vividly aware that her jacket, her little, filmy dress, her boots, her new nose ring all trod on the boundaries of the dress code. "Do sit down, please, Frances," Mrs. Peck said.

Mrs. Peck was wearing, of course, a well-made and proudly unflattering suit. On the walls around her were decorative, framed what-were-they-called, Francie thought—Wise Sayings. "I have something very, very sad, I'm afraid, to tell you, Frances." Mrs. Peck began.

Out, she was *out*. Francie's blood howled like a storm at sea; her heart pitched and tossed.

But Mrs. Peck's voice—what Mrs. Peck's voice seemed to be saying, was that Francie's mother was dead.

"What?" Francie said. The howling stopped abruptly, as though a door had been shut. "My mother's in the hospital. My mother broke her hip."

Mrs. Peck bowed her head slightly, over her folded hands. "EVERYTHING MUST BE TAKEN SERIOUSLY, NOTHING TRAGICALLY," the wall announced over her shoulder. "FORTUNE AND HUMOR GOVERN THE WORLD."

"My mother has a broken hip," Francie insisted. "Nobody dies from a broken fucking *hip*."

Mrs. Peck's eyes closed for a moment. "There was an embolism," she said. "Apparently, this is not unheard of. Patients who greatly exceed an ideal weight . . . That is, a Miss Healy called from the hospital. Do you remember Miss Healy? A student nurse, I believe. I understand you met each other when you went to visit your mother several weeks ago. Your mother must have tried to get up sometime during the night. And most probably—" Mrs. Peck frowned at a piece of paper and put on her glasses. "Yes. Most probably, according to Miss Healy, your mother wished to go to the toilet. Evidently, she would have fallen back against her pillow. The staff wouldn't have discovered her death until morning."

Bits of things were falling around Francie. "'Wouldn't have'?" she plucked from the air.

"This is, of course, a reconstruction," Mrs. Peck said. "Miss Healy came on duty this afternoon. Your mother wasn't there, and Miss Healy became concerned that perhaps no one had thought to notify you. A thoughtful young woman. I had the impression she was acting outside official channels, but . . ."

"But *all's well that ends well*," Francie said.

Mrs. Peck's eyes rested distantly on Francie. "I wonder," she said. "It might be possible, under the terms of your scholarship, to arrange for some therapy when you return." Her gaze wandered up the chattering wall. "A hospital must be a terribly difficult thing to administer," she remarked to it graciously. "I have absolutely no one to bring you to Albany, Frances, I'm afraid. I'll have to call someone in your family to come for you."

Francie gasped. "You can't!" she said.

Mrs. Peck frowned. She appeared to be embarrassed. "Ah," she said, no doubt picturing, Francie thought, some abyss of mortifying circumstances. "In that case . . ." she said. "Yes. I'll have Mr. Klemper cancel French tomorrow, and he—"

"Why can't I take the morning bus?" Francie said. "I've taken that bus a thousand times." She was going red, she knew; one more second and she'd cry. "Don't cancel French," she said. "I always take that bus. *Please*."

Mrs. Peck's glance strayed up the wall again, and hesitated, "HONI SOIT QUI MAL Y PENSE," Francie read.

Mrs. Peck took off her glasses and rubbed the bridge of her nose. "Miss Healy," she mused. "Such an unsuitable name for a nurse, isn't it. People must often make foolish remarks."

———————

HOW COULD it be true? How could Francie be on the bus now, when she should be at school? The sky hadn't changed since yesterday, the trees and fields out the window hadn't changed; Francie could imagine her mother just as clearly as she'd ever been able to, so how could it be true?

And yet her mother would have been dead while she herself had been asleep, dreaming. Of what? Of what? Of Mr. Davis, probably. Not of her mother, not dreaming of a little wad of blood coalescing like a pearl in her mother's body, preparing to wedge itself into her mother's heart.

If you were to break, for example, your hip, there would be the pain, the proof, telling you all the time it was true: *that's then and this is now.* But this thing—each second it had to be true all over again; she was getting hurled against each second. *Now.* And *now again—thwack!* Maybe one of these seconds she'd smash right through and find herself in the clear place where her mother was alive, scowling, criticizing . . .

Out the window, snow was draining away from the patched fields of the small farms, the small, failing farms. Rusted machinery glowed against the sky in fragile tangles. Her mother would have been dead while Francie got up and took her shower and worried about being late to breakfast and was late to breakfast and went to biology and then to German and then dozed through English and then ate lunch and then hid in the dorm instead of playing lacrosse and then quarreled with Jessica about a sock. At some moment in the night her mother had gone from being completely alive to being completely dead.

The passengers were scraggy and exhausted-looking, like a committee assigned to the bus aeons earlier to puzzle out just this sort of thing—part of a rotating team whose members were picked up and dropped off at stations looping the planet. How different they were from the team of sleek girls at school, who already knew everything they needed to know. Which team was Francie on?

Ha-ha. She glanced at the man across the aisle, who nodded com-miseratingly between bites of the vile-smelling food he lifted from a plastic-foam container on his lap.

All those hours during which her life (along with her mother) had gone from being one thing to being another, it had held its shape, like a car window Francie once saw hit by a rock. The rock hit, a web of tiny, glittering lines fanned out, and only a minute or so later had the window tinkled to the street in splinters.

The dazzling, razor-edged splinters had tinkled around Fran-cie yesterday afternoon in Mrs. Peck's voice. "Your family." "Have someone in your family come for you." Well, fine, but where on earth had Mrs. Peck got the idea there *was* anyone in Francie's family?

From Francie's mother, doubtless, the world's leading expert in giving people ideas without having to say a single word. "A proud woman" was an observation people tended to make, vague and flustered after encountering her. But what did that mean, "proud"? Proud of her poverty. Proud of her poor education. Proud of her unfashionable size. Proud of bringing up her Difficult Daughter, Without an Iota of Help. So what was the difference, when you got right down to it, between pride and shame?

Francie had a memory, one of her few from early childhood, that never altered or dimmed, however often it sprang out: her-self in the building stairwell with Mrs. Dougherty, making Mrs. Dougherty laugh. She could still feel her feet fly up as her mother grabbed her and pulled her inside, still hear the door slam. She could still see (and yet this was something she could never have seen, really) skinny Mrs. Dougherty cackling alone in the hall. "*How could you embarrass me like that?*" her mother said. The wave of shock and outrage and humiliation engulfed Francie again with each remembering; she felt her mother's fierce grip on her arm. Francie was an embarrassment. What on earth could she have been doing in the hall? An *embarrassment*. Well, *so be it.*

On the day she had brought Francie all the way from Albany to be interviewed at school, Francie's mother—wearing gloves!—had a private conversation with Mrs. Peck. Francie sat in the outer office and waited. Cynthia had been typing demurely, and occasionally other girls would come through—perfect girls, beautiful and beautifully behaved and sly. Francie could just picture their mothers. When she eventually did see some—Jessica's tall, chestnut-haired mother among them—it turned out that her imagination had not exaggerated.

Waiting in the outer office, Francie feared (Francie hoped) she was to be turned ignominiously away. Instead, she was confronted by Mrs. Peck's withering smile of welcome; Mrs. Peck was gluttonous for Francie's test scores. That Francie and her mother looked, each in her own way, so entirely *unsuitable* appeared to increase, rather than diminish, their desirability.

When her mother and Mrs. Peck emerged from the office together that afternoon, a blaze of triumph and contempt crackled behind the veneer of patently suspect humility on her mother's face. Mrs. Peck, on the other hand, looked as if she'd been bonked on the head with a plank.

Surely it was during that conference that Francie's family had been born. Her mother's gift (the automatic nuancing of the unspoken) and Mrs. Peck's mandate (to heap distinction upon herself) had intertwined to generate little tendrils of plausible realities. Which were now generating tendrils of their own: an imaginary church with imaginary relatives—*suitable* relatives—wavering behind viscous organ music and bearing with simple dignity their imaginary grief. Oh, her poor mother! Her poor mother! What possible business was it of Mrs. Peck's *when* her mother had wanted to go to the toilet for the last time?

Several companionable tears made their way down Francie's face, turning from hot to cold. The sensation consoled her as long as it lasted. When she opened her eyes, she saw the frayed outskirts of town.

FRANCIE CLIMBED the stairs cautiously, lest creakings draw the still gregarious Mrs. Dougherty to her peephole. She paused with her key in the lock before contaminating irreversibly the silence, her mother's special silence, which, she thought, a person had to shout to be heard over. Francie leaned her head against the door's cool plane, listening, then turned the key. The lock's tumbling sounded like a gunshot.

A little colorless sunlight had forced its way around the neighboring buildings and lay, exhausted, across the floor. A fine coating of city grime sealed the sills in front of the closed windows like insulation. Her mother's bed was tightly made; the bedspread was as mute as the surface of a lake into which a clue had been dropped long before.

The only disorder in the kitchen was a cup Francie had left in the sink when she'd come to see her mother in the hospital three weeks earlier, still full of dark liquid in which velvety spots had begun to blossom. Francie sat down at the table. The night she'd finally dared to ask her mother what had happened to her father they'd been in here, just finishing the dishes. Francie remembered: her mother was holding a white dish towel; she started to speak.

Too late, then, for Francie to retract the question—a question that had been clogging her mouth ever since the day, years before, when Corkie Patterson had pummeled into her the concept that every single person on earth had a father. As Francie clutched the wet counter her mother spoke of the sound—the terrible fused sound of brakes and the impact—the crowds out the window, which at first hid everything, the siren circling down on their block like a hawk. She did not use the word "blood," but when she finished her story and left the room without so much as a glance for Francie, Francie lifted her dripping fingers and stared at them.

After that, Francie's mother was even more unyielding, as though she were ashamed of her husband's death, or ashamed to have spoken of it. And Francie's father evaporated without a trace.

Francie had only cryptic fragments from before that night in the kitchen with which to assemble the story: her parents married at eighteen, she'd figured out. Had they loved each other? The undiminishing vigor of her mother's resentment toward absolutely everything was warming, in its way—there must have been love to produce all that hatred.

The bathroom, too, was clean—spotless, actually, except for a tiny smudge on the mirror. A fingerprint. Hers? Her mother's? She peered past it, into her own face. Had he even known there was to be a baby? Just think—things that you did went on and on, turning into situations, for example. Into people . . .

As little as Francie knew about him, it would be infinitely more than he could have known about her. There were no pictures, but if she were to subtract her mother's eyes . . . In just a few years, she would see changes in her face that her father had not lived to see in his.

"In a few years!" Bad enough she had to deal with "in a few minutes." *When you return*, Mrs. Peck had said. Well, sure, a person couldn't just stay at school, probably, when her mother died. But what on earth was she supposed to do here?

Her mother would have told her. Francie snatched open a drawer and out flew the fact of her mother's slippery, pinkish heap of underwear. Her mother's toothbrush sat next to the mirror in a glass. In the mirror, past the fingerprint, her mother's eyes lay across her own reflection like a mask.

THE HOSPITAL floated in the middle of a vast ocean of construction, or maybe it was demolition; a nation in itself, of which all humans were, at every moment, potential citizens. The inevitable false move, and it was wham, onto the gurney, with workers grabbing smocks and gloves to plunge into the cavity of you, and the lights that burned all night. Outside this building you lived as though nothing were happening to you that you didn't know about. But here, there was simply no pretending.

Cynthia had come up the hill, Mrs. Peck had sent Francie home, and now here she was—completely lost; she'd come in the wrong entrance. People passed, in small groups, not touching or speaking. The proliferating corridors and rotundas bloomed with soft noises—chiming, and disembodied announcements, and the muted tapping of canes and rubber shoes and walkers. The ceilings and floors were the same color and had the same brightness; metal winked, signaling between wheelchairs and bedrails. Francie tried to suppress the notion, which had popped up from somewhere like a groundhog, that her mother was still alive, lost here somewhere herself.

Two unfamiliar nurses sat at a desk at the mouth of the wing where Section E, Room 418, was. In their crisp little white hats they appeared to be exempt from error. They looked up as Francie approached, and their faces were blank and tired, as if they knew Francie through and through—as if they knew everything there was to know about this girl in the short, filmy dress and motorcycle jacket and electric-green socks, who was coming toward them with so much difficulty, as if the air were filled with invisible restraints.

But, as it turned out, when Francie tried to explain herself, using (presumably) key, she thought, words, like "Kathryn McIntyre," and "Room 418," and "dead," even then neither of the nurses seemed to understand. "Did you want to speak to a doctor?" one of them said.

A tiny, hot beading of sweat sprang out all over Francie. From the moment she was born people had been happy to tell her what to do, down to the most minute detail; Eds. Clarke & Melton knew just what was happening; there were admonitions and exhortations plastered all over the walls—this is how to behave, this is what to think, this is how to think it, that's then, this is now, this is where to put your sock—but no one had ever said one little thing that would get her through any five given minutes of her life!

She stared at the nurse who had spoken: *Say it*, Francie willed her, but the nurse instead turned her attention to a form attached to a clipboard. "Is Miss Healy around?" Francie asked after a minute.

The fact was, Francie would not have recognized Miss Healy; she'd hardly noticed the broad-faced, slightly clumsy-looking girl who'd been changing the water in a vase of flowers as Francie had listened to her mother describe, with somber gloating, the damage to her body, the shock of finding herself on the ice with her pork chop and canned peaches and so forth strewn around her, the pitiable little trickle of milk she had watched flow from the ruined carton into the filthy slush before she understood that she couldn't move.

"She never complained," Miss Healy was saying, in a melancholy, slightly adenoidal voice. "She was such a pleasant person. You could tell the terrible pain she was in, but she never said a word." Miss Healy directed her mournful recital toward Francie's elbow, as if she were in danger of being derailed by Francie's face. "And when the people from her office brought candy and flowers? She was just so *polite*. Even though you could see those things were not what she wanted."

Oh, great. Who but her mother could get someone to say that her pain was obvious but that she never complained? Who but her mother could get someone to say she was polite even though everyone could tell she didn't want their gifts? No doubt about it, the body they'd carted off almost a day and a half ago from Room 418 had been her mother's—Miss Healy had just laid waste, in her squelchy voice, to *that* last wisp of hope.

"The thing is," Francie said, "what am I supposed to do?"

"To do?" Miss Healy said. Her look of suffering was momentarily whisked away. "I mean, unfortunately, your mother's dead."

"No, I know," Francie said. "I get that part. I just don't know what to *do*."

Miss Healy looked at her. Clearly Francie was turning out to be, unlike her mother, *not a pleasant person*. "Well, you'll want to grieve, of course," Miss Healy said, as if she were remembering a point from a legal document. "Everyone needs closure." She frowned, then unexpectedly addressed, after all, Francie's problem. "I'll call downstairs so you can see her."

Fading smells of bodies clung to the air like plaintive ghosts, their last friendly overtures vanquished by the stronger smells of disinfectants. An indecipherable muttering came from other ghosts, sequestered in a TV suspended from the ceiling. Outside the window huge, predatory machines prowled among mounds of trash.

Miss Healy returned. "Mrs. McIntyre isn't downstairs. I'm really sorry—I guess they've sent her on."

They? On? If only there were someone around to take over. Anyone. Jessica, even. At least Jessica would be able to ask some sensible question. "On . . ." Francie began uncertainly, and Jessica gave her a little shove. "On where?"

"Oh," Miss Healy said. "Well, I mean, does your family use any in particular?"

Francie stared: Where would Jessica even begin with that one?

"Does your family have a particular one they like," Miss Healy explained. "Mortuary."

"It's just me and mother," Francie said.

Miss Healy nodded, as if this confirmed her point. "Uh-huh. So they'd have sent her on to whatever place was specified by the next of kin."

Francie felt Jessica start to giggle. "It's just me and mother," Francie said again.

"Just whoever your mother put down on the AN37-53," Miss Healy said. "Not literally the next of kin necessarily—she couldn't have used you, for instance, because you're a minor. But just, if there's no spouse, people might put down someone at their office, say. Or she might have used that nice friend of hers who came to visit once, Mrs. Dougherty."

Yargh. It wasn't enough that her mother had died—no, they had to toss her out, into that huge, melted mob, *the dead*, who couldn't speak for themselves, who were too indistinguishable to be remembered, who could be used to prove anything, who could be represented any way at all! "My mother *hates* everyone at her office," Francie said. "My mother *hates* Mrs. Dougherty. Mother calls Mrs. Dougherty that buggy Irish slut."

Miss Healy drew back. "Well, I guess your mom wasn't expecting to *die*, exactly, when she filled out that form," she said, and then recovered herself. "There, now. I'll call down again. Even *this* crazy morgue has files, I guess."

Out the window a wrecking ball swung toward a solitary wall. Miss Healy hesitated. She seemed to be waiting for something. "I called that lady at the school," she said. She stood looking at Francie, and Francie realized that she and Miss Healy must be almost the same age. "I just didn't figure there'd be some other way you'd know."

"HOW DID mother get all the way out here?" Francie asked the man who greeted her.

The man's little smile intensified the ruefulness of his expression. "We get a lot of folks out this way," he said. "You might be surprised."

"That's what I meant," Francie said. "I meant I was surprised."

The man jumped slightly, as if Francie had gummed him on the ankle, and then smiled ruefully again. "Serving all faiths," he explained, gesturing at a sign on the wall. *"Serving all faiths,"* Francie read. *"Owned and operated by Luther and Theodore T. Ade. When you're in need, call for Ade."* "Also," the man added, "competitive pricing. But mainly, first in the phone book."

He disappeared behind a door, and Francie jogged from foot to foot to warm herself—it had been a long walk from the last stop on the bus line. She looked around. Not much to see: a counter holding some file folders, a calendar and a mirror on the wall, several chairs, and a round table on which lay a dog-eared copy of *Consumer Reports*. So this was where her mother had got to—nowhere at all.

"Won't be another minute." The man was back in the room. "Teddy T.'s just doing the finishing touches."

Finishing touches? Francie blanched—she'd almost forgotten what this place was. "You're not using lipstick, are you?" she managed to say. "Mother hated it."

The man glanced rapidly at the mirror and then back at Francie.

"Lipstick," Francie said. "On her."

"'On her . . .'" the man said. As he stared at Francie, the room lost its color and flattened; swarming black dots began to absorb the table and the counter and the mirror. "I'm very sorry if that's what you had in mind, Miss, ah . . ." dots streamed out of the dot man to say. The riffling of file folders amplified into a deafening splash of dots, and then Francie heard, "I'm very, very sorry, because those were definitely not the instructions. I've got the fax right here—from your dad, right? Yup, Mr. McIntyre."

Francie's vision and hearing cleared before her muscles got a grip on themselves. She was on the floor, splayed out, confusingly, as her mother must have been on the ice, and the man was kneeling next to her, holding a glass of water, although, also confusingly, her hair and clothing were drenched—sweat, she noted, amazed.

"O.K. now?" the man asked. Next to him was a cardboard box, about two feet square, tied up with twine.

Francie nodded.

"Happens," the man said, sympathetically.

Francie finished the water slowly and carefully while the man fetched a little wooden handle and affixed it to the twine around the box. Things had gone far beyond misrepresentation now.

"And here's the irony," the man said. "We deliver."

ALL NIGHT long, Francie fell, plummeting through the air. When she finally managed to pry herself awake with the help of the pale wands of light along the blinds, she found herself sprawled forcefully back on her mattress, aching, as if she'd been hurled from a great height. On the kitchen floor was the cardboard box. Francie hefted it experimentally—yesterday it had been intolerably heavy; this morning it was intolerably light.

O.K., first in the phone book, true enough. ("See display ad, page 182.") "Hi," Francie said when the man answered. "This is Francie McIntyre. The girl who fainted yesterday? Could you—" For an instant, Miss Healy stood in front of her again, looking helpless. "First of all," Francie said. "I mean, thanks for the water. But second of all, could you give me my father's address, please? And, I guess, his name."

Kevin McIntyre—not all that amazing, once you got your head around the notion that he happened to be alive. And he lived on a street called West Tenth, in New York City. Francie looked out the window to the place where there had been for some years now a silently shrieking crowd and a puddle of blood, into which long, splotty raindrops were now falling. Strange—it was raining into the puddle, but at the level of the window it was snowing.

In the closet she found an old plastic slicker. She took it from the hanger and wrapped it around the cardboard box, securing it roughly with tape. Yes, everything had to be *just right*. But the only thing she'd actually *said* to Francie in all these sixteen years was a lie.

Francie looked around at the bluish stillness. "Hello hello," she called. Was that her voice? Was that her mother's silence, fading? What had become of everything that had gone on here? "Hello hello," she said. "Hello hello hello hello . . ."

THE BUS ticket cost Francie eighteen dollars. Which left not all that much of the seventy-three and a bit that she'd saved up, fortunately, to get her back to school and, in fact, Francie thought, to last for the rest of her life. "But, hey," Jessica returned just long enough to point out, "you'll be getting free therapy."

Francie put her box on the overhead rack and scrambled to a window seat. *West Tenth Street.* West of what? The tenth of how many? How on earth was she going to find her way around? If only her mother had let her go last year when Jessica invited her to spend Thanksgiving in New York with her family. But Francie's mother had been able to picture Jessica's mother just as easily as Francie had been able to. "Out of the question," she'd said.

". . . if *there's no spouse* . . ." So, her mother must have used his name on that form! They must never have got a divorce. Could he be a bigamist? Some people were. And he might think Francie was coming to blackmail him. He might decide to kill her right then and there—just reach over and grab a . . . a . . .

Well, one thing—he wasn't living on the street; she had his address. And he wasn't totally feebleminded; he'd sent a fax. Whatever he was, at least what he wasn't was everything except that. And the main thing he wasn't, for absolute certain, was a guy who'd been mashed by a bus.

"Would you like a hankie?" the lady in the seat next to Francie's asked, and Francie realized that she had wiped her eyes and nose on her sleeve. "I have one right here."

"Oh, wow," Francie said gratefully, and blew her nose on the handkerchief the lady produced from a large, shabby cloth sack on her lap.

Despite the shabbiness of the sack, Francie noticed, the lady was tidy. And pretty. Not pretty, really, but exact—with exact little hands and an exact little face. "Do you live in New York?" she asked Francie.

"I've never even been there," Francie said. "My roommate from school invited me to visit once, but my mother wouldn't let me go." Jessica's family had a whole apartment building to themselves, Jessica had told her; she'd called it a "brownstone." It was when Francie had foolishly reported this interesting fact that her mother put her foot down. "Actually," Francie added, "I think my mother was afraid. We had a giant fight about it."

"A mother worries, of course," the lady said. "But it's a lovely city. People tend to have exaggerated fears about New York."

"Yeah," Francie said. "Well, I guess maybe my mother had exaggerated fears about a lot of things. She—" The box! Where was the box? Oh, there—on the rack. Francie's heart was beating rapidly; clashing in her brain were the desire to reveal and the desire to conceal what had become, in the short course of the conversation, a secret. "Do you live in New York?" she asked.

"Technically, no," the lady said. "But I've spent a great deal of happy time there. I know the city very well."

Francie's jumping heart flipped over. "Have you ever been to West Tenth Street?" she asked.

"I have," the lady said.

Francie didn't dare look at the lady. "Is it a nice street?" she asked carefully.

"Very nice," the lady said. "All the streets are very nice. But it seems a strange day to be going there."

"It's strange for me," Francie said loudly. "My mother died."

"I'm terribly sorry," the lady said. "My mother died as well. But evidently no one was hurt in the accident."

"Huh?" Francie said.

"Amazing as it seems," the lady said, "I believe no one was hurt. Although you'd think, wouldn't you, that an accident of that sort— a blimp, simply sailing into a building . . ."

Francie felt slightly sickened—she wasn't going to have another opportunity to tell someone for the first time that her mother had died, to learn what that meant by hearing the words as she said them for the first time. "How could a blimp just go crashing into a building?" she said crossly.

"These are things we can't understand," the lady said with dignity.

Oops, Francie thought—she was really going to have to watch it; she kept being mean to people, and just completely by mistake.

"'How could such-and-such a thing happen?' we say," the lady said. "As if this moment or that moment were fitted together, from . . . bits, and one bit or another bit might be some type of mistake. 'There's the building,' people say. 'It's a building. There's the blimp. It's a blimp.' That's the way people think."

Francie peered at the lady. "Wow . . ." she said, considering.

"You see, people tend to settle for the first explanation. People tend to take things at face value."

"Oh, definitely," Francie said. "I mean, absolutely."

"But a blimp or a building cannot be a mistake," the lady said. "Obviously. A blimp or a building are evidence. Oh, goodness—" she said as the bus slowed down. She stood up and gave her sack a little shake. "Here I am."

"Evidence . . ." Francie frowned; Cynthia's red jacket flashed against the snow. "Evidence, of, like . . . the future?"

"Well, more or less," the lady said, a bit impatiently, as the bus stopped in front of a small building. "Evidence of the present, really, I suppose. You know what I mean." She reached into her sack and drew out some papers. "You seem like a very sensitive person— I wonder if you'd be interested in learning about my situation. This is my stop, but you're welcome to the document. It's extra."

"Thank you," Francie said, although the situation she'd really like to learn about, she thought, was her own. "Wait—" The lady was halfway down the aisle. "I've still got your handkerchief—"

"Just hold on to it, dear," the lady called back. "I think it's got your name on it."

The manuscript had a title, *The Triumph of Untruth: A Society That Denies the Workings of the World Puts Us at Ever Greater Risk*. "I'd like to introduce myself," it began. "My name is Iris Ackerman."

Hmm, Francie thought: Two people with situations, sitting right next to each other. Coincidence? She glanced up. The sickening thing was, there were a lot of people on this bus.

"My name is Iris Ackerman," Francie read again. "And my belief is that one must try to keep an open mind in the face of puzzling experiences, no matter how laughable this approach may subsequently appear. For many years I maintained the attitude that I was merely a victim of circumstance, or chance, and perhaps now my reluctance to accept the ugliness of certain realities will be considered (with hindsight!) willful obtuseness."

Francie's attention sharpened—she read on. "Certainly my persecution (by literally thousands of men, on the street, in public buildings, and even, before I was forced to flee it, in my own apartment) is a known fact. (One, or several, of these ruffians went so far as to hide himself in my closet, and even under my bed, when least expected.)

"Why, you ask, should so large and powerful an organization concentrate its efforts on tormenting a single individual? This I do not know. It is not (please believe me) false humility that causes me to say I do not consider myself to be in any way 'special.'"

Francie sighed. She rested her eyes for a moment on the weedy lot moving by out the window. Not much point, probably, trying to figure out what Iris had been talking about. Yup, she should have known the minute Iris said the word "blimp."

"I know only," the manuscript continued, "that there was a moment when I fell into the channel, so to speak, of what was ultimately to be revealed as 'my life': In the fall of 1965, when I was twenty years old, I encountered a mathematics professor, an older man, whom I respected deeply. I became increasingly fascinated by certain theories he held regarding the nature of numbers, but he, alas, misunderstood my youthful enthusiasm, and although he had a wife and several children, I was soon forced to rebuff him.

"I continued to feel nothing but the purest and most intense admiration for him, and would gladly have continued our acquaintance. Nevertheless, this professor (Doctor N.) terminated all contact with me (or affected to do so), going so far as to change his telephone number to an unlisted one. Yet, at the same time, he began to pursue me in secret.

"For a period of many months I could detect only the suggestion of his presence—a sort of emanation. Do you know the sensation of a whisper? Or there would sometimes be a telltale hardening, a *crunchiness*, near me. Often, however, I could detect nothing other than a slight discoloration of the atmosphere . . . And then, one day, as I was walking to the library, he was there.

"It was a day of violent heat. People were milling on the sidewalks, waiting. One felt one was penetrating again and again a poisonous, yellow-gray screen that clung to the mouth and the nostrils. I had almost reached the library when I understood that he was behind me. So close, in fact, that he could fit his body to mine. I had never imagined how hard a man's arms could feel! His legs, too, which were pressed up against mine, were like iron, or lead, and he dug his chin into my temple as he clamped himself around me like a butcher about to slash the throat of a calf. I cried out; the bloated sky split, and out poured a filthy rain. The faces of all the people around me began to wash away in inky streaks. A terrible thing had happened to me—A terrible thing had happened—*it was like water gushing out of my body.*

"Since then, my life has not belonged to me. Why do I not go to the authorities? Of course, I have done so. And they have added their mockery to the mockery of my tormentors: *Psychological help!* Tell me: Will 'psychological help' alter my history? Will 'psychological help' locate Dr. N.? Any information regarding my case will be fervently appreciated. Please contact: Iris Ackerman, P.O. Box 139775, Rochester, N.Y. Yours sincerely, Iris Ackerman."

ENCLAVES OF people wrapped in ragged blankets huddled against the walls of the glaring station. Policemen sauntered past in pairs, fingering their truncheons. Danger at every turn, Francie thought. Poor Iris—it was horrible to contemplate. And obviously love didn't exactly clarify the mind, either.

You had to give her credit, though—she was brave. At least she tried to figure things out, instead of just consulting, for example, the wall. To *really* figure things out, Francie blew her nose again. For all the good that did.

Any information regarding my case will be fervently appreciated. But this was not the moment, Francie thought, to lose her nerve.

The huge city was just outside the door, and there was no one else to go to West Tenth Street. There was no one else to hear what she had to hear. There was no one else to remember her mother with accuracy. There was no one else to not get the story wrong. There was no one else to reserve judgment. Francie closed one hand tightly around her new handkerchief, and with the other she gripped the handle on her box. The city rose up around her through a peach-colored sunset; now there was no more time.

The man who stood at the door of the apartment (K. McIntyre, #4B) was nice-looking. Nice-looking, and weirdly unfamiliar, as if the whole thing, maybe, were a complete mistake, Francie thought over and over in the striated extrusion of eternity (that was then and this is then; that was now and this is now) it had taken the door to open.

She was filthy, she thought. She smelled. She'd been wearing the same dress, the same socks, for days.

"Can I help you?" he said.

He had no idea why she was there! "Kevin McIntyre?" she said.

"Not back yet," he said. His gaze was pleasant—serene and searching. "Any minute."

He brought her into a big room and sat her down near a fireplace, in a squashy chair. He reached for the chain of a lamp, but Francie shook her head.

"No?" He looked at her. "I'm having coffee," he said. "Want a cup? Or something else—water? Wine? Soda?"

Francie shook her head again.

"Anyhow," he said. "I'm Alex. I'll be in back if you want me."

Francie nodded.

"Can I put your package somewhere for you, at least?" he asked, but Francie folded her arms around the box and rested her cheek against its plastic wrapping.

"Suit yourself," the man said. He paused at the entrance to the room. "You're not a very demanding guest, you know."

Francie felt his attention hesitate and then withdraw. After a moment, she raised her head—yes, he was gone. But then there he was again in the entranceway. "Strange day, huh?" he paused there to say. "Starting with the blimp."

The night before Francie left school, when she'd known so much more about her mother and her father than she knew now, she and Jessica had lain in their beds, talking feverishly. "Anything can happen at any moment," Jessica kept exclaiming. "Anything can just *happen*."

"It's worse than that," Francie had said (and she could still close her eyes and see Cynthia coming up that hill). "It's much, much worse." And Jessica had burst into noisy sobs, as if she knew exactly what Francie meant, as if it were she who had brushed against the burning cable of her life.

Her body, Francie noticed, felt as if it had been crumpled up in a ball—she should stretch. *Strange day*. Well, true enough. That was something they could all be sure of. This room was really nice, though. Pretty and pleasantly messy, with interesting stuff all over the place. Interesting, nice stuff . . .

Twilight was thickening like a dark garden, and paintings and drawings glimmered behind it on the walls. As scary as it was to be waiting for him, it was nice to be having this quiet time. This quiet time together, in a way.

Peach, rose, pale green—yes, poor guy; it might be a moment he'd look back on—last panels of tinted light were falling through the window. He might be walking up the street this very second. Stopping to buy a newspaper.

She closed her eyes. He fished in his pocket for change, and then glanced up sharply. Holding her breath, Francie drew herself back into the darkness. *It's your imagination*, she promised; he was going to have to deal with her soon enough—no sense making him see her until he actually had to.

DISASTER STAMPS OF PLUTO

Louise Erdrich

Louise Erdrich is the author of twelve novels as well as volumes of po-
etry, children's books, and a memoir of early motherhood. Her novel
Love Medicine won the National Book Critics Circle Award. *The Last Re-
port on the Miracles at Little No Horse* was a finalist for the National Book
Award. She lives in Minnesota with her daughters and is the owner of
Birchbark Books, a small independent bookstore.

The dead of Pluto now outnumber the living, and the cemetery
stretches up the low hill east of town in a jagged display of white
stone. There is no bar, no theater, no hardware store, no creamery
or car repair, just a gas pump. Even the priest comes to the church
only once a month. The grass is barely mowed in time for his visit,
and of course there are no flowers planted. But when the priest does
come, there is at least one more person for the town café to feed.

That there is a town café is something of a surprise, and it is
no rundown questionable edifice. When the bank pulled out, the
family whose drive-in was destroyed by heavy winds bought the
building with their insurance money. The granite facade, arched
windows, and twenty-foot ceilings make the café seem solid and
even luxurious. There is a blackboard for specials and a cigar box
by the cash register for the extra change that people might donate
to the hospital care of a local boy who was piteously hurt in a farming accident. I spend a good part of my day, as do most of the people

left here, in a booth at the café. For now that there is no point in keeping up our municipal buildings, the café serves as office space for town-council and hobby-club members, church-society and card-playing groups. It is an informal staging area for shopping trips to the nearest mall—sixty-eight miles south—and a place for the town's few young mothers to meet and talk, pushing their car-seat-convertible strollers back and forth with one foot while hooting and swearing as intensely as their husbands, down at the other end of the row of booths. Those left spouseless or childless, owing to war or distance or attrition, eat here. Also divorced or single persons like myself who, for one reason or another, have ended up with a house in Pluto, North Dakota, their only major possession.

We are still here because to sell our houses for a fraction of their original price would leave us renters for life in the world outside. Yet, however tenaciously we cling to yards and living rooms and garages, the grip of one or two of us is broken every year. We are growing fewer. Our town is dying. And I am in charge of more than I bargained for when, in 1991, in the year of my retirement from medicine, I was elected president of Pluto's historical society.

At the time, it looked as though we might survive, if not flourish, well into the next millennium. But then came the flood of 1997, followed by the cost of rebuilding. Smalls's bearing works and the farm-implement dealership moved east. We were left with flaxseed and sunflowers, but cheap transport via the interstate had pretty much knocked us out of the game already. So we have begun to steadily diminish, and, as we do, I am becoming the repository of many untold stories such as people will finally tell when they know that there is no use in keeping secrets, or when they realize that all that's left of a place will one day reside in documents, and they want those papers to reflect the truth.

MY OLD high school friend Neve Harp, salutatorian of the class of 1942 and fellow historical-society member, is one of the last of the original founding families. She is the granddaughter of the speculator and surveyor Frank Harp, who came with members of the Dakota and Great Northern Townsite Company to establish a chain of towns along the Great Northern tracks. They hoped to profit, of course. These townsites were meticulously drawn up into maps for risktakers who would purchase lots for their businesses or homes. Farmers in every direction would buy their supplies in town and patronize the entertainment spots when they came to ship their harvests via rail.

The platting crew moved by wagon and camped where they all agreed some natural feature of the landscape or general distance from other towns made a new town desirable. When the men reached the site of what is now our town, they'd already been platting and mapping for several years and in naming their sites had used up the few words they knew of Sioux or Chippewa, presidents and foreign capitals, important minerals, great statesmen, and the names of their girlfriends and wives. The Greek and Roman gods intrigued them. To the east lay the neatly marked-out townsites of Zeus, Neptune, Apollo, and Athena. They rejected Venus as conducive, perhaps, to future debauchery. Frank Harp suggested Pluto, and it was accepted before anyone realized they'd named a town for the god of the underworld. This occurred in the boom year of 1906, twenty-four years before the planet Pluto was discovered. It is not without irony now that the planet is the coldest, the loneliest, and perhaps the least hospitable in our solar system—but that was never, of course, intended to reflect upon our little municipality.

DRAMAS OF great note have occurred in Pluto. In 1924, five members of a family—the parents, a teenage girl, an eight- and a four-year-old boy—were murdered. A neighbor boy, apparently deranged with love over the daughter, vanished, and so remained the only suspect. Of that family, but one survived—a seven-month-old baby, who slept through the violence in a crib wedged unobtrusively behind a bed.

In 1934, the National Bank of Pluto was robbed of seventeen thousand dollars. In 1936, the president of the bank tried to flee the country with most of the town's money. He intended to travel to Brazil. His brother followed him as far as New York and persuaded him to return, and most of the money was restored. By visiting each customer personally, the brother convinced them all that their accounts were now safe, and the bank survived. The president, however, killed himself. The brother took over the job.

At the very apex of the town cemetery hill, there is a war memorial. In 1951, seventeen names were carved into a chunk of granite that was dedicated to the heroes of both world wars. One of the names was that of the boy who is generally believed to have murdered the family, the one who vanished from Pluto shortly after the bodies were discovered. He enlisted in Canada, and when notice of his death reached his aunt—who was married to a town-council member and had not wanted to move away, as the mother and father of the suspect did—the aunt insisted that his name be added to the list of the honorable dead. But unknown community members chipped it out of the stone, so that now a rough spot is all that marks his death, and on Veterans Day only sixteen flags are set into the ground around that rock.

There were droughts and freak accidents and other crimes of passion, and there were good things that happened, too. The seven-month-old baby who survived the murders was adopted by the aunt of the killer, who raised her in pampered love and, at great expense, sent her away to an Eastern college, never expecting that she would return. When she did, nine years later, she was a doctor—the first female doctor in the region. She set up her practice in town and restored the house she had inherited, where the murders had taken place—a small, charming clapboard farmhouse that sits on the eastern edge of town. Six hundred and forty acres of farmland stretch east from the house and barn. With the lease money from those acres, she was able to maintain a clinic and a nurse, and to keep her practice going even when her patients could not always pay for her services. She never married, but for a time she had a lover, a college professor and swim coach whose job did not permit him to leave the university. She had always understood that he would move to Pluto once he retired. But instead he married a girl much younger than himself and moved to Southern California, where he could have a year-round outdoor swimming pool.

MURDO HARP was the name of the brother of the suicide banker. He was the son of the town's surveyor and the father of my friend. Neve is now an octogenarian like me; she and I take daily walks to keep our joints oiled. Neve Harp was married three times, but has returned to her maiden name and the house she inherited from her father. She is a tall woman, somewhat stooped for lack of calcium in her diet, although on my advice she now ingests plenty. Every day, no matter what the weather (up to blizzard conditions), we take our two- or three-mile walk around the perimeter of Pluto.

"We orbit like an ancient couple of moons," she said to me one day.

"If there were people in Pluto, they could set their clocks by us," I answered. "Or worship us."

We laughed to think of ourselves as moon goddesses.

Most of the yards and lots are empty. For years, there has been no money in the town coffers for the streets, and the majority have been unimproved or left to gravel. Only the main street is paved with asphalt now, but the rough surfaces are fine with us. They give more purchase. Breaking a hip is our gravest dread—once you are immobile at our age, that is the end.

Our conversations slide through time, and we dwell often on setting straight the town record. I think we've sifted through every town occurrence by now, but perhaps when it comes to our own stories there is something left to know. Neve surprised me one day.

"I've been meaning to tell you why Murdo's brother, my uncle Octave, tried to run away to Brazil," she told me, as though the scandal had just occurred. "We should write the whole thing up for the historical newsletter."

I asked Neve to wait until we had finished our walk and sat down at the café, so that I could take notes, but she was so excited by the story beating its wings inside her—for some reason so alive and insistent that morning—that she had to talk as we made our way along. Her white hair swirled in wisps from its clip. Her features seemed to have sharpened. Neve has always been angular and imposing. I've been her foil. Her best audience. The one who absorbs the overflow of her excitements and pains.

"As you remember," Neve said, "Octave drowned himself when the river was at its lowest, in only two feet of water. He basically had to throw himself upon a puddle and breathe it in. It was thought that only a woman could have caused a man to inflict such a gruesome death upon himself, but it was not love. He did not die for love." Neve jabbed a finger at me, as though I'd been the one who kept the myth of Octave's passion alive. We walked meditatively on for about a hundred yards. Then she began again. "Do you remember stamp collections? How important those were? The rage?"

I said that I did remember. People still collect stamps, I told her.

"But not like they did then, not like Octave," she said. "My uncle had a stamp collection that he kept in the bank's main vault. One of this town's best-kept secrets is exactly how much money that collection was worth. When the bank was robbed in '34, the robbers forced their way into the vault. They grabbed what cash there was and completely ignored the fifty-nine albums and twenty-two specially constructed display boxes framed in ebony. That stamp collection was worth many times what the robbers got. It was worth almost as much money as was in the entire bank, in fact."

"What happened to it?" I was intrigued, as I hadn't known any of this.

Neve gave me a sly sideways look.

"I kept it when the bank changed hands. I like looking at the stamps, you see—they're better than television. I've decided to sell the whole thing, and that's why I'm telling the story now. The collection is in my front room. Stacked on a table. You've seen the albums, but you've never commented. You've never looked inside them. If you had, you would have been enchanted, like me, with the delicacy, the detail, and the endless variety. You would have wanted to know more about the stamps themselves, and the need to know and understand their histories would have taken hold of you, as it did my uncle and as it has me, though thankfully to a much lesser degree. Of course, you have your own interests."

"Yes," I said. "Thank God for those."

I would be typing out and editing Neve's story for the next month.

As we passed the church, we saw the priest there on his monthly visit. The poor man waved at us when we called out a greeting. No one had remembered, so he was cutting the grass. His parish was four or six combined now.

"They treat the good ones like simple beasts," Neve said. Then she shrugged and we pressed on. "My uncle's specialty, for all stamp collectors begin at some point to lean in a certain direction, was what you might call the dark side of stamp collecting."

I looked at Neve, whose excitements tend to take a shady turn, and thought that she had inherited her uncle's twist of mind along with his collection.

"After he had acquired the Holy Grails of philately—British Guiana's one-cent magenta, and the one-cent Z Grill—as well as the merely intriguing—for instance, Sweden's 1855 three-cent issue, which is orange instead of blue-green, and many stamps of the Thurn und Taxis postal system and superb specimens of the highly prized Mulready cover—my uncle's melancholia drew him specifically to what are called 'errors.' I think Sweden's three-cent began it all."

"Of course," I said, "even I know about the upside-down airplane stamp."

"The twenty-four-cent carmine-rose-and-blue invert. The Jenny. Yes!" She seemed delighted. "He began to collect errors in color, like the Swedish stamp, very tricky, then overprints, imperforate errors, value missings, omitted vignettes, and freaks. He has one entire album devoted to the seventeen-year-old boy Frank Baptist, who ran off stamps on an old handpress for the Confederate government."

Neve charged across a gravelly patch of road, and I hastened to stay within earshot. Stopping to catch her breath, she leaned on a tree and told me that, about six years before he absconded with the bank's money, Octave Harp had gone into disasters—that is, stamps and covers, or envelopes, that had survived the dreadful occurrences that test or destroy us. These pieces of mail, water-stained, tattered, even bloodied, marked by experience, took their value from the gravity of their condition. Such damage was part of their allure.

By then, we had arrived at the café, and I was glad to sit down and take a few notes on Neve's revelations. I borrowed some paper and a pen from the owner, and we ordered our coffee and sandwiches. I always have a Denver sandwich and Neve orders a BLT without the bacon. She is a strict vegetarian, the only one in Pluto. We sipped our coffee.

"I have a book," Neve said, "on philately, in which it says that stamp collecting offers refuge to the confused and gives new vigor to fallen spirits. I think Octave was hoping he would find something of the sort. But my father told me that the more he dwelt on the disasters the worse he felt. He would brighten whenever he obtained something valuable for his collection, though. He was in touch with people all over the globe—it was quite remarkable. I've got files and files of his correspondence with stamp dealers. He would spend years tracking down a surviving stamp or cover that had been through a particular disaster. Wars, of course, from the American Revolution to the Crimean War and the First World War. Soldiers frequently carry letters on their person, and one doesn't like to think how those letters ended up in the hands of collectors. But Octave preferred natural disasters and, to a lesser extent, man-made accidents." Neve tapped the side of her cup. "He would have been fascinated by the *Hindenburg*, and certainly there would have been a stamp or two involved, somewhere. And our modern disasters, too, of course."

I knew what she was thinking of, suddenly—those countless fluttering, strangely cheerful papers drifting through the sky in New York. . . . I went cold with dismay at the thought that many of those bits of paper were perhaps now in the hands of dealers who were selling them all over the world to people like Octave. Neve and I think very much alike, and I saw that she was about to sugar her coffee—a sign of distress. She has a bit of a blood-sugar problem.

"Don't," I said. "You'll be awake all night."

"I know." She did it anyway, then set the glass cannister back on the table. "Isn't it strange, though, how time mutes the horror of events, how they cease to affect us in the same way? But I began to tell you all of this in order to explain why Octave left for Brazil."

"With so much money. Now I'm starting to imagine he was on the trail of a stamp."

"You're exactly right," Neve said. "My father told me what Octave was looking for. As I said, he was fascinated with natural disasters, and in his collection he had a letter that had survived the explosion of Krakatoa in 1883, a Dutch postmark placed upon a letter written just before and carried off on a steamer. He had a letter from the sack of mail frozen onto the back of a New Hampshire mail carrier who died in the East Coast blizzard of 1888. An authenticated letter from the *Titanic*'s seagoing post office, too, but then there must have been quite a lot of mail recovered for some reason, as he refers to other pieces. But he was not as interested in sea disasters. No, the prize he was after was a letter from the year 79 AD."

I hadn't known there was mail service then, but Neve assured me that mail was extremely old, and that it was Herodotus whose words appeared in the motto "Neither snow, nor rain, nor gloom of night," etc., more than three hundred years before the date she'd just referred to—the year Mt. Vesuvius blew up and buried Pompeii in volcanic ash. "As you may know," she went on, "the site was looted and picked through by curiosity seekers for a century and a half after its rediscovery before anything was done about preservation. By then, quite a number of recovered objects had found their way into the hands of collectors. A letter that may have been meant for Pliny the Younger, from the Elder, apparently surfaced for a tantalizing moment in Paris, but by the time Octave could contact the dealer the prize had been stolen. The dealer tracked it, however, through a shadowy resale into the hands of a Portuguese rubber baron's wife, who was living in Brazil, a woman with obsessions similar to Octave's—though she was not a stamp collector. She was interested in all things Pompeian—had her walls painted in exact replicas of Pompeii frescoes, and so on."

"Imagine that. In Brazil."

"No stranger than a small-town North Dakota banker amassing a world-class collection of stamps. Octave was, of course, a bachelor. And he lived very modestly too. Still, he didn't have enough money to come near to purchasing the Pliny letter. He tried to leave the country with the bank's money and his stamp collection, but the stamps held him back. I think the customs officials became involved in questions regarding the collection—whether it should be allowed to leave the country, and so on. The Frank Baptist stamps were an interesting side note to American history, for instance. Murdo caught up with him a few days later, and Octave had had a breakdown and was paralyzed in some hotel room. He was terrified that his collection would be confiscated. When he returned to Pluto, he began drinking heavily, and from then on he was a wreck."

"And the Pompeii letter—what became of it?"

"There was a letter from the Brazilian lady, who still hoped to sell the piece to Octave, a wild letter full of cross-outs and stained with tears."

"A disaster letter?"

"Yes, I suppose you could say so. Her three-year-old son had somehow got hold of the Pompeii missive and reduced it to dust. So in a way it *was* a letter from a woman that broke Octave's heart."

There was nothing more to say, and we were both in a thoughtful mood by then. Our sandwiches were before us and we ate them.

NEVE AND I spend our evenings quietly, indoors, reading or watching television, listening to music, eating our meager suppers alone. As I have been long accustomed to my own company, I find my time from dusk to midnight wonderful. I am not lonely. I know I haven't long to enjoy the luxuries of privacy and silence, and I cherish my familiar surroundings. Neve, however, misses her two children and her grandchildren. She spends many evenings on the telephone, although they live in Fargo and she sees them often. Both Neve and I find it strange that we are old, and we are amazed at how quickly our lives passed—Neve with her marriages and I with my medical practice. We are even surprised when we catch sight of ourselves sometimes. I am fortunate in old age to have a good companion like Neve, though I have lately suspected that if she had the chance to leave Pluto she would do it.

That night, she had an episode of black moodiness, brought on by the sugar in her coffee, though I did not say so. She was still caught up in the telling of Octave's story, and she had also made an odd discovery.

Flanked by two bright reading lamps, I was quietly absorbing a rather too sweet novel sent by a book club that I belong to when the telephone rang. Speaking breathlessly, Neve told me that she had been looking through albums all evening with a magnifying glass. She had also been sifting through Octave's papers and letters. She had found something that distressed her: In a file that she had never before opened was a set of eight or nine letters, all addressed to the same person, with canceled stamps, the paper distorted as though it had got wet, the writing smudged, each stamp differing from the others by some slight degree—a minor flaw in the cancellation mark, a slight rip. She had examined them in some puzzlement and noticed that one bore a fifty-cent violet Benjamin Franklin issued two years after the cancellation mark, which was dated just before the sinking of the *Titanic*.

"I am finding it very hard to admit the obvious," she said, "because I had formed such a sympathetic opinion of my uncle. But I believe he must have been experimenting with forged disaster mail, and that what I found was no less than evidence. He was offering his fake letter to a dealer in London. There were attempts and rejections of certification letters, too." She sounded furious, as though he had tried to sell her the item himself.

I tried to talk Neve down, but when she gets into a mood like this all of her rages and sorrows come back to her and it seems she must berate the world or mourn each one. From what she could tell, all the other articles in Octave's collection were authentic, so after a while she calmed herself. She even laughed a bit, wondering if Octave's forgery would hold up if included in the context of an otherwise brilliant collection.

"It could improve the price," she said.

As soon as possible, I put the phone down, and my insipid novel as well. Neve's moods are catching. I have a notion I will soon be alone in Pluto. I try to shake off a sudden miasma of turbulent dread, but before I know it I have walked into my bedroom and am opening the chest at the foot of my bed and I am looking through my family's clothes—all else was destroyed or taken away, but the undertaker washed and kept these (kindly, I think) and he gave them to me when I moved into this house. I find the somber envelope marked "Jorghansen's Funeral Parlor" and slip from it the valentine, within its own envelope, that must have been hidden in a pocket. It may or may not be stained with blood, or rust, but it is most certainly a hideous thing, all schmaltz and paper lace. I note for the first time that the envelope bears a five-cent commemorative stamp of the Huguenot monument in Florida.

Sometimes I wonder if the sounds of fear and anguish, the thunder of the shotgun, is hidden from me somewhere in the most obscure corner of my brain. I might have died of dehydration, as I wasn't found for three days, but I don't remember that either, not at all, and have never been abnormally afraid of thirst or obsessed with food or water. No, my childhood was very happy and I had everything—a swing, a puppy, doting parents. Only good things happened to me. I was chosen Queen of the Prom. I never underwent a shock at the sudden revelation of my origins, for I was told the story early on and came to accept who I was. We even suspected that the actual killer might still be living somewhere in our area, invisible, remorseful. For we'd find small, carefully folded bills of cash hidden outdoors in places where my aunt or I would be certain to find them— beneath a flowerpot, in my tree house, in the hollow handles of my bicycle—and we'd always hold the wadded squares up and say, "He's been here again." But, truly, I am hard pressed to name more than the predictable sadnesses that pass through one's life. It is as though the freak of my survival charged my disposition with gratitude. Or as if my family absorbed all the misfortune that might have come my way. I have lived an ordinary and a satisfying life, and I have been privileged to be of service to people. There is no one I mourn to the point of madness and nothing I would really do over again.

So why, when I stroke my sister's valentine against the side of my face, and why, when I touch the folded linen of her vest, and when I reach for my brothers' overalls and the apron my mother died in that day, and bundle these things to my stomach together with my father's ancient, laundered, hay-smelling clothes, why, when I gather my family into my arms, do I catch my breath at the wild upsurge, as if a wind had lifted me, a black wing of air? And why, when that happens, do I fly toward some blurred and ineradicable set of features that seems to rush away from me as stars do? At blinding speeds, never stopping?

When Pluto is empty at last and this house is reclaimed by earth, when the war memorial is toppled and the bank/café stripped for its brass and granite, when all that remains of our town is a collection of historical newsletters bound in volumes donated to the regional collections at the University of North Dakota, what then? What shall I have said? How shall I have depicted the truth?

The valentine tells me that the boy's name should not have been scratched from the war memorial, that he was not the killer after all. For my sister loved him in return, or she would not have carried his message upon her person. And if he had had her love he probably fled out of grief and despair, not remorse or fear of prosecution. But if it was not the boy, who was it? My father? But no, he was felled from behind. There is no one to accuse. Somewhere in this town or out in the world, then, the being has existed who stalked the boys hiding in the barn and destroyed them in the hay, who saw the beauty of my sister and my mother and shot them dead. And to what profit? For nothing was taken. Nothing gained. To what end the mysterious waste?

AN EXTREMELY touchy case came my way about twenty years ago, and I have submerged the knowledge of its truth. I have never wanted to think of it. But now, as with Neve, my story knocks with insistence, and I remember my patient. He was a hired man who'd lived his life on a stock farm that abutted the farthest edges of our land. Warren Wolde was a taciturn crank, who nevertheless had a way with animals. He held a number of peculiar beliefs, I am told, regarding the United States government. On these topics, his opinion was avoided. Certain things were never mentioned around him— Congress being one, and particular amendments to the Constitution. Even if one stuck to safe subjects, he looked at people in a penetrating way that they found disquieting. But Warren Wolde was in no condition to disquiet me when I came onto the farm to treat him. Two weeks before, the farm's expensive blooded bull had hooked and then trampled him, concentrating most of the damage on one leg. He'd refused to see a doctor, and now a feverish infection had set in and the wound was necrotic. He was very strong, and fought being moved to a hospital so violently that his employers had decided to call me instead to see if I could save his leg.

I could, and did, though the means were painful and awful and it meant twice-daily visits, which my schedule could ill afford. At each change of the dressing and debridement, I tried to dose Wolde with morphine, but he resisted. He did not trust me yet and feared that if he lost consciousness he'd wake without his leg. Gradually, I managed to heal the wound and also to quiet him. When I first came to treat him, he'd reacted to the sight of me with a horror unprecedented in my medical experience. It was a fear mixed with panic that had only gradually dulled to a silent wariness. As his leg healed, he opened to my visits, and by the time he was hobbling on crutches he seemed to anticipate my presence with an eager pleasure so tender and pathetic that it startled everyone around him. He'd shuck off his forbidding and strange persona just for me, they said, and sink back into an immobilizing fury once I'd left. He never healed quite enough to take on all of his old tasks, but he lasted pretty well at his job for another three years. He died naturally, in his sleep one night, of a thrown blood clot. To my surprise, I was contacted several weeks later by a lawyer.

The man said that his client Warren Wolde had left a package for me, which I asked him to send in the mail. When the package arrived, addressed in an awkward script that certainly could have been Wolde's, I opened the box immediately. Inside were hundreds upon hundreds of wadded bills of assorted denominations, and of course I recognized their folded pattern as identical to the bills that had turned up for me all through my childhood. I could perhaps believe that the money gifts and the legacy were only marks of sympathy for the tragic star of my past and, later, gratitude for what I'd done. I might be inclined to think that, were it not for the first few times I had come to treat Wolde, when he reared from me in a horror that seemed so personal. There had been something of a recalled nightmare in his face, I'd thought it even then, and I was not touched later on by the remarkable change in his character. On the contrary, it chilled me to sickness.

THOSE OF you who have faithfully subscribed to this newsletter know that our dwindling subscription list has made it necessary to reduce the length of our articles. So I must end here. But it appears, anyway, that since only the society's treasurer, Neve Harp, and I have convened to make any decisions at all regarding the preservation and upkeep of our little collection, and as only the two of us are left to contribute more material to this record, and as we have nothing left to say, our membership is now closed. We declare our society defunct. I shall, at least, keep walking the perimeter of Pluto until my footsteps wear my orbit into the earth. My last act as the president of Pluto's historical society is this: I would like to declare a town holiday to commemorate the year I saved the life of my family's murderer. The wind will blow. The devils rise. All who celebrate it shall be ghosts. And there will be nothing but eternal dancing, dust on dust, everywhere you look.

Oh my, too apocalyptic, I think as I leave my house to walk over to Neve's to help her cope with her sleepless night. She will soon move to Fargo. She'll have the money to do it. Dust on dust! There are very few towns where old women can go out at night and enjoy the breeze, so there is that about Pluto. I take my cane to feel the way, for the air is so black I think already I am invisible.

REUNION

Richard Ford

Richard Ford is the author of six novels, most recently *The Lay of the Land*, and three collections of stories. Ford was awarded the Pulitzer Prize and the PEN/Faulkner Award for *Independence Day*, the first book to win both prizes. In 2001 he received the PEN/Malamud Award for excellence in short fiction.

When I saw Mack Bolger he was standing beside the bottom of the marble steps that bring travelers and passersby to and from the balcony of the main concourse in Grand Central. It was before Christmas last year, when the weather stayed so warm and watery the spirit seemed to go out of the season.

I was cutting through the terminal, as I often do on my way home from the publishing offices on Forty-first Street. I was, in fact, on my way to meet a new friend at Billy's. It was four o'clock on Friday, and the great station was athrong with citizens on their way somewhere, laden with baggage and precious packages, shouting goodbyes and greetings, flagging their arms, embracing, gripping each other with pleasure. Others, though, simply stood, as Mack Bolger was when I saw him, staring rather vacantly at the crowds, as if whomever he was there to meet for some reason hadn't come. Mack is a tall, handsome, well-put-together man who seems to see everything from a height. He was wearing a long, well-fitted gabardine overcoat of some deep-olive twill—an expensive coat, I thought, an

Italian coat. His brown shoes were polished to a high gloss; his trouser cuffs hit them just right. And because he was without a hat, he
seemed even taller than what he was—perhaps six-three. His hands
were in his coat pockets, his smooth chin slightly elevated the way a
middle-aged man would, and as if he thought he was extremely visible there. His hair was thinning a little in front, but it was carefully
cut, and he was tanned, which caused his square face and prominent brow to appear heavy, almost artificially so, as though in a peculiar way the man I saw was not Mack Bolger but a good-looking
effigy situated precisely there to attract my attention.

For a while, a year and a half before, I had been involved with
Mack Bolger's wife, Beth Bolger. Oddly enough—only because all
events that occur outside New York seem odd and fancifully unreal
to New Yorkers—our affair had taken place in the city of St. Louis,
that largely overlookable red-brick abstraction that is neither West
nor Middlewest, neither South nor North; the city lost in the middle, as I think of it. I've always found it interesting that it was both
the boyhood home of T. S. Eliot, and only eighty-five years before
that, the starting point of westward expansion. It's a place, I suppose, the world can't get away from fast enough.

What went on between Beth Bolger and me is hardly worth the
words that would be required to explain it away. At any distance
but the close range I saw it from, it was an ordinary adultery—
spirited, thrilling and then, after a brief while, when we had crossed
the continent several times and caused as many people as possible
unhappiness, embarrassment and heartache, it became disappointing and ignoble and finally almost disastrous to those same people.
Because it is the truth and serves to complicate Mack Bolger's un-
likeable dilemma and to cast him in a more sympathetic light, I will
say that at some point he was forced to confront me (and Beth as
well) in a hotel room in St. Louis—a nice, graceful old barn called
the Mayfair—with the result that I got banged around in a minor
way and sent off into the empty downtown streets on a warm, humid autumn Sunday afternoon, without the slightest idea of what

to do, ending up waiting for hours at the St. Louis airport for a midnight flight back to New York. Apart from my dignity, I left behind
and never saw again a brown silk Hermès scarf with tassels that my
mother had given me for Christmas in 1971, a gift she felt was the
nicest thing she'd ever seen and perfect for a man just commencing
life as a book editor. I'm glad she didn't have to know about my losing it, and how it happened.

I also did not see Beth Bolger again, except for one sorrowful
and bitter drink we had together in the theater district last spring,
a nervous, uncomfortable meeting we somehow felt obligated
to have, and following which I walked away down Forty-seventh
Street, feeling that all of life was a sorry mess, while Beth went
along to see *The Iceman Cometh*, which was playing then. We have
not seen each other since that leave-taking, and, as I said, to tell
more would not be quite worth the words.

But when I saw Mack Bolger standing in the crowded, festive
holiday-bedecked concourse of Grand Central, looking rather
vacant-headed but clearly himself, so far from the middle of the
country, I was taken by a sudden and strange impulse—which was
to walk straight across through the eddying sea of travelers and
speak to him, just as one might speak to anyone you casually knew
and had unexpectedly yet not unhappily encountered. And not to
impart anything, or set in motion any particular action (to clarify
history, for instance, or make amends), but simply to create an
event where before there was none. And not an unpleasant event,
or a provocative one. Just a dimensionless, unreverberant moment,
a contact, unimportant in every other respect. Life has few enough
of these moments—the rest of it being so consumed by the predictable and the obligated.

I knew a few things about Mack Bolger, about his life since
we'd last confronted each other semi-violently in the Mayfair.
Beth had been happy to tell me during our woeful drink at the
Espalier Bar in April. Our—Beth's and my—love affair was, of
course, only one feature in the long devaluation and decline in

her and Mack's marriage. This I'd always understood. There were two children, and Mack had been frantic to hold matters together for their sakes and futures; Beth was a portrait photographer who worked at home, but craved engagement with the wide world outside of University City—craved it in the worst way, and was therefore basically unsatisfied with everything in her life. After my sudden departure, she moved out of their house, rented an apartment near the Gateway Arch and, for a time, took a much younger lover. Mack, for his part in their upheaval, eventually quit his job as an executive for a large agribiz company, considered studying for the ministry, considered going on a missionary journey to Senegal or French Guiana, briefly took a young lover himself. One child had been arrested for shoplifting; the other had gotten admitted to Brown. There were months of all-night confrontations, some combative, some loving and revelatory, some derisive from both sides. Until everything that could be said or expressed or threatened was said, expressed and threatened, after which a standstill was achieved whereby they both stayed in their suburban house, kept separate schedules, saw new and different friends, had occasional dinners together, went to the opera, occasionally even slept together, but saw little hope (in Beth's case, certainly) of things turning out better than they were at the time of our joyless drink and the O'Neill play. I'd assumed at that time that Beth was meeting someone else that evening, had someone in New York she was interested in, and I felt completely fine about it.

"It's really odd, isn't it?" Beth said, stirring her long, almost pure-white finger around the surface of her Kir Royale, staring not at me but at the glass rim where the pink liquid nearly exceeded its vitreous limits. "We were so close for a little while." Her eyes rose to me, and she smiled almost girlishly. "You and me, I mean. Now, I feel like I'm telling all this to an old friend. Or to my brother."

Beth is a tall, sallow-faced, big-boned, ash blond woman who smokes cigarettes and whose hair often hangs down in her eyes like a forties Hollywood glamour girl. This can be attractive, although it often causes her to seem to be spying on her own conversations.

"Well," I said, "it's all right to feel that way." I smiled back across the little round blacktopped café table. It *was* all right. I had gone on. When I looked back on what we'd done, none of it except for what we'd done in bed made me feel good about life, or that the experience had been worth it. But I couldn't undo it. I don't believe the past can be repaired, only exceeded. "Sometimes, friendship's all we're after in these sorts of things," I said. Though this, I admit, I did not really believe.

"Mack's like a dog, you know," Beth said, flicking her hair away from her eyes. He was on her mind. "I kick him, and he tries to bring me things. It's pathetic. He's very interested in Tantric sex now, whatever that is. Do you know what that even is?"

"I really don't like hearing this," I said stupidly, though it was true. "It sounds cruel."

"You're just afraid I'll say the same thing about you, Johnny." She smiled and touched her damp fingertip to her lips, which were wonderful lips.

"Afraid," I said. "Afraid's really not the word, is it?"

"Well, then, whatever the word is." Beth looked quickly away and motioned the waiter for the check. She didn't know how to be disagreed with. It always frightened her.

But that was all. I've already said our meeting wasn't a satisfying one.

MACK BOLGER's pale gray eyes caught me coming toward him well before I expected them to. We had seen each other only twice. Once at a fancy cocktail party given by an author I'd come to St. Louis to wrest a book away from. It was the time I'd met his wife. And once more, in the Mayfair Hotel, when I'd taken an inept swing at him and he'd slammed me against a wall and hit me in the face with the back of his hand. Perhaps you don't forget people you knock around. That becomes their place in your life.

I, myself, find it hard to recognize people when they're not where they belong, and Mack Bolger belonged in St. Louis. Of course, he was an exception.

Mack's gaze fixed on me, then left me, scanned the crowd uncomfortably, then found me again as I approached. His large tanned face took on an expression of stony unsurprise, as if he'd known I was somewhere in the terminal and a form of communication had already begun between us. Though, if anything, really, his face looked resigned—resigned to me, resigned to the situations the world foists onto you unwilling; resigned to himself. Resignation was actually what we had in common, even if neither of us had a language which could express that. So as I came into his presence, what I felt for him, unexpectedly, was sympathy—for having to see me now. And if I could've, I would have turned and walked straight away and left him alone. But I didn't.

"I just saw you," I said from the crowd, ten feet before I ever expected to speak. My voice isn't loud, so that the theatrically nasal male voice announcing the arrival from Poughkeepsie on track 34 seemed to have blotted it out.

"Did you have something special in mind to tell me?" Mack Bolger said. His eyes cast out again across the vaulted hall, where Christmas shoppers and overbundled passengers were moving in all directions. It occurred to me at that instant—and shockingly— that he was waiting for Beth, and that in a moment's time I would be standing here facing her and Mack together, almost as we had in St. Louis. My heart struck two abrupt beats deep in my chest, then seemed for a second to stop altogether. "How's your face?" Mack said with no emotion, still scanning the crowd. "I didn't hurt you too bad, did I?"

"No," I said.

"You've grown a moustache." His eyes did not flicker toward me.

"Yes," I said, though I'd completely forgotten about it, and for some reason felt ashamed, as if it made me look ridiculous.

"Well," Mack Bolger said. "Good." His voice was the one you would use to speak to someone in line beside you at the post office, someone you'd never see again. Though there was also, just barely noticeable, a hint of what we used to call *juiciness* in his speech, some minor, undispersable moisture in his cheek that one heard in his *s*'s and *f*'s. It was unfortunate, since it robbed him of a small measure of gravity. I hadn't noticed it before in the few overheated moments we'd had to exchange words.

Mack looked at me again, hands in his expensive Italian coat pockets, a coat that had heavy, dark, bone buttons and long, wide lapels. Too stylish for him, I thought, for the solid man he was. Mack and I were nearly the same height, but he was in every way larger and seemed to look down to me—something in the way he held his chin up. It was almost the opposite of the way Beth looked at me.

"I live here now," Mack said, without really addressing me. I noticed he had long, dark almost feminine eyelashes, and small, perfectly shaped ears, which his new haircut put on nice display. He might've been forty—younger than I am—and looked more than anything like an army officer. A major. I thought of a letter Beth had shown me, written by Mack to her, containing the phrase, "I want to kiss you all over. Yes I do. Love, Macklin." Beth had rolled her eyes when she showed it to me. At another time she had talked to Mack on the telephone while we were in bed together naked. On that occasion, too, she'd *kept* rolling her eyes at whatever he was saying—something, I gathered, about difficulties he was having at work. Once we even engaged in a sexual act while she talked to him. I could hear his tiny, buzzing, fretful-sounding voice inside the receiver. But that was now gone. Everything Beth and I had done was gone. All that remained was this—a series of moments in the great train terminal, moments which, in spite of all, seemed correct, sturdy, almost classical in character, as if this later time was all that really mattered, whereas the previous, briefly passionate, linked but now-distant moments were merely preliminary.

"Did you buy a place?" I said, and all at once felt a widely spreading vacancy open all around inside me. It was such a preposterous thing to say.

Mack's eyes moved gradually to me, and his impassive expression, which had seemed to signify one thing—resignation—began to signify something different. I knew this because a small cleft appeared in his chin.

"Yes," he said and let his eyes stay on me.

People were shouldering past us. I could smell some woman's heavy, warm-feeling perfume around my face. Music commenced in the rotunda, making the moment feel suffocating, clamorous: "We three kings of Orient are, bearing gifts we traverse afar . . ."

"Yes," Mack Bolger said again, emphatically, spitting the word from between his large straight, white, nearly flawless teeth. He had grown up on a farm in Nebraska, gone to a small college in Minnesota on a football scholarship, then taken an MBA at Wharton, had done well. All that life, all that experience was now being brought into play as self-control, dignity. It was strange that anyone would call him a dog when he wasn't that at all. He was extremely admirable. "I bought an apartment on the Upper East Side," he said, and he blinked his eyelashes very rapidly. "I moved out in September. I have a new job. I'm living alone. Beth's not here. She's in Paris where she's miserable—or rather I hope she is. We're getting divorced. I'm waiting for my daughter to come down from boarding school. Is that all right? Does that seem all right to you? Does it satisfy your curiosity?"

"Yes," I said. "Of course." Mack was not angry. He was, instead, a thing that anger had no part in, or at least had long been absent from, something akin to exhaustion, where the words you say are the only true words you *can* say. Myself, I did not think I'd ever felt that way. Always for me there had been a choice.

"Do you understand me?" Mack Bolger's thick athlete's brow furrowed, as if he was studying a creature he didn't entirely understand, an anomaly of some kind, which perhaps I was.

"Yes," I said. "I'm sorry."

"Well then," he said, and seemed embarrassed. He looked to the blond girl standing in the crowd smiling. What he said was, "Wow-wee, boy, oh boy, do *you* look like a million bucks."

And I walked on toward Billy's then, toward the new arrangement I'd made that would take me into the evening. I had, of course, been wrong about the linkage of moments, and about what was preliminary and what was primary. It was a mistake, one I would not make again. None of it was a good thing to have done. Though it is such a large city here, so much larger than say, St. Louis, I knew I would not see him again.

RÊVE HAITIEN

Ben Fountain

Ben Fountain is the author of the story collection *Brief Encounters with Che Guevara*. His fiction has appeared in *Harper's*, *The Paris Review*, and *Zoetrope: All-Story*, and he has been awarded an O. Henry Prize, two Pushcart Prizes, and the PEN/Hemingway Award. He lives with his wife and their two children in Dallas, Texas.

In the evenings, after he finished his rounds, Mason would often carry his chessboard down to the Champ de Mars and wait for a match on one of the concrete benches. As a gesture of solidarity he lived in Pacot, the scruffy middle-class neighborhood in the heart of Port-au-Prince, while most of his fellow O.A.S. observers had taken houses in the fashionable suburb of Pétionville. Out of sympathy for the people Mason insisted on Pacot, but as it turned out he grew to like the place, the jungly yards and wild creep of urban undergrowth, the crumbling gingerbread houses and cobbled streets. And it had strategic position as well, which was important to Mason, who took his job as an observer seriously. From his house he could track the nightly gunfire, its volume and heft, the level of intent—whether it was a drizzle meant mainly for suggestive effect or something heavier, a message of a more direct nature. In the mornings he always knew where to look for bodies. And when war had erupted between two army gangs he'd been the first observer to know, lying in bed while what sounded like the long-rumored invasion raged nearby. Most of his colleagues had been clueless un-til the morning after, when they met the roadblocks on their way to work.

On Thursdays he went to the Oloffson to hear the band, and on weekends he toured the hotel bars and casinos in Pétionville. Otherwise, unless it had been such a grim day that he could only stare at his kitchen wall and drink beer, he would get his chess set and walk down to the park, past the weary peddler women chant-ing house-to-house, past the packs of rachitic, turd-colored dogs, past the crazy man who squatted by the Church of the Sacred Heart sweeping handfuls of dirt across his chest. There in the park, which resembled a bombed-out inner city lot, he would pick out a bench with a view of the palace and arrange his pieces, and within min-utes a crowd of mouthy street kids would be watching him play that day's challengers. Mason rarely won; that was the whole point. With the overthrow and exile of their cherished president, the me-thodical hell of the army regime, and now the embargo that threat-ened to crush them all, he believed that the popular ego needed a boost. It did them good to see a Haitian whip a *blan* at chess; it was a reason to laugh, to be proud at his expense, and there were evenings when he looked on these thrown games as the most constructive thing he'd done all day.

As his Creole improved he came to understand that the street kids' jibes weren't all that friendly. Yet he persisted; Haitians needed something to keep them going, and these games allowed him to keep a covert eye on the palace, the evening routine of the military thugs who were running the country—the de facto gov-ernment, as the diplomats and news reports insisted on saying, the de factos basically meaning anybody with a gun. Word got around about his evening games and the *zazous* started bringing chess sets for him to buy, the handcrafted pieces often worked in Haitian themes: the voodoo gods, say, or LeClerc versus Toussaint, or Baby Doc as the king and Michèle the queen and notorious Macoutes in supporting roles. Sometimes during these games the crowd grew so raucous that Mason feared drawing fire from the palace guards. And, regardless of the game, he always left in time to get home by dark. Not even a *blan* was safe on the streets after dark.

Late one afternoon he'd barely set up his board when a scrap of skin and bones came running toward him. *Blan!* the boy shouted, grinning wickedly, *veni gon match pou ou!* Mason packed up his set and followed the boy to a secluded corner of the park, a patch of trees and scrub screening it from the palace. There on the bench sat a mulatto, a young Haitian with bronze skin, an impressive hawk nose, and a black mass of hair that grazed his shoulders. His T-shirt and jeans were basic street, but the cracked white loafers seemed to hint at old affluence, also an attitude, a sexually purposed life that had been abandoned some time ago. He simply pointed to the spot where Mason should sit, and they started playing.

The mulatto took the first game in seven moves. Mason realized that with this one he was allowed to try; the next game lasted eleven moves. "You're very good," Mason said in French, but the mulatto merely gave a paranoiac twitch and reset his pieces. In the next game Mason focused all his mental powers, but the mulatto had a way of pinning you down with pawns and bishops, then wheeling his knights through the mush of your defense. This game went to thirteen moves before Mason admitted he was beaten. The mulatto sat back, eyed him a withering moment, then said in English:

"All of these nights you have been trying to lose."

Mason shrugged, then began resetting the pieces.

"I didn't think it was possible for anyone to be so stupid, even a *blan*," said the mulatto. "You are mocking us."

"No, that's not it at all. I just felt . . ." Mason struggled for a polite way to say it.

"You feel pity for us."

"Something like that."

"You want to help the Haitian people."

"That's true. I do."

"Are you a good man? A brave man? A man of conviction?"

Mason, who had never been spoken to in such solemn terms, needed a second to process the question. "Well, sure," he replied, and really meant it.

"Then come with me," said the mulatto.

HE LED Mason around the palace and into the hard neighborhood known as Salomon, a dense, scumbled antheap of cinderblock houses and packing-crate sheds, wobbly storefronts, markets, mewling beggars underfoot. Through the woodsmoke and dust and swirl of car exhaust the late sun took on an ocherous radiance, the red light washing over the grunged and pitted streets. Dunes of garbage filled out the open spaces, eruptions so rich in colorful filth that they achieved a kind of abstraction. With Mason half-trotting to keep up the mulatto cut along sidestreets and tight alleyways where Haitians tumbled at them from every side. A simmering roar came off the closepacked houses, a vibration like a drumroll in his ears that blended with the slur of cars and bleating horns, the scraps of Latin music shredding the air. There was something powerful here, even exalted; Mason felt it whenever he was on the streets, a kind of spasm, a queasy, slightly strung-out thrill feeding off the sheer muscle of the place.

It was down an alley near the cemetery, a small sea green house flaking chunks of itself, half-hidden by shrubs and a draggled row of saplings. The mulatto passed through the gate and into the house without speaking to the group gathered on the steps, a middle-aged couple and five or six staring kids. Mason followed the mulatto through the murk of the front room, vaguely aware of beds and mismatched plastic furniture, a cheesy New York-skyline souvenir clock. The next room was cramped and musty, the single window shuttered and locked. The mulatto switched on the bare light overhead and walked to an armoire that filled half the room. That too was locked, and he jabbed a key at it with the wrath of a man who finds such details an insult.

"Is this your house?" asked Mason, eyeing the bed in the corner, the soiled clothes and books scattered around.

"Sometimes."

"Who are those people out there?"

"Haitians," snapped the frustrated mulatto. Mason finally had to turn the key himself, which went with an easy click. The mulatto sighed, then pulled two plastic garbage bags out of the armoire.

"This," he announced, stepping past Mason to the bed, "is the treasure of the Haitian people."

Mason stood back as the mulatto began pulling rolls of canvas from the bags, stripping off the rag strings, and laying the canvases on the bed. "Hyppolite," he said crisply as a serpentine creature with the head of a man unfurled across the mattress. "Castera Bazile," he said next, "the crucifixion," and a blunt-angled painting of the nailed and bleeding Christ was laid over Hyppolite's mutant snake. "Philomé Obin. Bigaud. André Pierre. All of the Haitian masters are represented." At first glance the paintings had a wooden quality, and yet Mason, whose life trajectory had mostly skimmed him past art, felt confronted by something vital and real.

"Préfète Duffaut." The mulatto kept unrolling canvases. "Lafortune Felix. Saint-Fleurant. Hyppolite, his famous painting of Erzu-lie. There is a million dollars' worth of art in this room."

This was a lot, even allowing for the Haitian gift for puff. "How did you get it?" Mason felt obliged to ask.

"We stole it." The mulatto gave him an imperious look.

"You stole it?"

"Shortly after the coup. Most of the paintings we took in a single night. It wasn't difficult, I know the houses where they have the art. A few pictures came later, but most of the items we took in the time of the coup."

"Okay." Mason felt the soft approach was best. "You're an artist?"

"I am a doctor," said the mulatto, and his arrogance seemed to bear this out.

"But you like art."

The mulatto paused, then went on as if Mason hadn't spoken.

"Art is the only thing of value in my country—the national treasure, what Haiti has to offer to the world. We are going to use her treasure to free her."

Mason had met his share of delusional Haitians, but here were the pictures, and here was a man with the bearing of a king. A man who'd gutted his best chess game in thirteen moves.

"How are you going to do that?"

"There is a receiver in Paris who makes a market in Haitian art. He is offering cash, eighty thousand American dollars if I can get the paintings to Miami. A shameful price when you consider this is our treasure . . ." The mulatto looked toward the bed and seemed lost for a moment. "But that is the choice. The only choices we have in Haiti are bad choices."

"I guess you want the money for guns," said Mason, who'd been in-country long enough to guess. There were fantasts and rebels on every street corner.

"Certainly guns will have a role in this plan."

"You really think that's the solution?"

The mulatto laughed in his face. "Please, have you been drinking today?"

"Well." Like all the observers, Mason was touchy about appearing naive. "It took the army a couple of million to get Aristide out, and they already had the guns. You think you can beat the army with eighty thousand dollars?"

"You are American, so of course everything for you is a question of money. Honor and courage count for nothing, justice, *fear*—those people in the palace are cowards, okay? When the real fighting starts I assure you they will run. They will pack their blood money in their valises and run."

"Well, first you have to get the guns."

"First the paintings must be carried to Miami. You are an observer, this is the same as diplomatic immunity. If you take them no one will search your bags."

Mason laughed when he realized what was being asked, though the mulatto was right: the couple of times he'd flown out, customs had waved him through as soon as he flashed his credentials.

"What makes you think you can trust me?"

"Because you lost at chess."

"Maybe I'm just bad."

"Yes, it's true, you are very bad. But no one is that bad."

Mason began to see the backward logic of it, how in a weird way the chess games were the best guarantee. This was Haitian logic, logic from the mirror's other side, also proof of how desperate the mulatto had to be.

"You must," the mulatto said in a peremptory voice, and yet his eyes were as pleading as the sorriest beggar's. "For decency's sake, you must."

Mason turned as if to study the canvases, but he was thinking about the worst thing that had happened to him today. He'd been driving his truck through La Saline, the festering salt-marsh slum that stretched along the bay like a mile-wide lesion splitting the earth. At his approach, a thin woman with blank eyes had risen from her squat and held her baby toward him— begging, he thought at first, playing on his pity to shake loose some change, and then he saw the strange way the baby's head lolled back, the gray underpallor of its ropy skin. The knowledge came on like a slow electric shock: *dead*, that baby was dead, but the woman said nothing as he eased past. She simply held out her baby in silent witness, and Mason couldn't look at her, he'd had to turn away. With the embargo all the babies were dying now.

"Okay," he said, surprised at the steadiness of his voice. "I'll do it."

———

IT TURNED out that the mulatto wasn't really a doctor. He'd had two years of medical school at the University of Haiti before being expelled for leading an anti–Duvalier protest, "a stupid little thing," as he described it, he'd done much worse and never been caught. As far as Mason could tell, he eked out a living as a *dokté fey*, a kind of roving leaf doctor and cut-rate *houngan* who happened to have a grounding in Western medical science.

He'd cached stolen paintings all over town. Mason never knew when he'd turn up with the next batch, a bundle of wry Zephirins or ethereal Magloires to be added to the contraband in Mason's closet. But it was always after dark, almost always on the nights when the shooting was worst. He'd hear a single knock and crack open the door to find the mulatto standing there with a green trash bag, his hair zapping in all directions, eyes pinwheeling like a junkie's. Mason would give him a beer and they'd look at the paintings, the mulatto tutoring him on Haitian art and history.

"Something incredible is happening here," he might say as they sat in Mason's kitchen drinking beer, studying pictures of demons and zombies and saints. "Something vital, a rebirth of our true nature, which is shown so clearly in the miracle of Haitian art. '*Ici la renaissance*,' how strange that this was the name of the bar where Hyppolite was discovered. *Ici la renaissance*—it is true, a rebirth is coming in the world, a realization that the material is not enough, that we must bring equal discipline to the spiritual as well. And Haiti will be the center of this renaissance—this is the reason for my country, the only slave revolt to triumph in the history of the world. God wanted us free because He has a plan."

He could spiel in this elevated way for hours, forging text in his precision English like a professor delivering a formal lecture. If Mason kept popping beers, they'd eventually reach the point where paintings were scattered all over the house; then the mulatto would pace from room to room explaining tricks of perspective and coloration, giving historical reference to certain details. "But the dream is dying," he told Mason. "Those criminals in the palace are killing us. As long as they have the power, there will be no renaissance."

"They're tough," Mason agreed. "They've got all that drug money backing them up. The CIA too, probably."

"But they're cowards. Fate demands that we win."

He wouldn't tell Mason his name; he seemed to operate out of an inflated sense of the threat he posed to the regime. Some nights Mason was sure he'd fallen in with a lunatic, but then he'd think about the chess, or the reams of Baudelaire and Goethe the man could quote, or the cure he'd prescribed for Mason's touchy lower bowel—"You must drink a glass of rum with a whole clove of garlic." Mason did, and the next day found himself healed. If at times the mulatto seemed a little erratic, that might have something to do with being a genius, or the stress of a childhood spent in Duvalier's Haiti. One night Mason suggested a game of chess, but the mulatto refused.

"I don't play chess since I was a boy. The match with you, that was the first time in fifteen years."

"But you're brilliant!"

The mulatto shrugged. "I was third in the national championship the year I was twelve, and when my father found out he threw away my chess set and all my chess books. He said there is no place in the world for a Haitian chess player."

"But if you were good enough—"

"He said I would never be. And he was probably right, my father was a very smart man."

Mason hesitated; the past tense was always loaded in Haiti. "What was he?"

"Doctor. *Opthalmologiste.*"

Again Mason hesitated. "Under Duvalier most of the doctors left."

"My father stayed. He was an eminence. The last Haitian to deliver a paper to the International Congress of Opthalmology." He fell silent for a moment, seemed to gather himself. "If you were noted in your field, that could protect you, but this also meant that Duvalier perceived you as a threat. You could be famous but you could never slip, show that you were vulnerable in any way. One slip, and they'd take you." The mulatto paused again. "My father never slipped, but I think it made him a little crazy. He kept a gun in the house—we lived on the Champ de Mars, and at night we could hear the screams of people being tortured in the palace. One night he took this gun, my father, he held the bullets in his hand and he said to me: This bullet is for you. This one is for your brother. This one for your mama. And this one, for me. Because if they come they are not going to take us alive."

What could Mason say? Any sympathy or comfort he might try to offer would be false, because he'd lived such a stupid life. So he kept his mouth shut and listened, though on nights when the mulatto seemed especially bleak Mason insisted that he sleep on the couch. Sometimes he did; by morning he was always gone. Mason would straighten up the couch, eat his toast and mango jelly, then drive over to the office and get his detail for the day. Some days he drove around in his white 4Runner with the powder blue O.A.S. flag rippling in the breeze: "showing the blue" this was called, letting the de factos know that they were being watched, though after a time Mason realized this was a strategy that assumed some capacity for shame on their part. Other days he was assigned to the storefront office that took complaints of human-rights abuses. Not much happened on those days; it was common knowledge that the building was watched, and walk-in complaints were depressingly rare.

Once a week he'd drive over to Tintanyen and make a count of the bodies dumped out there, and often these were horrible days. Tintanyen was a wide plain of shitlike muck held together by a furze of rank, spraddling weeds. You entered through a pair of crumbling stone portals—the gates to hell, Mason couldn't help thinking—and stepped from your car into a pressure cooker, a blast of moist, dense, unwholesome heat, silent except for the whine of flies and mosquitoes. The mosquitoes at Tintanyen were like no others, an evil-looking, black-and-gray jacketed strain that seemed to relish the smell of insect repellent. Mason and his colleagues would tramp through the muck, sweating, swatting at the murderous bugs, hacking away the weeds until they came on a body, whatever mudcaked, hogtied, maggoty wretch the de factos had seen fit to drag out here. From the shade of the trees bordering the field a pack of feral dogs was always watching them, alert, anticipating a fresh meal. Those dogs, the Haitian driver once confided in a whisper, were de factos.

"The dogs?" Mason asked, wondering if his Creole had failed him again.

Sure, the driver explained. They were *zobop*, men who could change into animal form. Those dogs over there were de facto spies.

Mason nodded, squinting at the distant dogs. *M' tandé*, he said. I hear you.

Each week Mason photographed the bodies, drafted his report, and turned it over to his boss, the increasingly demoralized Argentine lawyer. They were all lawyers, all schooled in the authority of words, though as their words turned to dust a pall of impotence and futility settled over the mission. The weakest on the team gave themselves up to pleasure, taking advantage of their six thousand tax-free dollars a month to buy all the best art, eat at the best restaurants, and screw strings of beautiful, impoverished Haitian girls. The best lapsed into a simmering, low-grade depression: you had to watch, that was your job, to *observe* this disaster, a laughable, tragically self-defeating mission.

"What does it mean?" Mason asked the mulatto one night. They were sitting in Mason's kitchen during a blackout, studying Hyppolite's *Rêve Haitien* by candlelight. The picture was taped to the back of a kitchen chair, facing them like a mute third party to the conversation.

"It is a dream," said the mulatto, who was slumped in his chair with his legs thrown out. The first beer always went in a couple of gulps, and then he'd sag into himself like a heap of wet towels.

"Well, sure," said Mason, "*Haitian Dream,* you told me that." And the colors did have the blear look of a dream, the dull plasma blush of the alternating pinks, the toneless mattes of the blues and grays, a few muddy clots of sluggish brown. In the background a nude woman was sleeping on a wrought-iron bed. Closer in stood an impassive bourgeois couple, the man holding a book for the woman to read. The room was a homely, somewhat stilted jumble of curtains, tables and chairs, framed pictures and potted plants, while in the foreground two rats darted past a crouched cat. As in a dream the dissonance seemed pregnant, significant; the sum effect was vaguely menacing.

"I can't make heads or tails of it," said Mason. "And that thing there, by the bed," he continued, pointing out what looked like a small window casement between the bed and the rest of the room. "What's that?"

"That's part of the dream," said the mulatto, almost smiling.

"It looks like a window."

"Yes, I think you are right. Hyppolite puts this very strange object in the middle of his picture, I think he's trying to tell you something. He's telling you a way of looking at things."

On these nights the gunfire seemed diminished, a faint popping in their ears like a pressure change, though if the rounds were nearby the mulatto's eye would start twitching like a cornered mouse. Here is a man, Mason thought, who's living on air and inspiration, holding himself together by force of will. He was passionate about the art, equally passionate in his loathing for the people who'd ruined Haiti. You don't belong here, Mason wanted to tell him. You deserve a better place. But that was true of almost every Haitian he'd met.

"You know, my father thought Duvalier was retarded," the mulatto said one night. They were looking at a deadpan Obin portrait of the iconic first family, circa 1964; Papa Doc's eyes behind his glasses had the severe, hieratic stare of a Byzantine mosaic. "It's true," he continued, "they worked together treating yaws during the 1950s, every week they would ride out to Cayes to see patients. Duvalier would sit in the car wearing his suit and his hat and he would never say a word for six hours. He never drank, never ate, never relieved himself, he never said a word to anyone. Finally one day my father asked him, 'Doctor, is something the matter? You are always so quiet—have we displeased you? Are you angry?' And Duvalier turned to him very slowly and said, 'I am thinking about the country.' And of course, you know, he really was. Politically the man was a genius."

Mason shook his head. "He was just ruthless, that's all."

"But that's a form of genius too, ruthlessness. Very few of us are capable of anything so pure, but this was his forte, his true métier, all of the forms and applications of cruelty. The force of good always refers to something beyond ourselves—we negate ourselves to serve this higher thing. But evil is pure, evil serves only the self of ego, you are limited only by your own imagination. And this thing Duvalier conceived, this apparatus of evil, it's beautiful in the way of an elegant machine. An elegant machine that may never stop."

"I can see you've thought about it."

"Of course. In Haiti we are forced to think about it."

Which was true, Mason reflected as he made his rounds, Haiti shoved it in your face sure enough. During the day he'd drive through the livid streets and look for ways to make the crisis cohere. At night he'd lock his doors, pull down all the shades, spread twenty or thirty canvases around his house, and wander through the rooms, silently looking. After a while he'd go to the kitchen and fix a bowl of rice or noodles, and then he'd wander around some more, looking as he ate. It was like sliding a movie into the VCR, but this was better, he decided. This was real. With time the colors began to bleed into his head, and he'd find himself thinking about them during the day, projecting the artists' iridescent

greens and blues onto the streets outside his car, a way of seeing that seemed to charge the place with meaning. The style that
seemed so primitive and childish at first came to take on a sub-
versive quality, like a sly commentary on how the world had gone
the last five hundred years. In the flattened, skewed perspectives,
the faces' confrontational starkness, he began to get the sense of
a way of being that had survived behind the prevailing myths.
The direct vision, the thing itself without the softening filter of
technical tricks—the vision gradually became so real to him that
he felt himself clenching as he looked at the paintings, uneasy in
his skin, defensive. An obscure sophistication began to creep into
the art; they were painting things he only dimly sensed, but with
time he was starting to see a richness, a luxuriance of meaning
there that merged with the photos, never far from his mind, in the
mission's files of the Haitian dead.

Life here had the cracked logic of a dream, its own internal
rules. You looked at a picture and it wasn't like looking at a picture of a dream, it was passage into the current of the dream. And
for him the dream had its own peculiar twist, the dream of doing
something real, something worthy. A *blan*'s dream, perhaps all the
more fragile for that.

HE PACKED sixty-three canvases in a soft duffel bag and nobody laid
a hand on him. He had to face the ordeal all by himself, with not a
soul to turn to for comfort or advice. There hadn't even been the
consolation of seeing the mulatto before he left, the last sack of
paintings delivered by a kid with a scrawled one-word message: *Go.*
But Mason was white, and he had a good face; the whole thing was
so absurdly easy that he could have wept, though what he did do
on getting to his hotel room was switch on the cable to MTV and
bounce on the bed for a couple of minutes.

He'd gone from Haiti to the heart of chic South Beach. His
hotel rose off the sea in slabs of smooth concrete like a pastel-
colored birthday cake, but for a day Mason had to content

himself with watching the water from his balcony. When the call finally came, he gathered up the duffel bag and walked three blocks to The Magritte, an even sleeker hotel where the men were older, the women younger, the air of corruption palpable. Well, he thought, here's a nice place to be arrested, but in the room there was only the Frenchman and a silent, vaguely Asian type whose eyes never left Mason's face. There were no personal items about; they might have taken the room for an hour. Mason had to sit and watch while the Frenchman laid the paintings across the bed like so many bolts of industrial cloth. He was brisk, cordial, condescending, a younger man than Mason expected, with a broad, coarse face only slightly refined by a prissy mustache and goatee.

They wore dark, elegant suits. Their hair was smooth. They looked fit in the way of people who obsess over workouts and what they eat. New wave gangsters—Mason sensed a sucking emptiness in them, the void that comes of total self-absorption. It made him sick to hand the paintings over to these people.

"And the Bigaud?" the Frenchman asked in English, *"The Bathers?"*

"He couldn't get it."

A quick grimace, then a fond, forgiving smile; he was gracious in the way of a pro stuck with amateurs. He acted like a gentleman, but he wasn't—it was only since he'd lived in Haiti that Mason found himself thinking this way. Only since he'd met the first true gentleman of his life.

They gave him the money in a blue nylon bag, and he made them wait while he counted it. Later, perversely, he would think of this as the bravest thing he'd ever done, how he endured their stares and bemused sarcasm while he counted out the money. When it was finished and he'd zipped up the nylon bag, the Frenchman asked:

"What will you do now?"

Mason was puzzled, then adamant. "I'm going back, of course. I have to give him the money."

The Frenchman's cool failed him for the briefest moment. He seemed surprised, and in the silence Mason wondered. Is my honor so strange? And then the smile reengaged, with real warmth, it seemed, but Mason saw that he was being mocked.

"Yes, absolutely. They're all waiting on you."

AT THE house in Pacot he stuffed the cash up a ten-dollar voodoo drum he'd bought months earlier at the Iron Market. Then he settled in and went about his business, staying up late at night to listen for the door, going down to the park in the afternoons to take his daily drubbing at chess. He realized he was good at this kind of life, the lie of carrying on his normal routine while he kept himself primed for the tap on the back, the look from the stranger that said: *Come. Meet me.* Late at night he could hear machine guns chewing up the slums, a faint ghost-sound, the fear a kind of haunting. During the day he would look at the mountains above like huge green waves towering over the city, and he'd think, Let it come. Let it all crash down.

He missed the paintings with the same kind of visceral ache as he'd missed certain women who'd meant something to him. He missed the mulatto in a way that went beyond words, the man whose aura of purpose burned hot enough to fire even a cautious *blan*. My friend, Mason thought a hundred times a day, the phrase so constant that it might have been a prayer. My very good friend whose name I don't even know. The air felt heavy, thick with delay and anticipation, though the slow sway and bob of palm fronds seemed to counsel patience. Finally, one evening, he'd waited long enough. He carried his chess set past the park into the Salomon quarter, an awful risk that the mulatto would surely scold him for, but he couldn't help himself. He had trouble finding the street and had almost given up when it appeared in the ashy half-light of dusk. He turned and walked along it with a casual air. Just a glance at the house was all he needed: the green walls streaked with soot, the charred stumps of the trees, the blackened, empty windows like hollow eye sockets. Just a glance, and he never broke the swing of his stride, never lost the easy rhythm of his breathing.

The next day he went back with his truck and driver, poking around under the guise of official business. He knocked on doors and explained himself; the neighbors shuffled their feet, picked at their hands, glanced up and down the block as they talked. Lots of shooting one night, they said, people shooting in the street. Bombs, and then the fire, though no one actually saw it—they'd rolled under their beds at the first shot. The next morning they'd edged outside to find the house this way, and no one had gone near it since.

When did it happen? Mason asked, but now the elastic Haitian sense of time came into play. Three days ago, one man said. Another said a month. Back at the office Mason went through the daily logs and found an incident dated ten days earlier, the day he'd left for Miami. The text of the report filled a quarter of a page. They had the street name wrong but otherwise it fit, the shooting and explosions and ensuing fire, then the de factos' response to the O.A.S. inquiry. Seven charred bodies had been recovered from the house, none identified, all interred by the government. The incident was characterized as gang activity, "probably drug-related." Mason winced at the words. The line had grown to be a bad joke around the mission, the explanation they almost always got whenever a group of *inconnus* turned up dead.

Still, Mason hoped. He made his rounds each day through the stinking streets, past old barricades and army patrols and starving street kids with their furied stares, and every afternoon he wrote his report and watched storms roll down the mountains like the hand of God. Finally he felt it one day as he was driving home, he just knew: his glorious friend was dead. It caught him after weeks of silence, a moment when the cumulative weight of days reached in and pushed all the air from his chest, and when he breathed in again, there was just no hope. False, small, shabby, that's how it seemed now, the truth washing through him like sickness—he'd been a fool to think they'd had any kind of chance. Inside the house he got as far as the den, where he took the voodoo drum from its place on the shelf and sat on the floor. Wearily, slowly, he rocked the drum over and reached inside. The money was there, all that latent power stuffed inside the shaft—something waiting to be born, something sleeping. He cradled the unformed dream in his hands and wondered who to give it to.

THE GIRL ON THE PLANE

Mary Gaitskill

Mary Gaitskill is the author of the story collections *Bad Behavior* and *Because They Wanted To* and the novels *Two Girls Fat and Thin* and *Veronica*, a National Book Award finalist.

John Morton came down the aisle of the plane, banging his luggage into people's knees and sweating angrily under his suit. He had just run through the corridors of the airport, cursing and struggling with his luggage, slipping and flailing in front of the vapid brat at the seat assignment desk. Too winded to speak, he thrust his ticket at the boy and readjusted his luggage in his sticky hands. "You're a little late for a seat assignment," said the kid snottily. "I hope you can get on board before it pulls away."

He took his boarding pass and said, "Thanks, you little prick." The boy's discomfiture was made more obvious by his pretense of hauteur; it both soothed and fed John's anger.

At least he was able to stuff his bags into the compartment above the first seat he found. He sat down, grunting territorially, and his body slowly eased into a normal dull pulse and ebb. He looked at his watch; desk attendant to the contrary, the plane was sitting stupidly still, twenty minutes after takeoff time. He had the pleasing fantasy of punching the little bastard's face.

He was always just barely making his flight. His wife had read in one of her magazines that habitual lateness meant lack of interest in life or depression or something. Well, who could blame him for lack of interest in the crap he was dealing with?

He glanced at the guy a seat away from him on the left, an alcoholic-looking old shark in an expensive suit, who sat staring fixedly at a magazine photograph of a grinning blonde in a white jumpsuit. The plane continued to sit there, while stewardesses fiddled with compartments and women rolled up and down the aisles on trips to the bathroom. They were even boarding a passenger; a woman had just entered, flushed and vigorously banging along the aisle with her luggage. She was very pretty, and he watched her, his body still feebly sending off alarm signals in response to its forced run.

"Hi," she said. "I'm in the middle there."

"By all means." The force of his anger entered his magnanimity and swelled it hugely; he pinched his ankles together to let her by. She put her bag under the seat in front of her, sat down, and rested her booted feet on its pale leather. The old shark by the window glanced appraisingly at her breasts through her open coat. He looked up at her face and made smile movements. The stewardess did her parody of a suffocating person reaching for an air mask, the pilot mumbled, the plane prepared to assert its unnatural presence in nature.

"They said I'd missed my flight by fifteen minutes," she said. "But I knew I'd make it. They're never on time." Her voice was unexpectedly small, with a rough, gravelly undertone that was seedy and schoolgirlish at once.

"It's bullshit," he said. "Well, what can you do?" She had large hazel eyes.

She smiled a tight, rueful smile that he associated with women who'd been fucked too many times and which he found sexy. She cuddled more deeply into her seat, produced a *People* magazine, and intently read it. He liked her profile—which was an interesting combination of soft (forehead, chin) and sharp (nose, cheekbones)— her shoulder-length, pale-brown hair, and her soft Mediterranean skin. He liked the coarse quality in the subtle downturn of her lips, and the heavy way her lids sat on her eyes. She was older than he'd originally thought, probably in her early thirties.

Who did she remind him of? A girl from a long time ago, an older version of some date or crush or screw. Or love, he thought gamely.

The pilot said they would be leaving the ground shortly. She was now reading a feature that appeared to be about the wedding of two people who had AIDS. He thought of his wife, at home in Minneapolis, at the stove poking at something, in the living room reading, the fuzzy pink of her favorite sweater. The plane charged and tore a hole in the air.

He reviewed his mental file of girls he'd known before his wife and paused at the memory of Andrea, the girl who'd made an ass-hole of him. It had been twelve years, and only now could he say that phrase to himself, the only phrase that accurately described the situation. With stale resentment, he regarded her: a pale, long-legged thing with huge gray eyes, a small mouth, long red hair, and the helpless manner of a pampered pet let loose in the wilderness.

The woman next to him was hurriedly flipping the pages of *People*, presumably looking for something as engrossing as the AIDS wedding. When she didn't find it, she closed the magazine and turned to him in a way that invited conversation.

She said she'd lived in L.A. for eight years and that she liked it, even though it was "gross."

"I've never been to L.A.," he said. "I picture it being like *L.A. Law*. Is it like that?"

"I don't know. I've never seen *L.A. Law*. I don't watch TV. I don't own one."

He had never known a person who didn't own a TV, not even an old high school friend who lived in a slum and got food stamps. "You must read the newspapers a lot."

"No. I don't read them much at all."

He was incredulous. "How do you connect with the rest of the world? How do you know anything?"

"I'm part of the world. I know a lot of things."

He expelled a snort of laughter. "That's an awfully small perspective you've got there."

She shrugged and turned her head, and he was sorry he'd been rude. He glanced at her profile to read her expression and—of course; she reminded him of Patty LaForge, poor Patty.

HE HAD met Patty at Meadow Community College in Coate, Minnesota. He was in his last semester; she had just entered. They worked in the student union cafeteria, preparing, serving, and snacking on denatured food. She was a slim, curvy person with dark-blond hair, hazel eyes, and remarkable legs and hips. Her beauty was spoiled by the aggressive resignation that held her features in a fixed position and made all her expressions stiff. Her full mouth had a bitter downturn, and her voice was quick, low, self-deprecating, and sarcastic. She presented her beautiful body statically, as if it were a shield, and the effort of this presentation seemed to be the source of her animation.

Most of the people he knew at Meadow were kids he'd gone to high school and even junior high with. They still lived at home and still drove their cars around together at night, drank in the small bars of Coate, adventured in Minneapolis, and made love to each other. This late-adolescent camaraderie gave their time at Meadow a fraught emotional quality that was like the shimmering fullness of a bead of water before it falls. They were all about to scatter and become different from one another, and this made them exult in their closeness and alikeness.

THE WOMAN on the plane was flying to Kentucky to visit her parents and stopping over in Cincinnati.

"Did you grow up in Kentucky?" he asked. He imagined her as a big-eyed child in a cotton shift, playing in some dusty, sunny alley, some rural Kentucky-like place. Funny she had grown up to be this wan little bun with too much makeup in black creases under her eyes.

"No. I was born there, but I grew up mostly in Minnesota, near Minneapolis."

He turned away, registered the little shock of coincidence, and turned back. The situation compounded: she had gone to Redford Community College in Thorold, a suburb much like Coate. She had grown up in Thorold, like Patty. The only reason Patty had gone to Meadow was that Redford didn't exist yet.

He felt a surge of commonality. He imagined that she had experienced his adolescence, and this made him experience it for a moment. He had loved walking the small, neat walkways of the campus through the stiffly banked hedges of snow and harsh morning austerity, entering the close, food-smelling student union with the hard winter air popping off his skin. He would see his friends standing in a conspiratorial huddle, warming their hands on cheap cups of coffee; he always remembered the face of a particular girl, Layla, turning to greet him, looking over her frail sloped shoulder, her hair a bunched dark tangle, her round eyes ringed with green pencil, her perfectly ordinary face compelling in its configurations of girlish curiosity, maternal license, sexual knowledge, forgiveness, and femininity. A familiar mystery he had meant to explore sometime and never did, except when he grabbed her butt at a Halloween party and she smiled like a mother of four who worked as a porn model on the side. He loved driving with his friends to the Red Owl to buy alcohol and bagged salty snacks, which they consumed as they drove around Coate playing the tape deck and yelling at each other, the beautiful ordinary landscape unpeeling before them, revealing the essential strangeness of its shadows and night movements. He loved driving with girls to the deserted housing development they called "the Spot," loved the blurred memories of the girls in the back seat with their naked legs curled up to their chests, their shirts bunched about their necks, their eyes wide with ardor and alcohol, beer and potato chips spilled on the floor of the car, the tape deck singing of love and triumph. He getting out of the car for a triumphant piss, while the girl daintily replaced her pants.

In the morning his mother would make him "cowboy eggs," eggs fried on top of bacon, and he would go through the cold to Meadow, to sit in a fluorescent classroom and dream.

"DID YOU like growing up in that area?" she asked.

"Like it? It was the greatest time of my life." Some extremity in his voice made her look away, and as she did, he looked more fully at her profile. She didn't look that much like Patty; she wasn't even blond. But the small physical resemblance was augmented by a less tangible affinity, a telling similarity of speech and movement.

PATTY BELONGED to a different crowd at Meadow. They were rougher than the Coate people, but the two groups were friendly. Patty was a strange, still presence within her group, with her hip thrust out and a cigarette always bleeding smoke from her hand. She was loose even by seventies standards; she had a dirty sense of humor, and she wore pants so tight you could see the swollen outline of her genitals. She was also shy. When she talked she pawed the ground with her foot and pulled her hair over her mouth; she looked away from you and then snuck a look back to see what you thought of her. She was accepted by the Thorold people the way you accept what you've always known. The stiffness of her face and body contradicting her loose reputation, her coarse language expressed in her timid voice and shy manners, her beauty and her ordinariness, all gave her a disconnected sexiness that was aggravating.

But he liked her. They were often a team at work, and he enjoyed having her next to him, her golden-haired arms plunged in greasy black dishwater or flecked with garbage as she plucked silverware from vile plates on their way to the dishwasher. She spooned out quivering red Jell-O or drew long bland snakes of soft ice cream from the stainless-steel machine, she smoked, wiped her nose, and muttered about a fight with her mother or a bad date. Her movements were resigned and bitter, yet her eyes and her nasty humor peeked impishly from under this weight. There

was something pleasing in this combination, something congru-
ent with her spoiled beauty.

It was a long time before he realized she had a crush on him. All
her conversation was braided together with a fly strip of different
boys she had been with or was involved with, and she talked of all of
them with the same tone of fondness and resentment. He thought
nothing of it when she followed him outside to the field behind the
union, where they would walk along the narrow wet ditch, smoking pot and talking. It was early spring; dark, naked trees pressed
intensely against the horizon, wet weeds clung to their jeans, and
her small voice bobbed assertively on the vibrant air. The cold wind
gave her lips a swollen raw look and made her young skin grainy
and bleached. "So why do you let him treat you like that?" "Ah, I get
back at him. It's not really him, you know, I'm just fixated on him.
I'm working out something through him. Besides, he's a great lay."
He never noticed how often she came up behind him to walk him to
class or sat on the edge of his chair as he lounged in the union. Then
one day she missed work, and a buddy of his said, "Hey, where's
your little puppy dog today?" and he knew.

"DID YOU like Thorold?" he asked the girl next to him.

"No, I didn't." She turned toward him, her face a staccato burst
of candor. "I didn't know what I was doing, and I was a practicing
alcoholic. I kept trying to fit in and I couldn't."

"That doesn't sound good." He smiled. How like Patty to answer a polite question from a stranger with this emotional nakedness, this urgent excess of information. She was always doing that,
especially after the job at the cafeteria ended. He'd see her in a
hallway or the union lounge, where normal life was happening all
around them, and she'd swoop into a compressed communication,
intently twining her hair around her finger as she quickly muttered
that she'd had the strangest dream about this guy David, in which a
nuclear war was going on, and he, John, was in it too, and—

———

"WHAT DID you do after Redford?" he asked the girl next to him.

"Screwed around, basically. I went to New York pretty soon after that and did the same things I was doing in Thorold. Except I was trying to be a singer."

"Yeah?" He felt buoyed by her ambition. He pictured her in a tight black dress, lips parted, eyes closed, bathed in cheap, sexy stage light. "Didja ever do anything with it?"

"Not much." She abruptly changed expression, as though she'd just remembered not to put herself down. "Well, some stuff. I had a good band once, we played the club circuit in L.A. for a while six years ago." She paused. "But I'm mostly a paralegal now."

"Well, that's not bad, either. Do you ever sing now?"

"I haven't for a long time. But I was thinking of trying again." Just like Patty, she looked away and quickly looked back as if to check his reaction. "I've been auditioning. Even though . . . I don't know."

"It sounds great to me," he said. "At least you're trying. It sounds better than what I do." His self-deprecation annoyed him, and he bulled his way through an explanation of what he did, making it sound more interesting than selling software.

A stewardess with a small pink face asked if they'd like anything to drink, and he ordered two little bottles of Jack Daniel's. Patty's shadow had a compressed can of orange juice and an unsavory packet of nuts; their silent companion by the window had vodka straight. He thought of asking her if she was married, but he bet the answer was no, and he didn't want to make her admit her loneliness. Of course, not every single person was lonely, but he guessed that she was. She seemed in need of comfort and care, like a stray animal that gets fed by various kindly people but never held.

"Will you get some mothering while you're at home?" he asked.

"Oh, yes. My mother will make things I like to eat and . . . stuff like that."

He thought of telling her that she reminded him of someone he'd known in Coate, but he didn't. He sat silently, knocking back his whiskey and watching her roll a greasy peanut between two fingers.

OUT IN the field, they were sitting on a fallen branch, sharing a wet stub of pot. "I don't usually say stuff like this," said Patty. "I know you think I do, because of the way I talk, but I don't. But I'm really attracted to you, John." The wind blew a piece of hair across her cheek, and its texture contrasted acutely with her cold-bleached skin.

"Yeah, I was beginning to notice."

"I guess it was kind of obvious, huh?" She looked down and drew her curtain of hair. "And I've been getting these mixed signals from you. I can't tell if you're attracted to me or not." She paused. "But I guess you're not, huh?"

Her humility embarrassed and touched him. "Well, I am attracted to you. Sort of. I mean, you're beautiful and everything. I'm just not attracted enough to do anything. Besides, there's Susan."

"Oh. I thought you didn't like her that much." She sniffed and dropped the roach on the raw grass; her lipstick had congealed into little chapped bumps on her lower lip. "Well, I'm really disappointed. I thought you liked me."

"I do like you, Patty."

"You know what I meant." Pause. "I'm more attracted to you than I've been to anybody for two years. Since Paul."

A flattered giggle escaped him.

"Well, I hope we can be friends," she said. "We can still talk and stuff, can't we?"

"PATTY LAFORGE? I wouldn't touch her, man. The smell alone."

He was driving around with a carload of drunk boys who were filled with a tangle of goodwill and aggression.

"Ah, LaForge is okay."

He was indignant for Patty, but he laughed anyway.

"WERE YOU really an alcoholic when you lived in Thorold?" he asked.

"I still am, I just don't drink now. But then I did. Yeah."

He had stepped into a conversation that had looked nice and solid, and his foot had gone through the floor and into the basement. But he couldn't stop. "I guess I drank too much then too. But it wasn't a problem. We just had a lot of fun."

She smiled with tight, terse mystery.

"How come you told me that about yourself? It seems kind of personal." He attached his gaze to hers as he said this; sometimes women said personal things to you as a way of coming on.

But instead of becoming soft and encouraging, her expression turned proper and institutional, like a kid about to recite. "If I'm going to admit it to other alcoholics in the program, I can admit it in regular life too. It humbles you, sort of."

What a bunch of shit, he thought.

HE WAS drinking with some guys at the Winners Circle, a rough pickup bar, when suddenly Patty walked up to him, really drunk.

"John," she gasped. "John, John, John." She lurched at him and attached her nail-bitten little claws to his jacket. "John, this guy over there really wants to fuck me, and I was going to go with him, but I don't want him, I want you, I want you." Her voice wrinkled into a squeak, her face looked like you could smear it with your hand.

"Patty," he mumbled, "you're drunk."

"That's not why. I always feel like this." Her nose and eyelashes and lips touched his cheek in an alcoholic caress. "Just let me kiss you. Just hold me."

He put his hands on her shoulders. "C'mon, stop it."

"It doesn't have to mean anything. You don't have to love me. I love you enough for both of us."

He felt the presence of his smirking friends. "Patty, these guys are laughing at you. I'll see you later." He tried to push her away.

"I don't care. I love you, John. I mean it." She pressed her taut body against his, one sweaty hand under his shirt, and arched her neck until he could see the small veins and bones. "Please. Just be with me. Please." Her hand stroked him, groped between his legs. He took her shoulders and shoved her harder than he had meant to. She staggered back, fell against a table, knocked down a chair, and almost fell again. She straightened and looked at him as if she'd known him and hated him all her life.

HE LEANED back in his seat and closed his eyes, an overweight, prematurely balding salesman getting drunk on an airplane.

"Look at the clouds," said the girl next to him. "Aren't they beautiful?"

He opened his eyes and silently looked.

Shrewdness glimmered under her gaze.

"What's your name?" he asked.

"Lorraine."

"I'm John." He extended his hand and she took it, her eyes unreadable, her hand exuding sweet feminine sweat.

"Why do you want to talk about your alcoholism publicly? I mean, if nobody asks or anything?"

Her eyes were steadfast, but her body was hesitant. "Well, I didn't have to just now. It's just the first thing I thought of when you asked me about Thorold. In general, it's to remind me. It's easy to bullshit yourself that you don't have a problem."

He thought of the rows and rows of people in swivel chairs on talk-show stages, admitting their problems. Wife beaters, child abusers, dominatrixes, porn stars. In the past it probably was a humbling experience to stand up and tell people you were an alcoholic. Now it was just something else to talk about. He remembered Patty tottering through a crowded party on smudged red high heels, bragging about what great blow jobs she gave. Some girl rolled her eyes and said, "Oh, no, not again." Patty disappeared into a bedroom with a bottle of vodka and Jack Spannos.

He remembered a conversation with his wife before he married her, a conversation about his bachelor party. "It was no women allowed," he'd told her. "Unless they wanted to give blow jobs."

"Couldn't they just jump naked out of a cake?" she asked.

"Nope. Blow jobs for everybody."

They were at a festive restaurant, drinking margaritas. Nervously, she touched her tiny straws. "Wouldn't that be embarrassing? In front of each other? I can't imagine Henry doing that in front of you all."

He smiled at the mention of his shy friend in this context. "Yeah," he said. "It probably would be embarrassing. Group sex is for teenagers."

Her face rose away from her glass in a kind of excited alarm, her lips parted. "You had group sex when you were a teenager?"

"Oh. Not really. Just a gang bang once."

She looked like an antelope testing the wind with its nose in the air, ready to fly. "It wasn't rape," she said.

"Oh, no, no." Her body relaxed and released a warm, sensual curiosity, like a cat against his leg. "The girl liked it."

"Are you sure?"

"Yeah. She liked having sex with a lot of guys. We all knew her, she knew us."

He felt her shiver inwardly, shocked and fascinated by this dangerous pack-animal aspect of his masculinity.

"What was it like?" she asked.

He shrugged. "It was a good time with the guys. It was a bunch of guys standing around in their socks and underwear."

SOME KID he didn't know walked up and put his arm around him while he was talking to a girl named Chrissie. The kid's eyes were boyish and drunkenly enthusiastic, his face heavy and porous. He whispered something about Patty in John's ear and said, "C'mon."

The girl's expression subtly withdrew.

"What?" said John.

"Come on," said the kid.

"Bye-bye," said Chrissie, with a gingerly wag of her fingers.

He followed the guy through the room, seizing glimpses of hips and tits sheathed in bright, cheap cloth, girls doing wiggly dances with guys who jogged helplessly from foot to foot, holding their chests proudly aloof from their lower bodies. On the TV, a pretty girl gyrated in her black bra, sending a clean bolt of sex into the room. The music made his organs want to leap in and out of his body in time. His friends were all around him.

A door opened and closed behind him, muffling the music. The kid who'd brought him in sat in an armchair, smiling. Patty lay on a bed with her skirt pulled up to her waist and a guy with his pants down straddling her face. Without knowing why, he laughed. Patty twisted her legs about and bucked slightly. For a moment he felt frightened that this was against her will—but no, she would have screamed. He recognized the boy on her as Pete Kopiekin, who was thrusting his flat, hairy butt in the same dogged, earnest, woeful manner with which he played football. His heart was pounding.

Kopiekin got off her and the other guy got on; between them he saw her chin sticking up from her sprawled body, pivoting to and fro on her neck while she muttered and groped blindly up and down her body. Kopiekin opened the door to leave, and a fist of music punched the room. John's body jumped in shocked response, and the door shut. The guy on top of Patty was talking to her; to John's amazement, he seemed to be using love words. "You're so beautiful, baby." He saw Patty's hips moving. She wasn't being raped, he thought. When the guy finished, he stood and poured the rest of his beer in her face.

"Hey," said John lamely, "hey."

"Oh, man, don't tell me that. I've known her a long time."

When the guy left, he thought of wiping her face, but he didn't. She sighed fitfully and rolled on her side, as if there was something under the mattress, disturbing her sleep, but she was too tired to remove it. His thoughts spiraled inward, and he let them be chopped up by muffled guitar chords. He sat awhile, watching guys swarm over Patty and talking to the ones waiting. Music sliced in and out of the room. Then some guy wanted to pour maple syrup on her, and John said, "No, I didn't go yet." He sat on the bed and, for the first time, looked at her, expecting to see the sheepish bitter look he knew. He didn't recognize her. Her rigid face was weirdly slack; her eyes fluttered open, rolled, and closed; a mix of half-formed expressions flew across her face like swarming ghosts. "Patty," he said, "hey." He shook her shoulder. Her eyes opened, her gaze raked his face. He saw tenderness, he thought. He lay on her and tried to embrace her. Her body was leaden and floppy. She muttered and moved, but in ways he didn't understand. He massaged her breasts; they felt like they could come off and she wouldn't notice.

He lay there, supporting himself on his elbows, and felt the deep breath in her lower body meeting his own breath. Subtly, he felt her come to life. She lifted her head and said something; he heard his name. He kissed her on the lips. Her tongue touched his, gently, her sleeping hands woke. He held her and stroked her pale, beautiful face.

He got up in such a good mood that he slapped the guy coming in with the maple syrup a high five, something he thought was stupid and usually never did.

The next time he saw Patty was at a Foreigner concert in Minneapolis; he saw her holding hands with Pete Kopiekin.

Well, now she could probably be on a talk show about date rape. It was a confusing thing. She may have wanted to kiss him or to give Jack Spannos a blow job, but she probably didn't want maple syrup poured on her. Really, though, if you were going to get blind drunk and let everybody fuck you, you had to expect some nasty stuff. On the talk shows they always said it was low self-esteem that made them do it. If he had low self-esteem, he sure wouldn't try to cure it like that. His eyes rested on Lorraine's hands; she was wadding the empty nut package and stuffing it in her empty plastic cup.

"Hey," he said, "what did you mean when you said you kept trying to fit in and you couldn't? When you were in Thorold?"

"Oh, you know." She seemed impatient. "Acting the part of the pretty, sexy girl."

"When in fact you were not a pretty, sexy girl?"

She started to smile, then caught his expression and gestured dismissively. "It was complicated."

It was seductive, the way she drew him in and then shut him out. She picked up her magazine again. Her slight arm movement released a tiny cloud of sweat and deodorant, which evaporated as soon as he inhaled it. He breathed in deeply, hoping to smell her again. Sunlight pressed in with viral intensity and exaggerated the lovely contours of her face, the fine lines, the stray cosmetic flecks, the marvelous profusion of her pores. He thought of the stories he'd read in sex magazines about strangers on airplanes having sex in the bathroom or masturbating each other under blankets.

The stewardess made a sweep with a gaping white garbage bag and cleared their trays of bottles and cups.

She put down the magazine. "You've probably had the same experience yourself," she said. Her face was curiously determined, as if it were very important that she make herself understood. "I mean doing stuff for other people's expectations or just to feel you have a social identity because you're so convinced who you are isn't right."

"You mean low self-esteem?"

"Well, yeah, but more than that." He sensed her inner tension and felt an empathic twitch.

"It's just that you get so many projections onto yourself of who and what you're supposed to be that if you don't have a strong support system it's hard to process it."

"Yeah," he said. "I know what you mean. I've had that experience. I don't know how you can't have it when you're young. There's so much crap in the world." He felt embarrassed, but he kept talking, wanting to tell her something about himself, to return her candor. "I've done lots of things I wish I hadn't done, I've made mistakes. But you can't let it rule your life."

She smiled again, with her mouth only. "Once, a few years ago, my father asked me what I believed to be the worst mistakes in my life. This is how he thinks, this is his favorite kind of question. Anyway, it was really hard to say, because I don't know from this vantage point what would've happened if I'd done otherwise in most situations. Finally, I came up with two things: my relationship with this guy named Jerry and the time I turned down an offer to work with this really awful band that became famous. He was totally bewildered. He was expecting me to say 'dropping out of college.'"

"You didn't make a mistake dropping out of college." The vehemence in his voice almost made him blush; then nameless urgency swelled forth and quelled embarrassment. "That wasn't a mistake," he repeated.

"Well, yeah, I know."

"Excuse me." The silent business shark to their left rose in majestic self-containment and moved awkwardly past their knees, looking at John with pointed irony as he did so. Fuck you, thought John.

"And about that relationship," he went on. "That wasn't your loss. It was his." He had meant these words to sound light and playfully gallant, but they had the awful intensity of a maudlin personal confession. He reached out to gently pat her hand, to reassure her that he wasn't a nut, but instead he grabbed it and held it. "If you want to talk about mistakes—shit, I raped somebody. Somebody I liked."

Their gaze met in a conflagration of reaction. She was so close he could smell her sweating, but at the speed of light she was falling away, deep into herself where he couldn't follow. She was struggling to free her hand.

"No," he said, "it wasn't a real rape. It was what you were talking about—it was complicated."

She wrenched her hand free and held it protectively close to her chest. "Don't touch me again." She turned tautly forward. He imagined her heart beating in alarm. His body felt so stiff he could barely feel his own heart. Furiously, he wondered if the people around them had heard any of this. Staring ahead of him, he hissed, "Do you think I was dying to hear about your alcoholism? You were the one who started this crazy conversation."

He felt her consider this. "It's not the same thing," she hissed back.

"But it wasn't really a rape." He struggled to say what it was. He recalled Patty that night at the Winners Circle, her neck arched and exposed, her feelings extended and flailing the air where she expected his feelings to be.

"You don't understand," he finished lamely.

She was silent. He thought he dimly felt her body relax, emitting some possibility of forgiveness. But he couldn't tell. He closed his eyes. He thought of Patty's splayed body, her half-conscious kiss. He thought of his wife, her compact scrappy body, her tough-looking flat nose and chipped nail polish, her smile, her smell, her embrace, which was both soft and fierce. He imagined the hotel room he would sleep in tonight, its stifling grid of rectangles, oblongs, and windows that wouldn't open. He leaned back and closed his eyes.

The pilot roused him with a command to fasten his seat belt. He sat up and blinked. Nothing had changed. The woman at his side was sitting slightly hunched, with her hands resolutely clasped.

"God, I'll be glad when we're on the ground," he said.

She sniffed in reply.

They descended, ears popping. They landed with a flurry of baggage-grabbing. He stood, bumped his head, and tried to get into the aisle to escape, but it was too crowded. He sat back down. Not being able to leave made him feel that he had to say something else. "Look, don't be upset. What I said came out wrong."

"I don't want to talk."

Neither do I, he thought. But he felt disoriented and depressed amid these shifting, lunging, grabbing people from all over the country, who had been in his life for hours and were now about to disappear, taking their personal items and habits with them.

"Excuse me." She butted her way past him and into the aisle. He watched a round, vulnerable piece of her head move between the obstructions of shoulders and arms. She glanced backward, possibly to see if he was going to try to follow her. The sideways movement of her hazel iris prickled him. They burst from the plane and scattered, people picking up speed as they bore down on their destination. He caught up with her as they entered the terminal. "I'm sorry," he said to the back of her head. She moved farther away, into memory and beyond.

THE PAPERHANGER

William Gay

William Gay lives in Hohenwald, Tennessee. He is the author of the novels *The Long Home* and *Provinces of Night* and the short story collection *I Hate To See That Evening Sun Go Down*.

The vanishing of the doctor's wife's child in broad daylight was an event so cataclysmic that it forever divided time into the then and the now, the before and the after. In later years, fortified with a pitcher of silica-dry vodka martinis, she had cause to replay the events preceding the disappearance. They were tawdry and banal but in retrospect freighted with menace, a foreshadowing of what was to come, like a footman or a fool preceding a king into a room.

She had been quarreling with the paperhanger. Her four-year-old daughter, Zeineb, was standing directly behind the paperhanger where he knelt smoothing air bubbles out with a wide plastic trowel. Zeineb had her fingers in the paperhanger's hair. The paperhanger's hair was shoulder length and the color of flax and the child was delighted with it. The paperhanger was accustomed to her doing this and he did not even turn around. He just went on with his work. His arms were smooth and brown and corded with muscle and in the light that fell upon the paperhanger through stained-glass panels the doctor's wife could see that they were lightly downed with fine golden hair. She studied these arms bemusedly while she formulated her thoughts.

You tell me so much a roll, she said. The doctor's wife was from Pakistan and her speech was still heavily accented. I do not know single-bolt rolls and double-bolt rolls. You tell me double-bolt price but you are installing single-bolt rolls. My friend has told me. It is cost me perhaps twice as much.

The paperhanger, still on his knees, turned. He smiled up at her. He had pale blue eyes. I did tell you so much a roll, he said. You bought the rolls.

The child, not yet vanished, was watching the paperhanger's eyes. She was a scaled-down clone of the mother, the mother viewed through the wrong end of a telescope, and the paperhanger suspected that as she grew neither her features nor her expression would alter, she would just grow larger, like something being aired up with a hand pump.

And you are leave lumps, the doctor's wife said, gesturing at the wall.

I do not leave lumps, the paperhanger said. You've seen my work before. These are not lumps. The paper is wet. The paste is wet. Everything will shrink down and flatten out. He smiled again. He had clean even teeth. And besides, he said, I gave you my special cockteaser rate. I don't know what you're complaining about.

Her mouth worked convulsively. She looked for a moment as if he'd slapped her. When words did come they came in a fine spray of spit. You are trash, she said. You are scum.

Hands on knees, he was pushing erect, the girl's dark fingers trailing out of his hair. Don't call me trash, he said, as if it were perfectly all right to call him scum, but he was already talking to her back. She had whirled on her heels and went twisting her hips through an arched doorway into the cathedraled living room. The paperhanger looked down at the child. Her face glowed with a strange constrained glee, as if she and the paperhanger shared some secret the rest of the world hadn't caught on to yet.

In the living room the builder was supervising the installation of a chandelier that depended from the vaulted ceiling by a long golden chain. The builder was a short bearded man dancing about, showing her the features of the chandelier, smiling obsequiously. She gave him a flat angry look. She waved a dismissive hand toward the ceiling. Whatever, she said.

She went out the front door onto the porch and down a makeshift walkway of two-by-tens into the front yard where her car was parked. The car was a silver-gray Mercedes her husband had given her for their anniversary. When she cranked the engine its idle was scarcely perceptible.

She powered down the window. Zeineb, she called. Across the razed earth of the unlandscaped yard a man in a grease-stained T-shirt was booming down the chains securing a backhoe to a lowboy hooked to a gravel truck. The sun was low in the west and bloodred behind this tableau and man and tractor looked flat and dimensionless as something decorative stamped from tin. She blew the horn. The man turned, raised an arm as if she'd signaled him.

Zeineb, she called again.

She got out of the car and started impatiently up the walkway. Behind her the gravel truck started, and truck and backhoe pulled out of the drive and down toward the road.

The paperhanger was stowing away his T square and trowels in his wooden toolbox. Where is Zeineb? the doctor's wife asked. She followed you out, the paperhanger told her. He glanced about, as if the girl might be hiding somewhere. There was nowhere to hide.

Where is my child? she asked the builder. The electrician climbed down from the ladder. The paperhanger came out of the bathroom with his tools. The builder was looking all around. His elfin features were touched with chagrin, as if this missing child were just something else he was going to be held accountable for.

Likely she's hiding in a closet, the paperhanger said. Playing a trick on you.

Zeineb does not play tricks, the doctor's wife said. Her eyes kept darting about the huge room, the shadows that lurked in corners. There was already an undercurrent of panic in her voice and all her poise and self-confidence seemed to have vanished with the child.

The paperhanger set down his toolbox and went through the house, opening and closing doors. It was a huge house and there were a lot of closets. There was no child in any of them.

The electrician was searching upstairs. The builder had gone through the French doors that opened onto the unfinished veranda and was peering into the backyard. The backyard was a maze of convoluted ditch excavated for the septic tank field line and beyond that there was just woods. She's playing in that ditch, the builder said, going down the flagstone steps.

She wasn't, though. She wasn't anywhere. They searched the house and grounds. They moved with jerky haste. They kept glancing toward the woods where the day was waning first. The builder kept shaking his head. She's got to be *somewhere*, he said.

Call someone, the doctor's wife said. Call the police.

It's a little early for the police, the builder said. She's got to be here.

You call them anyway. I have a phone in my car. I will call my husband.

While she called, the paperhanger and the electrician continued to search. They had looked everywhere and were forced to search places they'd already looked. If this ain't the goddamnedest thing I ever saw, the electrician said.

The doctor's wife got out of the Mercedes and slammed the door. Suddenly she stopped and clasped a hand to her forehead. She screamed. The man with the tractor, she cried. Somehow my child is gone with the tractor man.

Oh Jesus, the builder said. What have we got ourselves into here.

THE HIGH sheriff that year was a ruminative man named Bellwether. He stood beside the county cruiser talking to the paperhanger while deputies ranged the grounds. Other men were inside looking in places that had already been searched numberless times. Bell-wether had been in the woods and he was picking cockleburs off his khakis and out of his socks. He was watching the woods, where dark was gathering and seeping across the field like a stain.

I've got to get men out here, Bellwether said. A lot of men and a lot of lights. We're going to have to search every inch of these woods.

You'll play hell doing it, the paperhanger said. These woods stretch all the way to Lawrence County. This is the edge of the Harrikin. Down in there's where all those old mines used to be. Aliens Creek.

I don't give a shit if they stretch all the way to Fairbanks, Alaska, Bellwether said. They've got to be searched. It'll just take a lot of men.

The raw earth yard was full of cars. Dr. Jamahl had come in a sleek black Lexus. He berated his wife. Why weren't you watching her? he asked. Unlike his wife's, the doctor's speech was impeccable. She covered her face with her palms and wept. The doctor still wore his green surgeon's smock and it was flecked with bright dots of blood as a butcher's smock might be.

I need to feed a few cows, the paperhanger said. I'll feed my stock pretty quick and come back and help hunt.

You don't mind if I look in your truck, do you?

Do what?

I've got to cover my ass. If that little girl don't turn up damn quick this is going to be over my head. TBI, FBI, network news. I've got to eliminate everything.

Eliminate away, the paperhanger said.

The sheriff searched the floorboard of the paperhanger's pickup truck. He shined his huge flashlight under the seat and felt behind it with his hands.

I had to look, he said apologetically.

Of course you did, the paperhanger said.

———

FULL DARK had fallen before he returned. He had fed his cattle and stowed away his tools and picked up a six-pack of San Miguel beer and he sat in the back of the pickup truck drinking it. The paperhanger had been in the Navy and stationed in the Philippines and San Miguel was the only beer he could drink. He had to go out of town to buy it, but he figured it was worth it. He liked the exotic labels, the dark bitter taste on the back of his tongue, the way the chilled bottles felt held against his forehead.

A motley crowd of curiosity seekers and searchers thronged the yard. There was a vaguely festive air. He watched all this with a dispassionate eye, as if he were charged with grading the participants, comparing this with other spectacles he'd seen. Coffee urns had been brought in and set up on tables, sandwiches prepared and handed out to the weary searchers. A crane had been hauled in and the septic tank reclaimed from the ground. It swayed from a taut cable while men with lights searched the impacted earth beneath it for a child, for the very trace of a child. Through the far dark woods lights crossed and recrossed, darted to and fro like fireflies. The doctor and the doctor's wife sat in folding camp chairs looking drained, stunned, waiting for their child to be delivered into their arms.

The doctor was a short portly man with a benevolent expression. He had a moon-shaped face, with light and dark areas of skin that looked swirled, as if the pigment coloring him had not been properly mixed. He had been educated at Princeton. When he had established his practice he had returned to Pakistan to find a wife befitting his station. The woman he had selected had been chosen on the basis of her beauty. In retrospect, perhaps more consideration should have been given to other qualities. She was still beautiful but he was thinking that certain faults might outweigh this. She seemed to have trouble keeping up with her children. She could lose a four-year-old child in a room no larger than six hundred square feet and she could not find it again.

The paperhanger drained his bottle and set it by his foot in the bed of the truck. He studied the doctor's wife's ravaged face through the deep blue light. The first time he had seen her she had hired him to paint a bedroom in the house they were living in while the doctor's mansion was being built. There was an arrogance about her that cried out to be taken down a notch or two. She flirted with him, backed away, flirted again. She would treat him as if he were a stain on the bathroom rug and then stand close by him while he worked until he was dizzy with the smell of her, with the heat that seemed to radiate off her body. She stood by him while he knelt painting baseboards and after an infinite moment leaned carefully the weight of a thigh against his shoulder. You'd better move it, he thought. She didn't. He laughed and turned his face into her groin. She gave a strangled cry and slapped him hard. The paintbrush flew away and speckled the dark rose walls with antique white. You filthy beast, she said. You are some kind of monster. She stormed out of the room and he could hear her slamming doors behind her.

Well, I was looking for a job when I found this one. He smiled philosophically to himself.

But he had not been fired. In fact now he had been hired again. Perhaps there was something here to ponder.

At midnight he gave up his vigil. Some souls more hardy than his kept up the watch. The earth here was worn smooth by the useless traffic of the searchers. Driving out, he met a line of pickup trucks with civil defense tags. Grim-faced men sat aligned in their beds. Some clutched rifles loosely by their barrels, as if they would lay to waste whatever monster, man or beast, would snatch up a child in its slaverous jaws and vanish, prey and predator, in the space between two heartbeats.

Even more dubious reminders of civilization as these fell away. He drove into the Harrikin, where he lived. A world so dark and forlorn light itself seemed at a premium. Whippoorwills swept red-eyed up from the roadside. Old abandoned foundries and furnaces rolled past, grim and dark as forsaken prisons. Down a ridge here was an abandoned graveyard, if you knew where to look. The paperhanger did. He had dug up a few of the graves, examined with curiosity what remained, buttons, belt buckles, a cameo brooch. The bones he laid out like a child with a Tinkertoy, arranging them the way they went in jury-rigged resurrection.

He braked hard on a curve, the truck slewing in the gravel. A bobcat had crossed the road, graceful as a wraith, fierce and lantern-eyed in the headlights, gone so swiftly it might have been a stage prop swung across the road on wires.

BELLWETHER and a deputy drove to the backhoe operator's house. He lived up a gravel road that wound through a great stand of cedars. He lived in a board-and-batten house with a tin roof rusted to a warm umber. They parked before it and got out, adjusting their gun belts.

Bellwether had a search warrant with the ink scarcely dry. The operator was outraged.

Look at it this way, Bellwether explained patiently. I've got to cover my ass. Everything has got to be considered. You know how kids are. Never thinking. What if she run under the wheels of your truck when you was backing out? What if quicklike you put the body in your truck to get rid of somewhere?

What if quicklike you get the hell off my property, the operator said.

Everything has to be considered, the sheriff said again. Nobody's accusing anybody of anything just yet.

The operator's wife stood glowering at them. To have something to do with his hands, the operator began to construct a cigarette. He had huge red hands thickly sown with brown freckles. They trembled. I ain't got a thing in this round world to hide, he said.

Bellwether and his men searched everywhere they could think of to look. Finally they stood uncertainly in the operator's yard, out of place in their neat khakis, their polished leather.

Now get the hell off my land, the operator said. If all you think of me is that I could run over a little kid and then throw it off in the bushes like a dead cat or something then I don't even want to see your goddamn face. I want you gone and I want you by God gone now.

Everything had to be considered, the sheriff said.

Then maybe you need to consider that paperhanger.

What about him?

That paperhanger is one sick puppy.

He was still there when I got there, the sheriff said. Three witnesses swore nobody ever left, not even for a minute, and one of them was the child's mother. I searched his truck myself.

Then he's a sick puppy with a damn good alibi, the operator said.

THAT WAS all. There was no ransom note, no child that turned up two counties over with amnesia. She was a page turned, a door closed, a lost ball in the high weeds. She was a child no larger than a doll, but the void she left behind her was unreckonable. Yet there was no end to it. No finality. There was no moment when someone could say, turning from a mounded grave, Well, this has been unbearable, but you've got to go on with your life. Life did not go on.

At the doctor's wife's insistence an intensive investigation was focused on the backhoe operator. Forensic experts from the FBI examined every millimeter of the gravel truck, paying special attention to its wheels. They were examined with every modern crime-fighting device the government possessed, and there was not a microscopic particle of tissue or blood, no telltale chip of fingernail, no hair ribbon.

Work ceased on the mansion. Some subcontractors were discharged outright, while others simply drifted away. There was no one to care if the work was done, no one to pay them. The half-finished veranda's raw wood grayed in the fall, then winter, rains. The ditches were left fallow and uncovered and half filled with water. Kudzu crept from the woods. The hollyhocks and oleanders the doctor's wife had planted grew entangled and rampant. The imported windows were stoned by double-dared boys who whirled and fled. Already this house where a child had vanished was acquiring an unhealthy, diseased reputation.

The doctor and his wife sat entombed in separate prisons replaying real and imagined grievances. The doctor felt that his wife's neglect had sent his child into the abstract. The doctor's wife drank vodka martinis and watched talk shows where passed an endless procession of vengeful people who had not had children vanish, and felt, perhaps rightly, that the fates had dealt her from the bottom of the deck, and she prayed with intensity for a miracle.

Then one day she was just gone. The Mercedes and part of her clothing and personal possessions were gone too. He idly wondered where she was, but he did not search for her.

Sitting in his armchair cradling a great marmalade cat and a bottle of J&B and observing with bemused detachment the gradations of light at the window, the doctor remembered studying literature at Princeton. He had particular cause to reconsider the poetry of William Butler Yeats. For how surely things fell apart, how surely the center did not hold.

His practice fell into a ruin. His colleagues made sympathetic allowances for him at first, but there are limits to these things. He made erroneous diagnoses, prescribed the wrong medicines not once or twice but as a matter of course.

Just as there is a deepening progression to misfortune, so too there is a point beyond which things can only get worse. They did. A middle-aged woman he was operating on died.

He had made an incision to remove a ruptured appendix and the incised flesh was clamped aside while he made ready to slice it out. It was not there. He stared in drunken disbelief. He began to search under things, organs, intestines, a rising tide of blood. The appendix was not there. It had gone into the abstract, atrophied, been removed twenty-five years before, he had sliced through the selfsame scar. He was rummaging through her abdominal cavity like an irritated man fumbling through a drawer for a clean pair of socks, finally bellowing and wringing his hands in bloody vexation while nurses began to cry out, another surgeon was brought on the run as a closer, and he was carried from the operating room.

Came then days of sitting in the armchair while he was besieged by contingency lawyers, action news teams, a long line of process servers. There was nothing he could do. It was out of his hands and into the hands of the people who are paid to do these things. He sat cradling the bottle of J&B with the marmalade cat snuggled against his portly midriff. He would study the window, where the light drained away in a process he no longer had an understanding of, and sip the scotch and every now and then stroke the cat's head gently. The cat purred against his breast as reassuringly as the hum of an air conditioner.

He left in the middle of the night. He began to load his possessions into the Lexus. At first he chose items with a great degree of consideration. The first thing he loaded was a set of custom-made monogrammed golf clubs. Then his stereo receiver, Denon AC3, $1,750. A copy of *This Side of Paradise* autographed by Fitzgerald that he had bought as an investment. By the time the Lexus was half full he was just grabbing things at random and stuffing them into the backseat, a half-eaten pizza, half a case of cat food, a single brocade house shoe.

He drove west past the hospital, the country club, the city-limit sign. He was thinking no thoughts at all, and all the destination he had was the amount of highway the headlights showed him.

IN THE slow rains of late fall the doctor's wife returned to the unfinished mansion. She used to sit in a camp chair on the ruined veranda and drink chilled martinis she poured from the pitcher she carried in a foam ice chest. Dark fell early these November days. Rain crows husbanding some far cornfield called through the smoky autumn air. The sound was fiercely evocative, reminding her of something but she could not have said what.

She went into the room where she had lost the child. The light was failing. The high corners of the room were in deepening shadow but she could see the nests of dirt daubers clustered on the rich flocked wallpaper, a spider swing from a chandelier on a strand of spun glass. Some animal's dried blackened stool curled like a slug against the baseboards. The silence in the room was enormous.

One day she arrived and was surprised to find the paperhanger there. He was sitting on a yellow four-wheeler drinking a bottle of beer. He made to go when he saw her but she waved him back. Stay and talk with me, she said.

The paperhanger was much changed. His pale locks had been shorn away in a makeshift haircut as if scissored in the dark or by a blind barber and his cheeks were covered with a soft curly beard.

You have grown a beard.

Yes.

You are strange with it.

The paperhanger sipped from his San Miguel. He smiled. I was strange without it, he said. He arose from the four-wheeler and came over and sat on the flagstone steps. He stared across the mutilated yard toward the treeline. The yard was like a funhouse maze seen from above, its twistings and turnings bereft of mystery.

You are working somewhere now?

No. I don't take so many jobs anymore. There's only me, and I don't need much. What has become of the doctor?

She shrugged. Many things have change, she said. He has gone. The banks have foreclose. What is that you ride?

An ATV. A four-wheeler.

It goes well in the woods?

It was made for that.

You could take me in the woods. How much would you charge me?

For what?

To go in the woods. You could drive me. I will pay you.

Why?

To search for my child's body.

I wouldn't charge anybody anything to search for a child's body, the paperhanger said. But she's not in these woods. Nothing could have stayed hidden, the way these woods were searched.

Sometimes I think she just kept walking. Perhaps just walking away from the men looking. Far into the woods.

Into the woods, the paperhanger thought. If she had just kept walking in a straight line with no time out for eating or sleeping, where would she be? Kentucky, Algiers, who knew.

I'll take you when the rains stop, he said. But we won't find a child.

The doctor's wife shook her head. It is a mystery, she said. She drank from her cocktail glass. Where could she have gone? How could she have gone?

There was a man named David Lang, the paperhanger said. Up in Gallatin, back in the late 1800s. He was crossing a barn lot in full view of his wife and two children and he just vanished. Went into thin air. There was a judge in a wagon turning into the yard and he saw it too. It was just like he took a step in this world and his foot came down in another one. He was never seen again.

She gave him a sad smile, bitter and one-cornered. You make fun with me.

No. It's true. I have it in a book. I'll show you.

I have a book with dragons, fairies. A book where Hobbits live in the middle earth. They are lies. I think most books are lies. Perhaps all books. I have prayed for a miracle but I am not worthy of one. I have prayed for her to come from the dead, then just to find her body. That would be a miracle to me. There are no miracles.

She rose unsteadily, swayed slightly, leaning to take up the cooler. The paperhanger watched her. I have to go now, she said. When the rains stop we will search.

Can you drive?

Of course I can drive. I have drive out here.

I mean are you capable of driving now. You seem a little drunk.

I drink to forget but it is not enough, she said. I can drive.

After a while he heard her leave in the Mercedes, the tires spinning in the gravel drive. He lit a cigarette. He sat smoking it, watching the rain string off the roof. He seemed to be waiting for something. Dusk was falling like a shroud, the world going dark and formless the way it had begun. He drank the last of the beer, sat holding the bottle, the foam bitter in the back of his mouth. A chill touched him. He felt something watching him. He turned. From the corner of the ruined veranda a child was watching him. He stood up. He heard the beer bottle break on the flagstones. The child went sprinting past the hollyhocks toward the brush at the edge of the yard, a tiny sepia child with an intent sloe-eyed face, real as she had ever been, translucent as winter light through dirty glass.

THE DOCTOR's wife's hands were laced loosely about his waist as they came down through a thin stand of sassafras, edging over the ridge where the ghost of a road was, a road more sensed than seen that faced into a half acre of tilting stones and fading granite tablets. Other graves marked only by their declivities in the earth, folk so far beyond the pale even the legibility of their identities had been leached away by the weathers.

Leaves drifted, huge poplar leaves veined with amber so golden they might have been coin of the realm for a finer world than this one. He cut the ignition of the four-wheeler and got off. Past the lowering trees the sky was a blue of an improbable intensity, a fierce cobalt blue shot through with dense golden light.

She slid off the rear and steadied herself a moment with a hand on his arm. Where are we? she asked. Why are we here?

The paperhanger had disengaged his arm and was strolling among the gravestones reading such inscriptions as were legible, as if he might find forebear or antecedent in this moldering earth. The doctor's wife was retrieving her martinis from the luggage carrier of the ATV. She stood looking about uncertainly. A graven angel with broken wings crouched on a truncated marble column like a gargoyle. Its stone eyes regarded her with a blind benignity. Some of these graves have been rob, she said.

You can't rob the dead, he said. They have nothing left to steal.

It is a sacrilege, she said. It is forbidden to disturb the dead. You have done this.

The paperhanger took a cigarette pack from his pocket and felt it, but it was empty, and he balled it up and threw it away. The line between grave robbing and archaeology has always looked a little blurry to me, he said. I was studying their culture, trying to get a fix on what their lives were like.

She was watching him with a kind of benumbed horror. Standing hip-slung and lost like a parody of her former self. Strange and anomalous in her fashionable but mismatched clothing, as if she'd put on the first garment that fell to hand. Someday, he thought, she might rise and wander out into the daylit world wearing nothing at all, the way she had come into it. With her diamond watch and the cocktail glass she carried like a used-up talisman.

You have broken the law, she told him.

I got a government grant, the paperhanger said contemptuously.

Why are we here? We are supposed to be searching for my child.

If you're looking for a body the first place to look is the graveyard, he said. If you want a book don't you go to the library?

I am paying you, she said. You are in my employ. I do not want to be here. I want you to do as I say or carry me to my car if you will not.

Actually, the paperhanger said, I had a story to tell you. About my wife.

He paused, as if leaving a space for her comment, but when she made none he went on. I had a wife. My childhood sweetheart. She became a nurse, went to work in one of these drug rehab places. After she was there awhile she got a faraway look in her eyes. Look at me without seeing me. She got in tight with her supervisor. They started having meetings to go to. Conferences. Sometimes just the two of them would confer, generally in a motel. The night I watched them walk into the Holiday Inn in Franklin I decided to kill her. No impetuous spur-of-the-moment thing. I thought it all out and it would be the perfect crime.

The doctor's wife didn't say anything. She just watched him.

A grave is the best place to dispose of a body, the paperhanger said. The grave is its normal destination anyway. I could dig up a grave and then just keep on digging. Save everything carefully. Put my body there and fill in part of the earth, and then restore everything the way it was. The coffin, if any of it was left. The bones and such. A good settling rain and the fall leaves and you're home free. Now that's eternity for you.

Did you kill someone, she breathed. Her voice was barely audible.

Did I or did I not, he said. You decide. You have the powers of a god. You can make me a murderer or just a heartbroke guy whose wife quit him. What do you think? Anyway, I don't have a wife. I expect she just walked off into the abstract like that Lang guy I told you about.

I want to go, she said. I want to go where my car is.

He was sitting on a gravestone watching her out of his pale eyes. He might not have heard.

I will walk.

Just whatever suits you, the paperhanger said. Abruptly, he was standing in front of her. She had not seen him arise from the headstone or stride across the graves, but like a jerky splice in a film he was before her, a hand cupping each of her breasts, staring down into her face.

Under the merciless weight of the sun her face was stunned and vacuous. He studied it intently, missing no detail. Fine wrinkles crept from the corners of her eyes and mouth like hairline cracks in porcelain. Grime was impacted in her pores, in the crepe flesh of her throat. How surely everything had fallen from her: beauty, wealth, social position, arrogance. Humanity itself, for by now she seemed scarcely human, beleaguered so by the fates that she suffered his hands on her breasts as just one more cross to bear, one more indignity to endure.

How far you've come, the paperhanger said in wonder. I believe you're about down to my level now, don't you?

It does not matter, the doctor's wife said. There is no longer one thing that matters.

Slowly and with enormous lassitude her body slumped toward him, and in his exultance it seemed not a motion in itself but simply the completion of one begun long ago with the fateful weight of a thigh, a motion that began in one world and completed itself in another one.

From what seemed a great distance he watched her fall toward him like an angel descending, wings spread, from an infinite height, striking the earth gently, tilting, then righting itself.

THE WEIGHT of moonlight tracking across the paperhanger's face awoke him from where he took his rest. Filigrees of light through the gauzy curtains swept across him in stately silence like the translucent ghosts of insects. He stirred, lay still then for a moment getting his bearings, a fix on where he was.

He was in his bed, lying on his back. He could see a huge orange moon poised beyond the bedroom window, ink-sketch tree branches that raked its face like claws. He could see his feet bookending the San Miguel bottle that his hands clasped erect on his abdomen, the amber bottle hard-edged and defined against the pale window, dark atavistic monolith reared against a harvest moon.

He could smell her. A musk compounded of stale sweat and alcohol, the rank smell of her sex. Dissolution, ruin, loss. He turned to study her where she lay asleep, her open mouth a dark cavity in her face. She was naked, legs outflung, pale breasts pooled like cooling wax. She stirred restively, groaned in her sleep. He could hear the rasp of her breathing. Her breath was fetid on his face, corrupt, a graveyard smell. He watched her in disgust, in a dull self-loathing.

He drank from the bottle, lowered it. Sometimes, he told her sleeping face, you do things you can't undo. You break things you just can't fix. Before you mean to, before you know you've done it. And you were right, there are things only a miracle can set to rights.

He sat clasping the bottle. He touched his miscut hair, the soft down of his beard. He had forgotten what he looked like, he hadn't seen his reflection in a mirror for so long. Unbidden, Zeineb's face swam into his memory. He remembered the look on the child's face when the doctor's wife had spun on her heel: spite had crossed it like a flicker of heat lightning. She stuck her tongue out at him. His hand snaked out like a serpent and closed on her throat and snapped her neck before he could call it back, sloe eyes wild and wide, pink tongue caught between tiny seed-pearl teeth like a bitten-off rosebud. Her hair swung sidewise, her head lolled onto his clasped hand. The tray of the toolbox was out before he knew it, he was stuffing her into the toolbox like a rag doll. So small, so small, hardly there at all.

He arose. Silhouetted naked against the moon-drenched window, he drained the bottle. He looked about for a place to set it, leaned and wedged it between the heavy flesh of her upper thighs. He stood in silence, watching her. He seemed philosophical, possessed of some hard-won wisdom. The paperhanger knew so well that while few are deserving of a miracle, fewer still can make one come to pass.

He went out of the room. Doors opened, doors closed. Footsteps softly climbing a staircase, descending. She dreamed on. When he came back into the room he was cradling a plastic-wrapped bundle stiffly in his arms. He placed it gently beside the drunk woman. He folded the plastic sheeting back like a caul.

What had been a child. What the graveyard earth had spared the freezer had preserved. Ice crystals snared in the hair like windy snowflakes whirled there, in the lashes. A doll from a madhouse assembly line.

He took her arm, laid it across the child. She pulled away from the cold. He firmly brought the arm back, arranging them like mannequins, madonna and child. He studied this tableau, then went out of his house for the last time. The door closed gently behind him on its keeper spring.

The paperhanger left in the Mercedes, heading west into the open country, tracking into wide-open territories he could infect like a malignant spore. Without knowing it, he followed the selfsame route the doctor had taken some eight months earlier, and in a world of infinite possibilities where all journeys share a common end, perhaps they are together, taking the evening air on a ruined veranda among the hollyhocks and oleanders, the doctor sipping his scotch and the paperhanger his San Miguel, gentlemen of leisure discussing the vagaries of life and pondering deep into the night not just the possibility but the inevitability of miracles.

CITY VISIT

Adam Haslett

Adam Haslett is the author of a collection of short stories, *You Are Not a Stranger Here*, which was a finalist for the Pulitzer Prize and the National Book Award and won the PEN/Winship Award. A recipient of the PEN/Malamud Award, Haslett is a graduate of the Iowa Writers' Workshop and the Yale Law School and has received fellowships from the Fine Arts Work Center in Provincetown, the Michener/Copernicus Society of America, and the Guggenheim Foundation. He lives in New York City, where he works part-time as a legal consultant and teaches a graduate creative writing workshop at Columbia's School of the Arts.

As they rose onto the bridge, Brendan leaned against the taxi window, gazing into the towers lit against the night sky, just as they are in the beginning of all the Miramax films, or the shots from the blimp when they show evening games at the U.S. Open—only now he could see the red-and-white streams of car lights rushing along the river's edge, beacons on the prows of ships jetting the waterway, a helicopter's taillights cruising down the glittering shore. His hand tightened on the wallet in his pocket, the $300 he'd saved from afternoon shifts at OfficeMax secured in the inner fold. This must be what it's like, he thought, for diplomats and stars—Roddick returning from another victory at Flushing, an actor weary from a foreign shoot, night travelers longing for the comfort of lovers and apartments back in the gilded city.

"I hope this man doesn't get us lost," his mother whispered across the back seat.

"Jesus, Mom. Like he's never been to the Plaza."

"What do you know about the Plaza Hotel?"

"I know what everyone else in the world knows, which is that it's at Fifty-ninth and Park Avenue, and it used to be owned by Donald Trump."

"Feeth," the driver said through the Plexiglas slot. "Thee Plaza eez on Feeth."

"Thank you, sir," his mother yelled.

Brendan glared at her, hardly able to stand the sight: tan sneakers, stonewashed jeans, a green fleece sweater. Under his rule her entire wardrobe would be drowned in a vat of black dye. But none of these dreadful choices came close to the offense of the item strapped to her waist. His eyes snared on the teal nylon of the fanny pack, and it felt as if all sixteen years of his life he'd worn her naivete through the streets like a crown of thorns. He'd pleaded with her since yesterday not to carry her valuables in that eyesore. He'd even recited the latest crime statistics; forced her to acknowledge that New York was one of the safest cities in the country, and that more people per capita had been murdered in their own state of Missouri than in the five boroughs last year. But still she wouldn't relent. Having to share his first entrance into a world-class hotel with that placard of ignorance struck him as more than anyone should have to bear.

"Won't you please take it off?" he implored again now, glaring down at her hand, which seemed to have unconsciously migrated to the defense of the wretched bulge.

A year ago she would have looked him in the eye and told him he was on thin ice. Now she just turned her head away and said, "Brendan, you need to calm down."

As if calm were an option! Every waking hour for two months had been burned up in anticipation of this weekend. The day his sad-sack, pale-faced, depresso father had finally moved out of the house and into an apartment closer to his job, his mother had got on the phone to his grandmother, and when she hung up she told Brendan he was getting the present he'd asked for each birthday and Christmas for the past two years: they were going to New York City, and they were staying in a hotel.

That same evening he'd sent an e-mail to Tom, the guy he'd spent so much time imagining since they'd met on the Web a few months before, whose pictures were so gorgeous: curly black hair, green eyes, a chest sculpted and smooth and strong. This wasn't one of those pathetic online non-affairs his friend Tanya was still having, where you fell in love with some 400-pound food-service worker in Jefferson City, believing he was Brad Pitt's nephew. Brendan had taken a bus to a few of those dates. The only relief they'd given him was the knowledge that some people on this earth were more desperate than himself. Sitting in the back row of Language Arts on the first day of school this year, the pothead desperadoes nodding beside him, he'd watched the teacher shift his saucer-sized red-plastic glasses up the bridge of his nose, and it seemed as obvious as the sentence diagrammed on the board that Brendan could become either a lonely, sad-assed middle-aged fag like Mr. Growley, up there in his cardigan, his perm, his yellowed moustache, as anxious and bitter an inmate of that place as the worst of them; or someone who got out, someone who lived in an apartment in a famous city.

Since Tom had replied, saying this weekend would be fine, his greatest fear had been that he would go all the way to New York City and be unable to lose his mother long enough to get down to the East Village on his own. To his surprise, what had seemed the most difficult step turned out to be the easiest. A week after she'd booked their tickets, he asked her if on the Saturday afternoon of their visit he could go to Tanya's nonexistent cousin's house, ten blocks from the hotel. He'd anticipated a grilling, and had a map ready to show her. But rather than asking questions, she'd kept on with the dinner dishes, this resigned look on her face, as if she'd expected him to ask such a thing.

As the cab descended from the bridge and turned on to the avenue, Brendan looked at his watch and realized he had less than twenty hours left to wait.

Life at the Plaza consisted mainly of trying to keep at least ten yards between him and his mother when they were not either in the room with the door closed or forced into proximity by a restaurant table. As soon as they'd pulled up, he'd leaped out of the taxi and ascended the steps past the doorman. As he looked back from the doorway, he could almost believe that the miserably attired woman looking frantically over her shoulder, as if bracing for the onslaught of al-Qaeda, was just some tourist one had to expect at such places. After she registered them and handed him a key, they rode the elevator to their floor and he walked well ahead of her down the plush hallway and into the room. The sound of her knocking after repeated failure to operate the lock properly led him to contemplate what she would do if he simply didn't respond. She would either begin one of her shouting whispers or call a manager, he decided, crossing to the door to let her in. "Well, I think it'll be very good," she said, when he protested her hotel-dining plans. "I'm sure a place as nice as this is very reliable." For two short days they would reside on an island with perhaps the greatest variety of food in the world. But no. Not for the Blankenburgs. The Blankenburgs would eat chicken Kiev in a foyer.

"You're just afraid you're going to be shot," he said. "You might as well take that fleece off and put on a bulletproof vest. At least it would be the right color."

As it turned out, the Oak Room was pretty fancy, and when he saw the prices of the entrees Brendan became alarmed. He waited for his mother to whisper something about how they might need to find another restaurant, but she said nothing. They weren't poor, but they didn't eat out and they didn't travel, and his mother was always stressed about the bank account, about any purchases more significant than groceries. It wasn't as if his dad could afford to pitch in, and his mother's job at the mall didn't pay much more than Brendan's at OfficeMax.

Ever since a year ago, when his father lost his sales job and started sleeping half the day, she'd gone sort of quiet, not even getting after Brendan to do his schoolwork the way she used to. She'd started going to church three or four days a week, and praying more at home. On the kitchen table he'd see the literature she brought back, encouraging people to support the marriage amendment because homosexuals were trying to undermine Missouri families. He couldn't remember her ever voting before, but she'd gone down to his old elementary school on primary day, back in August, and when she came home she sat at the kitchen table and cried. Brendan had paid for the pizza that night and rented her favorite movie, this old black-and-white thing she loved called *The Philadelphia Story*.

Their entrees arrived, and they ate together in silence in the windowless, paneled room, glancing around at the other diners. She shook her head no when the waiter asked if she'd like dessert, but said Brendan should go ahead if he wanted to. As he sometimes did when she became silent, he felt his chest go tight, a kind of caged feeling. He hadn't meant to yell at her so much today; it was just that he'd been so nervous.

"Thanks for the trip," he said. His twelve-dollar brownie sundae was placed before him in a white bowl set on a gold-rimmed plate.

She nodded, looking over his shoulder, sipping her Diet Coke.

After dinner they took a brief walk along Fifty-ninth Street, and he managed to drag her six yards into the bottom entrance to Central Park before she mentioned some woman who'd been raped while jogging at night and said, "You know, we really shouldn't." The fanny pack had been left in the room's safe, replaced by a hooded windbreaker tied around her waist in case of bad weather. Looking back at her in the lamplight as she peered into the trees, her head covered with a rain hat, Brendan felt the anger flaring again, that leading edge of the bitter promise to himself never to become her, never to stay in the middle of nowhere as she had, never to live like his family, with money so tight. His grandfather watched C-span in a nursing home in St. Louis, damning the spineless Democrats, telling Brendan whenever they visited that in the fifties the union knew how to get things done—crack a few heads when the time came, none of this liberal crap, solid people on a pay scale they were willing to stand up and defend. And when the set-piece tirade was over, he'd stare bewildered at his semi-employed, divorcing daughter as though she were some strange inhabitant of the ruined future. Hurrying back down those corridors of airless linoleum cells, Brendan felt like Sigourney Weaver in *Alien*, fleeing the menaced ship, life clarifying itself into the pure struggle for survival, only to get into the escape car with his mother and realize that the beast of anonymity and defeat remained nestled right there beside him.

He kept three steps ahead all the way back to the hotel.

At one o'clock the next day he carried all his outfit choices into the bathroom, locked the door, took a long, soapy shower, and then tried to decide. For the past week he'd been set on the plan of dark jeans, a gray sweatshirt, and a no-logo baseball cap. But now he saw that the sweatshirt came down too far past his waist, and tucked in it looked totally retarded. The blue button-down was cute in a way, preppy, which, given that Tom was a law student, seemed okay. But everything he'd read about the East Village made him think you should look as much like Lou Reed as possible, at least clothing-wise. He decided on a long-sleeved dark-blue T-shirt and his black waist-length zip-up jacket. He put some gel in his hair, but other than some moisturizer to keep his skin from flaking he couldn't do much about his face. At least the clothing covered his spindly body for now.

He grabbed his wallet from the bedside table and stuffed it deep in his pocket. Across the room his mother sat in one of the overstuffed chairs, facing out the window that overlooked the park.

"It's your grandmother you have to thank for all this, you know," she said. "She wanted to give us—you and me—she wanted to give us a treat after your father left. You're going to write her a thank-you note."

"Sure," he said, wishing she'd look at him when she spoke. "I'll be back later, okay?"

The white-brick building at 228 East Thirteenth Street stood five stories high, across from an empty lot. Steps led up to a silver panel of buzzers. Tom Fairly's name didn't appear on the list. Brendan had been told to expect this. A sublet, Tom had said. He just had to ring buzzer No. 12 and he'd be let in. He sat on a stoop a few doors down, not wanting Tom to see him out the window and think him a nerd for arriving early. Checking to make sure no one suspicious was looking on, he took out his wallet and counted the money again. Tom charged $200 for a date, but he'd brought the extra hundred just in case he wanted more, given Brendan's looks. The money helped pay for law school and Tom's debt from college.

Sounds like you just need to get your confidence going. I can be gentle like that. Don't worry. His breath went shallow at the memory of the words in the e-mail. He'd jacked off so many times to the idea of being kissed by Tom that he didn't know what he'd do when he got in there. The last minutes remaining between him and their meeting felt as if they would never pass. Then suddenly they had, and he was standing in the entryway holding his finger to the buzzer.

"Who is it?" a man's low, garbled voice asked through the speaker grate.

"Brendan. Brendan Blankenburg."

"All right. Come on up. Fourth floor."

He pushed the door open and walked down the black-and-white-tiled hall.

Every night for months he'd visited the Web site, read Tom's journals, looked at pictures of Tom in his baseball cap and Columbia

sweatshirt, or in the shower, water running down his smooth, rippling back. He'd met lots of guys in chat rooms who advertised
with homepages like Tom's, but most of them were older, and all
they had were pictures and a cell-phone number, maybe some lame
paragraph about how hot they were. Tom was the only one he'd
found who had a story: Growing up in a banker's family in Ohio.
His father discovering him with another boy senior year in high
school, cutting him off from the money. Coming to New York, finding a job working for a film director, putting himself through college and now law school. Some of the journal entries were dated a
while ago, but they talked about how hard it had been at first, not
knowing how the city worked, the parties and the clothes, how everyone seemed to know everything already and be bored with it.
Brendan knew from the site that Tom dated other guys in a normal,
romantic way; that he never mixed that up with dates like Brendan.
He kept reminding himself of this. A jolting, shaking motion rattled in his chest as he climbed the stairs.

The door of 4F stood slightly ajar. As he knocked, it swung farther open.

"Come on in," Tom said, stepping into the kitchen from the next
room. He reached out his hand and they shook, Brendan managing
through an extreme force of will to keep his arm steady. Tom wore
a pair of shiny red track pants with a white stripe running down
the leg, and a white T-shirt that hugged the muscles of his chest and
arms. He seemed a little older than in the pictures—maybe twenty-
six or twenty-seven, Brendan guessed—but just as beautiful, his
hair moist and curly, his eyes greener than on the Web, the lightly
tanned skin of his face perfectly smooth. No one in Moberly, Missouri, looked anything like this. Like they could be in a magazine.

"Thanks for having me over."

"No problem," he said, reaching behind Brendan to close the
door. "Want something to drink?"

Brendan looked quickly around the room for a cue about what
to request at three in the afternoon in the East Village. Finding

none, he said in a voice as casual as he could muster, "I'll have a Seven-and-Seven." Tom smiled. "Let's see. I don't think I have any Seagram's. How about a Tanqueray and tonic?"

"That's cool."

His host turned to the refrigerator, giving Brendan a chance to take in the apartment. The kitchen they stood in was tiny but immaculate, the counters nearly bare, the cabinets polished steel. Through the doorway Tom had emerged from Brendan could see into a small living room with a wood floor and a bright-red sofa, a modern-looking, colorful abstract painting on the wall above it. Beyond that, through another open door, was a large bed made up like the ones in the hotel—a beige comforter, lots of pillows arranged upright against the headboard. The place looked like a miniature version of something you'd see in a decorating magazine. He'd imagined Tom's apartment as a college dorm room: sports stuff lying around, sweatshirts and sneakers, law books, posters of his favorite bands on the wall. This seemed like an older person's home.

"This your first time in the city?" Tom asked, handing Brendan a glass.

"No, I came once with my dad when I was nine. We live in Missouri." Jesus! he thought. Could he say anything dorkier?

"Yeah, you mentioned that in your e-mail," Tom said. "Here, let's go in the other room." He led Brendan through and took a seat on the red couch. An armchair was on the other side of the coffee table. Brendan froze, not knowing where to go. Tom looked up at him and patted the couch with his hand. "Come over here." Feeling the shaking again, he perched on the opposite end of the sofa.

Since steeling his courage that evening two months ago to send Tom an e-mail asking for a date, he'd wondered again and again if his horny loneliness had driven him temporarily insane. Going to New York City and paying a guy to have sex? What the fuck was he doing? I think it's gutsy, Tanya had said in the cafeteria the day he told her. You're a freak, of course, but it's gutsy. The subway map and condoms she'd bought him as a going-away gift were tucked in the inside pocket of his jacket. Just don't let him murder you, okay?

Okay.

He took another swallow of his drink.

"So . . . have you ever been with a guy?" Tom asked.

He'd rehearsed an answer for this and, not looking up, managed to get it out without his voice breaking. "A couple times," he lied. "No serious boyfriend right now."

"It's cool either way. I've had guys come for their first time. I think it's hot."

He slid closer to Brendan and put an arm over his shoulders. "Come here," he said. "Give me a hug." Brendan put down his drink and leaned into him, his head over Tom's shoulder, Tom's arms coming around his back.

He'd never in his life been held like this before.

The sensation made him suddenly woozy. He thought he was going to pass out, but then the months of waiting burst inside and he had to scrunch his eyes closed and clench the muscles deep in his groin to prevent himself from coming in his jeans.

"This is, like, your exam period, right?" he whispered.

"How do you mean?" Tom asked softly in his ear.

They sat back from their hug, close together still, facing each other.

"On the Columbia Web site. It said you guys had your exams next week."

Tom put a hand on Brendan's bouncing knee. "You're cute," he said.

"Really?"

Tom nodded. Brendan could feel his cheeks burning, and he bowed his head. "It must be really hard to remember all the laws. My friend Tanya's stepdad's a lawyer, and he says they change all the time." Tom's hand touched the back of Brendan's neck, fingers brushing through his hair, pressing gently on his scalp.

"Is it all right," Brendan whispered even more quietly now, "is it all right if we don't go all the way?"

"Of course. Only what you want. Go ahead and finish up your drink."

Brendan drained the rest of his glass and looked back into Tom's face, which seemed more serious now, his lips closed in a flat line. "You go in there," he said, nodding toward the bedroom. "Take off your jacket and shoes. I'll be in in a minute."

Brendan walked into the bedroom and, doing as he was told, removed his jacket and laid it down on a chair in the corner. It would be all right, he told himself, looking at the tidy surface of the dresser: a bowl of change, keys, a tray of cufflinks, a bottle of what looked like some kind of fancy aftershave. Next to these lay a small, neat stack of envelopes. Glancing down, he saw the name Greg DeMarino printed above the address of the apartment. A boyfriend, probably? Someone who'd lived here once? Together there on the dark wood surface, the objects appeared so masculine somehow. It was nothing like his father's dresser, with its crumpled receipts and dog-eared copies of the catalogues he used to sell to his customers from. His mind leaped to the forbidden idea that Tom might be more of a man than his father: stronger, more powerful, richer. At that moment, more than wanting to be touched by Tom, Brendan wanted to be him, to live inside the sculpture of his body, inside the life he'd made here, surrounded by these clean things. When the older kids had pushed him against the lockers last year and started kicking, they kept saying she. "She's a pussy." "She's a fag." "Look at her." He couldn't forget that word: she. It wasn't true.

He took off his shoes and sat on the edge of the bed. From there he could see through into the kitchen, into the mirror on the back of the bathroom door, and in the mirror Tom standing at the sink, lighting a small pipe close to his mouth, tilting his head back and releasing a stream of white smoke. Brendan looked away, out the window, across an airshaft to a brick wall and a strip of sky above.

He was probably just smoking pot, which Brendan wouldn't have minded doing himself right now, but asking would be too awkward. When he looked back a minute later, Tom was standing in the doorway. He'd taken his T-shirt off and stood with his arms hanging at his sides, a little trail of dark hair leading down from his belly button into the waist of his track pants.

A lot of the pictures of sex that Brendan had seen on the Web left him scared or grossed out, especially the close-ups; they looked more like photographs out of some veterinary textbook than something two people would want to do together. The ones he liked were of two cute boys, their faces visible, some of their clothing still on—a T-shirt, or maybe their jeans, pulled down—kissing or about to kiss. On countless nights when he had nothing to do he'd spend hours searching for the right image, clicking again and again, waiting for the stupid dial-up connection so that he could download one gallery after another, scanning the faces and bodies, his brain twitching forward like some small caged animal trapped on an endlessly turning wheel, his saliva stale with impatience. And when he was done, he'd feel nothing but dull-headed and alone. He thought of all the men in the chat rooms, the ones who, excited by how young he was, wanted to meet up, and who wrote line after dirty line about all the things they wanted to do to him. Disgusting things, sometimes. Things he wished he didn't know lived in other people's hearts.

"You should take off your shirt," Tom said, coming to stand at the edge of the bed, between Brendan's legs. He could smell the musky, slightly perfumed warmth of Tom's bare stomach and chest. It was stupid, so stupid, but all he could think now was that if he took his shirt off, Tom would see his skinny body and never fall in love with him, never want Brendan to come back and help him study, or help him as he started out as a lawyer or tried one day to reconcile with his father, traveling back to the family in Ohio to let them know who he was and that he had a boyfriend now.

When Brendan made no move to lift his shirt off, Tom rested his hands on his shoulders.

"It's your first time, isn't it?"

Brendan nodded, looking down at the floor. "I guess it was different for you, being with that guy from high school. More natural, I guess."

For a moment Tom didn't say anything, and Brendan wondered if he had hurt him by reminding him of something painful.

"You're talking about the journals?"

He nodded again, looking up for the first time into Tom's eyes, which he noticed were now bloodshot.

"Brendan. Listen. A lot of guys who visit me, guys older than you, they like to pretend stuff, pretend they're different than they are. Or they like me to act a certain way. That homepage—it's one of the ones I keep up because some guys like that student thing. It turns them on. I'm not in law school or anything, but I've got all the sweatshirts—the undergrad ones, too. It's weird—some guys actually want to sleep with someone from a particular school. All I'm saying is, we don't need to do any of that. You seem like a sweet kid. You just need to know you look okay, and maybe you can learn how to suck a guy's cock so that when you get with someone, you won't be as nervous. Does that sound okay?"

Brendan fixed his eyes on the dresser: the polished cherry wood, the opaque glass of the aftershave bottle, the dark leather box that might once have contained cigars like the ones his grandfather wasn't allowed to smoke anymore. As Tom's words filtered into his mind, he felt as if a heavy serum that must have long been pooled beneath the crown of his head was beginning to soak down now into his brain, filling in around the backs of his eyes, pressing against his skull—some primitive inoculant against sudden loss.

He made no reply. Tom took Brendan's hand and pressed it against the bulge in his track pants.

"How does that feel?" he said in a low voice.

Frightening, actually, Brendan wanted to say, but didn't. The scent of Tom he'd noticed before was gone. Now it was as if he were watching the image before him on a monitor: a pretty man with a bare chest, a hand coming up from the bottom of the frame—an image he'd like if he found it late enough in his hunt and was tired of searching for the perfect kiss. No one in his life, except maybe Tanya, would recognize him now, sitting on this stranger's bed, about to have sex with a man. He didn't have to do it. He could get up and leave. But as soon as this thought occurred, he saw Mr. Growley, his teacher, in a room a thousand miles away, sitting in front of his own computer, pictures of naked men flashing on the surface of his giant lenses. Brendan wished he could reach into his mind and stab the image dead, but it persisted as he kept going, letting his other hand touch Tom's stomach.

"And what if I want to pretend?" he said.

Tom looked down at him with a curious tilt of the head. His expression had gone bleary, his pupils dilated.

The words Brendan had just uttered felt like the most adult he'd ever spoken, coldly thrilling, lonely in a new, more masculine way. He was hard now, very hard.

"We could do that, I guess," Tom said. "It's your hour."

"Kiss me, then," Brendan said. "Kiss me."

And then, with some of their clothes still on, the light from the window slanting across Tom's smooth muscled arm, the picture just about right, Brendan closed his eyes and waited.

Along Third Avenue twilight had fallen; people were speeding past him, carting grocery bags, or knapsacks slung over their shoulders. Some wore headsets; others talked into phones; two balding men in brown suits jabbered in some clipped foreign tongue, hands poking the cold air. The only people standing still were some Latino grocery boys smoking cigarettes by a stack of milk crates and, next to them, an old black man with a whitened beard mumbling at the pavement.

Brendan crossed Fourteenth Street with the light and stood under the bus shelter. Beside him was an ancient woman who came barely above his waist, her head covered with a polka-dotted scarf; under her arm she held a perforated box with a whining cat inside.

The bus arrived soon enough and carried them slowly up the avenue, block after block of restaurants, pet stores, pharmacies, as anonymous, it struck him, as the strip malls out on the highway near his school. Taller buildings began filling the view as they entered midtown, the sidewalks emptier here late on a Saturday afternoon. Through plate-glass windows he could see into darkened hair salons and sandwich shops, stools turned upside down on the counters. Every few blocks men in red-and-white vests were moving slowly past the storefronts, sweeping litter into little boxes dangling from the ends of poles. The old woman had fallen asleep in one of the handicapped seats at the front. Brendan moved by her as he stepped off the bus, and turned past Bloomingdale's toward the hotel.

He was halfway through the lobby when he realized he'd forgotten to notice what it felt like coming up the steps, past the doorman, through the revolving door on his own, a guest like any other. Recessed bulbs lit the plush hall; his footsteps were silent on the carpet. He inserted the key into its slot, opened the door to their room, and paused on the threshold.

If his mother had moved, she showed no sign of it. She was sitting in the same chair, facing the window, looking out at the expanse of bare trees in the park and the low, dimming sky. She hadn't turned at the sound of his entrance.

Back in the spring the vice-principal had called her the day Brendan was caught fighting with the kids who'd kicked him up against the lockers. Though he had no way of knowing what the man had reported to her, he sensed it was enough to blow whatever cover he'd managed until then. Her only child. But she'd never said anything, never demanded to know, never told him he had to go to church when he didn't want to. The men in the congregation were almost all married, and sometimes, when Brendan got tired of dogging in his own mind the awful suits his mother wore on Sunday mornings, he'd think it must sort of suck for her, too, how the others might look at her and feel pity.

"How was your visit?" she asked, still without turning to see him.

Could she ever know him now? After what he'd done? How could the raw facts of the past few hours of his life exist in the same world as her?

"Fine," he said. "It was fine."

"You know I'll always love you," she said.

To prevent himself from crying, he took a step backwards into the hallway and closed the door.

Opposite the elevators two chairs stood on either side of a table decked with flowers. He unzipped his jacket and sat, his legs stretched out in front of him, his head resting against the cushioned upholstery. At the apartment he'd left his $200 on the kitchen counter while the guy, whose name turned out to be Greg, was still in the shower, and then he'd shut the front door behind himself as he left. In the moments before he came, he'd experienced giddiness and this awful fear, a disbelief that someone so handsome would touch him along with the sensation that he was departing forever a world he understood. Lying on his back afterward, listening to the stranger wash his hands in the bathroom, a rectangle of the fading sky visible above the parapet, he'd thought of how invincible the glittering towers looked when they came over the bridge, how total seemed their promise of fame.

The elevator doors slid open before him and a couple in their thirties, dressed in elegant coats and scarves, emerged with bright cheeks and shopping bags. The man smiled and offered a nod as they passed by, and the thought occurred to Brendan that it probably gave this guy some small, barely recognized satisfaction to make such a gesture, to meet another person in this world of the hotel, to give and briefly gain the sense that yes, here is where we all belong.

TO THOSE OF YOU WHO MISSED YOUR CONNECTING FLIGHTS OUT OF O'HARE

Amy Hempel

Amy Hempel is a fiction writer whose publications include *Reasons to Live, At the Gates of the Animal Kingdom, Tumble Home,* and *The Dog of the Marriage. The Collected Stories* was one of the *New York Times* Ten Best Books of the Year and a finalist for the PEN/Faulkner Award. Hempel has received a Guggenheim Fellowship, United States Artists Fellowship, an Award for Literature from the American Academy of Arts and Letters, and an Ambassador Book Award.

To those of you who missed your connecting flights out of O'Hare, I offer my deepest apology.

What they did I had no way of knowing they would do because the last time this happened it was handled without the fuss. The last time it happened it affected no one else—I just walked off the plane before the stewardess locked the door, and my luggage, not me, was what reached my destination.

Did I know when I walked off Flight 841 that my suitcase would have to be pulled from the plane, a black fabric suitcase the handler had to find amidst the hundreds of other bags, and all of you passengers waiting?

And how about the pilot checking the toilets for a bomb, a stewardess doing likewise in the overhead compartment above what was, for maybe two minutes, my seat—6C.

I'm right about this—it didn't used to be this way. The agents on the ground, the ones who check you in, they used to see you coming off the plane and they knew what it meant and they knew you were not to blame and the looks that they gave you said, Better luck next time, and We hope you try again.

Now they are angry. The looks and accusations—making hundreds of passengers late!

That is when I told them that my husband was killed in a plane crash, the one in Tenerife.

There is precedent here for a lie of this kind, or rather, a lie at this time. On a talk show once, a comic told the story: how he boarded a plane to make a headline date in Vegas, but the plane that he boarded was a plane bound for Pittsburgh. When our comic finds out, the plane has begun its slow roll into position.

This man, this comic, was able to persuade the crew to return the plane to the gate. And how did he avoid the collective wrath of the passengers? When the plane came to a stop and the walkway was stretched to the door, the comic stood up and summoned a tone of voice. "I don't know about the rest of you," he said, "but I won't take this kind of treatment from an airline!"

The comic, looking indignant, then walked off the plane.

But you, the passengers of Flight 841, I want you to know the truth.

Starting with 6B, my would-be white-knuckle neighbor, buckling tight your seat belt as if it makes any goddamned difference. I mean—Sir, let me ask you a question: Do the newspapers ever say, "Whereas the survivors—the list follows—are those who buckled their seat belts"?

I want to take you, the passengers whom I have inconvenienced, into my confidence. Because if you are like me, you know that some of us are not the world, some of us are not the children, some of us will not help make a brighter day. Some of us are the silent sufferers of a noisy disease. And that is all I have to say about fear.

But! By making yourself scarce at the nation's airports, by deciding for the grounded comfort of a train, you will find yourself traveling through the City of Spires and the cities of steel, the country's richest pasture land and the Santa Fe Trail, across the Purgatoire River near the Sangre de Cristo range—just big sky and small talk and rhyming to yourself from a catalog of sights: pale deer at dawn on the edge of a lawn.

Past low pink tamarisk and Ponderosa pine, and Shoemaker Canyon lined with cottonwood trees that are home to wild turkeys beside the narrow Mora River.

Past the Forked Lightning Ranch that was once Greer Garson's home near the Sandia ("Watermelon") Mountains—they turn bright red at sunset and the trees on the side look like seeds.

Do I sound as if I work for the railroad?

The tragedy of the settlers on Starvation Peak—the Kneeling Nuns, a formation of rock.

It cost me some money to see this. You walk off a plane and even *think* about getting a refund! You get one—one—one trip for the price of two.

A five-hour flight works out to three days and nights on land, by rail, from sea to shining sea.

You can chalk off the hours on the back of the seat ahead. But seventy-some hours will not seem so long to you if you tell yourself first: This is where I am going to be for the rest of my natural life.

EMERGENCY

Denis Johnson

Denis Johnson is the author of five novels, a collection of poetry, and one book of reportage. He is the recipient of a National Book Award, a Lannan Fellowship and a Whiting Writers' Award, among many other honors for his work. He lives in northern Idaho.

I'd been working in the emergency room for about three weeks, I guess. This was in 1973, before the summer ended. With nothing to do on the overnight shift but batch the insurance reports from the daytime shifts, I just started wandering around, over to the coronary-care unit, down to the cafeteria, et cetera, looking for Georgie, the orderly, a pretty good friend of mine. He often stole pills from the cabinets.

He was running over the tiled floor of the operating room with a mop. "Are you still doing that?" I said.

"Jesus, there's a lot of blood here," he complained.

"Where?" The floor looked clean enough to me.

"What the hell were they doing in here?" he asked me.

"They were performing surgery, Georgie," I told him.

"There's so much goop inside of us, man," he said, "and it all wants to get out." He leaned his mop against a cabinet.

"What are you crying for?" I didn't understand.

He stood still, raised both arms slowly behind his head, and tightened his ponytail. Then he grabbed the mop and started making broad random arcs with it, trembling and weeping and moving all around the place really fast. "What am I *crying* for?" he said. "Jesus. Wow, oh boy, perfect."

I WAS hanging out in the E.R. with fat, quivering Nurse. One of the Family Service doctors that nobody liked came in looking for Georgie to wipe up after him. "Where's Georgie?" this guy asked.

"Georgie's in O.R.," Nurse said.

"Again?"

"No," Nurse said. "Still."

"Still? Doing what?"

"Cleaning the floor."

"Again?"

"No," Nurse said again. "Still."

BACK IN O.R., Georgie dropped his mop and bent over in the posture of a child soiling its diapers. He stared down with his mouth open in terror.

He said, "What am I going to do about these fucking *shoes*, man?"

"Whatever you stole," I said, "I guess you already ate it all, right?"

"Listen to how they squish," he said, walking around carefully on his heels.

"Let me check your pockets, man."

He stood still a minute, and I found his stash. I left him two of each, whatever they were. "Shift is about half over," I told him.

"Good. Because I really, really, really need a drink," he said. "Will you please help me get this blood mopped up?"

AROUND 3:30 A.M. a guy with a knife in his eye came in, led by Georgie.

"I hope *you* didn't do that to him," Nurse said.

"Me?" Georgie said. "No. He was like this."

"My wife did it," the man said. The blade was buried to the hilt in the outside corner of his left eye. It was a hunting knife kind of thing.

"Who brought you in?" Nurse said.

"Nobody. I just walked down. It's only three blocks," the man said.

Nurse peered at him. "We'd better get you lying down."

"Okay, I'm certainly ready for something like that," the man said.

She peered a bit longer into his face.

"Is your other eye," she said, "a glass eye?"

"It's plastic, or something artificial like that," he said.

"And you can see out of *this* eye?" she asked, meaning the wounded one.

"I can see. But I can't make a fist out of my left hand because this knife is doing something to my brain."

"My God," Nurse said.

"I guess I'd better get the doctor," I said.

"There you go," Nurse agreed.

They got him lying down, and Georgie says to the patient, "Name?"

"Terrence Weber."

"Your face is dark. I can't see what you're saying."

"Georgie," I said.

"What are you saying, man? I can't see."

Nurse came over, and Georgie said to her, "His face is dark."

She leaned over the patient. "How long ago did this happen, Terry?" she shouted down into his face.

"Just a while ago. My wife did it. I was asleep," the patient said.

"Do you want the police?"

He thought about it and finally said, "Not unless I die."

Nurse went to the wall intercom and buzzed the doctor on duty, the Family Service person. "Got a surprise for you," she said over the intercom. He took his time getting down the hall to her, because he knew she hated Family Service and her happy tone of voice could only mean something beyond his competence and potentially humiliating.

He peeked into the trauma room and saw the situation: the clerk—that is, me—standing next to the orderly, Georgie, both of us on drugs, looking down at a patient with a knife sticking up out of his face.

"What seems to be the trouble?" he said.

THE DOCTOR gathered the three of us around him in the office and said, "Here's the situation. We've got to get a team here, an entire team. I want a good eye man. A great eye man. The best eye man. I want a brain surgeon. And I want a really good gas man, get me a genius. I'm not touching that head. I'm just going to watch this one. I know my limits. We'll just get him prepped and sit tight. Orderly!"

"Do you mean me?" Georgie said. "Should I get him prepped?"

"Is this a hospital?" the doctor asked. "Is this the emergency room? Is that a patient? Are you the orderly?"

I dialled the hospital operator and told her to get me the eye man and the brain man and the gas man.

Georgie could be heard across the hall, washing his hands and singing a Neil Young song that went "Hello, cowgirl in the sand. Is this place at your command?"

"That person is not right, not at all, not one bit," the doctor said.

"As long as my instructions are audible to him it doesn't concern me," Nurse insisted, spooning stuff up out of a little Dixie cup. "I've got my own life and the protection of my family to think of."

"Well, okay, okay. Don't chew my head off," the doctor said.

The eye man was on vacation or something. While the hospital's operator called around to find someone else just as good, the other specialists were hurrying through the night to join us. I stood around looking at charts and chewing up more of Georgie's pills.

Some of them tasted the way urine smells, some of them burned, some of them tasted like chalk. Various nurses, and two physicians who'd been tending somebody in I.C.U., were hanging out down here with us now.

Everybody had a different idea about exactly how to approach the problem of removing the knife from Terrence Weber's brain. But when Georgie came in from prepping the patient—from shaving the patient's eyebrow and disinfecting the area around the wound, and so on—he seemed to be holding the hunting knife in his left hand.

The talk just dropped off a cliff.

"Where," the doctor asked finally, "did you get that?"

Nobody said one thing more, not for quite a long time.

After a while, one of the I.C.U. nurses said, "Your shoelace is untied." Georgie laid the knife on a chart and bent down to fix his shoe.

THERE WERE twenty more minutes left to get through.

"How's the guy doing?" I asked.

"Who?" Georgie said.

It turned out that Terrence Weber still had excellent vision in the one good eye, and acceptable motor and reflex, despite his earlier motor complaint. "His vitals are normal," Nurse said. "There's nothing wrong with the guy. It's one of those things."

AFTER A while you forget it's summer. You don't remember what the morning is. I'd worked two doubles with eight hours off in between, which I'd spent sleeping on a gurney in the nurse's station. Georgie's pills were making me feel like a giant helium-filled balloon, but I was wide awake. Georgie and I went out to the lot, to his orange pickup.

We lay down on a stretch of dusty plywood in the back of the truck with the daylight knocking against our eyelids and the fragrance of alfalfa thickening on our tongues.

"I want to go to church," Georgie said.

"Let's go to the county fair."

"I'd like to worship. I would."

"They have these injured hawks and eagles there. From the Humane Society," I said.

"I need a quiet chapel about now."

GEORGIE AND I had a terrific time driving around. For a while the day was clear and peaceful. It was one of the moments you stay in, to hell with all the troubles of before and after. The sky is blue and the dead are coming back. Later in the afternoon, with sad resignation, the county fair bares its breasts. A champion of the drug LSD, a very famous guru of the love generation, is being interviewed amid a TV crew off to the left of the poultry cages. His eyeballs look like he bought them in a joke shop. It doesn't occur to me, as I pity this extraterrestrial, that in my life I've taken as much as he has.

AFTER THAT, we got lost. We drove for hours, literally hours, but we couldn't find the road back to town.

Georgie started to complain. "That was the worst fair I've been to. Where were the rides?"

"They had rides," I said.

"I didn't see one ride."

A jackrabbit scurried out in front of us, and we hit it.

"There was a merry-go-round, a Ferris wheel, and a thing called the Hammer that people were bent over vomiting from after they got off," I said. "Are you completely blind?"

"What was that?"

"A rabbit."

"Something thumped."

"You hit him. *He* thumped."

Georgie stood on the brake pedal. "Rabbit stew."

He threw the truck in reverse and zigzagged back toward the rabbit. "Where's my hunting knife?" He almost ran over the poor animal a second time.

"We'll camp in the wilderness," he said. "In the morning we'll breakfast on its haunches." He was waving Terrence Weber's hunting knife around in what I was sure was a dangerous way.

In a minute he was standing at the edge of the fields, cutting the scrawny little thing up, tossing away its organs. "I should have been a doctor," he cried.

A family in a big Dodge, the only car we'd seen for a long time, slowed down and gawked out the windows as they passed by. The father said, "What is it, a snake?"

"No, it's not a snake," Georgie said. "It's a rabbit with babies inside it."

"Babies!" the mother said, and the father sped the car forward, over the protests of several little kids in the back.

Georgie came back to my side of the truck with his shirtfront stretched out in front of him as if he were carrying apples in it, or some such, but they were, in fact, slimy miniature bunnies. "No way I'm eating those things," I told him.

"Take them, take them. I gotta drive, take them," he said, dumping them in my lap and getting in on his side of the truck. He started driving along faster and faster, with a look of glory on his face. "We killed the mother and saved the children," he said.

"It's getting late," I said. "Let's get back to town."

"You bet." Sixty, seventy, eighty-five, just topping ninety.

"These rabbits better be kept warm." One at a time I slid the little things in between my shirt buttons and nestled them against my belly. "They're hardly moving," I told Georgie.

"We'll get some milk and sugar and all that, and we'll raise them up ourselves. They'll get as big as gorillas."

The road we were lost on cut straight through the middle of the world. It was still daytime, but the sun had no more power than an ornament or a sponge. In this light the truck's hood, which had been bright orange, had turned a deep blue.

Georgie let us drift to the shoulder of the road, slowly, slowly, as if he'd fallen asleep or given up trying to find his way.

"What is it?"

"We can't go on. I don't have any headlights," Georgie said.

We parked under a strange sky with a faint image of a quarter-moon superimposed on it.

There was a little woods beside us. This day had been dry and hot, the buck pines and what all simmering patiently, but as we sat there smoking cigarettes it started to get very cold.

"The summer's over," I said.

That was the year when arctic clouds moved down over the Midwest and we had two weeks of winter in September.

"Do you realize it's going to snow?" Georgie asked me.

He was right, a gun-blue storm was shaping up. We got out and walked around idiotically. The beautiful chill! That sudden crispness, and the tang of evergreen stabbing us!

The gusts of snow twisted themselves around our heads while the night fell. I couldn't find the truck. We just kept getting more and more lost. I kept calling, "Georgie, can you see?" and he kept saying, "See what? See what?"

The only light visible was a streak of sunset flickering below the hem of the clouds. We headed that way.

We bumped softly down a hill toward an open field that seemed to be a military graveyard, filled with rows and rows of austere, identical markers over soldiers' graves. I'd never before come across this cemetery. On the farther side of the field, just beyond the curtains of snow, the sky was torn away and the angels were descending out of a brilliant blue summer, their huge faces streaked with light and full of pity. The sight of them cut through my heart and down the knuckles of my spine, and if there'd been anything in my bowels I would have messed my pants from fear.

Georgie opened his arms and cried out, "It's the drive-in, man!"

"The drive-in . . ." I wasn't sure what these words meant.

"They're showing movies in a fucking blizzard!" Georgie screamed.

"I see. I thought it was something else," I said.

We walked carefully down there and climbed through the busted fence and stood in the very back. The speakers, which I'd mistaken for grave markers, muttered in unison. Then there was tinkly music, of which I could very nearly make out the tune. Famous movie stars rode bicycles beside a river, laughing out of their gigantic, lovely mouths. If anybody had come to see this show, they'd left when the weather started. Not one car remained, not even a broken-down one from last week, or one left here because it was out of gas. In a couple of minutes, in the middle of a whirling square dance, the screen turned black, the cinematic summer ended, the snow went dark, there was nothing but my breath.

"I'm starting to get my eyes back," Georgie said in another minute.

A general greyness was giving birth to various shapes, it was true. "But which ones are close and which ones are far off?" I begged him to tell me.

By trial and error, with a lot of walking back and forth in wet shoes, we found the truck and sat inside it shivering.

"Let's get out of here," I said.

"We can't go anywhere without headlights."

"We've gotta get back. We're a long way from home."

"No, we're not."

"We must have come three hundred miles."

"We're right outside town, Fuckhead. We've just been driving around and around."

"This is no place to camp. I hear the Interstate over there."

"We'll just stay here till it gets late. We can drive home late. We'll be invisible,"

We listened to the big rigs going from San Francisco to Pennsylvania along the Interstate, like shudders down a long hacksaw blade, while the snow buried us.

Eventually Georgie said, "We better get some milk for those bunnies."

"We don't have *milk*," I said.

"We'll mix sugar up with it."

"Will you forget about this milk all of a sudden?"

"They're mammals, man."

"Forget about those rabbits."

"Where are they, anyway?"

"You're not listening to me. I said, 'Forget the rabbits.' "

"Where are they?"

The truth was I'd forgotten all about them, and they were dead.

"They slid around behind me and got squashed," I said tearfully.

"They slid around *behind*?"

He watched while I pried them out from behind my back.

I picked them out one at a time and held them in my hands and we looked at them. There were eight. They weren't any bigger than my fingers, but everything was there.

Little feet! Eyelids! Even whiskers! "Deceased," I said.

Georgie asked, "Does everything you touch turn to shit? Does this happen to you every time?"

"No wonder they call me Fuckhead."

"It's a name that's going to stick."

"I realize that."

"'Fuckhead' is gonna ride you to your grave."

"I just said so. I agreed with you in advance," I said.

Or maybe that wasn't the time it snowed. Maybe it was the time we slept in the truck and I rolled over on the bunnies and flattened them. It doesn't matter. What's important for me to remember now is that early the next morning the snow was melted off the windshield and the daylight woke me up. A mist covered everything and, with the sunshine, was beginning to grow sharp and strange. The bunnies weren't a problem yet, or they'd already been a problem and were already forgotten, and there was nothing on my mind. I felt the beauty of the morning. I could understand how a drowning man might suddenly feel a deep thirst being quenched. Or how the slave might become a friend to his master. Georgie slept with his face right on the steering wheel.

I saw bits of snow resembling an abundance of blossoms on the stems of the drive-in speakers—no, revealing the blossoms that were always there. A bull elk stood still in the pasture beyond the fence, giving off an air of authority and stupidity. And a coyote jogged across the pasture and faded away among the saplings.

THAT AFTERNOON we got back to work in time to resume everything as if it had never stopped happening and we'd never been anywhere else.

"The Lord," the intercom said, "is my shepherd." It did that each evening because this was a Catholic hospital. "Our Father, who art in Heaven," and so on.

"Yeah, yeah," Nurse said.

The man with the knife in his head, Terrence Weber, was released around suppertime. They'd kept him overnight and given him an eyepatch—all for no reason, really.

He stopped off at E.R. to say goodbye. "Well, those pills they gave me make everything taste terrible," he said.

"It could have been worse," Nurse said.

"Even my tongue."

"It's just a miracle you didn't end up sightless or at least dead," she reminded him.

The patient recognized me. He acknowledged me with a smile. "I was peeping on the lady next door while she was out there sunbathing," he said. "My wife decided to blind me."

He shook Georgie's hand. Georgie didn't know him. "Who are you supposed to be?" he asked Terrence Weber.

SOME HOURS before that, Georgie had said something that had suddenly and completely explained the difference between us. We'd been driving back toward town, along the Old Highway, through the flatness. We picked up a hitchhiker, a boy I knew. We stopped the truck and the boy climbed slowly up out of the fields as out of the mouth of a volcano. His name was Hardee. He looked even worse than we probably did.

"We got messed up and slept in the truck all night," I told Hardee.

"I had a feeling," Hardee said. "Either that or, you know, driving a thousand miles."

"That too," I said.

"Or you're sick or diseased or something."

"Who's this guy?" Georgie asked.

"This is Hardee. He lived with me last summer. I found him on the doorstep. What happened to your dog?" I asked Hardee.

"He's still down there."

"Yeah, I heard you went to Texas."

"I was working on a bee farm," Hardee said.

"Wow. Do those things sting you?"

"Not like you'd think," Hardee said. "You're part of their daily drill. It's all part of a harmony."

Outside, the same identical stretch of ground repeatedly rolled past our faces. The day was cloudless, blinding. But Georgie said, "Look at that," pointing straight ahead of us.

One star was so hot it showed, bright and blue, in the empty sky.

"I recognized you right away," I told Hardee. "But what happened to your hair? Who chopped it off?"

"I hate to say."

"Don't tell me."

"They drafted me."

"Oh no."

"Oh yeah. I'm AWOL. I'm bad AWOL. I got to get to Canada."

"Oh, that's terrible," I said to Hardee.

"Don't worry," Georgie said. "We'll get you there."

"How?"

"Somehow. I think I know some people. Don't worry. You're on your way to Canada."

That world! These days it's all been erased and they've rolled it up like a scroll and put it away somewhere. Yes, I can touch it with my fingers. But where is it?

After a while Hardee asked Georgie, "What do you do for a job," and Georgie said, "I save lives."

DOUBLE EXPOSURE

Greg Johnson

Greg Johnson has published two novels, a study of Emily Dickinson, three critical works on Joyce Carol Oates, a book of poems, and three collections of short fiction. Johnson is a professor of English and a faculty member in the graduate writing program at Kennesaw State University and a frequent reviewer for such publications as the *New York Times Book Review*, the *Georgia Review*, and the *Atlanta Journal-Constitution*.

I

Her hair smelled bad.

The day we came to visit Mr. Thomas, that awful February, she happened to come downstairs—"just checking the mail," she said, with a half-apologetic smile—and after collecting a few envelopes she stalled a moment. That's when I noticed the smell, and focused my attention on the oily mane of darkish blond hair through which, I imagined, she had splayed her fingers many times. Though ten years old, I was an observant child, and passing my gaze downward I saw that her clothes looked cheap and not very clean. Her fingers had stains on them as of dark ink, or ashes.

My mother, with her middle-class American politeness, shook the woman's dirty hand without hesitation. From the smile she gave, she might have been meeting the queen. The woman kept looking back and forth between us, smiling eagerly, as my mother launched into a needlessly detailed explanation of our presence outside Mr.

Thomas's door. He was the great-uncle of a pilot's wife my mother had befriended while we still lived on the base, and Mrs. Fellowes had insisted we stop and meet the old man, since we were going to be his neighbors. The day before, my mother and I had moved into our own flat in the next block of Fitzroy Road, and though we hadn't finished unpacking she'd resolved that morning to fulfill her obligation promptly. She called it an "obligation," but I knew my mother was hungry to meet people—even a British woman's elderly uncle.

While my mother explained all this I stared at the woman, whose name was Sylvia. It struck me that Sylvia was just the kind of person my mother needed at that moment, for she was an intense, compassionate listener, expressing no impatience with my mother's volubility. That was the first time I guessed that Sylvia was lonely, too.

My mother kept talking. Within minutes she had told Sylvia the story she'd been giving everyone we met (our new landlord, neighbors she encountered in the hallway, even the elderly woman who owned the greengrocer's shop on the corner). The main details were these. Her husband, my father, was in the air force—which was true. He was stationed in London for another six months, at which time his term of service would end—also true. Though we'd been living on the base in quarters provided for married airmen, the U.S. government instead had provided a tiny flat in the Fitzroy Road for my father's dependents—a disappointing but temporary arrangement, my mother added quickly, for we'd all be returning home together in six months' time.

This last part was not true. The truth was my parents had split up, and my father had told us both, in separate, difficult conversations, that when we returned to America he planned to file for a divorce. My mother had moved us to the Fitzroy Road flat supposedly because she wanted, now that we were here, to "experience a different culture." It would be a fine learning experience for me, she said. We could stay in London (where I would follow a reading list sent by my fourth-grade teacher back in Atlanta) until August, when we'd have to return to America and my school. But the real reason we'd stayed in London, of course, was that my mother couldn't accept the separation—my father had met another woman—and was lingering in the hope that she'd get him back.

She hadn't told me this, in so many words, but I'd known what would happen in the way intelligent children know such dismal things. Perhaps I knew before she did, months earlier when my mother was still pretending to herself we were a happy little family about to conclude its British adventure.

Standing there in the freezing entryway with my mother and Sylvia, I'd begun fidgeting. I wanted to return to our flat, which at least was well-heated, and help my mother unpack, then read until dark and in that way make an end to another day against the time when we could finally return to America and a semblance of normalcy. But I fidgeted quietly; I was a polite boy. There was a baby's pram, empty, there in the vestibule, and I held the bar and moved the pram forward and back, forward and back, as though soothing an invisible child.

When my mother finally stopped talking, Sylvia related in a few, efficient sentences how she'd come to be here, occupying the two floors above Mr. Thomas's flat. He was such a nice and helpful man, she said; she knew we'd like him very much. By now, however, Sylvia had told us that Mr. Thomas had gone out for the day. He worked for an art museum, she said, and was an artist himself.

"Oh, really?" my mother exclaimed, as though delighted by this news.

Sylvia, ducking her head mischievously, cupped her mouth and stage-whispered, "But ringing the bell won't do, you know. He's deaf as a corpse."

"Oh, is he?" my mother said, sympathetically.

Sylvia laughed. "You have to bang and bang," she said, miming the action against Mr. Thomas's door. "Like you're trying to wake the dead. Literally."

My mother gave her most forced and gracious smile. "Really, I'll have to remember that."

Neither my mother nor Sylvia seemed to sense any awkwardness in their eager, serendipitous conversation here in this foyer—I saw that Sylvia was cold, too, the tips of her nose and ears a waxen pink—and now Sylvia was exclaiming over her "luck" in meeting another American woman living just a block away. They were about the same age, weren't they? She hoped they'd become good friends. Her babies were napping, or she'd have invited us upstairs to meet them, and make us a cup of tea.

"I've taken up all the British customs," Sylvia said, in her nasally half-Boston, half-British drawl. "I imagine you have, as well?"

My mother agreed because she was always agreeable, though she disliked tea. She swerved onto another subject, a tactic she often used just after committing a lie, then feeling her insincere, polite guilt about it. She latched onto another bit of information the woman had offered.

"You know, we've never met a real poet before," she said, admiringly. "Have we, honey?" she added, glancing down at me.

Uncomfortable beneath the gaze of the malodorous, poorly dressed Sylvia and my genteel-looking, perfumed mother—whom no one would recognize as a woman plunged into raving despair—I glanced away. I kept playing with the pram.

"No," I said quickly, fearing what would come next, as it did.

"You know, my son has written quite a few poems at school, back in the states," she said. "He goes to Catholic school, and the nuns read them aloud to the class."

"Is that so?" Sylvia said, staring down with renewed curiosity, her lips edging upwards in a smile.

I imagine that, to Sylvia, I looked much too well-fed and well-scrubbed to suggest a budding poet. Though I can't recall what I wore, I must have been nicely dressed, since my mother took great care with my clothes and grooming, knowing that my appearance reflected on her. In the coming days, after meeting Sylvia's

children, she would exclaim privately how she couldn't imagine a
woman not keeping her babies' nightgowns clean, their faces shining. Especially now when the weather had turned so brutally cold
and almost everyone you met had the flu.

The woman asked, "And what do you write about? You can't
have had any *deep* experiences." She gave her throaty laugh.

I shrugged; probably I blushed. "Just about . . . old houses and
forests, and sometimes ghosts. Things like that." I shouldn't have
been so specific, but unlike my mother I instinctively told the truth
when anyone asked a question.

Sylvia laughed again. "A budding Gothicist, are you?"

Neither my mother nor I knew what that meant, not then; but
we smiled as though she'd paid an extravagant compliment.

"I guess so," I mumbled.

My mother asked, blinking, "And how many poems have *you*
written?"

Sylvia's eyes chilled briefly at this gauche question. I saw the
disdain a "real poet" assumes in the face of someone ignorant of
poetry. But instantly her American cheerfulness returned.

"Oh, far too many!" she exclaimed. "I've been writing like a
fiend, these past few months."

Then came a silence. The awareness had grown, I suppose,
that here we stood in this frigid, dank-smelling entryway, talking pointlessly, when my mother and I should return to our
unpacking and Sylvia should get back to her children. It was Sylvia who broke the silence, her own politeness a bit forced, this
time.

"I'd offer to help you get settled in, but I can't leave with the
babies napping. The cabin fever I get inside here, though!—it gets
tiresome. But why don't the two of you stop over tomorrow, around
four? We'll have our tea then, and get acquainted."

I knew this invitation would not please my mother; for all her
loneliness, I could sense her dislike of Sylvia, with her shabby
clothes and intimidating vocabulary.

After my father left her, my mother seldom befriended any women, since it was a woman, after all, who'd broken up her marriage; she gravitated toward men, especially fatherly, even grandfatherly men. (Perhaps that was part of her eagerness to meet Mr. Thomas.) And I'm sure she was thinking tomorrow was too soon. After settling into our flat, no doubt she wanted to luxuriate in her misery, to weep for hours in her darkened bedroom with the door partway closed, and to make brief, anguished phone calls to my father, begging him to reconsider. Each time she did this, I hurried to my room, closed the door, and snapped on the radio. I didn't want to hear.

"I'd love that!" my mother cried. "Are you sure it's not too much trouble?"

Again that throaty laugh. "My version of 'tea' is pretty meager, I warn you. Just a few sweet rolls, but I *did* find a shop round the corner that sells the most wonderful Darjeeling. I think you'll like it." Another glance at me. "And there'll be an orangeade, of course, for our young Mr. Poe."

My mother smiled as if Darjeeling and Poe were part of her everyday discourse. "Thanks so much," she said, and then she looked at me, too. She added, in her shrilly polite voice, "Isn't it nice, honey, that we've met one of our neighbors?"

I gave a vague smile but could think of nothing to say.

"There aren't many Americans around here, I'm afraid," Sylvia said. "The people you see out in the streets—well, I love the British, but there's that intense reserve, you know, and eccentricity. Plenty of old widows with ill-tempered pugs, or retired bachelors who spend their evenings reading Kipling, drinking brandy until they pass out for the night."

My mother laughed. "Oh, dear," she said.

Sylvia bit her lower lip. "I shouldn't say that. I'm known to take a brandy myself, after my work's done in the evening and the children are in bed. I suppose it's my poetic license, enjoying a drink alone once in a while?"

There was something strange in her tone, as though my mother or I might contest this. But my mother simply repeated, touching my shoulder, "We've never met a *real* poet before, have we, honey?"

I started backing away, toward the glass-paned entrance door; someone must bring this overlong encounter to an end. My mother was too insanely polite and Sylvia, I sensed, too lonely; she'd be willing to stand out here for a long time, talking of anything at all.

"Well, I don't know how *real* a poet I am," she said, rolling her eyes.

I'd begun to appreciate the irony in her rich, throaty voice, and in the serious attention she gave to every inane remark my mother made. There was a kind of generosity there, I thought; or perhaps the loneliness was simply that desperate.

"I'm sure you're quite talented," my mother said.

"Well, my first collection came out not long ago—I'll be happy to give you an inscribed copy tomorrow, if you care for such things. And I've done some talks and things for the BBC, and an interview." She bit her lip. "I hope that doesn't sound pompous, but poets don't get much attention in this world—so we savor what little we get!"

"Interviewed on the BBC! Imagine that!" my mother said. She reached aside to touch my arm, only then realizing I'd retreated toward the door.

Sylvia made a quick, dismissive gesture with her hand. "Oh, it's nothing. Just a bunch of unanswerable questions to which I was obliged to give intelligent, long-winded answers."

My mother laughed. Sylvia laughed.

"Mommy, we'd better finish the unpacking," I said, in a plaintive tone. I sounded six rather than ten.

My mother nodded. Sylvia nodded. They said their good-byes quickly and reiterated their pleasure over finding each other, and their pleased anticipation of the next day's tea.

"But really, don't go to any trouble," my mother said, as she turned away. "And I do hope we'll hear some of your poems. I'd love that, and so would my son. We've never met—"

I'd winced, thinking surely she wouldn't repeat that phrase yet another time; fortunately, she'd caught herself.

"Don't worry, the tea will be modest. As for the poems, I don't think you'd care to hear them."

"Oh, but we *would*," my mother said.

"Oh, but you wouldn't," Sylvia said. "Believe me."

It was the only disagreeable thing she'd said—if to say something with a private reference may be called disagreeable—and it left my mother stranded in an awkward silence. The three of us stood there a few seconds longer, my nostrils twitching at the smell of Sylvia's hair, which reminded me of spoiled food, littered alleyways, the hamper of dirty laundry my mother sorted each Monday. Why didn't Sylvia shampoo her hair? I wondered. My mother still used the large green bottle of Prell she'd brought from home.

"Until tomorrow, then," my mother said, finally. "Shall I bring anything?"

Sylvia paused and lowered her eyes, in a way I recall as girlish. "No, just yourselves," she said. "Just the company."

She turned and vanished up the dark flight of stairs.

My mother whispered, angrily, "This is just our luck, isn't it."

I nodded. It surely was.

II

Her hair smelled worse.

And her face seemed discolored, the nostrils reddish-pink and raw, plum-dark shadows beneath her eyes. Even so, she gave that bright American smile when she greeted us. She wore a nicer outfit, I recall, some tight-fitting black Capri pants and a red velour sweater that looked new, but the hair had that same oily, much-fingered look, and ink stains still streaked her hands. I remember the side of her left hand, a large blotch as though it had rested on wet ink. I wondered why she didn't scrub them, why a grown woman wouldn't want her hair and hands clean. I confess I was in a foul mood—the kind children get when dragged somewhere they don't want to go—as I was fearful of my mother's embarrassing me. Otherwise I might not have minded, as Sylvia's being a poet had snagged my interest.

There were books and papers everywhere. After Sylvia let us in, she took my mother upstairs to see the babies, who'd been put down for their nap. But Sylvia said they were still awake and she wanted my mother to see them. She knew I had no interest in babies—she said this with the droll smirk she often gave me—so she invited me to "dig into" the pastries heaped on the tea table, arranged neatly on a ceramic plate. In retrospect it seems that Sylvia, too, no less than my mother, was trying to maintain an appearance of normalcy, even a determined conventionality, but in my boyishly harsh judgment her efforts had failed.

While they were upstairs, I shambled around the room, hands plunged into my pockets. My mother had insisted I wear my navy blazer; she'd also dug out my red bow tie from the preceding Easter. I passed my gaze along the desks and tables, pausing over each item like a miniature curator. There were so many heaps of papers, some an unsettling bright pink. So many books, too, stacked haphazardly: I stopped and glanced with my head turned sideways, reading titles before moving to another. I seem to remember books on history, including some on Napoleon (which struck me as odd). Memory is notoriously unreliable; it would be easy to claim that I recall reading, in Sylvia's spiky but legible hand, now-famous phrases like *White Godiva, I unpeel* or *I eat men like air*. I do remember seeing manuscript poems, neatly typed with many cross-outs and additions in the same spiky hand, but the only recollection I trust is my thinking that Sylvia had been right: my mother wouldn't like these poems.

Hearing them descend the stairs, I hurried to the table and sat down, examining the pastries as if I'd spent the entire time deciding which to eat. Sylvia had been modest in apologizing for the tea: the pastries were quite elaborate, some with fruit and cheese fillings, and it occurred to me that she'd spent a considerable sum on this little meal. Her furniture and belongings suggested she didn't have much money. The walls had been painted a stark white, and the sparse furniture included some plain bookcases and two uncomfortable-looking, vaguely Oriental chairs made of straw. I wondered if she couldn't afford to furnish the apartment properly or simply liked this spare, inhuman style. This thought, combined with the shadowy, chilly atmosphere of the rooms, made me wonder again if she was lonely.

Cheerfully, Sylvia approached the table, gesturing my mother toward an empty chair. "Don't they strike your fancy?" she asked me, smiling, "or are you just being polite?"

"I was just . . . waiting," I said.

My mother said, "He's never been one for sweets, actually. He's not like other children, that way."

"Oh?" Sylvia cocked her head, regarding me. "Try one of the cheese ones, then," she said, pointing an ink-stained finger at the very one, in fact, I'd planned to take. Delicately I lifted the pastry, took a small bite, and set the remainder on my plate. Both Sylvia and my mother stood watching me with anxious smiles, making me long to rise from my chair and rush back down Fitzroy Road to our own apartment. Of course, I did no such thing, and after pouring tea and getting settled in her chair Sylvia directed her attention to my mother, sending a volley of questions her way as if her guest— an ordinary-looking woman in a pale-blue dress with pleated skirt, and a conventional string of fake pearls—were the most fascinating person in England.

Since her separation from my father, my mother had mastered the art of giving courteous answers to people while providing very little concrete information. This was one skill of hers that I admired and soon enough deployed on my own (especially the next fall, back in Atlanta, when I returned to school). One thing I noticed was that neither Sylvia nor my mother talked about their husbands, as if honoring some tacit compact that such a disagreeable subject wouldn't do for polite teatime conversation. Once or twice Sylvia did refer to "my ex-husband," but only in a casual, glancing way, as you'd mention a pet now deceased, or a piece of furniture you'd thrown out; clearly, she no more wanted to talk about her marital disaster than did my mother—who now, perhaps fearing such a turn in the conversation, inevitably raised the subject I most dreaded.

"So, have you been writing poetry today, Mrs. Hughes?" she asked.

Sylvia reached out, playfully, and gave my mother a pretend slap on the arm. "Now really, do call me Sylvia," she said, for perhaps the third time. She withdrew the hand. Her smile vanished, her eyes seemed to retreat into shadow. "No, no—I really think I'm done writing poetry, for now."

My mother and I glanced up from our plates, surprised.

"But why is that?" my mother said. "If you've published a book, and been on the BBC—"

"I'm working on a novel," Sylvia said quickly. "It's called *Double Exposure*—at least at the moment!—and I'm enjoying it quite a lot. As for the poems, they—they seemed to come to a natural end, a few days ago. I put them together into a sequence, you see, so I suppose there'll be a new collection. . . ."

Her voice trailed off, as though she didn't quite believe this.

"*Double Exposure!*" my mother exclaimed, as I'd known she would. "What an excellent title. Are you interested in photography, Mrs.—oh, I'm sorry. Sylvia . . ."

Sylvia gave a deep, disdainful laugh. "No, no, it's about marriage—but especially about betrayal, infidelity. It's something else you wouldn't want to read!"

This silenced my mother; even she wouldn't deny the truth of this. Sylvia, chewing the last bite of her raspberry-filled scone, licked her stained fingers and shot a look at me.

"And how about you?" she asked. "Are you writing poetry these days?" I heard an ironic lilt to her voice, as though we shared a poets' complicity that excluded my mother.

I said, "No ma'am, not really. Only during school."

This was a lie, as I'd been writing small things here and there for weeks, late at night, after my mother had taken her sleeping pills; but I feared any questions from Sylvia about my writing. I kept the poems hidden in a drawer so my mother couldn't read them.

"Oh, but he reads a great deal," she said, recovering her ladylike smile. "Novels, mostly, but poetry as well—don't you, honey?"

I lowered my eyes. "Sometimes. At night," I said.

"When I was little," Sylvia said, in a gentler, nostalgic voice, "I'd memorize my favorite poems. They were short ones by Emily Dickinson, Edna St. Vincent Millay, and I loved walking round the house and saying them aloud—much to the consternation of my father. He was a college professor who mostly worked at home, and he did not like to be disturbed." She laughed angrily. "But poetry is such a *force* in my little world that I couldn't contain myself, at times."

My mother and I stared. Sylvia sounded as though she were talking to herself, not to us.

"In fact, I was about your age!" she said brightly, as if discovering a remarkable fact. Again she settled her red-rimmed gaze on me. "And you? Do you memorize poems, ever? Do you enjoy doing that?"

I winced, for I knew what my mother would say next.

"Oh yes, they had an assignment just last spring," she broke in. "They were each given a poem, and the next week they'd stand before the class and recite it. The teacher said *his* was the longest and he recited it beautifully, not only getting the words right but even the right pauses and rhythms, and so forth."

Sylvia's eyes were alight. "Do you still remember the poem? Would you recite it for us?"

"Oh, I couldn't now," I murmured.

"You little silly, of course you can!" my mother cried. "Remember, the other night at dinner I asked you?—and you recited it beautifully."

Sylvia's eyes had softened. She had sensed my embarrassment and regretted pursuing the topic. But my mother was adamant.

"Come on, now, recite the poem for Sylvia. And stand up, just like you did in the class. That should help you remember."

I did a quick mental calculation and reasoned it was easier simply to recite the poem than to refuse. I did remember it, so the ordeal would be over soon enough. Then I'd ask Sylvia to read some of her poetry and my mother would insist on that, too. They'd leave me alone for a while.

I stood, my legs wobbly as a newborn fawn's. Only then did I understand I was nervous. This woman, Sylvia, had published a book; she was an authentic poet; and what had seemed an excellent recital to my English teacher back in Atlanta might sound foolish and incompetent to her.

These anxieties mounted quickly; I felt my skittering heartbeat and tasted dry panic in my throat.

"Come *on*, honey," my mother prodded. "Don't keep us waiting all afternoon."

Sylvia's compassionate, pained stare is an image I'll never forget. It was the moment I first began to like her.

I swallowed; I licked my dry lips. I began: "'Joyce,' by Trees Kilmer . . ."

A moment passed before I caught the mistake. I noticed Sylvia's bent head, my mother rolling her eyes, and only then heard the quivering echo of my words. But doggedly I stumbled through the poem, transposing who knows how many words and lines, until I'd reached the end. I sat down.

Sylvia smiled. "I read that poem in school, too."

"You recited it much better the other night," my mother complained.

I saw that Sylvia was shivering. To change the subject I said, "Are you cold?" It wasn't the brightest question, for we all sat huddled around the table, hands in our pockets when we weren't eating. A small portable heater, glowing a faint orange in the room's corner, was the only source of warmth.

Sylvia looked rueful. "I've been cold ever since we moved to London. That's why the children and I have been sick so much—I'm sorry it's cold in here, but I keep the good heater in Nick and Frieda's room. You know, I was so thrilled to find a flat in this building, since Yeats lived here and I thought it would . . . inspire me, I suppose. But then this awful weather descended. There hasn't been a single day when I or the children—sometimes all three—haven't been sick. The flu, bronchitis, sinusitis, plain vanilla colds—you name it!"

My mother said, conversationally, "I read it's the coldest winter in London in more than a century. We didn't know what to expect, since it's our first trip abroad, but the snow, especially, *has* been awful."

"The frozen pipes are the worst," Sylvia said, answering my mother but still regarding me. "When I finally got plumbers to come out, they stood shaking their heads and said to pour hot water on the outdoor pipes. They said they'd come back the next day, and of course I'm still waiting. Everyone's pipes are frozen. Everything is paralyzed."

My mother frowned. "Really? I guess we're a bit luckier, in our building. We get the afternoon sun, and I suppose that helps."

"Yes," Sylvia said, absently. "I suppose it does."

During this brief impasse in the conversation, I sat remembering a poem by Yeats another student had memorized for her recitation. "The Folly of Being Comforted" was the title. I knew that my mother had no idea who Yeats was, and I also thought that our visit was providing no comfort to Sylvia.

When she offered my mother a second cup of tea, my mother placed her palm over the cup and exclaimed, "Oh, no, we've really got to be running! We're still living out of boxes, and I'm the type who can't rest until everything is put away. I like things neat and tidy."

I didn't think she intended a reference to the cluttered state of Sylvia's rooms—my mother was a frivolous, dishonest woman, but she wasn't mean-spirited—yet I saw Sylvia glance dolefully around.

"For us writers, nothing is ever tidy," she said, and added one of her throaty, enigmatic laughs. "Except," she said, turning to me and tweaking my bow tie, "for certain tidy young poets, perhaps I'm sure you'll grow up to write flawlessly rhymed sonnets and immaculate sestinas."

I dropped my eyes, embarrassed and pleased.

Laughing, my mother got to her feet. "For now, I'll be happy if he keeps his room straight." She held out her hand. "It was lovely meeting you, Sylvia. When we get our place in order, we'd love to have you over. But you *must* promise to read us some poems."

Walking us to the door, Sylvia seemed unexpectedly shy and girlish. "This went by so quickly," she said, and as I passed her slender form, which she seemed to drape along the edge of the open door, I caught again a whiff of her rank, unwashed hair. Since I'd grown to like her, I remembered that her pipes were burst and excused her on that account. During our tea she'd mentioned that she gave the babies sponge baths with water she carried several blocks from a store near Primrose Park.

Head bent, my mother adjusted her coat, pulled her gloves right; we said good-bye.

That was my last glimpse of Sylvia: standing behind her door, almost as if hiding, with her face and a shank of that dark blond hair hanging against the whitish gray light from inside her apartment. I can't remember if we stopped downstairs and spoke to Mr. Thomas, but it was he who gave us the news, several weeks later, that Sylvia was dead. My mother had thought to reciprocate Sylvia's hospitality and invite her for tea; she'd called Mr. Thomas because Sylvia had mentioned, with an air of apology, that she had no phone, but that Mr. Thomas occasionally would bring her messages upstairs.

I recall very clearly that phone conversation: as I stood listening, a cold lump of sorrow settled in my chest. After much talk of days and times, my mother and Mr. Thomas calculated that Sylvia had killed herself only a few days after our visit. He told her about the flurry of activity that had followed—the father coming to retrieve the children, the police coming and going, and their questioning Mr. Thomas about what he might have seen or heard. I got these details later, from my mother, for her side of the conversation that day was mostly, "Oh dear, oh dear! *Killed* herself? Really? But how did she— *Really?*" She was shouting, since Thomas was indeed partly deaf. Her tone was an odd mixture of dismay and quite audible relish. Another woman, she must have been thinking, had died because her husband had abandoned her, but she had survived. She still wept at night, she wrote and telephoned my father after drinking two or three gins to steady her nerves, but she hadn't killed herself.

"I suppose we all think of that at times, don't we," I remember her shouting to Mr. Thomas, as they were about to hang up. "The poor woman," she said, "and those poor, lovely children!" She put down the phone, then stared for a long moment at me.

"Tell me what happened," I said.

Almost a year passed before my mother's own suicide. We were back in Atlanta, the divorce had become final, and my father was sending monthly checks from England. He'd continued his affair and finally married the other woman—my stepmother to this day—and had returned to her in London, which he'd decided he preferred to the American Southwest where he'd grown up. But my mother stayed frozen in her grief, her rage, her self-pity. I remembered Sylvia's words, *Everything is paralyzed.*

I'd gone back to school, of course, and I remember dreading the bus trip home, knowing she'd still be wearing her housecoat, her eyes puffy from crying. The day I found her face down on the living room sofa, an empty container of pills and a coffee mug half-filled with gin on the table beside her, I wasn't really surprised. She'd left no note; unlike Sylvia, she lacked the consolations of language, much less of poetry. I shed a few tears and called my aunt Ruth, whose house was two blocks away and with whom I would live until I graduated high school.

Sylvia's prediction was correct, at least partly. I did try my hand at sonnets and sestinas, feeling drawn to fixed forms, but I suppose they weren't "immaculate" since magazines always rejected them and finally I gave up. In college, studying library science, I met a quiet girl who shared some of my classes and shortly after graduation we were married. We stayed in Atlanta and both got jobs in a major university library, sharing the same shift so we could spend our time at home together as well. Too late I discovered that I'd married my mother, for the girl had nothing of her own—nothing, that is, but me. Soon enough I felt stifled and began an affair with my wife's opposite number—a graduate student who did modeling on the side. I'd become, I suppose, a reasonably handsome young man, and my mistress was the catalyst for my trying to write poetry again. I remember reading Shakespeare's sonnets and trying to imitate them, including specific references to my mistress that delighted her. I asked my wife for a divorce, and after a few predictable scenes she agreed and moved back to rural Alabama to live with her mother.

Around the time of my second marriage, my new wife quit graduate school to start modeling full-time, and I stopped writing the poetry that nobody wanted to publish. I enjoyed—and still enjoy—being a librarian, and I always experience a small frisson of delight when a new book about Sylvia comes into the library. By now, there are many dozens, perhaps hundreds. My name has never appeared in the index of these books, though I've always been fearful that some intrepid biographer might track me down—as they did Mr. Thomas, who sometimes gave them interviews. (Recently Mr. Thomas, the only person who knew of my brief connection with Sylvia, passed away, forcing me to recall that in the mid-seventies, alarmed by the way Sylvia's legend was growing, I'd phoned him.

During that awkward, staticky, trans-Atlantic call, shouting so that he could hear, I'd extracted a promise that he'd never mention my name.) Nor did I tell anyone else, not even my wife, about my two encounters with Sylvia, though my wife occasionally mentions her in passing. She studied Sylvia's poetry at school.

All this has come to haunt me, I suppose, especially since I've understood that my second marriage, too, will soon come to an end. My wife, well past forty, no longer gets modeling assignments, and our intimate life together has shriveled to nothing. She's what people call a "well-preserved" woman, but no man can help the way he feels, after all. The difficulty, of course, will be telling her, going through the inevitable arguments with their tears and recriminations, and then finding a new place to live, a new life altogether. A first-year graduate student, who teases me about the "distinguished" streaks of gray in my hair, seems to find me attractive, but I'm not yet ready, I know, to marry again. That will take some time.

Yes, I do feel haunted by the ghosts of my past. Poor Sylvia, and my mother, and my first wife, and even my elegant second wife who seems already in my imagination part of the past though we still live together. (We never had children; I feel fortunate in that.) Sometimes at my desk, in an idle moment, I'll recall that image of Sylvia, peering around the door at me, bidding me good-bye. Or my first wife's moony, tear-stained face the night I turned my back on her forever. Or that famous television commercial in which my second wife appeared, shortly after we were married, a memory with a peculiar resonance I don't quite understand.

This was the mid-eighties, and we were particularly thrilled because it was her first commercial to go national. We would cuddle together under a quilt in our big four-poster, before or after making love, and replay the tape over and over.

I haven't seen the tape in years, but I remember it as clearly as I recall Sylvia's ink-stained fingers. It was an ad for a feminine product and my wife appears on horseback, first at a distance. She wears an elegant yellow sweater, brown jodhpurs and boots, her thick blond hair flying behind her; her body and the spectacular chestnut-colored mare are one, rippling through the sunlight and shadow. As the camera moves closer, we see her galloping along a dry, rutted lane overarched by the foliage of a spectacular New England autumn.

I have not cried since childhood but I did cry, or came close to crying, during the final seconds of that stupid commercial. The camera zooms in, showing my wife canted forward eagerly as she rides. My heart beats quickly, guiltily. For somehow, in that moment, she metamorphoses into the epitome of confident, glamorous womanhood, glorying in a fierce moment of power and vision with her hands clenching the bridle and her lovely hair flowing, springing behind her, wild and free.

OLD BOYS, OLD GIRLS

Edward P. Jones

They caught him after he had killed the second man. The law would never connect him to the first murder. So the victim—a stocky fellow Caesar Matthews shot in a Northeast alley only two blocks from the home of the guy's parents, a man who died over a woman who was actually in love with a third man—was destined to lie in his grave without anyone officially paying for what had happened to him. It was almost as if, at least on the books the law kept, Caesar had got away with a free killing.

Seven months after he stabbed the second man—a twenty-two-year-old with prematurely gray hair who had ventured out of Southeast for only the sixth time in his life—Caesar was tried for murder in the second degree. During much of the trial, he remembered the name only of the first dead man—Percy, or "Golden Boy," Weymouth—and not the second, Antwoine Stoddard, to whom everyone kept referring during the proceedings. The world had done things to Caesar since he'd left his father's house for good at sixteen, nearly fourteen years ago, but he had done far more to himself.

So at trial, with the weight of all the harm done to him and because he had hidden for months in one shit hole after another, he was not always himself and thought many times that he was actually there for killing Golden Boy, the first dead man. He was not insane, but he was three doors from it, which was how an old girlfriend, Yvonne Miller, would now and again playfully refer to his behavior. Who the fuck is this Antwoine bitch? Caesar sometimes thought during the trial. And where is Percy? It was only when the judge sentenced him to seven years in Lorton, D.C.'s prison in Virginia, that matters became somewhat clear again, and in those last moments before they took him away, he saw Antwoine spread out on the ground outside the Prime Property nightclub, blood spurting out of his chest like oil from a bountiful well. Caesar remembered it all: sitting on the sidewalk, the liquor spinning his brain, his friends begging him to run, the club's music flooding out of the open door and going *thumpety-thump-thump* against his head. He sat a few feet from Antwoine, and would have killed again for a cigarette. "That's you, baby, so very near insanity it can touch you," said Yvonne, who believed in unhappiness and who thought happiness was the greatest trick God had invented. Yvonne Miller would be waiting for Caesar at the end of the line.

HE CAME to Lorton with a ready-made reputation, since Multrey Wilson and Tony Cathedral—first-degree murderers both, and destined to die there—knew him from his Northwest and Northeast days. They were about as big as you could get in Lorton at that time (the guards called Lorton the House of Multrey and Cathedral), and they let everyone know that Caesar was good people, "a protected body," with no danger of having his biscuits or his butt taken.

A little less than a week after Caesar arrived, Cathedral asked him how he liked his cellmate. Caesar had never been to prison but had spent five days in the D.C. jail, not counting the time there before and during the trial. They were side by side at dinner, and neither man looked at the other. Multrey sat across from them. Cathedral was done eating in three minutes, but Caesar always took a long time to eat. His mother had raised him to chew his food thoroughly. "You wanna be a old man livin on oatmeal?" "I love oatmeal, Mama." "Tell me that when you have to eat it every day till you die."

"He all right, I guess," Caesar said of his cellmate, with whom he had shared fewer than a thousand words. Caesar's mother had died before she saw what her son became.

"You got the bunk you want, the right bed?" Multrey said. He was sitting beside one of his two "women," the one he had turned out most recently. "She" was picking at her food, something Multrey had already warned her about. The woman had a family—a wife and three children—but they would not visit. Caesar would never have visitors, either.

"It's all right." Caesar had taken the top bunk, as the cellmate had already made the bottom his home. A miniature plastic panda from his youngest child dangled on a string hung from one of the metal bedposts. "Bottom, top, it's all the same ship."

Cathedral leaned into him, picking chicken out of his teeth with an inch-long fingernail sharpened to a point. "Listen, man, even if you like the top bunk, you fuck him up for the bottom just cause you gotta let him know who rules. You let him know that you will stab him through his motherfuckin heart and then turn around and eat your supper, cludin the dessert." Cathedral straightened up. "Caes, you gon be here a few days, so you can't let nobody fuck with your humanity."

He went back to the cell and told Pancho Morrison that he wanted the bottom bunk, couldn't sleep well at the top.

"Too bad," Pancho said. He was lying down, reading a book published by the Jehovah's Witnesses. He wasn't a Witness, but he was curious.

Caesar grabbed the book and flung it at the bars, and the bulk of it slid through an inch or so and dropped to the floor. He kicked

Pancho in the side, and before he could pull his leg back for a second kick Pancho took the foot in both hands, twisted it, and threw him against the wall. Then Pancho was up, and they fought for nearly an hour before two guards, who had been watching the whole time, came in and beat them about the head. "Show's over! Show's over!" one kept saying.

They attended to themselves in silence in the cell, and with the same silence they flung themselves at each other the next day after dinner. They were virtually the same size, and though Caesar came to battle with more muscle, Pancho had more heart. Cathedral had told Caesar that morning that Pancho had lived on practically nothing but heroin for the three years before Lorton, so whatever fighting dog was in him could be pounded out in little or no time. It took three days. Pancho was the father of five children, and each time he swung he did so with the memory of all five and what he had done to them over those three addicted years. He wanted to return to them and try to make amends, and he realized on the morning of the third day that he would not be able to do that if Caesar killed him. So fourteen minutes into the fight he sank to the floor after Caesar hammered him in the gut. And though he could have got up, he stayed there, silent and still. The two guards laughed. The daughter who had given Pancho the panda was nine years old and had been raised by her mother as a Catholic.

That night, before the place went dark, Caesar lay on the bottom bunk and looked over at pictures of Pancho's children, which Pancho had taped on the opposite wall. He knew he would have to decide if he wanted Pancho just to move the photographs or to put them away altogether. All the children had toothy smiles. The two youngest stood, in separate pictures, outdoors in their First Communion clothes. Caesar himself had been a father for two years. A girl he had met at an F Street club in Northwest had told him he was the father of her son, and for a time he had believed her. Then the boy started growing big ears that Caesar thought didn't belong to anyone in his family, and so after he had slapped the girl a few times a week before the child's second birthday she confessed that the child belonged to "my first love." "Your first love is always with you," she said, sounding forever like a television addict who had never read a book. As Caesar prepared to leave, she asked him, "You want back all the toys and things you gave him?" The child, as if used to their fighting, had slept through this last encounter on the couch, part of a living room suite that they were paying for on time. Caesar said nothing more and didn't think about his eighteen-karat-gold cigarette lighter until he was eight blocks away. The girl pawned the thing and got enough to pay off the furniture bill.

Caesar and Pancho worked in the laundry, and Caesar could look across the noisy room with all the lint swirling about and see Pancho sorting dirty pieces into bins. Then he would push uniform bins to the left and everything else to the right. Pancho had been do-ing that for three years. The job he got after he left Lorton was as a gofer at construction sites. No laundry in the outside world wanted him. Over the next two weeks, as Caesar watched Pancho at his job, his back always to him, he considered what he should do next. He wasn't into fucking men, so that was out. He still had not decided what he wanted done about the photographs on the cell wall. One day at the end of those two weeks, Caesar saw the light above Pan-cho's head flickering and Pancho raised his head and looked for a long time at it, as if thinking that the answer to all his problems lay in fixing that one light. Caesar decided then to let the pictures remain on the wall.

Three years later, they let Pancho go. The two men had mostly stayed at a distance from each other, but toward the end they had been talking, sharing plans about a life beyond Lorton. The rela-tionship had reached the point where Caesar was saddened to see the children's photographs come off the wall. Pancho pulled off the last taped picture and the wall was suddenly empty in a most for-lorn way. Caesar knew the names of all the children. Pancho gave him a rabbit's foot that one of his children had given him. It was the way among all those men that when a good-luck piece had run out of juice, it was given away with the hope that new ownership would renew its strength. The rabbit's foot had lost its electricity months before Pancho's release. Caesar's only good-fortune piece was a key chain made in Peru; it had been sweet for a bank robber in the next cell for nearly two years until that man's daughter, walking home from third grade, was abducted and killed.

One day after Pancho left, they brought in a thief and three-time rapist of elderly women. He nodded to Caesar and told him that he was Watson Rainey and went about making a home for himself in the cell, finally plugging in a tiny lamp with a green shade, which he placed on the metal shelf jutting from the wall. Then he climbed onto the top bunk he had made up and lay down. His name was all the wordplay he had given Caesar, who had been smoking on the bottom bunk throughout Rainey's efforts to make a nest. Caesar waited ten minutes and then stood and pulled the lamp's cord out of the wall socket and grabbed Rainey with one hand and threw him to the floor. He crushed the lamp into Rainey's face. He choked him with the cord. "You come into my house and show me no respect!" Caesar shouted. The only sound Rainey could manage was a gurgling that bubbled up from his mangled mouth. There were no witnesses except for an old man across the way, who would occasionally glance over at the two when he wasn't reading his Bible. It was over and done with in four minutes. When Rainey came to, he found everything he owned piled in the corner, soggy with piss. And Caesar was again on the top bunk.

They would live in that cell together until Caesar was released, four years later. Rainey tried never to be in the house during waking hours; if he was there when Caesar came in, he would leave. Rainey's name spoken by him that first day were all the words that would ever pass between the two men.

A week or so after Rainey got there, Caesar bought from Multrey a calendar that was three years old. It was large and had no markings of any sort, as pristine as the day it was made. "You know this one ain't the year we in right now," Multrey said as one of his women took a quarter from Caesar and dropped it in her purse. Caesar said, "It'll do." Multrey prized the calendar for one thing: its top half had a photograph of a naked woman of indeterminate race sitting on a stool, her legs wide open, her pussy aimed dead at whoever was standing right in front of her. It had been Multrey's good-luck piece, but the luck was dead. Multrey remembered what the calendar had done for him and he told his woman to give Caesar his money back, lest any new good-fortune piece turn sour on him.

The calendar's bottom half had the days of the year. That day, the first Monday in June, Caesar drew in the box that was January 1 a line that went from the upper left-hand corner down to the bottom right-hand corner. The next day, a June Tuesday, he made a line in the January 2 box that also ran in the same direction. And so it went. When the calendar had all such lines in all the boxes, it was the next June. Then Caesar, in that January 1 box, made a line that formed an X with the first line. And so it was for another year. The third year saw horizontal marks that sliced the boxes in half. The fourth year had vertical lines down the centers of the boxes.

This was the only calendar Caesar had in Lorton. That very first Monday, he taped the calendar over the area where the pictures of Pancho's children had been. There was still a good deal of empty space left, but he didn't do anything about it, and Rainey knew he couldn't do anything, either.

THE CALENDAR did right by Caesar until near the end of his fifth year in Lorton, when he began to feel that its juice was drying up. But he kept it there to mark off the days, and, too, the naked woman never closed her legs to him.

In that fifth year, someone murdered Multrey as he showered. The killers—it had to be more than one for a man like Multrey— were never found. The Multrey woman who picked at her food had felt herself caring for a recent arrival who was five years younger than her, a part-time deacon who had killed a Southwest bartender for calling the deacon's wife "a woman without one fuckin brain cell." The story of that killing—the bartender was dropped head-first from the roof of a ten-story building—became legend, and in Lorton men referred to the dead bartender as "the Flat-Head In-sulter" and the killer became known as "the Righteous Desulter." The Desulter, wanting Multrey's lady, had hired people to butcher him. It had always been the duty of the lady who hated food to watch out for Multrey as he showered, but she had stepped away that day, just as she had been instructed to by the Desulter.

In another time, Cathedral and Caesar would have had enough of everything—from muscle to influence—to demand that some-one give up the killers, but the prison was filling up with younger men who did not care what those two had been once upon a time. Also, Cathedral had already had two visits from the man he had killed in Northwest. Each time, the man had first stood before the bars of Cathedral's cell. Then he held one of the bars and opened the door inward, like some wooden door on a person's house. The dead man standing there would have been sufficient to unwrap anyone, but matters were compounded when Cathedral saw a door that for years had slid sideways now open in an impossible fashion. The man stood silent before Cathedral, and when he left he shut the door gently, as if there were sleeping children in the cell. So Cathedral didn't have a full mind, and Multrey was never avenged.

THERE WAS an armed-robbery man in the place, a tattooer with home-made inks and needles. He made a good living painting on both muscled and frail bodies the names of children; the Devil in full re-galia with a pitchfork dripping with blood; the words "Mother" or "Mother Forever" surrounded by red roses and angels who looked sad, because when it came to drawing happy angels the tattoo man had no skills. One pickpocket had had a picture of his father tat-tooed in the middle of his chest; above the father's head, in medi-eval lettering, were the words "Rotting in Hell," with the letter "H" done in fiery yellow and red. The tattoo guy had told Caesar that he had skin worthy of "a painter's best canvas," that he could give Caesar a tattoo "God would envy." Caesar had always told him no, but then he awoke one snowy night in March of his sixth year and realized that it was his mother's birthday. He did not know what day of the week it was, but the voice that talked to him had the authority of a million loving mothers. He had long ago forgotten his own birthday, had not even bothered to ask someone in prison records to look it up.

There had never been anyone or anything he wanted commemorated on his body. Maybe it would have been Carol, his first girlfriend twenty years ago, before the retarded girl entered their lives. He had played with the notion of having the name of the boy he thought was his put over his heart, but the lie had come to light before that could happen. And before the boy there had been Yvonne, with whom he had lived for an extraordinary time in Northeast. He would have put Yvonne's name over his heart, but she went off to work one day and never came back. He looked for her for three months, and then just assumed that she had been killed somewhere and dumped in a place only animals knew about. Yvonne was indeed dead, and she would be waiting for him at the end of the line, though she did not know that was what she was doing. "You can always trust unhappiness," Yvonne had once said, sitting in the dark on the couch, her cigarette burned down to the filter. "His face never changes. But happiness is slick, can't be trusted. It has a thousand faces, Caes, all of them just ready to re-form into unhappiness once it has you in its clutches."

So Caesar had the words "Mother Forever" tattooed on his left bicep. Knowing that more letters meant a higher payment of cigarettes or money or candy, the tattoo fellow had dissuaded him from having just plain "Mother." "How many hours you think she spent in labor?" he asked Caesar. "Just to give you life." The job took five hours over two days, during a snowstorm. Caesar said no to angels, knowing the man's ability with happy ones, and had the words done in blue letters encased in red roses. The man worked from the words printed on a piece of paper that Caesar had given him, because he was also a bad speller.

The snow stopped on the third day and, strangely, it took only another three days for the two feet of mess to melt, for with the end of the storm came a heat wave. The tattoo man, a good friend of the Righteous Desulter, would tell Caesar in late April that what happened to him was his own fault, that he had not taken care of himself as he had been instructed to do. "And the heat ain't helped you neither." On the night of March 31, five days after the tattoo had been put on, Caesar woke in the night with a pounding in his left arm. He couldn't return to sleep so he sat on the edge of his bunk until morning, when he saw that the "e"s in "Mother Forever" had blistered, as if someone had taken a match to them.

He went to the tattoo man, who first told him not to worry, then patted the "e"s with peroxide that he warmed in a spoon with a match. Within two days, the "e"s seemed to just melt away, each dissolving into an ugly pile at the base of the tattoo. After a week, the diseased "e"s began spreading their work to the other letters, and Caesar couldn't move his arm without pain. He went to the infirmary. They gave him aspirin and Band-Aided the tattoo. He was back the next day, the day the doctor was there.

He spent four days in D.C. General Hospital, his first trip back to Washington since a court appearance more than three years before. His entire body was paralyzed for two days, and one nurse confided to him the day he left that he had been near death. In the end, after the infection had done its work, there was not much left of the tattoo except an "o" and an "r," which were so deformed they could never pass for English, and a few roses that looked more like red mud. When he returned to prison, the tattoo man offered to give back the cigarettes and the money, but Caesar never gave him an answer, leading the man to think that he should watch his back. What happened to Caesar's tattoo and to Caesar was bad advertising, and soon the fellow had no customers at all.

Something had died in the arm and the shoulder, and Caesar was never again able to raise the arm more than thirty-five degrees. He had no enemies, but still he told no one about his debilitation. For the next few months he tried to stay out of everyone's way, knowing that he was far more vulnerable than he had been before the tattoo. Alone in the cell, with no one watching across the way, he exercised the arm, but by November he knew at last he would not be the same again. He tried to bully Rainey Watson as much as he could to continue the facade that he was still who he had been. And he tried to spend more time with Cathedral.

But the man Cathedral had killed had become a far more constant visitor. The dead man, a young bachelor who had been Cathedral's next-door neighbor, never spoke. He just opened Cathedral's cell door inward and went about doing things as if the cell were a family home—straightening wall pictures that only Cathedral could see, turning down the gas on the stove, testing the shower water to make sure that it was not too hot, tucking children into bed. Cathedral watched silently.

Caesar went to Cathedral's cell one day in mid-December, six months before they freed him. He found his friend sitting on the bottom bunk, his hands clamped over his knees. He was still outside the cell when Cathedral said, "Caes, you tell me why God would be so stupid to create mosquitoes. I mean, what good are the damn things? What's their function?" Caesar laughed, thinking it was a joke, and he had started to offer something when Cathedral looked over at him with a devastatingly serious gaze and said, "What we need is a new God. Somebody who knows what the fuck he's doing." Cathedral was not smiling. He returned to staring at the wall across from him. "What's with creatin bats? I mean, yes, they eat insects, but why create those insects to begin with? You see what I mean? Creatin a problem and then havin to create somethin to take care of the problem. And then comin up with somethin for that second problem. Man oh man!" Caesar slowly began moving away from Cathedral's cell. He had seen this many times before. It could not be cured even by great love. It sometimes pulled down a loved one. "And roaches. Every human bein in the world would have the sense not to create roaches. What's their function, Caes? I tell you, we need a new God, and I'm ready to cast my vote right now. Roaches and rats and chinches. God was out of his fuckin mind that week. Six wasted days, cept for the human part and some of the animals. And then partyin on the seventh day like he done us a big favor. The nerve of that motherfucker. And all your pigeons and squirrels. Don't forget them. I mean really."

In late January, they took Cathedral somewhere and then brought him back after a week. He returned to his campaign for a new God in February. A ritual began that would continue until Caesar left: determine that Cathedral was a menace to himself, take him away, bring him back, then take him away when he started campaigning again for another God.

THERE WAS now nothing for Caesar to do except try to coast to the end on a reputation that was far less than it had been in his first years at Lorton. He could only hope that he had built up enough goodwill among men who had better reputations and arms that worked a hundred percent.

In early April, he received a large manila envelope from his attorney. The lawyer's letter was brief. "I did not tell them where you are," he wrote. "They may have learned from someone that I was your attorney. Take care." There were two separate letters in sealed envelopes from his brother and sister, each addressed to "My Brother Caesar." Dead people come back alive, Caesar thought many times before he finally read the letters, after almost a week. He expected an announcement about the death of his father, but he was hardly mentioned. Caesar's younger brother went on for five pages with a history of what had happened to the family since Caesar had left their lives. He ended by saying, "Maybe I should have been a better brother." There were three pictures as well, one of his brother and his bride on their wedding day, and one showing Caesar's sister, her husband, and their two children, a girl of four or so and a boy of about two. The third picture had the girl sitting on a couch beside the boy, who was in Caesar's father's lap, looking with interest off to the left, as if whatever was there were more important than having his picture taken. Caesar looked at the image of his father—a man on the verge of becoming old. His sister's letter had even less in it than the lawyer's: "Write to me, or call me collect, whatever is best for you, dear one. Call even if you are on the other side of the world. For every step you take to get to me, I will walk a mile toward you."

He had an enormous yearning at first, but after two weeks he tore everything up and threw it all away. He would be glad he had done this as he stumbled, hurt and confused, out of his sister's car less than half a year later. The girl and the boy would be in the backseat, the girl wearing a red dress and black shoes, and the boy in blue pants and a T-shirt with a cartoon figure on the front. The boy would have fallen asleep, but the girl would say, "Nighty-night, Uncle," which she had been calling him all that evening.

AN EX-OFFENDERS' group, the Light at the End of the Tunnel, helped him to get a room and a job washing dishes and busing tables at a restaurant on F Street. The room was in a three-story building in the middle of the 900 block of N Street, Northwest, a building that, in the days when white people lived there, had had two apartments of eight rooms or so on each floor. Now the first-floor apartments were uninhabitable and had been padlocked for years. On the two other floors, each large apartment had been divided into five rented rooms, which went for twenty to thirty dollars a week, depending on the size and the view. Caesar's was small, twenty dollars, and had half the space of his cell at Lorton. The word that came to him for the butchered, once luxurious apartments was "warren." The roomers in each of the cut-up apartments shared two bathrooms and one nice-sized kitchen, which was a pathetic place because of its dinginess and its fifty-watt bulb, and because many of the appliances were old or undependable or both. Caesar's narrow room was at the front, facing N Street. On his side of the hall were two other rooms, the one next to his housing a mother and her two children. He would not know until his third week there that along the other hall was Yvonne Miller.

There was one main entry door for each of the complexes. In the big room to the left of the door into Caesar's complex lived a man of sixty or so, a pajama-clad man who was never out of bed in all the time Caesar lived there. He *could* walk, but Caesar never saw him do it. A woman, who told Caesar one day that she was "a home health-care aide," was always in the man's room, cooking, cleaning, or watching television with him. His was the only room with its own kitchen setup in a small alcove—a stove, icebox, and sink. His door was always open, and he never seemed to sleep. A green safe, three feet high, squatted beside the bed. "I am a moneylender," the man said the second day Caesar was there. He had come in and walked past the room, and the man had told the aide to have "that young lion" come back. "I am Simon and I lend money," the man said as Caesar stood in the doorway. "I will be your best friend, but not for free. Tell your friends."

HE WORKED as many hours as they would allow him at the restaurant, Chowing Down. The remainder of the time, he went to movies until the shows closed and then sat in Franklin Park, at 14th and K, in good weather and bad. He was there until sleep beckoned, sometimes as late as two in the morning. No one bothered him. He had killed two men, and the world, especially the bad part of it, sensed that and left him alone. He knew no one, and he wanted no one to know him. The friends he had had before Lorton seemed to have been swept off the face of the earth. On the penultimate day of his time at Lorton, he had awoken terrified and thought that if they gave him a choice he might well stay. He might find a life and a career at Lorton.

He had sex only with his right hand, and that was not very often. He began to believe, in his first days out of prison, that men and women were now speaking a new language, and that he would never learn it. His lack of confidence extended even to whores, and this was a man who had been with more women than he had fingers and toes. He began to think that a whore had the power to crush a man's soul. "What kinda language you speakin, honey? Talk English if you want some." He was thirty-seven when he got free.

He came in from the park at two forty-five one morning and went quickly by Simon's door, but the moneylender called him back. Caesar stood in the doorway. He had been in the warren for less than two months. The aide was cooking, standing with her back to Caesar in a crisp green uniform and sensible black shoes. She was stirring first one pot on the stove and then another. People on the color television were laughing.

"Been out on the town, I see," Simon began. "Hope you got enough poontang to last you till next time." "I gotta be goin," Caesar said. He had begun to think that he might be able to kill the man and find a way to get into the safe. The question was whether he should kill the aide as well. "Don't blow off your friends that way," Simon said. Then, for some reason, he started telling Caesar about their neighbors in that complex. That was how Caesar first learned about an "Yvonny," whom he had yet to see. He would not know that she was the Yvonne he had known long ago until the second time he passed her in the hall. "Now, our sweet Yvonny, she ain't nothin but an old girl." Old girls were whores, young or old, who had been battered so much by the world that they had only the faintest wisp of life left; not many of them had hearts of gold. "But you could probably have her for free," Simon said, and he pointed to Caesar's right, where Yvonne's room was. There was always a small lump under the covers beside Simon in the bed, and Caesar suspected that it was a gun. That was a problem, but he might be able to leap to the bed and kill the man with one blow of a club before he could pull it out. What would the aide do? "I've had her myself,"

Simon said, "so I can only recommend it in a pinch." "Later, man," Caesar said, and he stepped away. The usual way to his room was to the right as soon as he entered the main door, but that morning he walked straight ahead and within a few feet was passing Yvonne's door. It was slightly ajar, and he heard music from a radio. The aide might even be willing to help him rob the moneylender if he could talk to her alone beforehand. He might not know the language men and women were speaking now, but the language of money had not changed.

IT WAS a cousin who told his brother where to find him. That cousin, Nora Maywell, was the manager of a nearby bank, at 12th and F Streets, and she first saw Caesar as he bused tables at Chowing Down, where she had gone with colleagues for lunch. She came in day after day to make certain that he was indeed Caesar, for she had not seen him in more than twenty years. But there was no mistaking the man, who looked like her uncle. Caesar was five years older than Nora. She had gone through much of her childhood hoping that she would grow up to marry him. Had he paid much attention to her in all those years before he disappeared, he still would not have recognized her—she was older, to be sure, but life had been extraordinarily kind to Nora and she was now a queen compared with the dirt-poor peasant she had once been.

Caesar's brother came in three weeks after Nora first saw him. The brother, Alonzo, ate alone, paid his bill, then went over to Caesar and smiled. "It's good to see you," he said. Caesar simply nodded and walked away with the tub of dirty dishes. The brother stood shaking for a few moments, then turned and made his unsteady way out the door. He was a corporate attorney, making nine times what his father, at fifty-seven, was making, and he came back for many days. On the eighth day, he went to Caesar, who was busing in a far corner of the restaurant. It was now early September and Caesar had been out of prison for three months and five days. "I will keep coming until you speak to me," the brother said. Caesar looked at him for a long time. The lunch hours were ending, so the manager would have no reason to shout at him. Only two days before, he had seen Yvonne in the hall for the second time. It had been afternoon and the dead lightbulb in the hall had been replaced since the first time he had passed her. He recognized her, but everything in her eyes and body told him that she did not know him. That would never change. And, because he knew who she was, he nodded to his brother and within minutes they were out the door and around the corner to the alley. Caesar lit a cigarette right away. The brother's gray suit had cost $1,865.98. Caesar's apron was filthy. It was his seventh cigarette of the afternoon. When it wasn't in his mouth, the cigarette was at his side, and as he raised it up and down to his mouth, inhaled, and flicked ashes, his hand never shook.

"Do you know how much I want to put my arms around you?" Alonzo said.

"I think we should put an end to all this shit right now so we can get on with our lives," Caesar said. "I don't wanna see you or anyone else in your family from now until the day I die. You should understand that, mister, so you can do somethin else with your time. You a customer, so I won't do what I would do to somebody who ain't a customer."

The brother said, "I'll admit to whatever I may have done to you. I will, Caesar. I will." In fact, his brother had never done anything to him, and neither had his sister. The war had always been between Caesar and their father, but Caesar, over time, had come to see his siblings as the father's allies. "But come to see me and Joanie, one time only, and if you don't want to see us again, then we'll accept that. I'll never come into your restaurant again."

There was still more of the cigarette, but Caesar looked at it and then dropped it to the ground and stepped on it. He looked at his cheap watch. Men in prison would have killed for what was left of that smoke. "I gotta be goin, mister."

"We are family, Caesar. If you don't want to see Joanie and me for your sake, for our sakes, then do it for Mama."

"My mama's dead, and she been dead for a lotta years." He walked toward the street.

"I know she's dead! I know she's dead! I just put flowers on her grave on Sunday. And on three Sundays before that. And five weeks before that. I know my mother's dead."

Caesar stopped. It was one thing for him to throw out a quick statement about a dead mother, as he had done many times over the years. A man could say the words so often that they became just another meaningless part of his makeup. The pain was no longer there as it had been those first times he had spoken them, when his mother was still new to her grave. The words were one thing, but a grave was a different matter, a different fact. The grave was out there, to be seen and touched, and a man, a son, could go to that spot of earth and remember all over again how much she had loved him, how she had stood in her apron in the doorway of a clean and beautiful home and welcomed him back from school. He could go to the grave and read her name and die a bit, because it would feel as if she had left him only last week.

Caesar turned around. "You and your people must leave me alone, Mister."

"Then we will," the brother said. "We will leave you alone. Come to one dinner. A Sunday dinner. Fried chicken. The works. Then we'll never bother you again. No one but Joanie and our families. No one else." Those last words were to assure Caesar that he would not have to see their father.

Caesar wanted another cigarette, but the meeting had already gone on long enough.

YVONNE HAD not said anything that second time, when he said "Hello." She had simply nodded and walked around him in the hall. The third time they were also passing in the hall, and he spoke again, and she stepped to the side to pass and then turned and asked if he had any smokes she could borrow.

He said he had some in his room, and she told him to go get them and pointed to her room.

Her room was a third larger than his. It had an icebox, a bed, a dresser with a mirror over it, a small table next to the bed, a chair just beside the door, and not much else. The bed made a T with the one window, which faced the windowless wall of the apartment building next door. The beautiful blue-and-yellow curtains at the window should have been somewhere else, in a place that could appreciate them.

He had no expectations. He wanted nothing. It was just good to see a person from a special time in his life, and it was even better that he had loved her once and she had loved him. He stood in the doorway with the cigarettes.

Dressed in a faded purple robe, she was looking in the icebox when he returned. She closed the icebox door and looked at him. He walked over, and she took the unopened pack of cigarettes from his outstretched hand. He stood there.

"Well, sit the fuck down before you make the place look poor." He sat in the chair by the door, and she sat on the bed and lit the first cigarette. She was sideways to him. It was only after the fifth drag on the cigarette that she spoke. "If you think you gonna get some pussy, you are sorely mistaken. I ain't givin out shit. Free can kill you."

"I don't want nothin."

"'I don't want nothin. I don't want nothin.'" She dropped ashes into an empty tomato-soup can on the table by the bed. "Mister, we all want somethin, and the sooner people like you stand up and stop the bullshit, then the world can start bein a better place. It's the bullshitters who keep the world from bein a better place." Together, they had rented a little house in Northeast and had been planning to have a child once they had been there two years. The night he came home and found her sitting in the dark and talking about never trusting happiness, they had been there a year and a half. Two months later, she was gone. For the next three months, as he looked for her, he stayed there and continued to make it the kind of place that a woman would want to come home to. "My own mother was the first bullshitter I knew," she continued. "That's how I know it don't work. People should stand up and say, 'I wish you were dead,' or 'I want your pussy,' or 'I want all the money in your pocket.' When we stop lyin, the world will start bein heaven." He had been a thief and a robber and a drug pusher before he met her, and he went back to all that after the three months, not because he was heartbroken, though he was, but because it was such an easy thing to do. He was smart enough to know that he could not blame Yvonne, and he never did. The murders of Percy "Golden Boy" Weymouth and Antwoine Stoddard were still years away.

He stayed that day for more than an hour, until she told him that she had now paid for the cigarettes. Over the next two weeks, as he got closer to the dinner with his brother and sister, he would take her cigarettes and food and tell her from the start that they were free. He was never to know how she paid the rent. By the fourth day of bringing her things, she began to believe that he wanted nothing. He always sat in the chair by the door. Her words never changed, and it never mattered to him. The only thanks he got was the advice that the world should stop being a bullshitter.

ON THE day of the dinner, he found that the days of sitting with Yvonne had given him a strength he had not had when he had said yes to his brother. He had Alonzo pick him up in front of Chowing Down, because he felt that if they knew where he lived they would find a way to stay in his life.

At his sister's house, just off 16th Street, Northwest, in an area of well-to-do black people some called the Gold Coast, they welcomed him, Joanie keeping her arms around him for more than a minute, crying. Then they offered him a glass of wine. He had not touched alcohol since before prison. They sat him on a dark green couch in the living room, which was the size of ten prison cells. Before he had taken three sips of the wine, he felt good enough not to care that the girl and the boy, his sister's children, wanted to be in his lap. They were the first children he had been around in more than ten years. The girl had been calling him Uncle since he entered the house.

Throughout dinner, which was served by his sister's maid, and during the rest of the evening, he said as little as possible to the adults—his sister and brother and their spouses—but concentrated on the kids, because he thought he knew their hearts. The grown-ups did not pepper him with questions and were just grateful that he was there. Toward the end of the meal, he had a fourth glass of wine, and that was when he told his niece that she looked like his mother and the girl blushed, because she knew how beautiful her grandmother had been.

At the end, as Caesar stood in the doorway preparing to leave, his brother said that he had made this a wonderful year. His brother's eyes teared up and he wanted to hug Caesar, but Caesar, without smiling, simply extended his hand. The last thing his brother said to him was, "Even if you go away not wanting to see us again, know that Daddy loves you. It is the one giant truth in the world. He's a different man, Caesar. I think he loves you more than us because he never knew what happened to you. That may be why he never re-married." The issue of what Caesar had been doing for twenty-one years never came up.

HIS SISTER, with her children in the backseat, drove him home. In front of his building, he and Joanie said good-bye, and she kissed his cheek and, as an afterthought, he, a new uncle and with the wine saying, *Now, that wasn't so bad,* reached back to give a playful tug on the children's feet, but the sleeping boy was too far away and the girl, laughing, wiggled out of his reach. He said to his niece, "Good night, young lady," and she said no, that she was not a lady but a little girl. Again, he reached unsuccessfully for her feet. When he turned back, his sister had a look of such horror and disgust that he felt he had been stabbed. He knew right away what she was thinking, that he was out to cop a feel on a child. He managed a good-bye and got out of the car. "Call me," she said before he closed the car door, but the words lacked the feeling of all the previous ones of the evening. He said nothing. Had he spoken the wrong language, as well as done the wrong thing? Did child molesters call little girls "ladies"? He knew he would never call his sister. Yes, he had been right to tear up the pictures and letters when he was in Lorton.

He shut his eyes until the car was no more. He felt a pained rumbling throughout his system and, without thinking, he staggered away from his building toward 10th Street. He could hear music coming from an apartment on his side of N Street. He had taught his sister how to ride a bike, how to get over her fear of falling and hurting herself. Now, in her eyes, he was no more than an animal capable of hurting a child. They killed men in prison for being that kind of monster. Whatever avuncular love for the children had begun growing in just those few hours now seeped away. He leaned over into the grass at the side of the apartment building and vomited. He wiped his mouth with the back of his hand. "I'll fall, Caesar," his sister had said in her first weeks of learning how to ride a bicycle. "Why would I let that happen?"

HE IGNORED the aide when she told him that the moneylender wanted to talk to him. He went straight ahead, toward Yvonne's room, though he had no intention of seeing her. Her door was open enough for him to see a good part of the room, but he simply turned toward his own room. His shadow, cast by her light behind him, was thin and went along the floor and up the wall, and it was seeing the shadow that made him turn around. After noting that the bathroom next to her room was empty, he called softly to her from the doorway and then called three times more before he gave the door a gentle push with his finger. The door had not opened all the way when he saw her half on the bed and half off. Drunk, he thought. He went to her, intending to put her full on the bed. But death can twist the body in a way life never does, and that was what it had done to hers. He knew death. Her face was pressed into the bed, at a crooked angle that would have been uncomfortable for any living person.

One leg was bunched under her, and the other was extended behind her, but both seemed not part of her body, awkwardly on their own, as if someone could just pick them up and walk away.

He whispered her name. He sat down beside her, ignoring the vomit that spilled out of her mouth and over the side of the bed. He moved her head so that it rested on one side. He thought at first that someone had done this to her, but he saw money on the dresser and felt the quiet throughout the room that signaled the end of it all, and he knew that the victim and the perpetrator were one and the same. He screwed the top on the empty whiskey bottle near her extended leg.

He placed her body on the bed and covered her with a sheet and a blanket. Someone would find her in the morning. He stood at the door, preparing to turn out the light and leave, thinking this was how the world would find her. He had once known her as a clean woman who would not steal so much as a needle. A woman with a well-kept house. She had been loved. But that was not what they would see in the morning.

He set about putting a few things back in place, hanging up clothes that were lying over the chair and on the bed, straightening the lampshade, picking up newspapers and everything else on the floor. But when he was done, it did not seem enough.

He went to his room and tore up two shirts to make dust rags. He started in a corner at the foot of her bed, at a table where she kept her brush and comb and makeup and other lady things. When he had dusted the table and everything on it, he put an order to what was there, just as if she would be using them in the morning.

Then he began dusting and cleaning clockwise around the room, and by midnight he was not even half done and the shirts were dirty with all the work, and he went back to his room for two more. By three, he was cutting up his pants for rags. After he had cleaned and dusted the room, he put an order to it all, as he had done with the things on the table—the dishes and food in mouseproof canisters on the table beside the icebox, the two framed posters of

mountains on the wall that were tilting to the left, the five photographs of unknown children on the bureau. When that work was
done, he took a pail and a mop from her closet. Mice had made a
bed in the mop, and he had to brush them off and away. He filled
the pail with water from the bathroom and soap powder from under the table beside the icebox. After the floor had been mopped,
he stood in the doorway as it dried and listened to the mice in the
walls, listened to them scurrying in the closet.

At about four, the room was done and Yvonne lay covered in
her unmade bed. He went to the door, ready to leave, and was once
more unable to move. The whole world was silent except the mice
in the walls.

He knelt at the bed and touched Yvonne's shoulder. On a Tuesday morning, a school day, he had come upon his father kneeling
at his bed, Caesar's mother growing cold in that bed. His father
was crying, and when Caesar went to him his father crushed Caesar to him and took the boy's breath away. It was Caesar's brother
who had said they should call someone, but their father said, "No,
no, just one minute more, just one more minute," as if in that next
minute God would reconsider and send his wife back. And Caesar
had said, "Yes, just one minute more." *The one giant truth . . .* , his
brother had said.

Caesar changed the bedclothing and undressed Yvonne. He got
one of her large pots and filled it with warm water from the bathroom and poured into the water cologne of his own that he never
used and bath-oil beads he found in a battered container in a corner beside her dresser. The beads refused to dissolve, and he had
to crush them in his hands. He bathed her, cleaned out her mouth.
He got a green dress from the closet, and underwear and stockings
from the dresser, put them on her, and pinned a rusty cameo on the
dress over her heart. He combed and brushed her hair, put barrettes
in it after he sweetened it with the rest of the cologne, and laid her
head in the center of the pillow now covered with one of his clean
cases. He gave her no shoes and he did not cover her up, just left her

on top of the made-up bed. The room with the dead woman was as clean and as beautiful as Caesar could manage at that time in his life. It was after six in the morning, and the world was lighting up and the birds had begun to chirp. Caesar shut off the ceiling light and turned out the lamp, held on to the chain switch as he listened to the beginnings of a new day.

He opened the window that he had cleaned hours before, and right away a breeze came through. He put a hand to the wind, enjoying the coolness, and one thing came to him: he was not a young man anymore.

HE SAT on his bed smoking one cigarette after another. Before finding Yvonne dead, he had thought he would go and live in Baltimore and hook up with a vicious crew he had known a long time ago. Wasn't that what child molesters did? Now, the only thing he knew about the rest of his life was that he did not want to wash dishes and bus tables anymore. At about nine-thirty, he put just about all he owned and the two bags of trash from Yvonne's room in the bin in the kitchen. He knocked at the door of the woman in the room next to his. Her son opened the door, and Caesar asked for his mother. He gave her the hundred and forty-seven dollars he had found in Yvonne's room, along with his radio and tiny black-and-white television. He told her to look in on Yvonne before long and then said he would see her later, which was perhaps the softest lie of his adult life.

On his way out of the warren of rooms, Simon called to him. "You comin back soon, young lion?" he asked. Caesar nodded. "Well, why don't you bring me back a bottle of rum? Woke up with a taste for it this mornin." Caesar nodded. "Was that you in there with Yvonny last night?" Simon said as he got the money from atop the safe beside his bed. "Quite a party, huh?" Caesar said nothing. Simon gave the money to the aide, and she handed Caesar ten dollars and a quarter. "Right down to the penny," Simon said. "Give you a tip when you get back." "I won't be long," Caesar said. Simon must have realized that was a lie, because before Caesar went out the door he said, in as sweet a voice as he was capable of, "I'll be waitin."

HE CAME out into the day. He did not know what he was going to do, aside from finding some legit way to pay for Yvonne's funeral. The D.C. government people would take her away, but he knew where he could find and claim her before they put her in potter's field. He put the bills in his pocket and looked down at the quarter in the palm of his hand. It was a rather old one, 1967, but shiny enough. Life had been kind to it. He went carefully down the steps in front of the building and stood on the sidewalk. The world was going about its business, and it came to him, as it might to a man who had been momentarily knocked senseless after a punch to the face, that he was of that world. To the left was 9th Street and all the rest of N Street, Immaculate Conception Catholic Church at 8th, the bank at the corner of 7th. He flipped the coin. To his right was 10th Street, and down 10th were stores and the house where Abraham Lincoln had died and all the white people's precious monuments. Up 10th and a block to 11th and Q Streets was once a High's store where, when Caesar was a boy, a pint of cherry-vanilla ice cream cost twenty-five cents, and farther down 10th was French Street, with a two-story house with his mother's doilies and a foot-long porcelain black puppy just inside the front door. A puppy his mother had bought for his father in the third year of their marriage. A puppy that for thirty-five years had been patiently waiting each working day for Caesar's father to return from work. *The one giant truth . . . Just one minute more.* He caught the quarter and slapped it on the back of his hand. He had already decided that George Washington's profile would mean going toward 10th Street, and that was what he did once he uncovered the coin.

At the corner of 10th and N, he stopped and considered the quarter again. Down 10th was Lincoln's death house. Up 10th was

the house where he had been a boy, and where the puppy was waiting for his father. A girl at the corner was messing with her bicycle,
putting playing cards in the spokes, checking the tires. She watched
Caesar as he flipped the quarter. He missed it and the coin fell to the
ground, and he decided that that one would not count. The girl had
once seen her aunt juggle six coins, first warming up with the flip
of a single one and advancing to the juggling of three before finishing with six. It had been quite a show. The aunt had shown the six
pieces to the girl—they had all been old and heavy one-dollar silver
coins, huge monster things, which nobody made anymore. The girl
thought she might now see a reprise of that event. Caesar flipped
the quarter. The girl's heart paused. The man's heart paused. The
coin reached its apex and then it fell.

ADINA, ASTRID, CHIPEWEE, JASMINE

Matthew Klam

Matthew Klam was named one of the twenty best fiction writers in America under forty by *The New Yorker*. His first book, *Sam the Cat and Other Stories*, a finalist for the Los Angeles Times Book Prize for first fiction, was named one of the best books of the year by the *New York Times*, *Esquire*, the *Los Angeles Times*, and the *Kansas City Star*, and was selected by Borders for its New Voices series. His work has been featured in *The New Yorker*, *Harper's*, *Allure*, *USA Weekend*, Nerve.com, the *Washington Post Magazine*, and the *New York Times Magazine*, where he is a contributing writer.

Saturday night Julia sat staring at a candle. It was after eight. She needed to eat.

She hadn't felt tired yet. She'd had a perfect pregnancy—no rashes, no fat feet, working full time, doing it all. A cartoonist couldn't have drawn a more adorable creature: rosy cheeks, pudgy nose, lime-green pregnancy pants drawn up over her stomach, white maternity smock.

Erica buzzed the front door with bags from the kebab place, and they set the coffee table and ate on the floor, with their backs against two ottomans. Erica wore fish-net stockings and a cotton cardigan that let her cleavage fall out, and told Julia about the sex she was having with her outlaw boyfriend, Malcolm—who couldn't commit, said he needed to "live monastically," then showed up at her house every night so riddled with guilt that she ended up comforting him on the rug in her foyer as he ripped her clothes off.

Julia ate too fast, choking on hummus, and accidentally drank what was left of Erica's wine. It tasted like cough syrup. She finished her kebab and rubbed a food stain off her shirt. Erica stared across the table at Julia as though she were trying to unscrew her own head.

Julia was embarrassed. It was mid-April. She was due June 17th. You were supposed to slip naturally into the new shape; you were supposed to love it. But she'd popped out hugely, and felt like a bear sipping tea. She was going to be a terrible mother.

After dinner, Malcolm arrived. He was tall and reddish, with a windburned face—he built houses for a living. He towered over them, touching them both, and invited Julia to join him and Erica at a party in the Palisades. Julia said she was too tired, and noticed him staring at her breasts and her belly, like a moron. When she kissed him good night, her face got hot. It was the wine, or hormones out of whack.

She got into bed but couldn't fall asleep. On TV, Brad Pitt was dressed in a black leather miniskirt, playing a warrior from ancient times who slept nude in animal skins. Lying there, she thought about Malcolm and his doglike stare. She used her vibrator, in an attempt to wear herself out, and accidentally broke her water. But she was two months shy of her due date and whatever came out, this little puddle, meant nothing to her. She wondered instead whether she'd finally hit her G-spot.

Sunday morning, she woke up with a warm physical pressure, almost like sadness, bearing down on her vagina. She was bleeding a little, but then it went away. By noon the pressure had shifted, and was sitting in her pelvis, where her bowels were. She left a message for Kevin at his hotel in Hartford, then another, until he called back. She ate some chicken, and then walked a mile and a half down Wisconsin Avenue to her gym, swam for an hour, and walked home.

At four that afternoon, she tried to nap, but her belly hurt. She gave up on napping and waited for Kevin to come home. Kevin spent the weekend shooting video of people speaking at a journalism conference—a Nixon-era geezer, a dopey mountaineer whose only training before typing up his best-seller had been a job painting boats. Nobody stuck to the subject, or laid out the fundamentals of writing Kevin needed for the video he had to put together. Famous people—Joyce Linden Fogg—whispered in a huge auditorium off the main lobby; Branson Kheils, a public-radio icon, rambled on about his first show in Minnesota (a pig slept in the yard behind the station) and brought down the house.

By Sunday afternoon, Kevin stood sagging under the weight of his twelve-pound camera; his overheating spotlight burned the side of his head as Dustin Christensen addressed the full session of two thousand to close the conference. Nothing about his latest project had been difficult, Christensen said, not the research or the writing. He'd infiltrated Afghani terrorists, slept beneath flying bullets. He'd used the proceeds from his blockbuster to build schools and roads in the mountains that once bred killers. Every word, every twitch transfixed the packed ballroom. It was the publicity tour that almost killed him, he said, and the Hollywood movie, and the luggage he'd lost on his way here. When the author finally took questions, Kevin slumped against the wall with the kind of exhausted relief you get from throwing up.

At last, back in his hotel room, Kevin wandered around in such a stupor that he packed too slowly and missed his plane. Waiting on standby at the airport, gazing at magazines at the newsstand as evening descended, he thought of all the things he'd never be, speeches he'd never give. He couldn't afford to buy a magazine because he was still waiting for the money from his last job, a heartwarming fund-raising film he'd shot for a fancy private high school. He felt so rotten he almost phoned Julia, but their last conversation warded him off.

"Sorry," he'd said when he finally reached her during the lunch break.

"Oh, God, Kevin," she'd said.

"What's wrong?"

"I just dropped a piece of chicken down my bra."

"I only have a second."

"Now I'm all covered with slime and grease on me. It's disgusting."

"It's O.K.," he'd said, because she was alone, and apparently bleeding, and seemed to be having some kind of problem. "I'm sorry you don't feel well."

"I drank wine last night by mistake," she said. "She's probably dead."

"My session is starting."

"Somebody get this thing out of me. Cut it out of me now."

Kevin had been out of college for two years when he got his first real job, writing press releases for an American gas company. He'd been living in cheap countries as an experiment, travelling to avoid working, but ended up in Japan, where people worked so hard they dropped dead on the sidewalk. It made the expat thing a little pointless. Back home, he spent nine years doing video production at a P.R. agency before starting his own business.

Nobody in his family had ever made a living in an imaginative career, and Kevin had no great store of talent, but, while at the agency, he began quietly working on his own film, a documentary. He'd read about this kid in the paper, a five-foot-six-inch basketball phenom named Durrell, who'd been beaten and starved as a child, and now played at a nearby college. Kevin politely stalked Durrell, and began making trips to his dorm room to tape these mindblowing stories of life in the Montclair, New Jersey, projects. Durrell's mom was a "roller," and his dad had gone to jail for hitting someone with a sledgehammer. He had a stoic way of speaking that made him look, onscreen, like he was falling asleep. But so what. Kevin met the foster family, and filmed their evening meals, and flew to road games at his own expense, and shot hundreds of hours of footage—of coaches on leafy strolls, of Durrell playing XBox and doing his raps. After almost three years, with no end in sight, he finally gained the trust of Durrell's twin sister, a single mother on welfare, who was killed sometime later in a random act of violence.

Durrell blew his knee out at the end of his junior year, and then flopped in a pro league in Europe, and stopped returning Kevin's calls. At about the same time, a film with an identical theme appeared in theatres, to huge acclaim, and Kevin sort of fell apart. Since then, he'd started a few other projects—documentaries, conceptual video art, screenplays, children's books—but had quit them all. Though he still dreamed of finishing the film, or at least editing a promo, or whatever you call it, or at least watching some of the footage, he felt that the time for his own dreams had ended, or would soon, because he'd be a father, and he'd have to stand aside for the next generation—while also remaining upright, embalmed, rotting, for eternity.

On the flight home, he sat in a broken seat by the toilet and stared out the window as the engine wobbled beneath the wing. If it fell off now, the plane would smash into the Jersey shore. Maybe, if he lived, he could make a documentary about that. He'd interview the survivors, teasing out his own story, then slowly turn the camera on himself to reveal the hideous burns all over his disfigured head! Or he could write some kind of magazine article about it, or a book, or novelize it, or try it as a feature-film script. . . . It would be easier just to die.

At five, Julia thought she had to poop. She tried to call Kevin and took half a Midol. At seven, it came in waves; it bent her in half. I'm just wound up, she thought. I'm hungover. Because she was seven months pregnant, she got out the midwife's card and called, apologizing for bothering her on a Sunday evening. The midwife said, "If you go to the emergency room, they'll give you stuff to calm your cramps."

"The emergency room?"

"We can't do anything for you here." The pamphlet from the midwife's office described warm baths, lavender butter smeared on your forehead. What the hell was the point if at the first sign of any-thing they sent you to the hospital?

"All I eat is chicken. Do you think I have food poisoning?"

"It's possible."

"If I did, would it hurt the baby?" The woman didn't know. Jesus.

By the time Julia got downstairs, she was walking like her Grandma Gertie before Gertie had both hips replaced. She breathed heavily, leaning on a stack of magazines by the front door. She had a little trouble deciding on her next move and panicked and called 911. When a voice answered, she apologized and walked outside to her car. She felt like she was being whacked with a two-by-four. Kevin landed at around seven and went straight to his office and dumped the footage onto his computer. The office was in a base-ment and his cell phone didn't ring down there; he ignored the reg-ular phone, because the sequence of the sixty-eight speeches had to be tagged correctly.

At nine o'clock, he called home and to his relief got the machine. He left a message saying that he still had more work to do and that Julia should go to sleep without him. Please, God, he thought. And now he had to go find somewhere to eat. He hated eating alone. He just wanted five minutes with somebody other than Julia—who was grossly pregnant and uncomfortable, and kept the fan turned on so high in the bedroom that he had to build a wall of pillows to keep from being blown onto the floor.

Times were hard, and bound to get harder. The sound of a key in the lock—anything triggered Julia's insomnia. She woke up if a bird flew past the window. Last week, a chunk of her hair fell out. She lost her wallet in the lining of her coat, and, when she found it, she closed the bathroom door and cried. Her belly was immense and her boobs were veiny and her nipples were brown. She smelled different—like cooked custard. And she had an attitude now: "Stand back, here I come." She passed many sleepless nights eat-ing nuts in bed, crunching with a squirrel's vigor. It altered their private business. Kevin loved sex, normally, anytime, anywhere. But now the sex was weird, because what exactly was going on down there? When he stared at that lump under the blanket, he felt self-conscious; he sensed an audience of skepticism and disapproval.

If he tried to talk to his sister or his mom about it, they got angry. If he said a word to his friends, the single guys acted horrified that a person could smell like custard, and the guys who had kids didn't care.

He and Julia got married three years ago, and right away they began trying. When nothing happened, he figured God was punishing him for something. They'd been together for almost a year before the wedding, and their early days had been filled, for him, with the excitement of loving her so much better than Roberta, his terrible last girlfriend, who'd slept on a horsehair mattress she inherited from her grandmother. Julia was by far the most beautiful woman Kevin had ever touched, and the most decent—passionate to the point of hysteria about a five-year plan for public charter schools. She was slight and wore the same T-shirt to bed every night and had a pretense of helplessness, which applied mainly to lifting the five-gallon water jug, but it made loving a skinny girl romantic, and he'd loved her in greater quantity than he'd ever loved anyone. He was in love; she was easy to love. He'd walk through the door every night and be, like, "I'm living with someone and I'm going to marry her."

She had a puffy little moonface, and Kevin loved to kiss the soft belly of each cheek, but within five minutes something always happened to ruin the moment. At first, he took the awkwardness between them for lack of experience, but that wasn't the problem. They just didn't like to talk to each other. She'd start a story in the middle, and if he asked a question she'd say, "What? Huh?," as if she needed a hearing aid. Any time they spent alone together, whenever one of them asked the question "How are you?" it was like writing a thank-you note to a grandparent in a nursing home. By the time those moments ended, Kevin was a wreck. But then he'd been in relationships with good conversations, too. Understanding killed attraction just as quickly. Here at least the mystery kept things primitive and charged.

Their conversations improved with practice, but when he couldn't knock her up the awkwardness returned. At some point, he decided to shut up more, so she shut up more, too, but that just made them strangers to each other. After a year, they found a clinic and she began making frequent trips to the doctor and they went ahead with it, not talking.

There was the Hawaiian porno tape he jerked off to at the clinic, the menstrual cycle on the refrigerator, the shots he gave her—big injections in her ass, little ones in her stomach. The pills she shoved in her pussy to make the lining more hospitable. The brave declarations they made as they faced the debate—donor egg versus flying to China.

Months passed, and it all became this tricky thing, like a blur in a photograph. She was blurring, smudging, not herself. Then there were the phone calls from the clinic—"Do it now"—the requisite screwing, the livestock feeling of it, the injunction against fiddling with himself, the creeping sensation that they were using up the last few drops he had, crawling toward the end.

She was ashamed. She starved herself on popcorn and soda and got too thin. He did everything he could to get away, staying late at work, eating dinner in a restaurant alone. A distance opened up between them. It was his failure, his weakness, but he couldn't tell anyone about it. He'd stopped loving Julia when he couldn't get her pregnant, but then, after two years of a humiliating and expensive twenty-nine-thousand-dollar fertility process, they'd succeeded, and now that she was pregnant he wished she was dead.

There'd been a case on television of a man who'd killed his pregnant wife, spawning special news reports. Tooling around the Internet, Kevin had learned that one in five pregnant women who died was murdered. A quarter of men who killed their wives killed them when they were pregnant. Women were strangled, bludgeoned, choked, drowned, burned alive, shot on the way home from a birthing class. Why didn't the guys just leave? Now he knew. He couldn't imagine actually strangling anyone, but the existence of the trend lofted him up on a dizzy little puff of curiosity. Watching Julia's belly grow, seeing her change, altered his world like a snowfall quieting everything. And yet he was nuts. He felt like he'd sawed off the top of his head. Instead of wondering how to fix it, he gave himself a gift: despair without shame. Freedom from the necessary revulsion with himself. Like some miserable Goth kid, his thoughts went straight to hell and made him stronger.

A paramedic took Julia up to the sixth floor in a wheelchair and one nurse put a bracelet on her wrist while another drew five vials of her blood. She liked all the attention. She got the feeling that they'd seen cramps like these before, which reassured her. Another nurse entered with papers to sign, and a fourth asked concerned, insightful questions. Two of the nurses were blond and wore diamond engagement rings, and another was worn out and motherly. The prettiest one put Julia in stirrups.

As a teen-ager, she'd spent some time in a hospital for bulimia and suicidal behavior, and she'd always looked back on it as the regimen that put order in her life, helped her collect herself and recover. The friends she'd made there, bound to her by their secret shame, remained the most important ones she had, to this day. Anyway, if she hadn't been locked up in that place she'd be dead.

Tonight she lay in the maternity ward of a teaching hospital, and the young doctor on call, a third-year resident, stepped into the examining room a little bleary, feeling his way around the room, blinking at her as though he'd come from somewhere dark. One side of his face was wrinkled where it appeared he'd been sleeping on it.

"You're having some pain," he said, and gloved up. "You need to maintain your fluids." He sat on a stool, and set a sealed plastic bag of metal instruments on top of her big bare stomach, and then began looking around, spinning on the stool. And then everyone had to laugh, because he was looking for the very bag that was right in front of him! He opened the bag and took out a speculum, which he stuck crookedly into her, accidentally cutting her. Her spasming innards rocketed into a worse state. She panicked. He twisted it around inside her.

"Yuh—you're in labor," he said loudly, "three centimetres," and his voice broke when he said it. "You're breech." He called for a sonogram and sent for the attending. When he withdrew the speculum, it had candy-apple-red blood on the end. There was blood on his glove, and he slid it off into the garbage as though it were covered with worms. He stared down at the floor and smiled apologetically, and the nurses rolled the sonogram machine into place and squirted gloop on Julia's belly.

The attending was a woman in her fifties with copper highlights in her hair. She held Julia's hand and spoke softly as she moved the sonogram thing around. She asked the young doctor what he saw on the screen. He studied the ghostly image. She turned to Julia and said, "Is there a possibility your water broke at some point in the last day or two?"

"My water?"

"Because there doesn't seem to be too much in there."

Julia remembered the stuff coming out the night before. "How much is missing?"

The attending wiggled the thing more. The contractions were seven minutes apart. Stopping them would be tricky, she said. Bringing the baby out now would be worse. More nurses came into the room. One asked if there was a family member Julia could call. She'd left messages for Kevin in three places. She gave them Erica's number.

They wheeled her into a room with a view of the plaza, and the attending put a clear bag of viscous-looking fluid called magnesium sulfate into the I.V. machine, assuring Julia that it was safe. "Some people don't love this drug," she explained. "But it helps the muscles to relax, to stop your contractions. We need to stop your contractions," she said, and left.

It hit her head first. Almost immediately, Julia went cross-eyed and half dead.

He called his buddy Ethan. He wanted to meet him at Schwann's, an old wood-panelled restaurant in Georgetown where Khrushchev had once sat with Nixon for a photo op, where the waiters were old men who wore smocks and kept their faces frozen while you ordered. Ethan understood what Kevin was going through; he was married, with three kids. But Ethan had a gigantic book contract that was killing him—he had to get some work done—so he told Kevin to stop by the house instead.

Ethan lived in this fucking mansion on P Street, a National Historic Landmark, according to the plate by the door. The doorknob was brass, and the size of a grapefruit. Trips to Ethan's house left Kevin feeling worthless and desperate, although Ethan's family had enough problems, the older girl with two-per-cent listening comprehension, the younger one shoplifting from stores on M Street, the three-year-old boy refusing to speak except in the broken English of the Guatemalan nanny. Ethan had written two decent books on politics and almost finished a third; and he had a good job talking on a cable news show. But he'd married Carrie, who was worth whatever the stock market did to the third of a billion dollars she'd inherited in 1990, and her wealth made it hard for him to keep his balls.

As Kevin came in, he could hear Ethan's girls screaming up the wide staircase, or maybe down in the ballroom they'd had painted like a jungle and filled with trampolines. If someone were being flayed alive it might have sounded the same way, that screaming, but Ethan just sighed and clucked his tongue, leading the way past fresh-cut flowers and oil paintings, until they entered the white-tiled kitchen with its endless counters, where a fat Rottweiler looked up to see what they were doing. Kevin could hear Carrie, somewhere, calling Ethan's name.

In the refrigerator were sodas and open wine bottles, a tray of wilted vegetables from a caterer, and part of a cake. They stood smearing butter on pieces of focaccia, listening to the screams. When a lull hit, Ethan yawned. Over the weekend, he and Carrie had hosted three parties: one for Carrie's grandmother, one for a nine-year-old, and one for Eliot Spitzer.

"I'm not gonna make it," he said, meaning the deadline for his book.

"You'll make it." There was a bottle of Scotch on the counter and they each had a shot. It tasted like gym socks soaked in gasoline. They had another. Soon the kitchen started to feel more like Schwann's.

"How was your thing in Hartford?"

"Fine."

"Julia O.K.? You ready? To become a father, a dad? You psyched?"

Kevin said yes.

"You're having a little girl."

"I know," Kevin said. "Here's to the greatest adventure a man can know."

"Aye, muchacho," Ethan said.

It sounded like furniture was being dragged across the floor upstairs. "Carrie!" Ethan yelled toward the dining room. "Honey, is everything O.K.?" They waited. "You'll be fine," he said to Kevin.

Carrie appeared in the back of the kitchen, having materialized from somewhere, like a ninja. She said hi to Kevin, but her lips were tight. "You're on for the rest of the night," she told Ethan, and filled a glass with water. "You haven't done a fucking thing all weekend." She walked out.

"Heh-heh," Ethan said. He walked to the foyer. "Don't leave."

"I should get going."

"I'm just gonna check on things."

"I'd better go."

Ethan called back. "Don't move."

"I'll see you later." Kevin let himself out as Ethan walked up the stairs.

An hour later, the young doctor threw the door open carrying a big yellow coffee mug with a smiley face on it and sort of skipped into the room as though he were kicking through rain puddles. "Doin' all right?" he asked, taking a drink from his mug. "How's the mag working out for ya?" He walked around, making notes on her chart. "Sometimes magnesium makes people irritable. It causes the heart to beat irregularly."

"Is this active labor?" She was shouting. "Is it stopping? Am I going to work tomorrow?" Her tongue tasted like aluminum.

"What do you mean by active labor?"

"My doctors told me to call if there was news. My midwife."

"We called them." He tapped her knees, her wrists, and her elbows, then her ankles and feet. No reflexes. The computer by Julia's head indicated that her contractions were getting stronger. "Let us know if you have any double vision," he said.

Julia said, "Yes, I do."

He made a note and turned the lights off and let the door bang shut.

On his way up Connecticut Avenue, Kevin stopped in Woodley Park, in front of the building where a woman named Cynthia lived. She was the ex-girlfriend of a guy named Artie, who'd made films for the Discovery Channel and had a shelf full of Emmys. She'd taken Artie's old job and brought Kevin in to help her with a two-hundred-page script she'd inherited on the birth of Islam. Together, they'd cut it down to four and a half scintillating minutes, to be aired one day on the channel's Web site. Over the last three months, they'd met half a dozen times in a tiny editing suite, a cockpit with carpeted walls, and in that warm, hushed darkness they'd chatted and commiserated and drunk soda and confessed.

They'd discovered that they were both dying to move to New York City to jump-start their careers. They'd both pitched the same guy at Showtime, with the same result. Cynthia had been a dancer in her youth, and had débuted at New York City Ballet at nineteen; two weeks later, she'd dislocated her hip—had to be lifted and hauled off-stage. Kevin completely understood, because of his own unfulfilled promise. She couldn't explain to anybody how it made her feel, but Kevin knew that an awful, unfixable thing would never stay buried.

She was a tall, thin woman with broad shoulders and a skinny neck and a scrunched-up little mouse face. She had huge brown eyes, and this heavy bosom, and she'd lean over and put her boobs on the table between them in the editing suite and scream back at Kevin about their sketchy luck and stare into his eyes like a maniac. He liked that.

It was late. He probably should've called first. She was the only woman he could think of within eighty miles who was single and answered her phone after nine o'clock at night.

He didn't want to go home yet. It was spring, and a velvety breeze touched his arms, and tender little green buds hung softly under the streetlights. There was only now, and that made living exquisite. And, anyway, he'd be dead someday and none of it would matter. Also, if he came in and woke Julia up she'd lie there, devastated, for the next six hours, sighing her ass off, and would blame him, and he'd take the blame, and feel terrible.

The only light in the room came from the monitor by her head, hooked to her belly, a sickly orange glow. The only sound came from the baby's pounding rhythm, amplified through the machine, like a little air compressor blasting away. *Choo-choo.* Julia turned her face to the wall when the pain came, and wrapped her hand around the rubber-coated railing on the bed, dug her nails into the rubber, squeezed her eyes shut, and opened her mouth wide, but there was no sound. Something flipped inside. During the gaps in the flipping, she let go. Her body had been built according to certain rules, but those rules had now been broken. If it got any worse, she would have to kill herself. She could crawl to the window and slide out. She dug into the rubber. When Kevin showed up, he would call everyone. She felt hopeless, lonely.

A soft, round, coffee-colored orb appeared near Julia's head. It was a face, powdery smooth, with trustworthy lines, and it spoke with an accent from somewhere—the Caribbean, maybe—partly reading in a breezy rhythm, from notes, ". . . serious complications, of course, the risks in bringing a baby out of the womb prematurely are known . . . cerebral palsy, neurologic disorders, developmental delays."

There was white stuff caked around the edge of Julia's mouth. Her gums were bleeding and she moved her tongue to try to find out where.

"Higher risks of retardation, asthma, and congenital aortic deformities . . . It's not uncommon for preemies to undergo a number of surgeries."

Then it was quiet, thank God, and the woman asked if Julia had any questions. Ha, yeah. When Julia shook her head, it thudded, and fell into thudding rhythm with the *choo-choo* of the heart monitor, and the two of them sailed off on a glassy blue bay. The woman wrote something with what looked like a turkey thermometer. Julia turned her face to the wall when the pain came. Scanning the face of the building for Cynthia's glowing windows, Kevin took a minute to think about what he'd say, then called from the street and told her how the man who ran publicity at the journalism conference had made him shoot the floral arrangements in the lobby, offering cinematic insights. "'Howzabout,'" Kevin said in a goofy voice, '"we drop that sunset over the Sheraton sign?'"

"You're kidding me!" Cynthia yelled. "Shut up!"

"I'm thinking about becoming a wedding videographer."

"Jesus, shut up!" she said.

"Hey, I have your lens," he said. "I didn't want to leave it in the office where somebody could swipe it. I'll drop it off on my way home."

He waited by his car on the corner, and a few minutes later Cynthia brought her dog, Jasper, downstairs. She wore a cute navy-blue miniskirt and a spangly T-shirt that said "Ciao Roma." They walked around the block and then back to the entrance to her building. In his mind, he was reporting these actions to someone. The dog, a white Yorkie with Milk Dud eyes, looked up at Kevin, and he took the leash from Cynthia's hand and ran his fingers over the dog's head.

Back in March, after a long night at the editing suite, Kevin had driven Cynthia home, but when he pulled up in front of her building she wouldn't get out. They'd been yakking all night. He hadn't had so much fun with anybody in five years. He'd wanted to do something. He shivered a little, and leaned over to say good night. She made an *oh* sound that caught in her throat, a garbage truck scared them, and they had a big laugh and she jumped out. Then, a few weeks later, they'd done the routine again, first talking exhaustively in the editing suite, getting that glow, then sitting in the car until he shivered. But there'd been no makeout session the second time, either, and that was it.

Cynthia had been seeing a guy in New York, and as they stood at the door she told Kevin that, since the last time she saw him, she'd been floored by the realization that the guy was a drunk. "I'm not afraid to be alone," she said. "And I'm not afraid I'll never find love."

"Of course," Kevin said. "You're thirty-two years old."

"I don't need any fuckhead boyfriend. I do what I want. I go out almost every night."

"You're living your life."

"You know what I made for dinner tonight?"

"What?"

"An egg-white omelette. With scallions. You know when I ate it? Nine o'clock."

"I envy your freedom."

Her skirt had a big plastic zipper on the front, and sat loosely on her hips, and as she talked he noticed that the skirt had slid around and now the zipper was on the side. During her glory days she'd taught ballet to Madonna, and dated a guy in the N.B.A. Kevin thought about those N.B.A. hands on her. He reached forward to give the leash back, and as she took it from him he tipped his head toward hers but she turned away, smiling.

He tried to explain. "I wanted to touch you in the car that night."

"I always love talking to you," she said.

"Me, too," he said.

She looked down. "Am I being too harsh?"

"What is this, ninth grade?" He took the lens out of his bag and handed it to her.

"You're a total freak," she said, smiling at him again and taking the lens. Then she got confused and stepped in and jangled him with a long soft hug, jamming herself against him.

He felt even more stupid now. "You sure you don't want to get one drink?"

"No, God, it's after eleven. I'm finished."

"Do you want to smoke a cigarette?"

"Don't give me all the power, Kevin. What do you think?"

"I think we should go upstairs."

"Right."

"Yeah."

"Don't look at me that way," she said. "I don't want to be the bad guy."

"You're just gonna go to sleep?"

"Go home to your pregnant wife."

Kevin stared at Cynthia. He had to hate her now. Maybe if he strangled somebody other than Julia he'd feel better. He blinked back tears and crumbled. "She ate three rotisserie chickens this week."

"That's good," Cynthia said sadly. "Fatten her up."

"She's fat enough. She looks like Tweedledee, with her preggo stretch pants pulled up to her armpits."

"That's cute."

"I'm gonna kill her in her sleep."

"What about the baby?"

"You think that would hurt the baby?"

"It might."

"See, that's the rub."

"It sounds like you don't like your wife."

"She has flaws."

"Well, God."

"Too many to name."

"Then she'll make an excellent mother."

It was almost midnight when Kevin got home. Julia's car was gone, the lights were on, and the front door was unlocked. What a fucking idiot. For a second he couldn't figure it out. But her book group met some Sundays and usually ran late. He wanted to slap her across the face with a brick.

He wanted her to go somewhere and never come back. He was so sick of this crap. If he left now . . . but that would be impossible. He had to find a way to get rid of her without getting rid of the baby. How could you do that?

He loved her, but he never wanted to see her again.

Kevin walked into the kitchen and without thinking began placing a stack of clean dishtowels into a drawer in color-coördinated piles.

Her face to the wall, her hand wrapped around the bedrail, she began to pant. Her eyes were fluttering behind her eyelids. Her cheeks puffed, her chin quivered. Then she gasped and her body stiffened. The nurse pushed her chair away from the bed and leaned over and placed her hand on Julia's forehead. The gesture startled Julia and big tears rolled down her face.

The young doctor stood at the foot of the bed. He clicked his penlight a few times and stared out the window at the plaza, at patients smoking cigarettes, trailing their I.V. poles. Against the weatherman's prediction, it had started to rain.

When the contraction ended, the nurse put Julia's bed down flat.

The young doctor said, "Heh-heh. I've just gotta, uh—" And

he moved to his place between Julia's legs. An old goat from the obstetrics department strode in with military purpose and introduced himself to Julia. The young doctor very carefully inserted his fingers. "Please stop moving," he said. He thought he was feeling the skull, but then realized that it was still the hip. "Still three," he said.

"*Talk to her,*" the old goat barked.

"You're still three centimetres dilated."

The old goat bent over and stuck his hand into Julia as though reaching for car keys that had fallen down the drain, and then cleared some phlegm from his throat. "Show me three." The young doctor held his index fingers about three centimetres apart. The old goat said, "That's five," and pulled the young doctor's hands apart. "That's eight. Slide over. Get out of the way."

Kevin carried his luggage upstairs and got undressed, glancing out the window for Julia's car. He thought back to his one big breakup after college, a relationship that had ended fairly well after five years, and he pictured that late-afternoon goodbye—he and Lisa had packed up the car, the car they'd bought together, and sat on the steps and split up the pictures in the photo album, then stood and hugged. Then she'd said something he never forgot, "Hey, you were good to me," and he said that she'd been good to him, too, and she drove away. And even now, after all this time, he missed her so much it ached to think about that day. He still talked to her every once in a while, and it was so easy to talk, easier than it had ever been with Julia. After she left, he'd gone upstairs to the empty apartment where they'd both been crying for weeks, and ordered Chinese food and turned on the TV and felt total relief. For a few months, he'd gone crazy, stayed out late, dated a cyclist named Jade, visited Cuba, and worked weekends. But he didn't establish anything with anyone, and he lived alone for a few years. There was the feeling of having been burned. By what, though? And now he had that feeling again, that lonely feeling, with Julia—he'd been burned by all of this, by his own hopes, and by his inability to do anything about the situation, to change the bad parts. Look at the mess, look at what he'd done. He was the only guy he knew who liked his wife and still tried to cheat on her every chance he got. That wasn't progress. It was nothing he'd recommend.

He felt, in the shower, as if he were washing off all the failures of the weekend. When he got out, she still wasn't home. The house was small and there was no other place for it, so one corner of the bedroom was being turned into a nursery. It had a stuffed penguin on the floor and a cardboard box of old baby clothes from his brother. The crib would be there in a month. Without unpacking his bag, Kevin got into bed and listened for Julia's car, but it had been a long day and he passed out.

The old goat hung his face at Julia and said, "We're getting a room ready. We're taking you in."

She felt herself going cold. The anesthesiologist pushed a pain-killing narcotic into the I.V. and inserted the epidural. Nurses in masks flowed about her. They dropped the bedrail, slid her onto a gurney, and suddenly she lay there, on the cold plate, chatty as hell, her euphoria ballooning.

"I'm not going to work tomorrow, that's for sure. I'm on maternity leave now, that's for sure."

People busied themselves around her. Finally, the young doctor said, "That's right."

"I'm a mom now. I will be in a minute," she said. The young doctor grabbed her I.V. as they turned her. She caught his stare and held it and said, "I already love her so much."

Bin Laden got her. Kevin should've known. She'd been buried, and he looked everywhere and found her, at last, in Georgetown, in the middle of the street, probably dead and covered with pavement, except for her face, and he looked down and saw that cute little face of hers. Who'd done this? Bin Laden. He had to get her out. There were alarms going, ringing out loud, the police. They'd come from headquarters and were going door to door, banging on the houses along M Street. And you could hear the *boom-boom* of construction crews down on Thirty-fifth, trying to break up the street to save her, but they weren't here yet and he didn't know who else they had to save and he would just have to wait and it was awful, terrible— they were calling Kevin's name.

Then, in the fuzzy air between dreaming and consciousness, he heard Julia screaming his name, whapping on the door, and he stood dizzily and was moving downstairs in his underwear. From the other side of the door, she screamed for him. She didn't have her keys, she must have lost her keys. No wonder he'd had to marry her—she was so stupid.

But it was Erica, Julia's friend from the nutso ward, looking weird. Kevin said, "Julia's not here."

"You have to come to the hospital."

"What?"

"You're having a daughter."

"You what?"

"She's at the hospital." It went on like that for another ten seconds before he got it. Julia said, "I was lying on the couch at seven o'clock tonight and I thought I had food poisoning."

"Uh-huh," the young doctor said. They were moving quickly, rolling her down the hall.

"I had the worst pain in my life and then it went away and five minutes later it came back. It never entered my mind I was in labor."

They stopped under the surgical lights inside the operating room. She could feel something cool, like ice water, across her belly.

"Can we wait a minute?" Julia asked. "He'll be here soon, I hope." The young doctor pulled his mask down and looked at the clock.

"I have to tell you," Julia said. "You're a doctor, so you'll know."

"I'm in medical school. I graduate in June."

"They had this movie on TV with Brad Pitt." She started to cry.

"It's O.K."

"I did something."

"All right."

"I wanted her out. I kept saying that, 'Get her out.'"

The young doctor waited another second. "You didn't mean it."

"I'm sorry."

"We're not machines," he said.

Erica pulled up to the hospital entrance and Kevin ran down the long corridor to the B-Wing elevator. Up on the sixth floor a nurse led him, shaking, into Labor and Delivery. It wasn't a heart attack so much as he'd strained the muscles that surrounded his heart. She gave him a paper suit and he shook as though he were freezing to death, putting each stitch of his own clothes in a plastic bag that she took from him, leading him into the operating room, where he squinted into the light, smiling at everyone, grinning madly.

"Look who we found," the nurse said, squeezing his arm. "It's Dad."

Julia's feet were toward the door. There were a dozen people around her. By her head, one guy fiddled with knobs on a bank of machines that Kevin, in his sleepy state, mistook for a film-editing system. Her legs were strapped down by two black seat belts. She'd been shaved. The skin above her stomach, painted a strange brown, was coated in some kind of wax paper. From her hip bones to her chest, the whole of her torso had been pulled open, a gaping bloody maw, pooling and flooding, stretched. A single band of gauze was tied, on one end, to a hook on the wall and on the other end to a small metal plate stuck in her skin that yanked her open, like something a sailor would rig up to hold a hatch in place. Naked of flesh, brimming with blood, her parts gushing, the pieces of her torso jiggled like gelatine. It looked like a torpedo had crashed through the roof and torn her in half.

Something like adrenaline moved him to the stool beside her head, where he sat behind a sheet that had been raised to hide the surgery from her, and took her hand and kissed it, and kissed her face.

"I feel so bad," he said, strangling off tears.

"Don't worry," she said. "Everything is O.K." She was gone, stoned, and so pale beneath her blueberry bonnet.

"Did you see anything?" she asked hopefully.

Kevin leaned over her disembodied head. He stroked her cheek. "Nothing. You're fine." He tried not to fall apart. His own stomach swam.

They had a little laugh then, in a bubbly, forced way, about the timing of it, how he would've been in Hartford if it had happened a night earlier. And laughed about the name they hadn't picked yet—Adina, Astrid, Chipewee, Jasmine. The people on the other side of the sheet clinked metal tools and mumbled and moved with urgent, clipped streams of nonsense. The old goat grunted epithets. The group fell into a rhythm.

Julia stopped mid-sentence, wincing, and Kevin lifted a bean-shaped plastic trough to her lips and she vomited into it. He glanced over the curtain and went a little cross-eyed at the sight of her. It was too much.

Two nurses placed their little bloody sponges on a tray and counted them in unison like children singing a nursery rhyme: *one, two, three,* touching each one, *four, five, six,* to twenty-five. Then they did it again, and then again.

When the baby came, screaming, Julia and Kevin stared at each other and froze, smiling dumbly. Finally the old goat said, "Dad, you can look," and Kevin glanced over the sheet and saw the young doctor holding the baby girl in his gloved hands. She was entirely fishlike and more purple than Kevin had feared, her tiny private parts swollen, her eyes sealed shut, and they wiped her face off as she tried to grab and hug the air in front of her. The doctor held the soft part of his pinkie to the roof of her mouth as the nurse rinsed her face. Then they whisked her away. Kevin kissed Julia and cried.

Without fanfare, Kevin was led to the baby, one room over, curled in a plastic tray under a heat lamp, writhing and screeching dryly and kicking her legs in the air. He examined her ears and lips and mottled purple skin. Oh, God, he thought as she screamed. Now there are two of them.

A tall, angular, dark-haired nurse strolled over, using the new familiar "Dad," and lifted the baby's foot. She needed blood and pricked it, and the baby screamed in a different way, and screamed and screamed, as the nurse calmly worked to bring blood to the glass tube, squeezing the little foot like a lemon, one drop, then another, bending the toes back against the shin, the little earthworm leg held up in the air. It appeared that, in her exuberance, the nurse had pinched off the blood flow to the foot by holding it this way, and Kevin felt sweat run down his back, as the white-hot rage of a thousand burning suns stoked his belly. He imagined himself kicking her, like Bruce Lee, in the head, until she finally released the foot. Because the baby had been in the breech position, her feet sprang up around her ears, and when the nurse pulled them down again they sprang back up and the nurse laughed as the baby screamed. She went to the other heel for blood, and then to a finger. In the end the baby was screaming so hard no sound came out.

Kevin sighed, covered in sweat, and smiled weakly at the nurse, who placed a tiny washcloth in his hand and suggested that he wash his baby. He put a hand on her chest and felt her soft kitten belly, her ribs like pasta. She looked a little like George Costanza.

It was sometime after three in the morning, on the fourteenth of April. Everything about this night reminded Kevin of powerful psychedelic drugs: his endless need to burn energy, his ultra-aware calmness, the sense of solace he found in his own oblivion, the way he moved among normal people, a changed human, unseen, and the feeling that he'd held back from learning all this until now. A torrent of new insights refused to recede. He checked in on Julia, then went back to the baby. He patrolled the sixth floor. He'd shifted his consciousness into a cosmic framework that no one on earth had experienced before. The lights were down in the neonatal I.C.U. The baby had two I.V.s and five wires connected to her, four on her chest, one on her ankle. The monitors glared above her. One was heart rate, one was respiration, one was oxygen level in the blood. He watched the beats. He watched and watched. He had nothing else in the world to do, and felt more peaceful and alert than he could ever remember. Beside him, in the dark room, a mother sat bleakly rocking in front of her glass case. Inside the case was a very tiny baby with a thin tube taped to its face, staring into space, dwarfed by its diapers, with a sock on its head, and huge, scary bug-out eyes. When he looked back, he realized that his baby was no bigger.

He watched his daughter's chest rising, a little hamster movement. He noticed that the tape holding the I.V. to the back of her ridiculous little hand was bloody. She slept peacefully, and her face shifted, and as it did she looked a little like his grandfather, then Jack Welch, and then Charlie Brown, snoozing by the window on a rainy afternoon.

He went back and sat at Julia's side. The lights were off there, too. He checked her chest, rising and falling, watched her breathe. She also wore a diaper. The temperature in the hospital was frigid. On her hand, he noticed a bloody piece of tape holding her I.V. in place and his heart ached for her and his throat burned. It came over him in a rush, in a moment, and he got rid of it just as quickly. She'd gone through it alone, and now she needed everything; she needed rest, she had to sleep. When she woke up, he'd be in this chair, with his two eyes open. A new motor inside him was running on high.

BABOONS

Sheila Kohler

Sheila Kohler is the author of six novels, *Bluebird, or the Invention of Happiness*; *Crossways*; *Children of Pithiviers*; *Cracks*; *The House on R Street*; and *The Perfect Place*. She has also written three books of short stories, *Stories from Another World*, *One Girl*, and *Miracles in America*. Her work received the O. Henry Award in 1988 and has received the Open Voice Award, the Smart Family Foundation Prize, and the Willa Cather Prize, and will be included in *The O. Henry Prize Stories* for 2008. Kohler was awarded the Dorothy and Lewis B. Cullman Center for Scholars and Writers Fellowship at the New York Public Library. She lives in New York City.

As they drive along the road to Oudtshoorn and draw near the house where the dinner is being held, Jan Marais tells his wife Kate that he is having an affair with Serge, his anesthetist.

Jan draws the car—the black Mercedes convertible his mother-in-law gave them as a wedding present—over onto the shoulder of the road, anticipating Kate's response. He wants to stop so that, if necessary, he can put his arms around his wife's shoulders and comfort her, should she weep in the car. The top is down, and Jan can see a small troop of brown-gray baboons by the side of the road. Big males and two or three smaller females with several young baboons around them are sitting on rocks or rooting in the earth under the wild fig and thorn trees. The sultry heat of the December evening is tempered only by the wind, which blows the branches about wildly.

Jan turns off the engine and the lights, but leaves the radio playing. A woman is singing softly: "Take me to your heart again . . ." Jan looks at his wife and waits for her reply, but she seems to be looking at the baboons.

"Baboons," she says incongruously, as though this were some sort of reply to what he has told her. Why can the woman not concentrate on the matter at hand? Jan thinks. This is one of the things which annoys him about Kate: the way she flits from subject to subject without any connection, the way she dithers, never able to make up her mind. He feels it is having an effect on him, on his work, where prompt decisions are a matter of life and death.

Kate is sitting beside him with her small hands in her lap, staring at the baboons. He notices how nicely the blue of her flowered dress reflects her star-shaped sapphire earrings. Kate has a way with color. She knows how to dress with understated elegance. He sees how flat the collar of this dress lies against her smooth white neck. She holds her small, dark head erect, and her lips turn down ever so slightly at the edges. Even in the fading light of day, he can see how her brown eyes glimmer in a hazy, dreamy way. He sees her luminous skin, the soft tinge in the cheeks which rises from her neck like a promise, and he smells her sweet odor of verbena and roses.

He asks her, "Don't you have anything to say?" but she does not answer.

Jan met Kate at a university party two years ago. When Jan left the small *dorp* in the Free State, where there is nothing much but dust and heat, to go to university in Cape Town to study medicine, his family was afraid he might marry a rich girl, and they would never see him again. But they have seen him more frequently since he married Kate, who often invites them to stay in their big house. Jan's mother, a clever woman, is from a French Huguenot family, the du Toits, and plays the organ in the Dutch Reformed Church.

When Jan was a boy, he would sit by her side and pump the organ.

Now he sits beside his wife, Kate, in the black Mercedes with the tan leather seats and the stick shift. He waits in the humid heat for her to say something, but she says nothing.

Besides the low voice on the radio and the barking of the baboons, there is only the lonely sigh of the wind in the branches. Kate seems to be gazing dreamily into the tangle of the wild trees.

KATE IS not saying anything, because her head is spinning. The tan leather of the car, the thick, dark mass of the trees, and the brown-gray bodies of the baboons with their dog-like muzzles are all spinning around her, alarmingly. For one terrifying moment, she has the sensation of leaving her body, abandoning herself; she can see herself from some distance: a pale woman with short, dark curls, sitting strangely still in a car.

As a child she sometimes felt this when she lay in the long dormitory at her Anglican boarding school near Cape Town. The narrow beds and the bare, whitewashed walls of the room would spin around her, and she would feel she was leaving herself behind. Sometimes she would say the prayer she had learned as a child: "Matthew, Mark, Luke, and John, God bless the bed that I lie on," and she would come back to herself. And there have been other moments in her life when she is not quite sure if she was dreaming or not.

Now she feels she must say something, anything, in response to what Jan has told her, if she is going to reclaim her discarded body, if she is to stop herself from floating out into the twilight. What comes to her from a distance is something in French, which Jan does not speak. She says, in her calm, gentle voice, *Tout lasse, tout passe, tout casse.*

KATE WAS studying art and languages at Cape Town University when she first met Jan. She liked his blond good looks, his good brain, and his frank and sometimes tactless manner, the way he said what he thought. Kate was taught as a child not to say things unless they were pleasant. She liked the fact that Jan was poor and from such a big family, and particularly that he was an Afrikaner, perhaps because it annoyed her widowed mother so much.

"You are all I have in the world now, darling," her mother said to Kate, her only child, when her husband died. During her studies at university, Kate continued to go home for the holidays, to drive her mother to church on Sundays, to sit and knit with her in the chintz-covered armchairs in the evenings, to fix her drink, and to go out to dinner at her mother's dull friends' houses, where no one ever said anything unpleasant.

Still, when Kate told her about Jan, her mother said, "Over my dead body will you marry a Boer!"

"Mother!" Kate said, appalled.

Her mother sighed and put her knitting needles down in her lap and said, more mildly, "He comes from such a different background, darling."

"That's why I like him," Kate said, rudely.

This altercation, highly unusual for Kate and her mother, may have strengthened Kate's resolve to marry Jan. Kate has her stubborn side.

Also, Kate liked the fact that Jan was studying to be a thoracic surgeon, that he would be saving lives. Kate herself has saved lives, though only those of a few wounded birds, two stray cats, a monkey which followed her around the garden for a while, before it turned vicious and bit her, and a puppy she once found half-drowned in a ditch.

Of course, Kate had not realized the long hours required to save lives, or she might have been less enthusiastic about Jan's work. She hadn't realized that Jan would come home late every night, his face gray, and so exhausted that all he could do was to throw himself, unwashed, smelling of sweat, into the big white bed where he slept as though nothing could wake him. She hadn't realized that he would be gone when she woke every morning, leaving the long corridors, the wide terrace, the smooth green lawn empty.

JAN SAYS harshly, "What did you say? What! What does that mean?" He is sweating slightly, and it seems to him that the sultry summer evening is growing warmer rather than cooler. Even the wind seems to be abating. Jan hates it when Kate speaks French or worse still, Italian, which seems affected to him. He hates the way she claps after a concert, lifting high her small hands and shouting out not "Bravo!" like everyone else but "Bravi!"

Jan speaks only English and Afrikaans. A scholarship boy, and captain of the rugby team, Jan was always first in his class, and the first in his family to go on to university. His father held a minor position on the South African railways, until he was dismissed because of something he did to a black man.

Besides, Jan doesn't understand how anyone would want to speak French at an important moment like this. He imagines Kate has said something condescendingly polite, which she often does, something calm and reassuring, when he is in a rage, in her low melodious English voice, something that by contrast reminds him all too well how his mother suddenly screamed at his father or at one of his little brothers or sisters in Afrikaans, or even at him, Jan, her pet, suddenly turning on him with cruelty, lashing out at him. It reminds him all too well how his mother would stride through their narrow house on a rampage, swiping with the hairbrush at any exposed limb or posterior in sight.

He turns his face toward Kate in the half-dark and asks again what she meant, but she does not bother to translate her foreign words. When she does not respond, he leans forward over the shiny wooden steering wheel, embracing it, clinging to it for support. He says, "I couldn't go on lying to you. I hate to lie to you. You cannot imagine how lonely it is to have to lie. I had to tell you the truth. And Serge will be there tonight. I've promised him I'll spend a weekend with him, so that we can sort this all out." He stops to wait for some response, but when Kate again says nothing, he goes on. "It has really no importance at all, to you and me, you understand. It doesn't mean anything has changed between us, that I don't love you still, which I do."

It is at that moment that the radio, which has been playing, goes off abruptly, and there is dead silence in the car.

HAVING SAID something to Jan, even if it was in French, and hearing Jan respond, saying something about love, Kate is now able to realize she is sitting there beside him in the car, slumped over a little, her hands still in her lap, the baboons on the rocks under the trees, the wind blowing her hair in her face.

She is thinking of what she wrote in her diary this morning. Kate keeps a little, blue leather diary diligently, as she does everything else. The people at the photography gallery where she works in Cape Town appreciate her diligence, her punctuality, her tact with their difficult clients, and her quiet unobtrusive presence. Her voice on the telephone is praised particularly. In her diary she writes down her weight, what exercise she has taken, what she has eaten (she tries to eat only fruit, vegetables, and whole-wheat grains), how many photographs she has sold for the gallery, a record of her periods, and, from time to time, even adds a few words about the weather. Today, exceptionally, she has written: "ran to beach; porridge for breakfast and an apple; a wild blue sky; perhaps a baby? How wonderful!" She has not had her period for six weeks and three days.

She was planning to give Jan this news, when he gave her his own. She looks at him. She has always liked to stare at his startlingly handsome face: the tanned skin, the determined chin, high cheek bones, and slightly slanting, almost yellow eyes—eyes the same color as his hair. She wonders if she should say something about the baby, but it does not seem to be the right moment. Instead, Kate remembers something Jan has told her about his life, which she has never quite believed. When Jan was telling her this, she thought of what her mother says about Afrikaners, that they are too emotional, that they exaggerate. Her mother thinks Afrikaners are all hysterical.

Jan told Kate, one evening, when he had drunk a whole bottle of wine on the terrace, that as a boy, a teacher of his, an older man who taught him Latin, had fallen in love with him. "In love with you? A teacher?" she had said. Jan nodded and said the man had been exceptionally good to him and taken a particular interest in his work. He had even visited his home to convince his parents to let Jan go on to university, which they might not have done otherwise. He had helped him acquire the scholarship which enabled him to continue his studies. One evening, the man had invited him to his house, and Jan had asked him to "show him," was what Jan had actually said, about sex. "I wanted to seduce him," Jan said.

Kate had not really believed this story or certainly had never given it much importance. All the necessary details to make the story believable seemed to be missing. When she questioned Jan, he did not remember the essentials: where the man's house was, what he looked like, if he were old or young, or even whether the man had complied or not with Jan's request, or what had happened to him after that. "I think he got fired," Jan said, when she questioned him.

"You think?" she said, and he shrugged, smiled, and explained that it was like a dream where you don't remember what happens *after* you have fallen down the cliff.

Now Kate stares at Jan, trying to imagine him with Serge. He is wearing the cream silk shirt with the high collar and the Gucci loafers with the tassels Kate bought him for his birthday, which, she supposes, Serge admires.

Kate thinks of Serge and realizes with a shock that he looks a little like her: a tall, dark, curly-haired, athletic man, with a sensuous mouth, and ears that stick out slightly. He did his medical training with Jan. She remembers Jan telling her that Serge caught him once when he passed out the first time they had to dissect a cadaver. She also remembers Serge telling her he read all of Proust in seventy-eight hours. For a moment she sees Serge as she saw him the last time, walking down the hospital corridor in his white coat, swinging his hips slightly, waving a hand, and calling out to her and Jan, "See you."

What Kate wonders now is how she could have known Jan for two years and not been aware of what he was thinking or feeling to this extent, how she could have ignored something so basic about him. She has always felt that the sexual side of their relationship was satisfactory. There were moments in the night when Kate reached out, and he made love to her passionately. Is it possible for a man to love both men and women? she wants to ask him, but feels it would not be appropriate. But she is truly curious about such a phenomenon. She has the impression now that she knows nothing at all about this man, her husband, and perhaps the father of her unborn child. She is no longer even sure that his long absences, which she has always tolerated, were caused by his work. Was he perhaps with Serge? Were there others? Were there women as well as men?

At this moment, she hears a loud barking sound and looks at the baboons which seem to be quarreling. One of them, a larger one with a dark muzzle, is baring its long teeth. A smaller, slender baboon leaves the troop and trots toward the car. It leaps easily and with surprising strength onto the bonnet of the car. The baboon lands lightly, its unsightly distended pink bottom lifted insolently, provocatively, toward their faces.

Jan blows the horn loudly and shouts out angrily, "Get off, God-damn it!" and the baboon, startled, jumps down onto the side of the road. With measured gait, it trots slowly, importantly, across the twilit road, on its flat black hands, going toward the other side, pink bottom swinging and dark tail held upwards, and then, as though it were broken, falling downwards.

Kate watches anxiously, as the animal makes its way safely across the road. Then, for some reason, it stops and turns and stares back at their car. It seems to be looking at them with curiosity in the half-dark. Perhaps it thinks they have something to eat? Yet it holds something up to its mouth in almost human hands—is it a wild fig? Do baboons eat figs?

Kate remembers reading somewhere that baboons will eat animals and even attack a small antelope. They are stronger than they look, apparently. This one appears to be nibbling on something. Then calmly it returns, going back from whence it came, going back to join its mates, who are barking in the dark thicket of the trees. As it crosses the road this second time, it is not as lucky. Though the baboon moves more quickly, a big blue car comes careening around the corner, and the animal, caught in its high beams, stops transfixed for a second too long, and is thrown brutally to one side.

Kate cries out loudly, "Oh no!" and puts her hands to her mouth and makes a little high-pitched sob.

Jan thinks that if she had said these words in response to his initial statement, if she had sobbed instead of speaking French, if the baboon had not jumped onto the bonnet of his car, he would probably have taken her into his arms, and things would not have gone any further.

Instead, he turns to her and hits her hard across her small, open mouth. He hits her with the back of his hand, so that his knuckles slam against her open lips, and he can feel her teeth. For a moment he thinks he might have dislodged one of them.

It is not the first time he has hit Kate in a moment of uncontrollable rage. Once, he had come in very late for dinner, after operating on a small boy. The child had bubble gum caught in his windpipe and lay on the operating table, gasping for breath. Jan had hesitated too long over an essential move, distracted for a second by something—the child's blond curls clinging to his white forehead, his little beating heart, and he had lost the boy's life. When Kate came out onto the terrace to greet him in her perfect pink dress, her single string of pearls, her dark curls fluffed up adorably around her pink cheeks, and complained about Jan's tardy arrival, he had simply hit her across her pretty face and left her standing there.

A placid, gentle woman, Kate, too, is capable of passion at unexpected moments. She is a surprisingly eager lover in his bed. Once, they had been at a party at the hospital, and she had drunk too much cheap wine. Waiting for the elevator, as they were leaving, Kate said, "I *saw* you putting your hand on that fat woman's leg," referring to one of his favorite night nurses, a good-humored, big-breasted Afrikaans nurse, who was sweating in her tight silk dress. Kate had hit Jan across the cheek, hard.

Now Kate takes out a tissue from her sequined handbag and spits a tooth into the kleenex and wipes the blood from her mouth. She says, "My tooth!" in an anguished tone, and he can see the tears in her dark eyes. Now, Jan thinks, she will weep as she should.

Jan feels suddenly calmer and for some reason, optimistic. Everything will work out with time, he thinks. Now that Kate knows about Serge, now that he has hit her, that she has even lost a tooth, he feels a certain relief. His hand throbs from the blow against her teeth which worries him somewhat, and he massages his knuckles, which hurt. His hands are very important to him, of course. He does not feel sorry for Kate at all, though he notices there is blood spattered on her blue dress, and he realizes they will not be able to go to the party now. So much the better, he thinks. The party was never a good idea.

THOUGH SHE has lost a tooth and tastes the blood in her mouth, though she feels her smarting lips and her throbbing gums, for a moment Kate is not absolutely certain that Jan has hit her. It does not seem possible. She can see no reason why he would have. She is the injured party, after all. What has she done to him? She thinks of the numerous advantages his marriage has conferred on him: the big white house with the tennis court and the smooth green lawns, the servants who cook and tend the garden and press his clothes, the important people she has introduced him to, even his job at the hospital, which was procured mainly because her mother knew the head of the department. She thinks of all the lavish affection she showers on him daily: the big bowls of flowers she arranges in his study, the clothes she buys him, the bills she pays, the nights she has sat up in the dusk, nibbling on nuts and sipping sweet sherry, waiting for him to come home, or, even worse, when he is home, watching him gulp down the fresh grilled fish and the healthful salads she has had prepared, in silence in the half-dark on the terrace, with only the sound of the crickets shrilling in the thick shrubbery and the candles flickering in the wind.

She wants to ask Jan if he regrets what he has done, if he is sorry for the harm he has caused her. But instead she looks at her tooth in the tissue and makes a tremendous effort to think of something that would comfort her.

Then she notices the poor baboon, which is making little pitiful cries at the side of the road. It has staggered up and seems confused, as if it has lost its way. It seems to want to cross the road. "Oh, help, please, look, it's alive!" she says impulsively, following her heart.

Jan glances at her with impatience and shakes his head, but he throws open the door of the car and jumps out into the warm night air. Besides, he is glad to be out of the car and away from her, glad to stretch his legs. He walks slowly along the side of the road in the darkness toward the animal. He stands with his hands in his pockets, kicks at the loose dirt, and peers down at the wounded baboon on the ground. He considers. He is not sure what to do about it. Probably better to put it out of its misery, he thinks, but remembers something about not touching a wounded animal. This one is probably a female, he thinks, and her young are near, though the rest of the troop seem to have scattered into the bush. He notices the arm of the baboon, which hangs pitifully broken and bleeding from its shoulder. He crouches down to observe.

It is turning almost completely dark now, the sun already beneath the horizon, only faint traces of pink remaining in the sky. He cannot see very clearly. He hears the crickets shrilling, as he stares down at the wounded animal, leaning a little closer to get a better look at the coarse, matted hair, the bleeding arm. The animal moves with such sudden speed and in such an unforeseen manner that Jan is unable to react. With its one good arm it reaches up and claws at him, tearing away the skin and the flesh from his shoulder so that it hangs down horribly.

Then Jan hears something else, the familiar sound of the Mercedes' engine revving up, and he is caught in the bright headlights. He staggers up into the road, transfixed, his hand to his bleeding shoulder, holding onto his flesh. As the car comes toward him, for a moment he thinks of Serge. Then he starts to spin, leaving his body behind, floating out into the dark.

ONCE IN A LIFETIME

Jhumpa Lahiri

Jhumpa Lahiri was born in London and raised in Rhode Island. She is the author of three books, most recently the story collection *Unaccustomed Earth*. Her debut collection of stories, *Interpreter of Maladies*, was awarded the Pulitzer Prize, the PEN/Hemingway Award, and *The New Yorker* Debut of the Year. Her novel *The Namesake* was a *New York Times* Notable Book and a Los Angeles Times Book Prize finalist, and was selected as one of the best books of the year by *USA Today* and *Entertainment Weekly*, among other publications. She lives in Brooklyn, New York.

I had seen you before, too many times to count, but a farewell that my family threw for yours, at our house in Inman Square, is when I begin to recall your presence in my life. Your parents had decided to leave Cambridge, not for Atlanta or Arizona, as some other Bengalis had, but to move all the way back to India, abandoning the struggle that my parents and their friends had embarked upon. It was 1974. I was six years old. You were nine. What I remember most clearly are the hours before the party, which my mother spent preparing for everyone to arrive: the furniture was polished, the paper plates and napkins set out on the table, the rooms filled with the smell of lamb curry and pullao and the L'Air du Temps my mother used for special occasions, spraying it first on herself, then on me, a firm squirt that temporarily darkened whatever I was wearing.

I was dressed that evening in an outfit that my grandmother had sent from Calcutta: white pajamas with tapered legs and a waist wide enough to gird two of me side by side, a turquoise kurta, and a black velvet vest embroidered with plastic pearls. The three pieces had been arrayed on my parents' bed while I was in the bath, and I stood shivering, my fingertips puckered and white, as my mother threaded a length of thick drawstring through the giant waist of the pajamas with a safety pin, gathering up the stiff material bit by bit and then knotting the drawstring tightly at my stomach. The inseam of the pajamas was stamped with purple letters within a circle, the seal of the textile company. I remember fretting about this fact, wanting to wear something else, but my mother assured me that the seal would come out in the wash, adding that, because of the length of the kurta, no one would notice it anyway.

My mother had more pressing concerns. In addition to the quality and quantity of the food, she was worried about the weather: snow was predicted for later that evening, and this was a time when my parents and their friends didn't own cars. Most of the guests, including you, lived less than a fifteen-minute walk away, either in the neighborhoods behind Harvard and MIT or just across the Mass Avenue Bridge. But some were farther, coming by bus or the T from Malden or Medford or Waltham. "I suppose Dr. Choudhuri can drive people home," she said of your father as she untangled my hair. Your parents were slightly older—seasoned immigrants, as mine were not. They had left India in 1962, before the laws welcoming foreign students changed. While my father and the other men were still taking exams, your father already had a PhD, and he drove a car, a silver Saab with bucket seats, to his job at an engineering firm in Andover. I had been driven home in that car many nights, after parties had gone late and I had fallen asleep in some strange bed or other.

Our mothers met when mine was pregnant. She didn't know it yet; she was feeling dizzy and sat down on a bench in a small park. Your mother was perched on a swing, gently swaying back and forth as you soared above her, when she noticed a young Bengali woman in a sari, wearing vermilion in her hair. "Are you feeling all right?" your mother asked in the polite form. She told you to get off the swing, and then she and you escorted my mother home. It was during that walk that your mother suggested that perhaps mine was expecting. They became instant friends, spending their days together while our fathers were at work. They talked about the lives they had left behind in Calcutta: your mother's beautiful home in Jodhpur Park, with hibiscus and rosebushes blooming on the rooftop, and my mother's modest flat in Maniktala, above a grimy Punjabi restaurant, where seven people existed in three small rooms. In Calcutta they would probably have had little occasion to meet. Your mother went to a convent school and was the daughter of one of Calcutta's most prominent lawyers, a pipe-smoking Anglophile and a member of the Saturday Club. My mother's father was a clerk in the General Post Office, and she had neither eaten at a table nor sat on a commode before coming to America. Those differences were irrelevant in Cambridge, where they were both equally alone. Here they shopped together for groceries and complained about their husbands and cooked at either our stove or yours, dividing up the dishes for our respective families when they were done. They knitted together, switching projects when one of them got bored. When I was born, your parents were the only friends to visit the hospital. I was fed in your old high chair, pushed along the streets in your old pram.

During the party it started snowing, as predicted, stragglers arriving with wet, white-caked coats that we had to hang from the shower curtain rod. For years, my mother talked about how, when the party ended, your father made countless trips to drive people home, taking one couple as far as Braintree, claiming that it was no trouble, that this was his last opportunity to drive the car. In the days before you left, your parents came by again, to bring over pots and pans, small appliances, blankets and sheets, half-used bags of flour and sugar, bottles of shampoo. We continued to refer to these things as your mother's. "Get me Parul's frying pan," my mother would say. Or, "I think we need to turn the setting down on Parul's toaster." Your mother also brought over shopping bags filled with clothes she thought I might be able to use, that once belonged to you. My mother put the bags away and took them with us when we moved, a few years later, from Inman Square to a house in Sharon, incorporating the clothes into my wardrobe as I grew into them. Mainly they were winter items, things you would no longer need in India. There were thick T-shirts and turtlenecks in navy and brown. I found these clothes ugly and tried to avoid them, but my mother refused to replace them. And so I was forced to wear your sweaters, your rubber boots on rainy days. One winter I had to wear your coat, which I hated so much that it caused me to hate you as a result. It was blue-black with an orange lining and a scratchy grayish-brown trim around the hood. I never got used to having to hook the zipper on the right side, to looking so different from the other girls in my class with their puffy pink and purple jackets. When I asked my parents if I could have a new coat they said no. A coat was a coat, they said. I wanted desperately to get rid of it. I wanted it to be lost. I wished that one of the boys in my class, many of whom owned identical coats, would accidentally pick it up in the narrow alcove where we rushed to put on our things at the end of the day. But my mother had gone so far as to iron a label inside the coat with my name on it, an idea she'd got from her subscription to *Good Housekeeping*.

Once I left it on the school bus. It was a mild late winter day, the windows on the bus open, everybody's outerwear shed on the seats. I was taking a different bus than usual, one that dropped me off in the neighborhood of my piano teacher, Mrs. Hennessey. When the bus neared my stop I stood up, and when I reached the front the driver reminded me to be careful crossing the street. She pulled back the lever that opened the door, letting fragrant air onto the bus. I was about to step off, coatless, but then someone cried out, "Hey, Hema, you forgot this!" I was startled that anyone on that bus knew my name; I had forgotten about the name tag.

———

BY THE following year I had outgrown the coat, and to my great relief it was donated to charity. The other items your parents bequeathed to us, the toaster and the crockery and the Teflon pots and pans, were gradually replaced as well, until there was no longer any physical trace of you in the house. For years our families had no contact. The friendship did not merit the same energy my parents devoted to their relatives, buying stacks of aerograms at the post office and sending them off faithfully every week, asking me to write the same three sentences to each set of grandparents at the bottom. My parents spoke of you rarely, and I imagine they assumed that our paths were unlikely to cross again. You'd moved to Bombay, a city far from Calcutta, which my parents and I never visited. And so we did not see you, or hear from you, until the first day of 1981, when your father called us very early in the morning to wish us a happy New Year and say that your family was returning to Massachusetts, where he had a new job. He asked if, until he found a house, you could all stay with us.

For days afterward, my parents talked of nothing else. They wondered what had gone wrong: Had your father's position at Larsen & Toubro, too good to turn down at the time, fallen through? Was your mother no longer able to abide the mess and heat of India? Had they decided that the schools weren't good enough for you there? Back then international calls were kept short. Of course, your family was welcome, my parents said, and marked the date of your arrival on the calendar in our kitchen. Whatever the reason you were coming, I gathered from my parents' talk that it was regarded as a wavering, a weakness. "They should have known it's impossible to go back," they said to their friends, condemning your parents for having failed at both ends. We had stuck it out as immigrants while you had fled; had we been the ones to go back to India, my parents seemed to suggest, we would have stuck it out there as well.

Until your return I'd thought of you as a boy of eight or nine, frozen in time, the size of the clothes I'd inherited. But you were twice that now, sixteen, and my parents thought it best that you occupy my room and that I sleep on a folding cot set up in their bedroom. Your parents would stay in the guestroom, down the hall. My parents often hosted friends who came from New Jersey or New Hampshire for the weekend, to eat elaborate dinners and talk late into the evening about Indian politics. But by Sunday afternoon those guests were always gone. I was accustomed to having children sleep on the floor by my bed, in sleeping bags. Being an only child, I enjoyed this occasional company. But I had never been asked to relinquish my room entirely. I asked my mother why they weren't giving you the folding cot instead of me.

"Where would we put it?" she asked. "We only have three bedrooms."

"Downstairs," I suggested. "In the living room."

"That wouldn't look right," my mother said. "Kaushik must practically be a man by now. He needs his privacy."

"What about the basement?" I said, thinking of the small study my father had built there, lined with metal bookcases.

"That's no way to treat guests, Hema. Especially not these. Dr. Choudhuri and Parul Di were such a blessing when we first had you. They drove us home from the hospital, they brought over food for weeks. Now it's our turn to be helpful."

"What sort of doctor is he?" I asked. Though I had always been in good health, I had an irrational fear of doctors then, and the thought of one living in the house made me nervous, as if his mere presence might make one of us sick.

"He's not a medical doctor. It refers to his PhD."

"Baba has his PhD and no one calls him a doctor," I pointed out.

"When we met, Dr. Choudhuri was the only one. It was our way of paying respect."

I asked how long you would be staying with us—a week? Two? My mother couldn't say; it all depended on how long it took your family to get settled and find a place. The prospect of having to give up my room infuriated me. My feelings were complicated by the fact that, until rather recently, to my great shame, I'd regularly slept with my parents on the cot in their room, and not in the room where I kept my clothes and things. My mother considered the idea of a child sleeping alone a cruel American practice and therefore did not encourage it, even when we had the space. She told me that she had slept in the same bed as her parents until the day she was married and that this was perfectly normal. But I knew that it was not normal, not what my friends at school did, and that they would ridicule me if they knew. The summer before I started middle school, I insisted on sleeping alone. In the beginning my mother kept checking on me during the night, as if I were still an infant who might suddenly stop breathing, asking if I was scared and reminding me that she was just on the other side of the wall. In fact, I was scared that first night; the perfect silence in my room terrified me. But I refused to admit this, for what I feared more was failing at something I should have learned to do at the age of three or four. In the end it was easy; I fell asleep out of sheer anxiety that I would not, and in the morning I woke up alone, squinting in the eastern light my parents' room did not receive.

THE HOUSE was prepared for your arrival. New throw pillows were purchased for the living-room sofa, bright orange against the brown tweed upholstery. The plants and the curios were rearranged, my school portrait framed and hung above the fireplace. The Christmas cards were taken down from around the front door, where my mother and I had taped them one by one as they came in the mail. My parents, remembering your father's habit of dressing well, bought robes to wear in the mornings, my mother's made of velour, my father's styled like a smoking jacket. One day I came home from school and found that the pink-and-white coverlet on my bed had been replaced by a tan blanket. There were new towels in the bathroom for you and your parents, plusher than the ones we used and a prettier shade of blue. My closet had been weeded, bare hangers left on the rod. I was told to clear out a couple of drawers, and I removed enough things so that I would not have to enter the room while you were in it. I took my pajamas, some outfits to wear to school, and the sneakers I needed for gym. I took the library book I was reading, along with the others stacked on my bedside table. I wanted you to see as few of my things as possible, so I cleared away my jewelry box full of cheap tangled chains and my bottles of Avon perfume. I removed the locked diary from my desk drawer, though I'd written only two entries since receiving it for Christmas. I removed the seventh-grade yearbook in which my photograph appeared, the endpapers filled with silly messages from my classmates. It was like deciding which of my possessions I wanted to take on a long trip to India, only this time I was going nowhere. Still, I put my things into a suitcase covered with peeling tags and stickers that had traveled various times back and forth across the world and dragged it into my parents' room.

I studied pictures of your parents; we had a few pasted into an album, taken the night of the farewell party. There was my father, his stiff jet-black hair already a surprise to me by then. He was dressed in a sweater vest, his shirt cuffs rolled back, pointing urgently at something beyond the frame. Your father was in the suit and tie he always wore, his handsome, bespectacled face leaning toward someone in conversation, his greenish eyes unlike anyone else's. The middle part in your mother's hair accentuated the narrow length of her face; the end of her raw-silk sari was wrapped around her shoulders like a shawl. My mother stood beside her, a head shorter and more disheveled, stray hairs hanging by her ears. They both appeared flushed, the color high in their cheeks, as if from drinking wine, even though all they ever drank in those days was tap water or tea, the bond between them clear. There was no evidence of you, the person I was most curious about. Who knows where you had lurked in that crowd? I imagine you sat at the desk in the corner of my parents' bedroom, reading a book you'd brought with you, waiting for the party to end.

My father went one evening to the airport to greet you. It was a school night for me. The dining table had been set since the afternoon. This was my mother's way when she gave parties, though she had never prepared such an elaborate meal in the middle of the week. An hour before you were expected, she turned on the oven. She had heated up a panful of oil and begun to fry thick slices of eggplant to serve with the dal, filling the room with a haze of smoke, when my father called to say that though your plane had landed, one of your suitcases had not arrived. I was hungry by then, but it felt wrong to ask my mother to open the oven door and pull out all the dishes for my sake. My mother turned off the oil and I sat with her on the sofa watching a movie on television, something about the Second World War, in which a group of tired men were walking across a dark field. Cinema of a certain period was the one thing my mother loved wholeheartedly about the West. She herself never wore a skirt—she considered it indecent—but she could recall, scene by scene, Audrey Hepburn's outfits in any given movie.

I fell asleep at her side, and the next thing I knew I was sprawled on the sofa alone, the television turned off, voices filling another part of the house. I stood up, my face hot, my limbs cramped and heavy. You were all in the dining room, eating. Pans of food lined the table, and in addition to the water pitcher there was a bottle of Johnnie Walker that only your parents were drinking, planted between their plates. There was your mother, her slippery dark hair cut to her shoulders, wearing slacks and a tunic, a silk scarf knotted at her neck, looking only vaguely like the woman I'd seen in the pictures. With her bright lipstick and frosted eyelids, she looked less exhausted than my mother did. She had remained thin, her collarbones glamorously protruding, unburdened by the weight of middle age that now padded my mother's features. Your father looked more or less the same, still handsome, still wearing a jacket and tie, a different style of glasses his concession to the new decade. You were pale like your father, long bangs combed over to one side of your face, your eyes distracted yet missing nothing. I had not

expected you to be handsome. I had not expected to find you appealing in the least.

"My goodness, Hema, already a lady. You don't remember us,
do you?" your mother said. She spoke to me in English, in a pleasant, unhurried way, with a voice that sounded amused. "Come,
poor thing, we've kept you waiting. Your mother told us you went
hungry because of us."

I sat down, embarrassed that you had seen me asleep on the
sofa. Though you had all just flown halfway across the world, it was
I who felt weary, despite my nap. My mother served me a plate of
food, but her attention was on you and the fact that you were refusing seconds.

"We had dinner before we landed," you replied, a faint accent
present in your English, but not the strong accent our parents
shared. Your voice had deepened, no longer a child's.

"It's remarkable, the amount of food you get in first class," your
mother said. "Champagne, chocolates, even caviar. But I saved
room. I remembered your cooking, Shibani," she added.

"First class!" my mother exclaimed, with an intake of breath.
"How did you end up there?"

"It was my fortieth birthday gift," your mother explained. She
looked over at your father, smiling. "Once in a lifetime, right?"

"Who knows?" he said, clearly proud of the extravagance. "It
could become a terrible habit."

Our parents spoke of the old Cambridge crowd, mine telling
yours about people's moves and accomplishments, the bachelors
who had married, the children who had been born. They spoke
about Reagan winning the election, all the ways that Carter had
failed. Your parents spoke of Rome, where you'd had a two-day
layover to tour the city. Your mother described the fountains, and
the ceiling of the Sistine Chapel you had stood three hours in line
to see. "So many lovely churches," she said. "Each is like a museum. It made me want to be a Catholic, only to be able to pray in
them."

"Do not die before seeing the Pantheon," your father said, and my parents nodded, not knowing what the Pantheon was. I knew— I was, in fact, in the middle of learning about ancient Rome in my Latin class, writing a long report about its art and architecture, all of it based on encyclopedia entries and other books in the school library. Your parents spoke of Bombay and the home you had left behind, a flat on the tenth floor, with a balcony overlooking palm trees and the Arabian Sea. "A pity you didn't visit us there," your mother said. Later, in the privacy of their bedroom, my mother pointed out to my father that we had never been invited.

After dinner I was told to show you the house and where you would sleep. Normally I loved to do this for guests, taking a proprietary pleasure in explaining that this was the broom closet, that the downstairs half-bath. But now I lingered over nothing, for I sensed your boredom. I was also nervous at being sent off with you, disturbed by the immediate schoolgirl attraction I felt. I was used to admiring boys by then, boys in my class who were and would remain unaware of my existence. But never someone as old as you, never someone belonging to the world of my parents. It was you who led me, climbing quickly up the stairs, opening doors, poking your head into rooms, unimpressed by it all.

"This is my room. Your room," I said, correcting myself.

After dreading it all this time, now I was secretly thrilled that you would be sleeping here. You would absorb my presence, I thought. Without my having to do a thing, you would come to know me and like me. You walked across the room to the window, opened it, and leaned out into the darkness, letting cold air into the room.

"Ever go out on the roof?" you asked. You did not wait for me to answer, and the next thing I knew you'd lifted the screen and were gone. I rushed over to the window, and when I leaned outside I couldn't see you. I imagined you slipping on the shingles, falling into the shrubbery, my being blamed for the accident, for standing by stupidly as you did such a brazen thing. "Are you okay?" I called out. The logical thing would have been to say your name, but I felt inhibited and did not. Eventually you came back around, seating yourself on the incline over the garage, gazing down at the lawn.

"What's behind the house?"

"Woods. But you can't go there."

"Who said?"

"Everyone. My parents and all the teachers in school."

"Why not?"

"A boy got lost in them last year. He's still missing." His name was Kevin McGrath, and he'd been two grades behind me. For a week we'd heard nothing but helicopters, dogs barking, searching for some sign of him.

You did not react to this information. Instead, you asked, "Why do people have yellow ribbons tied to their mailboxes?"

"They're for the hostages in Iran."

"I bet most Americans had never even heard of Iran before this," you said, causing me to feel responsible both for my neighbors' patriotism and for their ignorance.

"What's that thing to the right?"

"A swing set."

The word must have amused you. You faced me and smiled, though not kindly, as if I'd invented the term.

"I missed the cold," you said. "This cold." The remark reminded me that none of this was new to you. "And the snow. When will it snow again?"

"I don't know. There wasn't much snow for Christmas this year."

You climbed back into the room, disappointed, I feared, by my lack of information. You glanced at yourself in my white-framed mirror, your head nearly cut off at the top. "Where's the bathroom?" you asked, already halfway out the door.

That night, lying on the cot in my parents' room, wide awake though it was well past midnight, I heard my mother and father talking in the dark. I worried that perhaps you would hear them, too. The bed where you slept was just on the other side of the wall, and if I had been able to stick my hand through it, I could have touched you. My parents were at once critical of and intimidated by yours, perplexed by the ways in which they had changed. Bombay had made them more American than Cambridge had, my mother said, something she hadn't anticipated and didn't understand. There were remarks concerning your mother's short hair, her slacks, the Johnnie Walker she and your father continued to drink after the meal was finished, taking it with them from the dining room to the living room. It was mainly my mother who talked, my father listening and murmuring now and then in tired consent. My parents, who had never set foot in a liquor store, wondered whether they should buy another bottle—at the rate your parents were going, that bottle would be drained by tomorrow, my mother said. She remarked that your mother had become "stylish," a pejorative term in her vocabulary, implying a self-indulgence that she shunned. "Twelve people could have flown for the price of one first-class ticket," she said. My mother's birthdays came and went without acknowledgment by my father. I was the one who made a card and had him sign it with me on the first of every June. Suddenly my mother sat up, sniffing the air. "I smell smoke," she said. My father asked if she had remembered to turn off the oven. My mother said she was certain she had, but she asked him to get up and check.

"It's a cigarette you smell," he said when he came back to bed. "Someone has been smoking in the bathroom."

"I didn't know Dr. Choudhuri smoked," my mother said. "Should we have put out an ashtray?"

IN THE morning you all slept in, victims of jet lag, reminding us that despite your presence, your bags crowding the hallways, your toothbrushes cluttering the side of the sink, you belonged elsewhere. When I returned from school in the afternoon you were still sleeping, and at dinner—breakfast for you—you all declined the curry we were eating, craving toast and tea. It was like that for the first few days: you were awake when we slept, sleeping when we were awake; we were leading antipodal lives under the same roof. As a result, apart from the fact that I wasn't sleeping in my own room, there was little change. I drank my orange juice and ate my bowl of cereal and went off to the bus stop as usual. I spoke to no one of your arrival; I almost never revealed details of my home life to my American friends. As a child, I had always dreaded my birthdays, when a dozen girls would appear in the house, glimpsing the way we lived. I don't know how I would have referred to you. "A family friend," I suppose.

Then one day I came home from school and found your parents awake, their ankles crossed on top of the coffee table, filling up the sofa where I normally sat to watch *The Brady Bunch* and *Gilligan's Island*. They were chatting with my mother, who was in the recliner with a bowl in her lap, peeling potatoes. Your mother was dressed in a nylon sari of my mother's, purple with red dots in various sizes. Distressing news of your mother's missing suitcase had come: it had been located in Rome but had been placed on a flight to Johannesburg. I remember thinking that the sari looked better on your mother than on mine; the intense purple shade was more flattering against her skin. I was told that you were outside in the yard. I did not go out to look for you. Instead I practiced the piano. It was nearly dark by the time you came in, accepting the tea that I was still too young to drink. Your parents drank tea as well, but by six o'clock the bottle of Johnnie Walker was on the coffee table, as it would be every night that you stayed with us. You had gone out in only a pullover, your father's costly camera slung around your neck. Your face showed the effects of the cold, your eyes blazing, the borders of your ears crimson, your skin glowing from within.

"There's a stream back there," you said, "in those woods."

My mother became nervous then, warning you not to go there, as she had so often warned me, as I had warned you the night you came, but your parents did not share her concern. What had you photographed? they asked instead.

"Nothing," you replied, and I took it personally that nothing had inspired you. The suburbs were new to you and to your parents. Whatever memories you possessed of America were of Cambridge, a place that I could only dimly recall.

You took your tea and disappeared to my room as if it were yours, emerging only when summoned for dinner. You ate quickly, not speaking, then returned upstairs. It was your parents who paid me court, who asked me questions and complimented me on my manners, on my piano playing, on all the things I did to help my mother around the house. "Look, Kaushik, how Hema makes her lunch," your mother would say as I prepared a ham or turkey sandwich after dinner and put it in a paper bag to take to school the next day. I was still very much a child, while you, just three years older, had already eluded your parents' grasp. You did not argue with them and yet you did not seem to talk to them very much, either. While you were outside I'd heard them tell my mother how unhappy you were to be back. "He was furious that we left, and now he's furious that we're here again," your father said. "Even in Bombay we managed to raise a typical American teenager."

I did my homework at the dining table, unable to use the desk in my room. I worked on my ancient Rome report, something that had interested me until your arrival. Now it seemed silly, given that you'd been there. I longed to work on it in privacy, but your father talked to me at length about the structural aspects of the Colosseum. His civil engineer's explanations went over my head, were irrelevant to my needs, but to be polite I listened. I worried that he would want to see whether I had incorporated the things he said, but he never bothered me about that. He hunted through his bags and showed me postcards he'd purchased, and though it had nothing to do with my report, he gave me a two-lire coin.

WHEN THE worst of your jet lag had subsided we went to the mall in my parents' station wagon. Your mother needed bras, one item that she could not borrow from my voluptuous mother. At the mall our fathers sat together in a sunken area of benches and potted plants, waiting, and you were given some money and allowed to wander off while I accompanied our mothers to the lingerie department in Jordan Marsh. Your mother led us there, with the credit card your father had handed to her before they parted. Normally we went to Sears. On her way to the bras she bought black leather gloves and a pair of boots that zipped to the knee, never looking at the price before taking something off the shelf. In the lingerie department it was me the saleswoman approached. "We have lovely training models, just in," she said to your mother, believing that I was her daughter.

"Oh, no, she's far too young," my mother said.

"But look, how sweet," your mother said, fingering the style the saleswoman presented on a hanger, lacy white with a rosebud at its center. I had yet to get my period and, unlike many of the girls at school, still wore flower-printed undershirts. I was ushered into the fitting room, your mother watching approvingly as I took off my coat and sweater and tried on the bra. She adjusted the straps and attached the hook at the back. She tried things on as well, topless beside me without shame, though it embarrassed me to see her large, plum-colored nipples, the surprising droop of her breasts, the dark patches of underarm hair that gave off a faintly acrid but not altogether unpleasant smell. "Perfect," your mother said, running her finger below the elastic, along my skin, adding, "I hope you know that you're going to be very beautiful one day." Despite my mother's protests, your mother bought me my first three bras, insisting that they were a gift. On the way out, at the makeup counter, she bought a lipstick, a bottle of perfume, and an assortment of expensive creams that promised to firm her throat and brighten her eyes; she was uninterested in the Avon products my mother used. The reward for her purchases at the makeup counter was a large red tote bag. This she gave to me, thinking that it would be useful for my books, and the next day I took it to school.

———————

AFTER A WEEK your father began his new job, at an engineering firm forty miles away. At first my father got up early and dropped him off before returning to Northeastern to teach his economics classes. Then your father bought an Audi with a stick shift. You stayed home with our mothers—your parents wanted to wait until they'd bought their home to see which school you would go to. I was stunned, and envious—half a year without school! To my added chagrin, you were not expected to do anything around the house, never to return your plate or glass to the sink, never to make my bed, which I would see from time to time through the partly open door to my room in a state of total disarray, the blanket on the floor, your clothes heaped on my white desk. You ate enormous amounts of fruit, whole bunches of grapes, apples to their cores, a practice that fascinated me. I did not eat fresh fruit then; the textures and intensity of flavors made me gag. You complained about the taste, or lack of taste, but nevertheless decimated whatever my parents brought home from Star Market. I would find you, when I came home in the afternoons, always at the same end of the sofa, the toes of your thin bare feet hooked around the edge of the coffee table, reading books by Isaac Asimov that you'd picked off my father's shelves in the basement. I hated *Doctor Who*, the one show you liked on television.

I did not know what to make of you. Because you'd lived in India, I associated you more with my parents than with me. And yet you were unlike my cousins in Calcutta, who seemed so innocent and obedient when I visited them, asking questions about my life in America as if it were the moon, astonished by every detail. You were not curious about me in the least. One day a friend at school invited me to see *The Empire Strikes Back* on a Saturday afternoon. My mother said that I could go, but only if you were invited as well. I protested, telling her that my friend did not know you. Despite my crush, I didn't want to have to explain to my friend who you were and why you were living in our house.

"You know him," my mother said.

"But he doesn't even like me," I complained.

"Of course he likes you," my mother said, blind to the full implication of what I'd said. "He's adjusting, Hema. It's something you've never had to go through."

The conversation ended there. As it turned out, you were uninterested in the movie, not having seen *Star Wars* in the first place.

ONE DAY I found you sitting at my piano, randomly striking the keys with your index finger. You stood up when you saw me and retreated to the couch.

"Do you hate it here?" I asked.

"I liked living in India," you said. I did not betray my opinion, that I found trips to India dull, that I didn't like the geckos that clung to the walls in the evenings, poking in and out of the fluorescent light fixtures, or the giant cockroaches that sometimes watched me as I bathed. I didn't like the comments my relatives made freely in my presence—that I had not inherited my mother's graceful hands, that my skin had darkened since I was a child.

"Bombay is nothing like Calcutta," you added, as if reading my mind.

"Is it close to the Taj Mahal?"

"No." You looked at me carefully, as if fully registering my presence for the first time. "Haven't you ever looked at a map?"

On our trip to the mall you'd bought a record, something by the Rolling Stones. The jacket was white, with what seemed to be a cake on it. You had no interest in the few records I owned—Abba, Shaun Cassidy, a disco compilation I'd ordered from a TV commercial with my allowance money. Nor were you willing to play your album on the plastic record player in my room. You opened up the cabinet where my father kept his turntable and receiver. My father was extremely particular about his stereo components. They were off-limits to me, and even to my mother. The stereo had been the single extravagant purchase of his life. He cleaned everything himself, wiping the parts with a special cloth on Saturday mornings, before listening to his collection of Indian vocalists.

"You can't touch that," I said.

You turned around. The lid of the player was already lifted, the record revolving. You held the arm of the needle, resting its weight on your finger. "I know how to play a record," you said, no longer making an effort to conceal your irritation. And then you let the needle drop.

HOW BORED you must have been in my room full of a girl's things. It must have driven you crazy, being stuck with our mothers all day long as they cooked and watched soap operas. Really, it was my mother who did the cooking now. Though your mother kept her company, occasionally peeling or slicing something, she was no longer interested in cooking, as she had been in the Cambridge days. She'd been spoiled by Zareen, the fabulous Parsi cook you had in Bombay, she said. From time to time she would promise to make us an English trifle, the one thing she said she always insisted on making herself, but this didn't materialize. She continued to borrow saris from my mother and went to the mall to buy herself more sweaters and trousers. Her missing suitcase never arrived, and she accepted this fact calmly, saying that it gave her an excuse to buy new things, but your father battled on her behalf, making a series of irate phone calls to the airline before finally letting the matter go.

You were in the house as little as possible, walking in the cold weather through the woods and along streets where you were the only pedestrian. I spotted you once, while I was on the school bus coming home, shocked at how far you'd gone. "You're going to get sick, Kaushik, always wandering outside like that," my mother said. She continued to speak to you in Bengali, despite your consistently English replies. It was your mother who came down with a cold, using this as an excuse to stay in bed for days. She refused the food my mother made for the rest of us, requesting only canned chicken broth. You walked to the minimart a mile from our house,

bringing back the broth and issues of *Vogue* and *Harper's Bazaar.*
"Go ask Parul Mashi if she wants tea," my mother said one afternoon, and I headed upstairs to the guestroom. On my way I needed
to use the bathroom. There was your mother, wrapped up in a robe,
perched morosely on the edge of the bathtub, legs crossed, smoking
a cigarette.

"Oh, Hema!" she cried out, nearly falling into the tub, so startled that she crushed the cigarette against the porcelain and not
into the tiny stainless-steel ashtray she held cupped in her palm,
and which she must have brought with her from Bombay.

"I'm sorry," I said, turning to leave.

"No, no, please, I was just going," she said. I watched as she
flushed away the cigarette, rinsed her mouth at the sink, and applied fresh lipstick, blotting it with a Kleenex, which then fluttered
into the garbage pail. Apart from her bindi, my mother did not wear
makeup, and I observed your mother's ritual with care, all the more
impressed that she would go to such lengths when she was unwell
and spending most of her day in bed. She looked into the mirror intently, without evasion. The brief application of lipstick seemed to
restore the composure that my sudden appearance had caused her
to lose. She caught me looking at her reflection and smiled. "One
cigarette a day can't kill me, can it?" she said brightly. She opened
the window, pulled some perfume out of her cosmetics bag, and
sprayed the air. "Our little secret, Hema?" she said, less a question
than a command, and left, shutting the door behind her.

IN THE evenings we sometimes went house-hunting with you. We
took the station wagon; the beautiful car your father had bought
could not comfortably accommodate us all. My father drove, hesi-
tantly, to unknown neighborhoods where the lawns were all a little
bigger than ours, the houses spaced a little farther apart. Your parents searched first in Lexington and Concord, where the schools
were best. Some of the homes we saw were empty, others full of
the current occupants and their possessions. None, according to

the conversations I overheard at night as I tried to fall asleep, were the sort my parents could afford. They stepped to the side as your parents discussed asking prices with the real estate agents. But it wasn't money that stood in the way. The houses themselves were the problem, the light scant, the ceilings low, the rooms awkward, your parents always concluded, as we drove back to our house. Unlike my parents, yours had opinions about design, preferring something contemporary, excited when we happened to pass a white boxlike structure obscured by a thicket of tall trees. They sought an in-ground pool, or space to build one; your mother missed swimming at her club in Bombay. "Water views, that's what we should look for," your mother said, while reading the classified section of the *Globe* one afternoon, and this limited the search even further. We drove out to Swampscott and Duxbury to see properties overlooking the ocean, and to houses in the woods with views of private lakes. Your parents made an offer on a house in Beverly, but after a second visit they withdrew the bid, your mother saying that the layout was ungenerous.

My parents felt slighted by your parents' extravagant visions, ashamed of the modest home we owned. "How uncomfortable you must be here," they said, but your parents never complained, as mine did, nightly, before falling asleep. "I didn't expect it to take this long," my mother said, noting that almost a month had gone by. While you were with us there was no room for anyone else. "The Dasguptas wanted to visit next weekend and I had to say no," my mother said. Again and again I heard how much your parents had changed, how we'd unwittingly opened our home to strangers. There were complaints about how your mother did not help clean up after dinner, how she went to bed whenever it suited her and slept close to lunchtime. My mother said that your father was too indulgent, too solicitous of your mother, always asking if she needed a fresh drink, bringing down a cardigan if she was cold.

"She's the reason they're still here," my mother said. "She won't settle for anything less than a palace."

"It's no easy task," my father said diplomatically, "starting a new job, a new way of life all over again. My guess is she didn't want to leave, and he's trying to make up for that."

"You would never put up with that sort of behavior in me."

"Let it go," my father said, turning away from her and tucking the covers under his chin. "It's not forever. They'll leave soon enough and then all our lives will go back to normal."

SOMEWHERE, in that cramped house, a line was drawn between our two families. On one side was the life we'd always led, my parents taking me to Star Market every Thursday night, treating me to McDonald's afterward. Every Sunday I studied for my weekly spelling test, my father quizzing me after 60 Minutes was over. Your family began to do things independently as well. Sometimes your father would come home from work early and take your mother out, either to look at properties or to shop at the mall, where slowly and methodically she began to buy all the things she would need to set up her own household: sheets, blankets, plates and glasses, small appliances. They would come home with bags and bags, amassing them in our basement, sometimes showing my mother the things they'd bought, sometimes not bothering. On Fridays your parents often took us out to dinner, to one of the overpriced mediocre restaurants in town. They enjoyed the change of pace, having mysteriously acquired a taste for things like steak and baked potatoes, while my parents had not. The outings were intended to give my mother a break from cooking, but she complained about these, too.

I WAS the only one who didn't mind your staying with us. In my quiet, complicated way I continued to like you, was happy simply to observe you day after day. And I liked your parents, your mother especially; the attention I got from her almost made up for what I didn't get from you. One day your father developed the photographs from your stay in Rome. I enjoyed seeing the prints, holding them carefully by the edges. The pictures were almost all of you and your

mother, posing in piazzas or sitting on the edge of fountains. There
were two shots of Trajan's Column, nearly identical. "Take one for
your report," your father said, handing me one. "That should im-
press your teacher."

"But I wasn't there."

"No matter. Say your uncle went to Rome and took a snap for
you."

You were in the picture, standing to one side. You were looking
down, your face obscured by a visor. You could have been anyone,
one of the many passing tourists in the frame, but it bothered me
that you were there, your presence threatening to expose the secret
attraction I felt and still hoped would be acknowledged somehow.
You had successfully wiped away all the other crushes I harbored
at school, so that I thought only of being at home, and of where in
the course of the afternoon and evening our paths might intersect,
whether or not you would bother to glance at me at the dinner table. Long hours were devoted, lying on the cot in my parents' room,
to imagining you kissing me. I was too young, too inexperienced,
to contemplate anything beyond that. I accepted the picture and
pasted it into my report, but not before cutting the part with you
away. That bit I kept, hidden among the blank pages of my diary,
locked up for years.

YOUR WISH for snow had not been granted since you'd arrived. There
were brief flurries now and again, but nothing stuck to the ground.
Then one day snow began to fall, barely visible at first, gathering
force as the afternoon passed, an inch or so coating the streets by
the time I rode the bus home from school. It was not a dangerous
storm, but significant enough to break up the monotony of winter.
My mother, in a cheerful mood that evening, decided to cook a big
pot of khichuri, which she typically made when it rained, and for
a change your mother insisted on helping, standing in the kitchen
deep-frying pieces of potato and cauliflower, melting sticks of butter in a saucepan for ghee. She also decided that she wanted, finally,

to make the long-promised trifle, and when my mother told her that there weren't enough eggs your father went to get them, along with the other ingredients she needed. "It won't be ready until midnight," she said as she beat together hot milk and eggs over the stove, allowing me to take over for her when she tired of the task. "It needs at least four hours to set."

"Then we can have it for breakfast," you said, breaking off a piece of the pound cake she'd sliced, stuffing it into your mouth. You seldom set foot in the kitchen, but that evening you hovered there, excited by the promise of trifle, which I gathered you loved and which I had never tasted.

After dinner we crowded into the living room, watching the news as the snow continued to fall, excited to learn that my school would be closed and my father's classes canceled the next day. "You take the day off, too," your mother said to your father, and to everyone's surprise he agreed.

"It reminds me of the winter we left Cambridge," your father said. He and your mother were sipping their Johnnie Walker, and that night, though my mother still refused, my father agreed to join them for a small taste. "That party you had for us," your father continued, turning to my parents. "Remember?"

"Seven years ago," my mother said. "It was another life, back then." They spoke of how young you and I had been, how much younger they had all been.

"Such a lovely evening," your mother recalled, her voice betraying a sadness that all of them seemed to share. "How different things were."

In the morning icicles hung from our windows and a foot of snow blanketed the ground. The trifle, which we had been too tired to wait for the night before, emerged for breakfast along with toast and tea. It was not what I'd expected, the hot mixture I'd helped beat on the stove now cold and slippery, but you devoured bowl after bowl; your mother finally put it away, fearing that you would get a stomachache. After breakfast our fathers took turns with the shovel, clearing the driveway. When the wind had settled I was allowed to go outside. Usually, I made snowmen alone, scrawny and lopsided, my parents complaining, when I asked for a carrot, that it was a waste of food. But this time you joined me, touching the snow with your bare hands, studying it, looking happy for the first time since you arrived. You packed a bit of it into a ball and tossed it in my direction. I ducked out of the way, and then threw one at you, hitting you in the leg, aware of the camera hanging around your neck.

"I surrender," you said, raising your arms. "This is beautiful," you added, looking around at our lawn, which the snow had transformed. I felt flattered, though I had nothing to do with the weather. You began walking toward the woods and I hesitated. There was something you wanted to show me there, you said. Covered in snow on that bright blue-skied day, the bare branches of the trees concealing so little, it seemed safe. I did not think of the boy, lost there and never found. From time to time you stopped, focusing your camera on something, never asking me to pose. We walked a long way, until I no longer heard the sounds of snow being shoveled, no longer saw our house. I didn't realize at first what you were doing, getting on your knees and pushing away the snow. Underneath was a rock of some sort. And then I saw that it was a tombstone. You uncovered a row of them, flat on the ground. I began to help you, unburying the buried, using my mittened hands at first, then my whole arm. They belonged to people named Simonds, a family of six. "They're all here together," you said. "Mother, father, four children."

"I never knew this was here."

"I doubt anyone does. It was buried under leaves when I first found it. The last one, Emma, died in 1923."

I nodded, disturbed by the similarity of the name to mine, wondering if this had occurred to you.

"It makes me wish we weren't Hindu, so that my mother could be buried somewhere. But she's made us promise we'll scatter her ashes into the Atlantic."

I looked at you, confused, and so you continued, explaining that there was cancer in her breast, spreading through the rest of her body. That was why you had left India. It was not so much for treatment as it was to be left alone. In India people knew she was dying, and had you remained there, inevitably, friends and family would have gathered at her side in your beautiful seaside apartment, trying to shield her from something she could not escape. Your mother, not wanting to be suffocated by the attention, not wanting her parents to witness her decline, had asked your father to bring you all back to America. "She's been seeing a new doctor at Mass General. That's where my father often takes her when they say they're going to see houses. She's going to have surgery in the spring, but it's only to buy her a little more time. She doesn't want anyone here to know. Not until the end."

The information fell between us, as shocking as if you'd struck me in the face, and I began to cry. At first the tears fell silently, sliding over my nearly frozen face, but then I started sobbing, becoming ugly in front of you, my nose running in the cold, my eyes turning red. I stood there, my hands wedged up under my cheekbones to catch the tears, mortified that you were witnessing such a pathetic display. Though you had never taken a picture of me in your life, I was afraid that you would lift the camera and capture me that way. Of course, you did nothing, you said nothing; you had said enough. You remained where you were, looking down at the tombstone of Emma Simonds, and eventually, when I calmed down, you began to walk back to our yard. I followed you along the path you had discovered, and then we parted, neither of us a comfort to the other, you shoveling the driveway, I going inside for a hot shower, my red puffy face assumed by our mothers to be a consequence of the cold. Perhaps you believed that I was crying for you, or for your mother, but I was not. I was too young, that day, to feel sorrow or sympathy. I felt only the enormous fear of having a dying woman in our home. I remembered standing beside your mother, both of us topless in the fitting room where I tried on my first bra, disturbed that I had been in such close proximity to her disease. I was furious that you had told me, and that you had not told me, feeling at once burdened and betrayed, hating you all over again.

TWO WEEKS later, you were gone. Your parents bought a house on the North Shore, which had been designed by a well-known Massachusetts architect. It had a perfectly flat roof and whole walls of glass. The upstairs rooms were arranged off an interior balcony, the ceiling in the living room soaring to twenty feet. There were no water views but there was a pool for your mother to swim in, just as she had wanted. Your first night there, my mother brought food over so that your mother would not have to cook, not realizing what a favor this was. We admired the house and the property, the echoing, empty rooms that would soon be filled with sickness and grief. There was a bedroom with a skylight; underneath it, your mother told us, she planned to position her bed. It was all to give her two years of pleasure. When my parents finally learned the news and went to the hospital where your mother was dying, I revealed nothing about what you'd told me. In that sense I remained loyal. Our parents were only acquaintances by then, having gone their separate ways after the weeks of forced intimacy. Your mother had promised to have us over in the summer to swim in the pool, but as her health declined, more quickly than the doctors had predicted, your parents shut down, still silent about her illness, seldom entertaining. For a time my mother and father continued to complain, feeling snubbed. "After all we did for them," they said before drifting off to sleep. But I was back in my own room by then, on the other side of the wall, in the bed where you had slept, no longer hearing them.

SOME TERPSICHORE

Elizabeth McCracken

Elizabeth McCracken is the author of three books of fiction, *Niagara Falls All Over Again, The Giant's House,* and *Here's Your Hat What's Your Hurry.* She is the recipient of the Harold Vursell Award from the American Academy of Arts and Letters and the PEN/Winship Award. She has received grants from the Guggenheim Foundation, the Michener Foundation, the Fine Arts Work Center in Provincetown, and the National Endowment for the Arts. She was also honored as one of Granta's twenty best writers under forty.

1.

There's a saw hanging on the wall of my living room, a house key for a giant's pocket. It's been there a long time. "What's your saw for?" people ask, and I say, "It's not my saw. I never owned a saw."

"But what's it for?"

"Hanging," I answer.

By now if you took it down you'd see the ghost of the saw behind. Or—no, not the ghost, because the blue wallpaper would be dark where the saw had protected it from the sun. Ghosts are pale. So the room is the ghost. The saw is the only thing that's real.

These days, though it grieves me to say it, that sounds about right.

2.

Here's how I became a singer. Forty years ago I walked past the Washington Monument in Baltimore and thought, *I'll climb that*. It was first thing in the morning. They'd just opened up. As I climbed I sang with my eyes closed—"Summertime," I think it was. I kept my hand on the iron banister. My feet found the stairs. In my head I saw myself at a party, leaning on a piano, singing in front of a small audience. I climbed, I sang. I never could remember the words to "Summertime," largely because of a spoonerized version my friend Fred liked to sing—*Tummersime, and the iving is leazy/jifh are fumping, and the hiver is righ. . . .*

Then a man's voice said, "Wow."

In my memory, he leans against the wall two steps from the top, shouldering a saw like a rifle. But of course he didn't bring his saw to the Washington Monument. He was a big-boned, raw-faced blond man with a smashed Parker-house roll of a nose. His slacks were dark synthetic, snagged. His orange cardigan looked like it'd been used to scrub out pots then left to rust. A tiny felt hat hung off the back of his head. He was so big you wondered how he could have got up there—had the tower been built around him? Had he arrived in pieces and been assembled on the spot? "Wow," he said again, and clasped his hands in front of himself, bouncing on his knees with the syncopated jollification of a lovestruck 1930s cartoon character. I expected to see querulous lines of excitement coming off his head, punctuated by exclamation marks. He plucked off his hat. His hair looked like it had been combed with a piece of buttered toast.

"That was you?" he asked.

I nodded. Maybe he was some municipal employee, charged with keeping the noise down.

"You sound like a saw," he said. His voice was soft. I thought he might be from the south, like me, though later I found out he just had one of those voices that picked up accents through static electricity. Really he was from Paterson, New Jersey.

"A saw?" I asked.

He nodded.

I put my hand to my throat. "I don't know what that means."

He held up his big hands, one still palming his hat. *"Beautiful,"* he said. "Not of this earth. Come with me, I'll show you. Boy, you sure taught George Gershwin a lesson. Where do you sing?"

"Nowhere," I said.

I couldn't sing, according to my friends. The only person who'd ever said anything nice about my voice was my friend Fred Tibbets, who claimed that when I was drunk sometimes I managed to carry a tune. But we drank a lot in those days, and when I was drunk Fred was drunk, too, and sentimental. Still, I secretly believed I could sing. My only evidence was the pleasure singing brought me. Most common mistake in the world, believing that physical pleasure and virtue are in any way related, inversely or directly.

He shook his head. "No good," he said very seriously. "That's rotten. We'll change that." He went to take my hand and instead hung his hat upon it. Then I felt his hand squeeze mine through the felt. "You'll sing for me, OK? Would you sing for me? You'll sing for me."

He led me back down the monument, the hat on my hand, his hand behind it. My wrist began to sweat but I didn't mind. "Of course you'll sing," he said. He went ahead of me but kept stopping, so I'd half tumble onto the point of his elbow. "I know people. I'm from New York. Well, I live there. I came to Bawlmore because a buddy of mine, part of a trio, he broke his arm and needed a guitar player so there you go. There are 228 steps on this thing. I read it on the plaque. Also I counted. God, you're a skinny girl, you're like *nothing*, you're so lovely, no, you are, don't disagree, I know what I'm talking about. Well, not all the time, but right now I do. I'll play you my saw. Not everyone appreciates it but you will. What's your name? Once more? Oof. We'll change that, have to, you need something short and to the point. Take me, I used to be Gabriel McClonnahashem, there's a moniker, huh? Now I'm Gabe Mack. For you I don't know, let me think: Miss Porth. Because you're a chanteuse, that's why the Miss. And Porthkiss, I don't know. And Miss Kiss is just silly. Look at you blush! The human musical saw. There are all sorts of places you can sing, you don't know your own worth, that's your problem. I've known singers and I've known singers. I heard you and I thought, There's a voice I could listen to for the rest of my life. I'm not kidding. I don't kid about things like that. I don't kid about music. I was frozen to the spot. Look, still: goosebumps. You rescued me from the tower, Rapunzel: I climbed down on your voice. I'll talk to my friend Jake. I'll talk to this other guy I know. I have a feeling about you. I have a *feeling* about you. Are you getting as dizzy as me? Maybe it's not the stairs. Do you believe in love at first sight? That's not a line, it's a question. I do, of course I do, would I ask if I didn't? Because I believe in luck, that's why. We're almost at the bottom. Poor kid, you never even got to the top. Come on. For ten cents it's strictly an-all-you-can-climb monument. We'll go. Come on. Come on."

"I can sing?" I asked him.

He looked at me. His eyes were green, with gears of darker green around the pupils.

"Trust me," he said.

3.

I wasn't the sort of girl who'd climb a monument with a strange man. Or go back to his hotel room with him. Or agree to move to Philadelphia the next day.

But I did.

His room was on the top floor of The Elite Hotel, the kind of room you might check into to commit suicide: toilet down the hall, a sink in the corner of the room, a view of another building with windows exactly across from the Elite's windows.

"Musical saw," said Gabe Mack. He opened a cardboard suitcase that sat at the end of the single bed. First he took out a long item wrapped in a sheet. A violin bow. Then a piece of rosin.

"You hit it with that?" I asked.

"Hit it? What hit?" Gabe said.

"I thought—"

"Look," he said. The saw he'd hung in the closet with his suits. I'd thought a musical saw would be a percussion instrument. A xylophone, maybe. A marimba. He rosined the bow and sat on a chair on the corner. The saw was just a regular wood saw. He clamped his feet on the end of it and then pulled the bow across the dull side of the blade. You could hardly see the saw, the handle clamped between his feet, the end of the metal snagged in his hand: he was a pile of man with a blade at the heart, a man doing violence to something with an unlikely weapon.

It was the voice of a beautiful toothache. It was the sound of every enchanted harp, flute, princess turned into a tree in every fairytale ever written.

"I sound like that?" I said.

He nodded, kept playing.

I sound like that. It was humiliating, alarming, ugly, exciting. It was like looking at a flattering picture of yourself doing something you wished you hadn't been photographed doing. *That's me.* He was playing "Fly Me to the Moon."

He finished and looked at me with those Rube-Goldberg eyes. "That's you," he said. He flexed the saw back and forth and then dropped it to the ground. I knelt to look at it and saw my garbled reflection in the metal.

I picked it up. "You don't take the points off?"

"Nope," he said. "This is my second saw. Here. Give me." I lifted it by the blade and he caught it through the honey-colored handle. "First one I bought was too good. Short, expensive. Wouldn't bend. You need something cheap and with a good length to it. Eight points to an inch, this one. Teeth, I mean." He flexed it. The metal made that backstage thunder noise I'd imagined when he'd first said I sounded like a saw. "This one, though. It's right." He flipped it around and caught it again between his brown shoes and drew the bow against it. He'd turned on just one light by the hotel bed when we'd come into the room. Now it was dark out. I listed to the saw while I watched the corner sink. A spider came to the edge, tapping one leg on its edge like a blind man with a cane before clambering out, its shadow enormous. The saw sighed. Me too. Then he reached over with the bow and touched my shoulder. I flinched. I almost thought the bow had caught a case of sharp off the saw.

"That's you," he said again.

Maybe I loved Gabe already. What's love at first sight but a bucket thrown over you that smoothes out all your previous self-loathing, so that you can see yourself slick and matted down and cautionless and capable of nearly anything? Anyhow, I believed for the first time that I was capable of being loved.

Maybe I just loved the saw.

4.

We left for Philly the next day. The story of our success, and it wasn't much success, is pretty boring, as all success is. A lot of waiting by the phone. A lot of bad talent nights. One great talent night in which I won a box of dishes. The walk home from that night, Gabe carrying the dishes and smashing them into the gutter one by one. Don't do it, I said, those are mine—

He held one dish to my forehead, then lifted it up, then touched it down again, the way you do with a hammer to a nail before you drive it in.

Then he stroked my forehead with the plate edge.

"Don't tell me what to do," he said.

5.

He wrote songs. Before I met him I had no idea of how anyone wrote a song. His apartment on Samson Street smelled of burnt tomato sauce and had in the kitchen in place of a stove a piano that looked as though it had been through a house fire. Sometimes he played it. Sometimes he sat at it with his hands twitching over the keys like leashed dogs. *The Land Beyond the Land We Know. A Pocket Full of*

Pennies. Your Second Biggest Regret. Keep Your Eyes Out for Me. He was such a sly mimic, such a sneaky thief, that people thought these were obscure standards, if such a thing exists, songs they'd heard many times long ago and were only now remembering. He wrote a song every day. He got mad that sometimes I couldn't keep them straight or remember that. *That's A Hanging Offense. Don't You Care At All. Till the End of Us.*

We played them together. He bought me a green Grecian-draped dress that itched, and matching gloves that were too long, and lipstick, and false eyelashes—all haunted, especially the eyelashes.

History is full of the sad stories of foolish women. What was terrible is that I was not foolish. Ask anyone. Ask Fred Tibbets, who lied and said I could sing.

We cut a record called *Miss Porth Sings!* For a long time you could still find it in bins in record shops under *Vocals* or *Other* or *Novelty*. Me on the sleeve, my head tipped back. I wore red lipstick that made my complexion orange, and wore tiny saw-shaped earrings. My hair was cashew-colored.

That was a fault of the printing. In real life, in those days, my hair was the color of sand paper: diamond, garnet, ruby.

I was on the radio. I was on the Gypsy Rose Lee Show. Miss Porth, the Human Musical Saw! But the whole point was that Gabe's saw sounded human. Why be a human who only sounds like an inanimate object that sounds human?

6.

This is not a story about success. In the world we were what we'd always been. The love story: the saw and the sawish voice. We were two cripplingly shy, witheringly judgmental people who fell in love in private, away from the conversation and caution of other people, and then we left town before anyone could warn us.

In Philadelphia he began to throw things at me—silly, embarrassing, lighter-than-air things: a bowl full of egg whites I was about to whip for a soufflé, my brother's birthday card, the entire contents

of a newly opened bottle of talcum powder. For days I left white fin-
gerprints behind. Then he said it was an accident, he hadn't meant
to throw it at all.

And then he began to threaten me with the saw.

I don't think he could have explained it himself. He didn't
drink, but he would seem drunk. The drunkenness, or whatever it
was, moved his limbs. Picked up the saw. Brought it to my throat,
and just held it there. He never moved the blade, and spoke to the
terrible things he would do to himself.

"I'm going to kill myself," he said. "I will. Don't leave me. Tell
me you won't."

I couldn't shake my head or speak, and so I tried to look at him
with love. I couldn't stand the way he hated himself. I wanted to kill
the person who made him feel this way. Our apartment was bright
at the front, by the windows, and black and airless at the back,
where the bed was. Where we were now, lying on a quilt that looked
like a classroom map, orange, blue, green, yellow.

"My life is over," said Gabe. His summer freckles were fading. He had the burnt-tomato smell of the whole apartment.
"I'm old. I'm old. I'm talentless. I can see it, but you know, at the
same time, I listen to the radio all day and I don't understand.
Why will you break everyone's hearts the way you do? Why do
you do it? You're crazy. Probably you're not capable of love. You
need help. I will kill myself. I've thought about it ever since I was
a little kid."

The saw blade took a bite of me, eight tooth marks per inch.
Cheap steel, the kind that bent easily. I had my hands at the dull
side of the saw. *How did we get here,* I wondered, but I'd had the same
disoriented thought when I believed I'd fallen in love with him at
first sight, lying in the same bed: *how did this happen?*

"I could jump," he said. "What do you think I was doing up that
tower when you found me? Windows were too small, I didn't realize. I'd gotten my nerve up. But then there you were, and you were
so little. And your voice. And I guess I changed my mind. Will you

say something Marya? You've broken my heart. One of these days I'll kill myself."

I knew everything about him. He weighed exactly twice what I did, to the pound. He was ambitious and doubtful: he wanted to be famous, and he wanted no-one to look at him, ever, which is probably the human condition: in him it was merely amplified. That was nearly all I knew about him. Sometimes we still told the story of our life together to each other: why had I climbed the tower *that* day? Why had he? He almost stayed in New York. I'd almost gone back home for the weekend but then my great-aunt Marian died and my folks went to her funeral. If he'd been five minutes slower he wouldn't have caught me singing. If I'd been ten minutes later, I would have smiled at him as he left. We were lucky, we told each other, blind pure luck.

7.

One night we were at our standing gig, at a cabaret called Maxie's. It hurt to sing, with the pearls sticking to the saw cuts. The owner was named Marco Bell. He loved me. Marco's face was so wrinkled when he smoked you could see every line in his face tense and then slacken.

> *There's a land beyond the land we know,*
> *Where time is green and men are slow.*
> *Follow me and soon you'll know,*
> *Blue happiness*

My green dress was too big and I kept having to hitch it up. It wasn't too big a month ago. At the break, I sat down next to Marco. "How are you," I asked.

"My heart is broken," he answered. He leaned into the hand with the cigarette. I thought he might light his pomaded hair on fire.

"I'm sorry," I said.

"*You* break it, Miss Porth. With your—" He waved at the spot where I'd been standing.

I laughed. "They're not all sad songs."

"Yes," he said. There was not a joke in a five mile radius of the man. He had a great Russian head with bullying eyebrows. Three years earlier his wife had had a stroke, and sometimes she came into the club in a chevron-patterned dress, sitting in her wheelchair and patting the table top, either in time to the music or looking for something she'd put down there. "You're wrong. They are."

I said, "Sometimes I don't think I'm doing anyone any favors."

Then Gabe was behind me. He touched my shoulder lovingly. Listen: don't tell me otherwise. It was not nice love, it was not good love, but you cannot tell me that it wasn't love. Love is not oxygen, though many songwriters will tell you that it is; it is not a chemical substance that is either definitively present or absent; it cannot be reduced to its parts. It is not like a flower, or an animal, or anything that you will ever be able to recognize when you see it. Love is food. That's all. Neither better nor worse. Sometimes very good. Sometimes terrible. But to say—as people will—*that wasn't love.* As though that makes you feel better! Well, it might have been bad for me, but it sustained me for a while. Once I'd left I'd be as bad as any reformed sinner, amazed at my old self, but even with the blade against my neck, I loved him, his worries about the future, his reliable black moods, his reliable affection—that was still there, too, though sullied by remorse.

I stayed for the saw, too. Not the threat of it. I stayed because of those minutes on stage when I could understand it. Gabe bent it back and it called out, *oh, no, honey, help.* It wanted comfort. It wanted to comfort me. We were in trouble together, the two of us: the honey-throated saw, the saw-voiced girl. *Help, help, we're still alive,* the saw sang, though mostly its songs were just pronounced all stuck together, *I, we, mine, you, you, we, mine.*

Yes, that's right. I was going to tell you about the saw.

Gabe touched my shoulder and said, "Marya, let's go."

Marco said, "In a minute. Miss Porth, let's have a drink."

"Marya," said Gabe.

"I'd love one," I said.

Maxie's was a popular place—no sign on the front door, a private joke. There was a crowd. Gabe punched me. He punched me in the breast. A very strange place to take a punch. Not the worst place. I thought that as it happened: *not the worst place to take a punch.* The chairs at Maxie's had backs carved like bamboo. He punched me. I'd never been punched before. He said, "See how it feels, when someone breaks your heart?" and I thought, Yes, as it happens, I think I do.

I was on my back. Marco had his arms around Gabe's arms and was whispering things in his ear. A crowd had formed. People were touching me. I wanted them not to.

Here is what I want to tell you: I knew something was ending, and I was grateful, and I missed it.

8.

About five years ago in a restaurant near my apartment someone recognized me. "You're—are you Miss Porth?" he said. "You're Miss Porth." Man about my own age, tweed blazer, bald with a crinkly snub-nosed puppyish face, the kind that always looks like it's about to sneeze. "I used to see you at Maxie's," he said. "All the time. Well, lots. I was in grad school at Penn. Miss Porth! Good god! I always wondered what happened to you!"

I sitting at the bar, waiting for a friend, and I wanted to end the conversation before he arrived. The man took a bar stool next to me. We talked for a while about Philadelphia. He still lived there, he was just in town for a conference. He shook the ice in his emptied drink into his mouth, and I knew he was back there—not listening to me, exactly, just remembering who was at his elbow, and did she want another drink, and did he have enough money for another drink for both of him. All the good things he believed about himself then: by now he'd know whether he'd been right, and right or wrong knowing was dull. I didn't like being his time-travel device.

"I have your album," he said. "I'm a fan. Seriously. It's my field, music. I—Some guy hit you," he said suddenly. His puppy face looked over-sneezish. "I can't remember. Was he a drunk? Some guy in love with you? That's right. A crazy."

"Random thing," I said. "What were you studying?"

"Folklore," he said absentmindedly. "I always wondered something about you. Can I ask something? Do you mind?"

Oh, I thought, slide down that rabbit hole if you have to, just let go of my hem, don't take me with you.

"I loved to hear you," he said. Puppy tilt to his head, too. "You were like nothing else. But I always wondered—I mean, you seem like an intelligent woman. I never spoke to you back then." One piece of ice clung to the bottom of his glass and he fished it out with his fingers. "Did you realize then that people were laughing at you?"

Then he said, "Oh my God."

"I'm sorry," he said.

"Not me," he said, "I swear, you were wonderful."

I turned to him. "Of course I knew," I said. "How could I miss it?"

The line between pride and a lack of it is thin and brittle and thrilling as new ice. Only when you're young are you able to skate out onto it, to not care which side you end up on. That was me. I was innocent. Later, when you're old, when you know things, well, it takes all sort of effort, and ropes, and pulleys, and all kinds of tricks, to keep you from crashing through, if you're even willing to risk it.

Though maybe I did know back then that some people didn't take me seriously. But still: maybe the first time they came to laugh. Not the second. I could hear the audience. I could hear how still they were when I sang with my eyes closed. Oh, maybe some of them thought, *Who does she think she's fooling? Who does she think she is, with that old green gown, with those made-up songs?* But then they'd listen. It was those people, I think, the ones who thought at first they were above me, who got the wind knocked out of them. Who brought their friends the next week. Who bought my records. Who thought: *Me. No more, no less, she's fooling me.*

Later I got a letter asking for the right to put two songs from *Miss Porth Sings!* on a record called *Songs from Mars: Eccentrics and their Music.* The note said, *Do you know what happened to G. Mack? I need his permission too of course.*

9.

That night I went home with Gabe for the last time. Of course don't call the police, I told Marco. He was exhausted, repentant. I led him to the bed, to the faded quilt, and he fell asleep. From the kitchen I called his sister in Paterson, who I never met, and I told her Gabe Mack was in trouble and alone and needed help. Then I climbed into bed next to him. Gabe had an archipelago of moles on his neck I'd never noticed, and a few faint acne scars on his nose. His eyebrows were knit in dreamy thought. I loved that nose. He hated it. "Do I really look like that?" he'd ask, seeing a picture of himself. He'd cover his nose with his hand.

I didn't know what would become of him. I had to quit caring. It wasn't love and it wasn't the saw and it wasn't a fear of being alone that kept me there: it was wanting to know the end of the story, and wanting the end to be happy.

At five AM I left with a small bag, the saw, bamboo-patterned bruises on my back, and a fist-shaped bruise on my left breast. Soon enough I was amazed at how little I cared for him. Maybe that was worse than anything.

10.

Still, no matter what, I can't shake my first impression. Even now, miles and years away, the saw in my living room to remind me, when I think of Gabe, I see a 1930s animated character: the black pie-cut eyes, white gloved hands held flat against the background, dark long limbs without elbows and knees which do not bend but undulate. The cheap jazzy glorious music which, despite your better self, puts you in a good mood. Fills you with cheap jazzy hope. And it seems you're making big strides across the country on your spring-operated limbs, in your spring-loaded open car, in your jazzy pneumatic existence. You don't even notice that behind you, over and over in the same order, is the same tree, shack, street corner, mouse hole, table set for dinner, blown-back curtains.

COWBOY

Thomas McGuane

Thomas McGuane lives on a ranch in McLeod, Montana. He is the author of nine novels, three works of nonfiction, and two collections of stories.

The old fella makes me go into the house in my stocking feet. The old lady's in a big chair next to the window. In fact, the whole room is full of big chairs, but she's only in one of them—though, big as she is, she could fill up several. The old man says, "I found this one in the loose-horse pen at the sale yard."

She says, "What's he supposed to be?"

He says, "Supposed to be a cowboy."

"What's he doin in the loose horses?"

I says, "I was lookin for one that would ride."

"You was in the wrong pen, son," the old man says. "Them's canners. They're goin to France in cardboard boxes."

"Soon as they get a steel bolt in the head." The big old gal laughs in her chair.

Now I'm sore. "There's five in there broke to death. I rode 'em with nothin but binder twine."

"It don't make a shit," the old man says. "Ever one of them is goin to France."

The old lady don't believe me. "How'd you get in them loose horses to ride?"

"I went in there at night."

The old lady says, "You one crazy cowboy, go in there in the dark. Them broncs kick your teeth down your throat. I suppose you tried them bareback?"

"Naw, I drug the saddle I usually ride at the Rose Bowl Parade."

"You got a horse for that?"

"I got Trigger. We unstuffed him."

The old lady addresses the old man. "He's got a mouth on him. This much we know."

"Maybe he can tell us what good he is."

I says, "I'm a cowboy."

"You're a outta-work cowboy."

"It's a dying way of life."

"She's about like me—she's wondering if this ranch's supposed to be some kinda welfare agency for cowboys."

I've had enough. "You're the dumb honyocker drove me out here."

I think that'll be the end of it, but the old lady says, "Don't get huffy. You got the job. You against conversation or something?"

We get outside and the old sumbitch says, "You drawed lucky there, son. That last deal could've pissed her off."

"It didn't make me no nevermind if it did or didn't."

"She hadn't been well. Used to she was sweet as pudding."

"I'm sorry for that. We don't have health, we don't have nothin."

She must have been afflicted something terrible, because she was ugly morning, noon, and night for as long as she lasted—she'd pick a fight over nothing and the old sumbitch got the worst of it. I felt sorry for him, little slack as he cut me.

Had a hundred seventy-five sweet-tempered horned Herefords and fifteen sleepy bulls. Shipped the calves all over for hybrid vigor, mostly to the South. Had some go clear to Florida. A Hereford that still had its horns was a walking miracle, and the old sumbitch had a smart little deal going. I soon learned to give him credit for such things, and the old lady barking commands offen the sofa weren't no slouch neither. Anybody else seen their books might've said they could be wintering in Phoenix.

They didn't have no bunkhouse, just a LeisureLife mobile home that had lost its wheels about thirty years ago, and they had it positioned by the door of the barn so it'd be convenient for the hired man to stagger out at all hours and fight breech births and scours and any other disorder sent us by the cow gods. We had some doozies. One heifer got pregnant and her calf was near as big as she was. Had to reach in with a saw and take it out in pieces. When we threw the head out on the ground, she turned to it and lowed like it was her baby. Everything a cow does is designed to turn it into meat as fast as possible so that somebody can eat it. It's a terrible life.

The old sumbitch and I got along good. We got through calving and got to see them pairs and bulls run out onto the new grass. Nothing like seeing all that meat feel a little temporary joy. Then we bladed out the corrals and watched them dry under the spring sun at long last. Only mishap was when the manure spreader threw a rock and knocked me senseless and I drove the rig into an irrigation ditch. The old sumbitch never said a word but chained up and pulled us out with his Ford.

We led his cavvy out of the hills afoot with two buckets of sweet feed. Had a little of everything, including a blue roan I fancied, but he said it was a Hancock and bucked like the National Finals in Las Vegas, kicking out behind and squalling, and was just a man-killer. "Stick to the bays," he said. "The West was won on a bay horse."

He picked out three bays, had a keg of shoes, all ones and oughts, and I shod them best I could, three geldings with nice manners, stood good to shoe. About all you could say about the others was they had four legs each, and a couple, all white-marked from saddle galls and years of hard work, looked like no more summers after this. They'd been rode many a long mile. We chased 'em back into the hills and the three shod ones whinnied and fretted. "Back to work," the old sumbitch says to them.

We shod three 'cause one was going to pack a ton of fencing supplies—barb wire, smooth wire, steel T-posts, old wore-out Sunflower fence stretchers that could barely grab on to the wire, and staples—and we was at it a good little while where the elk had knocked miles of it down, or the cedar finally give out and had to be replaced by steel. That was where I found out that the old sumbitch's last good time was in Korea, where the officers at the front would yell over the radio, "Come on up here and die!" Said the enemy was coming in waves. Tells me all this while the stretcher's pulling that wire squealing through the staples. The sumbitch was a tough old bastard. "They killed a pile of us and we killed a pile of them." Squeak.

We hauled the mineral horseback, too, in panniers—white salt and iodine salt. He didn't have no use for blocks, so we hauled it in sacks and poured it into the troughs he had on all these bald hilltops where the wind would blow away the flies. Most of his so-called troughs were truck tires nailed onto anything flat—plywood, old doors, and suchlike—but they worked good. A cow can put her tongue anywhere in a tire and get what she needs, and you can drag one of them flat things with your horse if you need to move it. Most places we salted had old buffalo wallers where them buffalo wallered. They done wallered their last—had to get out of the way for the cow and the man on the bay horse.

I'd been rustling my own grub in the LeisureLife for quite some time when the old lady said it was time for me to eat with the white folks. This was not necessarily a good thing. The old lady's knee replacements had begun to fail, and both me and the old sumbitch was half afraid of her. She cooked as good as ever, but she was a bomb waiting to go off, standing bowlegged at the stove and talking ugly about how much she did for us. When she talked, the old sumbitch would move his mouth as though he was saying the same words, and we had to keep from giggling, which wasn't hard. For if the old lady caught us at that there'd a been hell to pay.

Both the old sumbitch and the old lady was heavy smokers, to where a oxygen bottle was in sight. So they joined a Smoke-Enders deal the Lutherans had, and this required them to put all their butts in a jar and wear the jar around their necks on a string. The old sumbitch liked this O.K. because he could just tap his ash right under his chin and not get it on the truck seat, but the more that thing filled up and hung around her neck the meaner the old lady got. She had no idea the old sumbitch was cheating and setting his jar on the woodpile when we was working outside. She was just more honest than him, and in the end she give up smoking and he smoked away, except he wasn't allowed to smoke in the house no more, nor buy ready-mades, 'cause the new tax made them too expensive and she wouldn't let him take it out of the cows, which come first. She said it was just a vice and if he was half the man she thought he was he'd give it up as a bad deal. "You could have a long and happy old age," she said, real sarcastic-like.

One day me and the old sumbitch is in the house hauling soot out of the fireplace, on account of they had a chimbley fire last winter. Over the mantel is a picture of a beautiful woman in a red dress with her hair piled on top of her head. The old sumbitch tells me that's the old lady before she joined the motorcycle gang.

"Oh?"

"Them motorcycle gangs," he says, "all they do is eat and work on their motorcycles. They taught her to smoke, too, but she's shut of that. Probably outlive us all."

"Looks to me she can live long as she wants."

"And if she ever wants to box you, tell her no. She'll knock you on your ass. I guarantee it. Throw you a damn haymaker, son."

I couldn't understand how he could be so casual-like about the old lady being in a motorcycle gang. When we was smoking in the LeisureLife, I asked him about it. That's when I found out that him and the old lady was brother and sister. I guess that explained it. If your sister wants to join a motorcycle gang, that's her business. He said she even had a tattoo—"Hounds from Hell," with a dog shooting flames out of his nostrils and riding a Harley.

That picture on the mantel kind of stayed in my mind, and I asked the old sumbitch if his sister'd ever had a boyfriend. Well, yes, quite a few, he told me, quite a damn few. "Our folks run them off. They was just after the land."

He was going all around the baler hitting the zerks with his grease gun. "I had a lady friend myself. She'd do anything. Cook. Gangbusters with a snorty horse, and not too damn hard on the eyes. Sis run her off. Said she was just after the land. If she was, I never could see it. Anyway, went on down the road long time ago."

Fall come around and when we brought the cavvy down two of them old-timers who'd worked so hard was lame. One was stifled, one was sweenied, and both had crippling quarter cracks. I thought they needed to be at the loose-horse sale, but the old sumbitch says, "No mounts of mine is gonna feed no Frenchman," and that was that. So we made a hole, led the old-timers to the edge, and shot them with a elk rifle. First one didn't know what hit him. Second one heard the shot and saw his buddy fall and the old sumbitch had to chase him around to kill him. Then he sent me down the hole to get the halters back. Lifting those big heads was some chore.

I enjoyed eating in the big house that whole summer until the sister started giving me come-hither looks. They was fairly limited except those days when the old sumbitch was in town after supplies. Then she dialled it up and kind of brushed me every time she went past the table. There was always something special on the town days—a pie, maybe. I tried to think about the picture on the mantel, but it was impossible, even though I knew it might get me out of the LeisureLife once and for all. She was getting more and more wound up, while I was pretending to enjoy the food or going crazy over the pie. But she didn't buy it—called me a queer and sent me back to the trailer to make my own meals. By calling me a queer, she more or less admitted what she'd been up to, and I think that embarrassed her, because she covered up by roaring at everyone and everything, including the poor old sumbitch, who had no idea what had gone sideways while he was away. It was two years before she made another pie, and then it was once a year on my birthday. She made me five birthday pies in all—sand cherry, every one of them.

I broke the catch colt, which I didn't know was no colt, as he was the biggest snide in the cavvy. He was four, and it was time. I just got around him for a couple of days, then saddled him gently as I could. The offside stirrup scared him, and he looked over at it, but that was all it was to saddling. I must've had a burst of courage, 'cause next minute I was on him. That was O.K., too. I told the old sumbitch to open the corral gate, and we sailed away. The wind blew his tail up under him, and he thought about bucking but rejected the idea and that was about all they was to breaking Olly, for that was his name. Once I'd rode him two weeks, he was safe for the old sumbitch, who plumb loved this new horse and complimented me generously for the job I'd did.

We had three hard winters in a row, then lost so many calves to scours we changed our calving grounds. The old sumbitch just come out one day and looked at where he'd calved out for fifty years and said, "The ground's no good. We're movin." So we spent the summer building a new corral way off down the creek. When we's finished, he says, "I meant to do this when I got back from overseas and now it's finished and I'm practically done for, too. Whoever gets the place next will be glad his calves don't shit themselves into the next world like mine done."

Neither one of us had a back that was worth a damn, and the least we could do was get rid of the square baler and quit hefting them man-killing five-wire bales. We got a round baler and a Dew-Eze machine that let us pick up a bale from the truck without laying a finger on it. We'd tell stories and smoke in the cab on those cold winter days and roll out a thousand pounds of hay while them old-time horned Herefords followed the truck. That's when I let him find out I'd done some time.

"I figured you musta been in the crowbar hotel."

"How's that?"

"Well, you're a pretty good hand. What's a pretty good hand doin tryin loose horses in the middle of the night at some Podunk sale yard? Folks hang on to a pretty good hand and nobody was hangin on to you. You want to tell me what you done?"

I'd been with the old sumbitch for three years and out of jail the same amount of time. I wasn't afraid to tell him what I done 'cause I had started to trust him, but I sure didn't want him telling nothing to his sister. I told him I rustled some yearlings, and he chuckled like he understood entirely. I had rustled some yearlings, all right, but that's not what I went up for.

The old man paid me in cash, or, rather, the old lady did, since she handled anything like that. They never paid into workmen's comp, and there was no reason to go to the records. They didn't even have my name right. You tell people around here your name is Shane and they'll always believe you. The important thing is I was working my tail off for that old sumbitch, and he knew it. Nothing else mattered, even the fact that we'd come to like each other. After all, this was a God damn ranch.

The old fella had several peculiarities to him, most of which I've forgotten. He was one of the few fellas I ever heard of who would actually jump up and down on his hat if he got mad enough. You can imagine what his hat looked like. One time he did it 'cause I let the swather get away from me on a hill and bent it all to hell. Another time a Mormon tried to run down his breeding program to get a better deal on some replacement heifers, and I'll be damned if the old sumbitch didn't throw that hat down and jump on it, right in front of the Mormon, causing the Mormon to get into his Buick and ease on down the road without another word. One time when we was driving ring shanks into corral poles I hit my thumb and tried jumping on my hat, but the old sumbitch gave me such an odd look I never tried it again.

The old lady died sitting down. I went in, and there she was, sitting down, and she was dead. After the first wave of grief, the old sumbitch and me fretted about rigor mortis and not being able to move her in that seated position. So we stretched her onto the couch and called the mortician and he called the coroner and for some reason the coroner called the ambulance, which caused the old sumbitch to state, "It don't do you no nevermind to tell nobody nothing." Course he was right.

Once the funeral was behind us, I moved out of the LeisureLife, partly for comfort and partly 'cause the old sumbitch falled apart after his sister passed, which I never would've suspected. Once she's gone, he says, he's all that's left of his family and he's alone in life, and about then he notices me and tells me to get my stuff out of the LeisureLife and move in with him.

We rode through the cattle pritnear ever day year round, and he come to trust me enough to show how his breeding program went, with culls and breedbacks and outcrosses and replacements, and took me to bull sales and showed me what to expect in a bull and which ones were correct and which were sorry. One day we's looking at a pen of yearling bulls on this outfit near Luther and he can't make up his mind and he says he wished his sister was with him and he starts snuffling and says she had an eye on her wouldn't quit. So I stepped up and picked three bulls out of that pen, and he quit snuffling and said damn if I didn't have an eye on me, too. That was the beginning of our partnership.

One whole year I was the cook, and one whole year he was the cook, and back and forth like that, but never at the same time. Whoever was cook would change when the other fella got sick of his recipes, and ever once in a while a new recipe would come in the AgriNews, like that corn chowder with the sliced hot dogs. I even tried a pie one time, but it just made him lonesome for days gone by, so we forgot about desserts, which was probably good for our health, as most sweets call for gobbing in the white sugar.

The sister never let him have a dog 'cause she had a cat and she thought a dog would get the cat. It wasn't much of a cat, anyhow, but it lived a long time, outlived the old lady by several moons. After it passed on, we took it out to the burn barrel and the first thing the old sumbitch said was "We're gettin a dog." It took him that long to realize that his sister was gone.

Tony was a Border collie we got as a pup from a couple in Miles City that raised them. You could cup your hands and hold Tony when we got him, but he grew up in one summer and went to work and we taught him "down," "here," "come by," "way to me," and "hold 'em," all in one year or less, 'cause Tony would just stay on his belly and study you with his eyes until he knew exactly what you wanted. Tony helped us gather, mother up pairs, and separate bulls, and he lived in the house for many a good year and kept us entertained with all his tricks. Finally, Tony grew old and died. We didn't take it so good, especially the old sumbitch, who said he couldn't foresee enough summers for another dog. Plus that was the year he couldn't get on a horse no more and he wasn't about to work no stock dog afoot. There was still plenty to do and most of it fell to me. After all, this was a God damn ranch.

The time had come to tell him why I went to jail and what I did, which was rob that little store at Absarokee and shoot the proprietor, though he didn't die. I had no idea why I did such a thing—then or now. I led the crew on the prison ranch for a number of years and turned out many a good hand. They wasn't nearabout to let me loose until there was a replacement good as me who'd stay a while. So I trained up a murderer from Columbia Falls, could rope, break horses, keep vaccine records, fence, and irrigate. Once the warden seen how good he was, they paroled me out and turned it all over to the new man, who was never getting out. The old sumbitch could give a shit less when I told him my story. I could've told him all this years before when he first hired me, for all he cared. He was a big believer in what he saw with his own eyes.

I don't think I ever had the touch with customers the old sumbitch had. They'd come from all over looking for horned Herefords and talking hybrid vigor, which I may or may not have believed. They'd ask what we had and I'd point to the corrals and say, "Go look for yourself." Some would insist on seeing the old sumbitch and I'd tell them he was in bed, which was pritnear the only place you could find him now that he'd begun to fail. Then the state got wind of his condition and took him to town. I went to see him there right regular, but it just upset him. He couldn't figure out who I was and got frustrated 'cause he knew I was somebody he was supposed to know. And then he failed even worse. The doctors told me it was just better if I didn't come round.

The neighbors claimed I was personally responsible for the spread of spurge, Dalmatian toadflax, and knapweed. They got the authorities involved and it was pretty clear that I was the weed they had in mind. If they could get the court to appoint one of their relatives ranch custodian while the old sumbitch was in storage they'd get all that grass for free till he was in a pine box. The authorities came in all sizes and shapes, but when they were through they let me take one saddle horse, one saddle, the clothes on my back, my hat, and my slicker. I rode that horse clear to the sale yard, where they tried to put him in the loose horses 'cause of his age. I told them I was too set in my ways to start feeding Frenchmen and rode off toward Idaho. There's always an opening for a cowboy, even a old sumbitch like me if he can halfway make a hand.

SAULT STE. MARIE

David Means

David Means is the author of *A Quick Kiss of Redemption, Assorted Fire Events*, and *The Secret Goldfish*. His stories have appeared in *The New Yorker, Harper's, Esquire, The O. Henry Prize Stories*, and *The Best American Short Stories*. He lives in Nyack, New York, and teaches at Vassar College.

Ernie dug in with the tip of his penknife, scratching a line into the plastic top of the display case, following the miniature lock system as it stepped down between Lake Superior and Lake Huron. At the window, Marsha ignored us both and stood blowing clouds of smoke at the vista . . . a supertanker rising slowly in the lock, hefted by water . . . as if it mattered that the system was fully functioning and freight was moving up and down the great seaway. As if it mattered that ore was being transported from the hinterlands of Duluth (a nullifyingly boring place) to the eastern seaboard and points beyond. As if it mattered that the visitor's center stood bathed in sunlight, while behind the gift counter an old lady sat reading a paperback and doing her best to ignore the dry scratch of Ernie's knife, raising her rheumy eyes on occasion, reaching up to adjust her magnificent hair with the flat of her hand.—I'm gonna go see that guy I know, Tull, about the boat I was telling you about, Ernie announced, handing me the knife. He tossed his long black hair to the side, reached into his pants, yanked out his ridiculously long-

537

barreled .44 Remington Magnum, pointed it at the lady, and said—
But first I'm going to rob this old bag.—Stick 'em up, he said, moving
toward the lady, who stared over the top of her paperback. Her face
was ancient; the skin drooped from her jaw, and on her chin bits of
hair collected faintly into something that looked like a Vandyke. A
barmaid beauty remained in her face, along with a stony resilience.
Her saving feature was a great big poof of silvery hair that rose like
a nest and stood secured by an arrangement of bobby pins and a
very fine hairnet.—Take whatever you want, she said in a husky
voice, lifting her hands out in a gesture of offering.—As a matter
of fact, shoot me if you feel inclined. It's not going to matter to me.
I'm pushing eighty. I've lived the life I'm going to live and I've seen
plenty of things and had my heart broken and I've got rheumatoid
arthritis in these knuckles so bad I can hardly hold a pencil to paper. (She lifted her hand and turned it over so we could see the claw
formation of her fingers.)—And putting numbers into the cash register is painful.—Jesus Christ, Ernie said, shooting you would just
be doing the world a favor, and too much fun, and he tucked the gun
back in his pants, adjusted the hem of his shirt, and went to find this
guy with the boat. Marsha maintained her place at the window, lit
another cigarette, and stared at the boat while I took Ernie's knife
from the top of the display case and began scratching where he left
off. Finished with the matter, the old lady behind the gift counter
raised the paperback up to her face and began reading. Outside, the
superfreighter rose with leisure; it was one of those long ore boats,
a football field in length, with guys on bicycles making the journey
from bow to stern. There was probably great beauty in its immen-
sity, in the way it emerged from the lower parts of the seaway, lifted
by the water. But I didn't see it. At that time in my life, it was just
one more industrial relic in my face.

A FEW minutes later, when Ernie shot the guy named Tull in the
parking lot, the gun produced a tight little report that bounced off
the side of the freighter that was sitting up in the lock, waiting for

the go-ahead. The weight line along the ship's hull was far above the visitor's station; below the white stripe, the skin of the hull was shoddy with flakes of rust and barnacle scars. The ship looked ashamed of itself exposed for the whole world to see, like a lady with her skirt blown up. The name on the bow, in bright white letters, was Henry Jackman. Looking down at us, a crew member raised his hand against the glare. What he saw was a sad scene: a ring of blue gun smoke lingering around the guy Ernie shot, who was muttering the word fuck and bowing down while blood pooled around his crotch. By the time we scrambled to the truck and got out of there, he was trembling softly on the pavement, as if he were trying to limbo-dance under an impossibly low bar. I can assure you now, the guy didn't die that morning. A year later we came face-to-face at an amusement park near Bay City, and he looked perfectly fine, strapped into a contraption that would—a few seconds after our eyes met—roll him into a triple corkscrew at eighty miles an hour. I like to imagine that the roller-coaster ride shook his vision of me into an aberration that stuck in his mind for the rest of his earthly life.

FOR WHAT it's worth, the back streets of Sault Ste. Marie, Michigan, were made of concrete with nubs of stone mixed in, crisscrossed with crevices, passing grand old homes fallen into disrepair— homes breathing the smell of mildew and dry rot from their broken windows. Ernie drove with his hand up at the noon position while the police sirens wove through the afternoon heat behind us. The sound was frail, distant, and meaningless. We'd heard the same thing at least a dozen times in the past three weeks, from town to town, always respectfully distant, unraveling, twisting around like a smoke in a breeze until it disappeared. Ernie had a knack for guiding us out of bad situations. We stuck up a convenience store, taking off with fifty bucks and five green-and-white cartons of menthol cigarettes. Then a few days later we hogtied a liquor-store clerk and made off with a box of Cutty Sark and five rolls of Michigan scratch-off Lotto tickets. Under Ernie's leadership, we tied up our victims with bravado, in front of the fish-eyed video monitors, our heads in balaclavas. We put up the V sign and shouted: Liberation for all! For good measure, we turned to the camera and yelled: Patty Hearst lives! The next morning the *Detroit Free Press* Sunday edition carried a photo, dramatically smudgy, of the three of us bent and rounded off by the lens, with our guns in the air. The accompanying article speculated on our significance. According to the article, we were a highly disciplined group with strong connections to California, our gusto and verve reflecting a nationwide resurgence of Weathermen-type radicals.—A place to launch the boat will provide itself, Ernie said, sealing his lips around his dangling cigarette and pulling in smoke. Marsha rooted in the glove box and found a flaying knife, serrated and brutal-looking, with a smear of dried blood on the oak handle. She handed it to me, dug around some more, and found a baggie with pills, little blue numbers; a couple of bright reds, all mystery and portent. She spun it around a few times and then gave out a long yodel that left our ears tingling. Marsha was a champion yodeler. Of course we popped the pills and swallowed them dry while Ernie raged through the center of town, running two red lights, yanking the boat behind us like an afterthought. Marsha had her feet on the dash, and her hair tangled beautifully around her eyes and against her lips. It was the best feeling in the world to be running from the law with a boat in tow, fishtailing around corners, tossing our back wheels into the remnants of the turn, rattling wildly over the potholes, roaring through a shithole town that was desperately trying to stay afloat in the modern world and finding itself sinking deeper into squalor beneath a sky that unfurled blue and deep. All this along with drugs that were, thank Christ, swiftly going about their perplexing work, turning the whole show inside out and making us acutely aware of the fact that above all we were nothing much more than a collection of raw sensations. Marsha's legs emerging beautiful from her fringed cutoff shorts—the shorts are another story—and her bare toes, with her nails painted cherry red, wiggling in the breeze from the window. The seaway at the bottom of the street, spread out in front of a few lonely houses, driftwood gray, rickety and grand, baking in the summer heat. They crackled with dryness. They looked ready to explode into flames. They looked bereft of all hope. In front of a Victorian, a single dog, held taut by a long length of rope, barked and tried to break free, turning and twisting and looping the full circumference of his plight. We parked across the street, got out of the truck, and looked at him while he, in turn, looked back. He was barking SOS. Over and over again. Bark bark bark. Bark bark bark. Bark bark bark. Bark bark bark. Bark bark bark. Until finally Ernie yanked his gun from his belt, pointed quickly, with both hands extended out for stability, and released a shot that materialized as a burst of blooming dust near the dog; then another shot that went over his head and splintered a porch rail. The dog stopped barking and the startled air glimmered, got brighter, shiny around the edges, and then fell back into the kind of dull haze you find only in small towns in summer, with no one around but a dog who has finally lost the desire to bark. The dog sat staring at us. He was perfectly fine but stone-still. Out in the water a container ship stood with solemnity, as if dumbfounded by its own passage, covered in bright green tarps.—We're gonna drop her right here, Ernie said, unleashing the boat, throwing back restraining straps, trying to look like he knew what he was doing. The water was a five-foot fall from the corrugated steel and poured cement buttress of the wall. The Army Corps of Engineers had constructed a breakwall of ridiculous proportions. We lifted the hitch, removed it from the ball, and wiggled the trailer over so that the bow of the boat hung over the edge. Then without consultation—working off the mutual energies of our highs—we lifted the trailer and spilled the boat over the edge. It landed in the water with a plop, worked hard to right itself, coming to terms with its new place in the world, settling back as Ernie manipulated the rope and urged it along to some ladder rungs. To claim this was anything but a love story would be to put

Sault Ste. Marie in a poor light. The depleted look in the sky and the sensation of the pills working in our bloodstream, enlivening the water, the slap and pop of the metal hull over the waves. The super-freighter (the one with green tarps) looming at our approach. To go into those details too much would be to bypass the essential fact of the matter. I was deeply in love with Marsha. Nothing else in the universe mattered. I would have killed for her, I would have swallowed the earth like an egg-eating snake. I would have turned inside out in my own skin. I was certain that I might have stepped from the boat and walked on the water, making little shuffling movements, conserving my energy, doing what Jesus did but only better. Jesus walked on water to prove a point. I would have done it for the hell of it. Just for fun. To prove my love. Up at the bow Ernie stood with his heel on the gunwale, one elbow resting on a knee, looking like the figurehead on a Viking ship. I sat in the back with Marsha, watching as she held the rubber grip and guided the motor with her suspiciously well-groomed fingers. I could see in the jit-teriness of her fingers that she was about to swing the boat violently to the side. Maybe not as some deeply mean-spirited act but just as a joke on Ernie, who was staring straight ahead, making little hoots, patting his gun, and saying,—We're coming to get you. We're gonna highjack us a motherfucking superfreighter, boys. I put my hand over Marsha's and held it there. Her legs, caught in the fringed grip of her tight cutoff jeans, were gleaming with spray. (She'd ampu-tated the pants back in a hotel in Manistee, laying them over her naked thighs while we watched, tweaking the loose threads out to make them just right.) Tiny beads of water clung to the downy hairs along the top of her thighs, fringed with her cutoff jeans, nipping and tucking up into her crotch. Who knows? Maybe she was look-ing at my legs, too, stretched against her own, the white half-moon of my knees poking through the holes in my jeans. When I put my hand over hers I felt our forces conjoin into a desire to toss Ernie overboard.

———————

TWO NIGHTS later we were alone in an old motel, far up in the nether regions of the Upper Peninsula, near the town of Houghton, where her friend Charlene had OD'ed a few years back. Same hotel, exactly. Same room too. She'd persuaded me that she had to go and hold a wake for her dead friend. (—I gotta go to the same hotel, she said.—The same room.) The hotel was frequented mainly by sailors, merchant-marine types, a defiled place with soggy rank carpet padding and dirty towels. In bed we finished off a few of Tull's pills. Marsha was naked, resting on her side as she talked to me in a solemn voice about Charlene and how much they had meant to each other one summer, and how, when her own father was on a rage, they would go hide out near the airport, along the fence out there, hanging out and watching the occasional plane arrive, spinning its propellers wildly and making tipping wing gestures as if in a struggle to conjure the elements of flight. Smoking joints and talking softly, they poured out secrets the way only stoner girls can—topping each other's admissions, one after the other, matter-of-factly saying yeah, I did this guy who lived in Detroit and was a dealer and he, like, he like was married and we took his car out to the beach and spent two days doing it. Listening to her talk, it was easy to imagine the two of them sitting out there in the hackweed and elderberry on cooler summer nights, watching the silent airstrips, cracked and neglected, waiting for the flight from Chicago. I'd spent my own time out in that spot. It was where Marsha and I figured out that we were bound by coincidence: our fathers had both worked to their deaths in the paint booth at Fisher Body, making sure the enamel was spread evenly, suffering from the gaps in their masks, from inhaled solvents, and from producing quality automobiles.

I WAS naked on the bed with Marsha, slightly buzzed, but not stoned out of my sense of awareness. I ran my hand along her hip and down into the concave smoothness of her waist while she, in turn, reached around and pawed and cupped my ass, pulling me forward against her as she cried softly in my ear, just wisps of breath, about nothing in particular except that we were about to have sex. I was going to roll her over softly, expose her ass, find myself against her, and then press my lips to her shoulder blades as I sank in. When I got to that point, I became aware of the ashen cinder-block smell of the hotel room, the rubber of the damp carpet padding, the walls smeared with mildew, and the large russet stains that marked the dripping zone inside the tub and along the upper rim of the toilet. Outside, the hotel—peeling pink stucco, with a pale blue slide curling into an empty pool—stood along an old road, a logging route, still littered with the relics of a long-past tourist boom. The woods across from the place were thick with undergrowth, and the gaps between trees seemed filled with the dark matter of interstellar space. When we checked in it was just past sunset, but the light was already drawn away by the forest. It went on for miles and miles. Just looking at it too long would be to get lost, to wander in circles. You could feel the fact that we were far up along the top edge of the United States; the north pole began its pull around there, and the aurora borealis spread across the sky. I like to think that we both came out of our skin, together, in one of those orgasmic unifications. I like to think that two extremely lonely souls—both fearing that they had just killed another human being—united themselves carnally for some wider, greater sense of the universe; I like to think that maybe for one moment in my life, I reached up and ran my hand through God's hair. But who knows? Who really knows? The truth remains lodged back in that moment, and that moment is gone, and all I can honestly attest to is that we did feel a deep affection for our lost comrade Ernie at the very moment we were both engaged in fornication. (That's the word Ernie used: I'd like to fornicate with that one over there, or I'm going to find me some fornication.) We lay on the bed and let the breeze come through the hotel window—cool and full of yellow pine dust—across our damp bellies. The air of northern Michigan never quite matches the freshness of Canada. There's usually a dull iron-ore residue in it, or the smell of dead flies accumulating between the stones onshore. Staring up at the ceiling, Marsha felt compelled to talk about her dead friend. She lit a smoke and took a deep inhalation and let it sift from between her teeth. (I was endlessly attracted to the big unfixed gap-tooth space between her two front ones.) Here's the story she told me in as much detail as I can muster:

CHARLENE WAS a hard-core drifter, born in Sarnia, Ontario, across the lake from Port Huron. Her grandmother on her mother's side raised her, except for a few summers—the ones in our town—with her deranged auto-worker father. She was passed on to her grandfather on her father's side for some reason, up in Nova Scotia. Her grandfather was an edgy, hard drinker who abused her viciously. Along her ass were little four-leaf-clover scar formations. She ran away from her grandfather, back to her grandmother in Sarnia, and then ran away from her and crossed the International Bridge to Detroit, where she hooked up with a guy named Stan, a maintenance worker at a nursing home, who fixed air conditioners and cleared dementia-plugged toilets. Stan was into cooking crank in his spare time. They set up a lab in a house near Dearborn, in a pretty nice neighborhood, actually. Then one day there was an explosion and Stan got a face full of battery acid. She left him behind and hooked up with another cooker, named King, who had a large operation in a house near Saginaw. She worked with him and helped out, but she never touched the stuff and was angelic and pious about it. Even King saw a kind of beauty in Charlene's abstinence, Marsha said. For all the abuse she had suffered she had a spiritual kind of calm. Her eyes were, like, this amazingly deep blue color. Aside from her scars and all, she still had the whitest, purest skin, Snow White skin, the kind that you just want to touch, like a cool smooth stone. She just got more and more beautiful until eventually the guy named King couldn't stand the gentleness in her eyes and, maybe to try to change things around, he started to beat her face like a punching bag. One afternoon, under the influence of his own product, he had a couple of friends hold her down while he struck her face with a meat pounder, just hammered it, until she was close to death—maybe actually dead. Maybe she left her body and floated above herself and looked down and saw a guy with long shaggy hair and a silver meat hammer bashing her face in and decided it just wasn't worth dying in that kind of situation and so went back into her body. (Marsha was pretty firm in her belief about this part.) Charlene's cheekbones were broken, her teeth shattered. It took about twenty operations on her jaw and teeth just to chew again. Even then, chewing never felt right; her fake teeth slipped from the roof of her mouth, she talked funny, and a ringing sounded in her ears when she tried to smile. When she laughed too hard, her mouth would clamp up and she'd hear a chiming sound, high in pitch, like bells, and then the sound of windswept rain, or wind in a shell, or wind through guy wires, or a dry, dusty windswept street, or the rustling of tissue paper, or a sizzling like a single slice of bacon in a pan, or a dial tone endlessly unwinding in her eardrum. Forever she was up over herself looking down, watching King go at her, the two guys holding onto her shoulders, her legs scissor-kicking, the flash of the hammer until it was impossible to know what was going on beneath the blood. When Marsha met her again—a year or so later, in the break room at Wal-Mart, she had this weirdly deranged face; the out-of-place features demanded some thought to put straight. I mean it was a mess, Marsha said. Her nose was folded over. The Detroit team of plastic and oral surgeons just couldn't put poor Charlene back together again. A total Humpty Dumpty. No one was going to spend large amounts of money on a face of a drifter, anyway. Marsha forced herself to look. Then Charlene told her the story of King, the reasons for the damage, and the whole time Marsha didn't remove her eyes from the nose, the warped cheeks, the fishlike mouth. She tried as hard as she could to see where the beauty had gone and what Charlene must've been like before King mashed her face, the angelic part, because she kind of doubted her on that part of the story. As far as she could remember, from their nights together getting stoned outside the airport fence, Charlene had been, well, just a normal-looking kid. But listening to her talk, she put the pieces together and saw that, yeah, yeah, yeah, maybe this mishmash of features had once been beautiful. Her eyes were certainly bright blue, and wide, and she had pale milky skin. That night after work they decided to go out together, not to a bar where she'd get hassled but just to buy some beer and go to Charlene's apartment and drink. She had some little pills she called goners, good God goners, something like that. So they went to her apartment, took the pills, drank some beer, and decided to watch *Blue Velvet*. Whatever transpired next, according to Marsha, was amazing and incredibly sensual; they were stoned together, watching the movie, and suddenly between them there grew a hugely powerful sense of closeness; when Marsha looked down at her on the couch, Charlene appeared to her too gorgeous not to kiss (that's how she put it, exactly). Her mouth was funny because her teeth were out, so it was just softness and nothing else, and then, somehow, they undressed—I mean it wasn't like a first for either of us, Marsha said—and she fell down between Charlene's knees, and made her come, and then they spent the night together. A few days later, Charlene quit her job and split for Canada, back over the bridge, and then the next thing Marsha heard she was up north at this hotel with some guys and then she OD'ed.

THE STORY—and the way she told it to me, early in the morning, just before dawn—as both of us slid down from our highs, our bodies tingling and half asleep, turned me on in a grotesque way. To get a hard-on based on a story of abuse seemed wrong, but it happened, and we made love to each other again, for the second time, and we both came wildly and lay there for a while until she made her confession.—I made that up, completely. I never knew a drifter named Charlene from Canada, and I certainly wouldn't sleep with a fuckface reject like that. No way. I just felt like telling a story. I felt like making one up for you. I thought it would be interesting and maybe shed some light on the world. The idea—the angelic girl, the perfect girl, the one with perfect beauty getting all mashed up like that. That's something I think about a lot. She sat up, smoking a cigarette, stretching her legs out. Dawn was breaking outside. I imagined the light plunging through the trees, and the log trucks roaring past. For a minute I felt like knocking her on the head. I imagined pinning her down and giving her face a go with a meat hammer. But I found it easy to forgive her because the story she made up had sparked wild and fanciful sex. I kissed her and looked into her eyes and noticed that they were sad and didn't move away from mine (but that's not what I noticed). What did I notice? I can't put words to it except to say she had an elegiac sadness there, and an unearned calm, and that something had been stolen from her pupils.—You weren't making that up, I said.—You couldn't make that shit up, she responded, holding her voice flat and cold.—So it was all true.—I didn't say that. I just said you couldn't make that shit up.

WE'RE GONNA get nailed for what we did, she said, later, as we ate breakfast. Around us truckers in their long-billed caps leaned into plates of food, clinking the heavy silverware, devouring eggs in communal silence. A waitress was dropping dirty dishes into the slop sink, lifting each of them up and letting them fall, as if to test the durability of high-grade, restaurant-quality plates.—We're gonna get nailed, I agreed. I wasn't up for an argument about it. The fact was, our stream of luck would go on flowing for a while longer. Then I'd lose Marsha and start searching for a Charlene. For his part, the world could devour plenty of Ernies; each day they vaporized into the country's huge horizon.—He's probably dead. He knew how to swim, but he didn't look too confident in his stroke.— Yeah, I agreed. Ernie had bobbed up to the surface shouting profanities and striking out in our direction with a weird sidestroke. His lashing hands sustained just his upper body. The rest was sunken out of sight and opened us up to speculation as to whether his boots were on or off. After he was tossed from the boat, he stayed under a long, long time. When he bobbed up, his face had a wrinkled, baby-ish look of betrayal. He blew water at us, cleared his lips, and in a firm voice said,—You're dead, man, both of you. Then he cursed my mother and father and the day they were born, Marsha's cunt and her ass and her mother and father and God and the elements and the ice-cold water of the seaway and the ship, which was about four hundred yards away (—come on, motherfuckers, save my ass). He kept shouting like this until a mouthful of water gagged him. We were swinging around, opening it up full-throttle, looping around, sending a wake in his direction and heading in. When we got to the breakwall we turned and saw that he was still out there, splashing, barely visible. The ship loomed stupidly in the background, oblivi-ous to his situation. A single gull spiraled overhead, providing us with an omen to talk about later. (Gulls are God's death search-ers, Marsha told me. Don't be fooled by their white feathers or any of that shit. Gulls are best at finding the dead.) Then we got back in Tull's truck and headed through town and out, just following roads north toward Houghton, leaving Ernie to whatever destiny he had as one more aberration adrift in the St. Lawrence Seaway system. For a long time we didn't say a word. We just drove. The ra-dio was playing an old Neil Young song. We turned it up, and then up some more, and left it loud like that, until it was just so much rattling noise.

RANCH GIRL

Maile Meloy

Maile Meloy is the author of the story collection *Half in Love* and the
novels *A Family Daughter* and *Liars and Saints*. Her stories have been
published in *The New Yorker*, *The Paris Review*, and *Ploughshares*, and
she was awarded a Guggenheim Fellowship in 2004. She was born and
raised in Montana, and lives in Los Angeles.

If you're white, and you're not rich or poor but somewhere in the
middle, it's hard to have worse luck than to be born a girl on a ranch.
It doesn't matter if your dad's the foreman or the rancher—you're
still a ranch girl, and you've been dealt a bad hand.

If you're the foreman's daughter on Ted Haskell's Running H
cattle ranch, you live in the foreman's house, on the dirt road between Haskell's place and the barn. There are two bedrooms with
walls made of particleboard, one bathroom (no tub), muddy boots
and jackets in the living room, and a kitchen that's never used. No
one from school ever visits the ranch, so you can keep your room
the way you decorated it at ten: a pink comforter, horse posters on
the walls, plastic horse models on the shelves. Outside there's an
old cow-dog with a ruined hip, a barn cat who sleeps in the rafters,
and, until he dies, a runt calf named Minute, who cries at night by
the front door.

You help your dad when the other hands are busy: wading after him into an irrigation ditch, or rounding up a stray cow-calf pair

when you get home from school. Your mom used to help, too—she sits a horse better than any of the hands—but then she took an office job in town, and bought herself a house to be close to work. That was the story, anyway; she hasn't shown up at the ranch since junior high. Your dad works late now, comes home tired and opens a beer. You bring him cheese and crackers, and watch him fall asleep in his chair.

Down the road, at the ranch house, Ted Haskell grills steaks from his cows every night. He's been divorced for years, but he's never learned how to cook anything except steak. Whenever you're there with Haskell's daughter Carla, who's in your class at school, Haskell tries to get you to stay for dinner. He says you're too thin and a good beefsteak will make you strong. But you don't like Haskell's teasing, and you don't like leaving your dad alone, so you walk home hungry.

WHEN YOU'RE sixteen, Haskell's ranch house is the best place to get ready to go out at night. Carla has her own bathroom, with a big mirror, where you curl your hair into ringlets and put on blue eye shadow. You and Carla wear matching Wranglers, and when it gets cold you wear knitted gloves with rainbow-striped fingers that the boys love to look at when they get drunk out on the Hill.

The Hill is the park where everyone stands and talks after they get bored driving their cars in circles on the drag. The cowboys are always out on the Hill, and there's a fight every night; on a good night, there are five or six. On a good night, someone gets slid across the asphalt on his back, T-shirt riding up over his bare skin. It doesn't matter what the fights are about—no one ever knows—it just matters that Andy Tyler always wins. He's the one who slides the other guy into the road. Afterward, he gets casual, walks over with his cowboy-boot gait, takes a button from the school blood drive off his shirt and reads it aloud: "'I Gave Blood Today,'" he says. "Looks like you did, too." Then he pins the button to the other guy's shirt. He puts his jean jacket back on and hides a beer inside it, his hand tucked in like Napoleon's, and smiles his invincible smile.

"Hey," he says. "Do that rainbow thing again."

You wave your gloved hands in fast arcs, fingers together so the stripes line up.

Andy laughs, and grabs your hands, and says, "Come home and fuck me."

But you don't. You walk away. And Andy leaves the Hill without saying good-bye, and rolls his truck in a ditch for the hundredth time, but a buddy of his dad's always tows him, and no one ever calls the cops.

Virginity is as important to rodeo boys as to Catholics, and you don't go home and fuck Andy Tyler because when you finally get him, you want to keep him. But you like his asking. Some nights, he doesn't ask. Some nights, Lacey Estrada climbs into Andy's truck, dark hair bouncing in soft curls on her shoulders, and moves close to Andy on the front seat as they drive away. Lacey's dad is a doctor, and she lives in a big white house where she can sneak Andy into her bedroom without waking anyone up. But cowboys are romantics; when they settle down they want the girl they haven't fucked.

WHEN HASKELL marries an ex-hippie, everyone on the ranch expects trouble. Suzy was a beauty once; now she's on her third husband and doesn't take any shit. Suzy reads tarot cards, and when she lays them out to answer the question of Andy Tyler, the cards say to hold out for him.

On the spring cattle drive, you show Suzy how to ride behind the mob and stay out of the dust. Suzy talks about her life before Haskell: she has a Ph.D. in anthropology, a police record for narcotics possession, a sorority pin and a ski-bum son in Jackson Hole. She spent her twenties throwing dinner parties for her first husband's business clients—that, she says, was her biggest mistake—and then the husband ran off with one of her sorority sisters. She married a Buddhist next. "Be interesting in your twenties," Suzy says. "Otherwise you'll want to do it in your thirties or forties, when it wreaks all kinds of havoc, and you've got a husband and kids."

You listen to Suzy and say nothing. What's wrong with a husband and children? A sweet guy, a couple of brown-armed kids running around outside—it wouldn't be so bad.

There's a fall cattle drive, too, but no one ever wants to come on it. It's cold in November, and the cows have scattered in the national forest. They're half wild from being out there for months, especially the calves, who are stupid as only calves can be. The cowboys have disappeared, gone back to college or off on binges or other jobs. So you go out with your dad and Haskell, sweating in heavy coats as you chase down the calves, fighting the herd back to winter pasture before it starts to snow. But it always snows before you finish, and your dad yells at you when your horse slips on the wet asphalt and scrapes itself up.

IN GRADE school, it's okay to do well. But by high school, being smart gives people ideas. Science teachers start bugging you in the halls. They say Eastern schools have Montana quotas, places for ranch girls who are good at math. You could get scholarships, they say. But you know, as soon as they suggest it, that if you went to one of those schools you'd still be a ranch girl—not the Texas kind, who are debutantes and just happen to have a ranch in the family, and not the horse-farm kind, who ride English. Horse people are different, because horses are elegant and clean. Cows are mucusy, muddy, shitty, slobbery things, and it takes another kind of person to live with them. Even your long curled hair won't help at a fancy college, because prep-school girls don't curl their hair. The rodeo boys like it, but there aren't any rodeo boys out East. So you come up with a plan: you have two and a half years of straight A's, and you have to flunk quietly, not to draw attention. Western Montana College, where Andy Tyler wants to go, will take anyone who applies. You can live cheap in Dillon, and if things don't work out with Andy you already know half the football team.

When rodeo season begins, the boys start skipping school. You'd skip, too, but the goal is to load up on D's, not to get kicked out or sent into counseling. You paint your nails in class and follow the rodeo circuit on weekends. Andy rides saddle bronc, but his real event is bull riding. The bull riders have to be a little crazy, and Andy Tyler is. He's crazy in other ways, too: two years of asking you to come home and fuck him have made him urgent about it. You dance with him at the all-night graduation party, and he catches you around the waist and says he doesn't know a more beautiful girl. At dawn, he leaves for spring rodeo finals in Reno, driving down with his best friend, Rick Marcille, and you go to Country Kitchen for breakfast in a happy fog, order a chocolate shake and think about dancing with Andy. Then you fall asleep on Carla's bedroom floor, watching cartoons, too tired to make it down the road to bed.

Andy calls once from Reno, at 2 A.M., and you answer the phone before it wakes your dad. Andy's taken second place in the bull riding and won a silver belt buckle and three thousand dollars. He says he'll take you to dinner at the Grub Stake when he gets home. Rick Marcille shouts "Ro-*day*-o" in the background.

There's a call the next night, too, but it's from Rick Marcille's dad. Rick and Andy rolled the truck somewhere in Idaho, and the doctors don't think Rick will make it, though Andy might. Mr. Marcille sounds angry that Andy's the one who's going to live, but he offers to drive you down there. You don't wake your dad; you just go.

THE DOCTORS are wrong; it's Andy who doesn't make it. When you get to Idaho, he's already dead. Rick Marcille is paralyzed from the neck down. The cops say the boys weren't drinking, that a wheel came loose and the truck just rolled, but you guess the cops are just being nice. It's your turn to be angry, at Mr. Marcille, because his son will live and Andy is dead. But when you leave the hospital, Mr. Marcille falls down on his knees, squeezing your hand until it hurts.

At Andy's funeral, his uncle's band plays, and his family sets white doves free. One won't go, and it hops around the grass at your feet. The morning is already hot and blue, and there will be a whole summer of days like this to get through.

Andy's obituary says he was engaged to Lacey Estrada, which only Lacey or her doctor father could have put in. If you had the guts, you'd buy every paper in town and burn them outside the big white house where Lacey took him home and fucked him. Then Lacey shows up on the Hill with an engagement ring and gives you a sad smile as if you've shared something. If you were one of the girls who gets in fights on the Hill, you'd fight Lacey. But you don't; you just look away. You'll all be too old for the Hill when school starts, anyway.

At Western, in the fall, in a required composition class, your professor accuses you of plagiarism because your first paper is readable. You drop the class. Carla gets an A on her biology midterm at the university in Bozeman. She's going to be a big-animal vet. Her dad tells everyone, beaming.

But the next summer, Carla quits college to marry a boy named Dale Banning. The Bannings own most of central Montana, and Dale got famous at the family's fall livestock sale. He'd been putting black bulls on Herefords, when everyone wanted purebreds. They said he was crazy, but at the sale Dale's crossbred black-baldies brought twice what the purebreds did. Dale stood around grinning, embarrassed, like a guy who'd beaten his friends at poker.

Carla announces the engagement in Haskell's kitchen, and says she'll still be working with animals, without slogging through all those classes. "Dale's never been to vet school," Carla says. "But he can feel an embryo the size of a pea inside a cow's uterus."

You've heard Dale use that line on girls before, but never knew it to work so well. Carla's voice has a dreamy edge.

"If I don't marry him now," Carla says, "he'll find someone else."

In his head, Haskell has already added the Banning acreage to his own, and the numbers make him giddy. He forgets about having a vet for a daughter, and talks about the wedding all the time. If Carla backed out, he'd marry Dale himself. For the party, they clear the big barn and kill a cow. Carla wears a high-collared white gown that hides the scar on her neck—half a Running H—from the time she got in the way at branding, holding a struggling calf. Dale wears a string tie and a black ten-gallon hat, and everyone dances to Andy's uncle's band.

Your mother drives out to the ranch for the wedding; it's the first time you've seen your parents together in years. Your dad keeps ordering whiskeys and your mother gets drunk and giggly. But they sober up enough not to go home together.

That winter, your dad quits his job, saying he's tired of Haskell's crap. He leaves the foreman's house and moves in with his new girlfriend, who then announces he can't stay there without a job. He hasn't done anything but ranch work for twenty-five years, so he starts day-riding for Haskell again, then working full-time hourly, until he might as well be the foreman.

WHEN YOU finish Western, you move into your mother's house in town. Stacks of paperwork for the local horse-racing board cover every chair and table, and an old leather racing saddle straddles an arm of the couch. Your mother still thinks of herself as a horsewoman, and buys unbroken Thoroughbreds she doesn't have time or money to train. She doesn't have a truck or a trailer, or land for pasture, so she boards the horses and they end up as big, useless pets she never sees.

Summer evenings, you sit with your mom on the front step and eat ice cream with chocolate-peanut-butter chunks for dinner. You think about moving out, but then she might move in with you—and that would be worse.

You aren't a virgin anymore, thanks to a boy you found who wouldn't cause you trouble. He drops by from time to time, to see if things might start up again. They don't. He's nothing like Andy. He isn't the one in your head.

When Carla leaves Dale and moves home to the Running H, you drive out to see her baby. It feels strange to be at the ranch now, with the foreman's house empty and Carla's little boy in the yard, and everything else the same.

"You're so lucky to have a degree and no kid," Carla says. "You can still leave."

And Carla is right: You could leave. Apply to grad school in Santa Cruz and live by the beach. Take the research job in Chicago that your chemistry professor keeps calling about. Go to Zihuatanejo with Haskell's friends, who need a nanny. They have tons of room, because in Mexico you don't have to pay property tax if you're still adding on to the house.

But none of these things seem real; what's real is the payments on your car and your mom's crazy horses, the feel of the ranch road you can drive blindfolded and the smell of the hay. Your dad will need you in November to bring in the cows.

Suzy lays out the tarot cards on the kitchen table. The cards say, Go on, go away. But out there in the world you get old. You don't get old here. Here you can always be a ranch girl. Suzy knows. When Haskell comes in wearing muddy boots, saying, "Hi, baby. Hi, hon," his wife stacks up the tarot cards and kisses him hello. She pours him fresh coffee and puts away the cards that say go.

THE NEW AUTOMATON THEATER

Steven Millhauser

Steven Millhauser is the author of numerous works of fiction and
was awarded the Pulitzer Prize for his novel *Martin Dressler*. His story
"Eisenheim the Illusionist" was the basis of the 2006 film *The Illusionist*, starring Edward Norton and Paul Giamatti. His work has been
translated into fourteen languages. He teaches at Skidmore College.

Our city is justly proud of its automaton theater. By this I do not
mean simply that the difficult and exacting art of the automaton
is carried by our masters to a pitch of brilliance unequaled elsewhere, and unimagined by the masters of an earlier age. Rather I
mean that by its very nature our automaton theater is deserving of
pride, for it is the source of our richest and most spiritual pleasure.
We know that without it our lives would lack something, though
we cannot say with any certainty what it is that we would lack. And
we are proud that ours is a genuinely popular theater, commanding
the fervent loyalty of young and old alike. It is scarcely an exaggera-
tion to say that from the moment we emerge from the cradle we fall
under an enchantment from which we never awake. So pronounced
is our devotion, which some call an obsession, that common wisdom distinguishes four separate phases. In childhood we are said
to be attracted by the color and movement of these little creatures,
in adolescence by the intricate clockwork mechanisms that give
them the illusion of life, in adulthood by the truth and beauty of

the dramas they enact, and in old age by the timeless perfection of an art that lifts us above the cares of mortality and gives meaning to our lives. Such distinctions are recognized by everyone to be fanciful, yet in their own way they expressed truth. For like our masters, who pass from a long apprenticeship to ever-greater heights of achievement, we too pass from the apprenticeship of childish delight to the graver pleasures of a mature and discriminating enjoyment. No one ever outgrows the automaton theater.

It must be confessed that the precise number of our theaters remains unknown, for not only are they springing up continually, but many of the lesser companies travel from hall to hall without benefit of permanent lodging. The masters themselves may exhibit at a single hall, or in several at once. It is generally agreed that well over eight hundred theaters are in operation throughout our city in the course of a single year; and there is no day during which one cannot attend some hundred performances.

Despite a great number of books on the subject, the origin of the automaton theater is shrouded in darkness. From the singing birds of Hero of Alexandria to Vaucanson's duck, every item of clockwork ingenuity has by some authority been cited as an influence; nor have historians failed to lay tribute to the art of Byzantium. Some scholars have gone so far as to lend a questionable authority to Johann Müller's fly, which legend tells us was able to alight on the hands of all the guests seated in a room before returning to its maker. Yet even if such tales should prove to be true, they would fail to explain our own more elegant art, which not only exceeds the crude imaginings of legend but is entirely explicable and demonstrable. One theory has it that our earliest clockwork artisans—about whom, it is admitted, little is known—were directly influenced by the dollhouse art of medieval Nürnberg, a conjecture to which a certain weight is lent by church records showing that fourteen of our ancestors were born in Nürnberg. What is certain is that the art of the miniature has long flourished in our town, and quite independently of the automaton theater. No home is without its cherrystone basket, its peachpit troll; and the splendid Hall of Miniatures in our Stadtmuseum is widely known. Yet I would argue that it is precisely our admirable miniatures which reveal their essential difference from our automaton theater. In the Stadtmuseum one can see such marvels of the miniature art as an ark carved from the pit of a cherry, containing three dozen pairs of clearly distinguishable animals, as well as Noah and his sons; and carved from a piece of boxwood one inch long, and displayed beneath a magnifying lens, the winter palace of the Hohenzollerns, with its topiary garden, its orchard of pear trees, and its many rooms, containing more than three hundred pieces of precise furniture. But when one has done admiring the skill of such miniature masterworks, one cannot fail to be struck by their difference from our automaton theater. In the first place, although it is called a miniature theater, these six-inch figures that lend such enchantment to our lives are virtual giants in comparison with the true masterpieces of miniature art. In the second place, the art of the miniature is in essence a lifeless art, an art of stillness, whereas the art of the automaton lies above all in the creation of living motion. Yet having said as much, I do not mean to deny all relation between the miniatures of our museums and the exquisite internal structures—the clockwork souls—of our automatons.

Although the origin of our art is obscure, and the precise lines of its development difficult to unravel, there is no doubt concerning the tendency of the art during the long course of its distinguished history. That tendency is toward an ever-increasing mastery of the illusion of life. The masterpieces of eighteenth-century clockwork art preserved in our museums are not without a charm and beauty of their own, but in the conquest of motion they can in no way compare to the products of the current age. The art has advanced so rapidly that even our apprentices of twelve exceed the earliest masters, for they can produce figures capable of executing more than five hundred separate motions; and it is well known that in the last two generations our own masters have conquered in their automatons every motion of which a human being is capable. Thus the mechanical challenge inherent in our art has been met and mastered.

Yet such is the nature of our art that the mechanical is intimately related to the spiritual. It is precisely the brilliance of our advance in clockwork that has enabled our masters to express the full beauty of living human form. Every gesture of the human body, every shade of emotion that expresses itself on a human face, is captured in the mobile forms and features of our miniature automatons. It has even been argued that these finely wrought creatures are capable of expressing in their faces certain deep and complex emotions which the limited human musculature can never hope to achieve. Those who blame our art for too great a reliance on mechanical ingenuity (for we are not without our critics) would do well to consider the relation between the physical and the spiritual, and to ask themselves whether the most poetic feeling in the soul of man can exist without the prosaic agency of a nervous system.

By its nature, then, our art is mimetic; and each advance has been a new encroachment on the preserves of life. Visitors who see our automatons for the first time are awed and even disturbed by their lifelike qualities. Truly our figures seem to think and breathe. But having acknowledged the mimetic or illusionistic tendency of our art, I hasten to point out that the realism of which I speak must not be misunderstood to mean the narrow and constricting sort that dominates and deadens our literature. It is a realism of means, which in no way excludes the fanciful. There is first of all the traditional distinction between the Children's Theater and the theater proper. In the Children's Theater we find as many witches, dragons, ghosts, and walking trees as may delight the imagination of the most implacable dreamer; but they are, if I may risk a paradox, real witches, real dragons, real ghosts, and real walking trees. In these figures, all the resources of clockwork art are brought to bear in the precise and perfected expression of the impossible. The real is used to bring forth the unreal. It is a mimesis of the fantastic, a scrupulous rendering of creatures who differ from real creatures solely by their quality of inexistence. But even the adult theater is by no means to be measured by the laughable banalities of our so-called realistic literature. For here too we can point to a great and pleasing variety of theatrical forms, which have evolved along with the evolving art of clockwork, and which are limited only by the special nature of the art itself. Being a speechless art, it relies entirely on a subtle expressivity of gesture—an apparent limitation that, in the hands of our masters, becomes the very means of its greatness. For these performances, which run from twenty to forty minutes, and are accompanied by such musical effects as may be required, seek no less than music itself to express the inexpressible and give precise and lasting shape to the deepest impulses of the human spirit. Thus some dramas may suggest the ballet, others the mime, still others the silent cinema; yet their form is their own entirely, various as the imagination, but all betraying a secret kinship.

But even aside from the great variety of our automaton theater this most realistic and mechanical of arts, which strives for an absolute imitation of Nature, cannot be called realistic without serious qualification. For in the first place, the automatons are but six inches high. This fact alone makes nonsense of the charge that our art is narrowly realistic in spirit and intention. The vogue of life-sized automatons, current some years ago, quite passed us by. Well known is the response evoked by the gross automatons of Count Orsini, upon the occasion of that worthy's much advertised visit to our city. One imagines the howls of laughter still ringing in his ears. But quite apart from the small size of our automatons is the nature of the pleasure of automaton art itself. It would be foolish to deny that this pleasure is in part a pleasure of imitation, of likeness. It is the pleasure of illusion fully mastered. But precisely this pleasure depends on a second pleasure, which is opposed to the first; or it may be that the pleasure of imitation is itself divisible into two opposing parts. This second pleasure, or this second half of the pleasure of imitation, is a pleasure of unlikeness. With secret joy we perceive every way in which the illusion is not the thing itself, but only an illusion; and this pleasure increases as the illusion itself becomes more compelling. For we are not children, we do not forget we are at the theater. The naturalness of the creatures moving and suffering on their little stage only increases our reverence for the masters who brought them into being.

These masters, of whom there are never more than twenty or thirty in a generation, are themselves the highest expression of a rigorous system of training that even on its lower levels is capable of producing works of superb skill and enchanting beauty; yet it is notable that despite occasional proposals the method has never cohered into a formal school. In somewhat arbitrary fashion the masters continue to take on apprentices, who move into the workshops and are expected to devote themselves exclusively to their art. Many of course cannot endure the rigors of such a life, which in addition to being narrow and arduous does not even hold out the promise of future prosperity. For it remains curiously true that despite public fervor the masters are, if not impecunious, at any rate far from prosperous. Many reasons have been adduced for this shameful state of affairs, one of the more fanciful being that the masters are so dedicated to their art that external comfort leaves them indifferent. But this can hardly be the case. The masters are not monks; they marry, they have children, they are responsible for maintaining a family with the additional burden of apprentices, not all of whom can pay even for their food. They are human beings like everyone else, with all the cares of suffering humanity, in addition to the burden of their rigorous art. Indeed the grave and sorrowing features of the older masters seem witness of a secret unhappiness. And so a far more plausible explanation of their lack of prosperity is that the laboriousness of the art far exceeds its capacity to pay. The theaters flourish, money pours in; but the construction of a single clockwork figure takes from six months to two or more years. Of course the masters are aided in large part by the higher apprentices, who are permitted to construct hands and feet, and even entire legs and arms, as well as the clockwork mechanisms of the less expressive portions of the anatomy. Yet even so the master automatist is entirely responsible for the face and head, and the final adjustments of the whole. And although the painting of the scenery on translucent linen—itself a labor of many months—is left almost entirely to the older apprentices, nevertheless the master automatist must provide the original sketches; and the same is true of many other matters, such as the elaborate lighting that, illuminating the beautiful translucencies, is so much a part of our automaton theater. And of course there is the drama itself, the choreography, the sometimes elaborate music. For all these reasons, our daily attendance at the theaters does not lead to prosperity for the masters, though the theater managers invariably live in the best part of town.

The mechanical skill of the masters, their profound understanding of the secrets of clockwork art, is impressive and even unsettling; but mechanical genius alone does not make a master. That this is so is evident from the fact that some apprentices as early as their thirteenth year are able to construct an automaton whose motions are anatomically flawless. Yet they are far from being masters, for their creatures lack that mysterious quality which makes the true masterpieces of our art seem to think and suffer and breathe. It is true that anatomical perfection is a high level of accomplishment and suffices for the Children's Theater. Yet when these same apprentices, impatient to be recognized, attempt several years later to start theaters of their own, the lack of spiritual mastery is immediately evident, and they are forced either to resign themselves to a life of service in the Children's Theater or else to return to the rigors of the higher apprenticeship. Even among those recognized as masters there are perceptible differences of accomplishment, though at a level so high that comparisons tend to take the form of arguments concerning the nature of beauty. Yet it may happen that one master stands out from the others by virtue of some scarcely to be defined yet immediately apparent quality, as our history demonstrates again and again; and as is the case at present, in the disquieting instance of Heinrich Graum.

For it is indeed of him that I wish to speak, this troubled spirit who has risen up in our midst with his perilous and disturbing gift; and if I have seemed to hesitate, to linger over other matters, it is because the very nature of his art throws all into question, and requires one to approach him obliquely, almost warily.

Like many masters, Heinrich Graum was the son of a watchmaker; like most, he displayed his gift early. At the age of five he was sent to the workshop of Rudolf Eisenmann, from which so many apprentices emerge as young masters. There he proved a talented but not precocious pupil. At the age of seven he constructed a one-inch nightingale capable of sixty-four motions, including thirty-six separate motions of the head, and exhibiting such perfect craftsmanship that it was used in the orchard scene of Eisenmann's *Der Reisende Kavalier.* This was followed almost a year later by a charming high-wire artist who climbed to the top of his post, walked with the aid of a balancing pole across the wire toward the opposite post, lost and regained his balance three times, fell and clung to the wire with one hand, climbed laboriously back up, and continued safely to the opposite post, where he turned and bowed. In all this there was nothing to distinguish young Heinrich from any talented apprentice; he was never a child prodigy, as has since mistakenly been claimed. A far greater degree of precocity is very frequent among the child apprentices, and is looked upon by the masters with a certain distrust. For in an art that more than any other demands a thorough mastery of mechanical details, a too-early success often leads the young apprentice to a false sense of ripeness. All too often the prodigy of seven is the mediocrity of fifteen, fit only for service in the Children's Theater. For it is not too much to say that the highest form of the automatist's art is entirely spiritual, though attained, as I have said, by mechanical means. The child prodigies display a remarkable technical virtuosity that is certainly impressive but that does not in itself give promise of future greatness, and that more often than not distracts them and other apprentices from their proper path of development. Young Heinrich was spared the affliction of precocity.

But he was highly talented; and a master always watches his talented apprentices for any sign of that indefinable quality which marks a pupil as doomed to mastery. In the case of young Heinrich it was his early interest in the human form and above all in the hands and face. At precisely the time when talented apprentices of ten and twelve are turning their attention to the dragons and mermaids of the Children's Theater, and reveling in the display of their considerable technical skills, Heinrich began to study the inner structure of Eisenmann's famous magician, capable of making a silver coin disappear, producing a bluebird from his hat, and shuffling and holding outspread in his hands a deck of fifty-two miniature cards. It was the mechanical problem that appears to have engaged young Heinrich's interest; it was the first problem he could not solve rapidly. For eight months during his twelfth year he dissected and reassembled the hands of the anatomical models that flourish in every workshop; the intricate clockwork structure of the thumb appears to have obsessed him. And in this too he distinguished himself from the child wonders, who move rapidly and a little breathlessly from one accomplishment to the next. At the end of eight months he was able to construct the precise duplicate of Eisenmann's magician—a feat that earned him the master's first serious attention. But what is more remarkable is that young Heinrich was still dissatisfied. He continued to study the structure of the hand (his series of sixty-three hands from this period is considered by some to be his first mature work) and shortly before his fourteenth birthday produced an Eisenmann magician capable of three new tricks never attempted before in automaton art. One of these tricks achieved a certain notoriety when it was discovered that no human magician was capable of duplicating it. Young Heinrich confessed to having improved the musculature of the hand beyond a merely human capacity; for this he was lightly rebuked.

The magician was followed quickly by his first original creation, the astonishing pianist capable of playing the entire first movement of the Moonlight Sonata on a beautifully constructed seven-inch grand piano. Heinrich had only a slight musical training, and the execution of the movement left much to be desired, but all agreed that the hands of the pianist displayed the mark of a future master.

Heinrich at fourteen was a large, slumped, serious boy, whose thick-fingered hands looked clumsy in comparison with the delicate clockwork hands of his creatures. Aside from his taciturnity, which even then was notable, he was in no way sullen or eccentric, as so many talented apprentices prove to be, and among his peers he had an unusual reputation for kindness. He seems to have slid awkwardly but without a struggle into young manhood, wearing his large and powerful body with an air of surprise.

It was immediately after the completion of the pianist that he began the study of the human face which was to have such profound consequences for his art and to make of him an acknowledged master by the age of twenty. For six long years he analyzed and dissected the automaton face, studying the works of the masters and trying to penetrate the deepest secrets of expressivity. During this entire period he completed not a single figure, but instead accumulated a gallery of some six hundred heads, many of them in grotesque states of incompletion. Eisenmann recognized the signs of maturing mastership, and allowed the stooped, grave youth to have his way. At the end of the six-year period Heinrich created in two feverish months the first figure since his pianist: the young woman whom he called Fräulein Elise.

Eisenmann himself pronounced it a masterpiece, and even now we may admire it as a classic instance of automaton art. This charming figure, who measures scarcely five inches in height, moves with a grace and naturalness that are the surest signs of mastership. Her famous walk, so indolently sensual, would alone have ensured the young master a place in the histories. She seems the very essence of girlhood passing into womanhood. But even in this early figure one is struck above all by the startling expressivity of the face. During her twelve minutes of clockwork life, Fräulein Elise appears to be undergoing a spiritual struggle, every shadow of which is displayed in her intelligent features. She paces her room now restlessly, now indolently, throwing herself onto her bed, gazing out the window, sitting up abruptly, falling into a muse. We seem to be drawn into the very soul of this girl, troubled as she is with the vague yearnings and dark intuitions of innocence on the threshold of knowledge. Every perfectly rendered gesture seems designed only to draw us more deeply inward; we feel an uncanny intimacy with this restless creature, whose mysterious life we seem to know more deeply than our own. The long, languorous, slowly unfolding, darkly yearning yawn that concludes the performance, as Elise appears to open like a heavy blossom, and draw us into the depths of her being, is a masterpiece of spiritual penetration, all the more remarkable in that Heinrich is not known to have been in love at this time. One fellow apprentice, a thin youth of eighteen, was so stirred by Elise that he was observed to study her twelve-minute life again and again. As the weeks passed his cheeks grew pale, a dark blueness appeared below his eyes; and it was said that he had fallen in love with the little Fräulein Elise.

The young master now entered upon a period of powerful creativity, which in four years' time led to his first public performance. The success of the Zaubertheater was immediate and decisive. His figures were compared to the greatest masterpieces of clockwork art; all commentators remarked upon their supple expressivity, their uncanny intensity. Here was an artist who at the age of twenty-four had not only mastered the subtlest intricacies of clockwork motion but, in an art where innovation was often disastrous, and always dangerous, had added something genuinely new. No one could ignore the haunting "inwardness" of his admirable creatures; it was as if Heinrich Graum had learned to shadow forth emotions never seen before. Even those who disdained all innovation as inherently destructive were compelled to offer their grudging admiration, for when all was said and done the young master had simply carried the art one step further in the honorable direction of scrupulous imitation. His difference was noted, and admired by those of most exacting taste; and he was pronounced to be in the classic tradition of the great masters, though with a distinctive modern flavor peculiarly and compellingly his own. Thus did it come about that he was admired equally by the older generation and the new.

It is one thing for a young master to earn his reputation; it is another for him to sustain it. Heinrich Graum was not one to ignore a challenge. In the course of the next twelve years the grave young master seemed to surpass himself with every new composition, each one of which was awaited with an eagerness bordering on fever. Audiences responded in kind to the peculiar intensity of his creatures; young women especially were susceptible to the strange power that glowed in those clockwork eyes. Well known is the case of Ilse Länger, who fell so desperately in love with his dark-eyed Pierrot that the mere sight of him would cause her to burst into fits of violent sobbing. One rainy Sunday, after a tormented night, the suffering girl left her house before dawn, walked along the gloomy avenue of elms north of the Schlosspark, and threw herself into the Bree, leaving behind a pitiful love-note and the fragment of a poem. Poor Ilse Länger was only an extreme and unfortunate instance of a widespread phenomenon. The tears of women were not uncommon at the Zaubertheater; young men wrote fiery poems to his Klara. Even sober critics were not above responses of the extreme kind, which sometimes troubled them, and which served as the basis of an occasional attack. It was noted that Graum's figures seemed more and more to be pushing at the limits of the human, as if he wished to express in his creatures not only the deepest secrets of the human soul but emotions that lay beyond the knowledge of men; and this sense of excess, which was at the very heart of his greatness, was itself seen to pose a danger, for it was said that his figures walked a narrow line dividing them from the grotesque. But such attacks, inevitable in an art of high and ancient tradition, were little more than a murmur in the thunder of serious applause; and the performances at the Zaubertheater were soon being called the triumph of the age, the final and richest flowering of the automatist's art.

It was perhaps the very extremity of these well-deserved claims that should have given us pause, for if an art has indeed been carried to its richest expression, then we may wonder whether the urge that impelled it in the direction of its fulfillment may not impel it beyond its proper limit. In this sense we may ask whether the highest form of an art contains within it the elements of its own destruction—whether decadence, in short, so far from being the sickly opposite of art's deepest health, is perhaps nothing but the result of an urge identical to both.

However that may be, the young master continued to move from triumph to triumph, shocking us with the revelation of ever-new spiritual depths, and making us yearn for darker and deeper beauties. It was as if his creatures strained at the very limits of the human, without leaving the human altogether; and the intensity of his late figures seemed to promise some final vision, which we awaited with longing, and a little dread.

It was at the age of thirty-six, after twelve years of uninterrupted triumph, that Heinrich Graum suddenly fell silent.

Now the silence of masters is not unusual, and is in itself no cause for alarm. It is well known that the masters undergo great and continual strain, for when we speak of mastering the sublime art of the automaton we do not mean a mastery that leads to relaxation of effort. It may indeed with more truth be said that the achievement of mastery is only the necessary preparation for future rigors. How else are we to explain the grave, melancholy countenances of our masters? The high art of the automaton demands a relentless and unremitting precision, an unwavering power of concentration, and a ceaseless faculty for invention, so that mastery itself must always struggle merely to maintain its own level. In addition there is the never acknowledged but always felt presence of the other masters. For there is a secret rivalry among them. Each feels the presence of the others, against whom he measures himself mercilessly; and although it may be that such rivalry is harmful to the health of the masters, yet without it there is every likelihood that the art would suffer, for a faint and scarcely conscious relaxation would inevitably set in. In addition to this rivalry, each master is a rival of the great masters of the past; and each is also a rival of himself, continually striving to surpass his own most superb achievements. Such pressures are more than sufficient to engrave deep lines on the faces of our masters, but there are in addition the continual threat of poverty, the burden of having to live in two worlds at once, and the common lot of suffering that no mortal can escape, and that often seems to the master, stretched as he always is to the highest pitch of a strained and exacting creativity, too much to bear. Thus it comes about that a master will sometimes fall into silence, from which he will emerge in six months or a year or two years as if born anew, while in his absence the theater is run by his leading apprentices. The striking feature of Heinrich Graum's case is therefore not the silence itself, nor even the suddenness of the silence, but rather its thoroughness and duration. For Graum remained silent for ten long years; and unlike all other masters who temporarily retire, he closed his theater and withdrew all his creatures from public performance.

The debate over the ten-year silence of Heinrich Graum will in all probability never cease. It has been compared in some quarters to Schiller's twelve-year silence between *Don Carlos* and *Wallenstein*, but perhaps I may be permitted to point out that Schiller began to compose poetry (if not drama) eight years after the completion of *Don Carlos*, that he worked steadily on *Wallenstein* from 1797 to 1799, and that in any case he was far from silent, since he published two full-length histories as well as numerous philosophical and esthetic essays during the very years of his dramatic silence. Graum's silence was complete. Moreover he released his apprentices. We have therefore no witnesses of his activity during this decisive period. He had married quietly during the triumphant years, and there is no cause whatever for connecting his silence in any way with his domestic life. During his silent years he is known to have made several trips in the company of his wife to various bathing resorts on the Nordsee; he was twice seen in a chair on the beach at Schev-eningen, a stooped giant of a man in brown bathing trunks, staring out gloomily at the water. But most of the time he appears to have remained shut up in his workshop on the Lindenallee. It is com-monly assumed that there he tirelessly took apart and recomposed clockwork creatures in the manner of his obsessive youth. Nothing can be proved to the contrary, for he has remained silent about this as about all other matters, but against the general assumption two objections may briefly be raised. First, no trace of any automaton from this period has ever been found. Second, the nature of the new automaton theater renders the theory of ceaseless experiment un-likely. It may be argued that he destroyed all his experiments; yet it should be remembered that he carefully preserved the sixty-three hands and more than six hundred heads of his apprenticeship. My own suggestion, which I offer after long and serious reflection, is that for ten years Heinrich Graum did nothing. Or to be more pre-cise: he did nothing, while thinking ceaselessly about the nature of his art. Had he been a man of letters, a Schiller, he might have of-fered to the world the fruits of his meditations; his genius being of the wordless kind, his thoughts were reflected only in the strange creatures that suddenly burst from him toward the end of this pe-riod, changing the nature of our automaton theater forever.

When the Zaubertheater first closed, we were disappointed and expectant. As the silence continued, our expectation diminished, while our disappointment grew. In time even our disappointment faded, returning only in stray eruptions of sadness or, on lavender summer evenings when the yellow streetlamps came on, a vague uneasiness, a restlessness, as if we were searching for something that had departed forever.

Meanwhile we threw ourselves into the automaton theater. It was a time of ripeness in the art; and it was said that never before had the skill of so many masters reached such a pitch of expres-sive brilliance, haunted as they all were by the memory of the old Zaubertheater.

The rumor of the great master's return was at first greeted with a certain reserve. He had vanished so completely that his possible reappearance among us was somehow disturbing. It was as if a beloved son, ten years dead, should suddenly return, long after one had made one's thousand little accommodations. An entire generation of apprentices had entered the workshops without having seen a single work of the legendary master; some were openly skeptical. Even we who had mourned his silence were secretly uncertain, for we had grown accustomed to things as they were, we had lost the habit of genius. In our timid hearts, did we not pray that he would stay away? Yet as the day drew near we became tense with expectancy; and in our pulses we could feel, like an eruption of fever at the onset of an unknown disease, a slow, secret excitement.

And Heinrich Graum returned; again the old Zaubertheater opened its doors. That long-awaited performance was like a knife flashed in the face of our art. Of those who remained during the full thirty-six minutes, some were openly enraged, others sickened and ashamed; a few were seized by the roots of the soul, though in a manner they could not understand and later refused to discuss. One critic stated that the master had lost his mind; others, more kindly though no more accurately, spoke of parody and the grotesque. Even now one still hears such charges and descriptions; the Neues Zaubertheater remains at the center of a passionate controversy. Those who do not share our love of the automaton theater may find our passions difficult to understand; but for us it was as if everything had suddenly been thrown into question. Even we who have been won over are disturbed by these performances, which trouble us like forbidden pleasures, like secret crimes.

I have spoken of the long and noble history of our art, and of its tendency toward an ever-increasing mimetic brilliance. Young Heinrich had inherited this tradition, and in the opinion of many had become its outstanding master. In one stroke his Neues Zaubertheater stood history on its head. The new automatons can only be described as clumsy. By this I mean that the smoothness of motion so characteristic of our classic figures has been replaced by the jerky abrupt motions of amateur automatons. As a result the new automatons cannot imitate the motions of human beings, except in the most elementary way. They lack grace; by every rule of classic automaton art they are inept and ugly. They do not strike us as human. Indeed it must be said that the new automatons strike us first of all *as automatons*. This is the essence of what has come to be called The New Automaton Theater.

I have called the new automatons clumsy, and this is true enough if we judge them from the standpoint of the masterpieces of the older school. But it is not entirely true, judged even from that standpoint. In the first place, the clumsiness itself is extremely artful, as imitators have learned to their cost. It is not a matter of simply reducing the number of motions, but of reducing them in a particular way, so that a particular rhythm of motions is produced. In the second place, the acknowledged master of expressivity cannot be said to have turned against the expressive itself. The new automatons are profoundly expressive in their own disturbing way. Indeed it has been noticed that the new automatons are capable of motions never seen before in the automatist's art, although it is a matter of dispute whether these motions may properly be called human.

In the classic automaton theater we are asked to share the emotions of human beings, whom in reality we know to be miniature automatons. In the new automaton theater we are asked to share the emotions of automatons themselves. The clockwork artifice, far from being disguised, is thrust upon our attention. If this were all, it would be startling, but it would not be much. Such a theater could not last. But Graum's new automatons suffer and struggle; no less than the old automatons do they appear to have souls. But they do not have the souls of human beings; they have the souls of clockwork creatures, grown conscious of themselves. The classic automatists present us with miniature people; Heinrich Graum has invented a new race. They are the race of automatons, the clan of clockwork; they are new beings, inserted into the universe by the mind of Graum the creator. They live lives that are parallel to ours but are not to be confused with ours. Their struggles are clockwork struggles, their suffering is the suffering of automatons.

It has become fashionable of late to claim that Graum abandoned the adult theater and returned to the Children's Theater as to his spiritual home. To my mind this is a gross misunderstanding. The creatures of the Children's Theater are imitations of imaginary beings; Graum's creatures are not imitations of anything. They are only themselves. Dragons do not exist; automatons do.

In this sense Graum's revolution may be seen to be a radical continuation of our history rather than a reversal or rejection of it. I have said that our art is realistic, and that all advances in the technical realm have been in the service of the real. Graum's new automatons offer no less homage to Nature. For him, human beings are one thing and clockwork creatures another; to confuse the two is to propagate the unreal.

Art, a master once observed, is never theoretical. My laborious remarks obscure the delicate art they seek to elucidate. Nothing short of attendance at the Neues Zaubertheater can convey the startling, disturbing quality of the new automatons. We seem drawn into the souls of these creatures, who assert their unreal nature at every jerk of a limb; we suffer their clumsiness, we are pierced by inhuman longings. We are moved in ways we can scarcely comprehend. We yearn to mingle with these strange newcomers, to pass into their clockwork lives; at times we feel a dark understanding, a criminal complicity. Is it that in their presence we are able to shed the merely human, which seems a limitation, and to release ourselves into a larger, darker, more dangerous realm? We know only that we are stirred in places untouched before. A dark, disturbing beauty, like a black sunrise, has come into our lives. Dying of a thirst we did not know we had, we drink from the necessary and tormenting waters of fictive fountains.

And the new automatons begin to obsess us. They penetrate our minds, they multiply within us, they inhabit our dreams. They waken in us new, forbidden passions we cannot name. Once again it is adolescent girls who have proved to be peculiarly susceptible to Graum's dark wizardry. In any audience one can see three or four of them, with their parted lips, their hungry eyes, their tense, hysterical attention. The tears that flow are not the tears of love, but quite different tears, deep, scalding tears torn up from unspeakable depths, tears that give no relief, tears wrung from nerves tormented by the crystalline harmonies of unearthly violins. Even our stern young men emerge from these dangerous performances with haunted eyes. Incidents of a pathological kind have been reported; the demonic pact between Wolfgang Kohler and Eva Holst must be passed over in silence. More troubling because more common are the taut, drained faces one sees after certain performances, especially after the terrifying dissolution scene in *Die Neue Elise*. The new art is not a gentle art; its beauties are of an almost unbearable intensity.

These are perhaps superficial signs; more profound is the new restlessness one feels in our city, an impatience with older forms, a secret hunger.

They are no longer the same, the old automatons. Gratefully we seek out the old theaters, but once we have felt the troubling touch of the new automatons we find ourselves growing impatient with the smooth and perfect motions of the old masters, whose brilliant imitations seem to us nothing but clockwork confections. So, rather guiltily, we return to the Neues Zaubertheater, where the new automatons draw us into their inhuman joys and sufferings, and fill us with uneasy rapture. The old art flourishes, and its presence comforts us, but something new and strange has come into the world. We may try to explain it, but what draws us is the mystery. For our dreams have changed. Whether our art has fallen into an unholy decadence, as many have charged, or whether it has achieved its deepest and darkest flowering, who among us can say? We know only that nothing can ever be the same.

PAPER LOSSES

Lorrie Moore

Lorrie Moore is the author of the story collections *Self-Help*, *Like Life*, and *Birds of America*, and the novels *Who Will Run the Frog Hospital?* and *Anagrams*. Her work has appeared in *The New Yorker*, *The Best American Short Stories*, and *The O. Henry Prize Stories*. She is a professor of English at the University of Wisconsin in Madison.

Although Kit and Rafe had met in the peace movement, marching, organizing, making no-nukes signs, now they wanted to kill each other. They had become, also, a little pro-nuke. Married for two decades of precious, precious life, she and Rafe seemed currently to be partners only in anger and dislike, their old lusty love mutated to rage. It was both their shame and demise that hate like love could not live on air. And so in this, their newly successful project together, they were complicitous and synergistic. They were nurturing, homeopathic, and enabling. They spawned and raised their hate together, cardiovascularly, spiritually, organically. In tandem, as a system, as a dance team of bad feeling, they had shoved their hate center stage and shone a spotlight down for it to seize. Do your stuff, baby! Who is the best? Who's the man?

"Pro-nuke? You are? Really?" Kit was asked by her friends, to whom she continued to indiscreetly complain.

"Well, no." Kit sighed. "But in a way."

"You seem like you need someone to talk to."

Which hurt Kit's feelings, since she'd felt that she was talking to *them*. "I'm simply concerned about the kids," she said.

Rafe had changed. His smile was just a careless yawn, or was his smile just stuck carelessly on? Which was the correct lyric? She did not know. But, for sure, he had changed. In Beersboro, they put things neutrally, like that. Such changes were couched. No one ever said that a man was now completely screwed up. They said, *The guy has changed*. Rafe had started to make model rockets in the base-ment. He'd become *a little different*. He was something of *a character*. The brazen might suggest, *He's gotten into some weird shit*. The rock-ets were tall, plastic, penile-shaped things to which Rafe carefully shellacked authenticating military decals. What had happened to the handsome hippie she'd married? He was prickly and remote, empty with fury. A blankness had entered his blue-green eyes. They stayed wide and bright but non-functional, like dime-store jewelry. She wondered if this was a nervous breakdown, the genuine arti-cle. But it persisted for months, and she began to suspect, instead, a brain tumor. Occasionally, he catcalled and wolf-whistled across his mute alienation, his pantomime of hate momentarily collapsed. "Hey, cutie," he'd call to her from the stairs, after not having looked her in the eye for two months. It was like being snowbound with someone's demented uncle: should marriage be like that? She wasn't sure.

She seldom saw him anymore when he got up in the morning and rushed off to his office. And when he came home from work he would disappear down the basement stairs. Nightly, in the anx-ious conjugal dusk that was now their only life together, after the kids had gone to bed, the house would fill up with fumes. When she called down to him about this, he never answered. He seemed to have turned into some sort of space alien. Of course, later she would understand that all this meant that he was involved with another woman, but at the time, protecting her own vanity and sanity, she was working with two hypotheses only: brain tumor or space alien.

"All husbands are space aliens," said her friend Jan.

"God help me, I had no idea," said Kit. She began spreading peanut butter on a pretzel and eating quickly. "In fact," said Jan, "my sister and I call them UFOs."

It stood for something. Kit hated to ask.

"Ungrateful fuckers," Jan said.

Kit thought for a moment. "But what about the *O*?" she asked. "You said UFO."

There was a short silence. "Ungrateful fuckeroos," Jan added quickly.

Kit sighed. "Rafe's in such disconnect. His judgment on matters is so bad."

"Not on the planet he lives on. On his planet, he's a veritable Solomon. 'Bring the stinkin' baby to me now!'"

"Do you think people can be rehabilitated and forgiven?"

"Sure! Look at Ollie North."

"He lost that Senate race. He was not sufficiently forgiven."

"But he got some votes."

"Yeah, and now what is he doing?"

"Now he's back to promoting a line of fire-retardant pajamas. It's a life!" Jan paused. "Do you fight about it?"

"About what?" asked Kit.

"The rockets back to his homeland."

Kit sighed. "Yes, the toxic military-crafts business poisoning our living space. Do I fight? I don't fight, I just, well, O.K.—I ask a few questions from time to time. I ask, 'What the hell are you doing?' I ask, 'Are you trying to asphyxiate your entire family?' I ask, 'Did you hear me?' Then I ask, 'Did you hear me?' again. Then I ask, 'Are you deaf?' I also ask, 'What do you think a marriage is? I'm really just curious to know,' and also, 'Is this your idea of a well-ventilated place?' A simple interview, really. I don't believe in fighting. I believe in giving peace a chance. I also believe in internal bleeding." She paused to shift the phone more comfortably against her face. "I'm also interested," Kit said, "in

those forensically undetectable dissolving plastic bullets. Have
you heard of those?"

"No."

"Well, maybe I'm wrong about those. I'm probably wrong.
That's where the Mysterious Car Crash may have to come in."

In the chrome of the refrigerator she caught the reflection of
her own face, part brunette Shelley Winters, part potato, the finely
etched sharps and accidentals beneath her eyes a musical interlude
amid the bloat. In every movie she had seen with Shelley Winters in
it, Shelley Winters was the one who died.

Peanut butter was stuck high and dry on Kit's gums. On the
counter, a large old watermelon had begun to sag and pull apart
in the middle along the curve of seeds, like a shark's grin, and she
lopped off a wedge, rubbed its cool point around the inside of her
mouth. It had been a year since Rafe kissed her. She sort of cared
and sort of didn't. A woman had to choose her own particular unhappiness carefully. That was the only happiness in life: to choose
the best unhappiness. An unwise move and, good God, you could
squander everything.

The summons took her by surprise. It came in the mail, addressed to her, and there it was, stapled to divorce papers. She'd
been properly served. The bitch had been papered. Like a person,
a marriage was unrecognizable in death, even buried in its favorite
suit. Atop the papers themselves was a letter from Rafe suggesting
their spring wedding anniversary as the final divorce date. "Why
not complete the symmetry?" he wrote, which didn't even sound
like him, though its heartless efficiency was suited to this, his new
life as a space alien, and in keeping generally with the principles of
space-alien culture.

The papers referred to Kit and Rafe by their legal names, Kath-
erine and Raphael, as if the more formal versions of them were the
ones who were divorcing—their birth certificates were divorcing!—
and not they themselves. Rafe was still living in the house and had
not yet told her that he'd bought a new one. "Honey," she said, trembling, "something very interesting came in the mail today."

Rage had its medicinal purposes, but she was not wired to sustain it, and when it tumbled away loneliness engulfed her, grief burning at the center with a cold blue heat. At the funerals of two different elderly people she hardly knew, she wept in the back row of the church like a secret lover of the deceased. She felt woozy and ill and never wanted to see Rafe—or, rather, Raphael—again, but they had promised the kids this Caribbean vacation, so what could they do?

This, at last, was what all those high-school drama classes had been for: acting. She had once played the Queen in "A Winter's Tale," and once a changeling child in a play called "Love Me Right Now," written by one of the more disturbing English teachers in her high school. In both of these performances, she had learned that time was essentially a comic thing—only constraints upon it diverted it to tragedy, or, at least, to misery. Romeo and Juliet, Tristan and Isolde—if only they'd had more time! Marriage stopped being comic when it was suddenly halted, at which point it became divorce, which time never disturbed and so the funniness of which was never-ending.

Still, Rafe mustered up thirty seconds of utterance in order to persuade her not to join them on this vacation. "I don't think you should go," he announced.

"I'm going," she said.

"We'll be giving the children false hope."

"Hope is never false. Or it's always false. Whatever. It's just hope," she said. "Nothing wrong with that."

"I just don't think you should go."

Divorce, she could see, would be like marriage: a power grab. Who would be the dog and who would be the owner of the dog?

What bimbo did he want to give her ticket to? (Only later would she find out. "As a feminist, you mustn't blame the other woman," a neighbor told her. "As a feminist, I request that you no longer speak to me," Kit replied.)

And months later, in the courtroom, where she would discover that the county owned her marriage and that the county was now taking it back like a chicken franchise she had made a muck of, forbidding her to own another franchise for six more months, with the implication that she might want to stay clear of all poultry cuisine for a much longer time than that, when she had finally to pronounce in front of the robed, robotic judge and a winking stenographer whose winking seemed designed to keep the wives from crying, she would have to declare the marriage "irretrievably broken." What second-rate poet had gotten hold of the divorce laws? She would find the words sticking in her throat, untrue in their conviction. Was not everything fixable? This age of disposables, was it not also an age of fantastic adhesives? Why "irretrievably broken" like a songbird's wing? Why not "Do you find this person you were married to, and who is now sitting next to you in the courtroom, a total asshole?" That would suffice, and be more accurate. The words "irretrievably broken" sent one off into an eternity of wondering.

She and Rafe had not yet, however, signed the papers. And there was still the matter of her wedding ring, which was studded with little junk emeralds and which she liked a lot and hoped she could continue wearing because it didn't look like a typical wedding ring. He had removed his ring—which did look like a typical wedding ring—a year before, because, he said, "it bothered him." She had thought at the time that he'd meant it was rubbing. She had not been deeply alarmed; he had often shed his clothes spontaneously—when they first met, he'd been something of a nudist. It was good to date a nudist: things moved right along. But it was not good trying to stay married to one. Soon she would be going on chaste geriatric dates with other people whose clothes would, like hers, remain glued to the body.

"What if I can't get my ring off?" she said to him now on the plane to La Caribe. She had gained a little weight during their twenty years of marriage, but really not all *that* much. She had been practically a child bride!

"Send me the sawyer's bill," he said. Oh, the sparkle in his eye was gone!

"What is wrong with you?" she said. Of course, she blamed his parents, who had somehow, long ago, accidentally or on purpose, raised him as a space alien, with space-alien values, space-alien thoughts, and the hollow, shifty character, concocted guileless-ness, and sociopathic secrets of a space alien.

"What is wrong with *you*?" he snarled. This was his habit, his space-alien habit, of merely repeating what she had just said to him. It had to do, no doubt, with his central nervous system, a silicon-chipped information processor incessantly encountering new linguistic combinations, which it then had to absorb and file. Rep-etition bought time and assisted the storage process.

More than the girls, who were just little, she was worried about Sam, her sensitive fourth grader, who now sat across the airplane aisle, moodily staring out the window at the clouds. Soon, through the machinations of the state's extremely progressive divorce laws—a boy needs his dad!—she would no longer see him every day; he would become a boy who no longer saw his mother every day, and he would scuttle and float a little off and away like paper carried by wind. With time, he would harden: he would eye her over his glasses, in the manner of a maître d' suspecting riffraff. He would see her coming the way a panicked party guest sees someone without a nametag. But on this, their last trip as an actual family, he did fairly well at not letting on.

They all slept in the same room, in separate beds, and saw other families squalling and squabbling, so that by comparison theirs—a family about to break apart forever—didn't look so bad. She was not deceived by the equatorial sea breeze and so did not overbake herself in the colonial sun; with the resort managers, she shared her moral outrage at the armed guards who kept the local boys from sneaking past the fence onto this white, white beach; and she rubbed a kind of resin into her brow to freeze it and downplay the creases—to make her appear younger for her departing hus-band, though he never once glanced at her. Not that she looked that good: her suitcase had got lost and she was forced to wear clothes purchased from the gift shop—the words "La Caribe" emblazoned across every single thing.

On the beach, people read books about Rwandan and Yugoslavian genocide. This was to add seriousness to a trip that lacked it. One was supposed not to notice the dark island boys on the other side of the barbed wire, throwing rocks.

There were ways of making things vanish temporarily. After making the protest, one could disappear oneself, in movement and repetition.

Sam liked only the trampoline and nothing else. There were dolphin rides, but he sensed their cruelty. "They speak a language," he said. "We shouldn't ride them."

"They look happy," Kit said.

Sam studied her with a seriousness from some sweet beyond. "They look happy so you won't kill them."

"You think so?"

"If dolphins tasted good," he said, "we wouldn't even know about their language." That the intelligence in a thing could undermine your appetite for it. That yumminess obscured the mind of the yummy as well as the mind of the yummer. That deliciousness resulted in decapitation. That you could only understand something if you did not desire it. How did he know such things already? Usually girls knew them first. But not hers. Her girls, Beth and Dale, were tough beyond Kit's comprehension: practical, self-indulgent, independent five-year-old twins, a system unto themselves. They had their own secret world of Montessori code words and plastic jewelry and spells of hilarity brought on mostly by the phrase "cinnamon M&M's" repeated six times, fast. They wore sparkly fairy wings wherever they went, even over cardigans, and they carried wands. "I'm a big brother now," Sam had said repeatedly to everyone and with uncertain pride the day the girls were born, and after that he spoke not another word on the matter. Sometimes Kit accidentally referred to Beth and Dale as Death and Bail, as they, for instance, buried their several Barbies in sand, then lifted them out again with glee. A woman on a towel, reading of genocide, turned and smiled. In this fine compound on the sea, the contradictions of life were grotesque and uninventable.

She went to the central office and signed up for a hot-stone massage. "Would you like a man or a woman?" asked the receptionist.

"Excuse me?" Kit said, stalling. After all these years of marriage, which *did* she want? What did she know of men—or women? "There's no such thing as 'men,' " her friend Jan used to say. "Every man is different. The only thing they have in common is, well, a capacity for horrifying violence."

"A man or a woman—for the massage?" asked Kit, buying time. She thought of the slow mating of snails, an entire day, being hermaphrodites and having it all be so confusing: by the time they had figured out who was going to be the girl and who was going to be the boy, someone came along with some garlic paste and just swooped them right up.

"Oh, either one," she said, and then knew she'd get a man.

Whom she tried not to look at but could smell in all his smoky aromas—tobacco, incense, cannabis—exhaling and swirling their way around him. A wiry old American pothead gone to grim seed. He did not speak. He placed hot stones up and down her back and left them there in a line up her spine. Did she think her belotioned flesh too private and precious to be touched by the likes of him? Are you crazy? The mad joy in her face was held over the floor by the massage-table headpiece, and at his touch her eyes filled with bittersweet tears, which then dripped out of her nose, which she realized was positioned perfectly by God as a little drainpipe for crying. The sad massage-hut carpet beneath her grew a spot. He left the hot stones on her until they went cold. As each one lost its heat, she could no longer feel it there on her back, and then its removal was like a discovery that it had been there all along: how strange to forget and then feel something only then, at the end. Though this wasn't the same thing as the frog in the pot whose water slowly heats and boils, still it had meaning, she felt, the way

metaphors of a thermal nature tended to. Then he took all the
stones off and pressed the hard edges of them deep into her back,
between the bones, in a way that felt mean but more likely had no
intention at all.

"That was nice," she said, as he was putting all his stones away.
He had heated them in a plastic electric Crockpot filled with water,
she saw, and now he unplugged the thing in a tired fashion.

"Where did you get those stones?" she asked. They were smooth
and dark gray—black when wet, she could see.

"They're river stones," he said. "I've been collecting them for
years up in Colorado." He placed them in a metal fishing-tackle
box.

"You live in Colorado?" she asked.

"Used to," he said, and that was that.

Kit got dressed. "Someday you, like me, will have done sufficient lab work," Jan had once said. "Soon you, like me, in your next
life, like me, will want them old and rich, on their deathbed, really, and with no sudden rallyings in the hospice. That would ruin
everything."

"You're a woman of steel and ice," Kit had said.

"Not at all," said Jan. "I'm just a voice on the phone, drinking a
little tea."

On the last night of their vacation Kit's suitcase arrived like a
joke. She didn't even open it. Sam put out the little doorknob flag
that said "WAKE US UP FOR THE SEA TURTLES." The doorknob
flag had a pre-printed request to be woken at 3 A.M. so that they
could go to the beach and see the hatching of the baby sea turtles
and their quick scuttle into the ocean, under the cover of night, to
avoid predators. But though Sam had hung the flag carefully, and
before the midnight deadline, no staff person woke them. And
by the time they got up and went down to the beach it was ten in
the morning. Strangely, the sea turtles were still there. They had
hatched during the night and then hotel personnel had hung on to
them, in a baskety cage, to show them off to the tourists who were
too lazy or deaf to have got up in the night.

"Look, come see!" a man with a Spanish accent who usually rented the scuba gear said. Sam, Beth, Dale, and Kit all ran over. (Rafe had stayed behind to drink coffee and read the paper.) The squirming babies were beginning to heat up in the sun; the goldening Venetian vellum of their wee webbed feet was already edged in desiccating brown. "I'm going to have to let them go now," the man said. "You are the last ones to see these little bebés." He took them over to the water's edge and let them go, hours too late, to make their own way into the sea. And that's when a frigate bird swooped in, plucked them, one by one, from the silver waves, and ate them for breakfast.

Kit sank down in a large chair next to Rafe. He was tanning himself, she could see, for someone else's lust.

"I think I need a drink," she said. The kids were swimming.

"Don't expect me to buy you a drink," he said.

Had she even asked? Did she now call him the bitterest name she could think of? Did she stand and turn and slap him across the face in front of several passers-by? Who told you *that*?

When they finally left La Caribe, she was glad. Staying there, she had begun to hate the world. In the airports and on the planes home, she did not even try to act natural: natural was a felony. She spoke to her children calmly, from a script, with dialogue and stage directions of utter neutrality. Back home in Beersboro, she unpacked the condoms and candles, her little love sack, completely unused, and threw it in the trash. What had she been thinking? Later, when she had learned to tell this story differently, as a story, she would construct a final lovemaking scene of sentimental vengeance that would contain the inviolable center of their love, the sweet animal safety of night after night, the still-beating tender heart of marriage. But, for now, she would become like her unruinable daughters, and even her son, who, as he aged stoically and carried on regardless, would come to scarcely remember— was it past even imagining?—that she and Rafe had ever been together at all.

STITCHES

Antonya Nelson

Antonya Nelson was born in 1961 in Wichita, Kansas. She is the author of five story collections, most recently *Some Fun*, and three novels. She has been awarded a Guggenheim Fellowship, a National Endowment for the Arts grant, and a Rea Award for the Short Story, and was named by *The New Yorker* as one of the "twenty young fiction writers for the new millennium" and by Granta as among the "best of the young American novelists." In addition to writing, Nelson also teaches, dividing her time between New Mexico State University and the University of Houston, where she shares a chair with her husband, the writer Robert Boswell.

"Mama?" she said. The word cut through every layer: the dark house, the late hour, the deep sleep, the gin still polluting her blood, the dream still spinning whimsically. All of it sliced away as if with a scalpel by her daughter's voice on the telephone.

"Baby." Ellen emerged from the murk: naked, conscious, attuned. "Baby?"

"I'm okay, Mama, but something happened, something happened here." *Here* was in her college town, two hours away from her parents' home, this her first semester. Ellen felt her heart beating.

"But you're okay?"

"I'm okay"

"Not hurt?"

"I'm okay. I'm scared."

Skeered, the children used to say, Tracy and Lonnie, Ellen's girl and boy. "Scared of what?" Ellen's house was lit only by the moon and a streetlamp, 3:30 in the morning, the worst of the witching hours. Without thinking she had brought the telephone from the hall to her son's room, where he slept, safe. Ellen had been dreaming about her ex-lover, whom she had been missing now for longer than the relationship itself had endured; this longing now felt normal, a facet of who she was. On the telephone her daughter was almost crying, as if to punish Ellen for her unfaithful dream: look what can happen if you aren't paying attention, if your affections go wandering. "Scared of what?"

"What's she scared of?" asked Ellen's husband, his breath bitter with sleep and age, his presence here at her elbow similar to his presence beside her in bed: she wanted to push him away, she wanted to pull him close. Sometimes she sunk her teeth into his shoulder and pretended it was erotic. He loved his daughter without hesitation, the way he loved his wife, his son. It was cloying, reassuring, inescapable, horrifying. Secure: like a safety belt or a prison sentence.

"Mama, I was *raped*." Now Tracy began to cry sincerely.

"What?" Ellen's husband shouted. They went back to their own bedroom and he was dressing, muttering, lights were igniting, drawers were slammed as Ellen clutched the phone with both hands as though it might leap through the air.

"Where *are* you?" she asked. "Where are you, darling?"

"In my . . . dorm," said her daughter, and that building erected itself, proud and institutional, enclosing the girl on its fourth floor, in her room full of posters and stuffed bears and empty beer cans.

"Police?" her husband asked, as he tried to extricate the phone.

"Not the police!" came Tracy's voice over the line, "it was someone I *know*." Now Ellen's husband was working pants over boxer shorts, the material bunching at his waist, storming from room to room in search of wallet and keys and eyeglasses and jacket, shirt flapping open like a flag.

"It was someone she knows," Ellen repeated for him.

"I heard," he said grimly. "I'm on my way," he added, tucking his shorts into his fly and zipping sharply. His decision had been made just as automatically as pulling a zipper; or, rather, his thinking had cleared a path through the fog of the night: blinding, exact, preemptory. Ahead of himself he saw only his daughter. Ellen had to marvel. "You stay on the phone," he told her. His hair was wild, his shoelaces trailing him as he slammed the door.

"Don't let him come here," her daughter had been saying, repeatedly. "*Please* don't let him come here." As if he could have been stopped.

"I'm going to talk to you, honey," said Ellen to her seventeen year old. A young college student, she was a girl who'd always been ahead of her years in some ways and behind them in others. Smart yet sentimental, maternal yet childlike, she was rounded and soft, dark, vaguely furred on her upper lip and forearms, the nape of her neck. She bore an uncanny resemblance to her maternal grandmother. Ellen would never escape that particular blend of bossiness and naivete. They book-ended her, her mother and her daughter, dark stocky peasants. Practical, conscientious, good: they exerted force from either side, like a flower press. Like a vise.

"Oh, why does he have to come here?" Tracy wailed rhetorically. And Ellen could easily envision her daughter's olive skin, wet with tears, as she wandered back into her son's room. His skin was exactly the opposite—fair, nearly hairless—and it covered a very different, knobby body. In his face you could see the child he'd been and the man he would become, lean and frail, charming and awkward. "Of course your father's coming, and we'll just talk until he gets there." The hundred miles between them appeared in Ellen's mind, the desert, the bright moon, and the animals as they blindly scurried out of his trajectory. His trip would be a clear shot, simple as a bullet from a gun. He had raised the garage door with enough force to make the lights in the house flicker.

But Lonnie hadn't woken up, twelve years old, skinny, innocent, eyelids almost translucent; he was sleeping the passionate sleep of an early teenager.

"Is he mad?" Tracy asked.

"Frightened," Ellen said. "Men get angry when they're frightened. He's mad at whoever raped you."

"Mama?" she sucked wetly in. "It wasn't exactly rape?"

"Tracy." Ellen pulled her bathrobe closer around her; the heater came on and the cat wandered to the floor vent beside Lonnie's guitar stand. When had she draped herself in her bathrobe? What had she been thinking, a few minutes ago, standing naked in her son's bedroom? She and her husband had had sex before going to sleep, she recalled now, which explained both her nudity and her dream of her ex-lover. "Trace. What do you mean, it wasn't exactly rape?" She was used to her daughter's amendments: the extremity, and then the backpedaling.

"I mean, I knew him, I know him, and he invited me to his house, and I went there, and I knew we were going to have sex. Don't keep saying my name," she added, stepping out of her tragedy for a moment to be irritated.

"There can still be rape—"

"I don't think it was rape. I agreed, I wanted it. I mean, I wanted some of it. He's my professor."

Ellen's heart hammered in a new kind of anger, the anger that comes after the fear, the anger that begins to refine itself, take shape in more intricate ways, like lace, like coral, around any extenuating circumstance. The worst thing, well, that wasn't what had happened to Tracy. It wasn't simple violence of the sort Ellen had envisioned. The man hadn't been a stranger in an alley, or a burglar in the dorm. He hadn't been a frat boy at a party, or one of a gang of drunks in a bar. Instead, it was a middle-aged man in a bed with a headboard, piles of books on the table beside it, floral sheets, prescription meds in the night table drawer, a room not unlike the room Ellen shared with her husband, filled with the familiar objects of comfort and respectable living, complication and texture, history. Instantly that house formed in Ellen's mind, growing swiftly from one fruitful word, *professor*, the divorced professor, the separated professor, the lecherous professor whose wife was out of town or teaching her own seminar, and Tracy there in that house, seduced by the older man's flattering attention to her. "Tell me," Ellen said to her daughter. "Tell me what happened."

"He's my movement teacher," she began, and what followed was not surprising, not to Ellen, who'd also been to college, who'd also developed crushes on professors, who knew all about the liberal arts. What was surprising, what had always surprised Ellen about this daughter of hers, was how she never failed to bring her female business to her mother. Breasts, boys, menstruation, makeup, cat fights, betrayal. It was unnerving to be this girl's mother. She was so *forthcoming*. So frankly healthy and unfucked-up. How had she gotten this way? Ellen felt somehow excluded from the process; she wasn't so healthy herself, still vaguely anorexic, still drinking too much and smoking occasionally, lying to her husband about her affections. She kept secrets—not in drawers or closets or diaries, but in her heart, behind her eyes, on her lips. Tracy's admirable openness seemed not to have been inherited from Ellen, so it must have come from her father.

"How old is this professor?" Ellen asked suddenly. Something Tracy had said made the image of the man shift. The bed, it was a *waterbed*.

"He's not actually a professor, per se," Tracy said. "He's more like the TA."

"Per se."

"What?"

"How old is the TA?"

"I dunno. Twenty-five?"

Ellen sighed. Not so much younger than her ex-lover. Now the professor's stately bedroom was devolving into her ex-lover's ratty apartment. Mattress on the floor, stolen silverware, chairs festooned with duct tape, disposable razors, wine in a box.

"He raped you? Or you had sex when you didn't want to? Or what?"

"Mama?"

"What, babe? What, Trace?"

"You know the most awful thing? The awfullest-seeming thing, the thing that's just really *really* hard to handle?"

"What, doll?" Ellen played with the phone's telescoping antenna, up and then down, patience a tone of voice she put on like a hat.

"A man crying," Tracy said. "I don't know why, but I can't take it."

Ellen thought of her husband's crying. When he had believed that their life together was over, he had wept. Tracy was right. It was an *awful* thing, it left her full of awe. Frightening, pathetic, to be patted on the head, to be avoided, shunned, locked out of the house. There was no good reaction to a man's crying, not one that would work. Men didn't know how to do it, how to modulate, how to breathe or minister to their own sudden emissions. Ellen thought that men would be inept at childbirth, as well: they were so ugly in pain, so bad at giving in to a force larger than themselves. She was remembering her ex-lover's contorted face, he'd been tearful a time or two, as well. "Baby," she said.

"It can just about kill you, watching a boy cry."

"Why was he crying? Why?"

"Because he hurt me."

Once more Ellen felt anger rise in her. Anger and empathy: these accompanied the guilt and the love she felt toward her daughter and always would. She paced the house's flowchart of a floor plan, hallway-kitchen-dining room-living room-hall, a smooth oval that her children used to chase around as if at a racetrack.

The cat, the same age as Tracy, watched her, blinking sagely and calmly. This man in distant Albuquerque kept shifting character in Ellen's mind, elastic as a superhero. She focused instead on the image of her husband, driving steadfastly through the desert, the bright moon beaming uncomplicatedly down upon him, both of his hands on the wheel. *He* was not a shape-changer. "*How* did he hurt you? What did he do?"

"Oh, it's embarrassing."

Ellen heard a near giggle in the girl's voice. Tracy always had frivolity just beneath the surface. She was a ticklish person, a jolly girl who liked to find things funny, who more than once had started laughing in the middle of a harsh scolding from her parents, so confident was she of their indulgence. Ellen could recall slapping her—how dare she mock her punishment?—and being glad to see that smirk disappear.

"Embarrassing how?" she asked, skeptical suddenly of the phone call, the tears. *Drama overdrive*, her son would have said. That was Tracy's M.O. She had a long history as a theater major. Even before she'd been in college she was majoring in it, back when no one had majors, just tendencies. She wanted her family members to prove their love; she wanted to sound an alarm in the middle of the night and see them jump. She depended on their willingness to play along.

"Like sex," Tracy said. "You know."

"I *don't* know. Tell me." The cat rolled onto its back on the dining room floor, splayed fat and relaxed, like a smiling drunk. Tracy was talking about her flirtation with her TA. His name was Henry Fielding.

"It is not," Ellen declared.

"It is so."

"Henry *Field*ing?"

"You've heard of him?"

"Tracy," she began, then thought better of it. Had she herself heard of Henry Fielding when she was seventeen? What had she

been doing at seventeen? Why was her daughter supposed to be doing something nobler?

"Everyone else calls him Hank, but I like Henry. Is Daddy really
coming here?"

"Of course he is. You call, he comes."

Tracy laughed, and it turned into tears. Ellen left the cat and
found a chair at the kitchen table, where the two halves of a squeezed
lime lay in a puddle of melted ice. She leaned over the telephone,
creating a pocket in which her ear and her daughter's mouth made
contact. "Sweetie," she said, "what happened?"

"Sometimes it's called 'deliveries in rear.' Coming in the back
door." She paused. "In my bottom?"

"Darling." Ellen shivered. She could not help imagining her
daughter's naked body, there before her as if in time-lapse photography, the grinning chubby baby, the naked little girl splashing in
the bathtub, the adolescent who ran on tiptoe from shower to bedroom with a towel clutched under her arms.

Tracy said, "So that wasn't actually rape, was it?"

"No?"

"No. It was more like . . ."

"Consensual?"

"Not exactly. More like a car wreck. Just. Out of control"

"Okay, honey. Out of control." Ellen fell into the echoing habit
of the shrink. She could be grateful for that simple trick, if nothing
else, from all of her tedious expensive sessions in therapy, all her
attempts to be cured of that ex-lover of hers, that obsession like a
virus, like a new life-form present in her body.

"And he said his waterbed might have had a leak."

"Waterbeds," Ellen recalled. "I thought those days were gone."

"It sloshed. Like being in a boat."

Ellen asked for the whole story. She had only one policy with
this girl: frankness. "I'll be the most angry if you lie." It had seemed
obvious to Ellen: the truth. But many people in fact did not want to
know it. Her husband didn't. He did not want to know that Ellen

loved someone else. He put his money on the wedding ring, on the indisputable evidence that every night he climbed into bed with Ellen, and she with him.

Tracy heaved a monumental sigh, backing up to the beginning of her evening. "First I went to a bar, with some friends. We had to cheer Tiffany up."

Ellen breathed evenly, trying to match her mood to the cat's. Beebee had survived, years and years, just by roaming calmly from room to room, meal to meal, allowing Tracy to come and go, love her and then forget her.

"So when I got to Hank's, I was kinda drunk. I had some beer."

"How did you get to his house?"

"I didn't drive, Mama, I walked. I walked there. It's a guest house behind a real house." Ellen's ex-lover's apartment now transformed into a tiny lighted cottage, and the revision was not unpleasant. What bothered her was her daughter drunk on Albuquerque's Central Avenue, wandering toward that cottage through the traffic and the whores and the roaming wolfish men.

When she got there, Tracy went on, Henry was listening to music.

"What kind?" her mother asked, thinking that this would define him, this movement class TA, his taste in music. But what kind would save him in her eyes? Classical? Jazz? Polka?

"I have no idea, some stuff, you know, like *guitars*. Henry's allergic to smoke, and I stank like the bar," Tracy went on. "You know how you stink after a bar?" As if she and her mother were now confidantes at the dorm, hanging their smelly clothing out the windows to air, hoping their underpants wouldn't wind up on the lawn below. Shouldn't a mother reprimand a girl who was four years too young to be at a bar? But where could she begin, with this reprimand? She herself had been to bars underage, to the homes of professors and married men, to the apartment of her ex-lover, and not so long ago. Ellen tossed the soggy limes into the sink and wiped her hand over the puddle, as if to erase her own evening of

drink. "So I took off my clothes and showered." They'd been flirting with each other in class, she reported. He was shy, awkward,
far from home, which was that famous daunting place, "Back East,"
a recent theater major himself, and he wanted to be an actor. An
actor! And she wanted to sing. Like that maternal grandmother
of hers, Tracy had an astonishingly strong voice, rising from her
ample chest, which housed her extraordinary heart. How could
Henry Fielding be worthy of that heart, Ellen wondered? Only her
husband was worthy, only Tracy's father. Again she featured him,
behind the wheel, completely untutored on the complexity of this
so-called rape. He was acquiring rage as he drove.

"Henry lended me one of his shirts. He wears these great old
button shirts . . ." *Lended?* What had happened to the SAT champ
they'd sent to college a semester early? "And then," Tracy continued, "then we started to kiss." She would have smelled like his Ivory
soap, her mother imagined. Boys often had Ivory soap, unperfumed,
familiar. His shower would be so ill-equipped that Tracy would
have had to use the soap on her hair, that thick wavy Italian hair
inherited from her grandmother. Ellen knew exactly how that hair
looked, damp. The tips of it saturated and dripping, like paint from
a brush, steady trails of water sliding down her cheek. She had beautiful plump purple lips, a gorgeous soprano singing voice, a quirky
sense of humor. She turned her eyes toward the people she loved, as
guileless and faithful as a puppy. She was a solid slow-moving girl,
heavy and sexy, her body utterly different from her mother's, her
nature sweeter, her keel evener, that sly funny girl. Yet innocent.
Would Henry Fielding have recognized her innocence, despite her
acting skill, her mature voice, her cleverness?

"He cooks," Tracy said, as if just to keep the line from going
silent for too long. "He likes to cook, a lot, he says. Like Dad. Remember when Lonnie said Dad's cooking all tasted like underarm
sweat?"

"Yes," Ellen said. She swelled at the memory. She loved her son
more purely than the others she loved. He'd told his father the food

tasted like underarm sweat, it was true, but it hadn't been an insult, just an observation. That was only one of the million things Ellen loved about Lonnie.

"I liked most of the sex," Tracy said as if reviewing a meal or movie. "It didn't hurt as much as I thought it would, the regular part."

"This was the first time?"

"Duh." Ellen, of course, would have been informed if it were otherwise.

"He *knew* it was the first time?"

"No. I lied." Now Tracy was crying again, the hiccuping variety of crying that would leave her eyes plumlike. Dark as she was, the underside of Tracy's eyes were nearly black, like her grandmother's. These shadows made her look older, wiser, than she was. She could fool bartenders and TAs with the bruisy rings beneath her eyes.

"I lied the other way, when I first had sex," Ellen said speculatively.

"Really?" Tracy snuffled. "You were nineteen, right? And the first time Daddy had sex he was fourteen."

"I'd forgotten that." She wasn't sure she'd ever known it.

"But I wonder, did anyone ever . . . does everyone have to . . ."

"Anal sex?" Ellen stalled while waiting for an answer to occur to her. What was the answer? *All men want it.* "I don't know a single woman who enjoys it," she said.

"I can see why," Tracy said, and then burst out afresh. Ellen let her. All those years ago, when she herself had been in college, calling home, her mother would never have let the line go unoccupied this way, silence and tears, dead air. In those days, with that generation, one was always aware of the ticking long-distance meter, the phone bill, the expense, the simple unease of intimate discussion, over the phone—or even in person. Her own mother absolutely refused to accept the human traits that weren't virtuous. She did not allow them in her loved ones. Ellen listened to her daughter cry with a kind of pride; she would let her cry for hours, if need be, hundreds of dollars' worth of tears.

"He didn't mean to put his penis there!" Tracy exclaimed. "It slipped, I think. He was confused," she sobbed. Oh, the confused penis, the slippage, the proximity of those two apertures, the slick bodies in the dark, the heated excitement of love, or its possible beginning. They were at sea in a leaky waterbed, it was a storm, an emergency, he'd made a mistake. Or not. If not, he was rough, unkind, piratical, dangerous. If not, then he did not care for Tracy, neither her pain nor her pleasure. Ellen didn't want to think of her daughter having sex at all, let alone painful sex, ambiguous sex. That body had been under Ellen's purview for a few years; she had been an exemplary steward. Who was this boy to use it so?

"It hurt, Mama, it hurt so bad."

Ellen involuntarily squeezed the muscles of her own but-tocks. *Sphincter*, she thought. She had no idea what to advise for her daughter's pain; whatever the damage, something as straight-forward as stitches was not the answer. Ellen could see the dorm room, its view of a nearby smokestack, the wheat fields, the little city at night. Except that had been her own dorm room, from twenty years ago, in winter, in Kansas. Freshman loneliness: it struck her with the force of a blow to the stomach. Loneliness never stopped stunning her; it was a lesson to learn again and again. "Baby, what can I do? I wish I could . . ." She wished she could take her pain, drain it from Tracy and absorb it herself. That was how her children's suffering always wounded her, her inability to suffer it for them.

"It's more psychological than . . . whatever," Tracy responded, "you know, else."

Ellen's head hurt. She had a hangover, she realized. Her daugh-ter's phone call had distracted her from it, but now it claimed her suddenly in a wash of dizzy nausea. Her own past evening was com-ing back: drinks, sex, passing out. Water, she thought, she needed water and a white slice of soft bread and some ibuprofen and a hot wet washcloth on her forehead. "Baby, did you bleed?" she asked, as she went in search of the components of her cure.

"A little," Tracy said.

"And do you still hurt, now?"

"Yeah. Two different kinds of hurts. I'm lying on my stomach, on my bed." She paused. "He used condoms," she added.

"Good," Ellen said, woozy at the use of the plural.

"Condoms *are* good," Tracy agreed. She was a girl who'd been educated early about their virtues, carrying one in her backpack since tenth grade, just in case.

Tipping the phone away from her mouth, swallowing water, Ellen thought, Hangover is crapulence. She thought of that word often on Sunday mornings, which this morning was. Sunday. *Crapulence*. It was the perfect word.

"I feel yucky," Tracy said. "I feel all wrong."

"Turn on the television," Ellen recommended. "TV is familiar." She headed now to the living room, to the enormous screen on which the family had watched movies the way their ancestors had sat in the glow of a hearth fire, communing. "Turn on Jack Hanna, honey." Wouldn't his golly-gee voice be a kind of comfort? Everything amazed and excited him: he was perpetually pleasantly surprised, like a kid. And *shouldn't* surprises be pleasant? Poor Tracy, with her bad date and awful surprise. "Liquor in the front, poker in the rear," Ellen recalled, a once-funny pun. "Jack Hanna's talking to elks," she said, watching the animals swing through the woods, knocking into trees with their heavy racks of antlers. A hangover felt like that, she thought, like a rack of antlers.

"I don't have cable," Tracy said flatly, "and Jack Hanna is dumb."

"Many men are dumb," her mother said. "But he's harmless, which a lot of men are not."

"Henry Fielding didn't even know how to get blood out of sheets," Tracy said. "That's how dumb he was. He was going to use hot water."

Ellen tried not to envision her daughter's blood on some boy's sheets. Ellen had spent a summer changing sheets, cleaning hotel rooms, in high school. People abandoned everything in hotel rooms: shame. Decency. Vomit. Pubic hairs. Leftover drugs, drink, food, clothing. She'd once pulled open a set of drapes over a large plate glass patio window to reveal a huge shattered piece of glass, cracked and distorted, appalling in its shocking violent intactness. But, mostly, at that hotel were the beds with bodily fluids on them, urine, semen, saliva, blood. The blood had never been enough to signal a murder. Just enough to suggest pain. A humiliation of some degree. The virginal. The menstrual. The reluctant anus. Ellen had wrapped them all into bundles, stuffed them deep into a trolley she would deposit downstairs, where the Mexican illegals would apply bleach. Onto those beds Ellen spread clean sheets, crisp and creased, tucked at the corners the way her mother had taught her, a neat fold like a sealed white envelope waiting to be undone.

"What will I tell Daddy?" Tracy said. "I don't want to tell Daddy about all this."

"Your father loves you," Ellen said, which was supposed to mean that Tracy could tell him anything.

"He'll think I'm a slut," Tracy cried.

"No, honey. No." But Ellen knew, as Tracy did, that her father would not be able to bear the details. "Just tell him it was the first time you had sex. He'll understand that. You don't have to lie about feeling upset. You are upset."

"I don't want to lie at all!"

"It's not lying to not tell him everything." That was Ellen's gift to her husband; she had saved him with it before. Listening to Tracy sniffle, Ellen was tempted to tell her daughter that her father loved her more than he loved anyone else. Was Tracy ready for that piece of parental honesty? To hear also that Ellen loved Lonnie that same way, *more*? Better? At what point was this blunt information fair game for her daughter? Her husband would never admit that he loved Tracy best. How could he admit something he didn't even know?

Ellen knew it for him.

"You and Daddy met in college," Tracy pleaded. "He was *your* TA."

"That's true."

"I want to meet someone, I wanted to, I thought . . ."

"You will." Would she? Ellen wondered. "You probably will, someone like Daddy. Someone who loves you."

"I know he loves me," Tracy said, "but I don't want him to know what happened."

"I understand," Ellen said. She walked once more to her son's room. There he lay, sprawled, wearing boxer shorts and a T-shirt in bed, just the way his father did. In the fly lay his boy's penis. He had one, his father had one, Henry Fielding had one. They got hard and wanted to fit somewhere. They had the power to harm. They stood out like vulnerable targets. A woman had cut her husband's off, thrown it in the street. There it must have lain, rootless and forsaken as a toadstool.

"Hear Lonnie snoring?" Ellen whispered.

"You know what, Mama?" Tracy whispered back. "Henry Fielding reminds me a little bit of Lonnie."

How could her heart not soften at that news? Her lover had reminded her of Lonnie, too.

"Yeah," Tracy went on dreamily, "you know, he has these clumsy big feet."

Ellen sighed. Her son was the one who had kept her from abandoning everything a few years earlier. He was a funny boy, prickly, eccentric, tearful one minute, punch-drunk the next. It didn't surprise Ellen to hear that Tracy had been attracted to a boy like her brother. Her son could someday make a mistake, put his penis someplace wrong, end up crying. Ellen's eyes filled. For Lonnie, for Tracy, for herself and her husband, for that lost lover, even for Henry Fielding, no doubt.

Ellen considered fixing herself a drink. The clock read 5:03. Never had she had a drink at this hour of the day. She'd had them at

4 A.M., and she'd had them at 9:00 A.M., but never at five in the morning. It was both too late and too early. Why not? she thought. This was what her bartender Paco said instead of "yes." "Why not?" in a bright exclamatory. Ellen adored her bartender. She visited him every evening, just the way her father had *his* bartender, when she was young. She and her father needed escape from the innocence that was their spouse—her mother, her husband, the placating good-hearted. Only a smoky bar would do, some days. If it were 5:00 P.M., that's where she would be headed.

"Mama," Tracy said now. It had been her first word, way back when. The next had been "Daddy."

"Baby."

Ellen returned to her bedroom. She had switched off the lights and muted Jack Hanna, and now settled her sore head on her pillow, daughter beside her. The cat jumped onto her feet and walked up her blanketed thighs.

"Now it'll be all weird in class," Tracy said forlornly. "It's not fair." She sounded weary, depleted, capable of falling into an exhausted sleep.

"No, it's not fair." This was what college would teach Tracy. It was, after all, the only lesson, and some people never learned it.

LANDFILL

Joyce Carol Oates

Joyce Carol Oates is a recipient of the National Book Award and the PEN/Malamud Award for Short Fiction. She has written some of the most enduring fiction of our time, including the national bestsellers *We Were the Mulvaneys*; *Blonde*, which was nominated for the National Book Award; and the *New York Times* bestseller *The Falls*, which won the 2005 Prix Femina. She is the Roger S. Berlind Distinguished Professor of the Humanities at Princeton University and has been a member of the American Academy of Arts and Letters since 1978. In 2003 she received the Common Wealth Award for Distinguished Service in Literature, and in 2006 she received the Chicago Tribune Lifetime Achievement Award.

Tioga County landfill is where Hector, Jr. is found. "Remains" buried in rubble, trash, raw garbage. Battered and badly decomposed and mouth filled with trash. Couldn't have protested if he'd been alive, buried in trash. Overhead, shrieking birds. In the vast landfill, dump trucks and bulldozers and a search team from the Tioga County Sheriff's Department in protective uniforms. Three weeks missing, in all the newspapers and TV. Most of his teeth broken at the roots but those that remain are sufficient to identify Hector Campos, Jr. of Southfield, Michigan. Nineteen years old, freshman engineering student, Michigan State University at Grand Rapids reported missing by his dormitory roommates in the late afternoon of Monday, March 27 but said to have been last seen around 2 A.M. of Saturday, March 25 in the parking lot behind the Phi Epsilon fraternity house on Pitt Avenue, Grand Rapids. And now in the early morning of April 17 Mrs. Campos who never sleeps answers the phone on the first ring. These terrible weeks her son has been missing, Mrs. Campos has answered the phone many times and made many calls as her husband has made many calls and now the call from the Tioga County Sheriff's Department they have been awaiting and dreading *Mrs. Campos? Are you seated? Is your husband there?* Mrs. Campos is not seated but standing uncertain and barefoot only partly clothed, shivering and her hair matted and eyes glazed, mouth tasting of scum from the hateful medication that has not helped her sleep, Mr. Campos, hurriedly descending the stairs close by, heavy-footed, in rumpled boxer shorts and sweated-through undershirt, says *Irene, what is it? Who is it? Give me that phone* rudely prying her icy fingers off the receiver Tioga County landfill, medical examiner, morgue. Identification, death certification. Approximately eighty miles from the Campos home: how quickly can Mr. and Mrs. Campos drive to the morgue to corroborate the identification?—except of course the body has "badly decomposed" and so at the morgue Mr. Campos views the body alone staring through a plate-glass partition that emits no smell while Mrs. Campos in a state of terror waits in another room. *Remains!* What is this strange, unfathomable word— *remains!* Mrs. Campos whispers aloud: "*Remains.*" She seems to have stumbled into a restroom, white-tiled walls, door locked behind her and the light switch triggering a fierce overhead fan releasing freezing antiseptic air. Why is Irene Campos here, why has this happened? Is this a public restroom? Where? Elsewhere, Mr. Campos observes the "remains" laid upon a table beneath glaring lights, most of the body shielded by a sheet so that only the head, or what remains of the head, is exposed. How is it possible, these "remains" are Hector, Jr. who'd once weighed one-seventy-five pounds of solid flesh just slightly soft at the waist, like his father Hector, Sr. squat-bodied, short-legged, with thick thighs, a wrestler's build (except Hector, Jr. who'd wrestled for Southfield High in his senior year had not made the wrestling team at Grand Rapids), five-feet-nine with wiry dark hair growing forward on his head, a low forehead, what remains now of Hector, Jr. could not weigh more than ninety pounds yet at once his father recognizes him, the shock of it like an electric current piercing his heart, the battered and mutilated and partially eaten-away face, the empty eye sockets, Oh God it is Hector: his son. Mr. Campos can barely murmur yes, turns away hunched and quivering with pain, yes that is Hector, Jr. Never the same man again, a man who has lost his son, his soul catheterized telling his anxious wife *Don't ask, don't speak to me please* even as Mrs. Campos loses control despite the medication she has been taking *Are you sure it's our son, I want to see him, what if there's a mistake, a tragic mistake, you know you make mistakes, why would Hector be in that terrible place, how has this happened, how has God let this happen, I want to see our son.* Hector, Jr. : called by school friends "Heck"—"Scoot." Within the Campos family, sometimes called "Junior" (which the boy came to hate, as soon as he was old enough to register the indignity) and sometimes "Little Guy" (until the age of twelve when Hector, Jr., chubby-solid at one hundred twenty pounds, five feet five, wasn't any longer what one would call little), more often just "Hector" even as his father was "Dad" within the family, or, less often, "James" (his baptismal name was Hector James Campos). Away at college Hector, Jr. was called "Hector" by his teachers, "Scoot" by his friends, "Campos" by the older Phi Epsilons he so admired and wished to emulate. *Campos was an O.K. guy, a good guy, great sense of humor, terrific Phi Ep spirit. Of the pledges, Campos was, like, the most loyal. Seems like a tragedy, a weird accident what happened to him but it didn't happen at the frat house, for sure.* On the Hill partying begins Thursday night, mostly you blow off your Friday classes which for "Scoot" Campos were classes he'd gotten into the habit of cutting: Intro Electrical Engineering taught by a foreigner (Indian? Pakistani? whatever) who spoke a rapid heavily accented English that baffled and offended the sensitive ears of certain Michigan-born students including Hector Campos, Jr. whose midterm exam was returned to him with the blunt red numeral 71, translating C-; and Intro Computer Technology in which, though the course was taught by a Caucasian-American male who spoke crisp clear English and though Hector, Jr. never got less than A- in his computer classes at Southfield High, here he was pulling C, C-, D+. *Probably yes Scoot had been drinking that night, maybe more than he could handle, not in the dorm here but over at the frat house, weekends he'd come back to the room here pretty wasted and, yes that was kind of a problem for us, but basically Scoot was a good kid just maybe in over his head a little, freshman engineering can be tough if you don't have the math and even if you do.* His roommates in Brest Hall reported him missing, finally late Monday afternoon they'd guessed something might be wrong, called the frat house but no answer, Scoot's things exactly as he'd left them sometime Saturday afternoon, it wasn't like Scoot to stay over at the frat house on a Sunday night, or through Monday, he was only just a pledge and didn't have a bed there, and he had four classes Monday he'd missed, had to be something was wrong. And weeks later signing forms in the Tioga County Morgue as through the twenty-two years of their marriage Mr. and Mrs. Campos have signed so many forms, mortgage papers, bank loans, home owners' insurance, life insurance, medical insurance, their son's college-loan application at Midland Michigan Bank. Hector Campos, Sr., one of the reliably high-performing salespersons at Southfield Chrysler, at least until recently, lies sleepless in his king-sized bed in the white-gleaming aluminim-sided colonial at 23 Quail Circle, Whispering Woods Estates of Southfield, Michigan as his wife sleeps beside him warmly fleshy and oblivious of his misery as by day Mrs. Campos is oblivious or in any case indifferent to her husband's misery, thoughts racing like panicked ants, his head hot and heavy ringing with the crazed demand for money, more money, always more money, more than you've computed, Mr. Campos!—more than the sum quoted by the university admissions office for tuition/room-and-board/text-books, "fees" for fraternity rush, for fraternity pledging, a star-tling high fee (payable in advance, Hector, Jr. has said) for fraternity initiation upcoming in May. *Send the check to me, Dad. Make it out to Phi Epsilon Fraternity, Inc. and send it to me, Dad. Please!* Mrs. Campos, lonely since Hector, Jr. has gone away to college if only seventy miles away, has taken up the campaign, excited and reproachful. Mrs. Campos is fierce in support of her son, pleads and argues, if you refuse Hector you will shame him in the eyes of his friends, you will break his heart, you know how hard he worked this summer, it isn't Hector's fault he couldn't earn as much as he'd hoped, you know how much a university education costs these days, even a state school like Grand Rap-ids, if you refuse him you will destroy him, this fraternity Pi Episom, Pi Epsilom?—this fraternity means more to Hector than anything else in his life right now, more even than the wrestling team, more even than that girl from Bloomfield Hills, this is Hector's new life, if you refuse him he will never forgive you *and I will never forgive you.* Yet: Mr. Campos gave in only when Mrs. Campos threatened to borrow the fifteen hundred dollars from her parents, suddenly then Mr. Campos gave in, disgusted, defeated, as so often through the years of a man's marriage, if he wishes to preserve the marriage, he gives in. *Married for love, does that mean for life? Can love prevail, through life?* Six months later in the chilled antiseptic air of the Tioga County medical examiner's office Mr. and Mrs. Campos are co-signing documents in triplicate that will release the "remains" of Hector Campos, Jr. for burial (in St. Joseph's Cemetery, South-field) after the medical examiner has filed his final report. Still, Mrs. Campos is stunned slow-speaking and her eyes shadowed in exhaustion blinking tears appealing to whoever will listen in

a reasonable voice *Must be some terrible mistake, a terrible accident, how did this happen, God help us to understand, why?* The
police investigation has yet to determine: had Hector died in
the early hours of March 25 in the steep-sided dumpster behind the Phi Epsilon frat house at 228 Pitt Avenue a few blocks
from the university campus where stains and swaths of blood
(identified as the blood of Hector Campos, Jr.) were discovered
in the interior of the trash bin as if made by wild-thrashing
bloody wings or had Hector died hours later, as long as forty-
eight hours later, deeply unconscious, possibly comatose from
brain injuries dying as late as Monday morning hauled away
unseen amid mounds of trash, cans, bottles, Styrofoam and
cardboard packages, rancid raw garbage, stained and filthy
clothing, paper towels soaked in vomit, urine, even feces,
dumped into the rear of the thunderous Tioga County Sanita-
tion Dept. truck at approximately 6:45 A.M. of March 27, from
228 Pitt Avenue hauled sixteen miles north of the city of Grand
Rapids to the Packard Road recycling transfer station to be
compacted amid tons of trash, rubble, raw garbage and subsequently hauled away to be dumped in the Tioga County landfill, a gouged, misshapen, ever-shifting landscape of trash-hills,
ravines and valleys, amid a grinding of dump trucks, bulldozers, cries of swooping and darting birds. These long-winged
birds, some of them gulls, some of them starlings, red-winged
blackbirds and crows, graceless turkey vultures, in a perpetual
frenzy of appetite and plunder. "Foul play" is not at the present
time suspected the Tioga County sheriff has said, carefully the
sheriff has explained that "foul play" has not been entirely
ruled out as a possibility, though the medical examiner has determined that the "massive injuries" to the body of Hector
Campos, Jr. are "compatible" with injuries that would have
been caused by the trash-compacting process. Yet a more complete autopsy may yield new information. Yet the police investigation will continue. And the university administration will

convene an investigating committee. As many as one hundred college students have been interviewed, Hector's roommates, classmates, Phi Epsilon pledges and brothers, even Hector's professors who take care to speak of him in neutral terms befitting one who has suffered a terrible but inexplicable—and blameless—fate. *Jesus! You have to hope that the poor bastard died right away, smashed out of his mind diving down the trash chute into the dumpster like breaking his neck on contact and never woke up.* Had Hector Campos, Jr. been "compacted" while alive no one wished to speculate, except police investigators. No one wished to contemplate. Before the discovery of the body in the landfill and the identification of the "remains" during the strain, anxiety, insomniac misery of the three-week search it was perceived how the mother of the missing boy never gave up hope, fierce and frantic with hope, a model mother, prayer vigils at St. Joseph's Church, family, relatives, neighbors, parish members, lighted votive candles, for God is a God of mercy as well as wrath, hiding her face in prayer, *God let Hector return to us, send Hector back to us, Hail Mary full of Grace the Lord is with thee blessed art thou among women pray for us sinners now and at the hour of our death Amen.* Angry that the medical examiner has released the autopsy report, "elevated" degree of alcohol in Hector, Jr.'s blood, "more than twice the legal limit" for driving a motor vehicle, both Mrs. Campos and her husband deny that their son had a drinking problem, not once had they seen their son drunk, if something happened to Hector at the fraternity party where were his friends, to help him? Why did his friends abandon him? Mrs. Campos is angry too with Mr. Campos who betrayed their son by giving in, after bloodstains were discovered in and near the dumpster, Mr. Campos is too quickly resigned to the worst, most terrible news a man can bear, in Hector, Sr.'s face that look of defeat, fury turned inward like cancer. *Why'd they wait so long. That call. Why hadn't anyone at the fraternity seen that Hector was missing, or might have needed help, where were his friends, why hadn't the search begun earlier!* Hector might have been still alive in the dumpster, those hours, injured and unconscious, but living, breathing, his life might have been saved. Mrs. Campos lives, relives, will forever relive the shock of that call out of nowhere: a male voice, identifying the caller as an assistant dean at the university. And Mrs. Campos says *Yes? Yes I am Hector's mother* drawing a quick short breath *Is something wrong?* In weak sick moments reliving the possibility of a phone call, bearing different news. The possibility of subsequent phone calls, bearing different news. For it is crucial, these days, these interminable stretches of (insomniac, openeyed, exhausted) time, to believe that Hector is alive, our son is alive, *he is alive!*—having only to shut your eyes to see him, Hector as he'd looked when he'd come home for a few days the previous month, his frowning smile, such a handsome boy, Mrs. Campos must always tell him how handsome he is, Hector has hated his "fat face" since puberty, his "beak nose," his "ape forehead, taking after Dad," Mrs. Campos winces at such words, pulls at Hector's hands when, unconsciously, he digs and picks at his nose, any serious discussion between them must be initiated by Mrs. Campos and then apologetically for her son so quickly takes offense, *Jesus Mom lighten up will you, you and Dad bugging me all the time, must've missed your call, what's the big deal, this crappy cell phone you bought me.* And Mrs. Campos cries *But I love you! We love you* but her words are muffled, she's sweating and thrashing in her sleep the nightmare has not lifted. Must keep the flame alive these terrible days, weeks. At Easter Sunday mass kneeling at the communion rail shivering in anticipation, shutting her eyes tight but this time seeing Hector, Jr.'s grimace, how he'd hated going to church, in recent years he'd refused altogether, even midnight mass on Christmas Eve he'd refused, Mrs. Campos had been so ashamed, so hurt, now kneeling at the

communion rail hiding her hot-skinned face in her hands
that feel like ice, ice-claws, blue veins on the backs of her
hands like the hands of an elderly woman, Mrs. Campos's
numbed lips are moving rapidly in prayer, dazed and desperate in prayer, snatching at prayer as you'd snatch at something to clutch, to grasp, to grip to keep your balance, the
tranquillizers she's been taking have affected her balance,
her sense of her (physical) self, numbness in her mouth, in
her head, buzzing in her head *Please help us please help us
please do not abandon us in our hour of need*, blindly she lifts
her head as the elderly priest makes his way to her, Mrs. Campos is next, craning her neck like a starving bird opening her
beak-mouth to take the doughy white communion wafer on
her tongue, how dry Mrs. Campos's tongue, how dry Mrs.
Campos's mouth, scum coating the interior of Mrs. Campos's mouth *This is my body, and this is my blood*. Half-fainting
then in ill-chosen patent leather pumps staggering away
from the communion rail, into the aisle, all eyes fixed upon
the heavily made-up woman with so clearly dyed-dark-red
hair, a middle-aged fleshiness to her face, bruise-like circles
beneath her eyes, quickly there comes Mr. Campos to help
the dazed-swaying woman back to the family pew, fingers
gripping her arm at the elbow. Hector Campos, Sr.! Father of
the missing boy! Swarthy-skinned, with dark wiry forward-
growing hair, low forehead criss-crossed with lines, large
oddly simian ears protruding from the sides of his head, a
grim set to the man's mouth, a flush of indignation, impatience as Mrs. Campos confusedly struggles with him as if to
wrench her arm out of his grip, as if Mr. Campos is hurting
her, making her wince, in the car driving home Mrs. Campos
will dissolve into hysteria screaming *You don't have faith!
You've given up faith, I hate you!* For it's crucial to believe, as
Mrs. Campos believes: nearly three weeks after Hector, Jr.
has "disappeared," he might yet be found, unharmed; might

yet call his anxious parents, after so many days of (inexplicably) not calling; might turn up at home, you know how
adolescents are, returning to surprise them on Easter Sunday, waiting in the house, in the kitchen, eating from the
refrigerator, when they return from St. Joseph's; or, somehow Hector has been injured and is "amnesiac"; or, has
been "abducted" but will escape his captor or be released
by his captor; has been wandering, drifting, who knows
where, hitch-hiking, left the university without telling anyone, quarreled with someone, he's upset, problems with a
girl, a girl he'd never told his parents about as he'd never
told them much about his personal life since sophomore
year of high school, since he'd put on weight, grew several
inches, became so involved with weight-lifting, and then
with wrestling, the fanatic weight-obsession of wrestling,
fasting, binge-eating, fasting, binge-eating, and maybe the
Phi Epsilons were putting pressure on Hector, maybe he
was made to feel inferior among the pledges, calling his
mother to say how crappy he felt never having enough
money, the other guys had money, *he* didn't, how shitty he
was made to feel, if the fraternity dropped him, didn't initi-
ate him with the other pledges, he'd kill himself, he would
he swore he'd kill himself!—and Mrs. Campos pleading
*Please don't say such terrible things, you don't mean what you
are saying, you are breaking my heart.* Mrs. Campos blames
Mr. Campos for coercing Hector into engineering, such
difficult courses, who could excell at such difficult courses,
it's no wonder that Hector has been so lonely, away from
home for the first time in his life. None of his Southfield
High friends were at Grand Rapids. His classes were too
large, his professors scarcely knew him. Twelve thousand
undergraduates at Grand Rapids. Three hundred residents
in ugly high-rise Brest Hall where poor Hector shared a
room with two other guys—"Reb" and "Steve"—who in

Hector's words "didn't go out of their way" to be friendly to him. In turn, Hector's roommates spoke vaguely, evasively, cautiously of him, when interviewed by Tioga County sheriff's deputies *Didn't know Scoot too well, kind of kept to himself, kind of obsessed about things, like the wrestling team last fall, he tried out but didn't make it but the coach encouraged him to try again he said so he was hopeful, you had to care a lot about Scoot's interests that's all he wanted to talk about in kind of a fast nervous way and he'd be like laughing, interrupting himself laughing, and, like, it was hard to talk to him, y'know? Fraternity rush was a crazed time for Scoot, he was really happy when he got a bid from the Phi Ep's, he'd had his heart set on that house and was really proud of his pledge pin and looking forward, he said, to living in the frat house next year if his dad OK'd it. Because there was some money issue, maybe. Or maybe it was Scoot's grades. He was having kind of a meltdown with Intro Electrical Engineering, also his computer course, some of the guys on the floor he'd ask for help which was mostly O.K— you had to feel sorry for him—but then Scoot would get kind of weird, and sarcastic, like we were trying to screw him up, telling him wrong things, there were times Scoot wouldn't speak to us and stayed away from the room and over at the frat house, hanging out there, Phi Ep's are known for their keg parties, kind of wild-party guys, there aren't many engineering majors up there on the Hill, anyway not in the Phi Ep house.* At 228 Pitt Street is a large, three-story Victorian house, a small mansion with peeling gunmetal-gray paint, moss growing in rain-gutters, rotting turrets, steep shingled roofs in need of repair. The Phi Epsilon house dates back to the early decades of the twentieth century when the Hill was Grand Rapids's most prestigious residential neighborhood, now the Hill is known as Fraternity Row, and Phi Epsilon exudes an air both derelict and defiant, its enormous metallic-silver Day-Glo ΦE above a listing portico. Scrub grass grows in the stunted front yard. Vehicles are parked in the cracked asphalt driveway, in the asphalt parking lot at the rear, in the weedy front yard and at the curb. Often, the dumpster at the rear of the house overflows and trash lies scattered at its base. It's a feature of the Phi Epsilon house that, warm weather or cold, its windows are likely to be flung open to emit high-decibel rock music, particularly at night; and that, out of the flung-open windows, begrimed and frayed curtains blow in the wind. Inside the house there's a pervasive odor of stale beer, fried foods, cigarette smoke, vomit and urine. The high-ceilinged rooms are sparely furnished with battered leather sofas and chairs, the decades-old gifts of alums. On the badly scarred hardwood floors are threadbare filth-stained carpets, on the walls torn and discolored wallpaper. Brass chandeliers have grown black with tarnish. There are rickety stairs and bannisters, gouged wood paneling, in the dining room a long battered table gouged by initials like fossil traces. In the basement is the enormous party room running the width of the house, with a stained linoleum floor, more battered leather furniture, leprous-green mold growing on the walls and ceiling, intensified odors. Scattered through the house are filth-splotched lavatories, in a room beyond the party room is an ancient, rattling oil furnace. For several years in the 1990s Phi Epsilon fraternity had been "suspended" from the university for having violated a number of campus and city ordinances: underage/illegal drinking on the premises, keg parties in the front yard, "operating a public nuisance," sexual assaults against young women and high-school-age girls and even, during a secret initiation ceremony in 1995, against a Phi Epsilon pledge who'd had to be rushed to a local emergency room with "rectal hemorrhaging." Bankrupt from fines, lawsuits, and a dwindling membership,

the fraternity had gone off-campus until in 1999 a group
of aggressive alums led by a Michigan state congressman
campaigned to get it reinstated, but by 2006 the fraternity
hadn't yet regained its pre-suspension numbers, with an
estimated twenty-six actives of whom one-third were on
academic probation. In the rush season that Hector Campos, Jr. became a pledge, the fraternity had needed at least
seventeen pledges; instead, only eight young men accepted bids: Zwaaf, Scherer, Tickler, Tuozzolo, Vreasy,
Feibush, Herker, Krampf, and Campos. Of these only the
first three were first-choices of the fraternity, the others
were accepted for practical, pragmatic reasons: to help fill
the membership. Hector "Scoot" Campus knew nothing
of this of course. None of the pledges knew of course.
Though drinking, you know how guys are when they're
drinking, it might've been, nobody can recall exactly,
might've been Herker's "big brother" who was pissed off
at Scoot Campos falling-down drunk belligerent and
more than usual asshole-behaving, who'd told Campos he
wasn't anybody's first-choice, for sure. *Fuck fuck you fuckhead* the guys yelled at each other, lurched at each other,
or maybe none of this happened, or didn't happen in this
way, interviewed by the Tioga County investigators none
of the guys would remember, or would say. *First we knew
Scoot was missing, it's the dean calling. Nobody knew he was
missing here. Must've gone back to his dorm and something
happened there or maybe he never went back. But whatever
happened to him didn't happen here.* Mrs. Campos tries to
take pride in this fact: Mr. Campos brought his family
from Detroit to live in the suburb of Southfield, in a white
aluminum-sided four-bedroom colonial at 23 Quail Circle
and no one in Irene Campos's family has so beautiful a
house, not her sisters, not her cousins, and no one in Mr.
Campos's family has so beautiful a house, living out their

lives on lower Dequindre, in mostly-black Detroit where for thirty-five years Cesar Campos worked for Gratiot Construction & Roofing, squatted and stooped on roofs in the blazing sun and drove a truck for the company, cement truck, dump truck hauling rubble from construction sites until his back gave out, died of heart failure at only sixty-seven, Irene Campos is terrified seeing in her husband's face the defeated look of the old father, resigned always to the worst, it's the peasant soul, bitter in resignation, dying before his time. *He has given up, he has lost hope we will see our son again, I will never forgive him*. But Mrs. Campos continues to have faith, just look at her! How many times she has called her son's cell phone though knowing Hector, Jr.'s cell phone was no longer in operation, no one knew where it was. (In the vast Tioga County landfill amid tons of rubble. Very likely. Where else?—Hector, Jr. kept his cell phone in the back pocket of his jeans, and that part of his clothing was torn from him.) *Mutations are the key to natural selection* he'd learned in Intro to Biology, his science-requirement course said to be the easiest of the science-requirement courses but Hector, Jr. wasn't finding it so easy, barely maintaining a C-average. *Natural selection is the key to evolution and survival* he'd written in wavering ballpoint fighting to keep his eyelids open, so very tired, wasted from the previous night, hanging out with the guys, he was trying to concentrate, unshaven and fattish smelling of his body, a taste of beer and pizza dough coming up on him even now hours later, *genes are the key to change, evolution is only possible through change, species change not by free will but blindly*. No idea what this meant, what any of the words meant. What the lecturer was saying. If words were balloons these words were floating up to bounce against the ceiling of the windowless fluorescent-lit lecture hall, collide with one another and drift about, stupidly. Would've used his laptop except his fucking laptop wasn't working right. E-mail seemed to be frozen, why's that? *No purpose only just chance, the pattern of scout-ants seeking food would look to a viewer like "intelligent design" but is really the result of the random haphazard trails of ants blindly seeking food.* Ants? No idea what the hell this guy's droning on about like it matters Jesus he's so bored!—thirsty for a beer, his throat is parched. Checks his cell and there's the text message sinking his heart PLEASE CALL MOM DARLING and with a stab of annoyance erases the message *What looks like "intelligent design" is merely random. Instinct and not intelligence any questions?* Meant to call his mother but Jesus why doesn't that woman get a life of her own, it's pledge-party weekend, Scoot Campos has other priorities. The girl he'd been planning to take to the party sent an e-mail something's come up, bitch he knew he couldn't trust, a girl one of the Phi Ep guys hooked him up with last time says thanks but she's out of town starting Friday, Scoot is damned disappointed, depressed, what's he going to have to do, pay for it? *Kind of earnest and boring when he was, like, sober, you got the impression Campos hadn't a clue how totally uninterested people were in things he'd talk about, the frat house, wrestling, his opinions on his courses, girls, me and Steve liked him O.K. at first it's cool we got a Hispanic roommate, or, what's it—Latino?—that's cool. But Campos, he's just some guy, nothing special about him you could pick up on, except he wanted to hang out with the frat guys, thought we were weird not to sign up for rush, after he pledged he'd start coming back to the room really late, stumbling around drunk like an asshole, mess up in here, piss on the toilet seat and the floor and next day act like it's some goddam joke, that last weekend he didn't come back, truth is that was great. That poor guy you have to feel sorry for but we didn't, much. It's a shitty thing to say, can't tell any adult but we don't miss Scoot. Can't tell anybody, it's, like, speaking ill of the dead, but we're fed up answering questions about him, we told all we know. Fed up with everybody assuming we were friends of his involved somehow, or responsible, fuck it we are not involved, and we are not responsible! And seeing his parents, Mrs. Campos is so sad and so pathetic, trying to smile at me, hugging me, and Steve, like we were Scoot's best friends, it's totally weird to realize that a guy like Scoot Campos, so pathetic, a loser, is somebody that is loved, by somebody.* At the party things were going O.K. in spite of the red-haired girl ditching him first chance she had hooking up with one of the older guys, O.K. Scoot could live with that but later there's some exchange of words, he's hot-faced trying not to show he's pissed at the guys taunting him, O.K. he's laughing to himself crawling—where? Upstairs, where? Can't think, his head is bombarded by deafening rock music, heavy-metal/industrial so high-decibel almost you can't hear it. Some kind of a joke, eager to make the guys laugh to show he isn't hurt by, who was it, that girl, blond girl, little-bitty tits, skinny little ass in jeans so tight it's all you can do not to trace the crack of her ass with your forefinger, maybe in fact somebody did just this, cracking up with laughter, braying belly-laughter so somebody slaps him, punches, kicks and he's on his knees, on his hands and knees crawling, needing to get to a toilet, and fast. Maybe it isn't funny, or—is it? Scoot Campos has fine-honed a reputation at the Phi Ep house as a joker, funniest goddam pledge, the other pledges are losers but Scoot Campos is a wrestler and he's witty, and wired. And good-looking, that kind of

swarthy-sexy Hispanic way, thick oily hair, thick solid
jaws and fleshy mouth. Funny like somebody on Comedy Central except Scoop makes it up himself, impro-
vised. A few beers, tequila, Scoot isn't tongue-tied and
sweating but witty, and wired. Chugging beers with
the guys, must be the ninth—tenth?—hour of the an-
nual pledge party, by coincidence it's Newman's Day
the twenty-fourth of the month named for the actor
Paul Newman, Scoot doesn't know why, nobody knows
why, the challenge is to chug twenty-four beers in some
record time, except at the party there's tequila, too.
Scoot has acquired a taste for tequila! If he'd known
about tequila in fucking high school, might've had a
God damn better time. Trying to remember what it
was, a few weeks ago, some crappy thing, humiliating,
hurt his feelings, middle of midterms he'd fucked up
the engineering exam, he knew, couldn't concentrate
studying for his next exam drinking with some of the
guys over at the frat house and (somehow) fell down
stairs somewhere, he'd been puking, and sort of passed
out, and somebody disgusted dragged him into a bathroom and turned on the shower and left him, and after
a while one of the guys came back and turned off the
shower and by this time Scoot had crawled out onto
the floor flopped over on his back and the guy kicks
him *Hey Campos, hey man how'ya doin* like meaning to
wake him, or turn him over, but did not so Scoot slept
off the drunk soaking wet and shivering in the cold
and next morning when he woke groggy and dazed
with a pounding headache, a taste of vomit in his
mouth, dried vomit all down his front, he'd been lying
flat on his back and had to think with the cruel clarity
of stone-cold sobriety *They left me here, to puke on my
back and choke and die, the fuckers.* His friends! His

fraternity brothers-to-be! Had to think *Never again! Not ever.* Meaning he'd depledge Phi Ep, and he'd stop drinking. But somehow, next weekend he'd come trailing back, couldn't stay away. These guys were his friends, Scoot's only friends. Except tonight, there's some kind of bad feeling again, Scoot's feelings are bruised, fuck he isn't going to show it, of the pledge class "Scoot" Campos is possibly the alums' favorite, he's been given to know. *Ethnic diversity! An idea whose time has come for Phi Epsilon.* At the top of the stairs he's out of breath, can't hold it back God damn is he pissing his pants?—can't help it, can't stop it, how'd this happen, if the girls downstairs learn of Scoot's accident they will be totally grossed-out and who can blame them, the guys are going to be disgusted, not the first time Scoot has pissed his pants too staggering-drunk to lurch to a toilet, or outside on the lawn, or too confused about where he is, if he's awake or in fact asleep, maybe this is a dream, one of those weird dreams it's O.K. to piss, nobody will scold it's O.K. to piss into some receptacle or crack in the floor, that hot wet sensation spreading in his groin, soaking his underwear and down his legs, strong-piss-smelling, quickly turning cold. A piss-trail following Scoot Campos up the stairs soaked into the carpet, he's laughing like a deranged little kid soaked his diaper on purpose, hell the carpets at the Phi Ep house are already (piss?) stained, what's the big deal? *Fuck you* he's saying, defending himself against some guy, or guys, stooping over him, cursing him calling him names, Scoot Campos is wired tonight, he's laughing in their faces, somebody dragging him where?—toward a window?—wide-open windows and curtains sucked outside and blowing/flapping in the rain, and there's a moon, Jesus!—glaring-white moon like a beacon, some kind of crazy eye peering into Scoot Campos's soul *How'ya doin Scoot hey man know what?—you're O.K.* This is God's eye, Scoot thinks. (Or maybe a street light? Outside on Pitt Avenue?) Cursing him somebody is lifting him he's thrashing and flailing his arms, laughing so any remaining dribble of piss is eked out and whoever it is grabbing Scoot in a hammerlock, one of the older-guy wrestlers, built like a tank and taut-jawed and giving off heat and that strong pungent smell of a male body meaning he's in fighting mode, cursing Scoot calling him asshole, dickhead, fuckhead, Scoot is being lifted, pushed into an opening in the wall, it's the trash chute, or maybe (if inadvertent witnesses are watching, from a short distance) the drunken pledge is crawling head-first into the chute of his own volition, and one of the guys grabs his ankles to pull him back, and Scoot is kicking, and yelling, and laughing, at least it sounds like laughter, with this wild-wired spic anything is possible. *Hey guys?—help me?—help me guys?* kicking like crazy so whoever has hold of his ankles has to let go, God damned dangerous Campos when he's been drinking, and Scoot's thick stocky body lurches down the trash chute, sounds like a pig squealing, a kid shooting down a slide in an amusement park, down-the-chute, down-the-chute into something soft to break your fall, at the end of the pitch-black stale-air chute there should be something soft except there isn't, with the impact of one hundred seventy-five pounds Scoot Campos strikes the edge of the trash bin, his forehead strikes the sharp metal edge of the bin, immediately he's bleeding, dazed, a terrible pounding

pain in his head, his neck has been twisted, his
spine, his legs are twisted weirdly beneath him, too
dazed to be panicked not knowing what has happened or where he is feebly he pleads *Hey guys?—
help me?* amid a confusion of rich, ripe, rotting
smells, something rancid, trash and garbage,
upside-down trying to turn, to twist his body
stunned and quivering like a mangled worm, trying to lift his head, to breathe, to open his mouth, a
terrible throbbing pain in his neck, in his upper
spine, like a gasping fish he opens his mouth but no
words, no sounds are uttered, can't call for help his
mouth is filled with trash, his brain shudders, and
is extinguished. For sure the guys will check on
Scoot, make their way downstairs shouting and
laughing like hyenas, craziest damn thing this
drunk pledge smashed out of his head slid down
the trash chute, not the first time a drunken pledge
or active at the Phi Ep house slid down the trash
chute, down into the dumpster, anyway there's the
intention that the guys will check on the pledge in
the dumpster, but amid party noise, a swarm of
people including high-school-age girls heavy-made
up and costumed in hooker mode, high-decibel
music pounding the ears, there's too many distrac-
tions. Later it will be claimed that a couple of guys
did in fact check the dumpster but Campos wasn't
there. Possibly Campos had been bleeding but
couldn't have been hurt seriously because evidently
he'd crawled out of the dumpster and gone away,
back to the dorm maybe, anyway nobody was in the
dumpster when they checked, they swore. Yet, the
guy had a weird sense of humor, everybody would
testify to Scoot Campos's weird sense of humor, he

might've returned and crawled back into the dumpster, like a little kid would do, like hide-and-seek,
except he fell asleep there, or he'd hurt his head and
passed out, and got covered in party trash, had to
be some freak accident like that, what other explanation is there? As Scoot's brain is bleeding, as
Scoot's mouth is filling with trash, as Scoot's heart
beats and lurches with a frantic stubbornness like
the heart of a partly dissected but still living frog
seventy miles to the east in Whispering Woods Estates, Southfield, Irene Campos lies awake in bed
uncomfortably perspiring, hot flushes in her face,
in her upper chest, her thoughts come confused
and slow and have something to do with the moon
veiled by curtains, or by high-scudding clouds, the
full moon is a sign of good luck and happiness or is
there something disquieting about the full moon
so whitely glaring, unless it's a neighbor's outside
light, Mrs. Campos isn't fully awake nor is she
asleep planning how next day she will insist to Mr.
Campos that they drive over to Grand Rapids to
visit with Hector, Jr. who hasn't been answering her
calls, hasn't even answered e-mail messages recently, beside her Mr. Campos is sleeping fitfully
on his back, twitches and thrashes in his smelly underwear she'll find, sometimes, kicked beneath the
bed or in a furtive mound in a corner of Mr. Campos's closet—why? Why would a man hoard soiled
underwear? And socks? Mr. Campos snores, snorts,
sounds like a drowning man, careful not to wake
him Mrs. Campos pokes and nudges him until he
rolls off his back, now grinding his back teeth but
facing away, at the edge of the bed. That day Mrs.
Campos sent Hector, Jr. a pleading text message

PLEASE CALL MOM DARLING for text messages are all the rage now, Mrs. Campos's woman
friends tell her, it's how young people communicate with one another but hours later Hector, Jr.
has not communicated with his mother, she has
become seriously worried. Oh, if only that college
hadn't been so aggressive sending brochures,
pamphlets, even a phone call, recruiting students
from Southfield High, not that the university was
going to offer Hector, Jr. a scholarship, not a
penny, his parents would be paying full tuition/
room-and-board/fees, if only Hector, Jr. had decided to go to Eastern Michigan University at Ypsilanti, no more than forty miles away, there's an
engineering school at Ypsilanti, too, and fraterni-
ties, but Hector, Jr. could live at home, at least, and
Mrs. Campos could take better care of him. Unconsciously caressing her left breast, clutching
her left breast in her right hand, lying on her side
clutching her large, warm, soft breast, how like a
sac of warm water it is, or warm milk, on the brink
of a dream of surpassing beauty and tenderness
Mrs. Campos shuts her eyes, why does Mr. Campos never caress her breasts any longer, why does
Mr. Campos never suck her nipples any
longer, Mrs. Campos runs her thumb over the
large soft nipple stirring it to hardness,
like a little berry, she is driving back from the
city, driving back from ugly Detroit to Whispering Woods Estates, such joy, such pride, turning
into the brick-gated subdivision off Southfield
Road, making her way floating along Pheasant
Pass, Larkspur Drive, Bluebell Lane and at last to
Quail Circle where, in the gleaming-white colonial at number 23, the Campos family lives.

ON THE RAINY RIVER

Tim O'Brien

Tim O'Brien received the 1979 National Book Award in Fiction for *Going After Cacciato*. His novel *The Things They Carried* won France's prestigious Prix du Meilleur Livre Etranger and the *Chicago Tribune*'s Heartland Prize; it was also a finalist for the Pulitzer Prize and the National Book Critics Circle Award. His most recent novel is *July, July*.

This is one story I've never told before. Not to anyone. Not to my parents, not to my brother or sister, not even to my wife. To go into it, I've always thought, would only cause embarrassment for all of us, a sudden need to be elsewhere, which is the natural response to a confession. Even now, I'll admit, the story makes me squirm. For more than twenty years I've had to live with it, feeling the shame, trying to push it away, and so by this act of remembrance, by putting the facts down on paper, I'm hoping to relieve at least some of the pressure on my dreams. Still, it's a hard story to tell. All of us, I suppose, like to believe that in a moral emergency we will behave like the heroes of our youth, bravely and forthrightly, without thought of personal loss or discredit. Certainly that was my conviction back in the summer of 1968. Tim O'Brien: a secret hero. The Lone Ranger. If the stakes ever became high enough—if the evil were evil enough, if the good were good enough—I would simply tap a secret reservoir of courage that had been accumulating inside me over the years. Courage, I seemed to think, comes to us in finite quantities, like an inheritance, and by being frugal and stashing it away and letting it earn interest, we steadily increase our moral capital in preparation for that day when the account must be drawn down. It was a comforting theory. It dispensed with all those bothersome little acts of daily courage; it offered hope and grace to the repetitive coward; it justified the past while amortizing the future.

In June of 1968, a month after graduating from Macalester College, I was drafted to fight a war I hated. I was twenty-one years old. Young, yes, and politically naive, but even so the American war in Vietnam seemed to me wrong. Certain blood was being shed for uncertain reasons. I saw no unity of purpose, no consensus on matters of philosophy or history or law. The very facts were shrouded in uncertainty: Was it a civil war? A war of national liberation or simple aggression? Who started it, and when, and why? What really happened to the USS *Maddox* on that dark night in the Gulf of Tonkin? Was Ho Chi Minh a Communist stooge, or a nationalist savior, or both, or neither? What about the Geneva Accords? What about SEATO and the Cold War? What about dominoes? America was divided on these and a thousand other issues, and the debate had spilled out across the floor of the United States Senate and into the streets, and smart men in pinstripes could not agree on even the most fundamental matters of public policy. The only certainty that summer was moral confusion. It was my view then, and still is, that you don't make war without knowing why. Knowledge, of course, is always imperfect, but it seemed to me that when a nation goes to war it must have reasonable confidence in the justice and imperative of its cause. You can't fix your mistakes. Once people are dead, you can't make them undead.

In any case those were my convictions, and back in college I had taken a modest stand against the war. Nothing radical, no hothead stuff, just ringing a few doorbells for Gene McCarthy, composing a few tedious, uninspired editorials for the campus newspaper. Oddly, though, it was almost entirely an intellectual activity.

I brought some energy to it, of course, but it was the energy that accompanies almost any abstract endeavor; I felt no personal danger; I felt no sense of an impending crisis in my life. Stupidly, with a kind of smug removal that I can't begin to fathom, I assumed that the problems of killing and dying did not fall within my special province.

The draft notice arrived on June 17, 1968. It was a humid afternoon, I remember, cloudy and very quiet, and I'd just come in from a round of golf. My mother and father were having lunch out in the kitchen. I remember opening up the letter, scanning the first few lines, feeling the blood go thick behind my eyes. I remember a sound in my head. It wasn't thinking, just a silent howl. A million things all at once—I was too *good* for this war. Too smart, too compassionate, too everything. It couldn't happen. I was above it. I had the world dicked—Phi Beta Kappa and summa cum laude and president of the student body and a full-ride scholarship for grad studies at Harvard. A mistake, maybe—a foul-up in the paperwork. I was no soldier. I hated Boy Scouts. I hated camping out. I hated dirt and tents and mosquitoes. The sight of blood made me queasy, and I couldn't tolerate authority, and I didn't know a rifle from a slingshot. I was a *liberal,* for Christ sake: If they needed fresh bodies, why not draft some back-to-the-stone-age hawk? Or some dumb jingo in his hard hat and Bomb Hanoi button, or one of LBJ's pretty daughters, or Westmoreland's whole handsome family—nephews and nieces and baby grandson. There should be a law, I thought. If you support a war, if you think it's worth the price, that's fine, but you have to put your own precious fluids on the line. You have to head for the front and hook up with an infantry unit and help spill the blood. And you have to bring along your wife, or your kids, or your lover. A *law,* I thought.

I remember the rage in my stomach. Later it burned down to a smoldering self-pity, then to numbness. At dinner that night my father asked what my plans were. "Nothing," I said. "Wait."

————————

I SPENT the summer of 1968 working in an Armour meatpacking plant in my hometown of Worthington, Minnesota. The plant specialized in pork products, and for eight hours a day I stood on a quarter-mile assembly line—more properly, a disassembly line—removing blood clots from the necks of dead pigs. My job title, I believe, was Declotter. After slaughter, the hogs were decapitated, split down the length of the belly, pried open, eviscerated, and strung up by the hind hocks on a high conveyer belt. Then gravity took over. By the time a carcass reached my spot on the line, the fluids had mostly drained out, everything except for thick clots of blood in the neck and upper chest cavity. To remove the stuff, I used a kind of water gun. The machine was heavy, maybe eighty pounds, and was suspended from the ceiling by a heavy rubber cord. There was some bounce to it, an elastic up-and-down give, and the trick was to maneuver the gun with your whole body, not lifting with the arms, just letting the rubber cord do the work for you. At one end was a trigger; at the muzzle end was a small nozzle and a steel roller brush. As a carcass passed by, you'd lean forward and swing the gun up against the clots and squeeze the trigger, all in one motion, and the brush would whirl and water would come shooting out and you'd hear a quick splattering sound as the clots dissolved into a fine red mist. It was not pleasant work. Goggles were a necessity, and a rubber apron, but even so it was like standing for eight hours a day under a lukewarm blood-shower. At night I'd go home smelling of pig. It wouldn't go away. Even after a hot bath, scrubbing hard, the stink was always there—like old bacon, or sausage, or dense greasy pig-stink that soaked deep into my skin and hair. Among other things, I remember, it was tough getting dates that summer. I felt isolated; I spent a lot of time alone. And there was also the draft notice tucked away in my wallet.

In the evenings I'd sometimes borrow my father's car and drive aimlessly around town, feeling sorry for myself, thinking about the war and the pig factory and how my life seemed to be collapsing toward slaughter. I felt paralyzed. All around me the options seemed to be narrowing, as if I were hurtling down a huge black funnel, the whole world squeezing in tight. There was no happy way out. The government had ended most graduate school deferments; the waiting lists for the National Guard and Reserves were impossibly long; my health was solid; I didn't qualify for CO status—no religious grounds, no history as a pacifist. Moreover, I could not claim to be opposed to war as a matter of general principle. There were occasions, I believed, when a nation was justified in using military force to achieve its ends, to stop a Hitler or some comparable evil, and I told myself that in such circumstances I would've willingly marched off to the battle. The problem, though, was that a draft board did not let you choose your war.

Beyond all this, or at the very center, was the raw fact of terror. I did not want to die. Not ever. But certainly not then, not there, not in a wrong war. Driving up Main Street, past the courthouse and the Ben Franklin store, I sometimes felt the fear spreading inside me like weeds. I imagined myself dead. I imagined myself doing things I could not do—charging an enemy position, taking aim at another human being.

At some point in mid-July I began thinking seriously about Canada. The border lay a few hundred miles north, an eight-hour drive. Both my conscience and my instincts were telling me to make a break for it, just take off and run like hell and never stop. In the beginning the idea seemed purely abstract, the word Canada printing itself out in my head; but after a time I could see particular shapes and images, the sorry details of my own future—a hotel room in Winnipeg, a battered old suitcase, my father's eyes as I tried to explain myself over the telephone. I could almost hear his voice, and my mother's. Run, I'd think. Then I'd think, Impossible. Then a second later I'd think, *Run*.

It was a kind of schizophrenia. A moral split. I couldn't make up my mind. I feared the war, yes, but I also feared exile. I was afraid of walking away from my own life, my friends and my family, my whole history, everything that mattered to me. I feared losing the respect of my parents. I feared the law. I feared ridicule and censure. My hometown was a conservative little spot on the prairie, a place where tradition counted, and it was easy to imagine people sitting around a table down at the old Gobbler Café on Main Street, coffee cups poised, the conversation slowly zeroing in on the young O'Brien kid, how the damned sissy had taken off for Canada. At night, when I couldn't sleep, I'd sometimes carry on fierce arguments with those people. I'd be screaming at them, telling them how much I detested their blind, thoughtless, automatic acquiescence to it all, their simpleminded patriotism, their prideful ignorance, their love-it-or-leave-it platitudes, how they were sending me off to fight a war they didn't understand and didn't want to understand. I held them responsible. By God, yes, I *did*. All of them—I held them personally and individually responsible—the polyestered Kiwanis boys, the merchants and farmers, the pious churchgoers, the chatty housewives, the PTA and the Lions club and the Veterans of Foreign Wars and the fine upstanding gentry out at the country club. They didn't know Bao Dai from the man in the moon. They didn't know history. They didn't know the first thing about Diem's tyranny, or the nature of Vietnamese nationalism, or the long colonialism of the French—this was all too damned complicated, it required some reading—but no matter, it was a war to stop the Communists, plain and simple, which was how they liked things, and you were a treasonous pussy if you had second thoughts about killing or dying for plain and simple reasons.

I was bitter, sure. But it was so much more than that. The emotions went from outrage to terror to bewilderment to guilt to sorrow and then back again to outrage. I felt a sickness inside me. Real disease.

Most of this I've told before, or at least hinted at, but what I have never told is the full truth. How I cracked. How at work one morning, standing on the pig line, I felt something break open in my chest. I don't know what it was. I'll never know. But it was real, I know that much, it was a physical rupture—a cracking-leaking-popping feeling. I remember dropping my water gun. Quickly, almost without thought, I took off my apron and walked out of the plant and drove home. It was midmorning, I remember, and the house was empty. Down in my chest there was still that leaking sensation, something very warm and precious spilling out, and I was covered with blood and hog-stink, and for a long while I just concentrated on holding myself together. I remember taking a hot shower. I remember packing a suitcase and carrying it out to the kitchen, standing very still for a few minutes, looking carefully at the familiar objects all around me. The old chrome toaster, the telephone, the pink and white Formica on the kitchen counters. The room was full of bright sunshine. Everything sparkled. My house, I thought. My life. I'm not sure how long I stood there, but later I scribbled out a short note to my parents.

What it said, exactly, I don't recall now. Something vague. Taking off, will call, love Tim.

I DROVE north.

It's a blur now, as it was then, and all I remember is a sense of high velocity and the feel of the steering wheel in my hands. I was riding on adrenaline. A giddy feeling, in a way, except there was the dreamy edge of impossibility to it—like running a dead-end maze—no way out—it couldn't come to a happy conclusion and yet I was doing it anyway because it was all I could think of to do. It was pure flight, fast and mindless. I had no plan. Just hit the border at high speed and crash through and keep on running. Near dusk I passed through Bemidji, then turned northeast toward International Falls. I spent the night in the car behind a closed-down gas station a half mile from the border. In the morning, after gassing up, I headed straight west along the Rainy River, which separates Minnesota from Canada, and which for me separated one life from another. The land was mostly wilderness. Here and there I passed a motel or bait shop, but otherwise the country unfolded in great sweeps of pine and birch and sumac. Though it was still August, the air already had the smell of October, football season, piles of yellow-red leaves, everything crisp and clean. I remember a huge blue sky. Off to my right was the Rainy River, wide as a lake in places, and beyond the Rainy River was Canada.

For a while I just drove, not aiming at anything, then in the late morning I began looking for a place to lie low for a day or two. I was exhausted, and scared sick, and around noon I pulled into an old fishing resort called the Tip Top Lodge. Actually it was not a lodge at all, just eight or nine tiny yellow cabins clustered on a peninsula that jutted northward into the Rainy River. The place was in sorry shape. There was a dangerous wooden dock, an old minnow tank, a flimsy tar paper boathouse along the shore. The main building, which stood in a cluster of pines on high ground, seemed to lean heavily to one side, like a cripple, the roof sagging toward Canada. Briefly, I thought about turning around, just giving up, but then I got out of the car and walked up to the front porch.

The man who opened the door that day is the hero of my life. How do I say this without sounding sappy? Blurt it out—the man saved me. He offered exactly what I needed, without questions, without any words at all. He took me in. He was there at the critical time—a silent, watchful presence. Six days later, when it ended, I was unable to find a proper way to thank him, and I never have, and so, if nothing else, this story represents a small gesture of gratitude twenty years overdue.

Even after two decades I can close my eyes and return to that porch at the Tip Top Lodge. I can see the old guy staring at me. Elroy Berdahl: eighty-one years old, skinny and shrunken and mostly bald. He wore a flannel shirt and brown work pants. In one hand, I remember, he carried a green apple, a small paring knife in the other. His eyes had the bluish gray color of a razor blade, the same polished shine, and as he peered up at me I felt a strange sharpness, almost painful, a cutting sensation, as if his gaze were somehow slicing me open. In part, no doubt, it was my own sense of guilt, but even so I'm absolutely certain that the old man took one look and went right to the heart of things—a kid in trouble. When I asked for

a room, Elroy made a little clicking sound with his tongue. He nodded, led me out to one of the cabins, and dropped a key in my hand.
I remember smiling at him. I also remember wishing I hadn't. The
old man shook his head as if to tell me it wasn't worth the bother.

"Dinner at five-thirty," he said. "You eat fish?"

"Anything," I said.

Elroy grunted and said, "I'll bet."

WE SPENT six days together at the Tip Top Lodge. Just the two of us.
Tourist season was over, and there were no boats on the river, and
the wilderness seemed to withdraw into a great permanent stillness. Over those six days Elroy Berdahl and I took most of our
meals together. In the mornings we sometimes went out on long
hikes into the woods, and at night we played Scrabble or listened to
records or sat reading in front of his big stone fireplace. At times I
felt the awkwardness of an intruder, but Elroy accepted me into his
quiet routine without fuss or ceremony. He took my presence for
granted, the same way he might've sheltered a stray cat—no wasted
sighs or pity—and there was never any talk about it. Just the opposite. What I remember more than anything is the man's willful, almost ferocious silence. In all that time together, all those hours, he
never asked the obvious questions: Why was I there? Why alone?
Why so preoccupied? If Elroy was curious about any of this, he was
careful never to put it into words.

My hunch, though, is that he already knew. At least the ba-
sics. After all, it was 1968, and guys were burning draft cards, and
Canada was just a boat ride away. Elroy Berdahl was no hick. His
bedroom, I remember, was cluttered with books and newspapers.
He killed me at the Scrabble board, barely concentrating, and on
those occasions when speech was necessary he had a way of com-
pressing large thoughts into small, cryptic packets of language.
One evening, just at sunset, he pointed up at an owl circling over
the violet-lighted forest to the west.

"Hey, O'Brien," he said. "There's Jesus."

The man was sharp—he didn't miss much. Those razor eyes. Now and then he'd catch me staring out at the river, at the far shore, and I could almost hear the tumblers clicking in his head. Maybe I'm wrong, but I doubt it.

One thing for certain, he knew I was in desperate trouble. And he knew I couldn't talk about it. The wrong word—or even the right word—and I would've disappeared. I was wired and jittery. My skin felt too tight. After supper one evening I vomited and went back to my cabin and lay down for a few moments and then vomited again; another time, in the middle of the afternoon, I began sweating and couldn't shut it off. I went through whole days feeling dizzy with sorrow. I couldn't sleep; I couldn't lie still. At night I'd toss around in bed, half awake, half dreaming, imagining how I'd sneak down to the beach and quietly push one of the old man's boats out into the river and start paddling my way toward Canada. There were times when I thought I'd gone off the psychic edge. I couldn't tell up from down, I was just falling, and late in the night I'd lie there watching weird pictures spin through my head. Getting chased by the Border Patrol—helicopters and searchlights and barking dogs—I'd be crashing through the woods, I'd be down on my hands and knees—people shouting out my name—the law closing in on all sides—my hometown draft board and the FBI and the Royal Canadian Mounted Police. It all seemed crazy and impossible. Twenty-one years old, an ordinary kid with all the ordinary dreams and ambitions, and all I wanted was to live the life I was born to—a mainstream life—I loved baseball and hamburgers and cherry Cokes—and now I was off on the margins of exile, leaving my country forever, and it seemed so impossible and terrible and sad.

I'm not sure how I made it through those six days. Most of it I can't remember. On two or three afternoons, to pass some time, I helped Elroy get the place ready for winter, sweeping down the cabins and hauling in the boats, little chores that kept my body moving. The days were cool and bright. The nights were very dark.

One morning the old man showed me how to split and stack fire-wood, and for several hours we just worked in silence out behind his house. At one point, I remember, Elroy put down his maul and looked at me for a long time, his lips drawn as if framing a difficult question, but then he shook his head and went back to work. The man's self-control was amazing. He never pried. He never put me in a position that required lies or denials. To an extent, I suppose, his reticence was typical of that part of Minnesota, where privacy still held value, and even if I'd been walking around with some horrible deformity—four arms and three heads—I'm sure the old man would've talked about everything except those extra arms and heads. Simple politeness was part of it. But even more than that, I think, the man understood that words were insufficient. The problem had gone beyond discussion. During that long summer I'd been over and over the various arguments, all the pros and cons, and it was no longer a question that could be decided by an act of pure reason. Intellect had come up against emotion. My conscience told me to run, but some irrational and powerful force was resisting, like a weight pushing me toward the war. What it came down to, stupidly, was a sense of shame. Hot, stupid shame. I did not want people to think badly of me. Not my parents, not my brother and sister, not even the folks down at the Gobbler Café. I was ashamed to be there at the Tip Top Lodge. I was ashamed of my conscience, ashamed to be doing the right thing.

Some of this Elroy must've understood. Not the details, of course, but the plain fact of crisis.

Although the old man never confronted me about it, there was one occasion when he came close to forcing the whole thing out into the open. It was early evening, and we'd just finished supper, and over coffee and dessert I asked him about my bill, how much I owed so far. For a long while the old man squinted down at the tablecloth.

"Well, the basic rate," he said, "is fifty bucks a night. Not counting meals. This makes four nights, right?"

I nodded. I had three hundred and twelve dollars in my wallet.

Elroy kept his eyes on the tablecloth. "Now that's an on-season price. To be fair, I suppose we should knock it down a peg or two." He leaned back in his chair. "What's a reasonable number, you figure?"

"I don't know," I said. "Forty?"

"Forty's good. Forty a night. Then we tack on food—say another hundred? Two hundred sixty total?"

I guess.

He raised his eyebrows. "Too much?"

"No, that's fair. It's fine. Tomorrow, though . . . I think I'd better take off tomorrow."

Elroy shrugged and began clearing the table. For a time he fussed with the dishes, whistling to himself as if the subject had been settled. After a second he slapped his hands together.

"You know what we forgot?" he said. "We forgot wages. Those odd jobs you done. What we have to do, we have to figure out what your time's worth. Your last job—how much did you pull in an hour?"

"Not enough," I said.

"A bad one?"

"Yes. Pretty bad."

Slowly then, without intending any long sermon, I told him about my days at the pig plant. It began as a straight recitation of the facts, but before I could stop myself I was talking about the blood clots and the water gun and how the smell had soaked into my skin and how I couldn't wash it away. I went on for a long time. I told him about wild hogs squealing in my dreams, the sounds of butchery, slaughterhouse sounds, and how I'd sometimes wake up with that greasy pig-stink in my throat.

When I was finished, Elroy nodded at me.

"Well, to be honest," he said, "when you first showed up here, I wondered about all that. The aroma, I mean. Smelled like you was awful damned fond of pork chops." The old man almost smiled. He made a snuffling sound, then sat down with a pencil and a piece of paper. "So what'd this crud job pay? Ten bucks an hour? Fifteen?"

"Less."

Elroy shook his head. "Let's make it fifteen. You put in twenty-five hours here, easy. That's three hundred seventy-five bucks total wages. We subtract the two hundred sixty for food and lodging, I still owe you a hundred and fifteen."

He took four fifties out of his shirt pocket and laid them on the table.

"Call it even," he said.

"No."

"Pick it up. Get yourself a haircut."

The money lay on the table for the rest of the evening. It was still there when I went back to my cabin. In the morning, though, I found an envelope tacked to my door. Inside were the four fifties and a two-word note that said EMERGENCY FUND.

The man knew.

LOOKING BACK after twenty years, I sometimes wonder if the events of that summer didn't happen in some other dimension, a place where your life exists before you've lived it, and where it goes afterward. None of it ever seemed real. During my time at the Tip Top Lodge I had the feeling that I'd slipped out of my own skin, hovering a few feet away while some poor yo-yo with my name and face tried to make his way toward a future he didn't understand and didn't want. Even now I can see myself as I was then. It's like watching an old home movie: I'm young and tan and fit. I've got hair—lots of it. I don't smoke or drink. I'm wearing faded blue jeans and a white polo shirt. I can see myself sitting on Elroy Berdahl's dock near dusk one evening, the sky a bright shimmering pink, and I'm finishing up a letter to my parents that tells what I'm about to do and why I'm doing it and how sorry I am that I'd never found the courage to talk to them about it. I ask them not to be angry. I try to explain some of my feelings, but there aren't enough words, and so

I just say that it's a thing that has to be done. At the end of the letter I talk about the vacations we used to take up in this north country, at a place called Whitefish Lake, and how the scenery here reminds me of those good times. I tell them I'm fine. I tell them I'll write again from Winnipeg or Montreal or wherever I end up.

ON MY last full day, the sixth day, the old man took me out fishing on the Rainy River. The afternoon was sunny and cold. A stiff breeze came in from the north, and I remember how the little fourteen-foot boat made sharp rocking motions as we pushed off from the dock. The current was fast. All around us, I remember, there was a vastness to the world, an unpeopled rawness, just the trees and the sky and the water reaching out toward nowhere. The air had the brittle scent of October.

For ten or fifteen minutes Elroy held a course upstream, the river choppy and silver-gray, then he turned straight north and put the engine on full throttle. I felt the bow lift beneath me. I remember the wind in my ears, the sound of the old outboard Evinrude. For a time I didn't pay attention to anything, just feeling the cold spray against my face, but then it occurred to me that at some point we must've passed into Canadian waters, across that dotted line between two different worlds, and I remember a sudden tightness in my chest as I looked up and watched the far shore come at me. This wasn't a daydream. It was tangible and real. As we came in toward land, Elroy cut the engine, letting the boat fishtail lightly about twenty yards off shore. The old man didn't look at me or speak. Bending down, he opened up his tackle box and busied himself with a bobber and a piece of wire leader, humming to himself, his eyes down.

It struck me then that he must've planned it. I'll never be certain, of course, but I think he meant to bring me up against the realities, to guide me across the river and to take me to the edge and to stand a kind of vigil as I chose a life for myself.

I remember staring at the old man, then at my hands, then at Canada. The shoreline was dense with brush and timber. I could see tiny red berries on the bushes. I could see a squirrel up in one of the birch trees, a big crow looking at me from a boulder along the river. That close—twenty yards—and I could see the delicate latticework of the leaves, the texture of the soil, the browned needles beneath the pines, the configurations of geology and human history. Twenty yards. I could've done it. I could've jumped and started swimming for my life. Inside me, in my chest, I felt a terrible squeezing pressure. Even now, as I write this, I can still feel that tightness. And I want you to feel it—the wind coming off the river, the waves, the silence, the wooded frontier. You're at the bow of a boat on the Rainy River. You're twenty-one years old, you're scared, and there's a hard squeezing pressure in your chest.

What would you do?

Would you jump? Would you feel pity for yourself? Would you think about your family and your childhood and your dreams and all you're leaving behind? Would it hurt? Would it feel like dying? Would you cry, as I did?

I tried to swallow it back. I tried to smile, except I was crying.

Now, perhaps, you can understand why I've never told this story before. It's not just the embarrassment of tears. That's part of it, no doubt, but what embarrasses me much more, and always will, is the paralysis that took my heart. A moral freeze: I couldn't decide, I couldn't act, I couldn't comport myself with even a pretense of modest human dignity.

All I could do was cry. Quietly, not bawling, just the chest-chokes.

At the rear of the boat Elroy Berdahl pretended not to notice. He held a fishing rod in his hands, his head bowed to hide his eyes. He kept humming a soft, monotonous little tune. Everywhere, it seemed, in the trees and water and sky, a great worldwide sadness came pressing down on me, a crushing sorrow, sorrow like I had never known it before. And what was so sad, I realized, was that Canada had become a pitiful fantasy. Silly and hopeless. It was no longer a possibility. Right then, with the shore so close, I understood that I would not do what I should do. I would not swim away from my hometown and my country and my life. I would not be brave. That old image of myself as a hero, as a man of conscience and courage, all that was just a threadbare pipe dream. Bobbing there on the Rainy River, looking back at the Minnesota shore, I felt a sudden swell of helplessness come over me, a drowning sensation, as if I had toppled overboard and was being swept away by the silver waves. Chunks of my own history flashed by. I saw a seven-year-old boy in a white cowboy hat and a Lone Ranger mask and a pair of holstered six-shooters; I saw a twelve-year-old Little League shortstop pivoting to turn a double play; I saw a sixteen-year-old kid decked out for his first prom, looking spiffy in a white tux and a black bow tie, his hair cut short and flat, his shoes freshly polished. My whole life seemed to spill out into the river, swirling away from me, everything I had ever been or ever wanted to be. I couldn't get my breath; I couldn't stay afloat; I couldn't tell which way to swim. A hallucination, I suppose, but it was as real as anything I would ever feel. I saw my parents calling to me from the far shoreline. I saw my brother and sister, all the townsfolk, the mayor and the entire Chamber of Commerce and all my old teachers and girlfriends and high school buddies. Like some weird sporting event: everybody screaming from the sidelines, rooting me on—a loud stadium roar. Hotdogs and popcorn—stadium smells, stadium heat. A squad of cheerleaders did cartwheels along the banks of the Rainy River; they had megaphones and pompoms and smooth brown thighs. The crowd swayed left and right. A marching band played fight songs. All my aunts and uncles were there, and Abraham Lincoln, and Saint George, and a nine-year-old girl named Linda who had died of a brain tumor back in fifth grade, and several members of the United States Senate, and a blind poet scribbling notes, and LBJ, and Huck Finn, and Abbie Hoffman, and all the dead soldiers back from the grave, and the many thousands who were later to die— villagers with terrible burns, little kids without arms or legs—yes, and the Joint Chiefs of Staff were there, and a couple of popes, and a first lieutenant named Jimmy Cross, and the last surviving veteran of the American Civil War, and Jane Fonda dressed up as Barbarella, and an old man sprawled beside a pigpen, and my grandfather, and Gary Cooper, and a kind-faced woman carrying an umbrella and a copy of Plato's *Republic*, and a million ferocious citizens waving flags of all shapes and colors—people in hard hats, people in headbands—they were all whooping and chanting and urging me toward one shore or the other. I saw faces from my distant past and distant future. My wife was there. My unborn daughter waved at me, and my two sons hopped up and down, and a drill sergeant named Blyton sneered and shot up a finger and shook his head. There was a choir in bright purple robes. There was a cabbie from the Bronx. There was a slim young man I would one day kill with a hand grenade along a red clay trail outside the village of My Khe.

The little aluminum boat rocked softly beneath me. There was the wind and the sky.

I tried to will myself overboard.

I gripped the edge of the boat and leaned forward and thought, *Now.*

I did try. It just wasn't possible.

All those eyes on me—the town, the whole universe—and I couldn't risk the embarrassment. It was as if there were an audience to my life, that swirl of faces along the river, and in my head I could hear people screaming at me. Traitor! they yelled. Turncoat! Pussy! I felt myself blush. I couldn't tolerate it. I couldn't endure the mockery, or the disgrace, or the patriotic ridicule. Even in my imagination, the shore just twenty yards away, I couldn't make myself be brave. It had nothing to do with morality. Embarrassment, that's all it was.

And right then I submitted.

I would go to the war—I would kill and maybe die—because I was embarrassed not to.

That was the sad thing. And so I sat in the bow of the boat and cried.

It was loud now. Loud, hard crying.

Elroy Berdahl remained quiet. He kept fishing. He worked his line with the tips of his fingers, patiently, squinting out at his red and white bobber on the Rainy River. His eyes were flat and impassive. He didn't speak. He was simply there, like the river and the late-summer sun. And yet by his presence, his mute watchfulness, he made it real. He was the true audience. He was a witness, like God, or like the gods, who look on in absolute silence as we live our lives, as we make our choices or fail to make them.

"Ain't biting," he said.

Then after a time the old man pulled in his line and turned the boat back toward Minnesota.

I DON'T remember saying goodbye. That last night we had dinner together, and I went to bed early, and in the morning Elroy fixed breakfast for me. When I told him I'd be leaving, the old man nodded as if he already knew. He looked down at the table and smiled.

At some point later in the morning it's possible that we shook hands—I just don't remember—but I do know that by the time I'd finished packing the old man had disappeared. Around noon, when I took my suitcase out to the car, I noticed that his old black pickup truck was no longer parked in front of the house. I went inside and waited for a while, but I felt a bone certainty that he wouldn't be back. In a way, I thought, it was appropriate. I washed up the breakfast dishes, left his two hundred dollars on the kitchen counter, got into the car, and drove south toward home.

The day was cloudy. I passed through towns with familiar names, through the pine forests and down to the prairie, and then to Vietnam, where I was a soldier, and then home again. I survived, but it's not a happy ending. I was a coward. I went to the war.

ESCORT

Chuck Palahniuk

Chuck Palahniuk is the bestselling author of numerous novels, as well as a nonfiction profile of Portland, Oregon, *Fugitives and Refugees*, published as part of the Crown Journeys series, and the nonfiction collection *Stranger Than Fiction*. He lives in the Pacific Northwest.

My first day as an escort, my first "date" had only one leg. He'd gone to a gay bathhouse, to get warm, he told me. Maybe for sex. And he'd fallen asleep in the steam room, too close to the heating element. He'd been unconscious for hours, until someone found him. Until the meat of his left thigh was completely and thoroughly cooked.

He couldn't walk, but his mother was coming from Wisconsin to see him, and the hospice needed someone to cart the two of them around to visit the local tourist sights. Go shopping downtown. See the beach. Multnomah Falls. This was all you could do as a volunteer if you weren't a nurse or a cook or doctor.

You were an escort, and this was the place where young people with no insurance went to die. The hospice name, I don't even remember. It wasn't on any signs anywhere, and they asked you to be discreet coming and going because the neighbors didn't know what was going on in the enormous old house on their street, a street with its share of crack houses and drive-by shootings, still nobody wanted to live next door to this: four people dying in the living room, two in the dining room. At least two people lay dying in each upstairs bedroom, and there were a lot of bedrooms. At least half these people had AIDS, but the house didn't discriminate. You could come here and die of anything.

The reason I was there was my job. This meant lying on my back on a creeper with a two-hundred-pound class-8 diesel truck drive-line lying on my chest and running down between my legs as far as my feet. My job is I had to roll under trucks as they crept down an assembly line, and I installed these drivelines. Twenty-six drive-lines every eight hours. Working fast as each truck moved along, pulling me into the huge blazing-hot paint ovens just a few feet down the line.

My degree in journalism couldn't get me more than five dollars an hour. Other guys in the shop had the same degree, and we joked how liberal arts degrees should include welding skills so you'd at least pick up the extra two bucks an hour our shop paid grunts who could weld. Someone invited me to their church, and I was desper-ate enough to go, and at the church they had a potted ficus they called a Giving Tree, decorated with paper ornaments, each orna-ment printed with a good deed you could choose.

My ornament said: Take a hospice patient on a date.

That was their word, "date." And there was a phone num-ber. I took the man with one leg, then him and his mother, all over the area, to scenic viewpoints, to museums, his wheelchair folded up in the back of my fifteen-year-old Mercury Bobcat. His mother smoking, silent. Her son was thirty years old, and she had two weeks of vacation. At night, I'd take her back to her Travelodge next to the freeway, and she'd smoke, sitting on the hood of my car, talking about her son already in the past tense. He could play the piano, she said. In school, he earned a degree in music, but ended up demonstrating electric organs in shopping-mall stores.

These were conversations after we had no emotions left.

I was twenty-five years old, and the next day I was back under trucks with maybe three or four hours sleep. Only now my own problems didn't seem very bad. Just looking at my hands and feet, marveling at the weight I could lift, the way I could shout against the pneumatic roar of the shop, my whole life felt like a miracle instead of a mistake.

In two weeks the mother was gone home. In another three months, her son was gone. Dead, gone. I drove people with cancer to see the ocean for their last time. I drove people with AIDS to the top of Mount Hood so they could see the whole world while there was still time.

I sat bedside while the nurse told me what to look for at the moment of death, the gasping and unconscious struggle of someone drowning in their sleep as renal failure filled their lungs with water. The monitor would beep every five or ten seconds as it injected morphine into the patient. The patient's eyes would roll back, bulging and entirely white. You held their cold hand for hours, until another escort came to the rescue, or until it didn't matter.

The mother in Wisconsin sent me an afghan she'd crocheted, purple and red. Another mother or grandmother I'd escorted sent me an afghan in blue, green, and white. Another came in red, white, and black. Granny squares, zigzag patterns. They piled up at one end of the couch until my housemates asked if we could store them in the attic.

Just before he'd died, the woman's son, the man with one leg, just before he'd lost consciousness, he'd begged me to go into his old apartment. There was a closet full of sex toys. Magazines. Dildos. Leatherwear. It was nothing he wanted his mother to find, so I promised to throw it all out.

So I went there, to the little studio apartment, sealed and stale after months empty. Like a crypt, I'd say, but that's not the right word. It sounds too dramatic. Like cheesy organ music. But in fact, just sad.

The sex toys and anal whatnots were just sadder. Orphaned. That's not the right word either, but it's the first word that comes to mind.

The afghans are still boxed and in my attic. Every Christmas a housemate will go look for ornaments and find the afghans, red and black, green and purple, each one a dead person, a son or daughter or grandchild, and whoever finds them will ask if we can use them on our beds or give them to Goodwill.

And every Christmas I'll say no. I can't say what scares me more, throwing away all these dead children or sleeping with them.

Don't ask me why, I tell people. I refuse to even talk about it. That was all ten years ago. I sold the Bobcat in 1989. I quit being an escort.

Maybe because after the man with one leg, after he died, after his sex toys were all garbage-bagged, after they were buried in the Dumpster, after the apartment windows were open and the smell of leather and latex and shit was gone, the apartment looked good. The sofa bed was a tasteful mauve, the walls and carpet, cream. The little kitchen had butcher-block countertops. The bathroom was all white and clean.

I sat there in the tasteful silence. I could've lived there.

Anyone could've lived there.

PEOPLE IN HELL JUST WANT A DRINK OF WATER

Annie Proulx

Annie Proulx is the acclaimed author of *The Shipping News* and three other novels, *That Old Ace in the Hole*, *Postcards*, and *Accordion Crimes*, and the story collections *Heart Songs*, *Close Range*, *Bad Dirt*, and *Fine Just the Way It Is*. She has won the Pulitzer Prize, a National Book Award, the Irish Times International Fiction Prize, two O. Henry Awards, and a PEN/Faulkner. She lives in Wyoming.

You stand there, braced. Cloud shadows race over the buff rock stacks as a projected film, casting a queasy, mottled ground rash. The air hisses and it is no local breeze but the great harsh sweep of wind from the turning of the earth. The wild country—indigo jags of mountain, grassy plain everlasting, tumbled stones like fallen cities, the flaring roll of sky—provokes a spiritual shudder. It is like a deep note that cannot be heard but is felt, it is like a claw in the gut.

Dangerous and indifferent ground: against its fixed mass the tragedies of people count for nothing although the signs of misadventure are everywhere. No past slaughter nor cruelty, no accident nor murder that occurs on the little ranches or at the isolate crossroads with their bare populations of three or seventeen, or in the reckless trailer courts of mining towns delays the flood of morning light. Fences, cattle, roads, refineries, mines, gravel pits, traffic lights, graffiti'd celebration of athletic victory on bridge overpass, crust of blood on the Wal-Mart loading dock, the sun-faded wreaths of plastic flowers marking death on the highway are ephemeral. Other cultures have camped here a while and disappeared. Only earth and sky matter. Only the endlessly repeated flood of morning light. You begin to see that God does not owe us much beyond that.

IN 1908, on the run from Texas drought and dusters, Isaac "Ice" Dunmire arrived in Laramie, Wyoming, at three-thirty in the dark February morning. It was thirty-four degrees below zero, the wind shrieking along the tracks.

"It sure can't get more worse than this," he said. He didn't know anything about it.

Although he had a wife, Naomi, and five sons back in Burnet County, for the sake of a job punching cows he swore to the manager of the Six Pigpen Ranch that he was single. The big spread was owned by two Scots brothers who had never seen the #6 and never wished to, any more than the owner of a slave ship wanted to look over the cargo.

At the end of a year, because he never went into town, saved his forty-dollar-a-month wages and was an indefatigable killer of bounty wolves, because he won at Red Dog more often than he lost, Ice Dunmire had four hundred dollars in a blue tin box painted with the image of a pigtailed sailor cutting a curl of tobacco from a golden plug. It wasn't enough. The second spring in the country he quit the #6 and went into the Tetons to kill wapiti elk for their big canine teeth, bought for big money by members of the B.P.O.E. who dangled the ivory from their watch chains.

Now he staked a homestead claim on the Laramie plain south of the Big Hollow, a long, wind-gouged depression below the Snowy Range of the Medicine Bows, put up a sod shanty, registered the Rocking Box brand. The boundary didn't signify—what he saw was the beautiful, deep land and he saw it his, aimed to get as much of it as he could. He bought and stole half a hundred cows, and with pride in this three-up outfit, declared himself a rancher. He sent for the wife and kids, filed on an adjoining quarter section in Naomi's name. His sudden passage from bachelor to family man with five little hen-wranglers, from broke cowpuncher to property-owning rancher, earned him the nickname of "Tricker" which some uneasily misheard as "Trigger."

What the wife thought when she saw the sod hut, ten by fourteen, roofed with planks and more dirt thrown on top, one window and a warped door, can be guessed at but not known. There were two pole beds with belly wool mattresses. The five boys slept in one and in the other Ice quickly begot on Naomi another and another kid as fast as the woman could stand to make them. Jaxon's most vivid memory of her was watching her pour boiling water on the rattlesnakes he and his brothers caught with loops of barbwire, smiling to see them writhe. By 1913, ridden hard and put away dirty, looking for relief, she went off with a cook-pan tinker and left Ice the nine boys—Jaxon, the twins Ideal and Pet, Kemmy, Marion, Byron, Varn, Ritter and Bliss. They all lived except Byron who was bitten by a mosquito and died of encephalitis. Boys were money in the bank in that country and Ice brought them up to fill his labor needs. They got ropes for Christmas, a handshake each birthday and damn a cake.

What they learned was livestock and ranchwork. When they were still young buttons they could sleep out alone on the plain, knees raftered up in the rain, tarp drawn over their heads listening to the water trickle past their ears. In the autumn, after fall roundup, they went up on Jelm Mountain and hunted, not for sport but for meat. They grew into bone-seasoned, tireless workers accustomed to discomfort, took their pleasure in drink, cigarettes, getting work done. They were brass-nutted boys, sinewy and tall, nothing they liked better than to kick the frost out of a horse in early morning.

"Sink them shittin spurs into his lungs, boy!" screamed Ice at a kid on a snorty bronc. "Be a man."

Their endurance of pain was legendary. When a section of narrow mountain trail broke away under Marion's horse, the horse falling with him onto rocks below, the animal's back broken and Marion's left leg, he shot the horse, splinted his own leg with some yucca stalks and his wild rag, whittled a crutch from the limb he shot off a scrub cedar, and in three days hopped twenty miles to the Shiverses' place, asked for a drink of water, swallowed it, pivoted on the cedar crutch, and began to hop toward the home ranch, another seven miles east, before George Shivers cajoled him into a wagon. Shivers saw then what he missed before—Marion had carried his heavy stock saddle the distance.

Jaxon, the oldest, was a top bronc buster but torn up so badly inside by the age of twenty-eight his underwear were often stained with blood; he had to switch to easy horses broke by other men. After a loose-end time he took over the daily operations of the Rocking Box and kept the books, stud records, but in summers turned all that back to his father while he ran as a salesman for Morning Glory windmills, bumping over the country in a Ford truck to ranches, fairs and rodeos. There was a hard need for cash. The Rocking Box had a hard need for cash. The jolting was enough that he said he might as well be riding broncs. He bought himself a plaid suit, then a roadster, hitched a rubber-tired trailer to the rear bumper. In the trailer bed he bolted a sample-sized Morning Glory windmill supplied by the company. The blades turned showily as he drove. He carried sidelines of pump rod springs, regulators and an assortment of Cowboy's Pal DeLuxe Calendars which featured campfires and saccharine verses or candy-tinted girlies kneeling on Indian blankets. The Morning Glory was a steel-tower, back-geared pumping mill. The blades were painted bright blue and a scallop-tailed vane sheet carried the message NEVER SORRY—MORNING GLORY.

"I got a advantage over those bums got nothin but the pictures and the catalogs. I show em the real thing—that main shaft goin through the roller bearins to the double-pinion gear. You can't show that in a picture, how them teeth mesh in with the big crank gears. The roller bearins are what makes it bite the biscuit. Then some old guy don't want a windmill he'll sure want a couple calendars. Small but it adds up."

He kept his say in ranch affairs—he'd earned the right.

Pet and Kemmy married and set up off the Rocking Box but the others stayed at home and single, finding ceaseless work and an occasional group visit to a Laramie whorehouse enough. Jaxon did not go on these excursions, claiming he found plenty of what he needed on his travels to remote ranches.

"Some a them women can't hardly wait until I get out a the truck," he said. "They'll put their hand right on you soon's you open the door. Like our ma, I guess," he sneered.

By the droughty depression of the 1930s the Dunmires were in everything that happened, their opinions based on deep experience. They had seen it all: prairie fire, flood, blizzard, dust storm, injury, sliding beef prices, grasshopper and Mormon cricket plagues, rustlers, scours, bad horses. They ran off hobos and gypsies, and if Jaxon whistled "Shuffle Off to Buffalo," in a month everybody was whistling that tune. The country, its horses and cattle, suited them and if they loved anything that was it, and they ran that country because there were eight of them and Ice and they were of one mind. But there builds up in men who work livestock in big territory a kind of contempt for those who do not. The Dunmires measured beauty and religion by what they rode through every day, and this encouraged their disdain for art and intellect. There was a somber arrogance about them, a rigidity of attitude that said theirs was the only way.

THE TINSLEYS were a different kind. Horm Tinsley had come up from St. Louis with the expectation of quick success. He often said that anything could happen, but the truth of that was bitter. He was lanky and inattentive, early on bitten by a rattlesnake while setting fence posts, and two months later bitten again at the same chore.

On the rich Laramie plain he ended up with a patch of poor land just east of the rain, dry and sandy range with sparse grass, and he could not seem to get ahead, trying horses, cattle, sheep in succession. Every change of season took him by surprise. Although he could tell snow from sunshine he wasn't much at reading weather. He took an interest in his spread but it was skewed to a taste for a noble rock or other trifling scenic vantage.

His failure as a stockman was recognized, yet he was tolerated and even liked for his kindly manner and skill playing the banjo and the fiddle, though most regarded him with contemptuous pity for his loose control of home affairs and his coddling of a crazy wife after her impetuous crime.

Mrs. Tinsley, intensely modest, sensitive and abhorring marital nakedness, suffered from nerves; she was distracted and fretted by shrill sounds as the screech of a chair leg scraping the floor or the pulling of a nail. As a girl in Missouri she had written a poem that began with the line "*Our life is a beautiful Fairy Land.*" Now she was mother to three. When the youngest girl, Mabel, was a few months old they made a journey into Laramie, the infant howling intolerably, the wagon bungling along, stones sliding beneath the wheels. As they crossed the Little Laramie Mrs. Tinsley stood up and hurled the crying infant into the water. The child's white dress filled with air and it floated a few yards in the swift current, then disappeared beneath a bower of willows at the bend. The woman shrieked and made to leap after the child but Horm Tinsley held her back. They galloped across the bridge and to the river's edge below the bend. Gone and gone.

As if to make up for her fit of destruction Mrs. Tinsley developed an intense anxiety for the safety of the surviving children, tying them to chairs in the kitchen lest they wander outside and come to harm, sending them to bed while the sun was still high for twilight was a dangerous time, warning them away from haystacks threaded with vipers, from trampling horses and biting dogs, the yellow Wyandottes who pecked, from the sound of thunder and the sight of lightning. In the night she came to their beds many times to learn if they had smothered.

By the time he was twelve the boy, Rasmussen, potato-nosed, with coarse brown hair and yellow eyes, displayed a kind of awkward zaniness. He was smart with numbers, read books. He asked complicated questions no one could answer—the distance to the sun, why did not humans have snouts, could a traveler reach China by setting out in any direction and holding steady to it? Trains were his particular interest and he knew about rail connections from study of the timetables, pestered travelers at the station to hear something of distant cities. He was indifferent to stock except for his flea-bitten grey, Bucky, and he threw the weight of his mind in random directions as if the practical problems of life were not to be resolved but teased as a kitten is by a broom straw.

When he was fifteen his interest turned to the distant sea and he yearned for books about ships, books with pictures, and there were none. On paper he invented boats like inverted roofs, imagined the ocean a constant smooth and glassy medium until Mrs. Hepple of Laramie spoke at an evening about her trip abroad, describing the voyage as a purgatory of monstrous waves and terrible winds. Another time a man worked for them five or six months. He had been in San Francisco and told about lively streets, Chinese tong wars, sailors and woodsmen blowing their wages in a single puking night. He described Chicago, a smoking mass shrugging out of the plains, fouling the air a hundred miles east. He said Lake Superior licked the wild shore of Canada.

THERE WAS no holding Ras. At sixteen this rank gangler left home, headed for San Francisco, Seattle, Toronto, Boston, Cincinnati. What his expectations and experiences were no one knew. He neither returned nor wrote.

The daughter, neglected as daughters are, married a cowboy with bad habits and moved with him to Baggs. Horm Tinsley gave up on sheep and started a truck garden and honey operation, specializing in canning tomatoes, in Moon and Stars watermelons. After a year or so he sold Ras's horse to the Klickas on the neighboring ranch.

In 1933 the son had been gone more than five years and not a word.

The mother begged of the curtains, "Why don't he write?" and saw again the infant in the water, silent, the swollen dress buoying it around the dark bend. Who would write to such a mother?—and she was up in the night and to the kitchen to scrub the ceiling, the table legs, the soles of her husband's boots, rubbing the old meat grinder with a banana skin to bring up the silvery bloom. A murderer she might be but no one could say her house wasn't clean.

JAXON DUNMIRE was ready to get back on the road with his Morning Glory pitch and bluster. They'd finished building a new round corral, branding was over, what there was to brand, forget haying— in the scorched fields the hay hadn't made. What in another place might have been a froth of white flowers here was alkali dust blooming in the wind, and a dark horizon not rain but another choking storm of dust or rising cloud of grasshoppers. Ice said he could feel there was worse to come. To save the ranchers the government was buying up cattle for nickels and dimes.

Jaxon lounged against a stall watching shaggy-headed Bliss who bent over a brood mare's hoof, examining a sand crack.

"Last year down by Lingle I seen Mormon crickets eat a live prairie dog," Jaxon said. "In about ten minutes."

"God," said Bliss, who had not tasted candy until he was fourteen and then spat it out, saying, too much taste. He enjoyed Jaxon's stories, thought he might like to be a windmill man himself sometime, or at least travel around a few weeks with Jaxon. "Got a little crack startin here."

"Catch it now, save the horse. We still got half a jar a that hoof dressin. Yeah, see and hear a lot a strange things. Clayt Blay told me that around twenty years ago he run into these two fellers in

Laramie. They told him they found a diamond mine up in the Sierra Madres, and then, says Clayt, both a them come down with the whoopin pox and died. Found their bodies in the fall, rotted into the cabin floor. But a *course* they'd told Clayt where their dig was before they croaked."

"You didn't fall for it." Bliss began to cut a pattern into the hoof above the crack to contain it.

"Naw, not likely anything Clayt Blay says would cause me to fire up." He rolled a cigarette but did not light it.

Bliss shot a glance into the yard. "What the hell is that stuff on your skunk wagon?"

"Aw, somebody's threwn flour or plaster on it in Rock Springs. Bastards. Ever time I go into Rock Springs they do me some mess. People's in a bad mood—and nobody got money for a goddamn windmill. You ought a see the homemade rigs they're bangin together. This one guy builds somethin from part of a old pump, balin wire, a corn sheller and some tie-rods. Cost him two dollars. And the son of a bitch worked great. How can I make it against that?"

"Oh lord," said Bliss, finishing with the mare. "I'm done here. I'll warsh that stuff off a your rig."

As he straightened up Jaxon tossed him the sack of tobacco. "There you go, brother boy. And I find the good shears I'll cut your lousy hair. Then I got a go."

A LETTER came to the Tinsleys from Schenectady, New York. The man who wrote it, a Methodist minister, said that a young man severely injured a year earlier in an auto wreck, mute and damaged since that time, had somewhat regained the power of communication and identified himself as their son, Rasmussen Tinsley.

No one expected him to live, wrote the minister, *and it is a testament to God's goodness that he has survived. I am assured that the conductor will help him make the train change in Chicago. His fare has been paid by a church collection. He will arrive in Laramie on the afternoon train March 17.*

The afternoon light was the sour color of lemon juice. Mrs. Tinsley, her head a wonderful frozen confection of curls, stood on the platform watching the passengers get down. The father wore a clean, starched shirt. Their son emerged, leaning on a cane. The conductor handed down a valise. They knew it was Ras but how could they know him? He was a monster. The left side of his face and head had been damaged and torn, had healed in a mass of crimson scars. There was a whistling hole in his throat and a scarred left eye socket. His jaw was deformed. Multiple breaks of one leg had healed badly and he lurched and dragged. Both hands seemed maimed, frozen joints and lopped fingers. He could not speak beyond a raw choke only the devil could understand.

Mrs. Tinsley looked away. Her fault through the osmosis of guilt.

The father stepped forward tentatively. The injured man lowered his head. Mrs. Tinsley was already climbing back into the Ford. She opened and closed the door twice, catching sudden sunlight. Half a mile away on a stony slope small rain had fallen and the wet boulders glinted like tin pie pans.

"Ras." The father put out his hand and touched the thin arm of his son. Ras pulled back.

"Come on, Ras. We'll take you home and build you up. Mother's made fried chicken," but looked at the warped mouth, sunken from lost teeth, and wondered if Ras could chew anything.

He could. He ate constantly, the teeth on the good side of his mouth gnashing through meats and relishes and cakes. In cooking, Mrs. Tinsley found some relief. Ras no longer tried to say anything after the failure at the train station but sometimes wrote a badly spelled note and handed it to his father.

I NED GIT OTE A WILE

And Horm would take him for a short ride in the truck. The tires weren't good. He never went far. Horm talked steadily during the drives, grasshoppers glancing off the windshield. Ras was silent. There was no way to tell how much he understood. There had been damage, that was clear enough. But when the father signaled for the turn that would take them back home Ras pulled at his sleeve, made a guttural negative. He was getting his strength back. His shoulders were heavier. And he could lift with the crooked arms. But what did he think now of distant cities and ships at sea, he bound to the kitchen and the porch?

He couldn't keep dropping everything to take Ras for a ride. Every day now the boy was writing the same message: I NED GIT OTE A WILE. It was spring, hot, tangled with bobolink and meadowlark song. Ras was not yet twenty-five.

"Well, son, I need a get some work done today. I got plants a set out. Weedin. Can't go truckin around." He wondered if Ras was strong enough to ride. He thought of old Bucky, fourteen years old now but still in good shape. He had seen him in Klicka's pasture the month gone. He thought the boy could ride. It would do him good to ride the plain. It would do them all good.

Late in the morning he stopped at Klicka's place.

"You know Ras come back in pretty bad shape in March. He's gainin but he needs to get out some and I can't be takin him twice a day. Wonder if you'd give some thought to selling old Bucky back to me again. At least the boy could get out on his own. It's a horse I'd trust him with."

He tied the horse to the bumper and led it home. Ras was on the porch bench drinking cloudy water. He stood up when he saw the horse.

"Ucka," he said forcefully.

"That's right. It's Bucky. Good old Bucky." He talked to Ras as though he was a young child. Who could tell how much he understood? When he sat silent and unmoving was he thinking of the dark breath under the trees or the car bucking off the road, metal screaming and the world tipped over? Or was there only a grainy field of dim images? "Think you can ride him?"

He could manage. It was a godsend. Horm had to saddle the horse for him, but Ras was up and out after breakfast, rode for hours. They could see him on the prairie against the sharp green, a distant sullen cloud dispensing lean bolts. But dread swelled in Mrs. Tinsley, the fear that she must now see a riderless horse, saddled, reins slack.

The second week after the horse's return Ras was out the entire day, came in dirty and exhausted.

"Where did you go, son?" asked Horm, but Ras gobbled potato and shot sly glances at them from the good eye.

So Horm knew he had been up to something.

Within a month Ras was out all day and all night, then away for two or three days, god knows where, elusive, slipping behind rocks, galloping long miles on the dry, dusty grass, sleeping in willows and nests of weeds, a half-wild man with no talk and who knew what thoughts.

THE TINSLEYS began to hear a few things. Ras had appeared on the Hanson place. Hanson's girls were out hanging clothes and suddenly Ras was there on the grey horse, his hat pulled low, saying garbled things, and then as quickly gone.

The party line rang four short times, their ring, and when Mrs. Tinsley answered a man's voice said, keep that goddamn idiot to home. But Ras was gone six days and before he returned the sheriff came by in a new black Chevrolet with a star painted white on the side and said Ras had showed himself to a rancher's wife way the hell down in Tie Siding, forty miles away.

"He didn't have nothin she hadn't see before, but she didn't preciate the show and neither did her old man. Unless you want your boy locked up or hurt you better get him hobbled. He's got a awful face on him, ain't it?"

When Ras came home the next noon, gaunt and starving, Horm took the saddle and put it up in the parents' bedroom.

"I'm sorry, Ras, but you can't go around like you're doin. No more."

The next morning the horse was gone and so was Ras.

"He's rid him bareback." There was no keeping him at home. His circle was smaller but he was on the rove again.

IN THE Dunmires' noon kitchen a greasy leather sofa, worn as an old saddle, stood against the wall and on it lay Ice Dunmire, white hair ruffed, his mouth open in sleep. The plank table, twelve feet long and flanked by pants-polished benches, held a dough tray filled with forks and spoons. The iron sink tilted, a mildew smell rose from the wooden counter. The dish cupboard stood with the doors off, shelves stacked with heavy rim-nicked plates. The beehive radio on a wall shelf was never silent, bulging with static and wailing voices. A crank telephone hung beside the door. In a sideboard stood a forest of private bottles marked with initials and names.

Varn was at the oven bending for biscuits, dark and bandy-legged, Marion scraping milk gravy around and around the pan and jabbing a boil of halved potatoes. The coffeepot chucked its brown fountain into the glass dome of the lid.

"Dinner!" Varn shouted, dumping the biscuits into a bowl and taking a quick swallow from his little whiskey glass. "Dinner! Dinner! Dinner! Eat it or go hungry."

Ice stretched and got up, went to the door, coughed and spat.

They ate without talk, champing meat. There were no salads or vegetables beyond potatoes or sometimes cabbage.

Ice drank his coffee from the saucer as he always had. "Hear there was some excitement down Tie Sidin."

"Didn't take you long to hear it. Goddamn Tinsley kid that come back rode into Shawver's yard and jacked off in front a the girl. Matter a time until he discovers it's more fun a put it up the old snatch."

"Do somethin about that. Give me the relish," said Jaxon. "Sounds like nutty Mrs. T. drownded the wrong kid." He swirled a piece of meat in the relish. "Goddamn, Varn, I am sure goin a miss this relish out on the road."

"Nothin a do with me. Buy yourself a jar—Billy Gill's Piccalilli. Get it at the store."

AROUND NOON one day in the wide, burnt summer that stank of grasshoppers, Mrs. Tinsley heard the measured beating of a truck motor in the yard. She looked out. A roadster with a miniature windmill mounted in the trailer behind it stood outside, the exhaust from the tailpipe raising a little dust. There was a mash of hoppers in the tire treads, scores more in various stages of existence clogging the radiator grille.

"The windmill man is out there," she said. Horm turned around slowly. He was just getting over a cold and had a headache from the dust.

Outside Jaxon Dunmire in his brown plaid suit came at him with a smile. His dust still floated over the road. A grasshopper leaped from his leg.

"Mr. Tinsley? Howdy. Jax Dunmire. Meaning a come out here for two years and persuade you about the Mornin Glory windmill. Probably the best equipment on the market and the mill that's saving the rancher's bacon these damn dustbowl days. Yeah, I been meanin a get out here, but I been so damn busy at the ranch and then runnin up and down the state summers sellin these good mills I don't get around the home territory much." The smile lay over his face as if it had been screwed on. "My dad and my brothers and me, we got five a these Mornin Glories on the Rockin Box. Water the stock all over, they don't lose weight walkin for a drink."

"I don't do no ranchin. Pretty well out a the sheep business, never did run cattle much. I just do some truck gardenin, bees. Plan a get a pair a blue foxes next year, raise them, maybe. We got the well. We got the crick close. So I guess I don't need a windmill."

"Cricks and wells been known a run dry. This damn everlastin drought it's a sure thing. More uses to a mill than waterin stock. Run you some electricity. Put in a resevoy tank. That's awful nice to have, fire protection, fish a little. You and the missis take a swim.

But fire protection's the main thing. You can't tell when your house is goin a catch fire. Why I seen it so dry the wind rubbin the grass blades together can start a prairie fire."

"I don't know. I doubt I could stand the expense. Windmills are awful expensive for somebody in my position. Hell, I can't even afford new tires. And those I need. Expensive."

"Well, sure enough, that's true. Some things are real expensive. Agree with you on that. But the Mornin Glory ain't." Jaxon Dunmire rolled a cigarette, offered it to Horm.

"I never did smoke them coffin nails." There was a ball of dust at the turnoff a quarter mile away. Windmills, hell, thought Horm. He must have passed the boy on the road.

Dunmire smoked, looked over the yard, nodding his head.

"Yes, a little resevoy would set good here."

Old Bucky rounded the corner, pounded in, lathered and tired and on him Ras, abareback, distorted face and glaring eye, past the windmill truck close enough for dirt to spatter the side.

"Well, what in the world was that," said Jaxon Dunmire, dropping the wet-ended butt in the dust and working the toe of his boot over it.

"That is Ras, that is my son."

"Packin the mail. Thought it might be that crazy half-wit got the women all terrorized wavin his deedle-dee at them. You hear about that? Who knows when he's goin a get a little girl down and do her harm? There's some around who'd as soon cut him and make sure he don't breed no more half-wits, calm him down some."

"That's your goddamn windmill, ain't it? It's Ras. Tell you, he was in a bad car wreck. There's no harm in him but he was real bad hurt."

"Well, I understand that. Sorry about it. But it seems like there's a part a him that ain't hurt, don't it, he's so eager a show it off."

"Why don't you get your goddamn windmill out a my yard?" said Horm Tinsley. "He was hurt but he's a man like anybody else."

Now they had this son of a bitch and his seven brothers on their backs.

"Yeah, I'll get goin. You heard about all I got say. You just remember, I sell windmills but I ain't full a what makes em go."

OUT IN the corral Ras was swiping at old Bucky with a brush, the horse sucking up water. A firm man would have taken the horse from him. But Horm Tinsley hesitated. The only pleasure the boy had in life was riding out. He would talk to him in a day or so, make him understand. A quick hailstorm damaged some young melons and he was busy culling them for a few days, then the parched tomatoes took everything he had hauling water from the creek, down to a trickle. The well was almost out. The first melons were ready to slip the vine when the coyotes came after the fruit and he had to sleep in the patch. At last the melons—bitter and small—were picked, the tomatoes began to ripen and the need for water slacked. It was late summer, sere, sun-scalded yellow.

RAS SAT hunched over in the rocking chair on the porch. For once he was home. The boy looked wretched, hair matted, hands and arms dirty.

"Ras, I need a talk to you. Now you pay attention. You can't go doin like you been doin. You can't show yourself to the girls. I know, Ras, you're a young man and the juice is in you, but you can't do like you been doin. Now don't you give up hope, we might find a girl'd marry you if we was to look. I don't know, we ain't looked. But what you're up to, you're scarin them. And them cowboys, them Dunmires'll hurt you. They got the word out they'll cut you if you don't quit pesterin the girls. You understand what I mean? You understand what I'm sayin to you when I say cut?"

It was disconcerting. Ras shot him a sly look with his good eye and began to laugh, a ghastly croaking Horm had not heard before. He thought it was a laugh but did not catch the cause of it.

He spoke straight to his wife in the dark that night, not sparing her feminine sensibilities.

"I don't know if he got a thing I said. I don't think he did. He laughed his head off. Christ, I wish there was some way a tell what goes on in his mind. Could a been a bug walkin on my shirt got him goin. Poor boy, he's got the masculine urges and can't do nothin about it."

There was a silence and she whispered, barely audible, "You could take him down a Laramie. At night. Them houses." In the dark her face blazed.

"Why, no," he said, shocked. "I couldn't do no such thing."

The following day it seemed to him Ras might have understood some of it for he did not go out but sat in the kitchen with a plate of bread and jam before him, barely moving. Mrs. Tinsley put her hand gingerly to the hot forehead.

"You've taken a fever," she said, and pointed him up to his bed. He stumbled on the stairs, coughing.

"He's got that summer cold you had," she said to Horm. "I suppose I'll be down with it next."

Ras lay in the bed, Mrs. Tinsley sponging his scarred and awful face, his hands and arms. At the end of two days the fever had not broken. He no longer coughed but groaned.

"If only he could get some relief," said Mrs. Tinsley. "I keep thinkin it might help the fever break if he was to have a sponge bath, then wipe him over with alcohol. Cool him off. This heat, all twisted in them sheets. I just hate a summer cold. I think it would make him feel better. Them dirty clothes he's still got on. He's full a the smell of sickness and he was dirty a start with when he come down with it. He's just burnin up. Won't you get his clothes off and give the boy a sponge bath?" she said with delicacy. "It's best a man does that."

Horm Tinsley nodded. He knew Ras was sick but he did not think a sponge bath was going to make any difference. He understood his wife was saying the boy stank so badly she could no longer bear to come near him. She poured warm water in a basin, gave him the snowy washcloth, the scented soap and the new towel, never used.

He was in the sickroom a long time. When he came out he pitched the basin and the stained towel into the sink, sat at the table, put his head down and began to weep, *hu hu hu*.

"What is it," she said. "He's worse, that's it. What is it?"

"My god, no wonder he laughed in my face. They already done it. They done it to him and used a dirty knife. He's black with the gangrene. It's all down his groin, his leg's swole to the foot—" He leaned forward, his face inches from hers, glared into her eyes. "You! Why didn't you look him over when you put him to that bed?"

The morning light flooded the rim of the world, poured through the window glass, colored the wall and floor, laid its yellow blanket on the reeking bed, the kitchen table and the cups of cold coffee. There was no cloud in the sky. Grasshoppers hit against the east wall in their black and yellow thousands.

THAT WAS all sixty years ago and more. Those hard days are finished. The Dunmires are gone from the country, their big ranch broken in those dry years. The Tinsleys are buried somewhere or other, and cattle range now where the Moon and Stars grew. We are in a new millennium and such desperate things no longer happen.

If you believe that you'll believe anything.

THE RED BOW

George Saunders

George Saunders is the author of three collections of short stories, *In Persuasion Nation*, *Pastoralia*, and *CivilWarLand in Bad Decline*, and the novella *The Brief and Frightening Reign of Phil*. He also wrote a children's book, *The Very Persistent Gappers of Frip*, which was a *New York Times* bestseller. In 2000 *The New Yorker* named him one of the best writers under forty. His work appears regularly in *The New Yorker*, *Harper's*, and *GQ*. Saunders teaches at Syracuse University.

Next night, walking out where it happened, I found her little red bow.

I brought it in, threw it down on the table, said: My God my God.

Take a good look at it and also I'm looking at it, said Uncle Matt. And we won't ever forget it, am I right?

First thing of course was to find the dogs. Which turns out, they were holed up back of the—the place where the little kids go, with the plastic balls in cages, they have birthday parties and so forth—holed up in this sort of nest of tree debris dragged there by the Village.

Well we lit up the debris and then shot the three of them as they ran out.

But that Mrs. Pearson, who'd seen the whole—well she said there'd been four, four dogs, and next night we found that the

669

fourth had gotten into Mullins Run and bit the Elliotts' Sadie and that white Muskerdoo that belonged to Evan and Millie Bates next door.

Jim Elliott said he would put Sadie down himself and borrowed my gun to do it, and did it, then looked me in the eye and said he was sorry for our loss, and Evan Bates said he couldn't do it, and would I? But then finally he at least led Muskerdoo out into that sort of field they call The Concourse, where they do the barbecues and whatnot, giving it a sorrowful little kick (a gentle kick, there was nothing mean in Evan) whenever it snapped at him, saying Musker Jesus!—and then he said, *Okay, now*, when he was ready for me to do it, and I did it, and afterwards he said he was sorry for our loss.

Around midnight we found the fourth one gnawing at itself back of Bourne's place, and Bourne came out and held the flashlight as we put it down, and helped us load it into the wheelbarrow alongside Sadie and Muskerdoo, our plan being—Dr. Vincent had said this was best—to burn those we found, so no other animal would—you know, via feeding on the corpses—in any event, Dr. Vincent said it was best to burn them.

When we had the fourth in the wheelbarrow my Jason said: Mr. Bourne, what about Cookie?

Well no I don't believe so, said Bourne.

He was an old guy and had that old-guy tenderness for the dog, it being pretty much all he had left in the world, such as for example he always called it *friend-of-mine*, as in: How about a walk, friend-of-mine?

But she is mostly an outside dog? I said.

She is almost completely an outside dog, he said. But still, I don't believe so.

And Uncle Matt said: Well, Lawrence, I for one am out here tonight trying to be certain. I think you can understand that.

I can, Bourne said, I most certainly can.

And Bourne brought out Cookie and we had a look.

At first she seemed fine, but then we noticed she was doing this funny thing where a shudder would run through her and her eyes would all of a sudden go wet, and Uncle Matt said: Lawrence, is that something Cookie would normally do?

Well, ah . . . , said Mr. Bourne.

And another shudder ran through Cookie.

Oh Jesus Christ, said Mr. Bourne, and went inside.

Uncle Matt told Seth and Jason to trot out whistling into the field and Cookie would follow, which she did, and Uncle Matt ran after, with his gun, and though he was, you know, not exactly a runner, still he kept up pretty good just via sheer effort, like he wanted to make sure this thing got done right.

Which I was grateful to have him there, because I was too tired in my mind and my body to know what was right anymore, and sat down on the porch, and pretty soon heard this little pop.

Then Uncle Matt trotted back from the field and stuck his head inside and said: Lawrence do you know, did Cookie have contact with other dogs, was there another dog or dogs she might have played with, nipped, that sort of thing?

Oh get out, get away, said Bourne.

Lawrence my God, said Uncle Matt. Do you think I like this? Think of what we've been through. Do you think this is fun for me, for us?

There was a long silence and then Bourne said well all he could think of was that terrier at the Rectory, him and Cookie sometimes played when Cookie got off her lead.

WHEN WE got to the Rectory, Father Terry said he was sorry for our loss, and brought Merton out, and we watched a long time and Merton never shuddered and his eyes remained dry, you know, normal.

Looks fine, I said.

Is fine, said Father Terry. Watch this: Merton, genuflect.

And Merton did this dog stretchy thing where he sort of like bowed.

Could be fine, said Uncle Matt. But also could be he's sick but just at an early stage.

We'll have to be watchful, said Father Terry.

Yes, although, said Uncle Matt. Not knowing how it spreads and all, could it be we are in a better-safe-than-sorry type of situation? I don't know, I truly don't know. Ed, what do you think?

And I didn't know what I thought. In my mind I was all the time just going over it and over it, the before, the after, like her stepping up on that footstool to put that red bow in, saying these like lady phrases to herself, such as, Well Who Will Be There, Will There Be Cakes?

I hope you are not suggesting putting down a perfectly healthy dog, said Father Terry.

And Uncle Matt produced from his shirt pocket a red bow and said: Father, do you have any idea what this is and where we found it?

But it was not the real bow, not Emily's bow, which I kept all the time in my pocket, it was a pinker shade of red and was a little bigger than the real bow, and I recognized it as having come from our Karen's little box on her dresser.

No I do not know what that is, said Father Terry. A hair bow?

I for one am never going to forget that night, said Uncle Matt. What we all felt. I for one am going to work to make sure that no one ever again has to endure what we had to endure that night.

I have no disagreement with that at all, said Father Terry.

It is true you don't know what this is, Uncle Matt said, and put the bow back in his pocket. You really really have no experience whatsoever of what this is.

Ed, Father Terry said to me. Killing a perfectly healthy dog has nothing to do with—

Possibly healthy but possibly not, said Uncle Matt. Was Cookie bitten? Cookie was not. Was Cookie infected? Yes she was. How was Cookie infected? We do not know. And there is your dog, who interacted with Cookie in exactly the same way that Cookie interacted with the known infected animal, namely through being in close physical proximity.

It was funny about Uncle Matt, I mean funny as in great, admirable, this sudden stepping up to the plate, because previously—I mean, yes, he of course loved the kids, but had never been particularly—I mean he rarely even spoke to them, least of all to Emily, her being the youngest. Mostly he just went very quietly around the house, especially since January when he'd lost his job, avoiding the kids really, a little ashamed almost, as if knowing that, when they grew up, they would never be the out-of-work slinking-around uncle, but instead would be the owners of the house where the out-of-work slinking uncle etc., etc.

But losing her had, I suppose, made him realize for the first time how much he loved her, and this sudden strength—focus, certainty, whatever—was a comfort, because tell the truth I was not doing well at all—I had always loved autumn and now it was full autumn and you could smell woodsmoke and fallen apples but all of the world, to me, was just, you know, flat.

It is like your kid is this vessel that contains everything good. They look up at you so loving, trusting you to take care of them, and then one night—what gets me, what I can't get over, is that while she was being—while what happened was happening, I was—I had sort of snuck away downstairs to check my e-mail, see, so that while—while what happened was happening, out there in the schoolyard, a few hundred yards away, I was sitting there typing—typing!—which, okay, there is no sin in that, there was no way I could have known, and yet—do you see what I mean? Had I simply risen from my computer and walked upstairs and gone outside and for some reason, any reason, crossed the schoolyard, then believe me, there is not a dog in the world, no matter how crazy—

And my wife felt the same way and had not come out of our bedroom since the tragedy.

So Father you are saying no? said Uncle Matt. You are refusing?

I pray for you people every day, Father said. What you are going through, no one ever should have to go through.

Don't like that man, Uncle Matt said as we left the Rectory. Never have and never will.

And I knew that. They had gone to high school together and there had been something about a girl, some last-minute prom-date type of situation that had not gone in Uncle Matt's favor, and I think some shoving on a ballfield, some name-calling, but all of this was years ago, during like say the Kennedy administration.

He will not observe that dog properly, said Uncle Matt. Believe me. And if he does notice something, he won't do what is necessary. Why? Because it's his dog. His dog. Everything that's his? It's special, above the law.

I don't know, I said. Truly I don't.

He doesn't get it, said Uncle Matt. He wasn't there that night, he didn't see you carrying her inside.

Which, tell the truth, Uncle Matt hadn't seen me carrying her inside either, having gone out to rent a video—but still, yes, I got his drift about Father Terry, who had always had a streak of ego, with that silver hair with the ripples in it, and also he had a weight set in the Rectory basement and worked out twice a day and had, actually, a very impressive physique, which he showed off, I felt—we all felt—by ordering his priest shirts perhaps a little too tight.

Next morning during breakfast Uncle Matt was very quiet and finally said, well, he might be just a fat little unemployed guy who hadn't had the education some had, but love was love, honoring somebody's memory was honoring somebody's memory, and since he had no big expectations for his day, would I let him borrow the truck, so he could park it in the Burger King lot and keep an eye on what was going on over at the Rectory, sort of in memory of Emily?

And the thing was, we didn't really use that truck anymore and so—it was a very uncertain time, you know, and I thought, Well, what if it turns out Merton really is sick, and somehow gets away and attacks someone else's—so I said yes, he could use the truck.

He sat all Tuesday morning and Tuesday afternoon, I mean not leaving the truck once, which for him—he was not normally a real dedicated guy, if you know what I mean. And then Tuesday night he came charging in and threw a tape in the VCR and said watch, watch this.

And there on the TV was Merton, leaning against the Rectory fence, shuddering, arching his back, shuddering again.

So we took our guns and went over.

Look I know I know, said Father Terry. But I'm handling it here, in my own way. He's had enough trouble in his life, poor thing.

Say what? said Uncle Matt. Trouble in his life? You are saying to this man, this father, who has recently lost—the dog has had *trouble in his life?*

Well, however, I should say—I mean, that was true. We all knew about Merton, who had been brought to Father Terry from this bad area, one of his ears sliced nearly off, plus it had, as I understood it, this anxiety condition, where it would sometimes faint because dinner was being served, I mean, it would literally pass out due to its own anticipation, which, you know, that couldn't have been easy.

Ed, said Father Terry. I am not saying Merton's trouble is, I am not comparing Merton's trouble to your—

Christ let's hope not, said Uncle Matt.

All's I'm saying is I'm losing something too, said Father Terry.

Ho boy, said Uncle Matt. Ho boy ho boy.

Ed, my fence is high, said Father Terry. He's not going anywhere, I've also got him on a chain in there. I want him to—I want it to happen here, just him and me. Otherwise it's too sad.

You don't know from sad, said Uncle Matt.

Sadness is sadness, said Father Terry.

Blah blah blah, said Uncle Matt. I'll be watching.

WELL LATER that week this dog Tweeter Deux brought down a deer in the woods between the TwelvePlex and the Episcopal church, and that Tweeter Deux was not a big dog, just, you know, crazed, and how the DeFrancinis knew she had brought down a deer was, she showed up in the living room with a chewed-off foreleg.

And that night—well the DeFrancini cat began racing around the house, and its eyes took on this yellow color, and at one point while running it sort of locked up and skidded into the baseboard and gave itself a concussion.

Which is when we realized the problem was bigger than we had initially thought.

The thing was, we did not know and could not know how many animals had already been infected—the original four dogs had been at large for several days before we found them, and any animal they might have infected had been at large for nearly two weeks now, and we did not even know the precise method of infection—was it bites, spit, blood, was something leaping from coat to coat? We knew it could happen to dogs, it appeared it could happen to cats—what I'm saying is, it was just a very confusing and frightening time.

So Uncle Matt got on the iMac and made up these fliers, calling a Village Meeting, and at the top was a photo he'd taken of the red bow (not the real bow but Karen's pinkish red bow, which he'd color-enhanced on the iMac to make it redder and also he had superimposed Emily's communion photo) and along the bottom it said FIGHT THE OUTRAGE, and underneath in smaller letters it said something along the lines of, you know, Why do we live in this world but to love what is ours, and when one of us has cruelly lost what we loved, it is the time to band together to stand up to that which threatens that which we love, so that no one else ever has to experience this outrage again. Now that we have known and witnessed this terrific pain, let us resolve together to fight against any and all circumstances which might cause or contribute to this or a similar outrage now or at any time in the future—and we had Seth and Jason run these around town, and on Friday night ended up with nearly four hundred people in the high school gym.

Coming in, each person got a rolled-up FIGHT THE OUTRAGE poster
of the color-enhanced bow, and also on these Uncle Matt had put
in—I objected to this at first, until I saw how people responded—
well he had put in these tiny teethmarks, they were not meant to
look real, they were just, you know, as he said, symbolic reminders,
and down in one corner was Emily's communion photo and in the
opposite corner a photo of her as a baby, and Uncle Matt had hung a
larger version of that poster (large as a closet) up over the speaker's
podium.

And I was sort of astonished by Uncle Matt, I mean, he was
showing so much—I'd never seen him so motivated. This was a guy
whose idea of a big day was checking the mail and getting up a few
times to waggle the TV antenna—and here he was, in a suit, his face
all red and sort of proud and shiny—

Well Uncle Matt got up and thanked everyone for coming, and
Mrs. DeFrancini, owner of Tweeter Deux, held up that chewed-up
foreleg, and Dr. Vincent showed slides of cross-sections of the brain
of one of the original four dogs, and then at the end I talked, only I
got choked up and couldn't say much except thanks to everybody,
their support had meant the world to us, and I tried to say about
how much we had all loved her, but couldn't go on.

Uncle Matt and Dr. Vincent had, on the iMac, on their own (not
wanting to bother me) drawn up what they called a Three-Point
Emergency Plan, which the three points were: (1) All Village animals must immediately undergo an Evaluation, to determine was
the animal Infected, (2) All Infected or Suspected Infected animals
must be destroyed at once, and (3) All Infected or Suspected Infected animals, once destroyed, must be burned at once to mini-
mize the possibility of Second-Hand Infection.

Then someone asked could they please clarify the meaning of
"suspected"?

Suspected, you know, said Uncle Matt. That means we suspect and have good reason to suspect that an animal is, or may be,
Infected.

The exact methodology is currently under development, said Dr. Vincent.

How can we, how can you, ensure that this assessment will be fair and reasonable though? the guy asked.

Well that is a good question, said Uncle Matt. The key to that is, we will have the assessment done by fair-minded persons who will do the Evaluation in an objective way that seems reasonable to all.

Trust us, said Dr. Vincent. We know it is so very important.

Then Uncle Matt held up the bow—actually a new bow, very big, about the size of a ladies' hat, really, I don't know where he found that—and said: All of this may seem confusing but it is not confusing if we remember that it is all about *This*, simply *This*, about honoring *This*, preventing *This*.

Then it was time for the vote, and it was something like 393 for and none against, with a handful of people abstaining (which I found sort of hurtful), but then following the vote everyone rose to their feet and, regarding me and Uncle Matt with—well they were smiling these warm smiles, some even fighting back tears—it was just a very nice, very kind moment, and I will never forget it, and will be grateful for it until the day I die.

AFTER THE meeting Uncle Matt and Trooper Kelly and a few others went and did what had to be done in terms of Merton, over poor Father Terry's objections—I mean, he was upset about it, of course, so upset it took five men to hold him back, him being so fit and all—and then they brought Merton, Merton's body, back to our place and burned it, out at the tree line where we had burned the others, and someone asked should we give Father Terry the ashes, and Uncle Matt said why take the chance, we have not ruled out the possibility of airborne transmission, and putting on the little white masks supplied by Dr. Vincent, we raked Merton's ashes into the swamp.

That night my wife came out of our bedroom for the first time since the tragedy, and we told her everything that had been happening.

And I watched her closely, to see what she thought, to see what I should think, her having always been my rock.

Kill every dog, every cat, she said very slowly. Kill every mouse, every bird. Kill every fish. Anyone objects, kill them too.

Then she went back to bed.

Well that was—I felt so bad for her, she was simply not herself—I mean, this was a woman who, finding a spider, used to make me take it outside in a cup. Although, as far as killing all dogs and cats—I mean, there was a certain—I mean, if you did that, say, killed every dog and cat, regardless of were they Infected or not, you could thereby guarantee, to 100 percent, that no other father in town would ever again have to carry in his—God there is so much I don't remember about that night but one thing I do remember is, as I brought her in, one of her little clogs thunked off onto the linoleum, and still holding her I bent down to—and she wasn't there anymore, she wasn't, you know, there, inside her body. I had passed her thousands of times on the steps, in the kitchen, had heard her little voice from everywhere in the house and why, why had I not, every single time, rushed up to her and told her everything that I—but of course you can't do that, it would malform a child, and yet—

What I'm saying is, with no dogs and no cats, the chance that another father would have to carry his animal-murdered child into their home, where the child's mother sat, doing the bills, happy or something like happy for the last time in her life, happy until the instant she looked up and saw—what I guess I'm saying is, with no dogs and no cats, the chance of that happening to someone else (or to us again) goes down to that very beautiful number of Zero.

Which is why we eventually did have to enact our policy of sacrificing all dogs and cats who had been in the vicinity of the Village at the time of the incident.

But as far as killing the mice, the birds, the fish, no, we had no evidence to support that, not at that time anyway, and had not yet added the Reasonable Suspicion Clause to the Plan, and as far as the people, well my wife wasn't herself, that's all there was to it, although soon what we found was—I mean, there was something prescient about what she'd said, because in time we did in fact have to enact some very specific rules regarding the physical process of extracting the dogs and/or cats from a home where the owner was being unreasonable—or the fish, birds, whatever—and also had to assign specific penalties should these people, for example, assault one of the Animal Removal Officers, as a few of them did, and finally also had to issue some guidelines on how to handle individuals who, for whatever reason, felt it useful to undercut our efforts by, you know, obsessively and publicly criticizing the Five- and Six-Point Plans, just very unhappy people.

But all of that was still months away.

I often think back to the end of that first Village Meeting, to that standing-ovation moment. Uncle Matt had also printed up T-shirts, and after the vote everyone pulled the T-shirt with Emily's smiling face on it over his or her own shirt, and Uncle Matt said that he wanted to say thank you from the bottom of his heart, and not just on behalf of his family, this family of his that had been sadly and irreversibly malformed by this unimaginable and profound tragedy, but also, and perhaps more so, on behalf of all the families we had just saved, via our vote, from similar future profound unimaginable tragedies.

And as I looked out over the crowd, at all those T-shirts—I don't know, I found it deeply moving, that all of those good people would feel so fondly toward her, many of whom had not even known her, and it seemed to me that somehow they had come to understand how good she had been, how precious, and were trying, with their applause, to honor her.

LESLIE AND SAM

Douglas Unger

Douglas Unger is the author of four novels, including *Leaving the Land*, a finalist for the Pulitzer Prize and Robert F. Kennedy Book Award, and *Voices from Silence*, a year's end selection by the *Washington Post Book World*. His most recent book is *Looking for War and Other Stories*. He is a cofounder of the MFA in Creative Writing International program and the Schaeffer Fellowship PhD with Creative Dissertation at the University of Nevada, Las Vegas.

They met in the Neurophysiology Lab. Carl and another new graduate student asked her to bring them one of the cats, a calico from a special breed with uniform dimensions of skulls and spines. They were on the research team doing a study on spinal cord regeneration. Carl invited her to stay and assist them—her first and only time assisting in surgery. A commanding way he had—as though there were never a question she would do what he asked—left her frustrated to the point of speechlessness. Some involuntary nervous response deep in her body started turning flips.

Masked and gowned as in an operating theater for humans, Leslie felt no squeamishness when Carl made his neat incision into the shaved skin patch in the fur of the anesthetized cat. She watched the pink and blue tissues dividing. She did her part—daubing with sterile gauze pads she gripped in forceps, soaking up the blood, impressed with how little bleeding there was and at Carl's deftly talented precision. But when he reached in with a tool like electrician's pliers and cut the exposed white spine—at the sickly crunching sound of living bone—she felt suddenly dizzy. There was a vague distant ringing in her ears. Then she was hovering in a hot sweat somewhere out of her body, seeing everything as if looking down from inside the intense mirrored lights.

"Damnit! Did she say she was a greenhorn? Get her out of here and I'll keep the cat under!"

Carl's masked face was leaning down close to hers, his muffled voice shouting, the one clear strip of his features showing cold blue eyes that could have murdered. The other student helped Leslie slowly off the floor and held her up as she staggered out of the surgery room. She sat with her head between her knees until she recovered.

"You OK?" he asked, later. "Sorry to lose it in there. It was just a little delicate, what we were doing."

"So you get off on maiming small animals?"

"Subcortical mechanisms of behavior," he said. "I'll spend a lifetime cutting up cats. That is if I ever get the Ph.D. and make it through M-school, too. Which in my case is like a shoo-in, if you get what I mean."

He had found her in her supply room office just off the animal labs, where she could often be found studying or at the computer, sitting at the beat-up metal desk hidden away among the pallet loads of animal feeds rising up around her like heavy walls. He was in bloody green scrubs, looking her up and down with that predatory expression of the habitual ass-grabber. Leslie fixed him with her own most malicious answering stare and shrugged.

"Hey, I mean it," he said. "I'll buy you dinner."

That tone again. Why was she always falling for this kind of arrogant bastard? Why did so many women choose the wrong men? But that was the way it had started. As an ambitious M.D.-Ph.D. student, Carl had a double schedule of classes and work in labs that would take up sixteen hours a day for six years before he was finished. Leslie wondered if he had just picked her out for convenience because she was so frequently in his path as he hurried from one place to another. He often slipped into her supply room office at any time as if just taking a break from his rushing around. They locked the door and spread out bags of monkey feed like a mattress. What bothered her the most was how she couldn't wait for the next of these flustered physical assaults on the job that came crashing into her serenity as would a carjacking. Then he snuck out like a thief and ran off on his rounds. But her girlfriends kept telling her what a catch he was. That she couldn't explain just how or why he had chosen her didn't change the fact that—outwardly and not knowing him better—Carl was the kind of guy most of them envied and desired.

The night he asked her to live with him, she arranged with her roommate for an evening to themselves. She cooked an elaborate, expensive dinner, a Salmon Joseph with wild rice and asparagus, to celebrate a difficult exam Carl had just finished taking in Biochemistry. He came in looking harried and exhausted, carrying a bottle of cheap brandy in a paper bag. Instead of sitting down to eat, he asked if he could fill her bathtub and take a bath first. As she was turning the burners down to warm and trying to save the fish from drying out, Carl pulled off his clothes, dropping them in a heap in the hallway. He carried his brandy into the bathroom and started filling the tub.

Minutes passed. Leslie heard the sound of his weeping, letting pain out in choking coughs he tried to swallow so no one could hear him. She ended up in the bathtub with him, holding him as he cried not with grief but from exhaustion. He had gotten an "A" on the exam and already knew he had. That was just the way he was— pretty much the way the whole relationship was going. Whatever he did, he did it all-out, full-time, non-stop, pushing himself to his limits until he finally broke down and collapsed into her arms.

Then she was there to comfort him, mothering him, all further resistance she might have felt toward him melting away with his head leaning on her shoulder, rocking him in the tepid water until it went cold.

EIGHT MONTHS later, Leslie came in to work one Monday morning at the lab and saw the order regarding Sam, in Carl's handwriting and signed with his name. It was waiting for approval by Dr. Oxnard, sitting on top of a stack of forms in the lab office in-box. "Euthanize for cross-section sampling," the order said.

There wasn't any more reason or urgency to it than that. Kill Sam just to kill him, because there was nothing more important to do this week. Kill Sam because "it was just his time" as Dr. Oxnard said. Or because no one could dream up any more reasons to keep feeding him.

Leslie found Dr. Oxnard and offered to pay for Sam's feed. Dr. Oxnard said there was no way even to process such a contribution into the laboratory budget. She pleaded that she could take Sam home and keep him there. That was out because of public health regulations, the fact that rhesus monkeys were notorious carriers of human disease, especially tuberculosis, and keeping them outside the laboratory was against the health laws. No. The decision had been made.

"I'll miss him, too. Clever old fellow, really," Dr. Oxnard said with his Cambridge accent. "But he's an old man already, not much longer before he just keels over in his cage. We have plans to clear out all the old monkeys for the new neuroprotein study connected to Alzheimer's. NIH grant just came through. Big opportunity for the lab," he said. "I'm sorry, dear, really I am. Remember what I told you about forming close attachments to the study subjects?"

It was true that with Sam, Leslie had done things she shouldn't have, getting closer to him than she had realized. But he had just been so unusual. For the four years Leslie had been working in the lab thirty hours a week—the highest paying student job on campus—Sam had always been there. His first records file had been lost in a disastrous computer crash long ago and nobody even knew how old he was. His beard was gray. He was large for a rhesus monkey when he stretched himself up. But mostly, he sat hunched over like an arthritic old man in his cage, his yellow eyes showing the milky haze of cataracts, one of his dangerous canine fangs broken off, most of his other teeth worn to ugly brown stumps he showed when he yawned.

Sam had been used in so many experiments that he was useless for any more. Years ago, behavioral researchers had taught him a series of arrangements of colored plastic symbols—stars, circles, squares and triangles in red, blue and green they actually called a "language." Sam was strapped into a highchair and coached to arrange the symbols on his tray in a certain order to get a piece of banana, another to get a grape, another for an apple bit, and so forth, though whether rhesus monkeys could actually understand what they were doing with such symbols was still a controversy.

After that training, Sam was enrolled in drug addiction studies. Heroine. Cocaine. THC. Speed. Alcohol. They strung him out on almost everything. The Ph.D. candidates in Biopsychology were looking for data on behavioral changes based on Sam's manipulation of the plastic toys on the tray. When each study was completed, they left him in his cage to go cold turkey so another Ph.D. candidate could write down observations of his withdrawals.

Lab lore had it that Sam was addicted and detoxed this way to various substances more than twenty times. He was soon discovered to be an unreliable subject, and kept around and alive because he was. No matter what drugs he was given, whether he was high, stoned, drunk, cold sober, he was able to perform his games with the plastic symbols exactly the same way, perfectly and without variation. This innate tolerance or learned resistance—whatever it was—caused some excitement for a while then even further cycles of forced addiction until the researchers could be sure of what they observed. When they put him back in his cage for detoxing, Sam took even that as routine. Leslie had been there for the last two of these. Sam rolled up into the same fetal crouch, covered himself with his wood shavings, refused to eat for two weeks, and she observed he had even perfected a technique of turning his head carefully to one side so he could projectile vomit through the wire mesh and not soil his cage.

Like most monkeys in addiction studies, Sam probably would have been euthanized long ago to look at damage to his brain if he hadn't by lucky chance—or his own cleverness—one day gotten loose in the lab and been discovered by Dr. Oxnard at the supply room computer playing with a joystick. Sam was standing in the desk chair, intently staring at the monitor screen and rapidly pressing the trigger button on the stick as though he were actually playing a game called "Space Invasion."

"Never saw anything like it," Dr. Oxnard used to tell the story. "There he was, shooting down spaceships like he knew just what the game was about. But we never could get him to do it again. So he was probably just momentarily fascinated by the noise the damn thing was making."

The student who had held the job before Leslie had spent most of his time playing computer games in the supply room office. He was eventually fired for it, and for having such a lax attitude toward his duties in the Gross Anatomy lab upstairs. He was caught intentionally mixing up parts of carefully numbered cadavers and just tossing them into one big bag for incineration. He then divided up the pile of ashes into individual boxes as though it made no difference whose remains were finally returned to the families.

One of the reasons the job paid so well was to ensure a painstaking attitude toward the cadavers. Both that and to compensate for the revulsion most people felt at working so closely with dead bodies and what the first-year medical students did to them. Part of Leslie's job each day was to wheel a stainless steel cart through the Gross Anatomy lab that was like a forest of bluish-gray cadavers lying on the tables, rows of bodies with legs and arms often held up and spread out in metal stirrups as if in some final offertory ritual. When she was hired, Dr. Oxnard had given her his standard medical school pep talk about "the revered science of anatomy" and respect for what he called "the humanity of human remains."

Leslie had recognized the cadavers right away for their beauty and fascination. After all, they were still in some way people. They had had names and real lives, hopes and dreams, and she had never thought of the bodies on the tables as anything less. Her girlfriends asked her how she could do what she did without it giving her nightmares. But she was grateful to be working this job that paid enough she could almost painlessly support herself through college. Her father was a high school math teacher and her mother worked part-time for the school administration office in not too far off Winnetka. She and her sisters were made aware almost since they were capable of speech of the sharp irony that a high school teacher wouldn't have the money to send his kids to college. So she was proud of this job, what it meant for her and for her family. She did everything with care and responsibility. Each morning, before the medical students came to class, as Leslie slowly pushed her cart between the rows of steel tables, alone in a dense silence among the dead, eyes watering from the formaldehyde as she carefully, religiously emptied and kept track of the dissecting pans, she felt mainly a sense of peace.

Working with dead people was the easiest part of her job. After that, she took the elevator down to the basement, where she put on an apron and a pair of heavy rubber gloves. There were about a hundred rat cage trays to pull out and scrape off into a garbage can, fresh pellets in the food dishes, water bottles to wash out and fill, the rat cages rotating on a once-every-three-days schedule. Then there were the cats. The cats sometimes really did give her nightmares, the ones that were subjects in experiments and left alive that way, electrode ports sticking up out of their heads like bizarre metal horns, some with their brains cut up so radically they were blind and deaf and flopped over in twitching, cage-thumping seizures. The cats in Carl's spinal nerve regeneration studies were even more pathetic, a bank of cages filled mostly with black and orange calicos left miserably dragging their useless hindquarters around. She had to remind herself these cats served a noble purpose, research to help human paraplegics one day recover more of their lives. Only once every two days on a set schedule was she able to lift them out of their cages, limp helpless cats she raised up one after the other in a kind of sling as they meowed in pain or protest or just a kittenish demand for attention, she was never sure, then she cleaned out their cages and washed off their fur with a foul smelling antiseptic solution. After the cats—the cats that would break her heart if she allowed herself to think about them or even to stop for a moment to scratch one behind the ears—she moved her caretaking chores into the monkey room.

Sam would be waiting. It was only for Leslie or Dr. Oxnard that he stuck one black palmed hand out through the cage mesh, letting it dangle there as if a kind of greeting. She discovered through experimentation that what he wanted in the way of greeting was to grip one of her fingers tightly in his paw. After a minute or two, he would shake her finger twice and let it go. Then with Leslie—only with her, it seemed—he would leave his paw sticking out through the cage wire in a beckoning way. Leslie would put her much larger hand around his as Sam looked shyly away in his cage, even using his other hand like a kind of visor to shield his eyes. What he actually wanted was to hold hands, some form of intimate touch, she had no doubts. She would talk to him as they did this, asking him how his night had gone, then before she let go and continued with her chores, she always dropped some grapes or a piece of apple into his cage. Sam very slowly and not at all greedily let her hand go, collected his treats and turned his back to her, not wanting her to watch him eating.

There were twenty-six other monkeys in the room. They weren't at all like Sam as Leslie filled their biscuit racks and cleaned their cages. The other monkeys were often raucous, loud, screaming, "ook-ooking" as she called it, their paws gripping the wire mesh like so many little prisoners as they rattled and shook their cages all together with what seemed earthquake force. Then, suddenly, they settled down and sat watching her all in a troop with an oddly rustling kind of quiet and with what she felt was a fierce and primitive form of interspecies hatred.

Sam really was different from the others, she kept thinking. He was an escape artist, for one thing. The standard spring latch contraption on his cage door he had managed to open, reaching it with his paws by squeezing his arms through the wire mesh and bending them in an astonishing contortion. The lab had tried a padlock, but that had been a hassle because of always having to keep track of the key, and Sam kept up a constant slapping at the lock that made an incessant noise hard to stand. Then one night, he proved determined enough to chew through the cage wire, breaking off pieces of some of his teeth. Besides, the times he did get loose, undoing the wire latch and just lifting up his sliding cage door, all he ever really did was wander around looking for bits of spilled biscuits from the other cages. Every once in a while, Leslie found him sitting in front of one of the female monkey's cages, both reaching out their paws, grooming each other, or using the hairy back of a paw to stroke each other's cheeks—Dr. Oxnard once told her whimsically that was the way monkeys kissed.

When Leslie found Sam loose in the monkey room—or even the times she had opened the door to her supply room office and let him come in and join her while she was studying—whenever Sam was loose for long enough, as though he were finished with what he wanted to do outside, he lazily stretched and yawned then crept off on all fours back into the monkey room where he would let himself back inside his cage, sliding his door closed behind him.

A monkey goes in search of its cage. What did that mean? Leslie often wondered. And thinking about Sam now—desperate fantasies of setting him free—she knew that even if she could just lead him out of the laboratory into the elevator and set him loose into the grass and trees of the hospital campus, or even if she could get him into a taxi and take him farther than that, out of the city to some large park or wild stretch of rivers and woods, no matter what Leslie could imagine doing, she knew that, in the end, since his birth knowing no other world, Sam was smart enough that he would eventually find his own way back like a lost dog returning home.

"What? You're kidding! That smelly old thing?"

This was Carl's reaction to her pleas to save Sam.

"Come on. Don't go anti-vivisectionist on me. We've got enough trouble with those freaks. Leslie, please," he said when it was clear she would only answer him with an enraged silence. "Don't be like this. You know the reality of what we're doing."

Finally, she told herself it wasn't Carl, that he wasn't in any way to blame—he was just the one there for the job. Still, the night she found out, she was upset enough that she found his bottle of sleeping pills he rarely used and took two to calm herself down. Later, in bed, she felt her skin flinching when Carl pulled her to him—how strong he was, the way he could just lift her around in bed as helpless as a monkey pinned by its arms. She lifelessly let him screw her while she pushed her fogging mind somewhere else.

"Don't be like this," Carl pleaded, softly.

She didn't answer. She turned her back to him. As she was slowly drifting into a drugged sleep, she sensed one of his strong competent hands gently feeling along the bones of her spine.

THE NEXT morning, the note Carl left stuck with a magnet to the refrigerator said only, *You've been avoiding me. We need to talk—C.*

She picked up his socks. She had never had a relationship with a man who didn't leave his socks on the floor. She gathered up his shirts, underwear and surgical greens piled on a chair. Collecting the laundry was part of her routine. For the past eight months, she had ended up doing his wash, the shopping, cooking what meals they shared increasingly mindful that he was probably only with her for the comforts she provided him. Carl could have any number of attractive girls. Nurses and technicians at the hospital were always throwing themselves at him. More and more, she felt an ache like a premonition of the deep hurt she would feel when he finally left her for one of them.

And now there was this problem over Sam. She realized she felt about Sam almost the same confused emotions she was feeling for Carl—how she looked at him now like he was already gone. How was it possible to go on living this way? Her own plans had very slowly and subtly changed, as though submerged into the daily patterns of this routine of life with him. She had once imagined she would receive her college degree then go on to graduate school in a field of environmental science—youthful visions she had conceived since high school of one day helping to preserve forests, riparian habitats, vanishing species. How had she managed to let most of this senior year go by without even applying? All of it came down to him—him, him, him, she realized. As she went out that morning into the grimy winter light of Chicago, she looked around their small shabby apartment with an awareness like a stab at the center of her being that everything would soon be a memory.

Sam. She went right to him, first thing, letting go her chores in the Gross Anatomy lab upstairs. There he was, waiting, his hand poking out through the wire mesh in that way he had. She let him grip her finger a long time, then she opened up his cage door and set a handful of grapes down in his wood shavings. Sam looked at the abundance of them a little warily. He slowly collected the grapes, one by one, like he was counting them, moving them around with his gnarled old paws, his wrists scarred like a suicide survivor's with multiple cuts, needle marks, slashes from so many times he had been hooked up to machines. He held a grape up to his nose and sniffed it then turned his back on her and ate it, as was his custom, as if too shy to let anyone see him eating.

Sam turned and faced her again. So unlike the other monkeys who took direct eye contact as a challenge, Sam could look any human being straight in the eyes as if fixing that person in his mind with his sharp yellow gaze. He did this to Leslie now. He curled his lip at her, a sign he wanted to play. He actually gestured with two fingers at his grapes, then he began arranging them in a star shape in the shavings.

"Not hungry?" she asked.

He looked at her again in that deep way. He arranged his grapes into a square and fixed on her again.

"Apple?" she asked. She pulled one from her lab coat pocket and held it out. He took the apple quickly, turned his back, and she watched the shifting, hunched-over movements as he greedily ate the whole thing. "Good for you, Sam. Good for you," she said.

She picked up her book. She had discovered on one of Sam's afternoons in the supply room office with her that he liked to hear her read. She had been reading sentences from one of her term papers off the computer screen to make sure of the rhythms and she had glanced over at Sam, finding him actually listening, his head cocked a little to one side, then as she kept on reading, she watched what looked like a pleased and tranquil mood come over him, his gray beard even nodding to the rhythm of her words as if to some gentle music. She experimented with this. Whenever she stopped reading, she noticed that Sam sat up and started shifting impatiently around, sniffing and poking his fingers at the bags of feed. Then when she started reading again aloud, he quit that and settled down, leaning back with what she thought was a pleasant, dreamy expression.

His apple finished, she watched as Sam turned again, facing her. He reached out through the open cage door with his paw as though waiting for her to let him grab and squeeze her finger all over again.

"No," she said. "I'll read to you now."

She was a senior, and like many Biology students, she had put off her core requirements in the Humanities as long as she could. The class was working its way through a *Masterpieces of World Literature: Volume One* anthology this semester. She opened the thick expensive book to the assignment for today and started reading: "Betwixt mine eye and heart a league is took / And each doth good turns now unto the other: / When that mine eye is famish'd for a look / Or heart in love with sighs himself doth smother / With my love's picture then my eye doth feast / And to the painted banquet bids my heart . . ."

It was the wrong thing to read. She couldn't go on. All she could do was keep repeating, though she wasn't sure the sounds she was making actually formed words, "I'm sorry, Sam . . . I'm sorry . . . I'm so sorry . . . I'm sorry . . . I'm sorry . . ."

She saw her future. Tomorrow, coming into the monkey room and finding Sam's cage empty. Then she saw the life ahead of her with Carl—how she would become even more attached, allied with him, cooking his meals, cleaning his place, picking up his socks and shirts. How he would pull her to him in the night and use her whenever he needed. And she would give him all he wanted, everything, see to all his comforts, see him through medical school, gladly, devotedly, more and more, until the day would come when his ambitious dreams were all she had left to call her own.

Sure, they might even get married—she was woman enough to keep him tied to the comforts she provided him so he would feel obliged to marry her and he would. He would get his degrees and make six figures in income. They would drive new cars and move into a beautiful house. She would put the house together for him, make his home her world. She would have his children. For a time, she would even be happy. But all the while, she would be waiting for a day like this one, the day Carl didn't come home, the day some nurse or lab-tech caught his eye on his hurrying way from one place to another and what she always sensed would happen would finally happen and that would be the end.

She would be alone, and, sure, missing the feel of his always rushing body, his delicate surgeon's touch, longing for his companionship and self-assured voice, the strong vanilla and medicine smell of him that was uniquely his no matter where he had been. Then she would be lost. Why it would never work out was the way she had already lost herself and would keep losing herself in him, dissolving into him like into some unstable absorbent solution until there was nothing left of herself, nothing of her own she could even recognize. That was it—she was already lost, and she knew this now, knew it as surely and certainly as she had ever known anything in her life.

No. Better to be alone now than let herself be destroyed by what was surely coming. And this job—she had worked it too long, she knew that much now, too. Once they killed Sam, she could never, ever set foot in this lab again. She would finish reading to him, yes, she would, read to him until he fell asleep or turned away in his cage. She would say her last good-bye then go to the supply room office to type up a letter of resignation to put on Dr. Oxnard's desk. From there, she would go directly home. She would pull out the empty boxes, suitcases and plastic bags and start packing. She would be gone to a friend's house before Carl turned up for dinner. She would leave a note for him on the refrigerator: *Let's not talk after all. I've decided to avoid you for the rest of my life.—L.*

Leslie sat there thinking all of this, seeing pictures in her mind in fast jumping images like a series of shaky disconnected scenes searching forward on a video. And now she was pushing the rewind button before the scenes ever had the chance to happen. She became suddenly aware of herself. Her eyes were closed, her body bent over and leaning against Sam's cage, her arms wrapped tightly around her middle as if to catch herself from the sensation she was falling. She was crying, making painful human sounds.

Suddenly, she stiffened. A sob caught still in her throat when she realized what it was, on the side of her face, such a light hairy sensation it almost tickled. Years later, she would describe what happened as one of the most tender and loving touches she ever experienced—how a monkey had once kissed her that way on the cheek.

THE BROWN CHEST

John Updike

John Updike was born in 1932, in Shillington, Pennsylvania. He graduated from Harvard College in 1954, and spent a year in Oxford, England, at the Ruskin School of Drawing and Fine Art. From 1955 to 1957
he was a member of the staff of *The New Yorker*, and since 1957 has lived
in Massachusetts. He is the father of four children and the author of
more than fifty books, including collections of short stories, poems,
essays, and criticism. His novels have won the Pulitzer Prize (twice),
the National Book Award, the National Book Critics Circle Award, the
Rosenthal Award, and the Howells Medal.

In the first house he lived in, it sat up on the second floor, a big
wooden chest, out of the way and yet not. For in this house, the
house that he inhabited as if he would never live in any other, there
were popular cheerful places, where the radio played and the legs of
grown-ups went back and forth, and there were haunted bad places,
like the coal bin behind the furnace, and the attic with its spiders
and smell of old carpet, where he would never go without a grown-
up close with him, and there were places in between, that were out
of the main current but were not menacing, either, just neutral,
and neglected. The entire front of the house had this neglected
quality, with its guest bedroom where guests hardly ever stayed; it
held a gray-painted bed with silver moons on the headboard and
corner posts shaped at the top like mushrooms, and a little desk

by the window where his mother sometimes, but not often, wrote letters and confided sentences to her diary in her tiny backslanting hand. If she had never done this, the room would have become haunted, even though it looked out on the busy street with its telephone wires and daytime swish of cars; but the occasional scratch of her pen exerted just enough pressure to keep away the frightening shadows, the sad spirits from long ago, locked into events that couldn't change.

Outside the guest-bedroom door, the upstairs hall, having narrowly sneaked past his grandparents' bedroom's door, broadened to be almost a room, with a window all its own, and a geranium on the sill shedding brown leaves when the women of the house forgot to water it, and curtains of dotted swiss he could see the telephone wires through, and a rug of braided rags shaped like the oval tracks his Lionel train went around and around the Christmas tree on, and, to one side, its front feet planted on the rag rug, with just enough space left for the attic door to swing open, the chest.

It was big enough for him to lie in, but he had never dared try. It was painted brown, but in such a way that the wood grain showed through, as if paint very thinned with turpentine had been used. On the side, wavy stripes of paint had been allowed to run, making dribbles like the teeth of a big wobbly comb. The lid on its brown had patches of yellow freckles. The hinges were small and black, and there was a keyhole that had no key. All this made the chest, simple in shape as it was, strange, and ancient, and almost frightening. And when he, or the grown-up with him, lifted the lid of the chest, an amazing smell rushed out—deeply sweet and musty, of mothballs and cedar, but that wasn't all of it. The smell seemed also to belong to the contents—lace tablecloths and wool blankets on top, but much more underneath. The full contents of the chest never came quite clear, perhaps because he didn't want to know. His parents' college diplomas seemed to be under the blankets, and other documents going back still farther, having to do with his grandparents, their marriage, or the marriage of someone beyond even them. There was a folded old piece of paper with drawn-on hearts and designs and words in German. His mother had once tried to explain the paper to him, but he hadn't wanted to listen. A thing so old disgusted him. And there were giant Bibles, and squat books with plush covers and a little square mottled mirror buried in the plush of one. These books had fat pages edged in gold, thick enough to hold, on both sides, stiff brown pictures, often oval, of dead people. He didn't like looking into these albums, even when his mother was explaining them to him. The chest went down and down, into the past, and he hated the feeling of that well of time, with its sweet deep smell of things unstirring, waiting, taking on the moldy flavor of time, not moving unless somebody touched them.

Then everything moved: the moving men came one day and everything in the house that had always been in a certain place was swiftly and casually uplifted and carried out the door. In the general upheaval the week before, he had been shocked to discover, glancing in, that at some point the chest had come to contain drawings he had done as a child, and his elementary-school report cards, and photographs—studio photographs lovingly mounted in folders of dove-gray cardboard with deckle edges—of him when he was five. He was now thirteen.

The new house was smaller, with more outdoors around it. He liked it less on both accounts. Country space frightened him, much as the coal bin and the dark triangles under the attic eaves had—spaces that didn't have enough to do with people. Fields that were plowed one day in the spring and harvested one day in the fall, woods where dead trees were allowed to topple and slowly rot without anyone noticing, brambled-around spaces where he felt nobody had ever been before he himself came upon them. Heaps and rows of overgrown stones and dumps of rusty cans and tinted bottles indicated that other people in fact had been here, people like those who had posed in their Sunday clothes in the gilded albums, but the traces they left weren't usable, the way city sidewalks and

trolley-car tracks were usable. His instinct was to stay in the little
thick-walled country house, and read, and eat sandwiches he made
for himself of raisins and peanut butter, and wait for this phase of
his life to pass. Moving from the first house, leaving it behind, had
taught him that a life had phases.

THE CHEST, on that day of moving, had been set in the new attic,
which was smaller than the other, and less frightening, perhaps because gaps in the cedar-shingled roof let dabs of daylight in. When
the roof was being repaired, the whole space was thrown open to
the weather, and it rained in, on all the furniture there was no longer room for, except up here or in the barn. The chest was too important for the barn; it perched on the edge of the attic steps, so
an unpainted back he had never seen before, of two very wide pale
boards, became visible. At the ends of each board were careless
splashes of the thin brown paint—stain, really—left by the chest-
maker when he had covered the sides.

The chest's contents, unseen, darkened in his mind. Once in a
great while his mother had to search in there for something, or to
confide a treasure to its depths, and in those moments, peeking in,
he was surprised at how full the chest seemed, fuller than he remembered, of dotted-swiss curtains and crocheted lap rugs and
photographs in folders of soft cardboard, all smelling of camphor
and cedar. There the chest perched, an inch from the attic stairwell,
and there it stayed, for over forty years.

Then it moved again. His children, adults all, came from afar
and joined him in the house, where their grandmother had at last
died, and divided up the furniture—some for them to carry away,
some for the local auctioneer to sell, and some for him, the only survivor of that first house, with its long halls and haunted places, to
keep and to assimilate to his own house, hundreds of miles away.

Two of the three children, the two that were married, had many
responsibilities and soon left; he and his younger son, without
a wife and without a job, remained to empty the house and pack

the U-Haul van they rented. For days they lived together, eating takeout food, poisoning mice and trapping cats, moving from crowded cellar to jammed attic like sick men changing position in bed, overwhelmed by decisions, by accumulated possessions, now and then fleeing the house to escape the oppression of the past. He found the iron scales, quite rusted by the cellar damp, whereon his grandmother used to weigh out bundles of asparagus against a set of cylindrical weights. The weights were still heavy in his hand, and left rust stains on his palm. He studied a tin basin, painted in a white-on-gray spatter-pattern that had puzzled him as a child with its apparent sloppiness, and he could see again his grandfather's paper-white feet soaking in suds that rustled as the bubbles popped one by one.

The chest, up there in the attic along with old rolled carpets and rocking chairs with broken cane seats, stacked hatboxes from the Thirties and paperback mysteries from the Forties, was too heavy to lift, loaded as it was. He and his younger son took out layers of blankets and plush-covered albums, lace tablecloths and linen napkins; they uncovered a long cardboard box labelled in his mother's handwriting "Wedding Dress 1925," and, underneath that, rumpled silk dresses that a small girl might have worn when the century was young, and patent-leather baby shoes, and a gold-plated horseshoe, and faithful notations of the last century's weather kept by his grandfather's father in limp diaries bound in red leather, and a buggy-whip. A little box labelled in his mother's handwriting "Haircut July 1919" held, wrapped in tissue paper, coils of auburn hair startlingly silky to the touch. There were stiff brown photographs of his father's college football team, his father crouching at right tackle in an unpadded helmet, and of a stageful of posing young people among whom he finally found his mother, wearing a flimsy fairy dress and looking as if she had been crying. And so on and on, until he couldn't bear it and asked his son to help him carry the chest, half unemptied, down the narrow attic stairs whose bare wooden treads had been troughed by generations of use, and then down the slightly broader stairs carpeted decades ago, and out the back door to the van. It didn't fit; they had to go back to the city ten miles away to rent a bigger van. Even so, packing everything in was a struggle. At one point, exasperated and anxious to be gone, his broad-backed son, hunched in the body of the U-Haul van, picked up the chest single-handed, and inverted it, lid open, over some smaller items to save space. The old thin-painted wood gave off a sharp *crack*, a piercing quick cry of injury.

THE CHEST came to rest in his barn. He now owned a barn, not a Pennsylvania barn with stone sides and pegged oak beams but a skimpier, New England barn, with a flat tarred roof and a long-abandoned horse stall. He found the place in the chest lid, near one of the little dark hinges, where a split had occurred, and with a few carefully driven nails repaired the damage well enough. He could not blame the boy, who was named Gordon, after his pater-nal grandfather, the onetime football player crouching for his pic-ture in some sunny autumn when Harding was President. On the drive north in a downpour, Gordon had driven the truck, and his father tried to read the map, and in the dim light of the cab failed, and headed him the wrong way out of Westchester County, so they wound up across the Hudson River, amid blinding headlights, on an unfathomable, exitless highway. After that egregious piece of guidance, he could not blame the boy for anything, even for failing to get a job while concentrating instead on perfecting his dart game in the fake pubs of Boston. In a way not then immediately realized, the map-reading blunder righted the balance between them, him-self and his son, as when under his grandmother's gnarled hands another stalk of asparagus would cause the tray holding the rusty cylindrical weights to rise with a soft *clunk*.

They arrived an hour late, after midnight. The unloading, in-cluding the reloading of the righted chest, all took place by flash-light, hurriedly, under the drumming sound of rain on the flat roof.

Now his barn felt haunted. He could scarcely bear to examine his inherited treasure, the chairs and cabinets and chinaware and faded best-sellers and old-fashioned bridge lamps clustered in a corner beyond the leaf-mulcher and the snow-blower and the rack of motorcycle tires left by the youngest son of the previous owner of the barn. He was the present owner. He had never imagined, as a child, owning so much. His wife saw no place in their house for even the curly-maple kitchen table and the walnut corner cupboard, his mother's pride. This section of the barn became, if not as frightening as the old coal bin, a place he avoided. These pieces that his infant eyes had grazed, and that had framed his parents' lives, seemed sadly shabby now, cheap in their time, most of them, and yet devoid of antique value: useless used furniture he had lacked the courage to discard.

So he was pleased, one winter day, two years after their wayward drive north, to have Gordon call and ask if he could come look at the furniture in the barn. He had a job, he said, or almost, and was moving into a bigger place, out from the city. He would be bringing a friend, he vaguely added. A male friend, presumably, to help him lift and load what he chose to take away.

But the friend was a female, small and exquisite, with fascinating large eyes, the whites white as china, and a way of darting back and forth like a hummingbird, her wings invisible. "Oh," she exclaimed, over this and that, explaining to Gordon in a breathy small voice how this would be useful, and that would fit right in. "Lamps!" she said. "I love lamps."

"You see, Dad," the boy explained, the words pronounced softly yet in a manner so momentous that it seemed to take all the air in the barn to give them utterance, "Morna and I are planning to get married."

"Morna"—a Celtic name, fittingly elfin. The girl was magical, there in the cold barn, emitting puffs of visible breath, moving through the clutter with quick twists of her denim-clad hips and graceful stabs of her narrow white hands. She spoke only to Gordon, as if a pane of shyness protected her from his hoary father—at this late phase of his life a kind of ogre, an ancestral, proprietorial figure full of potency and ugliness. "Gordon, what's this?" she asked.

The boy was embarrassed, perhaps by her innocent avidity. "Tell her, Dad."

"Our old guest bed." Which he used to lie diagonally across, listening to his mother's pen scratch as her diary tried to hold fast her days. Even then he knew it couldn't be done.

"We could strip off the ghastly gray, I guess," the boy conceded, frowning in the attempt to envision it and the work involved. "We *have* a bed," he reminded her.

"And this?" she went on, leaving the bed hanging in a realm of future possibility. Her headscarf had slipped back, exposing auburn hair glinting above the vapor of her breath, in evanescent present time.

She had paused at the chest. Her glance darted at Gordon, and then, receiving no response, at the present owner, looking him in the eyes for the first time. The ogre smiled. "Open it."

"What's in it?" she asked.

He said, "I forget, actually."

Delicately but fearlessly, she lifted the lid, and out swooped, with the same vividness that had astonished and alarmed his nostrils as a child, the sweetish deep cedary smell, undiminished, cedar and camphor and paper and cloth, the smell of family, family without end.

INCARNATIONS OF BURNED CHILDREN

David Foster Wallace

David Foster Wallace is the author of the novels *Infinite Jest* and *The Broom of the System*; the story collections *Girl with Curious Hair, Brief Interviews with Hideous Men,* and *Oblivion*; and the essay collections *A Supposedly Fun Thing I'll Never Do Again* and *Consider the Lobster*. His essays and stories have appeared in *Harper's, The New Yorker, Playboy, The Paris Review, Conjunctions, Premiere, Tennis, The Missouri Review,* and *The Review of Contemporary Fiction*. Wallace has received the Whiting Award, the Lannan Literary Award for Fiction, the *Paris Review* Prize for humor, the QPB Joe Savago New Voices Award, and an O. Henry Award.

The daddy was around the side of the house hanging a door for the tenant when he heard the child's screams and the Mommy's voice gone high between them. He could move fast, and the back porch gave onto the kitchen, and before the screen door had banged shut behind him the Daddy had taken the scene in whole, the overturned pot on the floortile before the stove and the burner's blue jet and the floor's pool of water still steaming as its many arms extended, the toddler in his baggy diaper standing rigid with steam coming off his hair and his chest and shoulders scarlet and his eyes rolled up and mouth open very wide and seeming somehow separate from the sounds that issued, the Mommy down on one knee with the dishrag dabbing pointlessly at him and matching the screams with cries of her own, hysterical so she was almost frozen. Her one knee and the bare little soft feet were still in the steaming pool and the Daddy's first act was to take the child under the arms and lift him away from it and take him to the sink, where he threw out plates and struck the tap to let cold well water run over the boy's feet while with his cupped hand he gathered and poured or flung cold water over his head and shoulders and chest, wanting first to see the steam stop coming off him, the Mommy over his shoulder invoking God until he sent her for towels and gauze if they had it, the Daddy moving quickly and well and his man's mind empty of everything but purpose, not yet aware of how smoothly he moved or that he'd ceased to hear the high screams because to hear them would freeze him and make impossible what had to be done to help his child, whose screams were regular as breath and went on so long they'd become already a thing in the kitchen, something else to move quickly around. The tenant side's door outside hung half off its top hinge and moved slightly in the wind, and a bird in the oak across the driveway appeared to observe the door with a cocked head as the cries still came from inside. The worst scalds seemed to be the right arm and shoulder, the chest and stomach's red was fading to pink under the cold water and his feet's soft soles weren't blistered that the Daddy could see, but the toddler still made little fists and screamed except now merely on reflex from fear, the Daddy would know he thought possible later, small face distended and thready veins standing out at the temples and the Daddy kept saying he was here he was here, adrenaline ebbing and an anger at the Mommy for allowing this thing to happen just starting to gather in wisps at his mind's extreme rear still hours from expression. When the Mommy returned he wasn't sure whether to wrap the child in a towel or not but he wet the towel down and did, swaddled him tight and lifted his baby out of the sink and set him on the kitchen table's edge to soothe him while the Mommy tried to check the feet's soles with one hand waving around in the area of her mouth and uttering objectless words while the Daddy bent in and was face to face with the child on the table's checked edge repeating the fact that he was here and trying to calm the toddler's cries but still the child breathlessly screamed, a high pure shining sound that could stop his heart and his bitty lips and gums now tinged with the light blue of a low flame the Daddy thought, screaming as if almost still under the tilted pot in pain. A minute, two like this that seemed much longer, with the Mommy at the Daddy's side talking sing-song at the child's face and the lark on the limb with its head to the side and the hinge going white in a line from the weight of the canted door until the first wisp of steam came lazy from under the wrapped towel's hem and the parents' eyes met and widened—the diaper, which when they opened the towel and leaned their little boy back on the checkered cloth and unfastened the softened tabs and tried to remove it resisted slightly with new high cries and was hot, their baby's diaper burned their hand and they saw where the real water'd fallen and pooled and been burning their baby all this time while he screamed for them to help him and they hadn't, hadn't thought and when they got it off and saw the state of what was there the Mommy said their God's first name and grabbed the table to keep her feet while the father turned away and threw a haymaker at the air of the kitchen and cursed both himself and the world for not the last time while his child might now have been sleeping if not for the rate of his breathing and the tiny stricken motions of his hands in the air above where he lay, hands the size of a grown man's thumb that had clutched the Daddy's thumb in the crib while he'd watched the Daddy's mouth move in song, his head cocked and seeming to see way past him into something his eyes made the Daddy lonesome for in a sideways way. If you've never wept and want to, have a child. Break your heart inside and something will a child is the twangy song the Daddy hears again as if the radio's lady was almost there with him looking down at what they've done, though hours later what the Daddy won't most forgive is how badly he wanted a cigarette right then as they diapered the child as best they could in gauze and two crossed handtowels and the Daddy lifted him like a newborn with his skull in one palm and ran him out to the hot truck and burned custom rubber all the way to town and the clinic's ER with the tenant's door hanging open like that all day until the hinge gave but by then it was too late, when it wouldn't stop and they couldn't make it the child had learned to leave himself and watch the whole rest unfold from a point overhead, and whatever was lost never thenceforth mattered, and the child's body expanded and walked about and drew pay and lived its life untenanted, a thing among things, its self's soul so much vapor aloft, falling as rain and then rising, the sun up and down like a yoyo.

CINNAMON SKIN

Edmund White

Edmund White's novels include *Hotel de Dream*, *Fanny: A Fiction*, *A Boy's Own Story*, *The Farewell Symphony*, and *A Married Man*. He is also the author of a biography of Jean Genet, a study of Marcel Proust, *The Flaneur: A Stroll Through the Paradoxes of Paris*, and a memoir, *My Lives*. Having lived in Paris for many years, he is now a New Yorker and teaches at Princeton University.

When I was a kid, I was a Buddhist and an atheist, but I kept making bargains with God: if he'd fulfill a particular wish, I'd agree to believe in him. He always came through, but I still withheld my faith, which shows, perhaps, how unreasonable rationality can be.

One of God's miracles occurred when I was thirteen. I was spending most of that year with my father in Cincinnati; my mother, a psychologist, thought I needed the promixity of a man, even though my father then ignored me and was uninterested in teaching me baseball or tennis, sports in which he excelled. My father and stepmother were going to Mexico for a winter holiday that would not, alas, fall during my Christmas school break, although it was unlikely that he would have invited me even if I had been free, since the divorce agreement specified nothing about winter vacations. One long weekend, I returned to Chicago to see my mother and sister, and fell on my knees beside my bed in the dark and prayed that I'd be invited to come along anyway. The next

morning my mother received a telegram from my father asking me
to join him in Cincinnati the following day for a three-week car trip
to Acapulco. He'd already obtained advance assignments from my
teachers; he would supervise my homework.

My mother had a phobia about speaking to my father, and spent
thirty-five years without ever hearing his voice. If vocal communication was forbidden, the exchange of cordial but brief tactical notes
or telegrams was acceptable, provided it didn't occur regularly. My
mother's generation believed in something called *character*, and it
was established through self-discipline. Anyway, my mother suggested that I phone my father, since court etiquette prevented her
from doing so.

The next day I took the train to Cincinnati; it was the James
Whitcomb Riley, named after the Hoosier Poet ("When the frost is
on the punkin," one of his odes begins). At the end of each car, there
were not scenes of rural Indiana, as one might have expected, but,
instead, large reproductions of French Impressionist paintings—
hayricks, water lilies, Notre-Dame, mothers and children *en fleurs*
. . . This train, which I took twice a month to visit my dad when I
was living with my mom, or to visit Mom when I was living with
Dad, was the great forcing shed of my imagination: no one knew
me; I was free to become anyone. I told one startled neighbor that
I was English and in America for the first time, affecting an accent
so obviously fabricated and snobbish that it eventually provoked a
smile. I told another I had leukemia but was in remission. Another
time I said that both my parents had just died in a car crash, and I
was going to live with a bachelor uncle. Once I chatted up a handsome young farmer, his face stiff under its burn, his T-shirt incapable of containing the black hair sprouting up from under it; he
inspired a tragic opera that I started writing the next week; it was
called "Orville."

On this trip, my imagination was busy with a thick guidebook
on Mexico I'd checked out of the public library. I read everything I
could about Toltecs, Aztecs, and Mayans; but the astrology bored

me, as did the bloody attacks and counterattacks, and one century blended into another without a single individual's emerging out of the plumed hordes—until the tragic Montezuma (a new opera subject, even more heartrending than Orville, whose principal attribute had been a smell of Vitalis hair tonic and, more subtly, of starch and ironing, a quality difficult to render musically).

THE YEAR was 1953; my father and stepmother rode in the front of his new, massive Cadillac—shiny pale-blue metal and chrome and, inside, an oiled, dark-blue leather with shag carpet—and I had so much space in the back seat that I could stretch out full length, slightly nauseated from the cigars that my father chain-smoked and his interminable monologues about the difference between stocks and bonds. While in the States, he listened to broadcasts of the news, the stock reports, and sporting events, three forms of impersonal entertainment that I considered to be as tedious as the Toltecs' battles.

I lay in the back seat, knocking my legs together in an agony of unreleased desire. My head filled with vague daydreams, as randomly rotating as the clouds I could see up above through the back window. In those days, the speed limit was higher than now and the roads were just two-lane meanders; there was no radar and no computers, and if a cop stopped us for speeding my father tucked a five-dollar bill under his license and instantly we were urged on our way with a cheerful wave and a "Y'all come back, yuh heah?" My father then resumed his murderous speed, lunging and turning and braking and swearing, and I hid so I wouldn't witness, white-knuckled, the near-disasters. As night fell, the same popular song, the theme song from the film *Moulin Rouge*, was played over and over again on station after station, like a flame being passed feebly from torch to torch in a casual marathon.

We stopped in Austin, Texas, to see my grandfather, who was retired and living alone in a small wooden house he rented. He was famous locally for his "nigger" jokes, which he collected in self-published books with titles such as *Let's Laugh*, *Senegambian Sizzles*, *Folks Are Funny*, and *Chocolate Drops from the South*, and he made fun of me for saying "Cue" Klux Klan instead of "Koo"—an organization he'd once belonged to, and accepted as a harmless if stern fraternity. He was dull, like my father, though my father was different: whereas my grandfather was gregarious but disgustingly self-absorbed, my father was all facts, all business, misanthropic, his racism genial and condescending, though his anti-Semitism was virulent and reeked of hate. He wanted as little contact as possible with other people. And while he liked women, he regarded them as silly and flighty and easy to seduce; they excited men but weren't themselves sexual, although easily tricked into bed. Men he despised, even boys.

MY STEPMOTHER, Kay, was "cockeyed and harelipped," according to my mother, although the truth was she simply had a lazy eye that wandered in and out of focus and an everted upper lip that rose on one side like Judy Garland's whenever she hit a high note. Kay read constantly, anything at all; she'd put down *Forever Amber* to pick up *War and Peace*, trade in *Désirée* for *Madame Bovary*, but the next day she couldn't remember a thing about what she'd been reading. My father, who never finished a book, always said, when the subject of literature came up, "You'll have to ask Kay about that. She's the reader in this family." He thought novels were useless, even corrupting; if he caught me reading he'd find me a chore to do, such as raking the lawn.

My father liked long-legged redheads in high heels and short nighties, if his addiction to *Esquire* and its illustrations was any indication, but my stepmother was short and dumpy, like my mother, though less intelligent. She'd been brought up on a farm in northern Ohio by a scrawny father in bib overalls and a pretty, calm, roundfaced mother from Pennsylvania Dutch country, who said "mind" for "remember." ("Do you mind that time we went to the caves in Kentucky?") Kay had done well in elocution class, and even now she could recite mindless doggerel with ringing authority—and with the sort of steely diction and hearty projection that are impossible to tune out. She could paint—watercolors of little Japanese maidens all in a row, or kittens or pretty flowers—and her love of art led her to be a volunteer at the art museum, where she worked three hours a week in the gift shop run by the Ladies' Auxiliary. Oh, she had lots of activities and belonged to plenty of clubs—the Ladies' Luncheon Club and the Queen City Club and the Keyboard Club.

Kay had spent her twenties and thirties being a shrewd, feisty office "gal" who let herself be picked up by big bored businessmen out for a few laughs and a roll in the hay with a good sport. She always had a joke or a wisecrack to dish up, she'd learned how to defend herself against a grabby drunk, and she always knew the score. I'm not sure how I acquired this information about her early life. Probably from my mother, who branded Kay a Jezebel, an unattractive woman with secret sexual power, someone like Wallis Simpson. After Kay married my father, however, and moved up a whole lot of social rungs, she pretended to be shocked by the very jokes she used to deliver. She adopted the endearingly dopey manner of the society matron immortalized in Helen E. Hokinson's *New Yorker* cartoons. Dad gave her an expensive watch that dangled upside down from a brooch (so that only Kay could read it), which she pinned to her lapel: a bow of white and yellow gold studded with beautiful lapis lazuli. Her skirts became longer, her voice softer, her hair grayer, and she replaced her native sassiness with an acquired innocence. She'd always been cunning rather than intelligent, but now she appeared to become naïve as well, which in our milieu was a sign of wealth: only rich women were sheltered; only the overprotected were unworldly. As my real mother learned to fend for herself, my stepmother learned to feign incompetence.

Such astute naïveté, of course, was only for public performance. At home, Kay was as crafty as ever. She speculated out loud about other people's motives and pieced together highly unflattering scenarios based on the slimmest evidence. Every act of kindness was considered secretly manipulative, any sign of generosity profoundly selfish. She quizzed me for hours about my mother's finances (turbulent) and love life (usually nonexistent, sometimes disastrous). She was, of course, hoping that Mother would remarry so Dad wouldn't have to pay out the monthly alimony. My sister was disgusted that I'd betray our mother's secrets, but Kay bewitched me. We had few entertainments and spent long, tedious hours together in the stifling Cincinnati summer heat, and I'd been so carefully sworn to silence by my mother that, finally, when one thing came out, I told all. I was thrilled to have a promise to break.

KAY AND my father fought all the time. She'd pester him to do something or challenge him over a trivial question of fact until he exploded: "God damn it, Kay, shut your goddam mouth, you don't know what the hell you're talking about, and I don't want to hear one more goddam word out of your mouth! I'm warning you to shut it and shut it now. Got it?"

"Oh, E. V.," she wailed (his nickname; his middle name was Valentine), "you don't have to talk to me that way, you're making me sick, physically sick, my heart is pounding, and, look, I'm sweating freely, I'm soaked right through, my underarms are drenched, and you know—my high *blood* pressure." Here she'd break off and begin blubbering. She had only to invoke her blood pressure ("Two hundred and fifty over a hundred and ten," she'd mysteriously confide) in order to win the argument and subdue my red-faced father. I pictured the two of them as thermometers in which the mounting mercury was about to explode through the upper tip. Kay constantly referred to her imminent death, often adding, "Well, I won't be around much longer to irritate you with my remarks, which you find so *stupid* and *ignorant*."

My father filled his big house with Mahler, and played it throughout the night; he went to sleep at dawn. And the more socially successful Kay became the less she conformed to his hours.

They scarcely saw each other. During the hot Cincinnati days, while Daddy slept in his air-conditioned room, Kay and I spent the idle hours talking to each other. I bit my nails; she paid me a dollar a nail to let them grow. When they came in, I decided I wanted them longer and longer and shaped like a woman's; Kay promised to cut them as I desired, but each time she tricked me and trimmed them short while I whined my feeble protests: "*C'mon*. I want them long and *pointy*. . . . Kay! You *promised!*" I danced for her in my underpants; once I did an elaborate (and very girly) striptease. As I became more and more feminine, she became increasingly masculine. She put one leg up and planted her foot on the chair seat, hugging her knee to her chest as a guy might. I felt I was dancing for a man.

Perhaps she watched me because she was bored and had nothing else to do. Or perhaps she knew these games attached me to her with thrilling, erotic bonds; in the rivalry with my mother for my affections, she was winning.

Or perhaps she got off on me. I remember that she gave me long massages with baby oil as I lay on the Formica kitchen table in my underpants, and I sprang a boner. Her black maid watched us and smiled benignly. Her name was Naomi and she'd worked for Kay one day a week ironing before Kay married; afterward she moved in as a full-time, live-in employee in my father's big house. She knew Kay's earlier incarnation as a roaring girl and no doubt wondered how far she'd go now.

In fact, she went very far. Once when I told her I was constipated she had me mount the Formica table on all fours and administered a hot-water enema out of a blue rubber pear she filled and emptied three times before permitting me to go to the toilet and squirt it out.

My whole family was awash with incestuous desires. When my real mother was drunk (as she was most nights), she'd call out from her bed and beg me to rub her back, then moan with pleasure as I kneaded the cool, sweating dough. My sister was repulsed by our mother's body, but I once walked in on her and my father in his study in Cincinnati. She must have been fourteen or fifteen. She was sitting in a chair and he stood behind her, brushing her long blond hair and quietly crying. (It was the only time I ever saw him cry.) Later she claimed she and Daddy had made love. She said she and I'd done it in an upper berth on the night train from Chicago to Cincinnati once, but I can't quite be sure I remember it.

When I was twelve, Kay was out of town once and Daddy took me to dinner at the Gourmet Room, a glass-walled dome on top of the Terrace Hilton. The restaurant had a mural by Miró and French food. Daddy drank a lot of wine and told me I had my mother's big brown eyes. He said boys my age were rather like girls. He said there wasn't much difference between boys and girls my age. I was thrilled. I tried to be warm and intuitive and seductive.

NOW, AS we approached the Mexican border, Kay started teasing me: "I hope you have on very clean underpants, Eddie, because the Mexican police strip-search every tourist and if they find skid marks in your Jockey shorts they may not let you in."

My father thought this was a terrific joke and with his thin-lipped smile nodded slowly and muttered, "She's serious, and she's a hundred percent right."

Although I worried about my panties, I half hoped that a brown-skinned, mustachioed guard in a sweat-soaked uniform would look into them, and at my frail, naked body: even though I was convinced that I'd never been uglier. I had a brush cut Kay had forced on me ("You'll be hot if you don't get all that old hair out of your face"), and my white scalp showed through it. I wore glasses with enormous black frames and looked like an unappealing quiz kid, without the budding intellectual's redeeming brashness. I was ashamed of my recently acquired height, cracking voice, and first pubic hairs, and I posed in front of the foggy bathroom mirror with a towel turban around my head and my penis pushed back and concealed between my legs. In public, I'd fold into myself like a Swiss Army knife, hoping to occupy as little space as possible.

But at the border the guards merely waved us through after querying my father about the ten cartons of Cuban cigars in the trunk (Dad had to grease a few palms to convince them the cigars were for his own use, not for resale). We drove down the two-lane Pan-American Highway from the Rio Grande through an endless flat cactus desert into the mountains. Kay encouraged me to wave at the tiny, barefoot Indians walking along the highway in their bright costumes, their raven-black hair hanging straight down to their shoulders. Sometimes they'd shake their fists at our retreating fins, but I seemed to be the only one who noticed.

From the highway, we seldom saw villages or even houses, although from time to time we noticed a red flag that had been tossed into the top of a mesquite tree. Daddy said the flag signified that a cow had just been slaughtered. "Since they don't have refrigeration," he informed us through a cloud of cigar smoke, his tiny yellow teeth revealed in a rare smile, "they must sell all the edible parts of the animal and cook them within a few hours." I don't know how he knew that, although he had grown up in Texas, worked summers as a cowboy, and must have known many Mexicans. I was struck by his equanimity in contemplating such shameful poverty, which would have disgusted him had we still been in the States; in Mexico, he smiled benignly at it, as though it were an integral part of a harmonious whole.

My father had a passion for travelling long hours and making record time. He also had ironclad kidneys. Kay had to stop to pee every hour. Perhaps her blood-pressure medicine was a diuretic. "Anyway," she whined, "I don't understand why we have to rush like this. What's the hurry? For Pete's sake, E. V., we're in a foreign country and we should take a gander at it. *No es problema*?"

Before her marriage, when she was still just my father's secretary and "mistress" (my mother's lurid, old-fashioned word), Kay would have said, "For Christ's sake." If she now replaced "Christ" with "Pete," she did so as part of her social beatification. She might actually have said "take a gander" when she was a farm girl in northern Ohio, but now it was placed between gently inverted commas to

suggest that she was citing, with mild merriment but without contempt, an endearingly rural but outdated Americanism. Like many
English-speaking North Americans, she thought foreign languages
were funny, as though no one would ordinarily speak one except as
a joke. "*No es problema?*" was her comic contribution to the mishap
of being in Mexico, the verbal equivalent of a jumping bean.

HALFWAY TO Mexico City we stopped at a beautiful old colonial-
style hotel that had what it advertised as the world's largest porch,
wrapped around it on all four sides. Meek Indian women were eter-
nally on all fours scrubbing tiles the garnet color of fresh scabs still
seeping blood. That night, Kay and Dad and I walked past banana
trees spotlit orange and yellow and a glowing swimming pool that
smelled of sulfur. "*Pee-you,*" Kay said, holding her little nose with
her swollen, re-nailed fingers.

"It's a sulfur spa, Kay," Dad explained. "The Mexicans think it
has curative powers."

We entered a roomy, high-ceilinged cave in which a band was
playing sophisticated rumbas. The headwaiter, broad and tall as a
wardrobe, wore a double-breasted jacket.

"*Uno* whiskey," Dad said once we were seated, showing off for
our benefit. "*Y* two Coca-Cola *por favorita.*"

"*Sí, señor!*" the headwaiter shouted before he reclaimed his dignity by palming the order off with lofty disdain on a passing Indian
busboy in a collarless blue jacket.

All the other guests at the hotel appeared to be rich Mexicans.
No one around us was speaking English. The most attractive people
I'd ever seen were dancing an intricate samba, chatting and smiling
to each other casually while their slender hips swivelled into and
out of provocative postures, and their small, expensively shod feet
shuffled back and forth in a well-rehearsed, syncopated trot.

Daddy was decked out in a pleated jacket with side tabs that
opened up to accommodate extra girth; I think it was called a Ha-
vana shirt. Suddenly both he and Kay looked impossibly sexless in

their pale, perspiring bodies. In my blood the marimbas had lit a crackling fire, a fiery longing for the Mexican couple before me, their bodies expert and sensual, their manner light and sophisticated—a vision of a civilized sexuality I'd never glimpsed before. Outside, however, the heavy sulfur smell somehow suggested an animal in rut, just as the miles of unlit rural night around the cave made me jumpy. There was nowhere to go, and the air was pungent with smoke from hearths and filled with the cry of cocks; in the distance were only the shadowy forms of the mountains.

IN MEXICO City, we stayed in a nineteen-thirties hotel on the Reforma. There were then only two million people in "México," as the citizens called their beautiful city, with a proud use of synecdoche. People swarmed over our car at each stoplight, proferring lottery tickets, but we kept our windows closed and sailed down the spacious boulevards. We saw the Ciudad Universitaria under construction outside town, with its bold mural by Diego Rivera—a lien on a bright future, a harbinger of progress. We visited the Museum of Modern Art and ate in a French restaurant, Normandie, a few blocks away. We ascended the hill to the fortress castle of Chapultepec, where the Austrian rulers, the lean Maximilian, the pale Carlota, had lived. We were poled in barques through floating gardens and climbed the Aztecs' step pyramids.

We were accompanied everywhere by one of Daddy's business associates and his wife. After I corrected this man ("Not the eighteenth century," I snapped, "that was in the *sixteenth*"), Daddy drew me aside and said, "Never contradict another person like that, especially someone older. Just say 'I may be wrong but I thought I read somewhere . . .' or 'What do I know, but it seems . . .' Got it? Best to let it just go by, but if you must correct him do it that way. And by the way, don't say you *love* things. Women say that. Rather, say you *like* things."

I had always been proud of noticing the fatuous remarks made by adults. Now I was appalled to learn that my father had been vexed by things I said. I was half flattered by his attention (he was looking at me, after all) but also half irritated at how he wanted me to conform to his idea of a man.

We went to Cuernavaca and saw the flower-heavy walls of its mansions, then to Taxco, where Kay bought a very thin silver bracelet worked into interlocking flowers. The heat made her heavy perfume, Shalimar, smell all the stronger; its muskiness competed with my father's cigar smoke. Only I had no smell at all. Daddy warned us to look for tarantulas in our shoes before we put them on.

We arrived at Acapulco, still a chic beach resort, not the paved-over fast-food hellhole it would become, and stayed at the Club de Pesca. I had a room to myself on a floor above my father and Kay's. The manager had delivered baskets of soft and slightly overripe fruit to our rooms; after a day, the pineapple smelled pungent.

One night we went to a restaurant in a hotel on top of a cliff and watched teen-age boys in swimsuits shed their silk capes and kneel before a spotlit statue of the Virgin, then plunge a hundred and fifty feet down into the waves flowing into and out of a chasm. Their timing had to be exact or they'd be dashed on the rocks. They had superb, muscled bodies, tan skin, glinting religious medals, and long black hair slicked back behind their ears. Afterward, the divers walked among the crowd, passing a hat for coins, their feet huge, their faces pale behind their tans, their haughty smiles at odds with the look of shock in their eyes.

The popular song that year in Mexico was "Piel Canela" ("Cinnamon Skin"), an ode to a beautiful mulatto girl. In the States, reference to color was considered impolite, although everyone told racist jokes in private; here, apparently, a warm brown color was an attribute of beauty. In the afternoons on the beach, young water-ski instructors stretched their long brown arms and legs, adjusting themselves inside their swimsuits, offering to give lessons to pale tourists, both male and female. We gringos had a lot to learn from them.

———————

A SINGER and movie star from Argentina, Libertad Lamarque, was staying in our hotel. When we rode up in the elevator with her, she was wearing a tailored white linen suit and had a clipped, snowy-white Chihuahua on a leash. It turned out that her room was next to mine. I became friendly with her daughter—I don't remember how we met. Although Libertad was in exile from Perón's Argentina, her daughter still lived most of the time in Buenos Aires, where she sang American ballads in a night club. One night she volunteered to sing "You Go to My Head" at the Club de Pesca—yes, that must be how I met her. I went up to congratulate her and was surprised to discover she scarcely spoke English, though she sang it without an accent.

Libertad's daughter must have found me amusing, or perhaps docile, or a convenient alibi for her midday mid-ocean pastimes. She invited me to go out on her speedboat late the next morning; after dropping anchor, she and the handsome Indian driver kissed and embraced for an hour. I didn't know what to do with my eyes, so I watched. The sun was hot but the breeze constant. That night I was so burned Kay had to wrap me in sheets drenched in cold water.

I moaned and turned for two days and nights in wet sheets. A local doctor came and went. My fever soared. In my confused, feverish thoughts I imagined that I'd been burned by the vision of that man and woman clawing at each other on the varnished doors that folded down over the speedboat's powerful motor.

The man who had accompanied Libertad's daughter on the piano was a jowly Indian in his late thirties. Perhaps he smiled at me knowingly or held my hand a second too long when we were introduced, but I honestly can't remember his giving me the slightest sign of being interested in me. And yet I became determined to seduce him. My skin was peeling in strips, like long white gauze, revealing patches of a cooked-shrimp pink underneath. My mirror told me the effect wasn't displeasing; in fact the burn brought out my freckles and gave me a certain raffishness. Perhaps soon I, too, would have cinnamon skin. Until now, I'd resembled a newly shorn sheep.

One night at ten, my well-sauced father, atypically genial, sent me off to bed with a pat on the shoulder. But, instead of undressing and going to sleep, I prepared myself for a midnight sortie. I showered in the tepid water that smelled of chlorine and pressed my wet brush-cut hair flat against my skull. From my chest I coaxed off another strip of dead skin; I felt I was unwinding a mummy. I soaked myself in a cheap aftershave made by Mennen and redolent of the barbershop (witch hazel and limes). I sprinkled the toilet water onto the sheets. I put on a fresh pair of white Jockey underpants and posed in front of the mirror. I rolled the waistband down until it revealed just a tuft of newly sprouting pubic hair. I danced my version of the samba toward the mirror and back again. I wriggled out of my undershorts, turned, and examined my buttocks. I kissed my shoulder, then stood on tiptoe and looked at my chest, belly button, penis.

At last, my watch told me it was midnight. I dressed in shorts and a pale-green shirt and new sandals and headed down toward the bar. My legs looked as long and silky as those of Dad's pinups. I stood beside the piano and stared holes through the musician; I hoped he could smell my aftershave. He didn't glance up at me once, but I felt he was aware of my presence.

He took his break between sets and asked me if I wanted to walk to the end of the dock. When we got there we sat on a high-backed bench, which hid us from view. We looked out across the harbor at the few lights on the farther shore, one of them moving. A one-eyed car or a motor scooter climbed the road and vanished over the crest of a hill. A soft warm breeze blew in over the Pacific.

Some people lived their whole lives beside the restless, changeable motions of the ocean, rocked by warm breezes night and day, their only clothing the merest concession to decency, their bodies constantly licked by water and wind. I who had known the cold Chicago winters, whose nose turned red and hands blue in the arctic temperatures, whose scrotum shrank and feet went numb, who could scarcely guess the gender, much less discern the degree of beauty, under those moving gray haystacks of bonnets, mittens, overcoats, and scarves—here, in Mexico, I felt my body, browned and peeled into purity, expand and relax.

The pianist and I held hands. He said, "I could come up to your room after I get off at four in the morning."

"I'm in Room 612," I said.

I looked over my shoulder and saw my very drunk father weaving his way toward me. When he was halfway out the dock, I stood up and hailed him.

"Hi, Daddy," I said. "I just couldn't sleep. I decided to come down and relax. Do you know Pablo, the pianist from the bar?" I made up the name out of thin air.

"Hello, Pablo." They shook hands. "Now you better get to bed, young man."

"O.K. Good night, Daddy. Good night, Pablo."

Back in my room, I looked at the luminescent dial on my watch as it crept toward two, then three. I had no idea what sex would be like; in truth, I had never thought about it. I just imagined our first embrace would be as though we were in a small wooden boat floating down a river by moonlight. Pablo and I would live here by the sea; I'd learn to make tortillas.

I woke to the sound of shouts in the hall. Oh, no! I'd given Pablo not my room number, 610, but that of Libertad Lamarque, 612. I could hear her angry denunciations in Spanish and Pablo's timid murmurs. At last, she slammed her door shut and I opened mine. I hissed for him to come in. He pushed past me, I shut the door, and he whispered curses in Spanish against me. He sat on the edge of the bed, a mountain that had become a volcano. I knelt on the floor before him and looked up with meek eyes, pleading for forgiveness.

I was appalled by the mistake in room numbers. In my fantasies love was easy, a costume drama, a blessed state that required neither skill nor aptitude but was conferred—well, on *me*, simply because I wanted it so much and because, even if I wasn't exactly worthy of it, I would become so once love elected me. Now my hideous error showed me that I wasn't above mishaps and that a condition of cinematic bliss wasn't automatic.

Pablo undressed. He didn't kiss me. He pulled my underpants down, spit on his wide, stubby cock, and pushed it up my ass. He didn't hold me in his arms. My ass hurt like hell. I wondered if I'd get blood or shit on the sheets. He was lying on top of me, pushing my face and chest into the mattress. He plunged in and out. It felt like I was going to shit and I hoped I would be able to hold it in. I was afraid I'd smell and repulse him. He smelled of old sweat. His fat belly felt cold as it pressed against my back. He breathed a bit harder, then abruptly stopped his movements. He pulled out and stood up. He must have ejaculated. It was in me now. He headed for the bathroom, switched on the harsh light, washed his penis in the bowl, and dried it off with one of the two small white towels that the maid brought every day. He had to stand on tiptoe to wash his cock properly in the bowl.

I sat on the edge of the bed and put my underpants back on. The Indian dressed and put one finger to his lips as he pulled open the door and stuck his head out to see if all was clear. Then he was gone.

A couple of years later, when my dad found out I was gay, he said, "It's all your mother's fault, I bet. When did it first happen?" He was obsessed with such technicalities.

"I was with *you*, Daddy," I said, triumphant. "It was in Acapulco that time, with the Indian who played the piano in the Club de Pesca."

A year later, after he'd made another trip with Kay to Acapulco, he told me he'd asked a few questions and learned that the pianist had been caught molesting two young boys in the hotel and had been shot dead by the kids' father, a rich Mexican from Mexico City. I never knew whether the story was true or just a cautionary tale dreamed up by Daddy. Not that he ever had much imagination.

RECENTLY I was in Mexico City to interview Maria Felix, an old Mexican movie star. She kept me waiting a full twenty-four hours while she washed her hair (as she explained). I wandered around the city, still in ruins from a recent earthquake. The beautiful town of two million had grown into a filthy urban sprawl of slums where twenty-four million people now lived and milled around and starved.

I returned to my hotel. My room was on the fifteenth floor of a shoddy tower. I had an overwhelming desire—no, not a desire, a compulsion—to jump from the balcony. It was the closest I ever came to suicide. I sealed the glass doors and drew the curtains, but still I could feel the pull. I left the room, convinced that I'd jump if I stayed there another moment.

I walked and walked, and I cried as I went, my body streaked by passing headlights. I felt that we'd been idiots back then, Dad and Kay and I, but we'd been full of hope and we'd come to a beautiful Art Deco hotel, the Palacio Nacional, and we'd admired the castle in Chapultepec Park and the fashionable people strolling up and down the Reforma. We'd been driving in Daddy's big Cadillac, Kay was outfitted in her wonderfully tailored Hattie Carnegie suit, with the lapel watch Daddy had given her dangling from the braided white and yellow gold brooch studded with lapis lazuli.

Now they were both dead, and the city was dirty and crumbling, and the man I was travelling with was sero-positive, and so was I. Mexico's hopes seemed as dashed as mine, and all the goofy innocence of that first thrilling trip abroad had died, my boyhood hopes for love and romance faded, just as the blue in Kay's lapis had lost its intensity year after year, until it ended up as white and small as a blind eye.

The title of the session let the cat out the bag. It advertised two false assumptions—that at some particular moment in time the jump shot had appeared, new and fully formed as Athena popping from the thigh of Zeus, and that a single individual deserved credit as inventor. "Who Invented the Jump Shot" will be a pissing contest. And guess who will win. Not my perpetually outnumbered, outvoted, outgunned side. Huh-uh. No way. My noncolored colleagues will claim one of their own, a white college kid on such and such a night, in such and such an obscure arena, proved by such and such musty, dusty documents, launched the first jump shot. Then they'll turn the session into a coming-out party for the scholar who invents the inventor. Same ole, same ole aggression, arrogance, and conspicuous consumption. By the end of the seminar's two hours they'll own the jump shot, unimpeachable experts on its birth, development, and death. Rewriting history, planting their flag on a chunk of territory because no native's around to holler, Stop, thief.

And here I sit, a colored co-conspirator in my lime-colored plastic contour chair, my transportation, food, and lodging complimentary, waiting for an answer to a question nobody with good sense would ask in the first place. Even though I've fired up more jumpers than all the members of the Association for the Study of Popular Culture combined, do you think anybody on the planning committee bothered to solicit my opinion on the shot's origins. With their linear, lock-step sense of time, their solipsism and bonehead priorities, no wonder these suckers can't dance.

Let's quietly exit from this crowded hall in a mega-conference center in Minneapolis and seek the origins of the jump shot elsewhere, in the darkness where my lost tribe wanders still.

Imagine the cramped interior of an automobile, a make and model extant in 1927, since that's the year we're touching down, on a snowy night inside, let's say, a Studebaker sedan humping down a highway, a car packed with the bodies of five large Negroes and a smallish driver whose pale, hairy-knuckled fingers grip the steering wheel. It's January 27, 1927, to be exact, and we're on our way from Chicago to Hinckley, Illinois, population 3,600, a town white as Ivory Snow, to play a basketball game against Hinckley's best for money.

Though he's not an athlete, the driver wears a basketball uniform under his shirt, you know, the way some men who are not women sport a bra and panties under their clothes, just in case. In any case, even if pressed into playing because the referee fouls out one of us, the driver's all business, not a player. A wannabe big-time wheeler-dealer but so far no big deal. Now he's got a better idea. He's noticed how much money white people will pay to see Negroes do what white people can't or won't or shouldn't but always wanted to do, especially after they see Negroes doing it. Big money in the pot at the end of that rainbow. Those old-time minstrel shows and medicine shows a goldmine and now black-faced hoofers and crooners starring in clubs downtown. Why not ball games. Step right up, ladies and gents. Watch Jimbo Crow fly. Up, up, and away with the greatest of ease. Barnstorming masters of thin air and striptease, of flim and flam and biff-bam-thank-you-mammy jamming.

Not the world-renowned Globies quite yet, and the jump shot not the killer weapon it will be one day, but we're on our way. Gotta start somewhere, so Mr. Abe the driver has rounded up a motley squad and the Globies' first tour has commenced humbly, if not exactly in obscurity, since we headed for Hinckley in daylight, or rather the dregs of daylight you get on overcast afternoons in gray, lakeside Chicago, 3:30 P.M. the time on somebody's watch when Pascal Rucker, the last pickup, grunts and fusses and stuffs his pivot man's bulk into the Studebaker's back seat and we're off.

Soon a flying highway bug *splat* invents the windshield. The driver's happy. Open road far as the eye can see. He whistles chorus after identical chorus, optimistically mangling a riff from a herky-jerky Satchmo jump. The driver believes in daylight. Believes in signing on the bottom line. Believes in the two-lane, rod-straight road, his sturdy automobile. He believes he'll put miles between Chicago and us before dark. Deliver his cargo to Hinckley on schedule. Mercifully, the whistling stops when giant white flakes begin to pummel us soundlessly. Shit, he mutters, shit, shit, then snorts, then announces, No sweat, boys. I'll get us to Hinckley. No sweat. Tarzan Smith twists round from the front seat, rolls his lemur eyes at me, *Right*, and I roll my eyes back at him, *Right*.

The Studebaker's hot engine strains through a colder than cold night. Occasional arrhythmic flutter-*fluups* interrupt the motor's drone, like the barely detectable but fatal heart murmurs of certain athletes, usually long, lean Americans of African descent who will suddenly expire young, seemingly healthy in the prime of their careers, a half-century later. *Fluups* worrying the driver, who knows the car's seriously overloaded. Should he pull over and let it rest. Hell, no, lunkhead. Just let it idle a while on the shoulder. Cut off the goddamn motor and who knows if it'll start up again. The driver imagines the carful of them marooned, popsicles stuck together till spring thaws this wilderness between Chicago and Hinckley. Slows to a creepy crawl. Can't run, can't hide. An easy target for the storm. It pounces, cuffs them from side to side of the highway, pisses great, sweeping sheets of snow spattering against the tin roof. How will he hear the next *fluup*. His head aches from listening. Each mile becomes minutes and minutes hours and hours stretch into an interminable wait between *one fluup* and the next. Did he hear the last one or imagine it. If *fluup*'s the sound of doom, does he really want to hear it again.

Some ungenerous people might suggest the anxious person hunched over the steering wheel obsesses on *fluups* to distract himself from the claustrophobia and scotophobia he can't help experiencing when he's the only white man stuck somewhere in the middle of nowhere with these colored guys he gets along with very well most of the time. C'mon. Give the driver a break. He rides, eats, drinks with them. To save money he'll sleep in the same room, the same bed, for Chrissakes, with one of them tonight. He'll be run out of godforsaken little midwestern towns with the players after they thump the locals too soundly. Nearly lynched when Foster grins back at a white woman's lingering Chessy-cat grin. Why question the driver's motives. Give the man the benefit of the doubt. Who are you, anyway, to cast the first brick.

Who handed you a striped shirt and whistle. In the driver's shoes—one cramping his toes, the other gingerly tapping the accelerator—you'd listen too. Everybody crazy enough to be out on the road tonight driving way too fast. As if pedal to the metal they can outrun weather, outrun accidents. You listen because you want to stay alive.

Or try to listen, try to stay alert in the drowsy heat of the car's interior, your interior hot and steamy too, anticipating a rear-end assault from some bootlegger's rattling, snub-nosed truck. Does he dare stomp harder on the gas. Can't see shit. The windshield ice-coated except for a semiclear, half-moon patch more or less the size of his soon-to-be roommate Smith's long bare foot. The driver leans forward, close enough to kiss the glass. Like looking at the world through the slot of one of those deep-sea diving helmets. Squinting to thread the car through the storm's needle eye makes his headache worse. Do his players believe he can see where he's going. Do they care. Two guys in the front seat trade choruses of snores. Is anybody paying attention. Blind as he is peering through snow-gritty glass, he might as well relax, swivel around, strike up a conversation if somebody's awake in the back.

It's fair to ask why, first thing, I'm inside the driver's head. Didn't we start out by fleeing a conference hall packed with heads like his. A carful of bloods and look whose brains I pick to pick. Is my own gray matter hopelessly whitewashed. Isn't the whole point of writing to escape what people not me think of me. In my defense I'll say it's too easy to feel what the players feel. Been there, done that. Too easy, too predictable. Of course not all players alike. Each one different from the other as each is different from the driver. But crammed in the Studebaker with someone not one of them at the wheel, players share a kind of culture, cause when you get right down to it, the shit's out of your hands, anybody's hands, ain't nowhere to go but where you're going so kick back and enjoy the ride. Or ignore the ride. Hibernate in your body, your good, strong, hungry player's body. Eat yourself during the long ride. Nourish your muscle with muscle, fat with fat, cannibalizing yourself to survive. Cause when the cargo door bangs open you better be ready to explode out the door. Save yourself. Hunker down. Body a chain and comfort. Body can be hurt, broken, disappear as smoke up a chimney, but because we're in this together, there's a temporary sense of belonging, of solidarity and weight while we anticipate the action we know is coming. Huge white flakes tumbling down outside, but you crouch warm inside your body's den, inside this cave of others like you who dream of winning or losing, of being a star or a chump, inventing futures that drift through your mind, changing your weatherscape, tossing and turning you in the busy land of an exile's sleep. If it ain't one thing it's another, raging outside the window, my brothers. Let it snow, let it snow, let it snow.

Whatever I pretend to be, I'm also one of them. One of us riding in our ancient, portable villages. Who's afraid of insane traffic, of howling plains, howling savages. *Howling. Savages.* Whoa. Where did those words come from. Who invented them. Treacherously, the enemy's narrative insinuates itself. Takes over before you realize what's going on. Howling savages. It's easy to stray. Backslide. Recycle incriminating words as if you believe the charges they contain. Found again. Lost again. *Howling savages.* Once you learn a language, do you speak it or does it speak you. Who comes out of your mouth when you use another's tongue. As I pleaded above, the mystery, the temptation to be other than I am disciplines me. Playing the role of a character I am not, and in most circumstances would not wish to be, renders me hyperalert. Pumps me up, and maybe I'm most myself not playing myself.

Please. If you believe nothing else about me, please believe I'm struggling for other words, my own words, even if they seem to spiral out of a mind, a mouth, like the driver's, my words, words I'm trying to earn, words I'm bound to fall on like a sword if they fail me. In other words I understand what it's like to be a dark passenger and can't help passing on when I speak the truth of that truth. What I haven't done, and never will, is be him, a small, pale, scared hairy mammal surrounded by giant carnivores whose dark bodies are hidden by darkness my eyes can't penetrate, fierce predators asleep or maybe prowling just inches away and any move I make, the slightest twitch, shiver, sneeze, *fluup* it's my nature to produce, risks awakening them.

Imagine a person in the car that snowy night, someone at least as wired as the driver, someone as helplessly alert, eyes hooded, stocking-capped hair hidden by a stingy brim, someone who has watched night fall blackly and falling snow mound in drifts taller than the Studebaker along fences bordering the highway, imagine this someone watching the driver, trying to piece together from the driver's movements and noises a picture of what the man at the wheel is thinking. Maybe the watcher's me, fresh from the Minneapolis conference, attempting to paint a picture of another's invisible thoughts. Or perhaps I'm still in my lime chair inventing a car-chase scene. You can't tell much by studying my face. A player's face disciplined to disguise my next move. Player or not, how can you be sure what someone else is thinking. Or seeing. Or saying. A different world inside each and every head, but we also like to believe another world's in there, a reasonably reliable facsimile of a reality we agree upon and pursue, a world the same for everyone, even though no one has been there or knows for sure if it's there. Who knows. Stories pretend to know. Stories claiming to be true. Not true. Both. Neither. Claiming to be inside and outside. Real and unreal. Stories swirling like the howling, savage storm pounding the Studebaker. Meaning what. Doesn't meaning always sit like Hinckley, nestled in darkness beyond the steamed peephole, meaning already sorted, toe-tagged, logged, an accident waiting for us to happen.

Since I've already violated Poe's rules for inventing stories, I'll confess this fake Studebaker's interior is a site suspiciously like the inside of whatever kind of car my first coach, John Cinicola, drove back in the day when he chauffeured us, the Shadyside Boys Club twelve-and-under hoop team, to games around Pittsburgh, Pennsylvania, fifty years ago, when *fluups* not necessarily warnings of a bad heart or failing motor but farts, muted and discreet as possible in the close quarters of anywhere from seven to ten boy bodies crammed in for the ride, farts almost involuntary yet unavoidable, scrunched up as our intestines needed to be to fit in the overpacked car. Last suppers of beans and wieners didn't help. Fortunately, we shared the same low-rent, subsistence diet and our metabolisms homogenized the odor of the sneaky, invisible pellets of gas nobody could help expelling, grit your teeth, squirm, squeeze your sphincter as you might. Might as well ask us to stop breathing or snoring. Collectively we produced a foul miasma that would have knocked you off your feet if you were too close when the Studebaker's doors flung open in Hinckley, but the smell no big deal if you'd made the trip from Chicago's South Side. A thunderhead of bad air, but our air, it belonged to us, we bore it, as we bear our history, our culture, just as everybody else must bear theirs.

In other words stone funky inside the car, and when the driver cracks the window to cop a hit of fresh air, he's lying if he says he ain't mixed up in the raunchiness with the rest of us. Anyway not much happening in the single-wagon wagon train crossing barren flatlands west of Chicago, its pale canvas cover flapping like a berserk sail, the ship yawing, slapped and bruised by roaring waves that crest the bow, blinding surges of spray, foamy fingers of sea scampering like mice into the vessel's every nook and cranny. A monumental assault, but it gets old after a while, even though our hearts pump madly and our throats constrict and bowels loosen, after a while it's the same ole, same ole splish-splash whipping, ain't it so, my sisters and brothers and we steel ourselves to outlast the storm's lashing, nod off till it whips itself out. Thus we're not really missing much if we break another rule and flash forward to Hinckley.

One Hinckley resident in particular anxiously awaits our arrival. A boy named Rastus whose own arrival in town is legendary. They say his mama, a hoboing ho like those Scottsboro girls,
so the story goes, landed in Hinckley just before her son. Landed
butt first and busted every bone in her body when the flatcar she'd
hopped, last car of a mile-long bluesy freight train, zigged when
she thought it would zag, whipping her off her feet, tossing her ass
over elbows high in the air. Miraculously, the same natural-born
talent that transforms Negroes into sky-walkers and speed burners
enabled this lady to regain her composure while airborne and drop
like an expertly flipped flapjack flat on her back. In spite of splitting her skull wide open and spilling brain like rotten cantaloupe
all over the concrete platform of Hinckley station, her Fosbury flop
preserved the baby inside her. Little Rastus, snug as a bug on the
rug of his mama's prodigiously padded booty, sustained only minor injuries—a slight limp, a lisp, a sleepy IQ.

Poor orphaned Rastus didn't talk much and didn't exactly walk
nor think straight either, but the townsfolk took pity on the survivor. Maybe they believed the good luck of his sunny-side-up arrival
might rub off, because they passed him house to house until he was
nine years old, old enough to earn his keep in the world, too old
to play doctor and nurse in back yards with the town's daughters.
Grown-up Rastus a familiar sight in Hinckley, chopping, hauling,
sweeping. A hired boy you paid with scraps from the table. Rastus grateful for any kind of employment and pretty reliable too if
you didn't mind him plodding along at his lazy pace. Given half a
chance, Rastus could do it all. If somebody had invented fast-food
joints in those days, Rastus might have aspired to assistant-manage
one. Rastus, Hinckley's pet. Loved and worked like a dog. No respect, no pussy, and nothing but the scarecrow rags on his back he
could really call his own, but Rastus only thirty-six. There's still
time. Time Rastus didn't begin to count down until the Tuesday he
saw on a pole outside Hinckley's only barbershop a flyer announcing the Harlem Globies' visit.

Of course Rastus couldn't read. But he understood what every-body else in town understood. The poster meant niggers coming. Maybe the word *Harlem*, printed in big letters across the top of the poster, exuded some distinctive ethnic scent, or maybe if you put your ear close to the poster you'd hear faint echoes of syncopated jazz, the baffled foot-tapping of Darktown strutters like ocean sound in seashells. Absent these clues, folks still get the point. The picture on the flyer worth a thousand words. And if other illiterates (the majority) in Hinckley understood immediately who was com-ing to town, why not Rastus. He's Hinckley if anybody's Hinckley. What else was he if he wasn't.

Rastus gazes raptly at the players on the flyer. He's the ugly duck-ling in the fairy tale discovering swans. Falls in love with the im-possibly long, dark men, their big feet, big hands, big white lips, big white eyes, big, shiny white smiles, broad spade noses just like his. Falls in love with himself. Frowns recalling the day his eyes strayed into a mirror and the dusty glass revealed how different from other Hinckley folks he looked. Until the mirror sneaked up, *Boo,* he had avoided thinking too much about what other people saw when they looked at him. Mostly people had seemed not to look. Or they looked through him. Occasionally someone's eyes would panic as if they'd seen the devil. But Rastus saw devils and beasts too. The world full of them, so he wasn't surprised to see the scary sign of one still sticking like a fly to flypaper on somebody's eyeballs.

After the mirror those devilish beasts and beastly devils horned in everywhere. For instance, in the blue eyes of soft-limbed, teasing girls who'd turn his joint to a fiery stone, then prance away giggling. He learned not to look too closely. Learned to look away, look away. Taught himself to ignore his incriminating image when it floated across fragments of glass or the surface of still puddles, or inside his thoughts sometimes, tempting him to drown and disappear in glowing beast eyes that might be his. Hiding from himself no cure, however. Hinckley eyes penetrated his disguise. Eyes chewing and swallowing or spitting him out wet and mangled. Beast eyes no matter how artfully the bearer shapeshifted, fooled you with fleshy wrappings make your mouth water.

Maybe a flashback will clarify further why Rastus is plagued by a negative self-image. One day at closing time his main employer, Barber Jones, had said, You look like a wild man from Borneo, boy. All you need's a bone through your nose you ready for the circus. Set down the broom and get your tail over here to the mirror, boy. Ima show you a wild cannibal.

See yourself, boy. Look hard. See them filthy naps dragging down past your shoulders. People getting scared of you. Who you think you is. Don King or somebody. Damned wool stinks worse'n a skunk. Ima do you a favor, boy.

Barber Jones yakkety-yakking as he yaks daily about the general state of the world, the state of Hinckley and his dick first thing in the morning or last thing at night when just the two of them in the shop. Yakkety-yak, only now the subject is Rastus, not the usual non-stop monologue about rich folks in charge who were seriously fucking up, not running the world, nor Hinckley, nor his love life, the way Barber Jones would run things if just once he held the power in his hands, him in charge instead of those blockheads who one day will come crawling on their knees begging him to straighten things out, yakking and stropping on the razor strop a Bowie knife he'd brought special from home for this special occasion, an occasion Rastus very quickly figures he wants no part of, but since he's been a good boy his whole life, he waits, heart thumping like a tom-tom, beside a counter-to-ceiling mirror while fat-mouth Jones sharpens his blade.

A scene from Herman Melville's *Benito Cereno* might well have flashed through Rastus's mind if he'd been literate. But neither the African slave Babo shaving Captain Delano nor the ironic counterpoint of that scene, blackface and whiteface reversed, playing here in the mirror of Jones Barbershop, tweaks Rastus's consciousness of who he is and what's happening to him. Mr. Melville's prescient yarn doesn't creep into the head of Barber Jones either, even though

Rastus pronounces "Barber" as *baba*, a sound so close to *Babo* it's a dead giveaway. Skinning knife in hand, Baba Jones is too busy stalking his prey, improvising Yankee-Doodle-like on the fly how in the hell he's going to scalp this coon and keep his hands clean. He snatches a towel from the soiled pile on the floor. He'll grab the bush with the towel, squeeze it in his fist, chop through the thick, knotty locks like chopping cotton.

Look at yourself in the mirror, boy. This the way you want to go round looking. Course it ain't. And stop your shakin. Ain't gon hurt you. You be thanking me once I'm done. Hell, boy, won't even charge you for a trim.

Lawd, lawd, am I truly dat nappy-haired ting in de mere. Am dat my bery own self, dat ugly ole pestering debil what don look lak nobody in Hinckley sides me. Is you me, Rastus. Lawd, lawd, you sho nuff tis me, Rastus confesses, confronting the living proof, his picture reversed right to left, left to right in the glass. Caged in the mirror like a prisoner in a cell is what he thinks, though not precisely in those words, nor does he think the word *panopticon*, clunkily Melvillean and thus appropriate for the network of gazes pinning him down to the place where they want him to stay. No words necessary to shatter the peace in Rastus's heart, to upset the détente of years of not looking, years of imagining himself more or less like other folks, just a slightly deformed, darker duck than the other ducks floating on this pond he'd learned to call Hinckley.

Boom. A shotgun blasts inside Rastus's brain, cold as the icy jolt when the driver cracks the Studebaker's window, as cold and maybe as welcome too, since if you don't wake up, Rastus, sleep can kill you. *Boom.* Every scared Hinckley duck quacks and flutters and scolds as it rises from the pond and leaves Rastus behind, very much alone. He watches them form neat, V-shaped squadrons high in the blue empyrean, squawking, honking, off to bomb the shit out of somebody in another country. You should have known long ago, should have figured it would happen like this one day. You all alone. Your big tarbaby feet in miring clay. You ain't them and they ain't

WHO INVENTED THE JUMP SHOT

John Edgar Wideman

John Edgar Wideman is the author of the short story collections *Damballah*, *Fever*, *The Stories of John Edgar Wideman*, *All Stories Are True*, and *God's Gym*. He is also the author of a memoir, *Brothers and Keepers*, and numerous novels and essays. He has twice received the PEN/Faulkner Award for Fiction. His other honors include the Rea Award for the Short Story, the American Book Award, the Lannan Literary Fellowship for Fiction, a MacArthur Fellowship, and the National Magazine Editors' Prize for Short Fiction.

> The native American rubber-ball game played on a masonry court has intrigued scholars of ancient history since the Spaniards redefined the societal underpinnings of the New World.
> —SCARBOROUGH AND WILCOX,
> *The Mesoamerican Ballgame*

The seminar room was packed. *Packed* as in crowded, *packed* as in a packed Supreme Court, *packed* as in a fresh-meat inmate getting his shit packed by booty bandits. In other words, the matter being investigated, "Who Invented the Jump Shot," (a) has drawn an overflow crowd of academics, (b) the fix is in, (c) I'm about to be cornholed without giving permission.

you. Birds of a different feather. You might mistake them for geese flying in formation way up in the sky, but you sure ain't never heard them caw-caw, boy. Huh-uh. You the cawing bird and the shotgun aimed for you ain't gon miss next time. Your cover's busted, boy. Here come Baba Jones.

You sure don wanna go around looking just so, do you boy.

Well, Rastus ain't all kinds of fool. He zip-coons outta there, faster than a speeding bullet. (Could this be *it*—not the instant the jump shot is invented, we know better than that, but one of many moments, each monumental, memorable in its own way, when Rastus or whoever chooses to take his or her game up another level— not a notch but a quantum leap, higher, hyper, hipper—decides to put air under her or his feet, jumpshoot-jumpstart-rise-transcend, eschew the horizontal for the vertical, operating like Frantz Fanon when he envisioned a new day, a new plane of existence, a new reality, up, up, and away.) Maybe he didn't rise and fly, but he didn't Jim Crow neither. No turning dis way and wheeling dat way and jiggling up and down in place. Next time the baba seen him, bright and early a couple mornings later, Rastus had shaved his skull clean as a whistle. Gold chains draping his neck like Isaac Hayes. How Rastus accomplished such a transformation is another story, but we got enough stories by the tail feathers, twisted up in our white towel—count 'em—so let's switch back to the moment earlier in the story, later in Hinckley time, months after Rastus clipped his own wings rather than play Samson to Jones's Delilah.

Rastus still stands where we left him, hoodooed by the Harlem Globies' flyer. Bald, chained Rastus who's been nowhere. Doesn't even know what name his mother intended for him. Didn't even recognize his own face in the mirror till just yesterday, Hinckley time. Is the flyer a truer mirror than the one in the barbershop, the mirror Rastus assiduously keeps at his back these days as he sweeps, dusts, mops. He studies the grinning black men on the poster, their white lollipop lips, white circles around their eyes, white gloved fingers, his gaze full of longing, nostalgia, more than a small twinge of envy and regret. He doesn't know the Globies ain't been nowhere neither, not to Harlem nor nowhere else, their name unearned, ironic at this point in time. Like the jump shot, the Globies not quite invented yet. Still a gleam in the owner/driver's eye, his wishful thinking of international marketing, product endorsements, movies, TV cartoon, prodigious piles of currency, all colors, sizes, shapes promiscuously stacking up. Not Globies yet because this is the team's maiden voyage, first trot, first road game, this trek from Chicago to Hinckley. But they're on their way, almost here, if you believe the signs tacked and glued all over town, a rain, a storm, a blizzard of signs. If he weren't afraid the flimsy paper would come apart in his hands, Rastus would peel the flyer off the pole, sneak it into the barbershop, hold it up alongside his face so he could grin into the mirror with his lost brothers. Six Globies all in a row. Because, yes, in spite of signs of the beast, the players are like him. Different and alike. Alike and different. The circle unbroken. Yes. Yes. Yes. And *whoopee* they're coming to town.

Our boy Rastus sniffs opportunity knocking and decides—with an alacrity that would have astounded the townsfolk—to become a Globie and get the hell out of Hinckley.

As befits a fallen world, however, no good news travels without bad. The night of the game Rastus not allowed in the armory. Hinckley a northern town, so no Jim Crow laws turned Rastus away. Who needed a law to regulate the only Negro in town. Sorry, Rastus, just white folks tonight.

I neglected to mention an incident that occurred the year before Rastus dropped into Hinckley. The town's one little burnt-cork, burnt-matchstick tip of a dead-end street housing a few hard-luck Negroes had been spontaneously urban-removed, and its inhabitants, those who survived the pogrom, had disappeared into the night, the same kind of killingly cold night roughing up the Studebaker. That detail, the sudden exodus of all the town's Negroes, should have been noted earlier in story time, because it helps you understand Hinckley time. A visitor to Hinckley today probably won't hear about the above-mentioned event, yet it's imprinted indelibly in the town's memory. Now you see it, now you don't, but always present. A permanent marker separating before and after. Hinckley truly a white man's town from that night on.

And just to emphasize how white they wanted their town to be, the night of the fires everybody wore sheets bleached white as snow, and for a giggle, under the sheets, blacked their faces. A joke too good to share with the Negroes, who saw only white robes and white hoods with white eyes in the eyeholes. We blacked up blacker than the blackest of 'em, reported one old-timer in a back issue of the Hinckley *Daily News*. Yes we did. Blacker than a cold, black night, blacker than black. Hauled the coloreds outdoors in their drawers and nightgowns, pickaninnies naked as the day they born. Told 'em, You got five minutes to pack a sack and git. Five minutes we's turnin these shacks and everythin in 'em to ash.

Meanwhile the wagons transporting the Globies into town have arrived, their canvas covers billowing, noisy as wind-whipped sails, their wooden sides, steep as clipper ships, splashed with colorful, irresistible ads for merchandise nobody in Hinckley has ever dreamed of, let alone seen. A cornucopia of high-tech goods and services from the future, Hinckley time, though widely available in leading metropolitan centers for decades. Mostly beads and baubles, rummage-sale trash, but some stuff packed in the capacious holds of the wagons extremely ancient. Not stale or frail or old-fashioned or used or useless. No, the oldest, deepest cargo consisted of things forgotten. *Forgotten?* Yes, forgotten. Upon which subject I would expand if I could, but forgotten means forgotten, doesn't it. Means lost. A category whose contents I'm unable to list or describe because if I could, the items wouldn't be forgotten. Forgotten things are really, really gone. Gone even if memories of them flicker, ghosts with more life than the living. Like a *Free Marcus* button you tucked in a drawer and lived the rest of your life not remembering it lay there, folded in a bloodstained head kerchief, until one afternoon as you're preparing to move the last mile into senior citizens' public housing and you must get rid of ninety-nine and nine-tenths percent of the junk you've accumulated over the years because the cubicle you're assigned in the high-rise isn't much larger than a coffin, certainly not a king-sized coffin like pharaohs erected so they could take everything with them—chariots, boats, VCRs, slaves, wives—so you must shed what feels like layers of your own tender skin, flaying yourself patiently, painfully, divesting yourself of one precious forgotten thing after another, toss, toss, toss. Things forgotten in the gritty bottom of a drawer and you realize you've not been living the kind of life you could have lived if you hadn't forgotten, and now, remembering, it's too late.

In other words, the wagons carried tons of alternative pasts—roads not taken, costumes, body parts, promises, ghosts. Hinckley folks lined up for miles at these canvas-topped depots crackling whitely in the prairie wind. Even poor folks who can't afford to purchase anything mob the landing, ooohing and ahhhing with the rest. So many bright lost hopes in the bellies of the schooners, the wagons might still be docked there doing brisk business a hundred years from now, the Globies in their gaudy, revealing uniforms showing their stuff to a sea of wide eyes, waving hands, grappling, grasping hands, but hands not too busy to clap, volleys of clapping, then a vast, collective sigh when clapping stops and empty hands drop to people's sides, sighs so deep and windy they scythe across the Great Plains, rippling mile after endless mile of wheat, corn, barley, amber fields of grain swaying and purring as if they'd been caressed when a tall Globie dangles aloft some item everybody recognizes, a forgotten thing all would claim if they could afford it, a priceless pearl the dark ballplayer tosses gratis into the crowd of Hinckleyites, just doing it to do it, and the gift would perform tricks, loop-de-looping, sparkling, airborne long enough to evoke spasms of love and guilt and awe and desire and regret, then disappear like a snowflake or a sentence grown too large and baroque, its own weight and ambition and daring and vanity ripping it apart before it reaches the earth. A forgotten thing twisting in the air, becoming a wet spot on fingers reaching for it. A tear inching down a cheek. An embarrassing drop of moisture in the crotch of somebody's drawers.

Wheee. Forgotten things. Floating through the air with the greatest of ease. Hang-gliding. Flip-flopping.

Flip-floppety-clippety-clop. The horse-drawn caravan clomps up and down Hinckley's skimpy grid of streets. Disappears when it reaches the abandoned, dead-end, former black quarter and turns right to avoid the foundation of a multiuse, multistory, multinational parking garage and amusement center, a yawning hole gouged deeper into the earth than the stainless steel and glass edifice will rise into the sky.

Is dat going to be the Mall of America, one of the Globie kids asks, peeking out from behind a wagon's canvas flap. A little Hinckley girl hears the little Globie but doesn't reply.

Then she's bright and chirrupy as Jiminy Cricket and chases after the gillies till she can't keep up, watching the last horse's round, perfect rump swaying side to side like Miss Maya's verse. Feels delicious about herself because she had smiled, managed to be polite to the small brown face poking out of the white sheet just as her mother said she must, but also really, basically, ignored it, didn't get the brown face mixed up with Hinckley faces her mother said it wouldn't and couldn't ever be. Always act a lady, honey. But be careful. Very careful. Those people are not like us. Warmed by the boy's soft voice, his long eyelashes like curly curtains or question marks, the dreamy roll of the horse's huge, split butt, but she didn't fall in love. Instead she chatters to herself in a new language, made up on the spot. *Wow. Gumby-o. Kum-bye-a. Op-poop-a-doop* . . . as if she's been tossed a forgotten thing and it doesn't melt.

She wishes she'd said yes to the boy, wishes she could share the good news.

Daddy said after the bulldozers a big road's coming, sweety-pie, and we'll be the centerpiece of the universe, the envy of our neighbors, Daddy said I can have anything I want, twenty-four seven, brother, just imagine, anything I want, cute jack-in-the-box, pop-up brown boys, a pinto pony, baby dolls with skin warm and soft as mine, who cry real tears. *Word. Bling-bling. Oop-poop-a-doop.*

After a dust cloud churned by the giant tires of the convoy settles, the little girl discovers chocolate drops wrapped in silver foil the chocolate soldiers had tossed her. In the noise and confusion of the rumbling vehicles, she'd thought the candies were stones. Or cruel bullets aimed at her by the dark strangers in canvas-roofed trucks her mother had warned her to flee from, hide from. Realizing they are lovely chocolate morsels, immaculate inside their shiny skins, she feels terrible for thinking ugly thoughts about the GIs, wants to run to the convoy and say *Danke, Danke* even though her mother told her, They're illiterate, don't speak our language. As she scoops up the surprises and stuffs them in her apron pocket, she imagines her chubby legs churning in pursuit of the dusty column. The convoy had taken hours to pass her, so it must be moving slowly. But war has taught her the treacherous distance between dreams and reality. Even after crash diets and aerobic classes her pale short legs would never catch the wagons, so she sits down, settles for cramming food into her mouth with both hands, as if she's forgotten how good food can be and wants to make up for all the lost meals at once. Licking, sucking, crunching, chewing. The melting, gooey drops smear her cheeks, hands, dimpled knees—chocolate stain spreading as the magic candy spawns, multiplies inside her apron pocket, a dozen new sweet pieces explode into being for every piece she consumes. She eats till she's about to bust, sweet chocolate coating her inside and out, a glistening, sticky tarbaby her own mother would have warned her not to touch. Eats till she falls asleep and keels over in the dusty street.

Dusty? What's up with this dusty. I thought you said it was snowing. A snowstorm.

Snowstorm. Oh yeah. Should have let you know that in expectation of a four-seasons mega-pleasure center, Hinckley domed itself last year.

Believe it or not, it's Rastus who discovers the girl. Since being refused entrance to the Globies' show, he's been wandering disconsolate through Hinckley's dark streets when suddenly, as fate would have it, he stumbles into her. Literally. Ouch.

Less painful than unnerving when Rastus makes abrupt contact with something soft and squishy underfoot. He freezes in his tracks. Instinctively his leg retracts. He scuffs the bottom of his shoe on the ground, remembering the parade earlier in the day, horses large as elephants. Sniffs the night air cautiously. Hopes he's wrong. Must be. He smells sugar and spice, everything nice, overlaid with the cloyingly sweet reek of chocolate. Another time and place he might have reared back, kicked the obstacle in his path, but tonight he's weak, depleted, the mean exclusion of him from the Globie extravaganza the final straw. Besides, what kind of person would kick a dog already down, and dog or cat's what he believes he'll see as he peers into the shadows webbing his feet.

Rastus gulps. His already overtaxed heart *fluups*. Chocolate can't hide a cherub's face, the Gerber baby plump limbs and roly-poly torso. Somebody's daughter lying out here in the gutter. Hoodooed. Stricken. Poor babygirl. Her frail—make up your mind—chest rises and falls faintly, motion almost imperceptible since they never installed streetlamps on this unpaved street when Negroes lived here, and now the cunning city managers are waiting for the Dutch-German-Swiss conglomerate to install a megawatt, mesmerizing blaze of glory to guide crowds to the omniplex.

Believe it or not, on this night of nights, this night he expected a new life to begin, riding off with the Globies, the players exhausted but hungry for another town tomorrow, laughing, telling lies, picking salty slivers of the town they've just sacked out their teeth, on this penultimate night before the dawning of the first day of his new life, Rastus displays patience and self-denial worthy of Harriet's Tom. Accepts the sudden turn of fate delaying his flight from Hinckley. Takes time out to rescue a damsel in distress.

One more job, just one more and I'm through, outta here. Trotting with the Globies or flying on my own two feet, I'm gittin out. Giddy-up. Yeah. Tell folks it was Rastus singing dis sad song, now Rastus up and gone.

Determined to do the right thing, he stoops and raises the girl's cold, heart-shaped face, one large hand under her neck so her head droops backward and her mouth flops open, the other hand flat against her tiny bosom. Figures he'll blow breath into her mouth, then pump her ribcage like you would a bellows till her lungs catch fire again. In other words Rastus is inventing CPR, cardiopulmonary resuscitation, a lifesaving technique that will catch on big in America one day in the bright future when hopefully there will be no rules about who can do it to whom, but that night in Hinckley, well, you can imagine what happened when a crowd of citizens hopped up and confused by Globie shenanigans at the armory came upon Rastus in the shadows crouched over a bloody, unconscious little white girl, puckering up his big lips to deliver a kiss.

To be fair, not everyone participated in the mayhem you're imagining. Experts say the portion of the crowd returning home to the slum bordering the former colored quarter must shoulder most of the blame. In other words, the poor and fragrant did the dirty work. The ones who live where no self-respecting white person would, an unruly element, soon themselves to be evicted when Consolidated Enterprises clears more parking space for the pleasure center, the same people, experts say, who had constituted by far the largest portion of the mob that had burned and chased all the Negroes out of town, these embarrassing undesirables and unemployables, who would lynch foreign CEOs too if they could get away with it, are responsible, experts will explain, for perpetrating the horror I'm asking you to imagine. And imagine you must, because I refuse to regale you with gory, unedifying details.

Clearly, not everyone's to blame. Certainly not me or you. On the other hand, who wouldn't be upset by an evening of loud, half-naked, large black men fast breaking and fancy dribbling, clowning and stuffing and jamming and preening for white women and kids screaming their silly heads off. Enough to put any grown man's nerves on edge, especially after you had to shell out your hard-earned cash to watch yourself take a beating. Then, to top it all off, once you're home, bone tired, hunkered down on your side of the bed, here comes your old lady grinning from ear to ear, bouncy like she's just survived a naked bungy-dive from the top of the god-damned pleasure center's twin-towers-to-be.

The Studebaker's wipers flop back and forth, bump over scabs of ice. The driver's view isn't improving. We inch along a long, long black tunnel, headlights illuminating slants of snow that converge just a few yards beyond the spot where a hood ornament would sit, if Studebakers, like Mercedes Benzes, were adorned with bowsprits in 1927. Bright white lines of force, every kamikaziing snowflake in the universe sucked into this vortex, this vanishing point the head-lights define, a hole in the dark we chug, chug behind, the ever receding horizon drawing us on, drawing us on, a ship to Zion, the song says.

Our driver's appalled by the raw deal Rastus received. During an interview he asserts, I'd never participate in something so mobbishly brutal. I would not assume appearance is reality. I would never presume truth lodges in the eyes of the more numerous beholders. After all, my people also a minority. We've suffered unjustly too. And will again. I fear it in my bones. Soon after the great depression that will occur just a few years from now, just a few miles down this very road we're traveling in this hot, *fluuping* car, some clever, evil motherfucker will say, Sew yellow stars on their sleeves. Stars will work like color. We'll be able to tell who's who. Protect our citizens from mongrels, gypsies, globetrotters, mi-grants, emigrants, the riffraff coming and going. Sneaking in and out of our cities. Peddling dangerous wares. Parasites. Criminals. Terrorists. Devils.

Through the slit in his iron mask the driver observes gallows being erected by the roadside. Imagines flyers nailed and taped all over town. Wonders if it had been wise to warn them we're coming.

SO WHO invented the jump shot. Don't despair. All the panelists have taken seats facing the audience. The emcee at the podium taps a microphone and a hush fills the vast hall. We're about to be told.

2. like the narration, told through anders but continues when aed

2. such an interesting character almost have to reread what he say)

3. The after, the scientific par fits w/ the rest, he is almost like the all science no "life"

4. what is significance of ladies, to give characterization of Anders

5. The ending that he remembers isnt grammatically correct, when he is in fact a critic.

BULLET IN THE BRAIN

Tobias Wolff

Tobias Wolff lives in Northern California and teaches at Stanford University. He has received the Rea Award for the Short Story, the Los Angeles Times Book Prize, and the PEN/Faulkner Award. His most recent book is *Our Story Begins: New and Selected Stories*.

Anders couldn't get to the bank until just before it closed, so of course the line was endless and he got stuck behind two women whose loud, stupid conversation put him in a murderous temper. He was never in the best of tempers anyway, Anders—a book critic known for the weary, elegant savagery with which he dispatched almost everything he reviewed.

With the line still doubled around the rope, one of the tellers stuck a "POSITION CLOSED" sign in her window and walked to the back of the bank, where she leaned against a desk and began to pass the time with a man shuffling papers. The women in front of Anders broke off their conversation and watched the teller with hatred. "Oh, that's nice," one of them said. She turned to Anders and added, confident of his accord, "One of those little human touches that keep us coming back for more."

Anders had conceived his own towering hatred of the teller, but he immediately turned it on the presumptuous crybaby in front of him. "Damned unfair," he said. "Tragic, really. If they're not chopping off the wrong leg, or bombing your ancestral village, they're closing their positions."

She stood her ground. "I didn't say it was tragic," she said. "I just think it's a pretty lousy way to treat your customers."

"Unforgivable," Anders said. "Heaven will take note."

She sucked in her cheeks but stared past him and said nothing. Anders saw that the other woman, her friend, was looking in the same direction. And then the tellers stopped what they were doing, and the customers slowly turned, and silence came over the bank. Two men wearing black ski masks and blue business suits were standing to the side of the door. One of them had a pistol pressed against the guard's neck. The guard's eyes were closed, and his lips were moving. The other man had a sawed-off shotgun. "Keep your big mouth shut!" the man with the pistol said, though no one had spoken a word. "One of you tellers hits the alarm, you're all dead meat. Got it?"

The tellers nodded.

"Oh, bravo," Anders said. *"Dead meat."* He turned to the woman in front of him. "Great script, eh? The stern, brass-knuckled poetry of the dangerous classes."

She looked at him with drowning eyes.

The man with the shotgun pushed the guard to his knees. He handed the shotgun to his partner and yanked the guard's wrists up behind his back and locked them together with a pair of handcuffs. He toppled him onto the floor with a kick between the shoulder blades. Then he took his shotgun back and went over to the security gate at the end of the counter. He was short and heavy and moved with peculiar slowness, even torpor. "Buzz him in," his partner said. The man with the shotgun opened the gate and sauntered along the line of tellers, handing each of them a Hefty bag. When he came to the empty position he looked over at the man with the pistol, who said, "Whose slot is that?"

Anders watched the teller. She put her hand to her throat and turned to the man she'd been talking to. He nodded. "Mine," she said.

"Then get your ugly ass in gear and fill that bag."

"There you go," Anders said to the woman in front of him. "Justice is done."

"Hey! Bright boy! Did I tell you to talk?"

"No," Anders said.

"Then shut your trap."

"Did you hear that?" Anders said. " 'Bright boy.' Right Out of 'The Killers.' "

"Please be quiet," the woman said.

"Hey, you deaf or what?" The man with the pistol walked over to Anders. He poked the weapon into Anders' gut. "You think I'm playing games?"

"No," Anders said, but the barrel tickled like a stiff finger and he had to fight back the titters. He did this by making himself stare into the man's eyes, which were clearly visible behind the holes in the mask: pale blue and rawly red-rimmed. The man's left eyelid kept twitching. He breathed out a piercing, ammoniac smell that shocked Anders more than anything that had happened, and he was beginning to develop a sense of unease when the man prodded him again with the pistol.

"You like me, bright boy?" he said. "You want to suck my dick?"

"No," Anders said.

"Then stop looking at me."

Anders fixed his gaze on the man's shiny wing-tip shoes.

"Not down there. Up there." He stuck the pistol under Anders' chin and pushed it upward until Anders was looking at the ceiling.

Anders had never paid much attention to that part of the bank, a pompous old building with marble floors and counters and pillars, and gilt scrollwork over the tellers' cages. The domed ceiling had been decorated with mythological figures whose fleshy, toga-draped ugliness Anders had taken in at a glance many years earlier and afterward declined to notice. Now he had no choice but to scrutinize the painter's work. It was even worse than he remembered, and all of it executed with the utmost gravity. The artist had a few

tricks up his sleeve and used them again and again—a certain rosy
blush on the underside of the clouds, a coy backward glance on the
faces of the cupids and fauns. The ceiling was crowded with various
dramas, but the one that caught Anders' eye was Zeus and Europa—
portrayed, in this rendition, as a bull ogling a cow from behind a
haystack. To make the cow sexy, the painter had canted her hips
suggestively and given her long, droopy eyelashes through which
she gazed back at the bull with sultry welcome. The bull wore a
smirk and his eyebrows were arched. If there'd been a bubble coming out of his mouth, it would have said, "Hubba hubba."

"What's so funny, bright boy?"

"Nothing."

"You think I'm comical? You think I'm some kind of clown?"

"No."

"You think you can fuck with me?"

"No."

"Fuck with me again, you're history. *Capiche?*"

Anders burst out laughing. He covered his mouth with both
hands and said, "I'm sorry, I'm sorry," then snorted helplessly
through his fingers and said, "*Capiche* oh, God, *capiche*," and at that
the man with the pistol raised the pistol and shot Anders right in
the head.

THE BULLET smashed Anders' skull and ploughed through his brain
and exited behind his right ear, scattering shards of bone into the
cerebral cortex, the corpus callosum, back toward the basal gan-
glia, and down into the thalamus. But before all this occurred, the
first appearance of the bullet in the cerebrum set off a crackling
chain of iron transports and neuro-transmissions. Because of their
peculiar origin these traced a peculiar pattern, flukishly calling to
life a summer afternoon some forty years past, and long since lost
to memory. After striking the cranium the bullet was moving at
900 feet per second, a pathetically sluggish, glacial pace compared
to the synaptic lightning that flashed around it. Once in the brain,

that is, the bullet came under the mediation of brain time, which gave Anders plenty of leisure to contemplate the scene that, in a phrase he would have abhorred, "passed before his eyes."

It is worth noting what Anders did not remember, given what he did remember. He did not remember his first lover, Sherry, or what he had most madly loved about her, before it came to irritate him—her unembarrassed carnality, and especially the cordial way she had with his unit, which she called Mr. Mole, as in, "Uh-oh, looks like Mr. Mole wants to play," and, "let's hide Mr. Mole!" Anders did not remember his wife, whom he had also loved before she exhausted him with her predictability, or his daughter, now a sullen professor of economics at Dartmouth. He did not remember standing just outside his daughter's door as she lectured her bear about his naughtiness and described the truly appalling punishments Paws would receive unless he changed his ways. He did not remember a single line of the hundreds of poems he had committed to memory in his youth so that he could give himself the shivers at will—not "Silent, upon a peak in Darien," or "My God, I heard this day," or "All my pretty ones? Did you say all? O hell-kite All?" None of these did he remember; not one. Anders did not remember his dying mother saying of his father, "I should have stabbed him in his sleep."

He did not remember Professor Josephs telling his class how Athenian prisoners in Sicily had been released if they could recite Aeschylus, and then reciting Aeschylus himself, right there, in the Greek. Anders did not remember how his eyes had burned at those sounds. He did not remember the surprise of seeing a college classmate's name on the jacket of a novel not long after they graduated, or the respect he had felt after reading the book. He did not remember the pleasure of giving respect.

Nor did Anders remember seeing a woman leap to her death from the building opposite his own just days after his daughter was born. He did not remember shouting, "Lord have mercy!" He did not remember deliberately crashing his father's car into a tree, or having his ribs kicked in by three policemen at an anti-war rally, or waking himself up with laughter. He did not remember when he began to regard the heap of books on his desk with boredom and dread, or when he grew angry at writers for writing them. He did not remember when everything began to remind him of something else.

This is what he remembered. Heat. A baseball field. Yellow grass, the whirr of insects, himself leaning against a tree as the boys of the neighborhood gather for a pickup game. He looks on as the others argue the relative genius of Mantle and Mays. They have been worrying this subject all summer, and it has become tedious to Anders: an oppression, like the heat.

Then the last two boys arrive, Coyle and a cousin of his from Mississippi. Anders has never met Coyle's cousin before and will never see him again. He says hi with the rest but takes no further notice of him until they've chosen sides and someone asks the cousin what position he wants to play. "Shortstop," the boy says. "Short's the best position they is." Anders turns and looks at him. He wants to hear Coyle's cousin repeat what he's just said, but he knows better than to ask. The others will think he's being a jerk, ragging the kid for his grammar. But that isn't it, not at all—it's that Anders is strangely roused, elated, by those final two words, their pure unexpectedness and their music. He takes the field in a trance, repeating them to himself.

The bullet is already in the brain; it won't be outrun forever, or charmed to a halt. In the end it will do its work and leave the troubled skull behind, dragging its comet's tail of memory and hope and talent and love into the marble hall of commerce. That can't be helped. But for now Anders can still make time. Time for the shadows to lengthen on the grass, time for the tethered dog to bark at the flying ball, time for the boy in right field to smack his sweat-blackened mitt and softly chant, *They is, they is, they is.*

PERMISSIONS

ALSO BY
JOYCE CAROL OATES

THE ECCO ANTHOLOGY OF CONTEMPORARY AMERICAN SHORT FICTION
ISBN 978-0-06-166158-7 (paperback)

A definitive, essential collection of the very best short stories by contemporary American masters, edited by Joyce Carol Oates, "the living master of the short story" (*Buffalo News*).

MY SISTER, MY LOVE The Intimate Story of Skyler Rampike
ISBN 978-0-06-154748-5 (hardcover)

"[Oates] reimagines the JonBenet case in New Jersey instead of Colorado, involving an ice-skating champion rather than a beauty queen. And Oates's imaginary version is so much more richly rewarding than what we know about what really happened that it ought to be true, and probably is." —*New York magazine*

THE GRAVEDIGGER'S DAUGHTER
ISBN 978-0-06-123682-2 (hardcover) • 978-0-06-123683-9 (paperback)

A sprawling, masterful epic about a young woman's struggle for identity and survival in post-World War II America.

"In her masterwork . . . Joyce Carol Oates combines gritty realism with a mesmerizing moment-by-moment creation of the title character's psyche."
—Sena Jeter Naslund, author of *Ahab's Wife*

BLACK GIRL/WHITE GIRL
ISBN 978-0-06-112564-5 (hardcover) • 978-0-06-112565-2 (paperback)

"Oates bravely grapples with the fallout of the Civil Rights movement, the early '70's backlash against Summer of Love optimism, and the well-intentioned but ultimately condescending antiracist piety of privileged white liberals." —*Publishers Weekly*

HIGH LONESOME Stories 1966-2006
ISBN 978-0-06-050120-4 (paperback)

Arranged by decade, this unprecedented volume gathers stories from Oates's seminal collections.

"If the phrase 'woman of letters' existed, Joyce Carol Oates would be, foremost in this country, entitled to it." —John Updike

MISSING MOM A Novel
ISBN 978-0-06-081622-3 (paperback)

Nikki Eaton, single, thirty-one, sexually liberated, and economically self-supporting, has never particularly thought of herself as a daughter. Yet, following the unexpected loss of her mother, she undergoes a remarkable transformation during a tumultuous year that brings stunning horror, sorrow, illumination, wisdom, and even a nurturing love.

"Her best ever—a masterpiece." —*Kirkus Reviews* (starred review)

THE FALLS A Novel
ISBN 978-0-06-072229-6 (paperback) • 978-0-06-156534-2 (paperback)
ISBN 978-0-06-074188-4 (cd)

A haunting story of the powerful spell Niagara Falls casts upon two generations of a family, leading to tragedy, love, loss, and, ultimately, redemption.

"*The Falls* . . . has the tension of suspense fiction and the melodrama of a gothic novel, but it's coupled with psychological insight and astute social commentary, proving that Oates, in her best work, continues to defy categorization." —*Los Angeles Times*

I AM NO ONE YOU KNOW Stories

ISBN 978-0-06-059289-9 (paperback)

A collection of 19 startling stories that bear witness to the remarkably varied lives of Americans of our time.

"These are small, hard gems, full of the same rich emotion and startling observation that readers of Oates's fiction have come to expect." —*New York Times Book Review*

THE TATTOOED GIRL A Novel

ISBN 978-0-06-113604-7 (paperback)

A celebrated but reclusive author reluctantly admits that he can no longer live alone and decides to hire an assistant. Considering at first only male applicants, he is dissatisfied with everyone he meets . . . then he encounters Alma.

"Oates takes a tricky look at the nature of hate and its sources. . . . *The Tattooed Girl* is a complicated, sometimes sweet story rife with misunderstandings and missteps, unintended hurts and deliberate forgiveness. It will leave a mark." —*Entertainment Weekly*

I'LL TAKE YOU THERE A Novel

ISBN 978-0-06-050118-1 (paperback)

Pitiless in exposing the follies of the time, *I'll Take You There* is a dramatic revelation of the risks—and curious rewards—of the obsessive personality, as well as a testament to the stubborn strength of a certain type of contemporary female intellectual.

"Young women who don't quite know where they fit in—and anyone who has known women like them—will find recognition and understanding in this latest piece in the novelistic quilt of one of America's most accomplished writers." —*St. Louis Post-Dispatch*

MIDDLE AGE A Romance

ISBN 978-0-06-093490-3 (paperback)

Joyce Carol Oates portrays a contemporary phenomenon rarely explored in literature and popular culture: the affluent middle-aged in America reinventing themselves romantically after the energies of youth have faded or become disillusioned.

"With wit and tenderness Oates takes us on the roller-coaster ride of middle age in pursuit of a last adventure, a last romance, a last defiance of the impending grave."
—*San Francisco Chronicle*

FAITHLESS Tales of Transgression

ISBN 978-0-06-093357-9 (paperback)

"*Faithless: Tales of Transgression* makes its brisk incisions into the themes of terror, female passion, collapsing male identity, loneliness, divorce, revenge and not a little gun ownership." —*New York Times Book Review*

BLONDE A Novel

ISBN 978-0-06-093493-4 (paperback)

Joyce Carol Oates reimagines the inner, poetic, and spiritual life of Norma Jeane Baker. Rich with psychological insight and disturbing irony, this mesmerizing narrative illuminates Baker's lonely childhood, wrenching adolescence, and the creation of "Marilyn Monroe."

"An overwhelmingly vivid and powerful rendering of a human being who outlived her life."
—*The Nation*

For more information about upcoming titles, visit www.harperperennial.com.

Visit www.AuthorTracker.com
for exclusive information on your favorite HarperCollins authors.

Available wherever books are sold, or call 1-800-331-3761 to order.

HARPER ◉ PERENNIAL